HIGH END

HIGH END

CAPT KEVIN P. MILLER USN (RET.)

Braveship
BOOKS

Aura Libertatis Spirat

HIGH END

Text Copyright © 2024 by Kevin P. Miller

Cover Image Copyright © 2024 by Wojciech Danecki

Braveship Books
www.braveshipbooks.com
Aura Libertatis Spirat

This book was edited by China DeSpain of Incantation Ink
incantationinkllc@gmail.com

Cover Art by Wojciech Danecki
Cover Design by Ivica Jandrijević

Back cover photo courtesy of *Rusty Buggy*

Map courtesy of University of Texas Libraries (Public Domain Resources)

Book layout by Alexandru Diaconescu
www.steadfast-typesetting.eu

ISBN-13: 978-1-64062-201-2
Printed in the United States of America

Dedicated to:
Dave, Joe, and Jack ... three great guys
in whom I am well pleased

Men have forgotten God; that's why all this has happened.

Alexandr Solzhenitsyn

Glossary of Jargon and Acronyms

1MC — ship's public address system

5MC — flight deck loudspeaker system

20mm — Twenty-millimeter cannon round, aka "twenty mike-mike."

AARGM — Advanced Antiradiation Guided Missile

AI — Artificial Intelligence

AIS — Automatic Information System (to monitor marine traffic)

Air Boss — Officer in Primary Flight Control (control tower) responsible for aircraft operations on deck out to five miles from ship.

AMRAAM — Advanced Medium Range Air-to-Air Missile (AIM-120)

Angels — altitude in thousands of feet. "Angels six" = 6,000 feet

AWACS — Airborne Warning and Control System; aka E-3 *Sentry* aircraft

Bandit — confirmed enemy airborne contact; also known as "'hostile."

Bingo — emergency fuel state divert from ship to shore base.

Bogey — unknown airborne contact

C4ISR — Command, Control, Communications, Computers, Intelligence, Surveillance, Reconnaissance

CAG — Carrier Air Wing Commander; formerly Commander, Air Group

CAP — Combat Air Patrol

Cat — catapult

CIC — Combat Information Center

COMAIR — Commercial Air Transportation

CoS — Chief of Staff

CSG — Carrier Strike Group

CVIC — Aircraft Carrier Intelligence Center

CVW — Carrier Air Wing

DDG — Guided Missile Destroyer

ELINT — Electronic Intelligence

EMCON — Emissions Control

ESM — Electronic Support Measures; used to detect and identify

EUCOM — U.S. European Command, Stuttgart, Germany

Flanker — NATO code name for Su-27-30 series aircraft

FLIR — Forward Looking Infra-Red.

g — the force of gravity. "4 g's" is four times the force of gravity.

GPS — Global Positioning System

Greyhound — Popular name for C-2 Carrier On-board Delivery aircraft, also known as the "COD."

Growler — popular name of EA-18G Airborne Electronic Attack aircraft, a *Super Hornet* variant.

Hawkeye — popular name for E-2 Early Warning aircraft, also known as the *Hummer.*

Helo — helicopter

Hornet — popular name for FA-18C Strike Fighter.

HSM — Helicopter Maritime-Strike Squadron flying MH-60R

HSC — Helicopter Combat Support Squadron flying MH-60S

ICS — Inter Cockpit Communication System

IR — Infra-Red

ISR — Intelligence, Surveillance, and Reconnaissance

JSF — Joint Strike Fighter; F-35 *Lightning II*

Knot — nautical mile per hour. One nautical mile is 2,000 yards or 6,000 feet.

LCS — Littoral Combat Ship

LSO — Landing Signal Officer, also known as "Paddles."

LRSAM — Long Range Anti-Ship Missile

NAVEUR — Naval Forces Europe

Nugget — first-cruise pilot

NVGs — Night Vision Goggles

OOD — Officer of the Deck

PIM — Position of Intended Movement

PLAT — Pilot Landing Aid Television; closed circuit video picture of flight deck operations.

Poseidon — popular name for P-8 Maritime Patrol Aircraft

Rhino — slang name for FA-18E/F *Super Hornet.*

ROE — Rules of Engagement

Romeo — slang name for MH-60R *Seahawk.*

RTB — Return to Base

SATCOM — Satellite Communications

SAM — Surface-to-air missile

SAR — Search and Rescue (CSAR is *Combat* Search and Rescue).

Seahawk — popular name for MH-60 series multi-mission helicopter.

Second Fleet — U.S. Navy numbered fleet responsible for North Atlantic Waters

Sixth Fleet — U.S. Navy numbered fleet responsible for European Waters

Sidewinder — popular name for AIM-9 infrared heat seeking air-to-air missile.

Sierra — slang name for MH-60S *Seahawk.*

SSBN — Nuclear-powered ballistic missile submarine, aka "boomer"

SSSC — Surface Subsurface Surveillance Control ("Triple-S, C")

SSN — Nuclear-powered attack submarine

SuCAP — Surface Combat Air Patrol

Super Hornet — popular name for upgraded FA-18E/F single seat or two-place Strike Fighter; also known as *"Rhino."*

TAO — Tactical Action Officer

Texaco — Comm brevity word for in-flight refueling tanker

Timber — Comm brevity word for Link-16

Tomahawk — Surface and subsurface-launched land-attack cruise missile

Trap — arrested landing

Triton — Popular name for MQ-4 unmanned surveillance aircraft

UAV — Unmanned Aerial Vehicle

VAQ — Fixed Wing Electronic Attack squadron flying EA-18G

VAW — Fixed Wing Early Warning squadron flying E-2D

VFA — Fixed Wing Fighter Attack squadron flying FA-18E/F

VLS — Vertical Launch System; missile launchers found on cruisers and destroyers.

WSO — Weapons Systems Officer

Winchester — out of ordnance

Acknowledgements

High End is the novel I thought I would write after publishing *Declared Hostile* in 2016. The concept was of a blue-water war-at-sea epic above the Arctic Circle with a resurgent Russia who had recently annexed the Crimea and flexed their military muscles in ways unseen since the late 1980's. My navalist friends directed my attention—rightly—to the pol/mil situation in the Western Pacific which became the idea for the third novel in the *Raven One* trilogy, *Fight Fight*.

In the 1980's and 90's I made two mini-deployments to the Norwegian Sea where I was able to enjoy—and sometimes endure in varsity conditions—some of the most memorable flying of my career, much of it above the Arctic Circle. It can be damn dangerous. The sea and sky are indeed different, and with every roll of the carrier (and they can bob like a cork up there) you know that you are "not in Kansas" anymore. While I lived on and flew from "the ship," my knowledge of flag spaces and the command-and-control networking of a battle group—today's strike group—was contained to glimpses while transiting the blue-tile area and just enough background to allow this junior officer a rudimentary understanding of my role in "the big picture."

Later in my career and especially in the careers of my friends and shipmates I was exposed to the inner workings of the ship's C2 suite and how warfare commander responsibilities broke out across the group. That said, the day-to-day life of a strike group commander and the command relationships at the highest level remained a mystery.

Researching my novels is a daunting yet enjoyable task, and none more enjoyable than sitting down with three friends who have experienced strike group command. Retired flag officers Admiral Bill Gortney, Vice Admiral Andy Lewis, and Rear Admiral Greg Nosal were generous with their time and provided keen insights and sea stories of their tours in this command position and observations about relationships with higher commands while operating on the North Atlantic. Many thanks to each of you with my deepest respect.

Retired U. S. Navy Captain Will Dossel, as he has with all my novels, provided invaluable background documentation on modern naval warfare and orders-of-battle. His sanity checks of my action scenes—from cockpit to pilothouse to flag suite—have benefitted readers in each novel. All of us, and especially me, are in his debt. Likewise, fellow retired Navy Captain John Stevenson has mentored me since I was a nugget, today with helpful text suggestions about place and readability. Thanks, J.R., for your loyal friendship, and for always watching over me.

As they have in the past, trusted shipmates DMB and Kwiff helped with my deck plate questions about things I never knew or had long forgotten. Thanks guys.

Special thanks to You Tube sensation—and another trusted shipmate—Commander Ward Carroll, USN (ret.), who asked me to tag along with him for a day at sea aboard a working CVN to observe our current warfighters and rekindle vivid memories of my years underway. Our sailors remain the best in the world.

This is my first novel without the services of longtime editor Linda Wasserman who is battling health challenges. While I miss Linda more than she knows, China DeSpain of Incantation Ink did a remarkable job stepping into the role of content and copy editor in a fictional (though real) world at sea steeped in jargon and acronyms. Her sharp eye caught the easy-to-miss punctuation errors but more importantly her suggestions on readability and character development were spot on and greatly appreciated. A hearty *well done* to you, China.

Jeff Edwards of Braveship Books remains my literary mentor as he has been for the past ten years and is always available with sage—and compelling—advice on any aspect of publishing. Thanks again, shipmate.

Thanks to renowned DCS developer Wojciech "Baltic Dragon" Danecki for his stirring cover art and his observations of Eastern European terms and mindset which adds so much to the reader experience. Many thanks to cover artist Ivica Jandrijević for another first-class book cover.

Formatter Alexandru Diaconescu adapted the manuscript to digital and print formats, accepting my last-minute changes with grace. Thanks, Alex.

My wife Terry has supported me throughout this journey, one that began almost 20 years ago when I first began to think about a character I would eventually call "Flip." I love you, Terry, more than ever.

At this writing, U.S. naval and air forces are not only deployed throughout the world as they have been for some 75 years but are actively engaged in two areas of responsibility with significant combat "firsts" in the past twelve months. *Europe* as a combat AOR is back as the tectonic pressures of tribal demographics in language, religion, culture (both ancient and modern) and history grind against the visions of a unified one-government continent—and a unified alliance. With the stakes of miscalculation higher than they've been in decades, the ability of the United States Navy to help deter and diplomatically signal with deployed naval forces is at capacity, and likely beyond. The men and women of our Navy and Marine Corps—depicted fictionally in these pages and in reality serving today on the four oceans of the world—will answer the call with what they have on hand.

Will it be enough?

CAPT Kevin Miller USN (Ret.)
Fall 2024

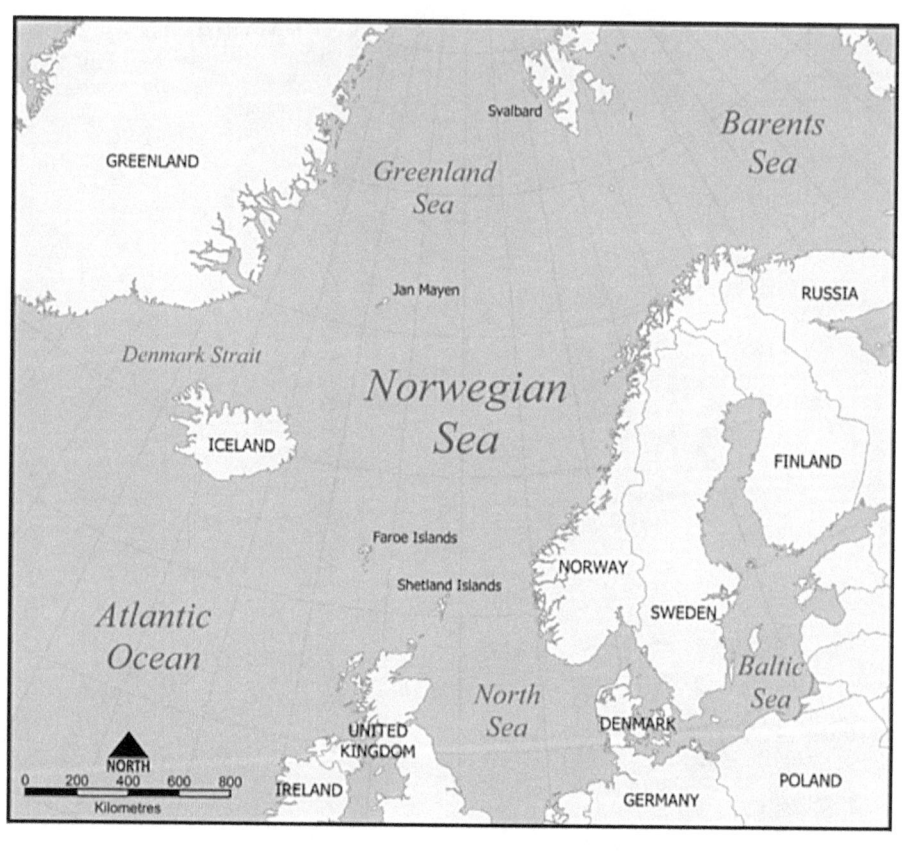

Part I

A bad peace is worse than war.
     – Tacitus

Chapter 1

MV *Konya K* 0130 June 2, 2024, Eastern Mediterranean Sea

Impatient, Aaghaa tugged on the quick-disconnect belt to Burak's jet suit as both men studied the Greek research vessel heading southeast on the darkened water. Satisfied it held, Aaghaa continued to check the suit as he spoke, while Burak kept his gaze on the brilliantly lit ship.

"Remember, you have three minutes to cross, ten minutes aboard, and three to get back. Zehab and Syed will follow in 15-second intervals, so once aboard clear the deck for them; there is no fuel for hovering."

Focused, Burak ran his index finger over his HK MP7A2 submachine gun safety. *Yes, Aaghaa, we've been over this!* With months of planning and practice behind them, Burak could do the op in his sleep. *Neutralize, set, activate, depart.* He knew every passageway and ladder of the MV *Nauticos Card*, and surprised himself at his anticipation to see it now personally and not on a screen.

Aaghaa glanced at his watch. "Two minutes!"

Burak lifted his head to the heavens, contemplating the swath the Milky Way made through the sky out here on the open sea, far from city lights. He flicked down his night vision goggles and scanned the horizon. To the southeast distant ships came into view, and turning his head left he saw a glow to the northwest, the cultural lighting of Crete. The dull glimmer from the bastard Greek island would serve as a guide for the return trip. Satisfied, he flicked the goggles up to save the batteries and his ambient night vision.

Zehab and Syed, having passed Aaghaa's inspection and mother hen fussing, lined up behind Burak on the fantail, the clearest deck aboard *Konya K*. The Turk operators, weapons strapped to their chests and belts, moved their arms in slow circles to check the free travel of their pack thrusters.

"One minute. *Burak!*"

Burak stepped to a clear part of the deck, free of obstructions but only three meters from the rail. He felt his heartbeat pound inside him, anticipating. *Focus on the mission.*

"Thirty seconds!" Aaghaa bellowed, and Burak reached up to energize his NVGs and pull them down in front of his face. His eyes focused on the deck as he waited, heart thumping as he thought of the mission and not the black water he was about to fly over.

"Ten seconds, *start!*"

With a press of his thumb, Burak energized his engine thrusters and felt the vibration on his back. With a slight squeeze of the handles to test, he felt light before he released them to feel his full weight on the deck. *Good.*

"Iyi!" he shouted his readiness.

"Iyi!" Aaghaa called back.

Head down, Burak waited for Aaghaa's countdown with fingertips light on the handles, like they had trained, *ready*, now impatient for Aaghaa's familiar cadence…just another night. Routine.

"Üç, iki, bir—Git!"

With increasing pressure Burak squeezed the handles and lifted off the deck. Over the roar of the thrusters, he heard Zehab and Syed cry *"God is great!"* as he slid over the rail and pivoted right, now lifting his eyes to the goggles as he stabilized on a heading to intercept.

At five meters, Burak could assess the texture of the waves below to maintain his altitude. The seas were calm and winds light. The waning moon would not be up for another two hours. *Good.*

Nauticos Card transited on a course that opened away from him, but by the geometry, he could aim for the bow to affect a smooth transition to a landing on the starboard bridge wing 15 meters above the surface. He held the cluster of lights steady on the horizon as he scanned the surface below in a practiced rhythm, his only visual cue of his rough altitude. He sensed that his comrades were now airborne behind him. *No turning back.*

The research vessel loomed ahead as its lights blazed, washing out Burak's NVG field of view, and he lifted his head to use his naked eyes. He estimated *Nauticos Card* to be one ship length away. Fighting the urge to slow his approach—his tendency in training—he bore in, timing his transition by a best-guess point at which he would rotate his arms forward to slow while adding power to climb, then stabilize to a precise landing on the bridge wing, like a bird to a branch. The giant crane on the lighted fantail slid by on his left, revealing no sailors on deck.

Now!

Burak moved his arms forward as he squeezed, slowing his approach to the massive steel wall before him as he ascended to above bridge level. With deft movements he floated across the bridge wing rail and plopped down on deck.

Through rote training, he opened the disconnects and pulled his pack to the pilothouse bulkhead to clear the deck for Zehab, who arrived seconds later. As Zehab doffed his pack, Burak engaged the elapsed timer feature of his watch and led with his weapon muzzle as he opened the hatch to the darkened bridge.

The mate, startled from his mindless cellphone scrolling, cried and lunged for the throttles, yanking them back as Burak placed his laser sight above his ear and pulled the trigger. The mate's head exploded as his body fell on the console and then the deck.

Blast, Burak thought as he moved to check the bridge for more crew. He was alone with the single dead man who had been on watch in the darkened bridge. However, with the ship engines at idle, the damage was done. *The crew is alerted.*

Zehab entered the bridge. "Syed is not here yet."

Burak thought quickly. Syed was to remain on the bridge to ensure they kept control while Burak and Zehab set and activated the charges in the engine room. They had a contingency. That Syed might be dead, having scraped himself off on the waves or struggled to free himself of the jet suit as it pulled him down, was secondary.

"No time, they are alerted. You go solo."

As Zehab went below, Burak remained and pushed the console throttles up to level 6, close to the half-ahead setting he surmised the ship maintained before the mate made the final move of his life.

Within seconds Burak heard the engines respond and checked his elapsed time: 1:15.

Zehab continued down the ladders—no sign yet of any crew—while Burak stopped at a non-tight door under the ladder well. As Burak turned the handle and burst inside, a woman screamed.

"What? Who are you?!" the frightened captain cried from the bed.

Without stopping, Burak grabbed the man as the hysterical woman wailed, cowering under the sheet.

"What!? Stop...ow!" the man screamed as Burak zip-tied his hands behind his back. The woman, gripped with fear, could only shriek in terror.

Exasperated, Burak stood and faced the woman. "Silence!" he snarled in Greek. When she continued out of control, he raised his weapon and placed a red laser point on her forehead. Cold realization now silenced the woman as her eyes widened in horror.

Burak squeezed the trigger, and a single suppressed round snapped her head back as a red spray exploded on the bulkhead behind her.

"NADIA! No! *No!*" the captain blubbered while prone on the floor, unable to comprehend the violence of the past minute.

Burak pulled him up and shoved him out and to the ladder, holding him by the collar to steady him as he descended, whimpering, with the weapon muzzle pressed against his back. From below they heard shots.

"My wife! Nadia!" the captain wept, gasping for breath.

"Silence!" Burak hissed, leading him down. At a ladder well he glanced at his watch. 4:10.

Zehab called from one deck below. "We are here, four remaining."

Burak wished Syed were here to bind them while Zehab set the charges. Three men and one woman stood hands up against the wardroom bulkhead, terrified, while a dead teenager lay on the deck in an expanding pool of his blood. Burak looked down in disgust. *We have no time.*

With sudden and precise movements, he put a single bullet into their chests in quick succession. The last man was able to lunge at Burak before the bullet drove him back. Surprised, Burak admired his courage. *The last one always thinks they will be spared.*

Horrified, the captain roared his grief and anguish as Zehab smacked him with the butt of his weapon. Burak pushed him out into the passageway and to the ladder and down as the man's whimpering increased.

At the engine room hatch, Burak pulled a knife from his shin scabbard and cut the zip tie while Zehab checked for intruders. "Open it, and you will be the one to tell the tale," Burak ordered in accented Greek. The anguished captain hesitated, and Burak put the tip of the knife under the man's chin, drawing blood as the terror-struck captain froze. "Do it *now* and I'll let you keep your balls!" Burak snarled. All but paralyzed with fear, the captain nodded and lifted his right hand to the code keypad while placing his left eye against the iris scanner.

"Now," Burak growled.

Holding his eye against the scanner, the captain entered four keystrokes on the covered pad. When the green light appeared above the door, Burak shoved the man toward Zehab, who spun him around and silently slit his throat with a waiting knife.

Burak entered and saw a slack-jawed man by an auxiliary generator, whom Burak dispatched with one shot. He checked his watch again. Four minutes left. Aaghaa would just have to wait.

Zehab followed and identified a lube oil pipe that fed one of the four main generators. With his hands bloodied, he attached a charge to it and set the timer as Burak scanned the engineering space for movement. Complete with the feed pipe, Zehab descended a ladder through the boiler plate and affixed a shaped charge to the hull at the forward engine room frame, timed to detonate four minutes and thirty-seven seconds after the feed pipe charge.

Burak glanced at his watch: 8:22.

"Now, we're late!"

Zehab scampered up the ladder and grabbed his weapon as Burak stepped to the hatch. Outside, he heard a voice.

Pushing the hatch open, he met a man, young, who froze at the sight of the black-clad intruder—and a muzzle pointed at him. Burak felled him with two shots and stepped over him before he retraced his steps to the passageway bulkhead and ladder. Zehab followed as they bounded up the ladders to the bridge. At the pilothouse Burak checked the time: 9:43—seventeen seconds left.

"Time's out, let's go."

He secured the access hatch to the ladders below as Zehab stepped out on the bridge wing to don his helmet and jet suit. From the observation deck above a shot fired and Zehab cried as he fell.

Burak lunged through the open bridgewing door and drew his weapon up to the shooter, a woman, transfixed on Zehab as she admired her shot. Burak's first round hit her hand on the weapon trigger and second below her armpit before she could cry out. Her lifeless body fell on the rail.

"Can you stand?" Burak asked.

Wincing and suppressing a cry, Zehab pulled himself up on the rail as he answered. "Yes, help me with the suit."

A pool of blood formed under Zehab's wounded leg as Burak helped him with his jet suit and cinched it down. Once on and secure, Burak donned his suit and stepped to Zehab to have him fasten it tight. Zehab held back groans of pain.

"In five minutes you'll be back with Aaghaa, who will scold you!" Burak joked to ease Zehab's mind. "Five more minutes. Can you do it?"

"Yes...I can...God willing."

"Goggles down, light off, and go when ready, around the stern and northwest."

Zehab wavered and took deep breaths.

"*Git!* Do it now!" Burak thundered.

Zehab lifted off and pivoted left, over the side. Once clear of the rail, Burak raised his weapon and fired twice. The first bullet hit the right thruster line which lost power at once. The left thruster, at full power, turned Zehab on his right side in midair; the second bullet hit the engine on his back. The operator cried out as he fell 12 meters to the dark surface with an audible splash and sudden silence.

Burak kicked his partner's weapon over the side as he justified his action. *We cannot risk this mission.*

Now minutes behind, he energized his own goggles and lit off his jet suit, squeezing the handles as soon as the engine spooled up behind him. With no time to lose he ascended at full power, slid left to clear the antennas and mast, and picked up *Konya K* in the distance. The ship transited perpendicular to his flight path, and he referenced a star ahead of it to hold course for intercept. He knew he had no margin for error.

Burak focused on maintaining his relative height as he sped over the waves at the steepest angle he dared. *Konya K* soon showed her outline, and he assessed her motion on the star. Knowing his fuel would soon run out, he would aim for the stern and do a half-buttonhook to a climb, stabilize over the deck, and down.

As the dark ship loomed up Burak corrected left and held it, ready for any engine sputter from fuel starvation. With the ship moving left to right in front of him he picked a spot on the stern as an aimpoint. When the bow wave slid under him, he felt a hiccup on the small of his back. *Now!*

Burak shifted his extended arms to the right and squeezed to the firewall stops. He veered right and climbed up alongside the ship's hull as he slid to the stern, transitioning his eyes under the goggles to assess his relative motion and landing point. Sliding two meters over the rail, he felt a chug and used the remaining thrust to stop his forward motion as he fell to the steel deck in a heap, breaking his fall with the left thruster and rolling on his back as if landing by parachute.

A waiting Aaghaa ran to him. "Burak! Are you okay? Hurry, let's clear the deck for the others."

Burak groaned as Aaghaa helped him to his feet. "Syed did not arrive. Did he leave?"

"Yes, he followed Zehab. Did Zehab make it?"

Burak nodded. "Yes. Together we completed the mission."

"Hurry then, he'll be here any second."

The operator shook his head. "No. He's dead."

Dumbfounded at the loss of two of his men, Aaghaa couldn't wait. "How?"

"He was shot by one we did not see. I took revenge for Zehab."

Aaghaa looked at *Nauticos Card* moving away to the southeast as he absorbed the news. He glanced at his watch. "Did you set the charges?"

"Yes. The bridge is secure and the ship steady on course."

"Good. Let's go below."

The men carried Burak's jet suit below and, after the operator changed into coveralls, went to the bridge to watch. Throughout, Aaghaa peppered him with questions, always coming back to the most important one.

"Are you sure the charges were set properly?"

"Zehab set them! And he's dead! He was like a brother, and he knew his business. We should see evidence any minute now."

Moody and ill at ease, Aaghaa paced on the darkened bridge as Burak lit a cigarette, watching the research vessel light cluster fall off and away on *Konya K's* starboard quarter. He thought of Zehab. *I had to; he would not have made it and we cannot risk capture. He would have done the same.*

Aaghaa checked his watch, then took a night vision device from its cradle on the helm console. "It's time."

The men watched *Nauticos Card* continue away as if it were the only vessel on the high seas. Aaghaa had the night vision device glued to his face.

"There," he murmured, not taking his eyes off the ship. Detectable on the device, the ship gave off a trail of smoke from the stern.

"The first charge worked, she's smoking," Aaghaa said with satisfaction.

Burak took the device from Aaghaa to see for himself. As he looked through the intensifiers, he noted a flash, then another one, on the superstructure.

"Fire. She's on fire."

"Already? Zehab did good work."

"How far do you say the ship is now?" Burak asked.

"Fifteen, maybe twenty kilometers."

The men watched the flickering lights from *Nauticos Card* on the horizon. Ahead of the ship were two merchantmen, their lights faint. Aaghaa was transfixed.

"It appears she's slowing—good."

Though barely visible on the horizon, *Nauticos Card* had stopped, smoke pouring from her superstructure as *Konya K* continued on her northeast course. Burak checked his watch. "The second charge should have gone off by now."

On *Nauticos Card*, the remaining crew, trapped in their berthing compartment as they tried to contact watch-standers on the bridge or engine room for rescue, cried when they heard a muffled explosion below. The ship wallowed on the sea, no longer making way. Minutes later, one of the terrified crew noted a list—that increased.

As Aaghaa and Burak watched from 10 miles away, *Nauticos Card*, her engine room on fire and taking water, settled by her stern as flooding progressed throughout the ship. Inside the compartment, the lights extinguished as the desperate crew beat on the bulkheads and screamed for help that would not come. Soon the deck angle increased by the stern in what the first mate knew was the final plunge. Begging for deliverance from a merciful God and crying their last wishes to live, the men and women slid to the aft bulkhead and huddled together, holding flashlights and contemplating their terrified faces as *Nauticos Card* groaned her last. The horrifying sound of water gurgling on the other side of the steel bulkhead raised a last-ditch cry for rescue. When water entered the compartment from forward and slid down the deck to them, they were seized by horror.

"No!" a woman sobbed as her boyfriend comforted her. *"This is not supposed to be happening!"*

As the bow of *Nauticos Card* slipped below the waves, bubbles and debris marked the spot on the dark waters of the Mediterranean.

Two miles to the northwest, a black special forces helmet with night vision goggles affixed bobbed on the surface.

Chapter 2

Hangar Bay Two, USS *Valley Forge*, June 3, 2024
Bay of Naples

Resplendent in his Service Dress White uniform, Rear Admiral Jim Wilson saluted and said, "I relieve you, sir."

Rear Admiral Mat Garretson, Commander, Carrier Strike Group Eighteen, returned Wilson's salute and held it. "I stand relieved."

With that, total responsibility for the eight warships and over 7,000 men and women of CSG-18 flowed from Garretson to Wilson. Dropping their salutes, the two admirals shook hands and turned to Admiral Richard Buffington, Commander, Naval Forces Europe-Africa. Upholding the nautical tradition handed down through the ages, Garretson spoke first.

"Sir, I have been properly relieved as Commander, Carrier Strike Group Eighteen."

Buffington returned his salute, then shook hands with Garretson. "Mat, well done, and we're going to miss you out here!"

Garretson smiled at Buffington's sentiment, at the same time relieved and wistful that the burden of command was no longer his. "Thank you, sir."

Buffington turned to Wilson, expectant.

"Admiral, I'm reporting aboard as Commander, Carrier Strike Group Eighteen."

"Jim, congratulations!" Buffington said as he grabbed Wilson's arm while pumping his hand. "Welcome aboard."

On cue, Wilson turned to the dais podium to address the 200 guests seated in the audience. In the front row sat Mary Wilson, with daughter Brittany and son Derrick seated beside her. Derrick wore the uniform of an ensign, commissioned the previous May from Auburn University. Beside Derrick sat Wilson's mother and father, bursting with pride at their son's achievement. Behind Mary sat the strike group brain trust of Captain Kristin Teel, Commander, Carrier Air Wing Four, the captain of *Valley Forge* Steve "Huey" Morrison, the "Commodore" of the Strike Group surface combatants Captain Bert Braud, and the captain of the cruiser *Manila Bay*, Bob Dolan.

Wilson adjusted the microphone. "Chief of Staff, put the staff at ease."

CSG-18 Chief of Staff Captain Mark Meadows, a surface warrior, saluted Wilson, performed an about-face, and ordered the staff at ease before returning to face Wilson.

Wilson glanced at his notecard, looked at his family, and began.

"Admiral Buffington, Admiral Garretson, Captain Morrison, Commodore Braud, Captain Teel, men and women of Carrier Strike Group Eighteen, distinguished guests, ladies and gentlemen. It is indeed an honor and privilege to assume to command of this 'tip-of-the-spear' strike group while on an extended deployment, and here aboard *Valley Forge*, a ship I once served aboard, and in these very waters. To my longtime friend, Admiral Mat Garretson, I and all in the strike group are indebted to you for your dedication and leadership during this tour and culminating with many successful multi-national exercises in this region as we work with our NATO Allies."

Wilson glanced at Mary, who smiled and nodded slightly at her husband. *Keep it brief, you haven't done anything yet...*

Wilson detected her message and continued.

"Mat, all of us here thank you and wish you fair winds…as you proceed to your next duty station at the five-sided wind tunnel, where you will surely receive lessons—administered daily—on why you wish to return to sea."

Knowing officers in the audience tittered at Wilson's reference to the Pentagon, where a thankful Wilson had just left. He glanced at the staff officers standing in ranks—and resumed his speech.

"To the men and women of Carrier Strike Group Eighteen, and especially to the assembled staff here today, I promise to do as Admiral Garretson did, to *take care of you* by ensuring that you have the tools and training to do your jobs well and faithfully in our shared service. It is an honor to be your shipmate on this magnificent flagship as together we preserve the peace and demonstrate our commitments to allies and deterrence to potential foes by our deployed presence here in this region. Admiral Buffington, Strike Group Eighteen remains ready, as it did upon arrival in the Mediterranean months ago, to answer the bell to any and all national tasking. But first, all of us can enjoy a few more days of liberty before we go back to sea, where sailors belong."

As Wilson returned to his seat, the crowd burst into applause, and Admiral Buffington rose to shake hands. "Nice job Jim, under five minutes!"

Wilson smiled. "I see all that food over there and I believe everyone else does too!"

After the benediction, Wilson took to the podium to dismiss the staff. "Chief of Staff, take charge and carry out the plan of the day!"

"Aye, aye, Admiral!" Meadows answered. As he turned to dismiss the staff, the ceremony ended, and the Navy Band struck the first notes of *Anchors Aweigh*. Waiting for Buffington to depart the dais first, Garretson stepped over to Wilson.

"Great words, Flip!"

"They were short."

"That's why they were great!" Garretson smiled. "I know you are going to have fun."

"It's a superb staff and strike group you are handing over, Mat. Thanks for making my job easier."

"Oh, don't mention it. Have fun."

The crowd mingled among their chairs as the three flag officers waded in to accept their well wishes and congratulations. Wilson accepted the handshakes and smiles as he kept Mary in his scan, moving toward her as he mingled with the guests and his parents. His father smiled as he approached.

"I'm so glad God let me live to see this day! So proud of you, James."

Wilson hugged him and kissed his beaming mother. "Thanks, Mom and Dad! So glad you're here!"

Mary had her back to her husband as she chatted with Olive, who came to attention and saluted as he approached. "Congratulations, sir."

Wilson returned her salute and shook Olive's hand as he embraced Mary with his free arm. She spun and hugged him.

"Well, *Flip*, you are back in your element. Good job, dear."

"Thanks for your secret coded message, delivered just in time. And Olive, here we are again, and look at you. *CAG Four* your own self! *Tomahawk*-freakin'-lead."

"*James!*" Mary scolded.

Olive smiled. "Admiral, welcome to our nice, calm, and *peaceful* summer Med cruise. I'll have you on the flight schedule once we get underway for an *uneventful* day hop."

"Thanks CAG. With you, I hope."

"So she can keep an eye on you?" Mary asked. Olive smiled at her and winked.

"It's her air wing." Wilson responded. "Hey, Ensign Wilson!"

Derrick saluted his father, who returned it before enveloping his son in a hug.

"Congratulations, Dad. Love going to your ceremonies, and your speech, Dad, was…oh my gosh, totally sick! Gettysburg address stuff, Dad. You slayed!"

"Get out!" Wilson laughed as he embraced Brittany, now 20 and almost as tall as him.

"So glad you are here, sweetie."

"Wouldn't miss it, Dad, especially in Italy!"

"That's the only reason?"

"No Dad…but it's sure nice."

As Wilson and his family accepted the congratulations of the guests, many of them strike group ship captains and Air Wing squadron commanders, the crowd moved to the buffet tables while mess specialists walked among them with trays of hors d'oeuvres. Mary chatted with Amie Garretson, whom she had known for years, while Derrick and Brittany caught up with Lieutenant Frank "Trigger" Rawley, a neighborhood friend during the Oceana years who was now a nugget pilot in the VFA-64 *Ravens*. Wilson enjoyed the company of familiar friends and new ones just made, while keeping an eye out for where his new boss, Admiral Buffington, was at all times. As the crowd thinned, Wilson found a moment with him.

"Jim, we're in an important operational theater. With the war in Ukraine, it's no longer just a liberty stop while transiting to and from the Suez Canal. It's more like the 70's and 80's when we operated two strike groups—we called them battle groups then—at a time here. This could always be a rough neighborhood, but the threat then was the Soviet Union. Now, it's the Russians whom we must contain up there in the Black Sea, the Israeli situation, and fights between all the nations of the eastern Med about undersea resources and economic advantage."

Wilson nodded. "May I call on you, sir, to get more before we depart next week?"

"Would love to, but I've gotta be in Brussels Monday and I'm slammed this weekend. We'll chat once you're underway and besides, I'd like to come out and visit at sea."

"Open invitation, sir."

"Naples duty is nice, and if I never see the Pentagon again I'll be fine, but a day spent at sea is a good day, and not many chances remain for me."

"Would you like to go flying with us once you come out to visit?"

Buffington smiled. "No, thanks! I'd be sinker the rest of the day! No, just meeting with you and your commanders, walking around and pressing the flesh with sailors is a day well spent."

"Look forward, sir."

Buffington looked at his watch. "Okay…shall we depart in thirty minutes for the beach?"

"Yes, sir. Let me check out with my CoS and herd the family to the fantail."

Wilson made eye-contact with Mary and gave her the two-finger run-up signal, her cue to say her good-byes and gather the family. He grabbed Derrick. "C'mon, time to go ashore, and we're not missing this boat."

Wilson led Derrick up to his in-port cabin, where they changed out of their uniforms and into civilian clothes. With a last check with the duty officer, Wilson led them back down to the hangar bay where Mary and Brittany waited.

"Ladies, let's go ashore."

At the fantail, Wilson spied the NAVEUR barge standing off, while a liberty ferry with hundreds of *Valley Forge* sailors cast off their lines for the trip to fleet landing. Alone to starboard was Mat Garretson, in civilian clothes with a backpack, an old sailor now, watching and waiting alone for one last trip ashore to end his final carrier deployment. As Mary and the kids enjoyed the view of the bay, Wilson walked up to him.

"Mat…tell me what it's like, now that it's over."

Garretson smiled. "Thirty-one years, nine deployments…and here I am standing on the fantail waiting to go ashore like I did when I was a jay gee…just yesterday."

"You'll be back."

"Yeah, maybe they'll give me another star, who knows, but any more times underway from here on out will be as a visitor."

Wilson smiled as he watched Garretson's eyes take in one last scene, and was reminded that in another year he, too, would be facing the end of his sea days.

With the ferry clear, the barge moved in to moor at the camel platform and take Admirals Buffington, Garretson, and Wilson ashore. As Wilson picked up his bag, his Flag Aide, Lieutenant Scott "Skweez" Toppel walked up. His eyes met those of Garretson.

"Admiral…"

"Skweez, whatever you've got…" Garretson pointed to Wilson.

"Forgive me, sir," the aide said. "Habit…Admiral Wilson, a Greek Research vessel sank last night about 200 miles east of the eastern tip of Crete. Search is ongoing, no survivors yet."

"Does Admiral Buffington know?"

"Yes, sir, his staff informed him."

"Very well, thanks."

After Skweez saluted and turned, Wilson looked at his watch. "Only took one hour for the first crisis."

"Easy day!" Garretson said smiling, then changed his tone. "Wonder if they got off a distress signal. Surprising they've found no survivors yet, the Med is full of traffic…someone would have seen a distress signal on the horizon."

"Yeah—maybe some kind of catastrophic explosion, or a chemical they were carrying."

"The Greeks have maintained an almost constant presence in that area since we've been here, as have the Turks. They are just two of the players—everyone around here wants what's on the sea floor."

The Officer of the Deck approached. "Admirals, we're boarding now."

The flag staff, Olive with several of her squadron CO's, and the Wilson family descended two decks to the floating platform "camel" to board the NAVEUR admiral's barge, a 40-foot covered fiberglass launch with kitchen and wet bar. Once ashore, the Wilsons planned to spend a few days in Sorrento.

Garretson and Wilson waited for Buffington, who finally arrived at the fantail.

"Gentlemen, my apologies. Jim, lead the way."

Wilson took the lead and stopped at the top of the ladder where the Officer of the Deck awaited.

Wilson came to attention. "I'm Admiral Wilson and I have permission to go ashore."

"Very well, sir!"

Wilson, followed by Garretson descended the ladder with their bags as the ship's 1MC sounded six bells followed by, "*Carrier Strike Group Eighteen, departing. Admiral, United States Navy, departing.*"

Buffington followed them down the ladder with his aide in front as eight bells sounded. "*Commander, U. S. Naval Forces Europe-Africa, departing.*"

The officers joined their wives, who with Olive and Mark Meadows waited in the stern as Derrick and Brittany sat with the junior officers up forward. *Valley Forge* line handlers cast off lines that the barge sailors pulled in as the coxswain backed off. Clear, he spun the wheel and gunned the engine that rumbled the cutter all the way to fleet landing.

After five minutes of small talk dominated by Buffington, he motioned Wilson to follow him up to the cockpit. "C'mon Jim, let's chat."

Pleasure craft darted about the sun-splashed Bay of Naples, most of them curious about *Valley Forge* as the great ship rode at anchor. Unable to keep their eyes off the long steel slab that bristled with airplane tails, Wilson and Buffington studied it for a moment before Buffington got down to business.

"Jim, you know that Greece and Turkey hate each other's guts, and this Greek research vessel situation has got me concerned, but we cannot show favoritism to either side in any of your dealings with them. You've got an exercise with the Greeks next week, and airspace is job one. If your flyboys and girls fly over something they shouldn't—and there are islands with 12-mile circles around them all over the Aegean—hot lava is going to be poured on me, followed quickly by you."

Wilson smiled and nodded. "Yes, sir."

"*Caesar's wife*, Jim. Decorum and diplomacy are job one, and that's your job, Admiral. If Greek or Turk flags contact you, don't delegate the response to your staff. *You* answer them, and *you* bow and scrape, *you* say mea culpa if there is any hiccup, and *you* are responsible to *me* for keeping relations with both of them friendly and accommodating. After the Greek exercise, you'll get a port visit to Antalya; you gladhand and be the gracious host, then an exercise with the Turks. And keep it all vanilla, Jim, don't show them anything."

"Aye, aye sir," Wilson answered, uneasy that Buffington had left out Wilson's immediate superior, his long-time mentor Vice Admiral Randy "The Big Unit" Johnson, who was unable to make the ceremony. Perhaps an oversight that Buffington neglected Johnson? Wilson's instincts thought not.

"You call me first if you have any questions. Oh, and another thing…I'm working with Norfolk to get two Littoral Combat Ships out here as part of your strike group, part of a rapid-deployment proof of concept. My people will coordinate with yours on the schedule and integration. Wish we had them for the exercise next week; they're outfitted with Naval Strike Missiles, and they are going to be a game-changer for the LCS, so get your staff smart on the NSM and put those ships through the ringer when they get here. We've gotta test this concept and Washington is watching."

"Aye, aye, sir, we'll stand by and look forward to integrating them."

Buffington turned to survey the glorious bay, with Mount Vesuvius towering over it and the city of Naples that rested on its slopes. "I sure do miss this…thanks for hosting me today, Jim. Let's go below to join the girls and no more shop talk."

As the men descended the small ladder to join the others, Wilson thought of Buffington's last comment. *Call* me *first*. He put it out of his mind as he sat next to Mary, enjoying Med liberty on his first day in command.

Hours later in the picturesque town of Sorrento, Jim and Mary Wilson sipped cappuccino at a café that overlooked the Bay of Naples. Riding at anchor, *Valley Forge* was over ten miles distant yet still dominated the harbor.

Wilson lowered his cup as he surveyed the expanse of blue sea. "Feels good to relax."

"You just took over!" Mary said, bemused.

"But I'm on liberty—with my wife!"

"Then be on liberty. That ship you can't take your eyes off of is far away now, and with good people in charge. They're fine, you're fine. See, it's not going anywhere. Now, you haven't said a word about my outfit."

"Love it!" Wilson quickly answered as Mary rolled her eyes in disdain. She then took the opportunity to ask a question she had long wondered about.

"Okay Flip Wilson…you made it. Strike Group Command. You're finally 'the admiral' now."

Wilson focused his attention on her as she smiled. She asked, "Has it been worth it?"

Wilson shifted his focus back to the sea.

"James, I'm not upset, but you're at twenty-nine years. You made flag…"

"It was never a goal…"

"I know, but here you are. Looking back…was it worth it?"

Wilson held eye contact with Mary as he considered his answer.

"Yes. And here's why. In every job I ever had I thought that if given the chance, I could do my boss's job."

"Better than him?"

"No…well, maybe…okay, yes…but I could do it. The Navy keeps promoting me, and this job—at sea—is a place where I can do some good."

Mary grinned. "We've been trying to get out of the Navy for the past 16 years."

"And failing big time," Wilson added.

They both looked out on the blue Tyrrhenian Sea and contemplated it. Wilson took another sip, forcing himself not to look at the carrier.

"James, honestly, what's next?"

Wilson grimaced and shifted in his chair. "Baby, I—we—just got here."

"No, *what do you want?* Four stars? It's okay if you do, if that's the path you want to go down, the path that I and the kids must also go down, but if you're just going along for the ride with no plan until the next set of orders…"

Wilson noticed the heat of the late afternoon sun on his chest. Soon it would be under the awning. He shifted his chair back to remain in the shade longer. Mary waited for an answer.

"I could retire next year, and we could live wherever we want."

"James, I know, know all that…but *what. Do. You. Want?*"

"I want a bottle of wine."

"I'm not letting you off the hook. I want to know for *my* sanity. Stay in Norfolk, back to Washington? Hawaii? Tampa? I can handle all that. And I can handle retirement, another exciting life. They are both exciting, but I just want to know what you are thinking and what to expect."

"They can fire me at any time for any reason."

"I know! Then retire."

When Wilson looked back out to sea, Mary shook her head.

"Okay, then stay. I'll support you either way, but I want to know what you are thinking now. I'm in this too."

Wilson turned to her and held her gaze.

"Okay. I want to stay until they tell me to go home. *Right now* that's what I want. And it could change. But *right now* I'm excited to be here. That's the truth! In a few days I'm going to say goodbye to you and the kids for the 100th time in my career and go out there, and I want to go. I love you no less, but I'm arrogant enough to think that I can have a positive impact on this Strike Group. We'll see what happens next year, and maybe—probably—I'll hate whatever shore staff duty they give me, but if it's still a fun challenge I'll play the game. So long as you play it with me. And baby, this is the last cruise. When it's over I'll miss it; Mat Garretson got a little emotional thinking about it this morning as he left, but just for a moment. He's excited to go home, as I will be when it's my time."

Mary smiled and placed her hands on the table. "Okay, then! I'm good. We'll play the game and let the chips fall where they may."

Wilson nodded. "You know that it's cutthroat now."

"Yep, and I'm certain that at least one friendship will be lost, but I'll move with you and go to the Navy League things and the spouse events. All I ask for is a front row seat."

Wilson gave her a look, unsure of her message.

"James, I mean it. I've been on this ride with you for 25 years, and I'm ready to keep going in this career. You just tell me when you stop playing the game, and we'll stop together."

"I will…deal."

"So…when are you going to order us some wine?"

"Right now," Wilson smiled.

He got the attention of the waiter, who soon poured them glasses of Sangiovese, leaving the bottle.

Just then, Derrick and Brittany appeared from inside the restaurant.

"What? Have you two been inside this whole time?"

"Yes, watching you and Dad," Derrick answered. "Are we moving again?"

Mary answered for Wilson. "Not this week...right, dear?"

Wilson nodded. "Not for the foreseeable future."

"Which is at least a month, great. Hey, we're going to join Trigger and some of the other guys from the *Ravens* over in Capri."

Wilson noticed Brittany's bare arms and the hemline of her sundress. Derrick carried a backpack.

"Who did you say?"

Derrick had anticipated this. "Our longtime family friend Lieutenant Frank Rawley and the new guy pilot and the intel ensign. Five of us, and *buddy system*, Dad. Brit's a big girl, and we'll come back before sunset."

"Okay, good, maybe we can go to dinner as a family. Dad's treat," Mary said.

"Thanks, Dad!" Brittany said as she kissed Wilson on his forehead, wheeling to follow her brother before any more questions were asked. They soon melted into the crowd as they headed toward the marina.

Wilson watched them, pensive. Mary detected what he was thinking.

"James, they're adults."

"Yeah, but our baby girl is going on liberty with the *Ravens?*"

"Something I should know about?"

"And probably wearing one piece of a two-piece bathing suit."

"James...we brought them up. Brittany knows what's right and wrong. They'll be back and we'll go out to dinner."

"The *Ravens* drank like fish in my day."

"Oh, do tell," Mary said as she inspected her husband.

"I'm just a dad, protective."

Mary touched his forearm. "We've known Frank since he was playing little league and mowing the lawn when you were gone, and I'm sure the other officers are safe. She's of drinking age here, and she's the daughter of the freaking admiral! She'll be lucky if any of the boys even *talk* to her!"

"Good," Wilson muttered.

"Oh, lighten the heck up...and pour me another glass, *Admiral Wilson.*"

Chapter 3

Waterfront, Antalya, Turkey, June 5, 2024

Burak sipped his espresso as the sun touched the western ridge above the harbor. *Konya K* was at the distant wharf, her self-loading crane lifting another container onto a waiting truck chassis. He was alone at the restaurant terrace that overlooked the bay and the Gulf of Antalya to the south, yellow orbs of the setting sun stationary on his dark sunglasses as he studied the activity at the port. He glanced at this watch.

Late. Was it too much to ask? Starving, Burak would give the courier two more minutes. If they missed the rendezvous, they could find him on Burak's time, not theirs. He needed a break from Aaghaa and cursed him; this meeting had his fingerprints of incompetence.

The courier arrived—*Selam!*—and Burak nodded in return as he motioned the younger man to join him. Burak forced a smile for appearances.

"Three minutes late," he said softly, his smile betraying his disgust. The courier ignored him and motioned to the waiter for espresso and water *sin* gas. Another reason to scorn the man, Burak thought. He orders like an American.

"Do you like this restaurant, *arkadasi?*"

Burak bristled. "Never been here before, but my patience is quite thin. May I suggest that you pass what you must and leave, and do not ever refer to me as *friend* again."

The courier showed no emotion as he lit a cigarette and scanned the horizon. Burak watched him—*he has no idea who he is dealing with*—yet was amused by the courier's smug manner. The thought of toying with the boy and inviting him for a stroll, where he could suddenly push the weakling into an alleyway and drive a fist into his solar plexus was appealing, but gnawing hunger precluded it. Another time.

"Do you have something for me?"

Saying nothing, the courier pulled a small envelope from his man-purse. Handing it to Burak, he took in the sunset view, avoiding eye contact. *An arrogant child,* Burak thought. *Children must learn.*

Burak glanced inside and saw a folded sheet of paper—instructions—accompanied by a money clip of ₺200 notes.

"Turkish lira?"

"5,000 lira. Pocket money for your meal and taxicab."

Burak nodded. "Two hundred euro. I am hungrier than that."

"You are to report to the address in the instructions, where you will receive further instructions."

"Very well. You may leave."

"*You* may leave," the courier muttered back, still not looking at him.

Burak smiled as took the envelope—and devised a new plan. Yes, his meal could wait. Leaving lire coins for the espresso, he stood and spoke. "It's on me. Good evening, *arkadasi.*"

The courier ignored Burak as he turned, and out of his peripheral vision ensured the operator left the restaurant. He sipped his espresso and contemplated Burak, who had snubbed him as an underling. *Dumb muscle*, the courier thought...*a mere soldier.* He would show the soldier who worked for whom.

Finished, he gathered his satchel and stepped out through the dining room and into the street, noting the admiring glances of the diners, pegging him as a man of means.

Stepping outside, his minibike was not where he had left it. Now panicked, he scanned left and right. *Nothing!*

Frantic with fear—*was it stolen?*—he set off down the hill to the left, scanning the street side to side at the minibikes parked outside the shops and cafés. In a side street he saw it, lying on the sidewalk.

Relieved, the courier strode to the bike and bent over to pick it up.

Sudden and searing pain to his spinal cord collapsed him on top of the handlebars. Before he could comprehend, he was lifted and shoved against the stucco wall of the doorway, knocking the wind out of him.

His mind raced, still unable to process what was happening. When Burak turned him, he received a punch to the kidney followed by a knee to the groin, which collapsed the courier a second time.

As the man gasped in pain, Burak zip-tied his hands in front of him. Delirious, the courier felt a cloth around his mouth and grunted when it was pulled tight, gagging him. Burak sat him up against the wall, and zip-tied his shoelaces.

"Your training is deficient, *arkadasi*, or you would not condescend to me as you would an small child." The courier, panting through the gag, could only watch him with wide eyes.

"Are you familiar with this infidel saying from the religion of Abraham? *When you sit down to dine with a ruler, note what is before you, and put a knife in your throat if you possess a great appetite.* Have you ever heard of this?"

The terrified courier nodded, struggling to breathe.

"Yes, but you seem to have forgotten this lesson, and only twenty minutes ago. You are a *courier* and nothing more. Do you think you will forget this?"

The man shook his head, his chest heaving.

"Good...but the lesson must be reinforced, for your own benefit."

Pulling a pair of hand-held cable cutters from his jacket's inside pocket, Burak grabbed the little finger of the courier's left hand and cut at the first knuckle.

Searing pain exploded into the courier's brain as he cried against the gag, his right hand holding his left to stop the bleeding. Burak lit a cigarette as the writhing courier whimpered in the fetal position.

"There now...a wound must be treated."

As he exhaled smoke into the courier's face, Burak stuck the end of the cigarette into the open finger, cauterizing the bleeding stump.

The courier gagged as his agony continued, tears exploding from his eyes as open nerve endings transmitted the pain to his brain stem.

Burak picked the fingertip out of the gutter and held it in front of the courier, who convulsed in torment.

"If you see a doctor soon, he may be able to repair this small mishap. Sadly, you must have gotten it caught in the wheel spokes...must be more careful. Yes, we *must* be more careful." He placed the bloody flesh next to the courier's face.

The courier panted through the gag and nodded his understanding.

"Next time, *arkadasi*, another body part. Do not let there be a next time."

Burak stood and smoothed his clothes as he looked down on the man. Lighting another cigarette, he walked to the street and down the hill toward the port.

"Gentlemen, the admiral."

Jim Wilson stepped into the *Valley Forge* flag mess as his staff pushed away from the table and stood at attention. He recognized two familiar faces.

"Seats, please," he said, and strode to his place at the middle of the table next to his Chief of Staff Mark Meadows as he and the others took their places. Meadows began.

"Admiral, welcome to Carrier Strike Group Eighteen. The staff is assembled, and the floor is yours, sir." Wilson nodded and remained seated.

"Thanks CoS, and ladies and gentlemen, good morning. Let me begin by congratulating you on a first-class ceremony last week. The staff looked sharp and the ceremony went off without a hiccup…or at least none that I am aware of."

Several at the table snickered, which Wilson expected.

"Yes, none that I am aware of," he added, smiling.

Helping to break the ice, Meadows jumped in. "Lots of paddling under the surface, sir."

"No doubt…regardless, it was a fine send off for Admiral Garretson and a great first impression for me.

Wilson brought his fingers to his lips as he gathered his thoughts.

"Right now, we are at the midpoint of this deployment, a routine summer Med cruise with another liberty port in two weeks. Once we run through Messina and get into the Ionian Sea, we'll exercise with the Greek Navy and Air Force, an exercise you've planned. I assure you I am not here to change it or take the controls or inject myself. My expectation is that you will maximize training for the strike group assets and the Greek forces we engage with; they need training too. My role is to engage with my Greek counterparts, and of course, we'll host them and do a bunch of dog-and-pony shows for them and whoever else Sixth Fleet tasks us to entertain. My job is to make your jobs easier, and so I ask to be kept informed. I've been around long enough to know that the first report is always wrong, and I'm quick to forgive honest mistakes, which we all make. That's all I've got, and I look forward to meeting and working with each one of you. CoS, take charge and carry out the plan of the day…and I need to see you."

"Aye, aye, sir," Meadows answered. As Wilson pushed away from the table, the others rose to attention.

"Seats please, everyone, I'm good. Relax and carry on."

Meadows motioned to the door that led to the conference room. "Admiral, we can meet in here. Would you like the *two* and the *three* to join us?"

"Yes, they need to hear this too."

As Meadows called over the staff Intel and Operations officers to the conference room, Wilson stepped inside and stood at his place at the head of the table, facing a large flat screen.

"Admiral, this is our Assistant Intel Officer, Lieutenant Commander Shane Duncan."

Wilson smiled and extended his hand. "Hello, shipmate."

Shane beamed as she shook hands. "Admiral Wilson, it's so nice to serve with you again!"

Meadows suppressed a grin. "Shane told me you had served together before, sir."

"Yes, in the *Firebirds* aboard *Coral Sea*. How long has it been Shane, twelve years?"

"Yes, sir!"

"And you're a commander now; to think that I knew you when."

Shane blushed. Wilson noted that her schoolgirl persona had not changed, despite the oak leaves she wore on her khaki uniform collar.

"A memorable time, sir. I'll never forget Commander Schofield."

"Yes," Wilson nodded. "None of us will ever forget Annie."

Meadows continued with the introductions.

"And Admiral, you already know our three, Captain Smoke Offenhausen."

Wilson beamed. "Hello Smoke, great to be with you again. How's Psycho?"

"You too, sir. She's doin' great and says hi."

"How many kids now?"

"Four, and the oldest is in ninth grade. And she hasn't lost a step, sir. They are in fear of her, and so am I most of the time."

Wilson chuckled at the thought of Psycho ruling the roost. "Please pass my hello."

"Will do, sir. Welcome aboard."

Mindful of the time, Meadows maneuvered Wilson to his seat.

"Admiral, please be seated. Shall we call up the status board?"

"Yes, please...an overhead of the eastern Med should do."

With Shane at the keyboard, soon a digital map of the Mediterranean appeared on the flat screen attached to the starboard bulkhead.

"Is this good, sir?" she asked.

"Yes, but please open it up...Crete to Israel."

The cursor formed a rectangle and once released, the chart showed lat/long gridlines as well as sea lanes and air navigation routes of the eastern Mediterranean Sea. With another click Shane brought up the Automatic Identification System (AIS) information of all the ships in the field of view, forming lanes of digital tracks that led to the Suez Canal and from Libya to the Aegean around Crete.

"Okay, that's good. Are we cleared secret?"

"Yes sir," Meadows answered. Wilson pulled out a folded white sheet of printer paper.

"Got this 'personal for' message from Admiral Buffington twenty minutes ago. Tensions between Turkey and Greece just spiked; that research ship that sank a few days ago…the Greeks blame Turkey."

Meadows returned to his seat. "Did they cite any proof in the P4, sir?"

"Admiral Buffington didn't say, and he and *we* may not know, but as far as we're concerned, we haf'ta walk a tightrope next week as we exercise with one NATO ally on the doorstep of another NATO ally who hates the first ally's guts. Smoke, where will we be?"

Smoke stepped to the screen and grabbed a pointer hanging next to it. "Admiral, we'll start the exercise with the Hellenic Air Force here in the Ionian west of Crete, work along the island's southern coast over two days, then go up past Rhodes and into the Aegean. Five days of ops up here."

A surprised Wilson saw Smoke point to the northern Aegean. "Up *there?* That's a little closet of sea space." Wilson said.

"And airspace sir. We must stay 12 miles off all these islands or the Greeks are going to lose their minds. We already know if we violate the airspace by so much as a wingtip they are going to Washington on a direct line—State Department—and then it's going to roll downhill."

"Until the hot lava is poured on us," Wilson surmised, remembering Buffington's warning.

"Yes, sir," Meadows added, "by Sixth Fleet. He's been livin' in our ass most of the deployment."

"Why is that?" Wilson asked, not letting on that he had served with Vice Admiral Johnson—*The Big Unit*—and held him in high regard.

"I think he's afraid of Admiral Buffington, sir, and—we can speak frankly—he would call us two or three times a week. *'What are you doing now? Why are you so close to Libya or Malta?'* We're on our published track and exercising as per the approved instruction, but he—or his staff—is nervous that they aren't in control of us and we are going to do something to get that lava poured on them."

"Doesn't sound like the Randy Johnson I know," Wilson said.

The room remained silent.

"Then it must be his staff. CoS, please write up a P4 message and invite him out here as we pass through Messina. Offer to send a *Rhino* to Sigonella and fly him out here in that. Will do him good."

"Aye, aye, sir."

Wilson continued.

"And regarding our two NATO allies, accusations are flying, tensions are rising, so Admiral Buffington wants us to be on our best behavior. That means do not mess with them, and especially the Turks who think we favor the Greeks. Don't let our subs surprise and embarrass them, defer to their tactical commanders when they have control of us, and don't let the air wing thump their small boys. Smoke, have you and Olive had this conversation?"

"We have sir, and she's going into each ready room to deliver this message and the airspace message personally."

"Great. Now Shane, I'd like to find out more about this research vessel that went down. Please make me smart on it and what everyone thinks they know about it tomorrow."

"Will do, sir."

Just then, the 1MC crackled, followed by the bosun's pipe. *"Ta-weet!* Underway, shift colors."

Wilson placed his palms on the table. "Alright, everyone. Great port call, and let's have a great at-sea period until the next one. I'm going to the flag bridge; Mark, could you please have a cup of black coffee delivered to me and a tech to teach me how to use that electronic display by my seat?"

"Aye, aye sir. I'll be up with the message board and…"

With a hand wave Wilson interrupted him. "No, you're welcome to come up, but I want to watch us head out to sea and think about the next two weeks."

"Aye, aye, sir," Meadows responded, wise enough to hold off on sending the technician so his new boss could think alone while he surveyed Naples Bay from the flag bridge, and contemplate his new role as Strike Group Commander.

Chapter 4

Naval Air Station Sigonella, Sicily, June 6, 2024

Following the linesman's directions, Captain "Olive" Teel taxied her FA-18F *Super Hornet* up to Base Ops as blazing sunlight shone on the Plain of Catania. With Mount Etna in the distance, she turned on the linesman signal and crept ahead on the yellow line to her parking spot. Shutting down the *Rhino's* left engine, she waited. On the flagpole yardarm she noted a blue flag with the three white stars of a vice admiral.

Soon the door to the ops building opened, and after a short delay, a large man in full flight gear with his helmet visor down walked through it, followed by a captain in summer whites. She watched the captain salute—returned by the larger man—and turn to a lieutenant holding a garment bag and speak in his ear, so as to be heard over the din of Olive's one turning engine. He took the garment bag, and with that in one hand and a worn helmet bag in the other, he walked toward Olive's jet, which had the boarding ladder down.

Behind Olive, a sailor prepared the backseat for the passenger before he descended the boarding ladder and stood at parade rest. As he approached the jet, Vice Admiral Randy Johnson smiled and waved at Olive. The sailor then came to attention and saluted Johnson, who returned it. Together they stowed his garment bag in an open avionics bay, before Johnson bounded up the boarding ladder and lowered himself into the *Rhino's* spacious backseat—without flight controls. The sailor followed to help hook up his connections and strap him in as Olive studied the Sigonella departure procedure.

Olive's headset clicked. "ICS check."

Olive keyed the ICS. "Loud and clear, Admiral, how me?"

"Gotcha the same. Hello, Olive."

"Welcome aboard, Admiral."

"How far is the ship?"

"About 100 miles...north of the Lipari Islands. We'll fly cyclic ops tonight and go through Messina early tomorrow."

"Great. Looking forward to a relaxing 24 hours at sea."

"Relaxing, sir?"

"When you have three stars, trust me, a day at sea is relaxing."

While they spoke, the linesman stowed the ladder and buttoned up the jet. On Olive's left side he signaled his readiness to start the left engine.

"Starting the left, sir," Olive said.

"Roger that," Johnson responded. Olive gave the two-finger run-up signal as she cranked the left engine.

Once Olive got the engine going, she again keyed the ICS. "Canopy."

"Clear," Johnson responded. At that, Olive lowered the canopy, and once down and locked, the environmental control system whooshed to life in their enclosed Plexiglas cocoon. In the back, Johnson energized the avionics displays the same way he had as a lieutenant flight instructor.

With the wheel chocks pulled, the linesman saluted and the aviators returned it as they taxied past and out to the taxiway. Olive keyed the mic.

"Sigonella Ground, Navy Alpha Hotel one-zero-zero taxi one *Super Hornet* from the Navy line, requesting clearance to USS ship."

A ground controller with an Italian accent responded. "Navy Alpha Hotel one-zero-zero, Sigonella Ground, turn right and taxi to hold short of runway one-zero left, cleared as filed. When you hold short, contact tower on UHF three-three-seven point six-zero, have a good day."

Olive read back the instructions to the ground controller, then, on the ICS, ran through the takeoff checklist. She got to the last item.

"Eject select—aft initiate."

Johnson answered. "Aft initiate...all set back here."

Cleared for takeoff on the right runway, Olive taxied into position and held the brakes as she went to 80% on the engines, which screamed behind them.

"Here we go, sir...eighty percent power...good oil, no flight control X'es...you good sir?"

"All set."

In one motion Olive released the brakes and pushed the throttles to max, the jet jumping ahead as pressure on their spinal cords registered 44,000 pounds of thrust from the two F-414 engines.

"Good nozzles," Olive said on the ICS, the sound of their breathing mixed in with the roar of the engines in burner behind them. Seconds later they had rolled 2,000 feet and were at rotation airspeed.

"Here we go..."

Olive lifted the nose and the jet gracefully climbed into the air. She slapped up the gear and flaps as she had hundreds of times in her long career, then commanded the radar into search before she had even broken 100 feet in altitude.

"Catania Departure, Navy Alpha Hotel one-zero-zero with you passing 500 out of Sigonella."

"Navy Alpha Hotel one-zero-zero, Catania, radar contact, turn left to heading zero-three-zero and climb and maintain ten thousand."

"Alpha Hotel one-zero-zero...and Catania, Alpha Hotel one-zero-zero canceling IFR at this time, request flight following until past Etna."

"Navy Alpha Hotel one-zero-zero, IFR cancelation received, proceed visual and we'll follow you until past Etna Mountain."

"Alpha Hotel one-zero-zero, thanks."

Responsible for her own aircraft avoidance, Olive steadied them toward the Strait of Messina as she leveled off at 11,500 feet with a full view of smoky Mt. Etna looming on their left side. Off hot mic, she engaged the ICS.

"Admiral, I wish I could give you the airplane."

"So do I, but I had my day," Johnson said, savoring another moment flying in a carrier jet, and conscious that it might be his last time, ever.

Olive pointed to their ten o'clock. "That's Mother on the TACAN, ninety-eight miles."

"Roger."

As bright sunlight filled their cockpit and radiated off the remaining patches of snow along the cone of the volcano, both aviators enjoyed the Sicilian countryside that featured tightly packed villages, whitewashed from centuries of sun, scattered among the green fields. Surrounding the island, dozens of vessels plied the blue water of the Mediterranean, many on their way to or from Messina as puffy white clouds hovered above. Over her right shoulder Olive noted the shoreline of Augusta Bay, where the great Athenian Empire was lost almost 2,500 years ago.

Olive took them over Messina as The Big Unit fiddled with the targeting FLIR. Ships choked the waterway going through it and across it. Olive studied the white tuft of smoke that emanated from Etna, sleeping now. At 300 knots indicated, they floated past the strait north of the island.

"When's our recovery time?" Johnson asked.

"Fifteen hundred, sir...we've got about thirty minutes and I would say two thousand pounds of play fuel."

"Okay, let's do some sight-seeing."

"Roger that, sir. Hang on."

Olive whipped the jet over on its left wing and pulled down, boresighting two of the smaller islands in the Lipari chain as she rolled out into a 20-degree dive.

"Sure have missed this, Olive. Enjoy it now…you never know."

In the descent, Olive checked in with Strike Control aboard *Valley Forge*, and leveled them at 500 feet above the waves. Ahead, a small fishing trawler motored away from them, unaware.

Olive offset left, and then rolled up on the right wing as they thundered past the boat, trailing seagulls and a seine net.

"Let's check out Stromboli," Johnson said. From the front seat, Olive nodded. It struck her that they were two senior aviators out enjoying the scene as they would have as lieutenants on a solo surface search hop away from the ship. *Screw around and call it training.* Alone in their thoughts, both realized it might indeed be Johnson's last opportunity to fly in a *Rhino*. Olive knew he was savoring every moment of this, which, for a short moment, gave her pause.

The dark volcanic cone of Stromboli loomed ahead, jutting out of the sea with small settlements clinging to the rocky edge. A ferry motored to the village of San Vincenzo on the island's eastern shore as the *Rhino* zipped over it, the obligatory airshow. Olive kept them off the beach a respectable distance but close enough to enjoy the stunning view. She held the turn until pointed at *Valley Forge*, 40 miles distant. White-hulled fishing boats and pleasure craft plied the waters all around them.

"Thanks for that, Olive."

"I won't tell anyone, sir."

"Yes, our little secret."

Olive climbed to 2,000 feet and slowed as she checked in with Marshal. On the northwest horizon at this distance the carrier appeared as a smudge, but unmistakable.

At ten miles, Olive radioed "see you at ten," and dropped the tailhook. Switching tower, they entered the overhead circle and looked for a formation of jets at their altitude, two *Rhinos* they would join on to come into the break.

Valley Forge steamed south as she trailed a wake in the light winds. On deck, sixteen jets lined up behind the catapults in a familiar pattern. Olive saw a section of *Rhinos* on her one o'clock.

"There they are sir; we'll join them as dash three. Skipper O'Donnell is leading."

"Irish O'Donnell? Does he know you went to get me?"

"He does, sir."

"Wow…he was just a nugget when we were in the *Bucs* together, after the 2008 cruise."

"All grown up now, and one of my stronger CO's."

"He was quick to learn."

Letting the formation float in front of them, Olive maneuvered to get on the bearing line of the two *Super Hornets* as the launch commenced below and more jets entered low holding in lazy fuel-saving turns as they all assessed the deck below and each other across the circle. Olive crossed under the wingman FA-18F, receiving a thumbs-up from the WSO in back, and flew a loose formation on the outside. In the lead jet, Commander Gary O'Donnell let his mask dangle as he smiled and waved at Olive and his former skipper Admiral Johnson in the back. With one more to go on the waist, Irish reattached his mask and motioned for a descent.

"Let the games begin," Johnson said.

With Olive and the wingman tightening into echelon parade formation, they accelerated in the easy descent aft of the ship as formations above them descended to follow them at interval into the break, tailhooks down. Approaching the initial, Olive saw Irish look over his right shoulder for traffic; see-and-avoid kept one alive.

Stable at 350 knots, they crossed the initial level at 800 feet, just offset of the ship's wake. Olive reached down and set a course line in the HSI to help align her downwind leg after the break. Holding parade, she peeked under the jets next to her and saw a *Rhino* launched off cat four. *Perfect.*

As the great carrier's bow receded from view, Irish kissed off the wingman and broke hard left, pulling to 5 g's. Olive maintained parade position on the wingman, probably a lieutenant who never expected to lead the Wing Commander with COMSIXTHFLET in the back seat.

The wingman kissed off Olive and broke left, and Olive checked the time; seventeen seconds later she would break.

'Ready, sir?"

"All set."

At 17 seconds, Olive snapped the jet left and pulled hard, retarding the throttles to idle as the *Rhino* bled off airspeed. Passing 250 knots she threw down the gear and flaps, and steadying out on the ship's reciprocal course, came up hot mic to do the landing checklist.

"Three down and locked, flaps full, hook down, antiskid off, harness locked."

"Roger, three green," Johnson confirmed.

Level at 600 feet, Olive slowed to her on-speed of 141 knots, assessing her abeam distance as the ship drew closer on the left. Irish was in the groove, and his wingman was already off the abeam. Another formation of *Rhinos* raced to the break.

Olive Teel had over 970 carrier arrested landings to her credit in 19 years of flying, yet she concentrated on this and all approaches as she did during her nugget cruise in the *Ravens*. She manipulated the controls without thinking, reflexively trimming out the stick forces, assessing the abeam distance, setting up her landing displays by rote muscle memory, *sensing* more than recognizing the minute corrections she made to fly the approach *perfectly*. Behind her, Johnson said nothing, his slow breathing on the ICS the only indication he was in the airplane. Like Olive, he couldn't help himself and followed her approach as if he were flying instead of just enjoying the sunny day and the professional spectacle of carrier aviation.

Olive also said nothing, her breathing measured and in control. Turning off the abeam, she flew the pattern as designed, the airplane responding to quick inputs to the controls and throttles. Soon after the "90" position, they saw a ball on the lens, slightly high. With the wingman aboard, she crossed over the wake and eased over to centerline. The LSO on deck activated the green cuts lights over the lens; *roger ball*.

The airplane twitched and buffeted as Olive made tight and aggressive corrections to stay on glideslope, on centerline, and on speed. Both pilots concentrated on the lens, the ball centered now as the ship grew larger. Johnson saw the foul line was clear and noted the bevy of LSOs on the platform watching them, as Olive concentrated on the ball, lineup, airspeed—and nothing else.

Crossing the ramp, both felt the jet sag and Olive corrected for it. Two seconds later they crashed down onto the deck and were thrown forward against the straps as the hook engaged a wire that wrestled them to a stop. Once Olive retarded the throttles to idle, Johnson spoke.

"Nice pass, CAG."

"A two-wire, but I'll take it."

In quick motions, also by rote, Olive raised the hook and folded the wings on signal, gave a thumbs-up to the maintenance personnel on deck, and retracted the flaps and reset the trim, her eyes never leaving the yellow shirt that taxied her clear of the foul line, then aft toward the island. Johnson saw the welcoming party: Flip Wilson and Huey Morrison. Behind them, "rainbow side boys"—two ranks of sailors in multi-colored flight deck jerseys—stood at attention on each side of a hatch that led to the island.

The yellow shirts led Irish and his wingman to parking spots on the bow as Olive was spun aft to park on the foul line near the island. As Wilson and Huey waited in cranials and float coats, blue shirts chocked and chained *Spartan* 100 as another *Rhino* trapped next to them, straining against the wire at full power. In the rear cockpit, Johnson unstrapped, and Olive shut down the jet on signal.

"Canopy," Olive prompted.

"Clear," The Big Unit bellowed.

The ear-piercing sounds of jet engines filled the cockpit as Olive raised the canopy. The plane captain dropped the boarding ladder, and Johnson pulled himself out of the aft cockpit. Before descending the ladder, he shouted a message to Olive.

"After you get out of your gear, join us."

At that moment a *Rhino* trapped next to them, and over the deafening roar, Olive could only nod her acknowledgment. Johnson descended the ladder, conscious of this moment in time, then turned to return the salute of the plane captain before he shook her hand and shouted *good jet!*

The side boys came to attention and saluted as Johnson lifted his hand to his visor as he strode through, smiling at Wilson and Huey, who waited by the hatch. Wilson stepped forward and saluted.

"Welcome home, Admiral!"

"Hey, Flip! Hello, Huey!" Johnson said as he returned their salutes and shook their hands. "Great to be back!"

Another *Rhino* slammed into the gear and slipped into burner as waves of sound felt in their chests enveloped them. "Let's go below!" Wilson shouted, and led him to the hatch, held open by the Air Transport Officer, who saluted. Inside, the ATO dogged the hatch behind them as the two admirals and Huey removed their helmets.

"The ship looks great, Huey. And your people on deck are sharp, everything suitcased."

"Thank you, sir, after three months they're confident and we've got great leadership out there."

Wilson sensed The Big Unit was ready to proceed. "Admiral, we have some refreshments in the flag mess. Huey, please lead the way."

As Huey led the admirals to Wilson's flag mess, Johnson gave them a preview. "Flip, I've asked Olive to join us, and get the surface commodore also. Want to expand on that message I sent you the other day."

"Yes, sir." Wilson looked over his shoulder to Skweez who nodded.

In the flag mess, Johnson removed his flight gear and handed the items to a waiting VFA-91 pararigger who took them to the squadron paraloft. The mess specialist had a charcuterie board of meats and cheeses on the table as the officers grazed.

"How was your flight, Admiral?" Wilson asked between bites. At that moment, Olive joined the group.

"Memorable and fun, ah, no, I mean we came straight here, no nonsense, by the book, per the brief. Right, CAG?"

"That's how I recall it sir," Olive deadpanned.

"Yes...well, Flip, why don't we step into your War Room and talk about this exercise."

"Right this way, sir."

Wilson led The Big Unit and the *Valley Forge* brain trust into the flag conference room. Shane was there with Smoke; behind them a digital projection of the Med showed on the flat screen.

"Admiral, you remember Smoke Offenhausen from the old *Raven* days, and this is our acting Intel Officer, Lieutenant Commander Shane Duncan."

"Hello Smoke, great to see you, shipmate!"

"You too, Admiral."

Johnson turned to Shane.

"Commander, pleasure to meet you."

"You too, sir!"

Wilson offered the fleet commander the head chair and sat on his right. The Big Unit surveyed the room and began.

"I'll guess, Admiral Wilson, that you've shared the P4 message with your staff. Basically, don't piss off the Greeks, and *really* don't piss off the Turks. We've got a canned exercise; it's not all that challenging, more for the command-and-control side with the Greeks taking tactical control of your ships and airplanes. You'll get some vanilla intercept and sea control training for the airwing and basic seamanship drills for the small boys. We'll establish a data link, then let them control it. No overland training. We cannot—*cannot*—fly over any Greek—or especially—Turkish airspace. If you must bingo a jet into Souda Bay or Izmir, that's different...but it would be better if it was Souda. If one of your guys violates Greek or Turkish airspace—I can't help them—or you."

Wilson nodded and glanced at Smoke. Their eyes met. *Message received.*

"Okay, this Greek research ship *Nauticos Card* that sank four days ago: the Greeks are absolutely convinced the Turks did it. If they have proof, they aren't sharing it. The Turks know the Greeks suspect them, and know that we know this. Of course they are denying it. We think sabotage but our proof is at the bottom of the Med, and the Greeks are looking to locate the wreck and find out. Regardless, we must track everything we can out here and maintain an airtight surface picture. Both Greek and Turkish drill ships have been turning off their automatic ID systems...but so have the Israelis, Egyptians, and Cypriots. The full extent of what's under the eastern Med is still not clear, but it's like a gold rush out here to get to it first. Everyone has staked a claim, and they overlap."

"Is Turkey the most aggressive player?" Wilson asked.

"I would say yes, but Greece is aggressively exploring, and frankly in areas that are much closer to Suez than Souda."

Shane manipulated the keyboard, and soon a graphic of eastern Mediterranean mineral claims appeared on the chart.

"Okay, good," Johnson said, then added, "You can see most of the exploration and claim activity is south and southwest of Cyrprus. Greece and Turkey may have the least proximity to the area but they are the most active, followed by the Israelis."

Huey spoke next.

"Admiral, we have an exercise track. When we get to the southeast of Crete would you like us to continue further southeast?"

The Big Unit looked up at the bulkhead as he thought. "Yes, but don't get in anyone's way, and search 360 degrees around the ship as a cover. If the Greeks ask why you're off your PIM, blame flight ops, or merchant traffic, or winds…the usual suspects."

"Lean fifty miles?"

"At the very most…so long as you have a cover story. Just don't tell me…and I didn't just answer."

"Admiral, do we know where *Nauticos Card* went down?" Wilson asked.

"Not really. We can extrapolate based on their DR track when the coastal stations last got an AIS hit on them, but once beyond that horizon it's best guess. It's ballpark, but not precise." Johnson referred again to the bulkhead flatscreen.

"The last time we were together, Flip, and you too, Olive, was in WESTPAC where our adversary claimed 'blue territory' in the South China Sea. It's the same situation here, with Turkey claiming sovereign rights—in most of the eastern Med. Blue territory—*mavi vatan* they call it—and hey, if it works for the Chinese in congested WESTPAC it can work here. The other countries follow suit, and all these interlocking 200-mile exclusion zones have one area in common: the patch of water southwest of Cyprus, the Bouri Field, where most of the proven oil and manganese reserves are located."

Johnson put his hands on the table, palm down.

"It's always something, isn't it, guys? So have a great exercise—do not do anything to piss off our allies who hate each other—and if you're good I'll let you go to Souda for liberty. Questions?"

Olive raised her hand. "Admiral, may we drop heavy inerts, strafe… chaff and flares?"

"Yes, anything inert you want to train with, but nothing live. You *may* load live weapons for CAP and SuCAP alerts, but have a high threshold to make that launch decision, and if you launch an alert, be very slow to arm up."

Wilson spoke next. "Thanks, sir. What would you like to do next on your vacation?"

"You know, I'd like to address the ship on the 1MC, give everyone a pat on the back and tell them why this at-sea period is important, then wander around the ship and press the flesh with sailors."

"Can do, sir, and allow me to send Skweez with you. He's yours to task for the duration of your visit."

"You mean my own personal manservant while your guest?"

Skweez smiled at the barb, used to it as a flag aide. Wilson played along.

"He *really* knows his way around the ship sir, especially the way to the flag mess or any wardroom." Skweez could only smile and shake his head.

"Perfect! Thanks, Flip. Huey, let's go."

CHAPTER 5

MV *Konya K*, Mediterranean Sea, 1600 June 8, 2024

Burak flicked the lighter open and brought the flame to his cigarette, inhaling deeply as the tobacco struggled to ignite in the light breeze. He gazed west to the horizon and exhaled; the sun flared orange as it sank into the sea. To the southwest—he estimated five kilometers—a pleasure yacht sailed into the sun under mainsail and jib. *Europeans,* he surmised. A rich executive and his young mistress—or two—saving the planet under the power of canvas. After the operation tonight, he hoped to come back here but knew Aaghaa wouldn't allow it. If the op was called off, the filthy hellhole of Alexandria awaited them. One day, maybe. One day a pleasure yacht, like a helpless fawn grazing in the open, blissfully unaware in these idyllic waters. Burak would come upon it on a clear night, climbing over the gunwale in silence, bursting into the cabin as the women shrieked in terror while the groggy executive tried to make sense of what was happening. The look on his face when he did. He thought of the master's wife last week. *That* look, but on faces 30 years younger.

Aaghaa interrupted his fantasy. "Burak, you should be asleep—we'll wake you in a few hours for dinner."

"I can sleep when I'm dead."

"My men need you at your best!"

The operator ignored him.

"Dinner in two hours, then we brief."

Burak nodded as he exhaled. *Old woman.*

Seven hours later, spray lashed Burak and the other three operators as their rigid hull inflatable bounded over the swells. Three hundred meters ahead, the 108-meter Greek supply vessel *Naciye Ram* motored at ten knots under a half-moon high above. The coxswain maneuvered the RHIB to the vessel's port quarter and eased through the wake to go alongside on the low freeboard in the after part of the ship.

In silence, the operators watched the vessel's white superstructure for signs of movement. Nothing. No night goggles tonight; between the moon and the ship lights that blazed bright they were not needed. The inflatable would not be needed once they boarded on this one-way mission that all understood.

The dark hull loomed alongside as one of the operators threw a grappling hook over. Once secure, he pulled hand-over-hand on a line that pulled the Jacob's ladder up to the locking device and felt it slam into place.

"Git!"

Burak was the first man over and moved to the cargo pallets as he waited for the others to join him in the shadows. When the fourth man was over, Burak said *git,* and in a low crouch they moved like phantoms to the port side ladder. No signs of alarm.

With faces darkened by camo paint and Burak in the lead, they raced up the ladder, with two operators stopping at the first deck berthing spaces while Burak and one other continued to the pilothouse. Burak opened the hatch and illuminated a flashlight on a young woman sitting at the helm console, who squinted at the sudden glare in the darkened space.

"What are you doing? Alexei?"

"Get away," Burak said in Greek, leveling his weapon muzzle at her face. Now terrified, she moved off the chair in wide-eyed shock as the second operator took the helm and turned it left. Burak had her raise her hands and turn away while placing the gun muzzle in the small of her back. He leaned in and whispered in his accented Greek.

"We are going below now, using the same way I entered, and you are free to use your hands to steady yourself, but if you make any sudden moves that alarm me, I will blow a hole through your spinal cord. Do you understand me?"

Breathing through her mouth in shock, the girl nodded.

"Go."

She moved to the port bridge wing and down the ladder with Burak following as *Naciye Ram* heeled right.

"Your cabin," Burak said, and she stopped after descending one deck and turned inboard.

An operator had the crew standing against the bulkhead with hands up, while the other gathered the watch-standers in the engine room. Burak pushed the girl into the arms of her shipmates as they trembled. *What is happening?*

Once the two mechanics arrived, Burak pushed them against the bulkhead. Nine crew: eight men and the woman.

"Who is your captain here?" Burak asked.

A gray-haired man of 45, eyes alert and not cowering like the others, stepped forward. "I am the captain, and..."

Burak raised his weapon and fired one round into the man's chest, dropping him to the deck.

"PAPA!" the girl cried, and rushed to him.

Burak walked toward the group as the girl bawled over her dead father.

"He did not answer my question correctly. Who is your captain here?"

The crew said nothing and just looked at him, some in fear, others in disgust.

"I will answer my own question then. I am your captain, and a captain's orders at sea are to be followed—to the letter, as they say. Put your hands together in front of you."

The crew did as they were told, except the girl, sobbing now.

"What is her name?" Burak asked.

"Corra," one answered. Burak nodded and looked at her.

"Corra...Corra, you must stand and do as you are told, now."

Through tears, she looked up at Burak with contempt. Coming to her feet, she suddenly lunged at him.

All flinched as another ear-splitting shot rang out. The girl lay at Burak's feet, also dead.

"Pity...such a spirited family, but they stepped toward me, and I feared for my life. You all saw it. Yes, I am afraid, and must defend myself from attack. Will anyone else attack me?"

The crew held his gaze in terrified silence.

"Good," Burak said, while motioning to his partner, who proceeded to zip-tie them and move below into the anchor windlass room.

The ship his, he contemplated the two dead bodies that lay in pools of blood. In a sudden spasm, the girl moved.

"Pity," Burak said as he placed the muzzle on the middle of her back and pulled the trigger.

At dawn, Burak sat in the captain's chair on the bridge and stared out to sea, recalling the operation and dreaming about the next one. *Naciye Ram* steamed north toward the Turkish coast, some 100 miles away—ten hours at their current speed. Antalya would be another two hours steaming, but Aaghaa would have the helicopter to drop off the prize crew and pick up Burak and the other operators once in sight of land. Burak hoped for the safe-house villa that overlooked the harbor of Finike that promised a few days of sun and good food, and returned to dreams of planning the next operation with another opportunity to kill again.

In the twilight, he spied a vessel on the western horizon. He watched it, and noted that it was approaching him. Far from a fat merchantman, it was narrow and appeared fast. Soon it showed the lines of a naval vessel, and as the sun rose higher, the gray color of one.

"Turn this vessel east and increase speed," Burak told the operator on the helm.

The man complied, and as *Naciye Ram* heeled left, Burak stepped outside to assess the ship, now trailing in his wake. The ship rested on a crest of white water under the bow, and he saw a helicopter lift from it.

Blast!

Pulling his satcom radio from his belt, Burak punched in the frequency he had memorized.

"What is it?" the familiar voice of Aaghaa said.

"A warship is pursuing us. It has a helicopter."

"I see you on my screen…help is to your southeast."

Burak stepped to starboard and scanned the horizon. A warship, bow-on with white water flaring from the bow, sped toward him. He estimated it to be 8 kilometers away and lifted the binoculars for a closer look. The gray-hulled ship flew a red flag. Turkish.

"Turn right, head for that ship!" Burak commanded. This contingency was not expected.

He stepped outside and peered through the binoculars at their pursuer. The flag flying from the ship appeared blue and white, and he estimated the helicopter to be inside one mile.

"Greek Navy. Everybody inside. Do not show your face!" he demanded as the rotor thrum of the helicopter filled the pilothouse. Through the aft window he studied the aircraft: American design, familiar to him in the skies of Iraq and Syria.

The Greek MH-70 *Aegean Hawk* flew low along their port side as *Naciye Ram* steadied on a course of southeast to close the friendly combatant—a dark shadow as the sun rose behind it—and Burak noted it was a frigate of similar design to the Greek. *Evenly matched.* Just then, the radio speaker blared in Greek.

"*Naciye Ram, Naciye Ram*, this is Hellenic Navy frigate *Agios Hiros*. Heave to and prepare for boarding."

Unsure if he should answer, the operator on the helm looked at Burak, who shook his head no.

"*Naciye Ram, Naciye Ram*, this is Hellenic Navy frigate. Turn left and heave to immediately."

The helicopter rotor blades dug into the air as it turned hard left for another pass alongside.

Now at 20 knots, *Naciye Ram* converged on the Turkish frigate that steamed toward it at flank speed in a race to block the Greek combatant and helicopter that desperately wanted to retake their supply ship. Burak moved from one side of the bridge to the other, assessing the relative motion of the three ships and their actions. With the Greek frigate closing on the starboard quarter, Burak heard the helicopter rotors change pitch. He bounded to the left side of the bridge and saw it enter a hover. The third operator looked at Burak for guidance.

"Stay here," he said.

Opening the bridge wing hatch, Burak pointed his automatic weapon in front of the slowing aircraft and pulled the trigger, kicking up spray ahead of the helicopter's flight path. The MH-70 reacted at once as the pilot dumped the nose and banked away to the left, accelerating away from the threat as the engines whined at full power. Burak bounded to the other side and studied the Greek ship through the binoculars. The gun muzzle on the bow pointed at him, and he exhaled when a flash and puff of white gun smoke erupted from it.

"They're firing on us," Burak said, resigned. He turned his head to the Turkish ship, now peeling off to meet their mortal enemy of three thousand years.

A single 5-inch shell landed 500 meters off *Naciye Ram's* starboard side, kicking up a geyser of water that fell back in a shimmering curtain of spray carried by the wind.

"*Naciye Ram, Naciye Ram*, this is Hellenic Navy warship! Heave to at once and cease firing!"

The Greek MH-70 gave a wide berth to both *Naciye Ram* and the Turkish frigate, who had its own 5-inch gun trained out to the Greek.

The operators, all three of whom were now with Burak in the pilot house, had not bargained for *this*, a running naval battle with them caught in the cross-fire. Burak observed the action with a smile forming on his lips. *What will happen?* To the west, the Greek gun flashed again, and again and again in quick succession.

"Turn left, now!" Burak shouted to the helmsman, who whipped the wheel over hard left.

Just as *Naciye Ram's* deck sloped to the right, the sound of a freight train filled the pilothouse as a 5-inch shell lifted a geyser of water high above the port bow.

"They are firing on us!" an operator cried, barely getting the words out before another roar and near miss lifted a column of white water ahead that *Naciye Ram* steamed into. The bridge windows shuddered from the shock wave which was followed by a wall of water that slammed into them, for a moment darkening the bridge as if the ship were suddenly submerged. The bow pitched as the ship entered the churned-up sea.

"Steady north!" Burak ordered, looking aft at the Turkish frigate as the seawater ran down the window. Its bow gun fired a round every five seconds at the Greek ship, which Burak saw turning hard left and not firing. Turkish shells landed well forward of the Greek that continued in its turn, its big gun no longer trained on them.

"Resume course, the Greek bastards are in retreat," Burak said, then added, "The cowards. Our countrymen in a like-sized vessel warned them away and they turned tail." The operators breathed easier but remained on edge. None had ever experienced heavy enemy artillery without bunkers in which to hide. To their south, the Turkish frigate continued in pursuit, the Greek helicopter shadowed them, and radio operators on both ships sent terse flash messages to Athens and Ankara dictated only moments earlier by their commanding officers, signifying the first military action between the belligerents since the Turkish invasion of Cyprus some fifty years before.

Chapter 6

USS *Valley Forge*, 0640 June 9, 2024

Wilson heard the J-dial phone buzz. He dabbed his wet face and placed the razor on the metal sink before he answered it.

"Admiral Wilson."

"Sir, it's Mark. We got word from SIXTH FLEET; the Greeks and Turks just engaged in a surface action thirty minutes ago, roughly 180 miles southeast of the eastern tip of Crete."

"How far from us now?"

"Three hun'red thirty."

"Any tasking yet?"

"No sir, but I expect some within the hour."

"I'll be there in a minute," Wilson said, and hung up.

As he buttoned his shirt and laced his shoes on autopilot, he thought. *Why? Intentional or accident? Who else knows? Will the exercise continue? Will this escalate and how much?*

Wilson exited his cabin and entered the War Room where Meadows, Smoke, and Shane stood in wait. Skweez placed a mug of coffee at Wilson's place at the head of the table.

"Seats, everyone. Okay, whatcha got?"

"Admiral, it appears that Turks have captured the Greek supply vessel *Naciye Ram* and a prize crew is taking it toward the Turkish coast. Shane."

Shane brought up the Link picture and a photo of *Naciye Ram* on the flat screen.

"A prize crew?" Wilson asked.

"That's what the Greeks believe. The vessel was enroute from Piraeus to supply the Greek rig *Kerkira Eclipse*, a semisubmersible in the disputed zone. The Greeks are convinced that it was boarded. They sent a frigate to chase it down and just as they intercepted it, the supply vessel turned and ran. They hailed it to heave to and when it didn't, the Greek frigate fired warning shots. That's when a Turkish frigate appeared and returned fire. Nothing was hit and all the ships withdrew, but the Greeks are pissed. At the current PIM, *Naciye Ram* has another six or seven hours before they get to Turkish waters."

Shane spoke up. "Admiral, my counterpart in Naples just emailed me on the high side. The Greeks are launching fighters out of Kasteli in Crete."

"Are they on the screen?" Wilson asked.

The group studied the link screen. After a moment, Smoke found their digital Air Traffic Control tracks. "Yep, airborne south of Heraklion…and heading east. F-16's…looks like two."

"They'll be on scene in twenty minutes," Wilson figured. "And probably with an air-to-air alert load. Smoke, what's on tap for us today?"

"Sir, we've got intercept training and a simulated war-at-sea with the Greeks south of Crete. Dissimilar air-combat-maneuvering with Greek *Vipers* out of Kasteli—maybe those guys. Lots of unit-level training for the airwing as we transit south of Crete before we turn north into the Aegean. Fairly vanilla."

Wilson studied the screen, and one contact stood out. "Well…what's this Russian friend doing today?"

Shane answered him. "Sir, that *Udaloy* got underway yesterday and is at sea off Tartus. If he makes 25 knots he could be on scene in roughly 15 hours."

The J-dial buzzed and Meadows picked it up, then turned to Wilson. "Admiral Johnson is on the line, sir."

"Put him through."

Wilson waited for Johnson to pick up. "Flip, Randy Johnson."

"Good morning, sir."

"Yes, and good morning to you too, a morning that just changed for both of us."

"I guessed that sir, and sir, I'm with my staff at the moment on an open line."

"Good; okay, here's the deal. The Greeks are spun up like we've never seen them, and Admiral Buffington just got tasking from Brussels. We are to proceed southeast of Crete and operate independently, getting between the Greeks and Turks and basically breaking up this fight before it escalates. No exercise events today. Your tasking is to operate as you would if you were just cruising, but do lots of SSSC and get a good surface plot on everyone. No live weapons *except*…for alert aircraft and I will let you determine your own alert posture."

"Roger, sir, and have you heard from your Greek counterpart yet?"

"No, have you?"

"No, sir, but I'll contact him and let him know that we are standing down from the exercise."

"Okay, good. So basically, try not to be too nosy—but be nosy. Out here."

"Aye aye, sir, out here."

As the line went dead, Olive and Huey entered.

"The ship and airwing team, and just in time," Wilson said, then added, "Our day just changed."

"We guessed sir," Olive answered. "This is all over cable news."

"Wow, they're fast. Okay, here's the tasking from NAVEUR: independent ops today—no exercise events—and Huey, take us southeast of Crete but no closer than 150 miles of where the incident took place. Two things: we want to fly SSSC from 50 to 200 miles out and get an ID on everything that floats. No ordnance—but buckets of chaff and flares would be good. Can you handle that, Huey?"

"With the first event in three hours, we'll make it happen, sir."

"Good. Next, an alert posture; four *Rhinos* loaded with *Maverick* for SuCAP and with self-defense missiles. Alert 30. When can you set that?"

Olive and Huey exchanged glances; Olive spoke first. "I can have crews ready in two hours; the jets will depend on the ordies to load."

"Will take us longer than that, sir, to break out weapons and get them to the roof," Huey said. "We'll press, Admiral, and we should have it set by lunchtime."

"Okay, good. Olive, contact your skippers, and I want you on TV to address the air wing. Do not mess with any Greek or Turkish combatants. Get close enough to ID them on your sensors or eyeballs and no closer. Non-threatening air speeds and avoid illuminating them."

"Aye aye, sir. Will this go 24 hours?"

Wilson pulled on his chin. "Let's see how the day goes and if we receive guidance from above."

"Roger that, sir," Olive replied, following Huey out to pass the word to their people.

After they left, Smoke asked Wilson a question. "Admiral, you're scheduled to fly this afternoon with the *Ravens*. Still want it?" Wilson considered it as Smoke and Meadows waited for his answer.

"Yes, I do. Mark, you've got it while I'm gone, and I'm only a radio call away."

"Aye, sir," Meadows replied.

"I'm going to call Admiral Patros now. Shane, find out what you can and give me an update in an hour."

"Yes, sir, Admiral," Shane said.

Wilson waited for Admiral Patros to join the line as Skweez listened with a notepad across the table.

"Admiral Wilson, this is Admiral Patros of the Hellenic Navy. How may I be of service?"

"Good morning, Admiral, and it is I who ask you this question," Wilson answered. "We have learned of your supply vessel capture and know that you have mobilized forces. We expect our exercise to be postponed today and are ready to resume at your direction."

"Thank you, Admiral Wilson. May I respond to you this evening while we attend to matters my government tasks me with?"

"Certainly, sir."

"We do ask that your forces do not close with us or forces belonging to Turkey. This is a matter best left to us to resolve."

"Admiral Patros, we understand your desires to handle this yourself and we do not question that. You understand that I must operate and scout the surface picture around me. Both of us, sir, must keep an eye on the Russian *Udaloy* off Syria. He could be a factor by midnight if he chooses."

"I do not object to that, but only request that you do not operate your forces east of 27 degrees longitude."

Skweez pointed to the chart on the table; 27 degrees east was 40 miles off the eastern tip of Crete. Wilson saw it was over 100 from the last datum of *Nicaye Ram.*

"Admiral, I have your request...but I cannot be constrained from searching outside my inner defenses for potential threats."

When Patros raised his voice, Wilson could detect that the reason was guidance from Athens.

"Admiral Wilson! We have taken fire from our ancient enemy for the first time in fifty years. As the officer in tactical command, I order you to remain west of 27 degrees east so Hellenic forces may handle this military situation unimpeded."

Wilson remained diplomatic, but firm. "Admiral, I understand your reticence to have any outside forces in this area of interest, but I must operate my forces in the manner that *I* must."

"You refuse my order?"

"Admiral Patros, you were designated OTC, er, Officer in Tactical Command, because of our exercise tasking which is no longer valid since our exercise is postponed. Admiral Patros...sir...I will do my best to follow your express desire to remain west of 27, but I cannot guarantee it."

"You will do your best?"

"Yes, sir," Wilson said, looking at Skweez who smiled. "I will do my best to scout the waters and airspace around my strike group and avoid the area of interest where possible."

A long pause followed. Wilson glanced at Skweez, then the chart.

With little choice, Patros broke.

"Wilson, as a fellow officer I take you at your word. But, if I see you...I will not be happy."

"You have my word, sir...I will do my best."

"Patros out."

After he heard the connection end, Wilson set down the receiver. "He's under pressure."

"You handled it well, sir."

Eyes down as he thought, Wilson said nothing. Skweez didn't know what to say in the awkward silence.

"When's my brief with the *Ravens*?" Wilson asked.

"Ten-thirty for a 1230 launch, sir."

Wilson returned to the chart and remained still in contemplation. Skweez watched him. He couldn't hold back.

"Admiral, I must ask. Are you going to send jets up there?"

Wilson nodded.

"Yes...out to 300 miles and beyond, if needed. Gonna scour the whole Eastern Med. I'm not even going to 'try' to avoid the datum at all."

Skweez nodded his understanding.

Wilson spoke. "He's not gonna trust me after today."

"You both have your tasking, sir."

Wilson could only nod. Patros knew Wilson was lying, and as Wilson relived the call, he considered how easy it had been to lie.

And that he had just taught his lieutenant to lie.

Burak sifted through the contents of the galley refrigerator when a sudden grinding noise from below and vibration on the deck jarred his senses. He slammed the door shut and bolted out and up to the bridge to investigate.

"What!?" he snarled at the operator on the helm, who looked perplexed at the engine console. Despite placing his engine at idle, the noise continued, but at a lower intensity.

"I don't know. We were going along with no difficulty until this sudden vibration. Let me try this..."

With the heel of his hand, he pushed on the throttle. At once the grinding and vibration intensified, and he retarded the throttle to idle.

Seething with frustration, Burak glowered at the man. "Can you fix it?"

"I don't know what the problem is, and I'm no engineer. Can *you* fix it?" The man stood his ground.

"Blast!" Burak muttered. To starboard, their Turkish escort continued ahead, and soon slowed.

"Get a crew man up here," Burak ordered. A voice came up on his radio.

"What is the difficulty?"

Burak pressed the transmit button. "We do not know. Engine trouble. We will get a crew man to fix it."

"What if he caused it?" the voice asked.

"They are secured away from the engine room. They cannot."

Burak fumed at the delay. The Turkish coast was less than 40 miles away. The man returned...with bad news.

"Burak, they have barricaded themselves inside."

The operator looked at him with contempt. "Show me!"

Arriving at the anchor windlass room, they could not budge the wheel of the watertight door. "Open it!" Burak roared, his frustration building while the men inside remained silent. Burak worked to control his breathing. Once inside he would rip them apart, engine repairs be damned!

"Blow it open," he said.

"With what? We have no C4."

Burak had run out of patience. *Must I do everything myself?*

"Blow. It. *Open!* And bring me the engineer," Burak growled before he stormed off to the bridge. Arriving there, the frigate stood close off his port bow, only two football pitches away. The radio came to life.

"He fouled your propeller."

Burak keyed the transmit button. "What do you mean?"

"Go up on the bow and look down. He used a mooring line to foul your propeller."

Burak and another operator went outside and strode to the bow, conscious of the eyes of the frigate crew on them. When they arrived at the forepeak they looked over the side. Coming out of the anchor hawsepipe was a manila mooring line, taut against the hull of the ship as it pointed aft to the water. The captured crew had fed it through in an effort to catch it in the turning propeller—and had succeeded. Across the water he heard sailors on deck laughing.

Burak held the man in front of him in cold contempt as he again keyed the hand-held transmit button while he scanned the horizon to the west.

"Tow us."

The frigate eased forward to clear *Naciye Ram*, and after several minutes turned back and crept up along the vessel's left side. A messenger line was shot over, and as Burak and his teammate pulled on it, a large towing line jerked its way across the water, then up and over *Naciye Ram's* side. A loudhailer from the frigate blared.

"Loop it on the bollard." Together the operators lifted the heavy line over the gunwale and looped it over a bollard as the frigate eased ahead. After several minutes of holding the loop on, the slack in the line tightened up and Burak stood clear as the line tension increased. "Let's go inside." As they entered the ship, Burak felt as slight tug. *We're moving.*

Back on the bridge, Burak had calmed down enough to assess the situation. The frigate had them in tow at three knots. Burak checked the chart. At least twelve hours at this speed. *Midnight.*

The captured crew was safe for the moment, but still captured, and Burak decided he could wait. Hungry and tired from a long night, he could wait till midnight when he and this ship were safe inside Turkish waters. The compartment would be opened, and Burak would be waiting on the outside once it was. He fell asleep in the captain's cabin bed, and dreamed of what he would do when they faced him in fear.

Chapter 7

Flight deck, USS *Valley Forge* 1255 June 9, 2024

Holding the nosewheel steering switch, Wilson stomped on the right rudder. The nose of *Raven* 400 swung hard right as it swept across the four-wire before the yellow shirt had him stop the turn and taxi his FA-18E ahead. Wilson complied as he had throughout his career, his eyes locked on the director who gave him a slight right signal, and Wilson's *Rhino* obeyed it as he was led to catapult 4. As he taxied behind the cat 3 jet blast deflector, he was given the "spread wings" signal, which he obediently followed.

He was *back* after years of staff toil in "the building," back at sea in the cockpit of a *Rhino* on a warm spring day in the Med. His Pentagon purgatory over, he could fly again—practically anytime he wanted to!—and day-only on easy, low stress hops like this, a surface search hop covering a sector of water to their east. Alone. Parked behind the waist cats, he suppressed a smile at the thought of a few hours of carrier aviation fun. He checked the divert field distance to Chania, Crete; 80 miles.

Valley Forge heeled hard to port as the bridge team maneuvered to put winds down the angle. Up on the bow, the CO of VFA-64, Commander "Comet" Halley waited on cat 2 in *Raven* 401 with his nugget wingman LTJG "Gigs" Gigliotti in 407 on cat 1. Wilson had briefed with them in the *Raven* ready room but would cover his own sector while the nugget stayed with his CO in their assigned sector. The white sky was the typical summertime Med light haze that Wilson remembered well, and in it a dozen jets from the previous event held in lazy left-hand turns, also watching and waiting for the action to begin on deck. The familiar voice of the Air Boss, Commander John Stevenson, came up on the radio.

"*Switchblade* six-one-six, winds down the angle at 21 knots, cleared to lift on LSE signal, cleared to cross the bow, take papa golf."

"Six-one-six, cleared to lift, cleared to cross, take papa golf, three-plus-zero-zero."

"Three-plus-zero-zero, roger."

At the top of the angle Wilson watched the yellow shirt LSE signal "lift" to the MH-60 *Sierra*, and seconds later the helicopter engines changed pitch and the aircraft struggled into an inelegant hover over the deck. The LSE pointed to port and saluted, and the *Sierra* gracefully slid left and gained airspeed as it climbed ahead of the bow and crossed right to its plane guard station.

Two minutes. The four catapult shuttles retracted to green shirts stationed on each cat to hook up four waiting jets screaming at idle power. Wilson loved this, the cadence of the launch sequence, the familiar procedures. Like he'd never left.

Wilson glanced to his left. Parked on El 4 were two *Rhinos* from the VFA-47 *Buccaneers*, loaded with live AIM-9's, an AMRAAM, and an IR *Maverick*. Two *Spartan* jets sat with identical loads on the starboard shelf. With this alert set, Wilson had options if he needed them.

No, Mark Meadows had options. While Wilson was airborne, he'd run the strike group, even though Wilson was only a radio transmission away.

Hours ago they had learned that the Greek vessel had broken down, and was under tow some 50 miles off the Turkish coast. Maybe they were headed for Antalya. Regardless, the Greeks shadowed them while Wilson's first SSSC event had given them plenty of room as they monitored the action over 200 miles away.

The *Rhino* on cat 3 came up on the power, then roared to life as the pilot cycled the controls under the watchful eyes of the troubleshooters. On the bow, Gigs also went into tension as a hurricane of jet blast flowed over the JBD. Wilson's jet bucked as it was bombarded by waves of sound and engine exhaust as the *Super Hornet* forward of him strained against the holdback.

The strike fighter roared down the deck as up forward Gigs accelerated along the cat 2 track. Both jets got to the ends of their strokes and turned away from one another in clearing turns to the left and right.

The *Rhino* on cat 4 howled at military power as the catapult went into tension, and this time Wilson bounced in his seat as his strike-fighter was pummeled by waves of F414 exhaust as the steel deflector shuddered only feet from his nose. Seconds later the jet thundered off the angle, disappearing as it did in a cloud of billowing steam released from the track that cascaded down the deck toward Wilson. On cat 1, Comet thundered away from the ship to catch Gigs as crews fed each catapult another jet, this time including Wilson.

Wilson waited with elbows on the canopy rails as the *Growler* on cat 3 went into tension, the back-seater looking over his shoulders at control surface movement as the pilot wiped out the controls. On deck next to the roaring monster, troubleshooters held their thumbs-up, and Wilson noted the pilot salute the catapult officer who returned it. Seconds after the officer knelt and pointed forward, the holdback released, and the EA-18G accelerated down the track with an audible *thunk* at the end as it leapt into the air.

Attention now turned to *Raven* 400, and Wilson felt it as he followed his director forward. He sensed all in the tower, those watching inside the ship on the PLAT, and most deck sailors amidships watching as "the admiral" was taken into readiness on cat 4. With his cockpit displays set, his eyes remained locked on the yellow shirt who looked up and down the track, then gave Wilson the take-tension signal.

Feeling his jet squat, Wilson ran the throttles to the military stops as he cycled the stick and rudder in the same methodical sequence he had developed since his lieutenant days, studying the engine instrument readings and FCS page for signs of trouble. With all in order, he looked at the catapult officer, waited for their eyes to meet, and popped a jaunty salute. The officer came to attention as he returned it, then checked the cat track and troubleshooters for signals of trouble as Wilson braced himself, locking his arms against the throttles and canopy towel rack.

Wilson bounced in his seat when the *Rhino* broke free and started its acceleration to flying speed as 4 g's pushed against his spine, slamming the throttles into burner as it did. The angled deck edge rushed up and under, releasing the g at once as Wilson took the stick and banked left, slapping up the gear and flaps in more near-reflexive motions, ingrained by over 20 years of shipboard experience. *Yes, free!*

He eased back to the right to parallel the ship's course as he leveled at 500 feet. A *Rhino* shot from the bow accelerated with him at his two o'clock as they raced ahead of *Valley Forge*. Wilson energized his APG-73 radar and targeting FLIR as he completed his after-launch checks.

At seven miles he reefed back on the stick and rocketed up, rolling left to steady on a heading of 060. His assigned sector was 060-090 from 100-200 miles while Comet and new guy Gigs searched 030-060 in section. As he climbed, the coastline of Crete come into view.

"*Knight*, four-zero-zero's up for checks."

"Four-zero-zero, *Knight*, you are up and up. Timber's sweet, fly your timber."

"Four-zero-zero," Wilson answered, checking his Link-16 steering and wondering if the controller in the *Hummer* knew that "the admiral" was flying 400.

The blue Mediterranean, blemished by the white wakes of merchants and island pleasure craft, glided below him as Wilson cruised to his first linked contact, 065 at 118 miles. Before he walked, he had learned that *Naciye Ram* was under tow some 40 miles from Turkish waters. Greek ships and aircraft kept a respectable distance as they shadowed it, and a Greek patrol boat south of Rhodes was en route to the scene. The Turks had F-16's up in Turkish airspace over Finike, 100 miles from the Greek Combat Air Patrol south of Rhodes; also F-16's fed updated ISR data from a *Pegasus* drone holding west of *Naciye Ram*.

A sudden transmission on the squadron tactical frequency surprised Wilson.

"Flip, Comet on tac."

"Go ahead," Wilson replied.

"Gigs has a right BLEED warning that's not going out. I'm going to stay with him as we talk to Mother and get him aboard this recovery."

"Roger that."

"If I can, I'll come out to play once he's on deck."

"Roger."

Gigs' engine bleed air malfunction was serious, but with the recovery still in progress Wilson expected he would be on deck soon. He also realized that he was the only jet covering the assigned *Raven* sectors.

After 20 minutes he came upon his linked track, a tanker headed northwest toward the Aegean. With the castle switch, he bump-locked it on the radar, and once locked the track showed a course of 303 at six knots. Wilson studied the ship on the FLIR display—typical Med oil/chemical tanker, maybe up from Suez. He checked his kneeboard card for the tanker ship codeword.

"*Knight, Raven* four-zero-zero...that track is a BASEBALL heading three-zero-three, ten knots."

"*Raven* four-zero-zero, *Knight*, roger...request you rig it before moving on."

"Four-zero-zero."

Wilson brought the throttles to idle and pointed at a spot aft of the tanker, keeping it just off his left nose as he descended. The ship had a black hull and white superstructure...a common color combo on a high seas' tanker anywhere in the world. With the early afternoon sun angle Wilson would come down the ship's port side to get the best look at it as he recorded his FLIR. On his kneeboard he scribbled the ship's course and speed, the time, and position.

Like an eagle swooping in low on the water, talons ready to grab an unsuspecting fish, Wilson steadily increased his g to align on the wake as he leveled at 500 feet and brought his throttles up to hold 300 knots. He would get a good look at the name on the fantail, port of registration, and flag. Approaching a mile, he eased lower as he scanned one more time to see if anyone else had the same idea.

Wilson found the flag on the mast truck…red. *Maybe this guy's Turkish*, he thought. As he approached along the wake, the name on the stern was easy to read: KADA TUNA. Seconds later he made out the registration port: ISTAN-BUL.

Yep, that's Turkish.

After he flew down the length of the vessel and found nothing unusual, he entered a climb and keyed the mic. "*Knight*, four-hundred marking on top; *Kada Tuna.*"

"*Raven* four-zero-zero, *Knight*, roger, next contact on timber, zero-three-eight, thirty-two."

"Four-zero-zero, roger," Wilson answered as he banked right, selecting SPARROW and popping the castle switch into AUTOACQ to lock whatever appeared on his air-to-air radar, actions of almost unconscious muscle memory.

Wilson headed northeast to the contact as he checked his HSI for the last *Naciye Ram* datum. This contact was 60 miles west of it. In the vicinity for sure, and Admiral Patros would not be happy, but Wilson would remain far from visual range of the Greek and Turkish shadowing forces with a valid cover story. Rhodes was over 30 miles away; he was safe in international airspace, and *Knight* watched his every move.

Chapter 8

Naciye Ram, South of Finike, Turkey
1400 June 9, 2024

Burak chafed in frustration as he paced the bridge. *Hurry up*.

On the bow, two of his operators wrestled with a new tow line trailed by the Turkish frigate. The first line had snapped with no warning; the frigate captain said he would have to slow their pace. So far it had delayed them almost an hour while *Naciye Ram* floated in calm seas, waiting for the replacement tow line. With Finike 41 miles away, they would not arrive until just before dawn. The safety of Turkish waters was roughly ten hours away, little solace to Burak in this botched mission.

The operators on the bow backed away as the line was tensioned. When it slowly lifted from the water, Burak felt a lurch, and the GPS display soon showed that they were moving.

He thought of the Greeks under the bow, barricaded for now. They could die of thirst for all Burak cared; any survivors he would dispatch himself tomorrow, after a nap and a meal.

The operators arrived on the bridge. "How much longer?" one asked.

Burak motioned to the frigate. "Up to him, but I estimate twelve hours, minimum. Find some food, and take turns sleeping."

"When do you wish to sleep?"

"I don't need it," Burak answered, lost in his thoughts.

He gazed west at the silhouette of a Greek warship on the horizon. Why hadn't they come? The maddening delay gave the enemy time to act. When would *he* come if the roles were reversed? Night, of course. The Greeks would come tonight, with a team of commandos. Burak guessed the time they would attack. An hour after sunset until they were safely inside Turkish waters was an acceptable window. Midnight, plus or minus, he figured. Maybe a nap *was* in order.

Above, he heard the rumble of a fighter engine. Stepping outside, he identified an F-16 high to the west, followed by another, both keeping outside the range of the Turkish guns. Greek or Turkish fighters? Could be either. He studied the frigate; sailors on deck craned their necks to get a better view of the jets. They did not seem concerned.

Wilson cruised at 10,000 feet in the milky Eastern Med sky. With his radar in SEA mode, he inspected the contacts on his display by bump-locking them, his FLIR slaving to the contact though the thin haze. A bulk carrier heading southeast, 20 miles distant. An island ferry heading west northwest. A containership. Toward the left edge of his screen he placed his cursor over a contact and bumped it. With a good lock, the course and speed data appeared: 085 at 22 knots. *Hmm*, Wilson thought, and once the FLIR settled down, his hunch was correct: a small surface combatant. He checked his kneeboard card, then called *Knight*.

"*Knight, Raven* four-zero-zero; showing a *desk lamp* at my ten o'clock heading east. Are you holding this track?"

"*Raven* four-zero-zero, *Knight*, affirm. Update course and speed."

Wilson complied, relieved that this combatant—probably Greek—was under the surveillance of the E-2. He would give the ship a wide berth, knowing that he was being monitored by *their* radar and wanting to avoid causing any heartburn to Admiral Patros. Just then *Knight* called, his voice elevated.

"*Raven* four-zero-zero picture, single group, BRA, three-five-five, thirty-two, twenty thousand, CAP, track southeast, hot. *Basket*."

Wilson studied the contact on his link display—nine o'clock at over 30 miles—and checked his kneeboard. *Basket* signified Greek F-16. He scanned the northern horizon through his helmet mounted display and saw the target designator box was over the tip of Rhodes. The Greek combat air patrol had committed on him. He keyed the mic.

"*Raven* four-zero-zero, roger. *Knight*, monitor that group."

"*Knight* monitor northern group."

As Wilson continued toward the assigned contact, he considered his options. The Greeks were running on him; if they didn't break off at 20 miles he would have to honor them. But *how*? Turn hard into them, fangs out? Or turn away in a non-threatening manner? They were Greeks, NATO allies. Besides, all he had was expendables and two drop tanks to "fight" with.

"*Raven* four-zero-zero, *Knight*, north group, BRA, three-five-zero 20 miles, 15 thousand, hot."

Wilson thought of Patros finding out that he was flying the American *Super Hornet* his fighters were running on. He banked right and added power, then answered *Knight*.

"*Raven* four-zero-four, roger. I'm coming right nose-cold; can you contact them and have them skip it?"

"They won't answer, sir."

Sir. Wilson guessed that the *Knight* crew had learned "the admiral" was flying 400. Did the Greeks know? Doubtful. With his nose passing through south he twisted his torso right to look over his shoulder as *Knight* called him.

"North group 15 miles, hot. Descending through twelve thousand."

Wilson kept the turn in and picked them up, two dots at his four o'clock long. Smoky engines and hauling the mail. *Uh, oh...*

He added power while remaining level, watching them rendezvous on the inside of this turn. His RWR aural tone came alive—as he expected—and the display showed him spiked at three o'clock. These guys weren't joining up on bearing line. *What are they doing?*

With the RWR *deedles* going off in his headset and the two dots growing larger, fast, Wilson was now alarmed and pushed the throttles to mil as he bunted slightly for airspeed. The Greek *Vipers* were not aligning their fuselages on Wilson's bearing line to join and signal him away. Looking down their intakes, Wilson remained padlocked on the fighters, missiles loaded on wing pylons now visible.

"*Knight, Raven* four..."

Wilson stopped, noting the decreasing range of the lead F-16 and co-altitude. *This guy's taking me right-to-right.* Wilson rolled away a bit, giving the Greek a clear indication that he was not a threat. Wilson's eyes got big when the *Viper* kept his nose on while holding a knife-edge, going belly up as he pulled lead.

Holy shit!

Wilson slammed the stick into the stops to avoid collision and shoved the throttles into burner. Outside, he heard and felt the sonic boom delivered less than 100 feet from his airplane. He stepped on bottom rudder and scooped down, lifting his head high to keep sight while maneuvering to place his lift vector on them. The lead F-16 dug down to engage, the trailer high nose off.

"*Knight*, four-hundred, they just thumped me! Engaged with two *Vipers*, Greek."

"Raven, Knight, your signal is RTB."

"No shit!" Wilson blurted under heavy g as he bottomed out of his impromptu loop. Carrying nothing but the drops on his pylons, he punched them off with EMERG JETT as his arm struggled against 5 g's of force. *Knight* called on GUARD frequency.

"Hellenic Air Force fighters this is U.S. Navy *Super Hornet* fighter. Cease maneuvering, I am friendly and operating with due regard in international airspace."

Not waiting for an answer, Wilson castled down into VERTACQ and locked the trailing fighter as the lead took his nose off at his three o'clock high. He maneuvered up to keep both in sight in his forward quadrant as they continued in a right-hand lead-trail, at that moment no longer a threat, the "fight" over before it had a chance to start.

Wilson descended and allowed his radar lock on the trailer to drift off the screen as the Greek fighters remained high above, the man in each cockpit monitoring the others. The Greeks turned in place left, putting them in a loose spread as they headed north to their CAP. Wilson figured they had a visual on him, and could reengage if Wilson's nose threatened.

"Knight, Raven four-zero-zero, they have disengaged and are transiting north."

"Raven four-zero-zero, *Knight,* roger. Mother sends RTB."

"Raven four hundred, wilco," Wilson answered, turning to place *Valley Forge's* TACAN needle on the nose. He had another question for *Knight.*

"Knight, four-hundred—are there any *Tomahawk* aircraft east of me?"

"Raven four-zero-zero *Knight,* negative. Mother just recalled the event."

Wilson could see Mark Meadows in flag plot calling Olive and Huey with that direction. Get everyone home, and especially the admiral.

"Raven four-zero-zero roger, switching Strike."

"Knight copies."

Ninety miles to the northeast, three Hellenic Air Force F-16's ripped over the waves at 550 knots, two of them carrying infrared AGM-65 *Mavericks.* Staying under the radar horizon, they weaved to avoid surface traffic as bridge-to-bridge comms of the ad hoc *tattletales* could alert the Turks to their presence—and intent. A daytime strike was bold, but this was merely a delaying action until the main assault was ready, still hours behind them.

"Action," the lead commanded, the first transmission since they had left Heraklion.

At forty miles from the datum they entered a shallow climb, the two *Maverick* birds setting their switches as the third *Viper* rode shotgun over them. The second missile jet took trail on the lead, both acquiring via radar-to-FLIR hand-off and then firing their missiles in sequence inside ten miles with a positive ID on *Naciye Ram.*

When they were inside thirty miles, the terrified Turkish operations specialists in the towing frigate's Combat Information Center thought the pop-up track to the west was inbound missiles, and confused orders were shouted by anxious watch officers to fire control radars for the missiles and close-in gun system.

Now at twenty miles and watched by the Greek shadowing vessel they roared over, the *Maverick* pilots locked their targets and handed them off to the missile display. They slewed their cursors onto *Naciye Ram's* bow and allowed the missile seeker to lock on the contrast.

"Lead good lock."

"Two good lock."

The *Vipers* bore down on their prey as surprised gunners scrambled to general quarters, the captain demanding—but not receiving—clear reports of what he was facing. He knew enough to rid himself of the cursed Greek vessel behind him, and bellowed for the tow line to be freed.

As his sailors raced aft, the first missile shot ahead from ten miles away, the pilot pulling off right.

The *Maverick* roared toward the target as the pilot egressed west. Thirty seconds later the second *Maverick* bird launched its missile, following the first as it howled off the rail.

The clear IR contrast of *Naciye Ram's* bow was all the missiles needed to maintain a track, and as they drew closer, the seeker heads focused on the vessels prow that slowly filled the imaged guidance system. While sailors on the frigate worked furiously to free the tow line, the missile "ran" on it until the cursor encountered an area of contrast, which held the seeker's attention.

The missile detonated on the manila tow line, cutting it 15 feet forward of the prow just as the sailors had freed it, dropping the precious line into the sea.

The second missile remained locked on *Naciye Ram's* forepeak, and one second before impact it "jumped" to lock on a mooring bit.

The explosion pelted the forecastle and superstructure, fragments ruining radio whips and the antenna of the S-band radar that rotated above. One shatterproof bridge window cracked like a spiderweb from a fragment.

Stunned by the sudden explosions, Burak and the others on the steel super-structure were unharmed by the missile's light warhead. But as Burak saw the tow frigate once again pull away without him, he did yet not realize he had a bigger problem.

Now obsessed with revenge, he wanted the Greeks up forward...if any were still alive.

CHAPTER 9

FLIGHT DECK, USS *VALLEY FORGE*, 1500 JUNE 9, 2024

Wilson deplaned on the foul line as the 120-decibel cacophony of the recovery continued next to him. Mark Meadows waited at the base of the ladder, his face grim under his cranial helmet. Wilson returned the salute of the young plane captain and turned to Mark.

"Anything going on here?" Wilson shouted above the din lightheartedly, knowing that much had certainly happened in the past hour. Mark wasn't smiling.

"The Greeks attacked their supply ship with F-16's—dead in the water now. The Turks are spun up," Mark shouted back, his eyes conveying the magnitude of their reaction. A surprised Wilson stepped back, not expecting this news. Now his Hellenic Air Force brushback made sense.

"And they know it was you, sir," Mark added. *Oh great*, Wilson thought, as a *Rhino* trapped aboard and thundered at full power next to them.

"Let's go below," Wilson shouted.

Entering the island at the Captain's Ladder, they went down one deck and followed the familiar blue tile to the flag spaces. Wilson thought of The Big Unit and Admiral Buffington. And the National Military Command Center deep in the Pentagon. He checked his watch: 0810 in Washington. Still drinking their first cup. They would drink gallons more coffee as this day unfolded. Skweez and a "pararigger" from the *Ravens* took Wilson's flight gear as he removed it, asking questions of Mark as he did.

"When did they hit the ship, and with what?"

"Greek F-16's, and just after the time you engaged with their CAP. We believe it was a guided missile, probably a *Maverick*."

"IR or laser?"

"Don't know yet, sir."

"Who's called?" Wilson asked as he unzipped his torso harness.

"Admiral Johnson's staff. The admiral wants to speak with you ASAP."

"Okay, set it up. What are we doing here?"

"I huddled with Olive and Huey. We are going to knock off for a few hours and maybe resume the flight schedule tonight, or maybe not. Double-cycle *Hummers* and helos will remain up in the interim."

"Good. Alright, let's get you, Smoke and Shane in the War Room for the call to SIXTHFLEET. Skweez, after you fill out the paperwork, join us."

"Aye, aye, sir."

Wilson stepped into the War Room and studied the current ops display. *Valley Forge* remained south of Crete, and the *Naciye Ram* datum had not moved since he launched, still fifty miles from Turkish coast. He noted that the Russian *Udaloy* was indeed moving west. Shane joined him.

Wilson pointed to the Russian track. "Shane, how long has this guy been moving?"

"About three hours, sir, and maintaining 25 knots."

"As you predicted. Is anyone bird-dogging him?"

"Yes sir, USS *Eugene Lindsey* has their *Romeo* up shadowing him. When they recover it we'll lose track; they are 50 miles south of the *Udaloy*, paralleling their course to the west."

Smoke and Mark entered.

"Admiral, SIXTHFLEET is on line one," Mark said.

Wilson picked up the receiver on the table-mounted phone. "Admiral Wilson." He heard a voice respond, "Yes sir, please standby for Admiral Johnson." Ten seconds passed.

"Flip, Randy Johnson."

"Good afternoon, sir. I've got my CoS and Ops/Intel with me."

"Roger that. How was your hop?"

Wilson glanced at Smoke. "Eventful, sir."

"Yes, I heard. How close did the guy get?"

"I'd say fifty feet; would'a been closer if I hadn't pushed away."

The Big Unit asked the question Wilson was waiting for.

"Flip, why *you*? Why were you there?"

"Admiral, the squadron CO briefed me along with his nugget wingman. They were to take the sector closest to the datum, but when his wingman had a right BLEED warning they RTB'ed in section and I moved up to cover it. I was under *Knight* control and the closest I got was maybe 75 miles to the datum. When the Greeks ran on me, I turned away and allowed them to rendezvous on my inside."

Wilson knew his excuses sounded lame. Johnson spoke next.

"Yeah, looks like they were there to shoo you away or worse. We got their comms; they came real close to arming up. Behind them the strikers came in low on the water and lofted two *Mavericks*. *Naciye Ram* is DIW last we heard, with Greeks and Turks moving forces to the area."

"We're watching that *Udaloy*, too, sir."

"Yes, and I want you to watch it. Keep *Eugene Lindsey* on him and send another small boy as a show of force. Show themselves, but no closer than ten miles. Helos stay outside three."

"Wilco, sir, and Admiral, we're not flying now, but I'm going to move us east and resume the night schedule, and probably keep an E-2 up all night."

"Good idea, and I'll see what ISR assets I can get for you so you don't crush your E-2 crews."

"Thank you, sir."

Despite his audience, Johnson had to address the elephant in the room.

"Flip, Patros is hopping mad. It's gone up to Brussels."

"Yes, sir," was all Wilson could say. He had a flashback of Cajun frowning at him when he handed him back a poorly written report.

"Look…you command your strike group, and you manage your time, but things will go a lot easier for both of us if one of your lieutenants is thumped next time, not that we are going to allow that again."

"Yes, sir."

"I'm protecting you, and I just counseled you. Matter closed."

"Yes, sir."

"Stay outside of 100 miles."

"Wilco, sir."

"Talk to you later, out here."

"Out here, sir."

Wilson set the receiver down in awkward silence. Mark broke it.

"Admiral, recommend we release another DDG, USS *O'Hare*, to help *Eugene Lindsey* track the Russian. *O'Hare* is carrying two *Romeos*, which will help."

"Good," Wilson said, grateful for the change in subject. "Can we get another *Romeo* to *Lindsey*?"

"I'll check with Olive, sir."

At that moment Olive appeared at the doorway.

"Admiral…we have a new shipmate that just arrived on the COD."

As Olive stepped aside, retired Captain Mike Hopper entered the room. Wilson beamed.

"Weed Hopper! Oh my gosh, we're going into combat now for sure. What are you doing here?" The men shook hands, then hugged.

"Kemosabe, I would ask you the same question, which I can now that I'm a civilian."

"Really, Weed, what brings you out here? I thought you were with the Council for Navy Studies."

"Still am, now on a field trip to assist Carrier Air Wing Four and analyze their deployed training matrix. I'm from CNS and I'm here to help!" Wilson looked at Olive.

"Admiral, I just found out when he darkened the door of CAG Office. We did not have him on the message."

Weed bailed her out. "You know, being a retired officer of my stature allows me to pull a few strings around the office. When I found out that Flip and Olive were at sea for this scheduled assist visit, I just had to jump on it."

"Karen let you go?"

"She packed my bags! After two plus years of me working from home, she's happy for the break. Besides, it's just for two weeks. When's the next port visit?" Weed noticed Smoke and stepped to him to shake hands.

"And Smoke's here! Wow, we've got the old band back together! Olive and Smoke are captains now; to think that we knew them when."

Mark Meadows and the rest of the staff were not sure what to make of the spontaneous reunion, but this newcomer had the admiral's trust and friendship. The sailors understood that. Wilson, however, still smarting, returned their focus.

"Okay, well, welcome aboard to Captain Hopper—Olive, he's all yours—but while you're here, Shane, let's get a quick look at the link and GCCS."

Shane maneuvered the mouse, and the screen split to show the Global Command and Control System screen next to the current ops display.

Wilson noted the datum stationary south of Turkey, then went to the *Udaloy*.

"Admiral, the Russian DDG has turned northwest, still at a high speed. It will be in the vicinity of the datum in six hours."

Olive spoke next.

"Sir, we can keep a *Hummer* airborne for the next 48 hours before we need to give the crews a rest."

Smoke chimed in. "And Admiral, there are two P-8's in Sig that are part of the exercise. We still have operational control of them, and my recommendation is to task them before SIXTHFLEET takes them back."

"Great idea, Smoke, let's keep OPCON for as long as we can. Okay, what are the Greeks doing?"

Shane answered.

"Open source has the F-16s back at Heraklion, but they've been flying quite a bit, about twenty sorties so far today. The Greeks are flowing in more fighters for bed down there, all F-16's."

"How about Turkish open source?" Wilson asked. Shane was ready.

"A squadron of F-16D's was moved to their reserve base at Antalya this morning, which is impressive and shows prior knowledge. They are flying F-16's out of Balikesir, Eskisehir, and Konya, and have a *Peace Eagle* AWACS up on this overland track north of Finike, which gives them an unimpeded view of the eastern Med. They are squawking IFF and not hiding their moves. It is probable, sir, that they have TB2 UAVs up near the datum, their *Shadow* and *Reaper* knockoffs that are quite capable in ISR and armed with laser guided bombs."

"Good, how about their ships?"

"This morning the corvette *Tahrihi Hadirga* left Marmaris and SIXTHFLEET believes it is enroute to the datum. No reports of anything else leaving the major Southern Sea Area bases of Izmir or Mersin."

Wilson studied the GCCS display. "How about the Hellenic Navy?"

"Everything they had at sea this morning is moving toward the datum: a frigate and two missile boats working the exercise in the Aegean. Open source shows underway preps in Salamis and Souda for two more missile boats."

"Subs?"

"All imaged in port sir, except one Greek boat last identified in the Aegean."

"Okay, thanks, Shane. Olive, thoughts."

"I'd like to resume flight ops in two hours and get in the three night events. We'll launch one *Hummer* on the last recovery and relieve it at 0400 and 0800, then resume with the schedule tomorrow. We'll swap out *Romeos* to keep one airborne all night. I'll coordinate all this with Huey, sir."

"Alert package?"

"Recommend four jets in alert thirty with two-and-one for air-to-air, and a *Maverick* and one laser guided bomb for anti-surface. I'll brief my squadrons to have jets airborne inside those 30 minutes."

"Will two 'winders and an AMRAAM be enough?"

"I think so sir; we are looking to defend ourselves, not engage anyone."

"Concur. Okay, we'll fly tonight. Mark ease us east but don't make a big show of it, and Olive, I want your E-2's to stay outside of 100 miles of the datum, but have a wingtip at 100.1 miles, if you know what I mean. Shadow the Russian and dispatch *O'Hare* to help."

"Aye, aye, sir."

The meeting broke up. Wilson motioned for Weed to remain behind.

"Good to see you, man. Glad you're here."

"And just in time to watch this *splendid little war* you've managed to become part of."

"I need to talk to Admiral Patros, if he'll take my call."

"What happened, did you dump fuel on one of their small boys, call Helen of Troy ugly?"

"The Greeks ran on me while I was searching my sector and minding my own business—*but not really*—and their radars practically burned a hole in my jet before they thumped me like I've never been thumped before. Had to push away to avoid a collision. But I'm not going to go high-and-right. *Mea culpa*, please forgive me, diffuse tension, your backyard, your imminent regional conflict, won't happen again."

"Such a politician."

"I'd like to think peacemaker."

"Flip Wilson, a *Great American Peacemaker*…no, sorry. Can't see it."

"Do you have a stateroom assigned?"

"Yes, Grand Central Station on the O-3 level under the cat 2 JBD."

"Ugh, I'll see what I can do."

"Sure is nice to have connections, thanks."

"Stow your gear and come back. And join us for dinner tonight, 1800." Wilson clasped his arm. "Glad you're here, Weed."

"A day at sea with Flip Wilson is always an exciting day."

"Souda Bay in a week!" Wilson answered, smiling.

"We'll see," Weed said, smiling back.

At that moment, some 250 miles away, *Konya K* took in mooring lines as she eased alongside the Alexandria containership wharf in Bab el-Arab Bay. She would unload ten containers and take on six more, a job made short with the large gantry crane that towered above the ship. After the transfer was complete, the crew would receive an hour to shop at the duty-free store before they would get underway with the evening tide for the return trip to Antalya—and another mission.

CHAPTER 10

NACIYE RAM 0030 JUNE 10, 2024

Burak checked his watch. The helicopter would arrive soon.

With two sailors sent over from the frigate and armed with an acetylene torch, they had opened the anchor windlass room to obtain another towing line. Unable to find one, the operators—out of sight of the Navy personnel—beat the captive crew with their rifle butts and fists. One of the thirsty Greeks had received a wound from the missile detonation despite a steel hull that had protected them from most of the force. That man took his beating with stoic resolve. Burak watched, impressed by his courage, then selected as his own victim a man who flinched from the blows with fear in his eyes. *That look…*Burak lived for that look.

Unable to be towed and vulnerable as the Greeks gathered their forces to the west, Burak surmised that *Naciye Ram* would soon be boarded. After coordination with Aaghaa, a helicopter would be sent at night. Burak ordered the crew to push cargo over the side to make an unobstructed deck for the aircraft. Their hands then tied to their waists, all the captives but one boarded the helicopter as its rotor blades thrashed the dark and humid sea air. After it lifted and turned north, Burak waited for the sound of its rotor blades to cease. On the dark fantail as a light breeze cooled them, the man panted with fear, not knowing why he was not with the others.

Burak motioned to the man, and one of the operators untied him. Burak nodded forward to the bridge, and the operator left them alone.

Pulling a cigarette from a pack, he placed it on his lips, then offered one to the man. "Go ahead, friend, it is alright. Can we not enjoy this spring evening?"

Trembling, the man did not understand Burak's Turkish but grasped the meaning, and with trepidation pulled a cigarette from the pack Burak held in front of him.

"There. Allow me to light it for you."

Burak flicked his lighter open and cupped his hand near the flame as he lit the man's cigarette. Burak was at his most vulnerable, alone on the open fantail at night with an enemy—part of the exhilaration—but a weakling he knew would not dare to take his only chance at life, or at least revenge. The cigarette lit, Burak extinguished the flame and returned the lighter to his pocket. He studied the man.

The Greek was in his late 20's, a mop of dark curly hair over a heavy day's growth of beard. He could pass for any Turk his age, any swarthy young man from southern Europe. Orthodox Christian, no doubt, but did he worship his savior, or had he abandoned religion like so many in the West? The man exhaled nervously as he took furtive glances at Burak, his eyes afraid to make contact, his heart palpitating in fear at what was to come—in greater fear of not knowing.

Burak realized that *he* did not yet know what he would do.

Aware of the time, and devising a plan, he flicked his cigarette butt into the sea.

"It is time, friend."

The man, his chest heaving in terror, saw Burak's knife blade flash in the moonlight. "Ohi, OHI!"

Toying with him, Burak showed him the blade and pointed at it. He then pointed at the dark water.

"You may choose, friend. Quick...or slow?" Burak again pointed at the knife. "Quick?" he repeated, then pointing at the sea, said, "or slow?"

The man shook his head. "Ohi! Eleos! *Parakalo!*"

Burak lunged as if to stab him and the man jumped back, balancing on the open deck edge with gentle sea lapping at the hull below him. "Eleos! Parakalo, *Parakalo!*"

When Burak held the knife as if to throw it, the man cried and jumped off the ship and into the water four meters below. Burak savored the moment: *that look*, a split second before he jumped. Sheathing his knife, he took his pistol from the holster and peered down from the deck edge. Below him the man looked up, gripped by a fear that showed even in the low light, babbling, begging for his life in Greek. Burak did not need a translation...each one understood the other perfectly.

Burak raised his pistol and fired. The man cried and turned from the splash next to him, swimming away from *Naciye Ram* with all his might. Burak fired again and laughed as the bullet splashed just above the boy's head, chuckling again as the Greek's arms and legs thrashed in wild panic to distance himself from both his tormentor and only refuge on the dark and open water. The man submerged and Burak waited in anticipation—*a sport!* When he surfaced, Burak fired, and the man turned to escape a nightmare that was inescapable. Burak stood and listened, hearing whimpers as the man treaded water thirty meters distant. Creatures of the deep would finish him off as he floated near the vessel, his terrified face now barely visible in the moonlight. Burak looked around the deck and saw a stray pallet of canned goods. He pulled out a can of meat—*perfect!*—and with his knife ripped open the top. He stepped to the rail and dumped the contents into the sea.

The thrum of distant rotor blades was again heard as the helicopter returned to take off Burak and the remaining operators. The Greek man, his face still visible, floated as before. Burak lifted his pistol and aimed, this time trying to hit him. The bullet lifted a column of water next to the man's right ear and again he dove away. *Sport.*

The rotors dug in as the pilot slowed to a hover and pedal-turned right in a graceful approach and landing to *Naciye Ram's* open fantail. Burak and his mates scrambled aboard, leaving the vessel—and one soon-to-be drowning man next to it—floating on the dark Mediterranean waters as had triremes and galleys and their terrified sailors over the millennia.

One hour later, the Greeks acted.

Two rigid hull inflatable boats of Greek special forces operators came upon *Naciye Ram* as the Turkish surface combatants abandoned it. Through night vision devices on a circling drone, the Greeks had watched the Turks depart it by helicopter with their hostages. They also watched as one man they deemed to be a hostage jumped off the ship, only to be fired upon as he swam for his life. The man was no longer tracked by the drone.

The team of ten operators came aboard at the fantail as the Turks had the night before, one group assigned to the bridge as another group went below into the engine room.

The bridge group was clearing it and the chartroom behind the helm when an explosion sounded below. For a moment they froze, until another explosion in the bowels of the ship prompted them into action.

They flew down the ladder, and while two men remained on deck to cover them, three reentered the ship where the first team had as smoke billowed out of the hatch. Hearing shouts from one deck below, the lead operator shone a flashlight down the ladder well. Rushing water covered the deck and rose toward them as the operators below scampered up the ladder.

The lead man then detected a list.

"Abort!"

They gathered outside as the lead called in the boats on the hand-held. Standing off from *Naciye Ram's* port quarter, they turned to go alongside the Jacobs Ladder. More explosions sounded from below, and the starboard list grew. At the port rail, the first men went over the ladder and down the side of the hull, now tilting at 20 degrees. Under them, the RHIB was bumped by *Naciye Ram's* bronze screw as it rose out of the water. One operator jumped aboard, breaking his ankle as he did.

The list increased and soon the starboard side was awash. The RHIBs could not get underneath the ladder as the ship continued to roll.

"Jump! Jump for your life!"

The six men remaining aboard tossed their weapons into the sea and ran down the sloping hull to fling themselves as far away from it as they could. Their life vests inflated by seawater contact, they swam to the nearest RHIB and pulled themselves aboard, then helped to pull the others to safety.

Naciye Ram rested on its starboard side and settled as the forward superstructure filled with water. Watching in fascination, the men took a roll call as they did, and the lead called to the corvette that launched them, the captain watching the scene from drone video real time with the rest of the Greek military command structure.

The vessel corkscrewed right and lifted its stern out of the water as the RHIBs moved off, the men unable to take their eyes off the spectacle. Great bubbles rose forward from where the hull slid deeper into the darkness. Then, without warning, *Naciye Ram* accelerated down and disappeared under the gurgling froth and spray that marked her final resting place.

The RHIBs came alongside one another, and the leader conducted another roll call to be sure. Satisfied all were accounted for, he motioned the coxswain to return as his men huddled in their soaked gear.

On the wind he heard something: *Boetheia! Boetheia!*

All heard it, and the coxswain turned to the sound. Shining a light, they saw a man, his arms lifting water up in the air as he cried for help in Greek. "Boetheia!"

The first RHIB came alongside him, and the operators, grabbing his arms and shirt, hauled the exhausted man over the side and into the boat. Pounding over the waves to the western horizon, the man shivered as the operators warmed him with a space blanket and their own bodies, learning that he was one of the vessel crewmen and left for dead by a sadistic Turkish terrorist. The man guzzled down a water bottle with one swig before he collapsed, reassured of his deliverance by the Hellenic Navy.

CHAPTER 11

USS *VALLEY FORGE* 0555 JUNE 10, 2024

Wilson awoke to the sudden sound of the phone buzzing by his head.

"Admiral Wilson."

"Sir, it's Mark in flag plot. *Naciye Ram* sank."

Wilson absorbed the news. "Okay…when and what else?"

"About five hours ago. Earlier the Turks took off about ten hostages on helos. Sometime later a Greek special forces team boarded the vessel and not long after they did, she started to take on water. The Greeks believe she was booby-trapped by the Turks and their team tripped an arming wire when they boarded it; she went down in minutes. They just sent video of the whole thing."

"Loss of life?"

"None reported, and they did get a survivor, one of the hostage crew that was floating in the water. He made his trousers into a flotation device after one of the terrorists made him walk the plank and then shot at him in the water. The Greeks have video of that, too."

"Wow. Is this on the media?"

"Social media, but not the networks yet. Sky News will probably run it within the hour—we're monitoring a feed—and it's almost 2200 in Washington."

"Anything from Naples?"

"Not yet, sir."

"The Russian DDG?"

"He's about 100 miles from the scene, sir. We're shadowing as before."

"Okay, I'll be there in five minutes. Is Shane with you?"

"No, sir, just the watch team, but I'll wake her."

"Good, see you in flag plot."

Wilson thought as he ran a razor over his stubble. *Greece and Turkey going at it big time, both mobilizing.* Wilson considered how Washington would react, and what tasking was coming from Brussels through Naples. Two NATO allies…why couldn't he contact his Turkish counterpart? Why would he, if not any business of the United States?

In his flight suit, Wilson walked through the War Room and into the Tactical Flag Command Center (TFCC), where Mark Meadows presided over the watch team monitoring the action around the Strike Group. "Admiral's in TFCC," a junior sailor sang out as Wilson stepped inside. Meadows stood behind the battle watch captain. Before them sat four stations of watch-standers on consoles, updating the large flat screens of GCCS and link data on the forward bulkhead.

"Good morning, Admiral. Here's the sitrep: we are 40 miles southeast of Crete and moving east at five knots. *Knight* 602's airborne and on station seventy miles east of us, and we've got OPCON of a P-8 out of Sigonella, *Tiger* 24, patrolling 200 miles east. *Lindsey* and *O'Hare* are shadowing the *Udaloy* west of Cyprus. He's been holding a 20-plus knot PIM all night and our small boys have been shadowing him with their *Romeos*. He's heading straight for the position where *Naciye Ram* went down, as are two Turkish combatants from Mersin. The frigate that was towing her is holding off in the Gulf of Antalya."

Wilson noted the Hellenic Navy vessels south of Rhodes. "Do the Greeks have anything airborne?"

"Just a patrol plane here, sir, over Rhodes now, and a UAV at the datum. The Turks haven't closed them since the sinking."

Who will make the next move? Wilson wondered. He was content to remain at this distance: near, but not intruding. Nothing from SIXTHFLEET; he would wait for tasking.

"Let's see the video," he requested.

The team called it up, and familiar FLIR video with a greenish tint emerged on the link screen of *Naciye Ram*, dead in the water, as the SOF team boarded her.

"We got this off social media, sir, after the Greeks leaked it."

"Roger," Wilson said.

Through grainy FLIR video they watched the team split up and enter the ship, then fast forwarded to when the first smoke appeared.

"Here comes the bridge team down...they return inside," Mark said, giving the play-by-play. "And now you can see more freeboard on the port side...and here they come."

They watched, spellbound as the RHIBs returned and the operators boarded them or jumped. Wilson was struck by how fast the ship rolled.

"They must have blown her whole bottom out," Wilson said, transfixed. They watched as *Naciye Ram* rolled over and lifted her stern high as the men struggled next to her. With the ship gone, the camera stayed on the RHIBs, one of which stopped and pulled an object from the water.

"There they are rescuing the survivor," Mark added.

Shane Duncan entered from the Supplemental Plot.

"Shane, have you seen this?" Wilson asked.

"Yes, sir, next door. Going viral, I reckon," Shane answered.

"What chatter are you hearing from Naples?"

"When I secured last night, they said the Greeks were recalling people from leave and flowing F-16s to Crete."

Wilson looked at the screen. "Any flying now?" Seeing none, he answered his own question. "No...okay, Mark, when does that P-8 have to RTB?"

"We've got him till 0800, sir."

Wilson could only smile. "Great, just when the *Udaloy* arrives...okay, we'll keep our *Romeos* and E-2 up, and when the flying day begins we'll fly as planned, monitor our NATO allies, but we need to stay out of their way. Alright...morning meeting at zero-seven...I want to hear your recommendations on how we should operate today at the meeting."

"Wilco, sir, we've got it."

The phone buzzed, and the watch captain answered it. "Admiral Wilson, Sixth Fleet himself wants to speak with you."

"Okay, thanks...Mark, let's take it in the War Room."

The men stepped next door to take the call as another day at sea began.

Wilson listened as Admiral Johnson went down the list of Russian forces moving to the eastern Med.

"So that makes four *Tu-22 Backfires* that just got to Hmeimim, Syria, and we're tracking four MiG-31's that are transiting from Central Russia that we expect this afternoon. Expect a *Bear* ELINT bird, a *Mainstay* for AEW, and an Il-38 to help with the surface picture. All at or heading to Hmeimim and we think will be available for tasking within the next 24 hours. And we just learned last night that the Russians sortied a *Grigorovich* class frigate out of Sevastopol and it's heading for the Bosporus and probably toward you—two days if they haul."

Wilson lifted his eyebrows. "Wow. Surprised they would spare anything from the Black Sea Fleet."

"Yes, my sentiments exactly," Johnson said.

"Why are they moving these forces, sir?" Wilson wanted to hear it from the admiral.

"Turkey is in trouble; the lira is about to collapse and they are spending a significant portion of their GDP on oil, much of it from Russia. Russia wants access to the Aegean and beyond, and despite the fact that the Bosporus and Dardanelles are international straits, the Turks do control them. With Turkey's belligerence in the eastern Med, the EU and NATO are spun up. We condemn their belligerence and by extension support Greece. That makes it all the easier for Russia to support Turkey; if we are for Greece and against Turkish overreach, they are *against* Greece and *for* Turkish overreach—anything to stick a thumb in our eye."

"What's NATO doing, sir?"

"The French are going to get *Charles de Gaulle* underway from Toulon tomorrow, and the Brits are looking to send *Prince of Wales* into the Med. Doubt the Brits will get her through Gibraltar in a week though, and I think it's an overreaction anyway. This tempest will blow over in a few days if we all play it cool and don't give them a reason to spin up."

Shane knocked lightly and cracked the door open. Wilson saw her and motioned her in. Smoke followed. One the other end of the line, Johnson continued.

"Flip, Turkey wants this to go hotter than it is right now; it helps them economically and politically at home. They want to show who's boss in the eastern Med, and they want to start drilling for oil and gas in the disputed seas where the proven reserves are. Cyprus is part of this too, by the way, and that's another reason the Turks aren't going to compromise; they can't back down after all their posturing."

Wilson took a yellow sticky from a pad on the table and wrote a message for Smoke sitting next to him:

Get Olive in here, and Weed

Johnson summarized the situation. "So, Flip, this is warming up, the Turks are going to try to pin these escalating tensions on the Greeks who are furious, the Russians are sending some serious force to support their Turkish client and remind everyone of their business interests in Northern Cyprus, the EU is spooked, NATO is puffing up their chest, and you are in the middle of it."

"Easy day."

"Yes, and it will go easier for you—and me, and Washington—if you operate with due regard and stay out of their hair. Your presence is the message Washington is sending, and I'm going to send you a DDG from Rota to beef up NATO's BMD posture, not sure which one yet, but one's coming to you tomorrow. More signaling. You are my air warfare commander and the strike commander, if it comes to that—and it shouldn't—but…"

"Submarines, sir?"

"I'm going to hang on to them, but you'll know where they are."

"Roger that, sir. I envision us flying normal cyclic ops, keep everyone in qual, routine training, but set an alert 15 CAP and SuCAP for any contingencies."

"Good call, and by sunset I am going to send you my intentions and concept of ops, from which you can publish your own CONOPS and intentions. I think we are in a lull for today, but when the MiGs arrive in Syria we'll see how they operate…and if they try to test you."

"We'll be ready and briefed for any and all."

At that moment, Olive entered the War Room, and Wilson motioned her to be seated at the table.

"Good," The Big Unit said. "Early on Olive needs to have some A-team players standing those alerts; they may go."

"Yes, sir, I'll pass that." Wilson nodded at Olive, who nodded back.

"Okay, Flip…you've got it, call me with anything, keep a reasonable distance from—but track—anything military, send me a SITREP this afternoon with your thoughts, and fly safe. Out here."

As Johnson hung up, Weed entered the War Room and faced Wilson.

"Reporting as ordered, sir."

"Weed—and Olive—we just wrapped it up with The Big Unit. Russia is sending *Backfires* and MiG-31's to Syria, a frigate from Sevastopol after they pay off the Turks, the Frogs and Brits are sending a carrier each this way, everyone from London to Ankara is bowing up for a fight, and we're going to Alert 15."

Olive spoke first. "Can't say I'm surprised. Heard about the Greek supply ship…just caught the story on Sky News."

"Everyone is spun up, and The Big Unit thinks the Turks like it that way and will continue to escalate tensions. Weed, is this in your geopolitics lane?"

"Yes, and concur that it will escalate, and no surprise given Ankara's irredentist policies of late."

Wilson narrowed his eyes at Weed. "Did you just say *irredentist*? What the hell is that?"

"Didn't you learn anything at War College, um, Admiral? For Turkey, this means they want to go back to the good ole days of the Ottoman Empire when they owned this little corner of paradise including this patch of water and every-thing underneath it. Their saber-rattling—and let's face it, they've got some quality sabers today—is them informing everyone that they're back. Their for-eign policy has been maximalist for the past decade, and this is the manifestation of it."

Wilson turned to Smoke. "Did he just say maximalist?"

Smoke nodded in embarrassment for his shipmate. "He did, sir, and then he said *manifestation*, too."

Recovering from his shock, Wilson could only look at his loyal wingman. "Weed, come back."

"Hey, this is what I'm reduced to after three years with the wine swilling and coat-and-tie wearing pol/mil geeks in the Beltway! Just give me a few days at sea; wait, I can feel the old vocabulary coming back. Seems like we're in a *shitstorm* out here—see, I've still got it!" Olive rolled her eyes. *Same old Weed.*

Ignoring the aviators' banter, Shane concentrated on her laptop screen. Wilson noticed her focus.

"Shane?"

She did not respond.

"Lieutenant Commander Duncan?"

Startled and flustered, Shane adjusted her glasses and recovered. "Oh, I'm sorry, Admiral, but I was just studying the shipping traffic using AIS data on the Maritime Trade website, tracking the vessels around the two Greek ships. There's a...coincidence, and maybe a suspect."

"Put it on the screen."

Shane manipulated the screen mirror controls, and seconds later her laptop image was projected on the bulkhead flatscreen.

"Admiral, here's the Greek research vessel *Nauticos Card* last week, with the track from Piraeus until her last known position. We can see how she maneuvered through the Aegean and then between Crete and the island of Kasos into the open Mediterranean on her way north of the Bouri Field. While she transited along the northern shore of Crete, she slowed due to traffic, then accelerated once free in the open, but made three course changes of 10-20 degrees over the next 12 hours to avoid traffic."

Shane fast-forwarded the AIS, which showed a blue line for the track of *Nauticos Card* as she transited.

"Admiral, I am now going to open up the screen and show a track of another ship, this one from the port of Derna, Libya, and bound for Antalya, Turkey, and at the same time."

Wilson and the others watched as the two blue track lines, surrounded by hundreds of maritime tracks that crisscrossed the Med, intersected close to the time contact on *Nauticos Card* was lost.

"Admiral, I'll freeze it at the last known position of *Nauticos Card*. There are many ships in the vicinity, and if we track them we can see how they encountered the Greek vessel at this time and location, but this ship from Derna did not maintain a steady course. We can see that at the points *Nauticos Card* made course and speed changes, roughly 15 minutes later this ship did too."

"What is the name of this ship?" Wilson asked.

"*Konya K*, sir, registered in Istanbul."

Wilson watched as the two tracks grew closer. Shane continued.

"Here is the last AIS hit on *Konya K*, approximately 30 miles from *Nauticos Card*. Perhaps they turned off the transceiver, or maybe the shore station missed them, but it came on an hour later, on basically the same course and speed. Nothing out of the ordinary, except for all the correlated course changes it made in the previous 24 hours."

"Where is it now?" Wilson asked.

"According to AIS, the ship is at sea; it left Alexandria seven hours ago."

Shane placed the computer mouse over the track. Smoke read off the information on the box.

"Bound for Antalya and making nine knots; ETA about noon tomorrow. By the photo it's a self-loading containership—probably doesn't leave the Med."

Shane had more to add. "And sir, it was transiting from Antalya to Alexandria two days ago. Approaching midnight on the eighth, it was 45 miles from *Naciye Ram*, and after midnight it sped up from 9 to 12 knots."

Wilson stared at the screen and thought. "So, you think this ship is involved."

"Sir, it was in the vicinity, and it made course and speed changes last week for seemingly no reason. Their changes were perfect to have it cross aft of *Nauticos Card* within visual distance. Could be luck or coincidence, but they could have been tracking the ship on AIS."

Wilson nodded. "Or receiving updated intercept info from a shore station. Okay, Shane, see what you can find out about it, and Olive, we need to get eyes on this thing."

"Yes, sir, and if they maintain this track and we keep to our PIM, at about noon they'll be roughly 180 miles away."

"That's not unreasonable for a sea surface search. Can we ensure an experienced aviator searches that sector?"

Olive smiled. "Can do, sir. I'll check the air wing flight schedules and put the right pilot on it."

"I'm sure you will. Nothing unusual, and ensure the *Knight* crew is briefed that we want to rig that track."

"Aye, aye, sir."

Before Wilson got up from the table, he went back to his Assistant Intel Officer. "Shane, what prompted you to research and develop this theory?"

"Sir, I just drew a circle of 50 miles from where *Nauticos Card* went down. None of the other tracks around it acted suspicious, but this one did."

Wilson got up from the table. "Good job, Shane. Make us smart on *Konya K*."

Chapter 12

Eastern Med, 1245 June 10, 2024

Captain Kristin "Olive" Teel, flying a VFA-64 *Ravens* FA-18E, held bearing line on the *Rhino* tanker as she joined up for 2,000 pounds. On altitude and on bearing line, she kept a steady closure on the tanker that orbited overhead *Valley Forge*. At 45 years old, Olive had joined on tankers for almost half of her life. Her rendezvous skill was such that she barely had to touch the controls now. Nearing the tanker, the hose began to trail from the refueling store as the pilot extended it into the airstream for the CAG. Olive reached down and extended the probe, clicking left wing down trim by habit and feeding rudder to align the fuselages and slow her closure. Stabilized on his left wing, the pilot gave her a thumbs-up and Olive slid in behind the basket. Again stabilized, she added power and held the sight picture as the probe slammed into the basket at 250 knots, and she was soon rewarded with a green light from the store: good flow.

Any second-cruise aviator could have handled this sector search, but Olive chose to take it herself. She would ensure the rigging of the contact-of-interest *Konya K* was done right, and if it wasn't, she would shoulder the blame. Who knew what the Greeks or Turks would do next? Or the Russians from Syria, even at 500 miles from the carrier.

The green light extinguished—*tank complete*—and Olive backed out to join the tanker's right wing as she retracted the probe. With more CVW-4 jets lined up for fuel, the tanker pilot gave her the kiss-off signal, and after a thumbs-up in return, Olive eased right and away from the others to clear the tanker and steady up on a heading of east to search her assigned sector.

Konya K was 180 miles from mother, heading 356 on a course for Antalya. Olive ducked into surface plot before she walked; between *Valley Forge* and *Konya K* were two tankers and a bulk carrier on a busy sea lane from Port Said to the Sea of Sicily, with more coming up from the Suez. *Plausible deniability.* She checked in with the *Knight* controller.

"*Knight, Raven* four-zero-three's up for your control."

"*Raven* four-zero-three, *Knight*, radar contact, fly timber."

"Four-zero-three."

Cruising at 14,000 feet, Olive coupled the flight controls to the assigned link heading of 110. Fifty miles. Seeing nothing air-to-air, she commanded the radar to surface search and found a contact 15 miles right of her nose. Peering over her dashboard, she saw it, a sailing vessel. She had never seen one before in this part of the Med, far from the Aegean islands they liked to frequent. Slewing her aiming diamond to it, she bumped the castle switch and her FLIR locked it. Single-masted sloop heading north. *Where is that guy coming from?* She made a mental note to rig it on the way home.

Her mind wandered back to the ship. Working for living-legend Flip Wilson again—the fourth time in her career—and during every sea tour. Two weeks ago she had received a good fitness report from Admiral Garretson, paper anyone would be proud of, but he gave Huey Morrison the top ticket. Both she and Huey were early in their tours, and Admiral Wilson would have to break them out again in the next reporting cycle. Wilson had known both of them for years; it would not be an easy thing to let down one of your friends with a career-ending report full of glowing praise.

Daydreaming as she floated to the east, she thought of her family. Her only child, Margaret, was finishing first grade and would enter second before Olive returned home to her. That she had dealt before with the guilt of her career choices did not make the separation any easier. If Flip gave her a shot next year, Washington duty would be next: the Pentagon...and hubby Chris would not be thrilled. Then who knew, except another move and more uncertainty. While contemplating the future, her eyes were drawn to the fuel display, as her eyes had when airborne for almost half of her life.

"*Raven* four-zero-three, *Knight* traffic one-two-seven, thirty-eight miles flight level two-two zero and climbing, heading three-one-three, probable CO-MAIR." Olive selected air-to-air and castled right into AUTOACQ. The radar locked the contact at once, and the FLIR soon revealed it was a two-engine airliner...probably out of Alexandria. Olive scanned around the canopy bow and saw it in her helmet-mounted sight.

"*Knight*, four-zero-three visual, COMAIR."

"Roger four-zero-three."

Olive went back to SEA mode and saw the linked contact off her nose. She switched out of autopilot and gently pushed, placing the ship in her HUD.

An LNG tanker, gray hull and the standard white superstructure. Up from Suez, no doubt. Olive recorded the course and speed, flew down the tanker's port side to identify it, and made her report to *Knight*.

Once more into the milky haze, she climbed to the east and set cruise power, her radar scanning as she inspected the contacts on her link page. She saw the link for *Konya K*, twenty miles beyond the link *Knight* commanded, on her nose. She would glide down to rig the interim contact, then stay low to intercept *Konya K*.

The ship was a bulk carrier with a blue hull, bound for the Aegean. Olive rigged it close, passing just down the vessel's port side at 300 feet. *Iho Sea* was registered in Panama and flew a Panamanian flag. Olive marked on top with *Knight*, and turned right as she leveled off at 1,000 feet and set the autopilot.

Konya K appeared out of the gloom, tracking north trailing a small wake. The black-hulled self-loader carried two cranes located forward and amidships, with an open fantail behind the typical white superstructure aft. Shipping containers were loaded forward of it, but not too high, and none aft. Olive bump-locked it with her radar and jotted down the course, speed, time, and lat/long. She then took a cut to the right, spacing herself to intercept the wake and fly up the port side with the sun high behind her. Hitting altitude hold, she prepared her hand-held camera and placed it in the right console before she took control of the jet.

Olive kept her eyes on the ship as she reversed her turn and eased down to 500 feet. One pass—*don't be conspicuous*—and she left her power up in the descent to have some smack on the jet as she flew past. Rolling out three miles aft, she flew next to the wake as she leveled off, and commanded her FLIR to track the ship, which at this close range filled the display.

With her eyes outside she focused on the fantail; KONYA K was easily visible in big white letters against the black hull. Sensing movement on the portside bridge wing, she inspected her FLIR display. A white object moved toward the pilothouse. *A person!* she thought, and detected another white-hot object at the tip of the bridge wing. Looking through her windscreen, she could not make it out as human.

At 350 knots and inside one mile, she held the *Rhino* at one degree nose up, slightly right wing down, and hit attitude hold. She readied her camera while she took another look at the open fantail. No helipad markings, but metal chassis to hold containers were set side-by-side. Under KONYA K the port of registration ISTANBUL was now visible.

Once the ship became visible aft of her canopy bow, she snapped photos as she whizzed past, taking care to get the fantail, superstructure, and deck. Over her right shoulder, she snapped the name KONYA K next to the anchor hawsepipe before her wing obstructed the ship from view.

She took the stick, entered a gentle climb, and keyed the mic.

"*Knight, Raven* four-zero-three mark on top, *armrest*," she transmitted, using the codeword for a self-loading containership…the only one in the vicinity.

"*Raven* four-zero-three, *Knight*, roger, follow your timber." Olive rogered the transmission and turned left to intercept the next linked contact some twenty miles north.

She had leveled off at 1,000 feet and hit altitude hold when *Knight* broke in.

"*Raven* four-zero-three *Knight*, skip it, snap east to intercept single group, 084, three-three-zero miles, one-six thousand, hot. Probable *placemat*."

What?

Olive turned and climbed as she repeated back the directions from the E-2. *Three hundred and thirty miles? What's a* placemat?

Established in her climb to intercept, Olive dug into her kneeboard pack and found the codeword *placemat*: Tu-160 *Blackjack*.

Electrified, Olive continued up as she contemplated what this meant. A Russian bomber, their biggest and fastest, heading out to sea from Syrian airspace toward her, and most importantly, *Mother* behind her. The carrier was already in a cruise missile launch window…if the bomber had targeting data. In the traffic-choked Med that would complicate things. Russia and the United States were far from war, but the ship would not allow unescorted overflight. Olive checked her kneeboard again and found the codeword for deck-launched intercept.

"*Knight*, four-zero-three, interrogative *flowerpot*."

"*Raven* four-zero-three, *Knight*, expect that."

Wilson was at his desk when the 1MC sounded.

"*This is the TAO. Now launch the alert five fighters, initial vector zero-niner-zero. Now launch the alert five fighters, initial vector zero-niner-zero.*"

Wilson bolted from his desk and into the Tactical Flag Control Center, where the TFCC watch officer was on the phone amid a flurry of activity among the console operators. On the big board he found his airwing aircraft tracks, and among the many COMAIR tracks, an unidentified track far to the east. The watch officer LCDR Dave Snell noticed him standing behind his chair.

"Admiral's in TFCC!" he sang out.

"What's goin' on, Dave?" Wilson asked.

"Russian *Blackjack* inbound, sir. We followed it on civilian flight following from the Caspian, normal squawk, and heading for Hmeimim in Syria. Normal enroute descent to landing, then it leveled off at ten-thousand feet and sped up to the west as it went feet wet."

Wilson saw the track off the coast heading further out to sea south of Cyprus.

"It's still squawking sir, holding 420 knots, and *Knight* is vectoring *Raven* four-zero-three to it now."

Wilson suspected who the pilot was, but needed to be sure.

"Who's in four-oh-three?"

Snell pulled up the Air Ops page. "CAG Teel, sir."

Wilson nodded as he suppressed a smile. *The Big Unit is going to be shaking his head.*

On the PLAT, the first FA-18F taxied to cat three as the wingman followed. With this mid-cycle alert launch, the flight deck was thrown into disorder and confusion that surpassed the norm, and one deck above Wilson heard the Air Boss bark orders on the 5MC.

"Where did it come from?" Wilson asked.

"Engels Air Base, sir, on the eastern shore of the Caspian."

"Has SIXTH FLEET been informed?"

"Yes, sir, battle watch at least."

Wilson returned to the big board as the first *Rhino* was placed in tension, the roar from its two F414 engines filling the space. On the PLAT he watched the pilot salute, and seconds later the jet was shot off the angle as the crew lowered the JBD for the wingman. The *Blackjack* they would intercept was already in a launch window.

Was a satellite bird about to overfly them? Were any of the merchant ships visible on the horizon? Tattletales feeding them tipper info? Was the bomber coordinating with the Udaloy? Did the Turks have an ISR drone nearby that the strike group had not yet detected? Tensions in the region were high, and the alert launch was standard procedure, but Wilson wanted and needed answers to these questions.

"Engels," Wilson muttered to himself but so Snell could hear. "A long way... and makes a statement."

Olive monitored her link display as the *Blackjack* track held steady on a heading of west as it skirted just south of Akrotiri, Cyprus at 17,000 feet. Had the RAF launched an alert from the airfield? No heads-up from *Knight*. In Range-While-Search mode she monitored the civil air traffic, the high stuff likely from the Persian Gulf and India, while the lower altitudes held flights climbing out of

Ben Gurion and Amman or crossing the sea from Cairo. At 80 miles from the track, she got a radar hit on the bomber but did not yet lock it.

"*Raven* four-zero-three, *Knight*; *flowerpot* inbound."

"*Raven* four-zero-three."

Olive opened up her link display and saw the *Rhinos* depart Homeplate some three hundred miles behind her. Keeping a respectable distance from the Russian, she would intercept the *Blackjack* first with the *Rhinos* arriving about 20 minutes after that.

She was one of only a handful of aviators who had ever intercepted one of the massive swing-wing bombers, escorting a flight of two north of Puerto Rico when she was in the *Firebirds*. Tensions were high then too, but with two Greek vessels sunk under mysterious circumstances and Greece and Turkey on a war footing, the regional tension now was much higher. She found the *Udaloy* on her display, northwest of her and not a factor.

At sixty miles she slaved the FLIR to her helmet-mounted sight and scanned the horizon off her nose. Too much haze. Leaving the radar in RWS she monitored the civil traffic, and noted that the coast of Cyprus was now just discernable in the low visibility.

The link vector showed the Russian holding slight left aspect, and Olive allowed the lateral separation to build in order to stern convert on the bomber's left wing. She noted the sun high to her right and considered a climb to get above the bomber's altitude to join from out of the sun, but soon rejected it. No need to alarm them on this innocent intercept in international airspace.

Inside forty miles the Tu-160—despite its white paint job in a white sky—became visible, and after Olive found it on the FLIR she bump locked it. She fiddled with the return to see it better and ensured her recorder was on. Opening up, then narrowing the focus, she ensured there were no escort fighters snuggled close.

"*Knight, Raven* four-zero-three has a tally on the track; *placemat*."

"Roger, four-zero-three, join in escort."

"Four-zero-three."

Decrementing to twenty miles, she locked it on radar, and once she obtained a course and speed, she sweetened her intercept heading and broke lock.

"*Raven* four-zero-three, *Knight*, mother just launched mission *Texaco*."

"*Raven* four-zero-three, roger, ten miles and the *placemat* is steady two-seven-three, one-seven thousand."

Approaching ten miles and satisfied with the lateral separation, Olive rolled into a left bank, allowing the bomber to cross in front of her as she joined, unsure if the Russians yet knew she was there. Out of habit she checked her belly for traffic—or threat fighters—and then resumed.

Up close now, the *Blackjack* impressed Olive as it had 12 years ago, and as she joined from below, she studied its wings and underside for any ordnance or open bomb bay. No ECM indications from it—everyone on their best behavior. The wings were swept back slightly as it cruised at 350 indicated. Olive had never flown formation on an American B-1B, but the lines were similar. She reported joined.

"*Knight, Raven* four-zero-three in escort; steady 270, angels seventeen."

"Roger, four-zero-three, *flowerpot* is on your nose for one hundred."

Olive rogered the *Knight* controller and eased acute on the bomber's left wing. The pilot, eyes covered by a helmet visor, looked at her; after a moment she realized he was staring at her. No friendly wave, no turning away to monitor the cockpit. She studied the small window aft of the pilot—nothing. On the fuselage were written large Cyrillic letters she did not understand. Keeping plenty of distance—her Puerto Rican experience with one of these maneuverable monsters fresh in her memory—she snapped photos as the pilot continued to stare a hole in her.

Wishing to remain predictable, she avoided any sudden moves and held on the *Blackjack's* left bearing line as the alert fighters joined. They checked in with the *Knight*.

"*Knight, Spartan* one-zero-five, flight of two, checking in, low state nine-point-nine, zero, two, and one, good timber."

"*Spartan* one-zero-five, *Knight*, fly your timber; *Raven* four-zero-three joined in escort."

"*Spartan* one-zero-five."

Olive glanced at her link display and saw them at sixty miles, offset slightly left for a classic stern conversion. The bomber continued ahead.

Then it didn't, pushing over slightly as it held course. Olive keyed the mic.

"*Knight, Raven* four-zero-three; the bogey has entered a slight descent."

"*Knight* copies."

"*Spartan* copies."

The *Blackjack* pilot no longer looked at Olive as the jet ramped down in a shallow dive, maintaining course as airspeed built. *Just like Puerto Rico,* she thought. On the Nav display, Mother was 200 miles away—and they were going right at her. She checked her fuel—acceptable.

"*Knight, Spartan* one-zero-five has a tally, visual."

She picked up the *Spartans* visually and slid behind the Tupolev to take station on the right wing. The *Spartans* flew a solid intercept and rolled out next to the bomber on its left wing. Olive took photos of the *Rhinos* next to the big jet as they all descended at two degrees nose down.

Two hundred miles. Olive thought of Flip, Mark, Huey, the controllers aboard *Manila Bay*—and the entire strike group tactical brain trust—watching this drama unfold. Underneath she spied a drill ship dead in the water as a service vessel approached it. The Bouri Field. Nearby merchants dotted the sea as they had through the millennia, oblivious.

Minutes passed, and passing ten thousand, the *Blackjack* hadn't budged as if in attitude hold. Olive selected the MARK she had hit at launch time; her velocity vector was right on it. With her TACAN radiating, *Valley Forge* was near the MARK as the event launch time neared. The Russian, now leading three American fighters, was bringing Olive back to her nest in time for her own recovery…but she was under no illusions. Her velocity vector was right on the ship; what did the Russians know? She assessed all she could from the jet and the demeanor of the cockpit crew, who had not looked at her in five minutes, as if they had blinders on.

One hundred miles, holding 450 knots, and going right at the ship like riding a laser beam, the *Blackjack* added power to maintain closure speed in the dense air near the surface. *What is this guy doing?* she thought as her eyes danced from the bomber to the range to her ship, falling fast.

CHAPTER 13

FLAG PLOT, USS *VALLEY FORGE*, 1345 JUNE 10, 2024

With the secure radio transceiver held firm against his ear, Wilson studied the tactical picture as he conversed with Captain Bob Dolan aboard the cruiser USS *Manila Bay* riding shotgun ahead of the carrier.

"Admiral, the track is behaving as I would expect it to. He knows where we are, and we aren't trying to hide. He's going to do a low flyby and dust us off to announce his presence or just flip us the bird for general purposes and return—maybe back to Engels, or maybe he'll duck into a Syrian base. They operated there in the 2010's. Recommend weapons hold, sir. Over."

Wilson nodded while watching the *Blackjack* and his escorts jump closer with each computer-generated update. "Bob, I'm inclined to agree, and despite the fact that I have fighters on him, do you have any constraints or reservations about him? Over."

"None, sir. We can hand him off right now and engage on your orders or continue tracking if you want your fighters to take him, but we're not there, sir, in my view. At fifty miles, which is going to be in three minutes, I intend to warn him on GUARD. Over."

"Concur, and so you know, I'm in the middle of a launch and then recovery of the event airborne. My people are telling me if he holds he's going to overflight in about 15 minutes. Call him on the early side of fifty. Thanks, Bob. Out."

"Will do, sir. Out."

Wilson cradled the receiver and turned to Mark Meadows. "Ever seen a *Blackjack*?"

"No, sir, not in the flesh."

"Okay, let's watch this live from the flag bridge. Shane, you too. This is once-a-career."

"Thank you, sir!" Shane beamed, thankful to get out of the drudgery of SUPPLOT and see some sunshine.

Wilson led the way through the labyrinth of passageways to the flag ladder, followed by a five-deck climb to the flag bridge on the O-8 level, each step ingrained from almost thirty years of operating from *Nimitz*-class carriers. As they climbed each ladder, deafening roars, one after another, enveloped them as *Valley Forge* shot jets from three catapults.

Hazy sky met a sharp blue horizon when they arrived on the deserted flag bridge, and Wilson checked the flight deck progress before he walked to the starboard side to inspect the screening ships on the southern horizon. Mark and Shane still marveled at the flight deck action, unfamiliar with it yet enthralled by the power and seeming order amid the ear-splitting chaos on the other side of the heavy bullet-proof glass.

Wilson returned and took his chair, punching in the direct line to the Captain one deck above. At his feet he monitored the tactical feed from CDC.

"Captain," Huey answered.

"Huey, it's Flip one deck below you. Are you monitoring our potential visitor?"

"Yes, sir. Have you been in touch with Bob Dolan?"

"Just got off the phone with him. He said he'd call on GUARD at around fifty miles."

"He made that call, sir, and I show them inside fifty now. Let's see…we've got three more to shoot and fifteen fixed-wing to recover. I've got a sweet tanker overhead with give and I've got crossing traffic on my nose at eight miles; I'd like to maneuver to cross behind him after the recovery if I can recover them now."

Wilson was torn.

"This guy might thump us in the middle of the recovery. Can we delta everyone and bet on the come?" As Wilson spoke, cat three flung a *Growler* into the air.

"Admiral, if this guy breaks ten miles we'll delta the pattern and resume once he passes."

"Okay, sounds good. Out here."

Mark pointed at the display. "Admiral."

Olive fell back as sudden flame became visible from the burner cans of the four big engines. *Holy crap! There he goes!* she thought as she shoved her engines into burner to maintain position and bunted to gain some knots, her eyes padlocked on the bomb-bay doors. The *Spartans* were on it.

"*Knight, Spartan*, the bogey just went into burner."

"*Knight* copies."

"Weapons status…?"

"Standby."

As the Air Wing Commander and senior on scene, Olive did not know if the *Spartan* flight lead knew it was her in *Raven* 403.

"*Spartan* one-zero-five; *Tomahawk* actual is in four-oh-three."

After a moment, the *Spartan* lead responded.

"Roger, four-zero-three."

USS *Manila Bay* transmitted on GUARD.

"Russian warplane, Russian warplane, this is U.S. Navy warship transmitting on GUARD. I am operating due regard in international waters. Turn left one-eight-zero and state your intentions." The E-2 ratcheted up the tension.

"*Spartan* one-zero-five, *Knight*; weapons tight."

"*Spartan* one-zero-five, weapons tight."

Valley Forge steamed 45 miles ahead as the four airplanes passed through eight thousand feet, and Olive wasn't sure what Flip Wilson—or Bob Dolan in *Manila Bay*—was thinking. The Russian bomber was flying aggressively, ignoring radio calls…and ignoring her on their right wing. Not a routine encounter, and the *Blackjack* did not appear to be intimidated. Her mind assessed the situation as she held position. *Who* was weapons tight? The *Spartan* fighters or *Manila Bay*? And who would take a shot if one was called for?

Forty miles: five minutes to the ship, but as airspeed built it would be more like four. Olive knew this was a "manhood" check…the *Spartans* would have downed the bomber at the moment the bomb bay doors opened, despite the countries not being in a state of war. All the airplanes had a right to be there, and the Russian had a right to thump the carrier if it wanted, but this had not happened in recent years, maybe ever. At thirty-four miles the indicated airspeed rose above 550-600 knots over the ground. Olive took the lead.

"*Knight, Spartan, Raven* four-zero-three; I've got the lead. *Knight*, status."

"*Raven, Knight*, roger…they're figuring it out."

"Four-zero-three," Olive replied, then added, "*Spartans* take trail, weapons tight," as she moved away from the bomber, expecting something unusual, and giving herself room to react.

Wilson's eyes remained on the link repeater as he waited for Dolan to pick up.

"Captain Dolan, sir."

"Bob, if it comes to it in the next 90 seconds, how should we handle this?"

"Your call, sir. I've got him and can take him with two birds if you pull the fighters off, or they can. It's then missile transit time, and their time will be shorter."

Wilson considered it. At this range two SM-2's from *Manila Bay* could arrive thirty seconds after launch, the escort fighter missiles in ten. Both types could destroy the *Blackjack*. The seconds counted down as Wilson wrestled with his decision.

"Twenty-five miles sir, ten miles a minute," Mark said. Shane's eyes darted from Wilson to the eastern sky and back.

"Weapons hold," Wilson said.

"Weapons hold aye, sir, WEAPONS HOLD," Dolan bellowed to his cruiser watch team. Wilson kept the line open.

Now at 20 miles and passing 2,400 feet on the display, Wilson studied the horizon to pick them up visually as the recovery continued. Overhead he noted a section of *Rhinos* enter the break. He buzzed the bridge.

"*Yessir.*"

"Huey, he's not breaking off and will be here in a minute, signal delta."

"Aye, aye, sir," Huey said, remaining on the line as he called the Air Boss to convey the order.

"There they are," Mark announced.

Wilson picked them up, a dot at fifteen miles with three faint dots near it. He checked the altitude readout; *1,600, 1,500, 1,400.* He heard Olive on the land/launch frequency.

"Boss, *Raven* four-zero-three, see you at ten escorting the *Blackjack*, recommend you clear the pattern."

"Already done, *Raven*. Ninety-nine *Tomahawk* stay well clear of Mother, *Blackjack* inbound at ten from the east."

Huey returned to Wilson.

"We've got a good track sir, RAM and CIWS armed, weapons hold."

"Roger!" Wilson answered, tense.

You do not have to take the first hit, Wilson thought. Was it already too late? Not at war, nothing on the wings, bomb bay closed with an armed section to blow it out of the sky the second the doors moved.

The *Blackjack* bore in, now approaching *Manila Bay* on its way to *Valley Forge* without giving the cruiser a thought, not moving on Wilson's bridge window, not showing any bearing drift, as if its flightpath were held on it, *on him,* a modern-day kamikaze, determined, accelerating *in anger* to its death and the deaths of hundreds.

Eight miles and below 500 feet! He had never seen or heard of this. Two huge intakes under the wing grew larger, and his mind flashed an image of Hariri and the *Flatpack*. Mark stepped toward him as Shane took a nervous breath.

Enough!

The first to flinch, Wilson brought the receiver to his ear, ready to order *Hostile! Weapons tight!* when the bomber veered left.

Still descending toward the deck, Wilson froze as the Tupolev leveled at 100 feet, practically at his eye level as vapor jumped off its wings and those of the escorting *Rhinos*. All on the flight deck and in the island were entranced as the formation roared past just off the port side.

He watched them recede to the west, and the four entered a gentle climb, then a steep climb as the bomber showed planform with its wings still swept, ignoring the jets overhead—if he even knew they were there. Forgetting he was still on the freq., Wilson jumped as Dolan spoke.

"Admiral, how was your airshow? Looked great from where we sat."

"As close as I ever want to get, and if he sets up for another run like that, I will end it much earlier."

"If the fighters need to recover, I've got him sir."

"Yes, and one in particular. Olive Teel is flying that lead *Rhino* and I'll meet her at her jet when she lands."

"Yes, sir, look forward to hearing her story…and Huey's!"

"I'm getting on the horn to Sixth Fleet and sending an OPREP. Will stay on my bridge until this guy leaves, and you stay on him as long as you can. Out here."

"Aye, aye, sir. Out."

Wilson got up from his chair. "Mark, get Admiral Johnson for me and start the OPREP message. Bring me a draft in fifteen minutes."

"Yes, sir," Meadows replied.

"I'll help you, sir," Shane said, and went below while Meadows stayed behind to arrange the call.

Wilson watched the *Blackjack* as it steadied up and climbed to the east. A *Rhino* came into the break above him and the recovery resumed.

He replayed the incident in his mind…and knew that he had hesitated. A Rolling Airframe Missile launched from the bow would have gotten there just before the first 20mm *Phalanx* close-in weapon system bullet arrived. Would they together have stopped the near-supersonic behemoth? Even if wounded, it could have careened into the ship—at the island, removing virtually all the carrier's command and control—in mere seconds.

I put this crew at risk, he thought, and the more he thought, the more he realized he had put the United States at risk with his late decision, which the Russians certainly had interpreted and were now reporting as *no-decision*.

Alone on his flag bridge, Wilson struggled with the burden of command.

"Damn," he muttered as he left to go below.

Chapter 14

Flag cabin, USS *Valley Forge*, 1530 June 10, 2024

Weed listened as Wilson caught him up on the day's excitement.

"So Olive traps and I meet her at the jet on the foul line. Unflappable Olive; she's the coolest. Escorting a kamikaze *Blackjack*, almost getting shot by us…just another routine hop."

"But you should never go on a routine hop…" Weed quipped.

"Exactly, and we come down here where Shane and half the ship and air wing intel officers are ready with their questions. First, she rigged the Turkish ship, *Konya K*—nothing unusual. We should get the images soon. Then *Knight* vectors her east to intercept the *Blackjack*, which had a flight plan to Syria, normal ATC handoffs, filed IFR for anyone to monitor, and approaching Hmeimim it breaks its enroute descent and heads here, another 400 miles."

"Another *Blackjack* intercept to add to her belt. Some girls get all the luck."

"She said these guys weren't all friendly waves. The way they stared at her and then ignored her was unnerving, she said, but the most unnerving thing is that when the jet started down, it was as if it was tied to the ship. The controls didn't budge as it let down right on us as if riding a laser beam."

"TACAN on?" Weed asked.

"Yes, ops normal, but even if they have the freq., they rode that beam or just eyeballed it from over 100 miles. She said she couldn't have done it that flawlessly, no human could."

"And when it got here?"

"I was on the flag bridge, and once I picked it up it did not move on the glass, like it was coming for me personally. Zero drift, which is not all that impressive from a visual pickup, but at range Olive said it was as if they could see us and just coupled their autopilot."

"Maybe they can see us."

"Yes…maybe they have a new optic gizmo…but to fly a perfect ramp-down all the way here…where do I get whatever they have?"

"Would you use it tactically? Just fly straight at something in three dimensions? What's the value?"

Wilson nodded. "Concur…but they have something that allows them to couple up on something. My TACAN beam, tipper offset from something, multispectral detection and tracking…with unheard of accuracy."

"Where did the *Blackjack* go, Hmeimim?"

"No, Engels on the Caspian Sea."

"That's a hike."

"Yep…and a 6,000-mile *FU* to us."

Wilson's phone buzzed and he picked it up. "Admiral Wilson."

"Sir, Skweez here. Admiral Buffington is on the line, and not his staff. It's really him."

Wilson sat up. *Whoa! NAVEUR himself.* "Put him through at once—and stay on."

"Yessir," Skweez said.

Wilson whispered to Weed, *"Admiral Buffington."* Weed raised his eyebrows in surprise, and Wilson heard the connection go through.

"Admiral Wilson, sir."

"Wilson! What's going on?"

"Good afternoon, sir. We're still collecting all the data…"

"What the fuck are you doing launching that CAP? *Do you want to start World War Three?"*

Stunned by Buffington's tone, Wilson's eyes met those of Weed, who could only hear one side of the conversation. "Sir, we launch CAPs for high-interest bogeys as a matter of routine. We are always going to intercept and escort them—"

"Bullshit! You sent two snot-nosed lieutenants with live missiles, two *kids* who do not have the judgment to make a weapons call if things go south. Bob Dolan in *Manila Bay* does, because he can track them from longer range and put the right weapon on him if it comes to that, all backed up with his over 20 years at sea. In situations like these, *Admiral,* he is the man who has a better picture and more amplifying information in his combat spaces than a kid on a joyride."

Dismayed, Wilson grabbed for a lifeline.

"Admiral, the Air Wing Commander herself was the first to intercept the bomber, and was right on his wing, taking the lead and directing the CAP."

"I don't give a fuck about that or her! NO aviator in a cockpit has a better picture than Dolan with a proven combat system and his decades of experience on when to shoot and when not to shoot. Your fliers don't have that!"

"Admiral…my *senior aviator* was on the bomber's wing, reporting real time, directing the CAP. It doesn't get any better." Wilson immediately regretted that last crack.

"Dammit Wilson, that was pure dumb luck and you know it. Your CAG can't be on every intercept to hold the hands of your JO's. Bob Dolan, whether he's reading the message traffic or sleeping or taking a piss, can be in combat in minutes, *seconds*, and direct the track and assess firing decisions with authority, with reach back, and with experience. When did you go weapons tight?"

Wilson struggled to remember. *Did I go weapons ti -*

"WHEN?" Buffington bellowed. Wilson flinched from the blast, and Weed strained to hear what he could.

"Admiral, I'm not sure we did. We—"

"Not sure? Not sure? You've made my point, Wilson. That thing could have cleaned your clock, and even if you went weapons tight in the end game it would be too late. Admiral, you are paid to command that strike group, and you are paid to make smart decisions, smarter than vacillating when a decision is called for. Jim, your cruiser captain over in *Manila Bay* can make these decisions better because he's seen them before. It's not your fault that you haven't. You've been flying around all these years and yes, you've seen your share of aerial action, but you are new to this, and smart commanders empower their people and trust their people. I strongly suggest that you trust Bob the next time this happens. Now, where are you?"

"Southeast of Crete, sir. We—"

"Yes, dammit, I can see you. Where *should* you be, admiral?"

Wilson looked past Weed with pursed lips. *Are we playing stump the dummy now?*

"Admiral, I'm over 150 miles from the datum, closer to 200…"

"I can see where you are, Wilson! I'll spell it out for you: MOVE WEST. Now! Recover your damned airplanes and go. Lower the temperature out there and operate smart. I expect my strike group commander to make command decisions at sea, but I do not expect them to make things worse. You've got a steep learning curve and I'll cut you some slack after only being in the seat for a week, but this is the big leagues, Jim. Need your A-game every day. Trust Bob and your surface warfare leadership to take care of you, and call me with any questions. Out here."

Setting the receiver in its bulkhead cradle, Wilson took a deep breath, expecting Weed to break the silence. He did not disappoint.

"Friendly chat with a four-star. How was it? Any tidbits to pass?"

"Whoa…"

Weed waited.

"That was a fleet ass-ripping…wow. Do I still have my arms and legs?"

Skweez knocked twice, then opened the door, his face ashen. Wilson motioned him in.

"Come in and have a seat."

"Admiral, Captains Meadows and Teel, plus Commander Duncan, are waiting outside to see you."

"Okay, let's go to the War Room," Wilson answered. With his heart rate still elevated, he and Weed entered from his stateroom door, the rest entering from the main door.

Once the officers entered the War Room and took seats, Wilson began.

"Okay, to bring you all up to speed, I just got off the phone with Admiral Buffington." Meadows raised his eyebrows, but the others remained expressionless.

"It was a one-way conversation, the gist of which is that I waited too long to make a decision that would have given us a chance to not absorb the first shot."

Olive spoke.

"Admiral, we had two armed *Rhinos* one mile in trail. One false move…"

"I know, and you and I and Mark must have a sidebar about how we'll handle this the next time, but for now we need to move west. Mark, call Huey—and now, please—to call everyone airborne back, recover them, and head west at 20 knots."

"Aye, aye, sir," Meadows said as he stood to contact the bridge.

"And the DDGs birddogging the *Udaloy*. Everyone to the west."

"Roger, sir."

As Meadows departed, Wilson turned to Olive.

"Okay. Do we have pictures of *Konya K*?"

"Yes, sir, that's why we're here." Olive said. Shane handed Wilson a folder of stills. After he studied two of the photos Olive took of the ship, he asked, "What am I looking for here?"

Olive answered.

"Admiral, look at this one just as I'm approaching the fantail. On the port bridge wing you can see this blob…and look at this near the pilot house door."

Wilson nodded. "Okay…"

"And this next one, sir. That 'blob' is a man, hiding his face, and you can see that the pilot house door is just open, open because someone scurried inside as I approached."

"And the guy hiding his face?"

"Admiral, have you ever seen that? First, I've never seen anyone on a weather deck of any ship I've rigged in my career. And today when I do, which must be a rare experience for the merchant sailors too, one runs away and the other hides his face."

Wilson made a face.

"Circumstantial evidence? I mean, any evidence? Do they think they are under attack? Sun too bright?"

"Admiral, here they are on the high seas, hour after hour of mind-numbing routine, and a fighter shows up to give them the obligatory airshow right down their port side. And instead of ooh-ing and ah-ing and waving, they run inside or hide? Struck me as odd...but there's more sir."

Olive dug out a photo and handed it to Wilson.

"Sir, Shane caught this. Look at this SEA BOX container."

Wilson pored over the image of *Konya K's* bow area. A familiar brown container with the SEA BOX livery was stacked on the port side, forward of the crane.

"Now look at this close up."

Wilson held the photo with two hands as he looked for anything unusual. Then he saw it.

"That is a seam—for a door. A big door."

"Yes, sir," Shane replied. "We went over each container that Captain Teel had an image of. This is the only one with a door, and there are other SEA BOX containers on top of other stacks aboard *Konya K*."

Olive jumped in.

"Admiral, Shane found more evidence. First, this SEA BOX container has nothing behind it. Okay, containers can be stacked haphazardly, but look at this close up."

Wilson studied the close-up image of the container doors, facing aft.

"What am I missing?"

"Down here, sir, left-hand door. No metal identification plate that is found on all other containers. Shane looked. Every container with this door visible that I took a photo of has such a plate, except this one."

Wilson nodded. Maybe this container carried a *Klub* cruise missile.

"*Klub*-in-a-box?"

"Yes, sir," Shane answered. "The export version of the Russian SS-N-27 *Sizzler*, also known as *Klub*."

Wilson pulled on his chin. "Okay, this concept has been around for some time. But who has it, a demonstrated or postulated anti-ship missile in a shipping container?"

"Sir, in the Mediterranean, Algeria has *Klubs* in their navy, but no sir, nothing fielded in a shipping container anywhere that we are aware of. It would not be too hard, though. And sir, some of these containers may carry a search-and-track radar or a UAV. Or targeting info from a satellite download to the ship fed into the launch computer."

"How many crew to operate this system?"

"Roughly ten, sir, but maybe more." Wilson nodded. *Konya K* had plenty of room for riders.

"So Turkey bought a Russian export anti-ship cruise missile. Does Sixth Fleet have this yet?"

"We're going to send it now, sir."

"Okay, good. Everyone is dismissed except CAG and Mister Hopper."

Once Shane and Skweez departed the space and closed the door, Wilson began.

"Okay, we're moving west at the order of Admiral Buffington to lower the temperature out here. Fine. He ripped me a new one for launching the CAP and not letting *Manila Bay* take the lead on tracking and potential shooting."

Olive spoke up.

"Admiral, are you going to tell The Big Unit that Buffington called?"

Wilson exhaled.

"I'm wrestling with it, but yes. *I* didn't call NAVEUR, he called me, and I thought he was going to pat me on the back. The Big Unit needs to know the boss isn't happy and I'll come clean about my late decision."

"You've never played chicken with a *Blackjack* before," Weed said.

"And I don't plan to again. I want to run west all night then stop southwest of Crete and fly tomorrow. Vanilla stuff. Basic squadron training. But I want an alert 5 and I want us to think that with our two NATO allies squaring off we need to operate at a heightened sense of caution. Olive, tell the airwing that we don't need to poke the hive, any hive. Give combatants a wide berth, and if a threat appears, withdraw if able but honor it if you must. Inert bombs and missiles…except for the alert."

"Aye, aye, sir."

"I'll pass this to Huey and the warfare commanders," Wilson added.

Above them they heard the Air Boss on the 5MC, the sound penetrating the armored steel flight deck, direct the re-spot. All three of them glanced at the PLAT as they did.

Wilson rubbed his eyes. *Let Mark pass it to the warfare commanders.*

Skweez reentered the room, his eyes focused on Wilson.

"Admiral, Captain Meadows wants you in TFCC."

"Be right there," an impatient Wilson responded, still looking at Olive's photos.

"Sir…recommend ASAP. The Greeks torpedoed *Konya K.*"

"*Ho-lee shit,*" Weed said under his breath, as a stunned Wilson absorbed the news.

CHAPTER 15

FLAG PLOT, USS *VALLEY FORGE*, 1555 JUNE 10, 2024

Wilson burst into TFCC, his eyes drawn to the big screen and the datum of *Konya K*, assessing at once the range to him. A watch-stander sang out.

"*Admiral's in TF—*"

Wilson waved his hand. "Enough! Mark, what's up?"

"We just got this, sir, from Naples. A Greek boat launched an electric torpedo at *Konya K*. Explosion, but no indication that it sank."

"I thought that boat was in the Aegean. Did it move that far, that fast?"

"The boat we're tracking in the Aegean is still there, sir. This is one we weren't tracking."

Wilson shook his head. *Good grief.* Blame could be assessed later.

"How do we know?"

"USS *Trigger* heard the torpedo and impact."

"How far?"

Meadows turned to Wilson and whispered the range so that the watch-standers could not hear.

Wilson shook his head in perplexed amazement. "Do the Greeks know we have a boat nearby?"

"If they do, *I* do not know that, sir."

Wilson nodded. Where The Big Unit and Buffington placed submarines was not his problem. But they had lost track of a Greek boat in what was now a full-fledged shooting war. He hoped that *Trigger* was moving west as *Eugene Lindsey* and *O'Hare* were. Above them he heard the Boss on the 5MC. *Make a ready deck*, Rhinos *in the break.*

Meadows glanced at Weed, and Wilson sensed his uneasiness. "He's good, Mark."

Olive leaned in. "Admiral, I'm going up to visit Huey and fill him in."

"Good…get everyone aboard, pivot west and sprint, and Mark, get the rest of the strike group moving west at best speed. Keep *Manila Bay* in shotgun."

The two captains *aye aye'd* Wilson as they departed, leaving him with Weed as they both examined the link picture and status board.

"I better call The Big Unit."

"What are you going to tell him?" Weed asked.

"Well, first that I'm moving west at best speed, and then the reaming by Buffington…then the *Blackjack* dust off. How's that?"

"Hard to know where to start, isn't it, Kemosabe?"

Wilson smiled. "He'll want to hear about Buffington first."

"Yeah, and I can hear him now: *Tell me about the bomber some other time; why is my boss pissed at you?*"

"I still don't know *why* Buffington called, other than he just feels he can jump a chain because at four stars he can, and I don't know if The Big Unit or anyone on his staff knows. Anyway…want to sit in on this call too?"

"Oh, you bet I do! Can Flip Wilson push Randy Johnson, the nicest guy in naval aviation, over the edge? He's already apologized to an admiral for you once this week."

Get out of the port catwalk! the Air Boss bellowed above them. They both looked at the PLAT as another *Rhino* rolled into the groove. Wilson turned to Skweez, who hovered next to his stateroom door.

"Skweez, get Admiral Johnson for me."

"Aye, aye, sir. Stateroom?"

"Yes, and bring me a cola, please." Wilson led Weed into his stateroom and waited.

With the door closed behind them, Weed began.

"You know Buffington hates aviators, don't you?"

"I've heard."

"And why not? They fly into bad-guy country and get Navy Crosses and Silver Stars that he could never get. The press, the movies, not to mention the girls hanging on them in those wrinkled flight suits. And then they just blow off their paperwork and still get promoted to flag. Not fair, doncha know."

Skweez poked his head inside. "Standby, sir."

"Stay," Wilson ordered, and Skweez closed the door and sat next to Weed. The connection rattled.

"Admiral Wilson," Wilson said, looking down at the table as he waited. Ten seconds later, The Big Unit picked up.

"Flip, Randy Johnson. What have you got for me?"

"Quite a day here, sir, and while I don't know where to start, I'll say that I'm moving us west after we recover this event, and about thirty minutes ago NAVEUR called me."

"I know, he just got off the phone with me."

"Yes, sir."

"Said he had to train you."

"I consider myself trained, sir."

"Is this a clear line?"

"My aide is with me, sir," Wilson answered in another half-truth.

"Look, I'm sorry he went off on you, and I have a pretty good sense of what he said. Let the *Aegis* cruiser handle the air picture and you and your airplanes get out of the way, right?"

"In so many words, yes, sir."

"Yeah, I'll bet. Okay, as your immediate superior I asked to pass along future ass-rippings, but he enjoys them too much to delegate. Don't worry about it; now, tell me about the *Blackjack*."

"Olive and a CAP of *Rhinos* were on it, and she said that from about 100 miles it ramped down on us as if it were riding a laser. She said it did not twitch in attitude or course—just sped up and went by us just under the number."

"How did you do?" Wilson anticipated the question.

"Sir…I struggled, I mean…tensions are high but we're not at war. Shoot too early, shoot too late…international airspace…kind of threatening, but bomb bay closed."

"Would you shoot him next time?"

Wilson glanced at Weed as he considered the question.

"Admiral…I don't know, except to say that I'd probably act ten seconds sooner."

The Big Unit chuckled. "The proverbial ten seconds. You give yourself a mile and a half extra range at that speed."

"I'll take it, sir. I mean, do you have guidance?"

"Flip, I really don't. You are on scene with your gut, and none of us, including Buffington, have ever had our doors blown off by a *Blackjack*. I'm not second-guessing."

"He gave me the full-up wire brush, sir, and toward the end of the conversation I was expecting relief for cause." Wilson heard The Big Unit exhale.

"Flip, he does this. With me daily, *hourly*, and it's part of my job. Hot lava off a duck's back. But he reaches over me to Strike Group Commanders that deploy here, and I wouldn't be surprised if he has already been on the horn with your cruiser CO. It's his style, we don't like it, and he picks on aviators especially, so don't take it personally. I have your back. Just let me know when it happens, but I can't control him."

"Thank you, sir," Wilson said as he eyed Weed's grin.

"Don't mention it. Now, *Konya K*: what do you know?"

"Well, we got a report from *Trigger* that a Greek sub torpedoed her."

"That is true."

"Did she sink?"

"No. The Turks launched an anti-torpedo torpedo at it…and it worked."

"*Konya K* has this?"

"Yep."

"So…it's a Turkish combatant?"

"Nope, it's a privateer, with a letter of marque. In the service of Turkey. And it looks like her service is coming to an end now that everyone knows what she is."

"A *privateer*? Pressed into service?" Wilson repeated.

"Yes, and good job by Olive and your intel people getting that imagery to us. We found two containers with *Klubs*, and she has anti-torpedo launchers on her port and starboard. Fired automatically…these days you only have seconds."

"How did she know to launch it?"

"Probably has a towed array, and our first guess is below the waterline. We believe it is highly modified inside. My people tell me she was laid up in dry dock for a year three years ago…needles of information in the daily haystack of data. "

"My intel officer said it was near the *Nauticos Card* last week."

"Yes, and we're pulling all the AIS data on her, but the Greeks are ahead of us and not sharing anything."

Wilson needed more. "Why don't they shoot again? Something is bound to get through."

"They may have detected *Trigger* and got spooked, or had a mechanical failure, or maybe there is a Turkish boat they're worried about. I'd sure have one near *Konya K*. Regardless, she's kicked it up to eighteen knots and is making a beeline for Antalya. Bottom line, we're getting out of there."

"Where do you want me, sir?"

"Head toward Sicily and orbit east for now," The Big Unit answered. "I may even bring you into Augusta Bay and ride at anchor to show the world we are not in the middle of this and want no part of it, but we're ready for tasking within hours. How are you doing on fuel?"

"We're scheduled to go alongside tonight."

"Perfect. Fill up and get your small boys topped off. I'll give you tasking later tonight: Augusta Bay or go through Messina and operate north of Sicily. Be ready for either. Out here."

"Thank you, sir, out."

"Ohppp…it's Buffington. I'm putting you on hold."

"Yes, sir."

As The Big Unit took the call from NAVEUR, Wilson informed the others.

"Buffington just called him and I'm on hold." Skweez nodded and waited. Weed looked away to the bulkhead in thought.

"A Navy Cross…guess you have to be in the right place at the right time. You know, *I* can't even get a Navy Cross when I'm on your wing."

"Will you shut up?" Wilson growled in mock annoyance.

"Or even on the same *ship*, come to think of it. What a career I could have had if not for you."

Wilson smiled. "Timing is everything."

"My detailer told me that and I've always hated him for it."

Skweez grinned as the two old salts bantered. The speaker crackled, and the three focused again.

"Flip, I'm back. New development. The Turks sank the Greek sub, verified by *Trigger*. They are pulling the rods and running west, and that's what I want you to do now. And there's more; we've got tipper info that the Russians are mobilizing their Northern and Baltic Sea Fleets."

"Wow. What's Brussels doing, sir?"

"Having an aneurism, because this escalates and expands this outside the Med, where everyone thought this could be contained. It's their boomers, Flip. If they put them all to sea even in a show of force, then it's game on, and this fight between Greece and Turkey is a sideshow."

"Roger that," Wilson said. Weed looked at the table in grave contemplation of what this could mean. The Big Unit had more.

"And you guys remain the only deployable carrier on both sides of the Atlantic. *Coral Sea* is out of her complex overhaul but nowhere near ready. *John Adams* is going in behind her but needs a month—Fleet Forces is going to give her two weeks to prep for sea. *Tinian* and her ARG are deploying in three days for CENTCOM—my guess is they'll turn north once clear of Cape Henry."

The gravity of Johnson's words caused Wilson's heart to beat faster, and he glanced at the PLAT as the E-2 rolled into the groove. The Big Unit had one more tasker.

"We've got allied warships sinking in the Med and need to hold the line in the North Atlantic, so get to Gibraltar, now. We'll refuel you passing Rota. Run."

Part II

Any ruler that has but ground troops has one hand,
but one that has also a navy has both.

– Peter the Great

CHAPTER 16

SEVEROMORSK, RUSSIA 0845 JUNE 11, 2024

Kapitan Second Rank Dmitry Petrov stepped out of the Destroyer Division Headquarters Building and turned left to take the shortcut through the woods down to the piers, the brilliant sun shining as it had been since late May. To Petrov, the short Kola Peninsula summer had already arrived with the forecast a balmy 18C temperature. Other ship kapitans had their sailors drive them the one-kilometer trip from the piers to HQ to make a show of getting out of the car from the backseat as their drivers held open the doors of their own personal Ladas. They always offered him rides—*join me, Dmitry Ivanovich*—but he declined. *Pompous asses* Petrov thought, embarrassed to be one of their number, and unwilling to wedge his tall frame into the backseat of a vehicle suited more for women and children. With skies clear and calm under a rare ridge of high pressure, Petrov anticipated enjoying his short walk back to his ship as he contemplated the electrifying news he had just received.

The shaded asphalt footpath to the wharf curved downhill and offered glimpses of Russia's Red Banner Northern Fleet as it lay moored along Vaenga Bay, a sight Petrov never tired of. The carrier *Admiral Kuznetsov* dominated the waterfront, sitting tied to his pier as he had been for years. *Building Sixty-Three* the tin-can sailors called the ship. Scaffolding covered his superstructure, and the flight deck was a jumble of shipyard equipment. He would not get underway for many more months or years. *Wasteful plaything*, Petrov thought. No one would miss him.

At the pier he walked across the road through the open fence to where his ship, the *Udaloy II* guided missile destroyer *Admiral Alekseyev* lay moored to his port side. Returning the salute of a young *leytenant* from the ship on the other side, he absentmindedly scanned the hull of his ship, the only *Udaloy II* assigned to the Northern Fleet, for paint blemishes and rust. Out of the corner of his eye he noticed the Junior Officer of the Deck on the quarterdeck watching him. Mladshiy Leytenant Federov...barely old enough to shave.

He swung himself up and on to the gangway, first facing aft and saluting the Russian ensign, then at the top saluting a fearful Federov who snapped to attention.

"Kapitan Vitorogo Ranga Petrov, reporting my return aboard."

Trembling while at stiff attention, Federov saluted at the same time, catching his visor and knocking the combination cover from his head. Mortified, he caught his breath as an unamused Petrov waited.

"Per-mission granted, Kapitan!" he rasped. Petrov noticed the man's lip quivering, a human reflex of someone who knows they are about to die. Through superhuman effort the quarterdeck orderlies held in their laughter, one biting his cheek even after he tasted the salty blood.

"It is customary to just say 'aye aye,' for the kapitan, Federov. Now pick up your cover and have the executive officer gather all the officers not on watch in the wardroom in ten minutes."

"Yes, sir, Kapitan, I mean *aye, aye* Kapitan." Federov's face had gone white, and the sailors visibly struggled to maintain their composure.

Petrov turned and walked to the forward ladder, climbed to the O-1 level, and crossed to the starboard side to enjoy the bay and the magnificence of the morning as he journeyed forward, thinking about his orders. *At long last, we are getting underway!*

In his cabin, he traded his windbreaker for a sweater and scanned again the orders he kept folded in his pocket. Sortie the day after tomorrow with the tide at 1900, following the *Slava* guided missile cruiser *Marshal Yermolov* and leading the division into the Barents Sea. The two big guns, the nuclear-powered battlecruiser *Pyotr Velikiy* and carrier *Kuznetzov*, would miss it, mired in engineering maintenance work. Again Petrov sniffed; *more trouble than they are worth anyway.*

And from the submarine base at Skalisty, the remaining *Delta* boats, two *Oscar* cruise missile boats, and all but one of the fleet's *Akula* attack boats would join them in the most powerful fleet assembled in Russian Federation history, the most powerful since the Tsar sent the Imperial fleet halfway around the world to its annihilation at Tsushima.

Despite his excitement, Petrov held reservations, as all seafaring men did. *What is Moscow doing?* he thought. He checked his watch: three minutes. He re-read the tasking message from fleet headquarters to pass the time, already knowing what he would say as he'd rehearsed it on the walk down the hill.

They had been waiting a minute when Petrov stood, checked his face in the mirror over his sink, and exited his stateroom.

Entering the wardroom, the two dozen officers came to attention. Once quiet returned, Petrov commanded, "seats." The officers, all men, took their seats, and as they did Petrov pulled out a cigarette, and, motioning to the group, said, "please." With permission granted, several of the men lit cigarettes. Petrov turned to the XO, Kapitan-Leytenant Yevgeny Kuzmin.

"Mister Kuzmin, are we all present?"

"Kapitan, all but Federov on the quarterdeck."

"Very well...*Admiral Alekseyev* is in good hands," Petrov said, well aware of his audience, two of whom he caught smirking at his feigned trust of Federov.

Petrov began.

"I have called you from your duties to tell you that the situation in our fascist republic of Ukraine is dire. The West continues to feed them with arms and materiel, and casualties continue to mount. Who here has lost a friend or loved one in the past two years?"

Four of the men raised their hands, including Kuzmin, whom Petrov knew had lost his brother in the Ukraini mud. He acknowledged the men and continued.

"The Motherland can no longer ignore the existential threat from the West that gathers on our borders and whose sanctions are a source of hardship here at home. We must relieve the pressure, and with every bit of our national strength." For effect, Petrov pulled the folded orders from his pocket and held them for the group to see.

"We are to get underway with the fleet."

A whoop went up in the wardroom as the joyous men pumped their fists into the air and clasped each other's shoulders. *Finally!*

"In two days," Petrov said, barely audible in the din.

The men stopped and looked at him. Petrov detected what they were thinking. *Two days?*

"Nineteen hundred local time, day after tomorrow. *Marshal Yermalov* as the flagship, with us leading the destroyer division. Every submarine that Skalisty can put to sea. Once in the open, we'll be given our orders."

The officers mulled this news. Going to sea was exciting, but two days? And with potential combat against the West in the offing? The preparations, the provisioning. Their women and children. Hushed, they returned their eyes to Petrov.

"Between that time and now, we must paint the ship. All of it, and with this new color."

He held up a paint chip for the men to see, causing the junior leytenants at the end of the table to squint to see it. Kuzmin broke the baffled silence.

"Is that—*pink*, Kapitan?"

"*Camoutint*, I'm told, but pink if you wish. We must paint the entire ship—from the waterline up—in this low-visibility color by the time we cast off."

Dumbfounded, the men sat and stared at Petrov and the chip he held, some with open mouths.

"Cans of this paint and painting scaffolds will be delivered by the end of the hour, and Mister Kuzmin, no leave until the job is complete."

"Aye, aye, Kapitan; will others in the division also paint their ships this color?"

"No, just us.

The men slumped back into their chairs in disgust. *Pink? We'll be the laughingstock of the whole Northern Fleet.* Petrov would have none of it.

"You officers will LEAD!" he snapped, then added, "And convey to your sailors that this shade will aid us in avoiding optical detection, *especially* by submarines. Along with the infrared cloaking panels we already have on the ship, we will be almost immune to EO and IR detection. All we must worry about is radar and sonar, which is more than enough."

Petrov had made reference to the IR panels that covered the exposed skin of *Admiral Alekseyev*, rendering the ship almost invisible in the infrared spectrum at range, and strange to a seeker head in the end game. Sadly, it was the only ship in the Russian Federation Navy so fitted.

"Kapitan, will the paint hurt the IR countermeasures?" Leytenant Medvedev asked.

"No, because the panels only mimic the air temperature, and they are already painted gray—I do not anticipate a problem from submarines or surface ships. Airplanes of course we will continue to avoid wherever possible, and I anticipate our orders will take us far from any air threat."

Petrov saw that his men remained unconvinced, and the possibility of no liberty before a no-notice sortie put them in a foul mood.

"Once the news media is alerted and reports our preparations to go to sea, we can think about a last moment of liberty...but not before. Mister Kuzmin, this will be an all-hands effort on the paint scaffolds, with only the commissary ratings exempt as they take on and secure stores, and the gunnery mates only when small ammunition is delivered to the pier. Get in your coveralls, but first inform your *michmen* so they can prepare the men. With no further questions, dismissed. We have...fifty-seven and one-half hours. Now, *dismissed*."

The officers came to their feet and filed through the doors and into the passageways. Through a porthole Petrov saw a truck with pallets of paint parked near the quarterdeck gangway.

"Better get to the quarterdeck Kuzmin, and supervise before Fedorov orders them off the pier."

"Aye, aye, Kapitan," the XO answered before he exited through the aft door.

Alone in the wardroom, Petrov contemplated Arina and nine-year-old Sasha. He hadn't been away for months at a time since Sasha was just a baby. That too was a "combat" cruise to Syria, but this one, with Russia at war along its western border against a former republic supported by NATO, would be a *real* combat cruise. Against the Americans, probably the Brits and Norwegians, and maybe all of NATO. *Arina.* He wouldn't tell her. *Just a small exercise, we'll be back in a few days.*

The state of *Admiral Alekseyev* dominated his thoughts. Petrov considered his missile tubes. Anti-ship missiles: only five of eight P-270 *Moskits* loaded. ASW weapons: only one SS-N-15 *Starfish*. Three Type-53 war shot torpedoes. His 130mm gun with an assisted range out to 25 miles had only half a magazine. And only three SAN-9 SAMs to deal with the air threat. Petrov demanded from headquarters two Kamov Ka-27 *Helix* helicopters or more *Starfish* missiles. He'd get the helos, but probably no more 130mm rounds as all manner of artillery was needed in the south. He'd have to make do.

He thought of the open Atlantic, the unpredictable weather from the North Cape to the coast of Ireland…no, Bermuda! Norwegian patrol planes dogging him, *Penguin* missiles detected seconds from impact amid shouts of terror on the bridge. British sea-skimmers emerging among the dense oil rigs in the North Sea. Hell, a Yankee *Virginia* class boat could be lurking outside the sea buoy even now, and one could appear with no warning at any time. He expected air cover from the fleet Sukhoi's for the first half of the North Cape transit—what else would they do without a ship to take them to sea?—but they could not help far from home south of Vestafjord, into the teeth of *dozens* of NATO fighters with trained airmen from Norway, Scotland, and Iceland.

He would have to spend days on end in Combat, groggy eyes trying to make sense of computer-generated contacts with a nervous and untrained crew looking to him for salvation. *I've not experienced this myself!* he thought, cursing all the division staffs that gun-decked the "training" he had received during scripted exercises on every ship he had served. He once witnessed a *Moskit* launch on a target rock in the Kara Sea, but as a wide-eyed junior-officer-of-the-deck on the bridge. His crew had seen the same launch only in training films.

Admiral Alekseyev had some advantages. The IR tiles alone could delay detection or confuse weapon tracking, but for how long? Long enough to get in the first shot? Because it would have to be first shots that saved him and the ship. And this new camouflage paint? Would he truly be *invisible*? To human eyes? And at what range? Regardless, against NATO, facing fully loaded airplanes and submarines, he needed every arrow the Motherland could give him. Paint the damn ship pink, then; you eggheads had better be right.

The division staff would be into their vodka in a matter of hours, celebrating the glorious victory to come while his crew painted his entire ship. What could he do for them in the remaining hours to give them their best chance of survival? He needed everything and had only promises. Walking athwartship to the starboard side, he gazed through the porthole into the bay. As promised, two paint barges pushed by skiffs approached, sailors on them ready to throw mooring lines to his crew. *They did what they said they would* he thought. Paint—and pink paint at that—to combat NATO.

Without time to load big missiles and without additional gun rounds, Petrov wasn't going to trade salvos with anyone. He had to dodge and deflect, remaining covert as he snuck up on a target to deliver a warning blow. The Motherland depended on the Red Banner Fleet—and Dmitry Petrov aboard the most capable surface combatant in the division—to deliver it.

CHAPTER 17

PILOTHOUSE, USS *VALLEY FORGE*, 1800 JUNE 12, 2024

"Admiral's on the bridge!"

Huey turned in his Captain's Chair to see Wilson amble up from the portside passageway. Off the bow, *Manila Bay* led *Valley Forge* toward a setting sun as the strike group ships sped to the west.

"Good afternoon, Admiral."

"Hey, Huey. How goes it?"

"Steaming as before…holding roughly sixty miles off the coast of Algeria at 28 knots. Still in the open now that we've cleared Sardinia but tomorrow this time we're going to be in that funnel of traffic in the Alboran Sea leading into and coming out of Gibraltar."

Wilson noted a gaggle of junior pilots tramping up to the bow, leaning hard into the strong gusts. The PLAT monitor over Huey's bridge window showed 43 knots. On the flight deck, the aircraft were buttoned up with heavy tie downs and panels closed as gale-force winds pummeled them. Wilson thought of tomorrow's underway replenishment with USNS *Chattahoochee*.

"What do you think about the UNREP tomorrow?" he asked Huey.

"Going to be okay if he can rendezvous with us at dawn, and once we're alongside, we'll be good until about noon. After that the traffic is going to pick up big time."

"The small boys need it now…how about you?"

"Sir, we've got 68% aviation fuel, and depending on your tasking, that's good or not good. Pay me now or pay me later. Now, we would prefer to go alongside here in the Med and avoid the Atlantic swells. I'd hate to pass by *Chattahoochee* and bet on the come that USNS *Gene Cernan* can provision us as we pass Rota. Let's see…she's transiting just north of the Azores in sea state seven…that's fifteen-foot seas."

Wilson studied the GCCS display. Both *Valley Forge* and *Gene Cernan* were 1,000 miles from Gibraltar, with the carrier closing it at twice the speed. His surface combatants needed fuel to make steam more than *Valley Forge* needed it to fly, and time alongside *Chattahoochee* would be precious even before the strike group entered the choked sea approaches to the strait. He needed to get out of the Med, and needed to fill his strike group tanks.

"Huey, can we sprint ahead and go alongside *Chattahoochee* early? I really want to come out of here as a full-up strike group."

Huey checked GCCS and did a mental calculation. "Admiral, we can pull the rods and sprint, which I think will buy us 50 miles. That's about three hours alongside before *Manila Bay* and the rest show up. We won't have a shotgun for most of that time, and it's going to beat up the jets."

Wilson had already considered it as his gaze returned to the flight deck. Fifty knot winds and spray would lash the planes spotted forward, precluding maintenance, and having to roust his exhausted sailors in the wee hours to prepare for refueling was not preferred. However, *Chattahoochee* was a bird in hand. Huey then made it easier.

"Sir, let's run ahead now in light seas, top off from *Chattahoochee*, wait for the rest, then sprint through the strait as a group in the early morning hours the following day. We'll put you there anytime you want, but the traffic will be lighter then—not absent but lighter, certainly the cross-strait traffic."

"Okay. Good. You sure? What do you need from *Gene Cernan*?"

"We'll game it tonight sir and manage the risk. What I hope he has is lots of food and bomb bodies with kits. If he has AMRAAMs and ARGMs, we'll take them."

"How many LRASMs do we have?"

"A handful last time I checked, sir."

"Okay, please get me a real number. I'm going to ask for more, and maybe they can get them to us passing Rota. We are going to get another two DDGs from there, bringing us up to six plus *Manila Bay*."

Both officers looked at *Manila Bay* three miles ahead. "OOD!" Huey barked.

"Aye, aye, sir!" the lieutenant responded.

"Give me flank speed, and pass *Manila Bay* 1,000 yards on her starboard side. Tell her with blinking light."

As the lieutenant *aye-ayed* Huey and issued orders to the bridge team, Huey turned to Wilson.

"The sea-and-anchor detail going through the strait is going to be sporty, sir. With the Chinese in Tangier, I'm expecting a curve-ball of some kind."

"Yes," Wilson nodded. "I'm considering flying a CAP as we go through."

"Even more sporty!"

"Check with Olive and give me a plan tomorrow."

"Aye, aye, sir," Huey said, smiling.

Aboard *Admiral Alekseyev*, the loudspeaker sounded: *"Red Banner Northern Fleet, arriving."*

Hands clasped behind his back, Petrov stood at ease as the admiral's sedan came to a stop adjacent to *Admiral Alekseyev's* gangway. A *leytenant* called the eight side boys in dress uniforms first to attention, and then *present arms* as the admiral's aide stepped out of the sedan and opened the door for the fleet commander, Admiral Konstantin Platonov, who spent a moment surveying the ship—and its distinctive camouflage color—before passing through the side boys, holding a salute as he did. Aboard the destroyer, topside personnel stood at attention in their paint-stained coveralls.

Petrov, with Kuzmin behind him, stepped to the top of the gangway to greet his former kapitan, who had commanded this very ship some twenty years before. The admiral smiled as he bounded up to the quarterdeck, turned aft to salute the St. Andrew's Cross on the fantail, and saluted Petrov.

"Request permission to come aboard, Kapitan Petrov."

Petrov returned his salute. "Granted with pleasure, Admiral. Welcome back; *Admiral Alekseyev* has missed you."

Petrov's quarterdeck sailors stood at rigid attention as the admiral and their kapitan embraced in a bear hug. Following Platonov was his Chief of Staff, Vitse-Admiral Dushenov, and his tall aide, a *kapitan-leytenant*. Petrov led the visitors to the wardroom as Kuzmin trailed behind. Platonov asked Petrov about his ship on the way, as his staff followed in silence.

"How goes the painting, Dmitry Ivanovich?"

"We have all the starboard side hull complete, Admiral, and only the sections you see on the port side to go. Upper works is a tedious challenge, but the men have worked through the night and we should be complete within six or so hours."

"Will you sortie on schedule?"

"Provisioning is complete, admiral. We have magazine space for more weapons if they may be loaded pier side, but we will sortie on time."

"Good, good. I'll see what may be spared. Regardless, tomorrow will be a day of glory for the Red Banner Fleet."

Petrov led them into the wardroom where the steward had tea, espresso, and coffee with coffee cake. The senior officers took seats as Platonov's aide poured black coffee for his admiral, adding two heaping spoonsful of sugar.

"Kapitan, you may excuse your messman."

Petrov nodded to the man, who left at once.

Platonov waited in silence, then motioned to his aide. *"Zakryto."*

The aide stepped to the porthole curtains and closed them, and then checked the two doors to the room, ensuring they were locked before he returned to stand behind Platonov.

"Kapitan Petrov, all of the Russian Federation depends on the success of our mission."

"We are ready, Admiral."

"Please be seated, both of you."

Petrov and Kuzmin took seats next to one another at the wardroom table, unsure of Platonov's intent. The admiral stepped to the bulkhead behind him to admire a painting of *Admiral Alekseyev*, then returned his focus to the DDG kapitan.

"You will sortie as planned with our surface action group, leading the division out behind the flagship, but once in the open you will be released with orders to escort a merchant past the gap and into the open Atlantic."

"Aye, aye, Admiral."

Platonov motioned, and Dushenov pulled out a folder. Opening it, he placed a photograph in front of Petrov, a photograph of the self-loading containership *Vitac*.

"Actually, Kapitan, this merchant is your shield and your connection with me. You will escort it from a position on its quarter, a close position."

Petrov nodded that he understood.

"Two hundred meters," Platonov said, his eyes holding Petrov's as the surprised kapitan absorbed this order. Did Petrov hear correctly? *Two hundred meters! Over the entire Atlantic?* He glanced at tight-lipped Kuzmin, whose eyes remained on the photograph of the containership. After a pause, Platonov continued.

"And not one meter further. Two hundred meters, Dmitry Ivanovich, which keeps you inside his radar return and allows you to communicate through semaphore, and semaphore only. No blinking light and certainly no bridge-to-bridge. We will communicate with *Vitac* through SATCOM and HF as any merchant would—a team of communicators and signalmen will sail with him to relay my orders to you and to relay your communications to me. The rest of the fleet to include you will be under strict radio silence, but you...will be able to respond if required."

Petrov nodded and said "yes, sir." *Two hundred meters!* He and Kuzmin would have to spend all their time on the bridge to ensure separation, and once past Iceland, darkness would return to the nighttime hours. *Night station keeping on an unpredictable single-screw containership.*

Platonov was far from done.

"Kapitan…I now ask you and your executive officer to fold your hands and place them in your lap under the table." Puzzled, Petrov and Kuzmin nonetheless complied.

"Thank you. A single sheet of paper with your orders will now be placed in front of you. You will not touch it, but merely read it. Once both of you have read the order and understand it fully, you are to indicate that to me by stating, 'I understand my orders, admiral.' Do you have questions?"

"No questions, Admiral." Petrov felt his heart race. *What is going on?*

"Very well. Admiral…"

Dushenov pulled another sheet from the folder and placed it in front of Petrov, who lowered his eyes to read it. On the top and bottom of the sheet was the red stamp: EYES ONLY

```
FROM: NORTHERN FLEET JOINT STRATEGIC COMMAND
TO:   ADMIRAL ALEKSEYEV DDG-651

SUBJ: WEAPON AUTHORIZATION

1. UPON RECEIPT OF AUTHENTICATED ORDER, AFTER DE-
   TECTION AND POSITIVE TARGET IDENTIFICATION OF
   ENEMY SURFACE COMBATANT WITHIN 30-80% LAUNCH AC-
   CEPTABILITY REGION OF ON-BOARD P-270 MOSKIT ASCM,
   ENGAGE WITH ON-BOARD P-270 MOSKIT ASCM SER. NO.
   31917186-S AS PART OF THREE MISSILE SALVO. COM-
   PLY WITH ALL MISSILE LAUNCH ACQUISTION PARAME-
   TERS AND TACTICAL DOCTRINE. WEAPON SELECT OPTION
   A. FUSING: INST.
```

Petrov raised his eyes to Platonov, who did not blink. A low-yield tactical nuclear weapons launch order. Petrov controlled his breathing. A first-strike option as both men knew the Motherland could one day employ. He slid the sheet to Kuzmin, who read it.

"Do you understand, Dmitry Ivanovich, because there is more."

"I understand, Admiral."

"Do you know in which tube this serial number is loaded?"

"Yes, Admiral."

"Do you understand the minimum and maximum launch ranges?"

"Yes, Admiral."

"Do you understand the number of weapons required in this salvo?"

"Yes, Admiral."

"Do you understand the weapon select option ordered?"

"Yes, Admiral."

Platonov asked Kuzmin the same questions, receiving the same responses.

"Very well, gentlemen. Dushenov."

Admiral Dushenov grabbed the sheet from in front of Kuzmin and returned it to the folder. He picked up another sheet and waited.

"You will now receive the code word authorizing launch of this serial number." Platonov motioned to Dushenov, who placed it face up in front of Petrov.

Petrov glanced at it…and froze.

ARINA

Platonov watched Petrov recognize the single word. "Kapitan Petrov, do you understand that when you receive this codeword you are to respond with the codeword we will now provide you?"

"Yes, Admiral." Petrov slid the sheet to Kuzmin, who read it.

"Very well."

Platonov nodded, and Dushenov replaced the sheet with another, also written with only a single word. Petrov breathed hard through his nose.

SASHA

"Do you understand the authentication response, Kapitan Petrov?"

Petrov nodded. "Yes, Admiral." Again he slid the sheet to his executive officer who acknowledged it. Dushenov retrieved the sheet and placed it back in the folder with the others. Platonov took a long drink of his coffee before returning it to the saucer.

"I have one more question, Dmitry Ivanovich…are you willing?"

Petrov nodded at once. "I am, admiral."

Platonov faced Kuzmin. "Yes, Admiral," Kuzmin replied, his voice firm.

Platonov studied both men. "It is imperative that you remain hidden for us to use this option. It is an *option*, and one that will come to me through the President himself. If it is used—and we hope that the fleet sortie will cause NATO to withdraw, hold their fire, and stop supporting the enemy republic to our south—but *if* it is used…we know that we can expect a response. The enemy response may be de-escalation once they see our resolve, or it may be *escalation*, and on a scale mankind has not ever seen, but only imagined."

Platonov's aide had not moved a muscle, his eyes searing into Petrov, un-blinking.

"Admiral, I have a question," Petrov said.

"Please."

"Admiral, are we the only kapitan and executive officer receiving this brief-ing?"

"It is a fair question, Dmitry Ivanovich, but one that I am afraid I cannot answer. I cannot confirm or deny that."

Both men held each other's gaze in the awkward silence. *I will not even know if a mushroom cloud on the horizon is ours or theirs,* Petrov thought.

"Thank you, Admiral. *Admiral Alekseyev* and I are prepared for this battle."

"You *must* avoid detection, Dmitry. We have cloaked you with the electro-optical and infrared wizardry the Motherland has provided us. I only wish that the whole destroyer division were so equipped. You will receive two helicopters, a *Helix* and a *Hokum-B* attack aircraft. *Do not* let them be detected before the commencement of hostilities—if—hostilities commence."

"Are you hopeful, Admiral?"

Platonov considered the question.

"Dmitry Ivanovich, I wish to one day bounce my grandchildren upon my knee, and to teach them about Jesus, and to return sanity to this world. Alas, my children have no interest in children, and I will probably die without that joy. But if I—and we all—can strike a blow to prevent our enemies from conquering us so Russian children and their children can live in peace, then I am willing to die for the chance of eliminating the threats to our borders and our waters so we may thrive as the West does. My headquarters is certainly targeted by *Amerikanskiy,* and British, and even French warheads, as is this very pier. All of us who remain ashore know this, and I accept it, knowing full well what may occur if I send you that codeword if called to do so. For now, we will demonstrate and perhaps even skirmish on the high seas. If the West pushes us hard enough, we will do what we must to de-escalate, and, God help us, if this goes full scale…we will die with honor rather than live as their slaves as we did in the 1990's. We will not go back to that."

Petrov nodded. Could he send back to Platonov the name of his only son?

Deep inside he knew that yes…he could.

Five hours later, Petrov lay awake next to Arina, also awake.

Sasha had gone to his room early, understanding in only a basic sense that his father would be gone at sea for an undetermined but long time, yet more concerned about spending tomorrow night with friends after school. The no-notice deployment was a shock to Arina's method of easing Petrov out of her daily life as the sailing date approached. Sasha did not understand the gravity of the world situation. Arina did...but did not really. Her husband was a warship kapitan in the Red Banner Fleet, full of prestige and privilege, but tomorrow the bill that she never thought she would ever have to pay would come due. *War*, a kind that that had not been fought since The Great Patriotic War 80 years earlier...black and white pictures in an elementary school history book. Their room was only semi-dark despite heavy window shades; the sun never set this time of year, and she did not even have the comfort of darkness to help her mind try to make sense of this. *Why?*

Hours earlier, their last-night-at-home lovemaking had been passionless and mechanical. Expected. Both of their minds were elsewhere: Petrov scanning the horizon from his kapitan's chair, and Arina in an empty house counting down the hours, days, and weeks, but this time for news. How would the news come? A call? A wife who heard something she shouldn't have? How would she react? How would she tell Sasha? *What would become of them?*

Petrov exhaled through his nose.

"Are you awake?" she asked, already knowing.

"Yes."

They remained quiet, both formulating words they had only hours left to say to one another. After a minute, Arina spoke.

"Dima, have you already gone to sea?"

Petrov said nothing for a long time. He took her hand.

"I'll miss you."

"I'll miss you, too," Arina said softly. She then asked the question that she knew she should not.

"Will you return?"

Petrov remained silent for a time before he answered her.

"Yes," he said, without a hint of confidence.

"When you do, let's leave here."

"For where?" he said.

"St. Petersburg."

"We've done a tour there already. Timing won't allow it."

"Then back to Kaliningrad."

"It's a stuffy closet. Why?"

"Because it's in *Europe!*"

"Murmansk *is* Europe!" Petrov protested, releasing her hand.

"No it's *not*. This is *Siberia!* Isolated, and everyone in everyone else's business. At least Kaliningrad is *next* to Europe!"

Petrov didn't answer, the tension building between them.

"Sevastopol, Kaliningrad, here…I'm tired of living in these military districts! At least the Crimea had nice weather!"

Petrov exhaled. "Moscow will be next for me, the Duma," he said.

"Nooo! Stuffed in a three-room flat, and again, *with everyone in everyone else's business. No,* Dima."

"When I make first rank, we'll rate a dacha."

Petrov felt Arina shake her head.

"A run-down hovel in the countryside! *Ha!* And *if* the staff will let you use it after your 14-hour days in the Duma with the jackals. Please, St. Petersburg, *please,* Dima."

Petrov remained silent. A tour in St. Petersburg now was not on the career path. "Maybe one day I can command the Baltic Fleet."

"Your fellow kapitan wives smile and flash their lashes at the fleet commander at every chance so *their* husbands will have a chance to command it while they entertain in the fancy house. I can't cheapen myself…even for orders to St. Petersburg."

"Don't want you to."

"They'll do *anything,* Dima. I've heard them."

"Don't want you to."

Tired of fighting, Arina sighed. "Besides…fleet command is over ten years from now, isn't it?"

Moscow duty was next, and Arina knew it too, but she grasped for something to dream of now, only hours before her husband had to wake up, eat his breakfast, and say goodbye to his wife and son. For who knew how long. Both had to face the larger unknown; what would the Red Banner Fleet find out there?

Arina thought of her man struggling for his life in the icy ocean. Desperate to think of something else, she could not get the thought out of her mind. She had no idea of what her husband's ship could do, or the weapons from the West they would face. NATO had so much—did the fleet even have a chance against all of Europe and America? This was suicidal madness, all driven by the egos in Moscow! The bastards! *Don't go, Dmitry!*

"Do you love me?" she whispered.

"Yes, you know I do, and I will think of you daily."

"And Sasha?"

"Of course, Sasha, our good son."

"Will you return to him to be his father?"

"Yes, Arina, and to you to be your husband. Do not worry." Petrov himself was worried but could not let her know about the British torpedoes or *Amerikanskiy* anti-ship missiles—*missile inbound, starboard side!*—that dominated the thoughts of each man aboard. Each man looked to him for salvation. Could he do it? He thought of Platonov, and one word. *ARINA*.

Arina rolled toward him, pressing herself close.

"Then I will not worry. You are a fine kapitan of a fine ship, with a fine crew, the best of the Motherland serving in the finest fleet of the Russian Navy. Kill them, Dima, now. Every one of them. Every gun and bomb you have. I *hate* the Americans and what they've done to us all our lives. *Drown them.* Drown them without pity, and never let another night like this come to us. Come back, my love, in victory, and I will follow you wherever you wish."

Petrov held her hand as she spoke. She did not know what she was asking. If NATO opposed them and this went hot, many Northern Fleet ships would sink before the end of the month...but the fleet would take enemy ships with them. *Many* of them, and maybe an American aircraft carrier. The attack boats had the best chance to bag one, but fate and the equipment he carried would present him with the opportunity to bring glory to the Navy on the high seas that was denied it at Tsushima, and in all the Cold War flare ups of the last century. *Over one hundred years* of humiliation as the Americans and bastard British operated with impunity on Russia's very shores! Yes, Arina, no quarter. And no warning in this modern age. Close to maximum range and fire before he can, our only chance. *An American supercarrier...*they would be forced to withdraw. He imagined a burning American carrier lift its stern out of the water as he witnessed it from his bridge, awestruck.

Unable to sleep, they held hands and laid next to each other for the next hour in silent thought, each contemplating what one did not understand, while the other understood all too well to speak of it now. Petrov carried an additional burden Arina could never know about. In missile tubes two and five he held the destructive power of five Hiroshimas, and the fleet commander himself had told him to be ready to employ it. At a date and time of the President's choosing.

Alone with her thoughts, Arina finally drifted off, but Petrov could not shake the possibility that through his actions not only a world war but a *world-ending* war was possible…no, likely. The Americans would respond, oh yes. Would it be proportional? A ship or ships for a ship or ships? Or would they, as Platonov said, hit military targets in the Motherland? A military target was less than two kilometers from where he lay. *Arina and Sasha.* Did he on the high seas or his family here have a greater chance of survival?

Arina stirred. Petrov imagined she was awake, but did not disturb her. *Maybe she'll go back. Sleep. Please God, let me sleep on this, my last night ashore.*

But he could not as his life, his blessed and fortunate life, flashed before his eyes. His last night ashore. Ever.

Unknown to Petrov, Arina Petrova was also awake, and together in bed they contemplated alone the remaining hours they had, the sea raging in their minds.

Chapter 18

RFS *Admiral Alekseyev*, Severomorsk, 1710 June 13, 2024

Petrov checked his watch. Late. The flagship *Marshal Yermolov*, the fleet's only *Slava* class cruiser, passed in front of his bow as he stood out, but also late. Petrov was to fall in 500 meters in trail as he led the rest of the division, but only now his sailors attached the tow line from the tug to the bollard. He hoped that the cruiser's kapitan saw *Admiral Alekseyev* still moored and reduce speed to help him.

"Single up lines on the bow and stern," the OOD Nikitin commanded. An impatient Petrov strode to the starboard wing and saw the aft tug had already taken up his slack as the forward tug moved off, lifting the line out of the water at a measured pace. He returned inside and spoke in a low voice next to his *leytenant*, who displayed evidence of stress on his face. "Expedite, Mister Nikitin."

With the tug tow lines taut, *Admiral Alekseyev* eased away from the pier. On Nikitin's order, line handlers cast off the remaining manila mooring lines that dropped into the water of Kola Bay as men on the pier hauled them ashore with muscled pulses of energy. In a flurry of activity, the colors were shifted and both tugs pulled the destroyer off parallel to the pier with a clear lane to open water and his station behind the cruiser.

"Rudder amidships. All ahead dead slow," Nikitin ordered under Petrov's watchful eye. The helm and lee helm repeated his orders, and Petrov felt a sense of calm in the ordered activity of the bridge. *Underway.* Life was simpler underway.

Free of the pier, *Admiral Alekseyev* cast off the tow lines and moved into position. From the adjacent pier, tugs pulled the *Udaloy* I destroyer *Severomorsk* off to take his station behind Petrov.

Petrov used his seaman's eye to estimate when Nikitin should begin his turn to line up behind the flagship. He appeared timid, letting too much separation build...a common trait of *leytenants*. Petrov walked behind him so only Nikitin could hear.

"Drive this ship, Mister Nikitin. Put him where he needs to be. Sharp, crisp, and expeditious."

"Aye, aye, Kapitan."

"Do not overshoot—I would put my rudder at right standard now."

Nikitin gave the order as Petrov walked to his chair on the port side, acting uninterested as he observed everything. His exec Kuzmin entered the bridge from the weather deck behind him.

"Well done to the mates, Yevgeny Sergeevich. Flawless underway."

"The tugs were late and apologized. One kapitan cried *dasvidaniya and go with God* before he departed."

Petrov smiled.

"After his crew whistled at our, um, dress," Kuzmin added.

"We will be protected and surprise our enemy in this *dress*. And, soon we will join our escort for the evening."

Kuzmin, nodded.

"Did you see the merchant that stood out this morning from the commercial wharf?"

"Yes, Kapitan…is that him?"

"Yes…let me supervise this first…Mister Nikitin! Maintain in his wake and 500 meters."

By the time the division passed Ostrov Island, nine ships of the missile and anti-submarine divisions had sortied and fallen in as ordered. Now in the narrowest part of the channel Petrov stood behind his chair and watched, waiting for the flagship to commence his turn to the north and signal a speed change to seven knots.

Stately and elegant, the surface ships of the Red Banner Fleet wended their way through the tight channel, barren shorelines on either side, typical of the rocky Murmansk Oblast topography. No small craft saw them off; sightseeing of the fleet at any time was strictly prohibited.

Admiral Alekseyev's four gas turbines whined in the background as the ship made the turn behind the cruiser. Satisfied and with the channel wider, Petrov returned to Kuzmin.

"The merchant is a containership crewed by Russians under the flag of Panama. It is a legitimate containership, and is capable of 20 knots, but his speed of advance will be thirteen."

Kuzmin nodded his understanding but was skeptical. *Escorting a lumbering merchant at hailing range through the entire Norwegian Sea?*

"Have you learned where is it bound for?"

Petrov smiled. "It is bound for Murmansk, and my intention once our mission is complete—if we are given *that* mission—is to keep it next to us and continue to use our disguise for as long as we can. We have been given control over it, and I won't relinquish it until ordered."

Kuzmin nodded again. *Mutual support* for a change. He would welcome it. "When will we tell the officers?"

Petrov had thought about it. "No big announcement. I'll order the OOD to come alongside him and remain there. We'll relieve the watches as normal."

With little choice, Kuzmin nodded, accepting, but still unsure they could maintain it. "Two-hundred meters...and for what, six or seven days to the gap?"

"We *will* remain in his radar cell to give us every advantage, and acoustically the enemy will have difficulty identifying our gas turbines next to his diesel-electrics."

Kuzmin remained a skeptic. *Maintain two-hundred meters for a week? In North Atlantic sea states?*

"And think of it, Yevgeny Sergeevich. An enemy missile will have a decision to make."

The XO grinned at the thought. "We must then thank our seafaring brothers for their service to the Red Banner Fleet."

"Indeed," Petrov said.

The open Barents Sea became visible on the horizon as they continued north, passing the auxiliary pier at Polyarny on their left. Petrov, and all the sailors that could, took glances at a gathering of people along the cliffside just north of the port buildings. Sailor families—*the women always knew*—gathered there each time a ship stood out, and the gathering this day was the largest Petrov had ever seen, probably 200. Though the bridge team required strict attention to duty, even the helmsman snuck in a quick glance. Petrov caught him but seemed not to notice.

Stepping out on the bridge wing, Petrov studied the group. On the cliff-side, only one kilometer away, families waved and cried out to their men. The high-pitched cries of one overweight woman—already drunk on vodka—carried across the water. He noted some men in the group—probably retired veterans—pointing at *Admiral Alekseyev*. Sudden laughter broke out here and there. As the crowd receded from view, a young woman lifted her top, drawing the ire of nearby wives who scolded her. On the foredeck, Petrov's seamen pointed and laughed at the scene. Moments after they passed, Petrov heard a roar from *Severomorsk* astern of him as the young woman played to a new audience.

Arina and Sasha were not there—they never were. Petrov thought just maybe this time, but no. Arina had already steeled herself. After breakfast she took Sasha to school and did not say goodbye. She always kissed him goodbye...

Breaking free of the rocky shore, the surface fleet entered the broad expanse of the Barents. *Marshal Yermolov* signaled for a speed change, followed by a defensive screen with the cruiser in the center. Holding a northeasterly course to confuse the *Amerikanskiy* satellite timed to pass overhead, the flotilla sped toward a clear horizon as the crews settled into their shipboard routines. Petrov stayed on the bridge as *Admiral Alekseyev* fell back into station while the trailing ships sprinted ahead. Above them, twin-tailed Sukhois of the fighter regiment bore holes in the sky as they escorted the flotilla into the open ocean. One group of two fighters swooped low alongside and thundered past, no doubt curious about Petrov's new paint job. He held his ears and scoffed at the show-offs. *They'll stop "escorting" us before we even round the North Cape.* The Russians could then expect a Norwegian escort of armed F-35's. Petrov contemplated what that would mean. *Who will fire first?* Sending the entire fleet to sea sent a statement, but would NATO consider it a hostile act?

He glanced south, then focused, surprised that already he could no longer see the coast, only inland peaks of familiar yet distant mountains along the horizon in the unlimited visibility. Arina and Sasha were there between him and the mountains, safe in the bosom of Mother Russia. The loudspeaker blared.

"Flight quarters, flight quarters, all personnel man your flight quarters station."

Petrov scanned the horizon and saw them, ten naval aviation helicopters. He would get a *Helix* and one of the new *Hokum-B* attack birds. He hoped they had weapons loaded. Enjoying the balmy weather—he had never experienced such a pleasant "evening" in the Barents—he remained on the bridge wing to watch. When the formation split up, a *Helix* carrying a torpedo flew toward him and entered a hover as it approached the fantail, while the Ka-52 *Katran*—Russian for "Mud Shark"—circled the ship, the pilots gawking at it. He saw weapons hanging from its pylon stations. *Good.*

He stepped inside and into the Navigation Room behind the bridge to check the plot. A turn soon, to the northwest to intercept an arc keeping them 100 miles off the coast of Europe before they entered the approaches to the GIUK gap. Petrov did not yet know which part of the "gap" they would penetrate, or even if they would, but first he had to intercept the containership. Checking the AIS display, he found the MV *Vitac*, northwest of them at 20 miles. At this rate, he would fall in with him around midnight while the rest of the fleet continued on course, leaving him alone with his new friend.

Returning to the bridge wing to take one last look at the Motherland, he noticed that the temperature had dropped, the sun now obscured by a ledge of clouds from the southwest. Scanning the southern horizon again, he searched for evidence of land, of home. He squinted hard but could not see it.

Dmitry Petrov stood on a steel deck on the open ocean where he belonged, part of the most powerful surface action group the Russians had put to sea in modern times. As the formation steamed northwest, he vainly searched the horizon to the south, convincing himself of the fact that this was really happening.

CHAPTER 19

FLAG BRIDGE, USS *VALLEY FORGE*, 0200 JUNE 14, 2024

Wilson awoke to his alarm clock and silenced it. He had caught a few hours of sleep in his O-8 level sea cabin to be ready for the transit of Gibraltar in two hours. Running his hand over the stubble of his beard, he rejected the idea of a shave. *No one will notice during darken ship.*

Hearing rotor blades on the flight deck below him, he flicked on the PLAT as he put on his uniform. The black-and-white image of two *Sierras* and a *Romeo* turned on spots three, four, and five, still tied down. Each of the *Sierras* carried two *Hellfire* on one wing and an APKWS pod on the other. The big GAU-21 .50 cal. and smaller M240 free guns protruded from the open cabin doors. The PLAT showed 38 knots of wind, and on the horizon the lights of many ships. He checked the ship's internal navigation display: twenty-five knots. Huey had a head of steam on as he entered one of the busiest and most traffic-clogged waterways in the world.

Stepping outside his cabin he found himself alone on the flag bridge, with only the screen of his flag chair tactical display illuminating the space like a nightlight. Scanning the horizon ahead were the masthead and running lights of dozens more ships coming into and out of Gibraltar.

Punching in his direct-line phone number, Wilson summoned Mark Meadows to the flag bridge and checked the GCCS display. His strike group ships followed the carrier single file after a long day alongside *Chattahoochee* topping off their tanks. In the Atlantic, USNS *Gene Cernan* was only 300 miles closer to Gibraltar. He checked the SIPRNET. Nothing yet from SIXTHFLEET to *Cernan* to expedite the rendezvous with Wilson. He'd ping them for an update after he was free and clear in the Atlantic.

Hours earlier The Big Unit had informed him that the Russian Northern Fleet had sortied. The *whole* fleet. Everything not in dry dock or covered in scaffolding. Their carrier *Kuznetsov* and *Kirov*-class cruiser were in deep maintenance and had not. Regardless, a dozen nuke boats of every type, even a *Kilo* diesel boat, got underway at the same time. NAVEUR had never seen anything like it.

One of their *Oscar* boats was already deployed, and last found days ago south of the GIUK gap, its position now unknown. Could it be outside Gibraltar, waiting? Wilson doubted it—from the last datum it would have had to run submerged at full speed making a racket—but that was a possibility no one could discount.

Wilson exited aft into the abandoned passageway bathed in red light, went up a ladder to the bridge, and opened the door. The bridge was unlit as the flight deck sodium vapor lights were secured for this strait passage. Wilson came upon the dark form of a watch-stander and spoke in a low tone.

"Good morning, shipmate; I'm Admiral Wilson."

"Admiral's on the bridge!" the startled sailor bellowed so the bridge team could hear, and from his chair, the silhouette of Huey turned to greet Wilson.

"Good morning, sir. Just in time for the special sea and anchor detail. I'm expecting Olive to join me as we get closer."

"Great. I'll be one deck below you, but what are you looking at now?"

Huey brought up the AIS on his display.

"Sir, we're about 40 miles from Gibraltar…here's the Rock. But the narrowest part of the strait is here, another five miles past it. It's eight miles across, and we can expect crossing ferry traffic, even now. Much of it at this hour are illegals crossing from Africa to Europe."

Wilson nodded. "Do you just blow through, or is there a gameplan?"

Huey pulled up a screen on the AIS. "Admiral, we've selected auto transit, giving the software our desired speed and heading parameters. We've given it 23 to 29 knots with two degrees of heading change and to remain clear of all traffic by 500 yards. With that, it sees the traffic around us and calculates the best course and speed to avoid traffic and get through in the most efficient manner. It recommends sir…the Navigator and his team still give orders to the helm and we are not wedded to it."

Wilson nodded his understanding.

"We also know when the ferries are scheduled to cross and when a vessel not scheduled leaves a ferry port—so long as everyone is transmitting AIS. We have lookouts posted fore and aft with goggles, gunners on the bow and stern quarter fifties with goggles, and of course the *Sierras*."

"When do they launch?" Wilson asked.

Huey checked the Air Plan. "Any minute, sir."

From outside they heard the Air Boss on the 5MC call away the launch, and from inside the bridge they heard him inform the pilots on the radio.

"*Switchblades* and *Talon,* you are cleared to launch on LSE signal, winds down the angle at thirty-six knots, cleared to cross the bow, remain within ten miles of mother."

The pilots rogered him, and the first helicopter illuminated his lights and lifted into a hover as the yellow shirt pointed his wands forward. The *Sierra* dipped its nose as the pilot pulled power and climbed away, followed by the wingman and then the *Romeo,* each securing their position lights as they cleared the ship. Behind on their AIS track, the Officer of the Deck shouted an order to increase turns as *Valley Forge* plowed ahead. Aft on the flight deck shelf, three *Rhinos* started up, two CAP birds and a tanker. Aware of the OOD nearby, Wilson spoke in a low tone.

"Huey, I'll be watching this transit one deck below you, but what concerns you now?"

"Admiral, weaving our way through the regular strait traffic at night is always a challenge, but a small craft—particularly a speedboat crossing in front of us or just coming at us—is a worry. Our *Sierras* are controlled from Combat and I'll have an open line to them. With the SA I've got here, and inputs from the lookouts on my quarters, I expect that I'll be very hands-on in their employment."

"Good. Are you comfortable with the ROE?"

"Yes, sir. Once the helos get a PID hostile and relay it, Combat will then direct the action, and if the action is kinetic, I fully understand it's your call, sir, not mine. Are you going to have Mark there?"

"Yes, and all of us will be in touch real time."

"What if a threat gets inside 1,000 yards, sir?"

Wilson considered the question. Huey's .50 cal gunners could easily take a contact at that range. All the gunners, in the aircraft and in the catwalks, were highly qualified enlisted men.

"I expect that the *Sierras* will be on a contact before that, but yes, if the contact gets by them and is a threat to you, we'll have you open fire. Clear as mud?"

"We'll be ready, sir," Huey replied.

Wilson scanned ahead off the bow, the horizon dotted with the running lights of merchants entering and leaving the Med. One large bulk carrier transited in the opposite direction down their port side.

Wilson scanned again off the bow. The lighted coastlines of Spain and Morocco were not yet in view.

"Are your gunners on goggles?"

"Yes, sir. My A-team."

"Alright. Have a good transit, and I'll keep in close touch."

"Yes, sir."

Wilson exited the bridge into a passageway of darken-ship red lighting and descended the ladder. Olive, on her way up to the bridge, waited for him at the base of it.

"Good morning, sir."

"Olive, let's chat for a moment." Wilson led them into the flag bridge, where Mark Meadows studied the link display in front of Wilson's chair. Wilson walked to the middle of the bridge as Olive followed, the merchant traffic on the horizon providing the only light.

"What's the latest, CAG?"

"We're ready, sir. Huey's tanks are topped off and we got two *Rhino* engines from the beach that the mechs are installing tonight in *Raven* and *Spartan* jets. Pilots are current, and they're boning up on their Russian recce; they're in good spirits."

"Are they ready for EMCON? It's gonna be like our time on *Hanna* once we break free in two hours. We must not emit if we can help it."

"Yes, sir, and we've talked about no satellites…which I expect we'll lose before long."

"I think so too. And there's an *Oscar* boat out there south of the GIUK gap; we could encounter him in another 24 hours."

"Have we been tasked, Admiral?"

"Yes. Transit north of Iceland and await tasking. But with the Russians rounding the North Cape at their best speed, we'll intercept them someplace in the gap, so I expect tasking sooner."

"Sir, what's the latest from Norfolk?"

"*Tinian* should be underway today or tomorrow, and it's going to be a "Lightning Carrier" with 20 F-35's with some *Cobras* and—I hope—*Sierras*. Still being hashed out and the Marines are pissed about kicking off their heavy-lift helos."

"*Romeo's?*" Olive asked.

"I'd like some more too, and we've asked for four if they can ferry them to us. And did you see we're getting three DDGs from Rota tomorrow?"

"Yes, sir, each with two *Romeos*."

"Right, and they aren't officially ours…but I want you to think of them as ours."

"Wilco."

Outside, the first *Rhino* taxied up to cat 3.

"Who's flying tonight?" Wilson asked.

"Comet and his Ops Officer Smitty. The first team."

Wilson nodded. He and *Valley Forge* were ready for any surface or airborne threat. In two hours he would be free, sprinting west into the open Atlantic as the sun rose behind him. *The Russians.* How fast are they coming down? What's their plan? What are The Big Unit and Buffington thinking; what's *their* plan? As he thought about what would meet him in the Atlantic, he noted coastal lights from Spain, and, scanning southwest, saw a glow from Morocco. *Who is going to surprise us?*

Wilson walked to the link screen that Mark monitored. "Let's see where the Russians are."

Meadows called up the link picture. "The surface combatants have not yet rounded the North Cape, sir. Eighteen knot speed of advance."

"Subs?"

Meadows manipulated another screen. Only two were tracked on link, both *Delta* ballistic missile boats near the Russian surface action group. Lots of boats missing…

Wilson exhaled. "The *Oscar?*"

Meadows punched in a series of keyboard commands. A colored wedge appeared, with the apex south of Iceland and extending to an arc that ran from the North Sea to Cork at the bottom of Ireland to the tip of Greenland.

"That's from the last datum two days ago, sir. Tomorrow at this time our furthest-on circle will extend into the Bay of Biscay, and if we run at flank we'll be entering it."

Wilson nodded. He would extend further into the Atlantic before heading north…if Naples would let him.

"Okay. What's the weather tomorrow?"

"Should be fair, sir. Low overcast, better than seven miles vis, three-foot seas."

Wilson looked at Olive. "The deck will be moving, and it will *stay* moving from when we pass the strait till we see the Cape Henry light. Ever operate up in the Norwegian Sea?"

"Sir, I've been with you my whole career—no."

"Well, get ready for severe pitching deck; even in the summer this thing will bob like a cork."

Ahead of them a containership plodded toward Gibraltar, and Huey maneuvered to pass him on the right. With their position lights off, no one on the bridge could see the airborne helos.

Raven 401, the first *Rhino* on the waist, went into tension, and Wilson watched as the pilot wiped out the controls, keeping his head down as he monitored the engine instruments. Soon the external lights came on, signifying readiness as the troubleshooters held their wands high. Wilson checked the PLAT: Comet. Seconds later the *Super Hornet* roared down the track, flung into the darkness by superheated steam power that slammed the shuttle into the water brake, shaking the deck underneath them four levels above it. Wilson checked the PLAT wind over the deck readout: 44 knots. Huey had pulled the rods.

"Admiral, I'm going below to take station in Combat. Nothing is going to come within five miles of us that the *helos* don't identify, and I'm confident with the ROE. Will be in touch, sir."

"Good, Mark, I'll be right here."

As Meadows left, Wilson invited Olive to stay.

"Olive, do ya want to watch the action here?"

"Do you expect action, sir?"

The second *Rhino* went into tension and Wilson waited for it to launch. After it called airborne, Wilson answered. "Yes."

"What kind? Small boat? Plane?"

"Yes."

As was her nature, Olive remained silent. Wilson continued.

"I'll be spring loaded for action this time, pushing my engagement envelope out there. The whole world knows we're blowing through here and why. Just like on a city street; if you're out there at 4am nothing good will come of it."

Olive stepped toward the port side to view the tanker taxiing over the cat 3 JBD. "All these merchants just reported that we have aircraft airborne. The Moroccans and the Chinese in Tangier know."

"Yes, and they'd be smart not to mess with us...but I'm paid to think that they will; frankly, I'm more worried about European crazies on the Spanish side."

"The antifa types?"

"Yeah. Regardless, the threat is ahead of us now, but as we approach the Rock it will be all around us."

"And above us...and below," Olive added. Both contemplated the lights of two continents now visible on the horizon, an unbroken line of light.

The *Super Hornet* tanker went into tension as the two senior aviators watched, each assessing the performance of the sailors on deck and the pilot in the cockpit. Without the sodium vapor lights, the activity on the usually well-lit flight deck was difficult to follow, making the most dangerous workplace in the world that much more dangerous. Once the jet illuminated its lights, the catapult safety observer pointed his wand forward. Seconds later, the tanker roared down the track as it was flung into the air with another *boom* that reverberated throughout the ship.

Eight miles ahead, *Talon* 720, an MH-60 *Romeo*, detected a radar contact.

As one of the MH-60 *Sierras* was called to assist, the two *Romeo* pilots identified the contact on their FLIR as a fishing boat of roughly 50 feet, transiting west toward the strait. On their night vision goggles they saw a single stern light.

The contact—assigned track number 1182—was linked and tracked in the carrier's Combat Information Center. Meadows noted the "skunk" would pass south of their track with a CPA just inside a mile.

Switchblade 610 flew to it, also identifying it on their FLIR and NVGs as a trawler, running west to the strait at fifteen knots. Meadows received this information and did a quick calculation in this head. *Valley Forge* and the rest of the strike group would overtake the boat in under an hour, as they entered the strait. By its heading, Meadows expected track 1182 would veer southwest toward the Spanish enclave of Ceuta by the time the carrier passed it.

Meanwhile, ships flowed in and out of the strait as the American aircraft patrolled among them, monitoring their progress.

With 30 minutes to the narrowest part of the strait, Wilson had a clear view of Gibraltar to his right and the enclave of Ceuta to the left. Olive monitored her aircraft on the link display. Lights of commercial shipping—entering and exiting the strait as if on a two-lane highway—blazed bright against the black backdrop of the open western horizon.

"Huey's been weaving around these guys for hours and we're still on his planned PIM," Olive said.

"Yeah...Let's see how he goes by this guy," Wilson replied, studying the stern light of the tanker one mile in front of them.

"Hey, why didn't you fly tonight?" he asked.

Olive kept her head down in the display. "Let the kids do it. Comet is my go-to, and the helo crews are led by strong department heads. Can't fly all the missions of interest."

"Can't argue with that."

"I'm still losing sleep!" she said.

"Yes…all of us heavies are awake."

Suddenly, Wilson saw a light above the horizon moving left to right and crossing in front of their track.

"What's this?"

Olive checked the link display. "Nothing on the link."

The light stopped in front of carrier and remained stationary, as if hovering. Wilson picked up the phone and dialed Huey direct.

"Captain."

"Huey, Flip; do you see that light in front of us?"

"Yes, sir, and I don't have a range on it. I'm going to jump in and send a *Switchblade* to investigate."

"Roger, I'm calling Mark in Combat, out here."

As Huey called a *Sierra* to investigate, Wilson phoned Mark.

"Mark, this is the admiral. Off our nose we've got a light hovering in front of us, and we don't have a good handle on the range. Huey's sending one of the *Sierras* to investigate…wait."

As Wilson spoke, another light, then more, and a then growing stream of lights raced toward the hovering light.

"What the fuck…" Wilson muttered to himself.

The lights formed rows under the hovering light; Wilson surmised 50 lights per row, and once a row was complete, the lights streamed to form another row on top of the last, and another, and another as the lights surged in from a void off the port bow. The rows filled in where the hovering light was and continued building.

"Sir?" Mark asked.

Transfixed, Wilson and Olive watched the lights continue to stream in and form rows until a giant square of lights, hundreds of them, floated in front of *Valley Forge's* track as the ship raced toward them at 27 knots.

"Mark, we've got a swarm of lights forming a square in front of us, smack on our nose. I think drones."

"Yes, sir, and I'm hearing chatter from the helo pilots."

At that moment, one light departed the upper left corner of the square and flew counterclockwise. Dozens of lights from the square—and finally all of them—followed forming a spiral. The lights then changed color and pulsed.

"I do *not* like this," Wilson muttered, struggling with how to respond to this unknown.

Alarmed, Olive stepped toward Wilson. "Sir, that looks hostile to me, whoever's doing it."

Before Wilson could answer, the lights moved into a jumble before they formed the outline of a young woman's portrait, with other lights moving in to form the eyes, nose, and mouth.

With excited radio chatter in the background, Wilson was mesmerized by the display. *Is that?* Wilson wondered, sensing the image was familiar.

The left eye then "winked," and the image dissolved into a jumble of lights for a few seconds before they flew into ordered letters, forming a word.

Brittany

Wilson heard Olive catch her breath, and the phone buzzed.

"Admiral Wilson," he answered, not taking his eyes off the drones.

"Sir, it's Huey; recommend weapons free on the drones off our bow!"

Wilson's heart pounded as he focused on the word: *Brittany.*

"Admiral! Request weapons free on the drones!"

Snapping out of it, Wilson heard himself answer, as if not there himself.

"Those drones are hostile. Weapons free on the drones off our bow."

"Aye, aye, sir!"

Huey hung up, and the drones morphed into an image of an American supercarrier, then a map of the continental United States. Olive had seen enough.

"Admiral, I'll be in Combat."

"Roger," Wilson said absentmindedly, still trying to grasp what the display meant—and who was controlling it.

The 1MC sounded: *General Quarters, general quarters, all hands man your battle stations!*

Chapter 20

Switchblade 610, 0330 June 14, 2024

Lieutenant Commander Ed Weiler pulled collective as he rolled the MH-60S toward the pulsing light display to the west.

"Okay, weapons free. Gunners, to your mounts!" he directed. The co-pilot, Lieutenant "Hoff" Brennan, checked their flight path.

"Clear left!"

"Hoff, try to slave the FLIR on the drones once I'm stabilized," Weiler added.

"Roger."

Behind Brennan in the cabin, Petty Officer Parker Stover switched on the M240 chain gun that protruded from the left cabin door. On the right door, Aircrewman Tom Pruter maneuvered the barrels of the big GAU-21 for action.

The drones continued with their impressive LED light show, moving from one image to the next as if in animation. One moment they formed a bull charging a matador, the next, a bird landing on a branch. As the *Sierra* flew toward it, the drones appeared to widen their field of display.

"Guys, can you see the drone formations ahead of us?" Weiler asked the gunners over the ICS.

"Got it, sir," Stover answered. "Tally," Pruter added.

"Okay…Petty Officer Stover, I'm going to get closer and enter a hover with a pedal turn right. When I clear you, I want you to spray them with the 240. Just spray 'em."

The drones whirled in a spiral, then the lights on all extinguished.

"Roger sir, and I still have them on my goggles."

In unison, the drones illuminated themselves and formed a dolphin jumping out of the water. The lights washed out the NVGs of all in the aircraft. Weiler directed his aircrewmen and co-pilot.

"Guys, look under your goggles if you have to. Climbing to angels one; Stover, I want look-down shots, nothing above the horizon even if you see drones there."

"Aye, aye, sir!"

"Hoff, watch the torque; I'm lifting us up to angels one as fast as I can. We recording this?"

"Ninety-one percent, ninety-two, slowing through sixty knots. Yep, FLIR record on," Hoff answered.

The radio was alive with calls as the ship directed the *Sierras* to engage the drones now only two miles ahead of the carrier. The second *Sierra*, *Switchblade* 612, converged on the lighted swarm from the south. Weiler needed to direct traffic.

"610 is leveling at angels one, engaging the swarm with the door gun."

"Copy, 610," his wingman replied.

In the cabin, Weiler speculated that they were 500 feet from the drones... which now formed an MH-60 *Sierra*. "Holy shit," Brennan muttered as Weiler pedal-turned into a hover.

"Petty Officer Stover, standby...standby...open fire on the drone swarm nine-o'clock!"

Stover's M240 spit a torrent of bullets that he sprayed at the drones below the horizon, now whirling into a new image.

"Don't hit a ship!" Weiler cried, aware of nearby merchants but now unsure of the action from his right seat.

The lights on the drones extinguished, but Stover could still make out glowing wisps of them with his NVGs against the black surface. After five seconds, Stover let the gun barrels cool off.

"Pruter, you ready?" Weiler asked.

"Affirm, sir!"

Holding the hover, Weiler pedaled left and away, giving Pruter a clear lane of fire unobstructed by the wing.

"GAU-21; open fire! Look down shots only!"

At that moment, the drones illuminated and, as one, charged them. Pruter got off a short burst before he was forced to stop as they flew past the *Sierra*. Several rounds were sprayed above the horizon as the surprised gunner reacted more than aimed.

Weiler flinched as several of the lighted wisps came at him before they were pushed down and away by the rotor wash. Dozens met the same fate. However, one did not.

A tiny drone, weighing only ten ounces, managed to fly into the open cabin and bounce off the ceiling bulkhead and into Stover's leg.

"Whoa!" Stover cried as he reacted to the sudden slap on his flight suit. The broken quadcopter light pulsed as it lay motionless on the cabin deck.

"We got one inside! It's a little quadcopter, practically fits in my hand!" he exclaimed.

Checking the engine instruments for any signs of damage, Ed Weiler wasn't taking chances and dumped the nose to gain airspeed as he cleared to the south.

"Okay, safe up, we're clearing to reassess. Hoff, watch for traffic and gunners stay on your weapons." Weiler keyed the UHF.

"*Switchblade* 612, 610 had a small midair and is clearing south. You're cleared on any leakers."

Helpless as he watched alone in his flag bridge, Wilson observed the drones scatter until they—in unison—extinguished their lights. His two *Sierra* helicopters were in the middle of them, invisible until a sudden burst of tracers from the door guns illuminated them as they charged into an unseen enemy that, without warning, could foul their rotors and crash the helos in front of the carrier entering the narrowest part of the strait at flank speed.

If they really were an enemy.

Without anything to see or shoot, both aircraft cleared to the south. He breathed easier, but perceived the threats on this strait transit were far from over. He called Huey.

"Huey, what's your assessment?"

"Admiral, I've got a clear lane now and there's a ferry about to leave Tarifa that I want to get by, so I've ordered a flank bell. We're going to leave the small boys behind for a moment, but they can catch up to us on the other side."

"Roger; what do you think that light show was?"

"It was meant for us, no doubt. Not sure where they came from or how they had a strong enough signal to control them."

"Good job with the *Sierras*; recover that one if there's any question, and don't think twice about taking the first shot. I'm going below to Combat if you need me."

Wilson exited the bridge and flew down five ladders in the same manner he had as a lieutenant. *The Big Unit needs a call in the next five minutes.*

With purpose, he strode through the red darken-ship passageways into Combat and saw Mark on the phone with Olive next to him. Watch-standers in battledress monitored the displays and spoke into radio telephone handsets.

"Mark, what do you know?"

"Admiral, we're not sure and may not be for a while. A neural network of the type that controlled those drones needs bandwidth and power, and with our closest point of approach to land of four miles, my sense is that they had help with one of the skunks next to us. We're rigging the crap out of them now, to include three *Romeos* from the combatants in trail. We are sniffing them and collecting everything we can."

"Did you see it down here? It was like something you'd see in the Olympics or Super Bowl."

"It was grainy and blurred on the PLAT, and not much better from the FLIR of that *Sierra* that engaged them."

Wilson was impatient. "Okay…I've got to call Sixth Fleet with what I have now."

"Yes, sir, and Smoke is working on a flash message."

"Where's Shane?"

"She's in SUPPLOT, sir, and I'm sure she'll have the latest open-source info, which is probably out on social media as we speak."

"Good. You've got this, and after I call Sixth Fleet, I'm going to hang out here until we break free into the Atlantic."

Wilson departed through the backdoor into his flag ops spaces and his stateroom. Smoke met him with the flash message draft that Wilson scanned. The message was addressed to Sixth Fleet, and informed NAVEUR, EUCOM, and NATO.

Gibraltar passage, time, lat/long, unidentified drone swarm, sudden threat on CVN track, engaged with MH-60S door guns, threat disappeared, no damage, no casualties.

"Good," Wilson said. "Let's let Norfolk know too. Info Fleet Forces, Second Fleet, and Naval Air Forces. With those edits you are authorized to release."

Skweez appeared. "Admiral, Sixth Fleet is ready to patch you through to Admiral Johnson. Open line in the War Room."

"Yep, let's go."

One minute later, Wilson heard the line rattle.

"Flip, what's up?" The Big Unit asked, groggy from sleep.

"Sorry to disturb you sir, but we're passing Gibraltar now and we engaged with a drone swarm about ten minutes ago."

"Whoa," Johnson said, now more awake. "Give me the run down."

"A swarm of drones, lighted like you'd see in a Super Bowl halftime display, appeared without warning on our track, about two miles off our bow—I was on the flag bridge. Under my orders the MH-60 *Sierras* we had up engaged them with their door guns and the drones dispersed. Last we saw them they headed south."

"Toward Morocco?"

"Yes, sir, or maybe the Spanish enclave of Ceuta."

"Damage?" The Big Unit asked.

"One of the *Sierras* reported a midair with one of them, but they are reported small—actually, I'm watching that bird recover now. We still have a *Sierra* and *Romeo* up, as well as two CAP fighters."

"Did the helos spray bullets on any merchant ships?"

"No reports about that, sir."

"Do the Brits or Spanish know?"

"If they do, I haven't told them," Wilson answered, then added, "We are sending a Flash message now to you, informing NAVEUR, EUCOM, and NATO. The ship is in GQ and we'll stay in it until clear."

"Okay, I'm going to HQ. Your people stay in touch with my staff with a running play-by-play. I'll call in thirty minutes."

Skweez handed Wilson a scrap of paper, indicating that it was urgent.

"Roger, sir…oh, wait one…okay, one of the drones flew into the *Sierra* cabin. They say it's something you'd get at any electronics store and fits in your hand."

"Roger that, thanks. Okay, I'm calling my watch team and coming in. Will be in touch soon, out here."

Valley Forge charged through Gibraltar at thirty knots, Huey weaving the 100,000 tons of inertia around the merchants with one degree heading changes as the helos patrolled for threats in front of him. Overhead, the CAP fighters hung on the blades, ready for anything.

Returning to Combat, Wilson surveyed the display of linked merchant traffic on the western side the strait. Most of it flowed along the Spanish coast to round Cape St. Vincent, Portugal on their way to or from the English Channel. Near Rota, he noticed two of the three guided missile destroyers The Big Unit was sending him to augment the strike group, giving him a cruiser and six DDGs. The Rota ships, ballistic missile defense capable, also carried five MH-60 *Romeos* between them. Combined with his own surface combatants, Wilson had almost 700 VLS tubes at his disposal, plus the *Harpoon* canisters each ship carried. With full magazines and topped-off fuel, Wilson was about to take operational control of the most powerful strike group in recent memory.

The radio chatter had died down to routine, and with "The Rock" passing down their starboard quarter, Huey was now on a course to open water and a point some 300 miles to the west-southwest with sparse traffic to avoid the clogged artery along the continent. Just after noon they would rendezvous with *Gene Cernan* as the group then turned northwest to a point 400 miles west of Ireland. After taking every weapon from *Cernan's* hold that his strike group magazines could stow, they would head north. Two days in the expected sea states. The Northern Fleet vanguard would be nearing the GIUK gap then, if the seas cooperated.

Olive entered from the starboard passageway with something in her hand. Shane followed.

"Admiral, this is what flew into the *Sierra* cabin."

In the dimlit space, Wilson took the quadcopter and inspected it, one rotor missing.

"Made in China, sir, and you can get them online for about $25."

Wilson turned it over and found the sticker. MADE IN CHINA

"What isn't made in China these days?" he asked, not actually expecting an answer.

Shane had one anyway.

"Sir, the Chinese control the port of Tangier, but that does not mean they're behind this. Could be them, or an anti-NATO group in Spain, or some rich guy who wants to get in the news."

Wilson nodded, impatient for more. "Okay…all true, but I want answers, so get with Sixth Fleet and get reach-back to Washington. Wake somebody up. I want to know more before noon. Who could do this and why. And as soon as this is on social media, let me know."

"Aye, aye, Admiral," Shane replied, and departed for SUPPLOT. Olive remained behind.

"Admiral, we may have sprayed a merchant."

Wilson looked at her as he absorbed it. "You gotta be shittin' me."

"Wish I were sir, but our gunner is afraid he may have flinched when he had the hammer down and lofted some rounds. He could see ships in the distance during the engagement."

Wilson shook his head in disgust. "Great. Do we know *anything*? Have a recording of the link picture, their FLIR, anything?"

"We'll piece it together, sir, and I'll get it to you soonest."

"Look—he's a kid; is it a *he*?"

"Yessir, a squared-away sailor by every account."

"Okay…I'm not going to go high and right, and I'm not going to tell anyone. Chances are that if a ship was hit it doesn't even know. So find out—but quietly."

"Aye, sir. Thought you'd say that," Olive said, smiling.

She left, and Wilson stood alone, contemplating the link picture amid the buzz of activity in Combat. The screen had his aircraft, the clutter of surface "skunk" tracks, the dozens of COMAIR tracks. The watch-standers spoke into handsets and pointed at the screen at a contact of interest. Despite the hum of activity in the space, the tension had subsided.

His eyes fell on the coastline. *Faro de Trafalgar.* Cape Trafalgar. He smiled to himself that an epic sea battle had occurred in these very waters. He thought of Nelson. *No captain can do very wrong if he places his ship alongside that of the enemy.*

Wilson would leave the legacy of Trafalgar behind as he sped west, but he wondered how Nelson would have reacted to the modern fact that today, stumbling upon an enemy on the horizon might be too late.

He had to scout ahead, just like Nelson, to find the enemy at range, an enemy at that moment still undeclared.

Chapter 21

RFS *Admiral Alekseyev*, 100 miles off the North Cape, 0700 June 14, 2024

Petrov read the classified dispatches from the fleet HQ. A Yankee carrier group led by USS *Valley Forge* had departed the Mediterranean hours ago, while another prepared to get underway in Norfolk. American destroyer sorties from Rota, Spain, and squadrons of P-8 maritime patrol planes and F-15E's deployed to Iceland. Reports of American attack boats departing New London and Norfolk to add to who-knew-how-many they already had deployed along the GIUK gap. Royal Navy and Royal Norwegian Navy surface combatant sorties, to include the Brit carrier with F-35s. Both navies had submarines at sea, and a Norwegian diesel boat could be tracking him now.

Where are our planes? Petrov thundered in his mind. Still well within range of their airfield at Severomorsk, he hadn't seen a Sukhoi or a MiG in eight hours. *Had the prima donnas slept all night?*

He glanced up at *Vitac*, leading them off his port bow as he had since they rendezvoused ten hours earlier. *Admiral Alekseyev* held steady on the plodding containership in the gentle swells, maintaining 150-200 meters as it had for hours, and, to ensure his watch-standers maintained that distance, he had spent the night in his chair. To the west, Petrov could barely make out the superstructures of the division combatants as they eased ahead with the attack boats. In another hour or so, they would disappear over the horizon, leaving him alone with his black-hulled disguise under a familiar low overcast above a slate-gray sea.

Vitac's radar dish spun, the information data linked to Petrov, along with what was detected by a *Mainstay* early warning plane the Air Force had up north of him. How much longer would the fleet enjoy this level of tactical awareness before they had to energize their own emitters? At some point in the next two days the Air Force support would end, followed soon by the satellites. As he had all night, he studied *Vitac* and detected no relative motion. *Good.*

His Exec, Kuzmin, approached his chair with a cup of espresso.

"Here, Kapitan, so you'll make it through the next watch."

"*Spasibo,* Yevgeny Sergeevich. I'll need it and many more."

"When will you sleep?"

Petrov didn't answer him as he sipped.

"You *must* get some rest, Kapitan, especially now that we are in our own waters. Maybe you should not drink this."

"*Are* we in our own waters? The border of Norway is due south of us, and an American submarine could have been waiting outside the sea buoy and trailing in our wake now."

Kuzmin frowned, then smiled. "Kapitan, I'll rephrase my question; when will you let me monitor the bridge team and get some experience?"

Petrov smiled in return; Kuzmin had a point.

"Very well, XO. Let me assess the oncoming watch first, then you take it."

Kuzmin surveyed the horizon as he took another sip. He then leaned in and murmured.

"*Let me,* Kapitan."

Petrov turned and their eyes met; Kuzmin needed to win this one or lose confidence.

In the background, the OOD gave an order to the helm. Petrov checked *Vitac* before he answered in a low tone.

"Fedorov is the next watch."

Kuzmin nodded a slow reassurance. "He'll be under close observation, and all will be well, Kapitan."

Petrov looked back at the containership. "Officer of the Deck, range to the lead ship!"

After checking the angle to *Vitac's* top mast, he calculated it.

"One hundred thirty-nine meters, Kapitan!"

"You are telling me, then, that you are out of position! I want one-fifty!"

"Aye, aye, Kapitan!" the nervous OOD replied, and turned to the helmsman at once.

Petrov's gaze went back to *Vitac.* "I can do that too, Kapitan," Kuzmin insisted.

Resigned, Petrov lifted his stiff body out of the chair. "Very well, Yevgeny Sergeevich. You've got the deck. I'll be in the wardroom or my cabin if you need me."

"Yes, sir, Kapitan."

Departing the bridge, Petrov made eye contact with the boatswain and nodded.

"Kapitan Petrov is off the bridge!"

Two-thousand seven-hundred miles south, an exhausted Wilson rubbed his eyes.

Clear of Gibraltar—and after securing from General Quarters—*Valley Forge* pounded through the increasing seas toward a rendezvous with USNS *Gene Cernan*. Even with thirty knots of natural wind in their face and whitecaps visible on the PLAT screen, the carrier rode the swells with ease. Wilson's seven surface combatants were having a sportier time, and the seas would only get worse once they turned north.

What was *that?* Wilson thought. Still shaken by it, the lighted swarm with Brittany's image and name dominated his thoughts. While the drones were harmless—another one had been found in the port catwalk—the ship could have been in danger if they'd carried even a small explosive. He had called Mary at almost midnight in Virginia Beach to warn her of the expected social media storm that had not yet happened. Brittany slept soundly in her bedroom. Mary said she would wake her up early to inform her.

Then what? Would Fleet Forces provide protection for his family? Did they need it?

Skweez knocked twice.

"Enter."

"Sir, Admiral Buffington is on the line," Skweez said, pointing at the phone.

"Him or his staff?" Wilson asked, uneasy.

"The admiral *actual*, sir," Skweez replied, then added. "He's hot, sir."

"Pick up out there," Wilson said, and directed him to close the door. He picked up the receiver.

"Admiral Wilson, sir."

"WILSON, YOU STUPID DUMB SONOFABITCH! DO YOU WANT TO START WORLD WAR THREE!"

Wilson felt a shot of cortisol to his heart.

"Admiral…"

"WHAT are you doing shooting up the whole frickin strait at a bunch of toys? If someone finds a spent round or cartridge on a merchant, there will be hell to pay! EUCOM is already living in my ass because I can't control my forces who go *right to kinetic* because of a damn *light show?* But I haven't got to the best part yet!"

Wilson waited.

"WHAT were you thinking adding NATO on that flash message? EUCOM just ripped me like I haven't been ripped since I was a plebe because of *your* attention-grabbing and self-serving bullshit! Dammit Wilson, I have fuckin' told you to get your act together and command that strike group like a flag officer in the United States Navy, but that was *your* fuckup and *your* responsibility…and I'm paying for it!"

Speechless, Wilson waited for Buffington to finish his tirade. He'd been warned after he selected for admiral…*there will be moments like this.*

"WILSON! What do you have to say for yourself?" Buffington roared.

Wilson opened his mouth but no words came out. He forced himself.

"Admiral…regarding the message, we are transiting in international waters between the territory of two NATO allies, Spain and Britain, so because bad news does not get better with age…"

"WILSON, that is *total bullshit! I* will tell them, *NOT YOU!* And *I* will tell Spain and Britain and not fuckin' Croatia and Luxembourg and *especially* Greece after your episode last week!"

Wilson thought of Skweez listening. "Sir, I apologize…"

"Why the *fuck* didn't you inform AFRICOM? Huh? Why? Right there next to you, may be in his lane, and is at least an American, but NO, you tell all of Europe about our U.S. Navy fuckup with a flash message at the top of your lungs!"

Wilson fought to get his footing as Buffington raged. Maybe he made mistakes—and more than one—during the transit, but Buffington was completely out of control. Regardless, his heart pounded as his body experienced a natural fight-or-flight response.

"Now, I don't care who you are with all your flyboy medals and press for just doing your damn job, but *one more hiccup* and I'm on the phone to Washington to get your relief! Meanwhile, the LCS's I promised to send you are underway and heading across the pond to you. These are missile shooters and you need to deploy them smart, so get with your surface warrior brain trust and *no more fuckups!* Out here!"

Wilson set the receiver down and remained motionless. Skweez knocked on the door.

"Come in," Wilson snapped.

His aide looked ashen. "Sir, Captain Hopper is outside to see you."

"Did you hear it all?"

Skweez nodded.

"Let him in…you too."

Weed entered and Skweez closed the door behind him. Weed sensed the dejection from the lieutenant and found Wilson staring intently at something on the bulkhead.

"What's going on?" Weed asked.

"Admiral Buffington and I just had a conversation—pretty much one-way, but a conversation."

"And?"

"Shooting the drone swarm was a bad idea."

"Okay…protecting your ships from an unknown. Last week he shit on you for not doing it."

Wilson remained silent.

"Care to share the gory details?" Weed asked.

"And including NATO on the flash message was a bad idea…he may have a point there."

"Reamed out by 'Big Dick' Buffington. Lesser men have lived to tell the tale."

"And better men have been relieved for cause, and after that call I'm pretty sure I have one foot in that category."

"Kemosabe, he's not going to relieve you. Flip Wilson, the one-man air force? The toast of the Washington Navy Yard? No way. He's bluffing."

Wilson shook his head. "That's not how I heard it. And we all know that no one's indispensable."

Weed waved his hand in disbelief. Wilson studied Skweez, who looked at the floor, deflated.

"How're you doin'?" Wilson inquired.

Skweez looked up and for a moment could not find the words.

"Admiral…I'm fine, but *that*…hurt me. So maybe I'm not fine."

"I fucked up. Deserved it."

"Sir…no one deserves *that*. I mean, I haven't even heard of a sailor who *deserves* a tongue lashing get a flaming like that. I'm just stunned, sir."

Wilson nodded. "Skweez, you are privy to things here. Yes, he jumped the chain again, and he's embarrassed again. I'm his outlet, and he's probably talking with Admiral Johnson right now. Regardless, this is small stuff, and when you are in this seat 20 years from now—which I hope you are if you pursue a career—you may experience it too. I just got some training. Message received—now we'll press on."

Weed wasn't buying it. "He's a wild card, Flip; you are a successful aviator and a threat."

Wilson raised his hand. "Enough, please."

"I'm retired and can say what I want."

"Not here, you can't," Wilson shot back.

Skweez took that as a cue. "Excuse me, sir," he said, and closed the door behind him. Wilson held the gaze of his friend in the tense silence.

"I need you, Weed, but I don't need that, not in front of him."

"He's a big boy; that's why you hired him."

"He's a holdover from Mat until I get my own guy, but I may keep him. Regardless—no more of that. I mean it."

Weed frowned as he looked at the bulkhead, then exhaled through his nose. "I'm sorry, man. Won't happen again."

"I know. Now...what do I do the next time? Am I going to see these things now that we are entering blue water, away from any cell towers? Controlled from a ship or ships or satellite? Are they conditioning me with plastic toys that I'll ignore after a while—then hit me?"

Weed waited for Wilson to answer his own question.

"Yes, concur. I'll have Huey blow them out of the sky with the CIWS, no questions asked, and if there are suspicious merchants nearby, I'm going to board them."

"Even after Big Dick told you not to?"

"Yes...with the Russians clearing out the waterfront in Murmansk, it's different now."

"No argument from me. What's next on your agenda?"

"Food, then sleep, then meetings with my brain trust, then food, then sleep."

"Just like the old days."

Wilson studied the PLAT camera that showed an open horizon off the bow. "I'm feeling freer already. And I need to decompress."

"Hop in a jet tomorrow. Blue water ops in the middle of nowhere, low ceilings, probable pitching deck, threat of world war...it will do you good."

Wilson nodded. "Yes, I believe I will."

Chapter 22

Flight deck, USS *Valley Forge*, 0720 June 15, 2024

In full flight gear, Wilson stepped out of the island and walked to *Raven* 400 on the fantail as the crisp salt air and warm sunshine caressed his face. *Valley Forge* rose and fell in slow motion as he scanned the horizon. Unlike his hop days earlier, this one, after the incident at Gibraltar, was an important piece of the scouting effort the strike group needed to ensure unimpeded sailing ahead. To the west, a low overcast hovered over the surface, but it was a glorious day to fly a hop he wanted to fly. The trap would also be Wilson's 300th of his career aboard the carrier.

Assigned a section of water to the west, Wilson would fly out some 300 miles and identify what he came across on the surface, diving down to rig contacts of interest and report all back to *Knight* and the ship. EMCON. No emitting, or even talking, until clear of Mother, and then only to the E-2. At this point in his career, it was a mission Wilson could handle. The hard-core tactical flying was to be done by his air wing aviators, and with the threat to the north and northeast, Wilson's assigned sector was considered unimportant...one "the admiral" could handle, the thought of which made Wilson smile as he walked to his jet.

A 19-year-old plane captain waiting for Wilson at the ladder stood at parade rest, confident of his jet and of himself. Wilson walked straight to him, and the sailor came to attention and saluted.

"Good morning," a smiling Wilson said, returning his salute. "What's your name?"

"Airman Parham, sir."

Wilson extended his hand. "Airman Parham, I'm Admiral Wilson. How's the jet?"

"Good to go, sir!" The young man smiled as they shook hands.

"Alright, let me stow this and I'll be right back."

His preflight inspection complete, Wilson climbed into the cockpit of the *Super Hornet* the same way he had over the past 25 years. Parham followed and began hooking up his g-suit and mask as Wilson attached the ejection seat leg restraints.

"Sir, what are you doing today?"

"All of us are going to check for surface contacts around the ship. I'm going west about three, maybe four hundred miles depending on what's out there. The captain wants to know, so I've got to tell him!"

Parham slammed home the left shoulder Koch fitting. "Alright, sir. Have a good flight."

At a break during the busy start-up litany, with Wilson's hands outside the cockpit as Parham checked the jet, Wilson's mind wandered.

During the past 24 hours, Wilson's strike group had prepared for the real possibility of combat with the Russian Northern Fleet, the lead elements of which were detected by satellite imagery to be some 500 miles from the GIUK gap. They were not emitting, and the Americans could not either, now that they had headed northwest to meet them. Merchants that had originated from the Kola Peninsula—Russian flagged or not—were out there south of the gap, potential tattletales that the air wing had to find and track hundreds of miles ahead and then avoid as the strike group proceeded north.

Accompanied by two escorts, the Royal Navy carrier HMS *Queen Elizabeth*, outfitted with 27 F-35B's and detachments of *Apache* attack helos and Augusta Westland AW159 *Wildcats*, was to get underway with the tide out of Portsmouth and potentially join Wilson at sea tomorrow. Wilson had mulled that in his mind since he had learned of it last night. Who would have operational control of the Brits? Would Naples give OPCON of Wilson's strike group to a British admiral? No doubt a food-fight Buffington and The Big Unit were involved in at some level. He'd find out after he got back from the hop, just a single-cycle surface search.

Outside, a sailor with the position board appeared and held it high so Wilson could read it. NEAREST LAND: NORDESTE 231/320. Wilson scribbled the info on his kneeboard card. In the brief, Wilson noted that Portugal was another 150 miles further than that to his east. If any of the event airplanes got in trouble and could not tank, the Azores it would be, with Lajes now bearing 250 at 380 miles, almost an hour's flight time over the trackless—and cold, even at this time of year—open ocean.

Despite launching into the bluest of "blue water," Wilson did, in fact, need this hop to clear his mind. His uneasiness about what was coming down from the Arctic Circle and NATO command-and-control was eclipsed by Buffington's tirade. He couldn't get it out of his head. Some thirty-six hours ago he had been "attacked" in restricted waters with unknowns on both sides of the strait and only 2,000 yards away, in the form of multiple passing and crossing merchants. That the drones were little more than toys did not change the fact that, with tensions high, he had to consider they weren't. Naples and Brussels and Washington were commanding Wilson's strike group from their swivel chairs while he had to make decisions in real time. He admitted to himself that adding the NATO collective to the message was a mistake, causing one four-star to yell at another, the aftermath cascading downhill in a sequence as old as time. Lesson learned; Albania and Bulgaria could find out later.

With post-start checks complete and a good jet, Wilson returned Parham's salute as the yellow shirt led him out of his spot and to cat 3.

He checked the time; seven minutes to go. With her rudders amidships, *Valley Forge* now steadied on a heading of east.

The launch commenced, and red-shirted ordies walked up to arm him, Wilson lifting his hands so they could see them in familiar routine. He carried two *Sidewinders* on his wingtips and 400 rounds of 20mm in his nose, a reflection of the air wing mindset to *scout*, and nothing more.

From Wilson's vantage point on cat 3, long swells lifted the bow of the carrier above the horizon and held it there for a moment before it gracefully fell back, revealing the blue Atlantic streaked by high winds on the sunlit sea. He'd seen worse, but the forecast was for the ceilings to lower after lunch, four hours away. Six hundred miles west of Lisbon, *Valley Forge* led the strike group as it launched the first event of the day: fourteen *Rhinos* to search the waters around her and scout ahead of the planned northwest track.

The yellow shirt stiffened to attention—*here it comes*—and gave Wilson the take-tension signal. Wilson slammed the throttles up to the detent and raised the launch bar switch. The *Rhino* on the bow also thundered to life as smoking waves of exhaust billowed over the JBD. Wilson cycled the controls in the same deliberate manner he had done over each catapult launch of his career, and scanned the engines and flight control page. *Good.* He turned to the yellow shirt, and when their eyes met, popped him a salute. Ahead of Wilson, *Valley Forge* had her nose buried, showing him blue water before it slowly rose to the horizon.

Shoot me. Shoot me, now.

As the bow broke the horizon, 4-g's slammed Wilson back in his seat as the deck edge rushed up and 400 was thrown into the air. At the same time a *Spartan* FA-18F was launched from cat 2, and as if part of a formation, the two *Super Hornets* banked away from one another and into an impromptu combat spread as they cleaned up and accelerated.

His airspeed building, Wilson leveled at 500 feet and energized his FLIR. His radar could wait until a safe distance from the ship. Both jets sprinted east of the carrier's course, and the *Spartan* was first to lift his nose and veer right. Wilson then rolled and pulled left, trading his knots for altitude as he rocketed up and back to the west under bright sunshine.

Leveling at 17,000, he selected altitude hold and set the power as he headed toward his assigned sector of 270-300. Far below him, *Valley Forge* continued to shoot the first event jets. He'd be back in 85 minutes, and held 450 indicated to run out to 300 miles from Mother quickly and then race back home in time for the recovery.

To the west, a blanket of cloud hugged the surface to the horizon, but with holes and fissures, he could duck through to get a look at a contact. The *Spartan* he had launched with floated a few thousand feet underneath him as it took its station to the northwest. Above him, he spied the contrails of a twin-engine jet heading east, and guessed it to be an airliner. To verify, he lifted his nose to unmask his FLIR and locked it. Yes, probable airliner. He glanced back at *Valley Forge*, and wondered if a sharp-eyed passenger could identify her at this range.

With little to do on the transit west, his thoughts returned to the ship. Was his strike group ready for this? Was he? They had to scout, to identify and track everything hundreds of miles ahead of their PIM and on their flanks for hundreds of miles. Anything on the surface was a threat until it was identified friendly, and, like his combat deployment to WESTPAC aboard *Hancock,* an "innocent" airliner could pose a threat, reconnaissance or kinetic. Wilson studied the jet high above—white fuselage—and figured that it could belong to any number of passenger carriers. He scribbled down his time and position.

At the required distance, he contacted the E-2.

"*Knight, Raven* four-zero-zero up for your control."

"*Raven* four-zero-zero, *Knight,* proceed as briefed. Timber sour."

"Four-zero-zero, wilco," Wilson replied.

No data link, Wilson thought. Was it the E-2 black box or something more ominous? The ship depended on the link picture, and without it, Wilson and the other pilots would have to provide snapshots of what they found in their sectors to be relayed to the ship by the *Hummer.* He hoped it would come up soon as he sped west at almost 500 knots ground speed.

At that moment, 12,000 miles above Newfoundland, a Russian intercept vehicle neared an American GPS satellite. With both travelling at 14,000km/hour, the vehicle eased up next to the satellite and, when stabilized two meters away, a mechanical arm grabbed it. Once secure, a thruster fired for three seconds, nudging the satellite out of orbit toward the atmosphere. With the Russian vehicle locked on the American bird in a death grip, the two machines hurtled toward the Indian Ocean as the alarm was sounded at Peterson Space Force Base in Colorado Springs. Frantic controllers notified the National Military Command Center duty desk in Washington, and within minutes, the secretary and key members of the joint staff were informed.

In what was mankind's first armed space-to-space attack, the doomed satellite and intercept vehicle burned up together over Perth, Australia, appearing as a brief shooting star in the night sky. Over the next two hours, six more satellite intercept/destructions of American space-based assets were accomplished, including one of a radar reconnaissance satellite and a vital naval communications bird.

The Russian Federation had taken the first shot.

CHAPTER 23

RAVEN 400, NORTH OF THE AZORES, 0830 JUNE 15, 2024

"*Raven* four-zero-zero, *Knight*, potential contact on your nose for sixty-five."

Wilson dropped a MARK, then keyed the mic.

"*Raven* four-zero-zero."

He scanned the horizon ahead of him. The layer underneath seemed to break in the distance, allowing Wilson to perhaps see the contact without having to radiate first. He'd ramp down now to slip through an opening and come up to it on the deck. Identifying the contact without being detected was his goal, but a correct identification was job one.

A ship type was good enough; the air crews had been briefed not to "rig" a contact and alert it that an American carrier was nearby, and to treat everything as a potential threat. He checked the sun: high even at this hour in late spring and still climbing. He offset 10 degrees left to allow him to approach the contact up sun and use what concealment it offered to avoid detection.

Now hundreds of miles from the carrier and opening, Wilson checked Lajes as his divert waypoint. Inside 200 miles. Below, the sea surface temp was 62 degrees Fahrenheit. Though far from comfortable, it was survivable—for probably 24 hours in a raft, and a handful of hours without one. State 13.3—fat on gas.

"*Raven* four-zero-zero, *Knight*."

"*Knight*, *Raven* four hundred, go ahead."

"*Raven* four-zero-zero, we had a jet north of you RTB single-engine and he's escorted. Could you work north after you ID this skunk and stay for the next cycle? Expect *Texaco*."

Wilson pondered the request. First, escorting back a single-engine jet hundreds of miles from Homeplate was the right call, but it left the northwest sector open. Less critical than the north-northwest sector, it was still important. Mark Meadows and the staff wouldn't miss him, and who could refuse more flight time on this gorgeous day?

"*Raven* four-zero-zero, wilco."

"Roger that, *Raven* four-zero-zero, and after you ID the skunk fly three one zero."

"Four hundred, roger that," Wilson answered.

Wilson checked the range from the mark: 45 miles. Able to see the surface 5,000 feet below, he maneuvered through an opening in the undercast with the sun at his back. Just touching the cloud deck's ceiling, he came upon a clear sea underneath and continued down. Under 1,000 feet, he saw it: a car carrier with a blue hull headed west. Wilson turned right to skirt its port quarter, lessening the opportunity for the single bridge watch-stander to notice a fighter at range and remaining too far to hear. He referenced the code word for car carrier.

"*Knight, Raven* four-zero-zero mark on top *french door*, two five zero at ten."

"Copy all, *Raven*, vector three one zero, range unknown."

Wilson checked his fuel. 12.1. With the next recovery in 2.5 hours, he'd need at least 6K if he didn't waste it. Despite the promise of a tanker to meet him on station, he couldn't bet on it, and motored northwest at max endurance fuel flow to conserve fuel until the tanker showed up. He elected to stay low to see underneath the layer—now overcast—that floated above him at 1,000 feet. The sharp horizon would highlight anything around him.

Wilson headed into a part of the Atlantic far from the sea lanes, now over 1,000 miles west of Ferrol, Spain. All around him was empty water. *The vastness,* he thought, alone as he was in the North Atlantic. Keeping his radar off, he brought the FLIR seeker head to the horizon and slewed left. No indentations on it. *Empty.*

Random radio chatter from other air wing aircraft kept him company as he droned ahead into the abyss. Every so often a *Spartan* or *Buccaneer* checked in with a contact, all merchant sightings. Routine. Wilson expected that in these latitudes, and was glad there was nothing of interest, but that would change. This afternoon? Tonight? Tomorrow?

Tomorrow. Along the expected PIM, his scouts would likely find something just south of the gap. Unless the Russians had slowed. American P-8's from Iceland and Royal Air Force *Poseidons* from Scotland would detect the attack boats first. The *Oscar.*

Why hadn't they found that yet? When would this turn hot? What indication or warning would they receive? Would he receive it first?

Wilson flew on, spending more time monitoring his fuel, as every carrier pilot did. Over 500 miles from Mother; had he ever been this far from the ship by himself? He was opening on Lajes, now over 400 miles from the only sure thing in the eastern Atlantic. He didn't expect to sweat fuel on this hop, not in a *Rhino*. In the *Hornet*, it was a way of life, and using lessons learned over a lifetime, Wilson managed his throttles to maximize the efficiency of every pound of fuel.

Something ahead, twenty degrees left. Wilson slewed the FLIR to it. A merchant outline, unusual with the superstructure amidships. Maybe it was a light-loaded containership. It appeared bow on, and Wilson gently banked right and descended to 500 feet to arc around it and study it from the aft quarter.

"*Knight, Raven* four-zero-zero has a contact on my nose about 15 miles, investigating."

The E-2 did not answer.

Wilson wondered if the *Hummer* crew knew that he was piloting 400. Not that it mattered. He was happy to help—and at this moment, lead—Carrier Strike Group Eighteen from the front. The pace would pick up, oh, yes, and he lamented that he'd be tied to TFCC or Combat for the next 96 hours. At minimum.

Abeam the contact, Wilson studied it closer. It was a general-purpose cargo ship of 400-500 feet. Black hull with large white superstructure amidships. Heading south. He checked the bearing to Lajes. Not going there. *What is this guy doing?*

His headset whistled, and Wilson's eyes were drawn immediately to the left DDI. Some caution had just flashed, but what? He checked his engine instruments and flight control page. All good. *What caused that*, he thought as he continued on. *Spurious input.*

Arcing right to keep the ship at ten miles, he was now behind it as he came upon the remnant of its light wake. Less than ten knots, he guessed. Crossing the wake, he looked down his wing line at the vessel and determined the heading: 200. *Must be headed for South America.*

He noticed movement on the FLIR. A dot near it...*what is that?* He lifted his visor up, but was unable to see it with his naked eye. He banked into it and tried to lock it on the FLIR, but the object was too small to hold it. He tightened his turn to decrease the range, and setting attitude hold, tried the FLIR again. Success! The FLIR locked a dot that moved closer to the ship, presenting the outline of it in the background. Perfect. He scribbled notes for his report to *Knight*: the time and lat/long.

Wilson's eyes were drawn again to the left DDI.

HYD 2A

Wilson froze, and his heart jumped in his rib cage before the aural caution sounded. *Fuck!*

He rolled out and pulled up the FCS page. Before he could even scan it, another caution appeared, followed by an aural *Flight Controls, Flight Controls*:

HYD 2B

Mother of God!

His pulse pounding, Wilson turned easy left in the most direct route to east, ignoring the merchant while pulling the emergency checklist out of his g-suit pocket. The right leading-edge flap degrade could wait; losing the hydraulic system powered by his right engine—hundreds of miles from home—could very soon become catastrophic. Almost 600 miles from the ship, he checked his fuel: 9.6.

With his eyes open wide as adrenaline coursed through him, Wilson lifted his visor to better study the tiny hydraulic pressure gauge by his right knee. The steam gauge confirmed it: HYD 2 pressure was near zero. He noticed his breathing was irregular and shallow. *Don't panic and fly the airplane!*

He steadied on a heading of 110—close enough for now—and climbed at a shallow angle holding 300 knots as he entered the overcast. Before he did, he searched over his right shoulder for evidence of a fluid leak, streaks of red on the wing, or a wispy trail behind him. Nothing, and soon he entered the clouds.

Wilson fought to control himself as his fingers fumbled to open the pocket checklist. Then it dawned on him: *get the probe out!*

He extended the refueling probe, hoping for any residual pressure to force it out into the airstream. The door opened and the probe slowly extended—then stopped. Wilson couldn't believe it.

Sonofabitch!

Without the probe, Wilson was in deep trouble.

Fly the damn airplane! Aviate!

Selecting to fly a bingo emergency fuel profile, Wilson pushed down to increase airspeed as he referenced the pocket checklist. He knew that operating the engine without fluid in the hydraulic reservoir was a recipe for fire, but he needed to get fast in the climb. *Calm down*, he told himself, controlling his breathing and focusing.

The procedure called for the jettison of unwanted ordnance, and Wilson pushed the station 4 and 8 tiles, armed up, and hit SELECT JETT. With a familiar shudder as the CADs actuated, he watched his left tank fall away and checked his right wing to see it too was clean. Wilson then watched the probe for any signs of life, wishing and hoping it could lock itself in full extension. Now with 360 knots—extension speed be damned—he kicked the left rudder hard in an effort to yaw it open. The half-extended probe didn't budge. *Dammit!*

Navigate.

Wilson headed for the spot from which *Valley Forge* had launched him some 90 minutes earlier. Waypoint zero was 592 miles away! He berated himself for not hitting a MARK on the cat. He *always* did that, a habit of 25 years of carrier flying. Preoccupied, he had neglected to. *Screw it.* The E-2 would give him a steer. He checked Lajes; 453 miles at 165.

Passing 10,000 feet, the uneasiness Wilson felt about his right engine built inside him. He had to shut it down; it had been several minutes since the caution appeared and operating at military power most of that time. Even with both engines, he was well over an hour from landing. He'd have to fly home single engine, and Wilson—methodically and deliberately—retarded the right throttle to off, feeding in left rudder trim to remain in balanced flight and hold 250 knots in the climb.

Communicate.

"*Knight, Raven* four-zero-zero."

Wilson waited a normal time for a response. He hadn't heard *Knight* for a while. After a longer than average wait, he tried again.

"*Knight, Raven* four-zero-zero."

Nothing. He then heard a *Buccaneer* jet call *Knight*, and they seemed to be having a conversation that Wilson could only hear one side of. Checking his climb progress, he keyed the mic.

"*Cutlass,* three zero seven, *Raven* four-zero-zero, how do you read?"

After several seconds, the *Rhino* pilot answered. "Go ahead, *Raven.*"

Yes!

"*Cutlass, Raven* four-zero-zero, I've experienced a HYD 2 failure and am RTB single engine. Trying to get *Knight* to give me a steer but no joy, please relay."

The pilot was on top of it. "Roger that, four hundred, stand by."

Wilson listened to the pilot relay his message and waited. With his left engine at military power, he assessed his profile. The single engine bingo table only went out to 200 miles. Passing 17,000 feet on the way to 25K, he checked the fuel required: almost 4K to go 200 miles! Wilson had to go at least 500 on his total fuel remaining of 8.3, and his heart rate increased again.

"*Raven, Cutlass* three zero seven."

"Go ahead."

"Ah…the *Knight* is searching but can't find you."

Staring at the combined operational picture during a routine visit to Combat, a surprised Olive couldn't believe it.

"The *admiral* is on a double cycle out of radio contact? What are you guys thinking?"

The watch officer, a surface warfare lieutenant, didn't understand.

"Ah…ma'am, I'm not sure what you are talking about?"

Olive shook her head in disbelief. "The *pilot* of *Raven* four-zero-zero; that's Admiral Wilson."

The watch officer studied the status board and checked the roster as he formed an answer. "Ah…yes…we had a jet go down in the 300 sector and asked if four hundred could take it, and the E-2 said he could."

"The E-2 sent him? Is there a tanker enroute?"

The harried lieutenant, not versed in the ways of airplanes, didn't have an answer. If a pilot accepted tasking, what more was required?

Olive picked up the phone to call Huey.

"Huey, Olive in combat…do you know the admiral is out there alone someplace hundreds of miles from us?"

Huey checked the status board. "No…isn't he on this recovery?"

"No, they double-cycled him because a *Spartan* fell out, that single engine RTB."

"Oh, yeah…but he accepted it, right?"

"Don't know, but anyway, that's where he is and he won't make the 1130 meeting in the War Room."

"I'm fine if we cancel it."

"Me too, but even in this quasi-combat—I just don't like anyone being out that far, and especially him. We have to search wide, I get it, and keep jets up, but…"

"I know, but he's got more air sense than anyone in the wing…present company excepted."

"Huey, he's not really current, not on the step," Olive replied, then lowered her voice. "And…he's different."

"I know; he's only been in the seat two weeks, and yesterday shook him up."

Olive nodded to herself, but what could be done? Flip Wilson was her boss—again—and arguably the finest pilot airborne now, despite being past his prime. When *was* his prime? The old *Raven* days?

"Yeah…okay, he made an airborne call. I'll get a status on him; meanwhile, how are the seas doing?"

"Picking up, which you can probably feel. And the weather in Lajes is going down, not that we want to send anyone there."

"Can we fly the rest of the day?"

"Yes, but it's going to deteriorate. Your LSOs will have their hands full."

"Great. Okay, roger all, talk to you later."

"Out here," Huey said.

CHAPTER 24

RAVEN 400, NORTH OF THE AZORES 0950 JUNE 15, 2024

Leveling at 25,000, Wilson milked the left throttle to hold 250 knots. With a fuel flow of 3,900 pounds, and fighting a slight headwind, his groundspeed was 290 knots. At this rate he'd have two hours, and would make up some fuel in the descent. He tried the E-2 again.

"*Knight, Raven* four-zero-zero..."

As he waited for an answer, he checked his groundspeed; a dismal 285 against a quartering headwind of 136 at 48. He needed a break.

Why couldn't the damn *Hawkeye* see him? Though he did not know the position of the E-2, he expected it would be ahead of the ship's track. With the sun on his right shoulder, he could only continue east and wait to be picked up.

It dawned on him. *Blow the probe out!* He activated the emergency extend switch. *Nothing!*

Fighting against rising panic, Wilson had just used his last chance to extend the probe, still halfway open and doing nothing but increasing his drag. Blue water with no ability to tank and maybe two looks at the deck once he arrived on the ball...Wilson forced himself to remain calm as he breathed through his nose under his oxygen mask. He was behind the airplane, and he knew it.

Lajes was on his right shoulder, showing 450 miles. Diverting there was an option. *A sure thing!* But was it? Recovering there would be bad, and tip off any spies in the hills that *Valley Forge* was nearby. Wrestling with his options, Wilson rejected the concern. *The whole world knows* Valley Forge *just went through Gibraltar!* He peered south; a white blanket to the horizon. Unable to see anywhere near 400 miles, he had to *know* before he made a decision. And, he needed to admit he'd pressed it.

"*Cutlass* three-zero-seven, *Raven* four hundred."

"Go ahead, *Raven.*"

"I'm estimating five hundred plus from mother on the single engine RTB. Declaring an emergency and I need an escort."

"Roger, four-zero-zero. I'm inbound to *Texaco* and should be plugged in ten mikes. I'll get an extra 3K and buster on out to you. *Knight* has relayed."

"Four-zero-zero."

Wilson imagined the ship losing their minds. *The admiral's single engine with a HYD 2 failure and beyond radar range!* He'd become visible to them before long…but what about Lajes?

"Three zero seven, ask them for current conditions and forecast at Lajes."

"Wilco, four hundred."

Wilson could only wait as he monitored the fuel and groundspeed. On the fuel page, he dipped below 8K. Five hundred miles at 285 ground: 1+26 hours. He crunched the numbers again: 5,600 pounds. He'd have 2,300 pounds of fuel when he got to the ship, and would "make money" on the idle descent. *If* the ship had a ready deck. Assessing the time, he'd be late for the event two recovery, but not too bad if he could keep the ground speed up in the descent. Nearing the ship he'd call; Huey would make a ready deck. Unable to do anything more, he checked his pocket checklist to refresh himself on the single engine landing procedure if restarting the right was not in the cards.

"*Raven* four-zero-zero, *Cutlass*."

"Go ahead."

"Mike Four Alpha has you; steer one two five at five sixty."

Wilson was shocked—and alarmed. Five hundred and *sixty* miles! His NAV page showed waypoint zero just inside 500. More math…an extra 12 minutes and 800 pounds. The ship must have moved east for the launch and recovery winds…but sixty miles? Regardless, Mike Four Alpha—the DDG *Eugene Lindsey* to the west of Mother—had him and could vector *Cutlass* 307—or somebody—to escort. *Cutlass* 307 chimed in again.

"*Raven* four hundred, current conditions at Lajes; one half mile in rain and fog, lowering to one quarter. Braking action poor, altimeter 29.78."

Great, Wilson thought. Dog squeeze weather over a single runway nestled in mountainous terrain. And even if he broke out, poor braking with carrier pressure tires. No, he'd take a pitching deck he could see over fixed but wet concrete in the goo.

"*Cutlass* three-zero-seven, copy all. I'm pressing to the ship and expect to be on the ball with one point five. Probe is inop—unable to tank."

"Roger that, four-zero-zero, will pass."

The broken layer Wilson had flown over two hours earlier had consolidated into an overcast. Thankfully, no convective activity on this late-spring day. Yet.

He scanned the horizon, then looked up and saw an airliner overtaking him at his nine o'clock high, probably in the high thirties some five miles away…what passed for human contact.

"*Raven* four-zero-zero, *Knight*."

Yes! Wilson thought, grateful that the E-2 finally had him.

"*Knight, Raven* four-zero-zero has you loud and clear, on a single-engine RTB to mother, request steer."

"*Raven* four-zero-zero, radar contact. Understand declaration of emergency?"

"Affirm," Wilson replied.

"Roger that, *Raven*, your steer one-one-niner, five-one-zero miles."

Wilson rogered the E-2, frustrated that he was still outside 500 miles of the ship. He crunched the numbers again…he'd have 1.5 on the ball if he was lucky, especially if he restarted the right engine for landing. He'd get three looks at the deck with that—*if* he was lucky.

Wilson breathed through his nose as his eyes darted from the horizon to the fuel page.

Scanning the horizon ahead of him, Huey took the call from Combat. Outside his port window, an MH-60S slid over the angle to spot three.

"He's at 500 miles on a single engine profile? Okay, get a tanker to him."

"He says he can't tank, sir."

"Why not?"

"Not sure, sir, but my understanding is that he can't."

Huey said okay, then hung up and called Olive.

"Olive, Huey…okay, we've got him at 500 miles and he can't tank. Single engine…I'm thinking HYD 2 failure."

"That's exactly what he just reported, probe stuck," Olive answered. On that profile, he's more than 90 minutes away."

"Concur, but maybe we can shave that. With this *Switchblade* on deck I'm going to run west as fast as I can and maybe gain 25-30 miles. Let me go, I'll be in touch."

Huey cradled the receiver and barked, "OOD!"

"Aye, aye, sir!"

"Turn us west as tight as you can and once out of the turn, all-ahead flank."

"Aye, aye, sir!"

As the OOD shouted orders, Huey assessed the seas. *Building.* He called up the weather page on his bridge chair display. Low overcast with surface winds out of the west.

This should work.

Booop.

Wilson picked up the hit on his RWR display. *Spartan* 105, pulled off his SSSC sector, approached on his left side. Searching visually, Wilson soon picked up the speck, highlighted against the white horizon. Though far from secure, Wilson now had an escort—and a potential on-scene commander.

Three hundred and eighty miles to go. Wilson had agonized over every second of the last 300, over an hour since the HYD 2 caution illuminated. Left engine good, flight controls good. The only drawback—a potentially fatal drawback—was the inability to tank. Obsessed as any carrier pilot, he compared the groundspeed and fuel flow. He'd have a low fuel light on the ball, which brought additional problems.

Alone, despite the *Spartan* joining on the left bearing line, he second-guessed himself as he had the past hour. *I shouldn't have accepted the tasking. I should have put the probe out the moment the caution illuminated, blown the damn thing out earlier.* Berating himself now was not productive; there would be time later, and he returned to the task of squeezing every pound of thrust from every drop of fuel.

The two-seat *Rhino* joined on his wing in parade, the pilot lifting a thumbs-up. Wilson nodded and followed with his fuel state, then gave him the signal for cruise formation. The *Rhino* slid back and under Wilson to his right side as he checked his jet for any signs of damage.

Wilson thought back to the last merchant he intercepted. Was it Russian? It did have Eastern European lines. Bulk carriers, containerships, tankers, and car carriers were found everywhere on the high seas...but a general-purpose merchant ship with large superstructure amidships was rare. And that dot! A small helo or drone; Wilson figured it was the latter. Why would that guy be operating a drone? Out in the middle of nowhere? *If* it was his. Wilson hadn't seen anything else near the contact, but stopped looking as soon as the HYD cautions appeared.

"*Raven* four-zero-zero, *Knight*; we've got your squadron rep on relay."

"Go ahead," Wilson replied.

"Four-zero-zero, rep." Wilson recognized the voice of Comet, the *Raven* CO.

"Rep from four hundred…got a HYD 2A and 2B caution, rapid loss of HYD 2 pressure. Right engine shut down, probe stuck halfway out and I was unable to blow it out."

"Roger that, four-zero-zero, what's your state?"

Wilson glanced at the engine instruments. "Five-point-six, holding thirty-nine hundred pounds per hour."

"Copy that."

"Punched the tanks off."

"Roger; standby."

Wilson saw the contrails of another airliner in the distance, this one coming at him. It had probably overflown the carrier. Sea routes, commercial airways, satellite orbits—how could he keep the strike group hidden? He put his FLIR on it—a four engine jet, rare these days. Comet called him.

"*Raven* four-zero-zero, rep."

"Go ahead."

"Sir, we're going to catch you with a ready deck, and *Knight* will call your descent and vector you for a visual straight in. We request you hold four thousand foot per minute in the descent at 250 indicated, and we recommend you start the right engine and fly a normal approach; I'll be here to back you up on the checklist."

"Roger all; is the expected BRC easterly?"

"Affirm."

"Roger; what's the weather?"

"Right now, ceiling one thousand over, winds out of the east at 35 knots, gusting to 45. Expect a four-degree glideslope and half flaps."

"Roger, how's the deck?"

Comet didn't answer at first, then said, "It's movin' a little."

Wilson knew at once what that meant. It's moving…*a lot.*

Chapter 25

USS *Valley Forge* 1030 June 15, 2024

White spray exploded off the bow of *Valley Forge* as she buried herself into another rising wave crest. The hammer blow shook the ship and crew, and no one more than Huey Morrison.

He surveyed the western horizon: whitecaps and darkening skies. He had never operated this far north in the Atlantic but had heard the stories. The weather changes within the hour...and less. Three miles to port, *Manila Bay* lifted her bow high as she traversed a swell, and Huey watched as she then fell to meet another one, generating an eruption of spray that travelled the length of the ship. Huey would gladly bash in his hull plates and those of the strike group to get Flip aboard, but how many dousings of salt water could the *Rhinos* parked on the bow take? He had to slow down in this increasing sea state. On the bright side, the surface winds had shifted to the west.

At best he could buy Flip 15 miles. Maybe save him 300 pounds. With the weather lowering and the sea state picking up, all the air wing jets would have to penetrate through likely icing conditions before they faced a pitching deck—and a low boarding rate. Huey surmised the ceiling to be 1,000 feet. Tankers would have to get underneath it to hawk the low state jets, or just send the low-states back up through it to find the tanker someplace on top. With no TACAN radiating to help the pilots effect a rendezvous, that evolution would take time and precious fuel.

He thought about radiating. No hostilities—yet—and relatively low in latitude, the Russian surface ships were at least 1,500 miles north of him. His main concern was the known unknown of the *Oscar* attack boat, which would have to surface to sniff out his TACAN. It would have to be in his vicinity, which he thought unlikely. Thinking through options, his phone buzzed.

"Cap'n."

"Huey, Mark Meadows in TFCC. Do you know we just lost GPS?"

"No," Huey answered, scanning his tactical display for signs. "When?"

"We just lost it, but NAVEUR contacted me on the high side saying they have indications that the Russians have nudged several birds out of orbit. My sense is that we'll lose SATCOM before noon."

Huey froze at this news. *Holy fuckin' shit!*

"Whoa...okay, what are you thinking?"

"My sense is to get the admiral and everyone else aboard, ride out this storm as we assess, and maybe pick it back up this afternoon after we get more guidance from above. Bottom line is that we cannot radiate; they just escalated big time and we need a huddle before we go back out there in this new satellite-denied environment. I think more will be downed."

"Concur. Okay...are you watching these seas?"

"Yeah...the pilots can fly in this?"

"Yes, and even worse, and at night, but the danger is ratcheted up."

Meadows made himself clear. "We still have a need to scout ahead of us, and an hour ago the airplanes *helped* that effort, but after this...they *are* the effort."

"I hear you...Okay, I like that plan. Let's get the admiral and everyone aboard. First, I'm beating us up in these seas and gotta take some turns off, which is going to decrease my ability to meet the admiral."

"Okay, your call, but..."

Huey waited.

"We gotta get the admiral back."

"Mark, no argument, but are you asking me to radiate to help in that effort?"

"No...yes."

"I want him too, and the jet, and all the kids and jets."

"Okay; I didn't ask...this is yours and I'm stepping back. Whether you radiate or not, I'll support you."

"Roger that. He can handle the pitching deck once he shows up, but he's got a sick bird and it's going to be delicate. Job one, get him here."

The call complete, Huey cradled the receiver. *No GPS and probably no SAT-COM.* The Russians had fired the first shot. That they had made it easier, in a way. *War footing.* On the other hand, they had fired knowing full well they were taking on the United States—and NATO. Why did they?

As word spread throughout *Valley Forge—the frickin' Russians are blowing up our satellites!*—Huey contemplated what it meant as his ship pounded against the relentless swells.

War. World War...holy fuckin' shit...

"*Raven* four-zero-zero, begin descent."

Wilson rogered the E-2's command and pushed over, setting the attitude for a 4,000 foot-per-minute descent. He puckered the left nozzle to get what he could in range, trusting the E-2 that he would not have to dive through the clag right on top of the ship. Below him was a broken layer, with another layer visible under that. Not knowing *exactly* where the carrier was gnawed at him.

"Four-zero-zero, expected BRC is west."

Wilson rogered the call; the winds were out of the west now…which meant he had to hook-in behind the ship. Without a TACAN and unable to radiate his own radar, he had to blindly follow the E-2's vectors and altitude assignments, a descent he could manage so much better if he *knew* where the ship was and its heading. Holding 950 pounds per hour on his left engine, he figured what he would have in five minutes: 2.3. A fuel state that meant little without *knowing*.

Passing 18,000 feet, he felt his heart rate increase. He was flying into a box of his own making. No link. The decision to accept double cycle. Late getting the probe out, and the pneumatic mechanism inop. Of all the times! And now unforecast worsening weather. He was afraid to ask himself what was next. Keeping himself busy, he checked the leading edges for icing and the engine inlet temp. Clear.

Trapping with his fuel remaining was his only chance. Ejecting from fuel starvation—with 105 next to him to call away the SAR—was another chance at life, if a helo could get to him in the next hour. He could squeeze thirty minutes of flight time with what he had…on deck or in the water. Less than thirty minutes either way.

Wilson had reached his limit.

"*Knight, Raven* four-zero-zero…you are going to have to set me up five miles aft on course, and I'll accept cherubs six to break out and proceed VFR, but you've got to help me manage this fuel."

"Roger, sir…standby."

Wilson looked over at 105 on his left wing…as blind as he was.

"*Raven* four-zero-zero, check your descent to three thousand, fly heading zero eight three."

"Four-zero-zero," Wilson answered.

So he *had* been needlessly chewing up altitude in the descent. He did some more math: thirty miles at this groundspeed. Roughly 100 pounds, but with the ship heading at him he'd have to do a 180 to intercept the final bearing…once he broke out and saw it. Wilson energized his SPN-41 receiver on the off chance the ship would radiate it for him.

Did he need the right engine? With the deck pitching at launch time, it could not be any better with probable high winds. In these conditions, he needed a wave off capability—at least he was light. Starting the right engine with a dead HYD 2 system would increase the chance of fire. And double the fuel flow. In the clag while passing angels ten, he wrestled with his options and set his radar altimeter warnings. He checked 105 next to him; the outline of the *Rhino* was just visible in the goo.

Breaking into the clear, he got a peek at the surface below him, dark gray with whitecaps. The ceiling looked to be enough for VFR underneath. *Thank you.*

"*Raven* four-zero-zero, on this heading and descent rate, Mother should be at your nine o'clock when you break out."

Still unsure, Wilson held his tailhook to avoid even that added drag. Scanning the horizon, he noted a dot against the gray backdrop of clouds at his eleven o'clock and figured it to be over ten miles. Maybe the duty tanker. He placed his FLIR on it—a *Rhino* as he suspected, and in a left-hand orbit. He passed through angels six, holding a 3,000 fpm rate of descent as directed.

He had his pocket checklist open to the landing gear emergency extension procedure. He'd blown the gear down before in his career, but not in a *Rhino*. *Slow below 180, gear handle down, rotate 90 clockwise, pull to detent.* Next to him, *Spartan* 105 had dropped his hook. Wilson did likewise, and exhaled his relief when 105's pilot raised his thumb up high.

They entered a wisp of cloud, broke free, then back in it. Wilson held his rate of descent as his eyes danced among the HUD and engine instruments. 2,500 pounds…he made his decision.

"*Knight, Raven* four-zero-zero, I'm going to bring it aboard single engine."

"Roger four-zero-zero, will pass. We'll switch you to Tower when you have a see-me."

"Four-zero-zero."

The LSO's were using MOVLAS: Manually Operated Visual Landing Aid System. Wilson figured the ship must be bobbing like a cork as he flew his instruments in the thickening clag. *Should I start the right?*

At 1,000 feet he broke free and looked left. There she was, *Valley Forge* some five miles away, with a jet in the groove and white spray off the bow!

He checked his fuel: 2.4.

"*Knight, Raven* four-zero-zero and *Spartan* one-oh-five see you at ten, low state two point four."

"Roger, *Raven*, switch Tower button one."

"Roger, switching, and thanks."

Wilson eased the formation left and tapped his helmet to switch up button one. After he punched it in, he waited for a moment, as he had throughout his career.

"Power...*power!*...wave off pitching deck."

Wilson watched the *Rhino* wave off as another lined up for his approach. Below him, whitecaps streaked the cobalt water and Wilson could see the marks they left on the swells. The LSO called.

"Workin' forty-eight knots, slightly axial."

Despite having flown the previous 500 miles, Wilson was only halfway home; he had to get the gear down...and hope for a steady deck once he got to the ramp.

Chapter 26

Pri Fly, USS Valley Forge 1115 June 15, 2024

Olive entered Primary Flight control and dogged the hatch behind her. One of the airmen noticed her and sang out: "CAG's in Pri Fly."

The Air Boss Commander Stevenson acknowledged her and pointed to the south. "We've got him in sight, CAG, about five miles south." Comet stood next to him with the NATOPS manual open.

"What's his state?" Olive asked. Comet answered.

"He hasn't checked in yet, but last we heard it was two point five, ma'am. I'm guessing he'll have two-oh on the ball."

Olive nodded just as the LSO transmitted on the UHF speaker: "Wave off, pitching deck." Olive looked left in time to see a *Rhino* climb away in front of them and reenter the pattern for another try. Stevenson turned to her.

"CAG, I'm watching him and the pattern and when he gets lined up at three miles I'll have everyone Delta." Olive nodded her approval. They heard Wilson transmit.

"Tower, *Raven* four-zero-zero five miles aft, single engine, state two point one, unable to tank."

Stevenson answered him at once.

"Four-zero-zero, roger, report 3 miles for a straight in, your rep is here."

"Four-zero-zero."

Comet edged closer to the Boss as Olive listened.

"Boss, he's going to have to blow the gear down and he won't be able to taxi."

"Roger that, and he's going to have a fuel-low caution any minute…I expect he'll have a one point six on the ball."

"Sounds about right," Olive said.

"Here, talk to him," Stevenson said, handing Comet the mic.

Keeping his eyes on Wilson, Comet spoke. "*Raven* four-zero-zero, Rep."

"Go ahead," Wilson answered.

"Four hundred, we're standing by for emergency gear extension."

Wilson glanced down at the steps in his pocket checklist. "Roger that, I'm going to hold off and keep flaps in AUTO till I get closer to final bearing."

"Roger, sir, we're standing by."

In the Tower, the phone buzzed and Stevenson picked it up. The captain.

"Yes, sir," Stevenson answered as Olive listened. "Yes, sir…wilco."

Setting the receiver down, he informed everyone. "Okay, the captain is going to accelerate a little to see if he can steady the deck any. We gotta get these guys aboard."

Olive could only let the captain, the air boss, Comet, and the LSOs do their jobs. She considered leaving Pri Fly…if an accident was imminent…but she couldn't. She'd stay and watch from here. Wilson's voice came over the loudspeaker.

"Dirtying up now."

Comet responded. "Roger…slow below 180, gear handle down, rotate 90 right and pull. Flaps half."

Stevenson picked up the binoculars. "*Spartan* one-oh-five is still with him, good…okay, gear coming down…looks like he's on a five mile arc."

He surveyed the pattern. "Okay, we'll take two more, then Delta everyone for the admiral." The loudspeaker crackled again, another transmission from Wilson.

"Got an unsafe left main."

Everyone in the tower froze.

"Oh shit," Comet said under his breath.

Wilson porpoised his nose to get 105 to join closer. As he waited, he tested his gear indicator lights—good. *Dammit.* He may *really have* an unsafe gear. With 105 close enough for signals, Wilson made the landing gear signal followed by a thumbs-up. How do they look? When the *Spartan* didn't respond, he transmitted.

"One-zero-five, how do they look?"

"They appear to be three down, sir."

Wilson responded with a thumbs-up. The procedure called for a min-sink-rate landing—not going to happen today on a carrier, and especially with the deck moving. And he couldn't blow the gear down again. He glanced at his fuel: 1.9. To his left, *Valley Forge* pitched in the white-capped swells as Wilson approached what remained of its wake.

"Tower, four hundred has an unsafe left main but visual inspection appears down. Four miles turning in."

"Roger, four-zero-zero continue, traffic is a *Rhino* approaching the ninety. *Rhino* at the ninety, say your side."

"Three-one-zero."

"Roger, three-one-zero, you continue; break, ninety-nine the rest of the pattern *Delta Easy, Delta Easy*, taking a low-state single engine *Rhino* at four miles. Break, break, *Raven* four-zero-zero, keep the power up after the trap, we'll tow you out."

"Four-zero-zero, wilco."

In his cockpit, Wilson trimmed out the control forces and maintained on speed. Left of course, he would remain at 600 feet and intercept the glideslope at two miles. Four degrees. Winds—what were they? He waited for the *Rhino* to trap before he transmitted.

"Say winds."

The LSO was on it. "Working forty-nine knots."

Good grief, Wilson thought. *Maybe I* should *start the right engine.*

Too late. He was committed to this approach and continued to burn fuel as he approached the glideslope. The FUEL LO caution illuminated in his left display. *I know!*

At half flaps, *Spartan* 105 remained near him, ready to render assistance as the rest of the pattern held at max endurance. Even at midday, the gray ceiling made the ocean the color of slate, marred by hundreds of whitecap streaks on the surface. Wilson held on speed and slid right to intercept the centerline. On the lens, the yellow light appeared next to the green datums; the LSO's had him. The Air Wing LSO transmitted.

"Workin' fifty knots, slightly axial."

Wilson bunted the nose then reset to start himself down, manipulating the throttle manually. Glancing inside, the left main was still unsafe and his fuel still low: now 1.7. At least he'd be light if he had to wave off.

Suddenly he was lined up right; the ship made a correction for winds. Hoping Huey would leave it alone for now, he corrected and called the ball.

"Four-zero-zero, *Rhino* ball, single-engine, one point six."

"Roger balllll, deck's movin' a little, you're high."

Wilson *was* high and gave the stick a little pop to correct it. In his peripheral vision he saw *Valley Forge* lift her bow; the angled deck ahead of him transformed into a steel wall. He watched the ball, now coming down, and corrected for it and lineup—still right of center. The LSO called.

"Comin' down now, on glideslope…on centerline." In the background Wilson could hear the phone talker shout *Clear deck, Rhino!*

Ten seconds from touchdown, the deck came up, showing him a flat plate that led down to the sea. Froth erupted from the port side of the hull—the carrier's massive screws coming out of the water.

"Onnnn glideslope…you're a *lit-tle* slow."

Wilson fought the winds and anticipated the ball movement. He observed the deck fall away—*fast*—and doubted Paddles would take him much further as the LSO raised the ball above the datums.

"A lit-tle high…"

Wilson pulled a handful of power, then reset it as the ramp continued to fall away, once again showing him in a steep dive.

"Wave-off, pitching deck."

He crammed the left throttle forward and maintained on speed, easing in left rudder to maintain balanced flight as he flew up the angled deck, flying right by the island with the Air Boss and Huey, whom he knew were padlocked on him. As Wilson climbed away, he noted a *Rhino* in the pattern on downwind.

"Four hundred, cleared downwind, the pattern's yours, say state."

Wilson eased left as he climbed to 600 feet and glanced down at his fuel.

1.4

"One point four."

"Roger," Stevenson answered. The CAG LSO then transmitted.

"Four-zero-zero, Paddles."

"Go ahead," Wilson answered.

"Deck didn't cooperate, sir, we'll get'cha this time, but we're workin' fifty knots slightly axial—watch out for that burble in close."

"Copy," Wilson said as he studied the *Rhino* on downwind that he was cutting out. With collision not imminent, he ignored him as he turned to the abeam. With his single engine, Wilson flew a wider pattern than usual and took care not to get slow. At military power he burned fuel he didn't have—couldn't be helped. He had only minutes of it left.

Leveling, he glanced at the ship before a caution tone in his headset brought him back inside: L FUEL HOT. He keyed the mic.

"Just got a left fuel hot, state one point three."

The Air Boss answered. "Roger, four hundred, continue."

Stevenson turned to Comet. "Left fuel hot?"

"Yes, sir, expected with his low state, just don't horse the jet around and bring it aboard."

"Barricade?"

"Too late for that," Olive said, then stepped toward Stevenson. "That's the captain's call, of course, but my emphatic recommendation is normal attempts until he flames out. Besides, we've got six more jets to recover."

"How much time do you think he has?"

"I'd say eight minutes, ten if we're lucky."

"We could rig it in five."

"Recommend against...we're trying to catch the admiral and not clobber the deck, and we made that decision twenty minutes ago."

"He's at barricade fuel, below it."

Olive stood her ground. "That's my point; either catch the admiral in a barricade and have six emergency low-states, or work him the best we can, and we already made the decision to work him the best we can. It's the captain's decision, but I recommend no." Olive's eyes held Stevenson's for effect. Comet said nothing as the phone buzzed.

Stevenson handed the mic to Comet. "Talk to him; *'be easy with the jet.'*" He answered the phone. "*Yessir.*" Olive tried to listen as the Air Boss nodded.

"Sir, the CAG is here and recommends against because we'll then have six low-states with one sweet tanker airborne...yessir...I'll have *Switchblade* snuggle up—he probably already is. Yes, sir."

"Okay, no barricade."

Olive nodded. "Good. Let me talk to Paddles." Stevenson punched up the J-dial circuit to the platform and handed it to Olive.

Her CAG LSO answered, shouting above the noise of fifty knots of wind and a nearby *Rhino* at idle that filled Olive's receiver. "Platform, Lieutenant Commander Elsken."

"Elmo, CAG. I'm in Pri Fly; just work him the best you can and do what the captain and boss tell you; I've got your back."

"Roger that, ma'am."

"How is it out there?" Olive asked.

The LSO hesitated, then answered. "I've never seen this, ma'am."

"Roger, will let you work him. Out here."

Olive looked southeast at Wilson, flying a deep pattern to ensure he was set up on speed and under control. She exhaled through her nose.

He has two looks left.

Small raindrops spotted Wilson's windscreen before they ran aft and disappeared under his 150-knot airspeed as he leveled at 600 feet, two miles aft and easing toward centerline. He knew he was in extremis, but no matter how well he flew, the deck would either be in a position to take him…or not. Glancing at the ship, he saw the *Switchblade* plane-guard hovering next to it to starboard. *A vulture.* Wilson imagined that *Vulture's Row* was full, then put it out of his mind.

"Workin' fifty-three knots, slightly axial."

Wilson couldn't believe it. *Fifty-three knots!…axial! What is Huey doing?*

Valley Forge continued to struggle to get the winds down the angle. Despite the high winds, her wake was noticeable yet ragged as the ship changed courses in her effort to place the headwind component perfectly. To the west, a thin veil of rain looked like a door, one that the ship headed toward. Wilson would happily take axial winds if he could have a steady deck. The ball came up from the bottom of the lens and showed him on. He glanced at his fuel: 1.1.

"Four-zero-zero, *Rhino* ball, one point one, single engine."

"Roger ball, fifty-four knots axial, you're onnnn glideslope."

Wilson was on, but felt high and steep as he worked to remain on-speed in the gusts. The rain fell light on his canopy, forming streaks as he concentrated on the ball, his HUD velocity vector a source of stability on the heaving and pitching flight deck. The jet suddenly settled and he flashed a slow chevron, correcting at once as he drifted left.

"You're a lit-tle slooow, deck's steady."

Wilson overcorrected and drove himself high. He popped the stick and reset the attitude, fighting to find a steady power setting.

"You're high…power to catch it."

In close, Wilson sensed the deck coming up as he gave it a shot of power, but not enough. Elsken was on it.

"Power! *POWER!*"

As the ramp lifted ever higher, Wilson was at military power as the jet slammed down hard in front of the one-wire. The force of the blow drove the nose down and compressed the strut as the jet seemed to bounce back up in the air. The tailhook skittered over the first three wires and ticked the number four cross deck pendant as Wilson roared down the angle trailing a shower of sparks, the hook trying in vain to grab something. He knew when his nose-gear buried itself on a *hard* landing; *dammit!*

At military on the good engine, Wilson climbed away and banked easy left, flying the airplane back into the pattern for another try. He glanced again at his fuel: eight hundred pounds. At least his left main was down and locked.

One more chance, *maybe* two—if the fuel indication was correct.

Flying with his left hand, he removed his kneeboard from his right knee and stowed it on the console—just in case.

Chapter 27

USS *Valley Forge*, North Atlantic
1125 June 15, 2024

The 5MC flight deck loudspeaker boomed with the voice of the Air Boss. "Paddles, call the captain."

On the windswept LSO platform, Elmo handed the pickle switch to one of the nearby LSOs and dialed the bridge. Huey picked up and answered with a terse, "Cap'n."

"Sir, it's Elmo on the platform."

"Paddles, we gotta get him aboard. Talk to him early and often, and I've been fighting these winds the whole recovery. If the winds are out of limits, take him. If the deck is doing some wild hiyacka, take him. Do you understand?"

"*Understood, sir!*" Elmo shouted into the handset to be heard over the din of the flight deck.

"Out here," Huey said.

Elmo returned to the MOVLAS station and took the pickle switch. *Raven* 400 approached the ninety position. He pressed the transmit button.

"At the ninety, say your state."

He heard Admiral Wilson's voice respond. "Eight hundred pounds."

Elmo turned to his backup LSO, Craze.

"Okay, this is from the bridge. We're taking him no matter what the winds or deck is doing. Back me up on lineup especially. No wave off unless he's about to smack the ramp, got it?"

"Roger, that...and he's probably got two looks with eight hundred pounds."

"Craze, we're taking him...I'm taking him. This pass."

"Roger that, I'm backing you up. You've got control, and here he comes."

The phone talker sang out: "Gear set, *Rhino*, foul deck."

Holding the pickle switch high, Elmo looked over his left shoulder at the deck. Men inspected one of the wires.

"Boss had better get those guys outta there!" he said to no one, concentrating on Wilson as he neared the wake. *Fifty-five knots!* an amazed Elmo thought as the cold wind whipped around his flight suit legs. *You gotta be shittin' me!*

"Four-zero-zero *Rhino* ball, point six, single engine."

"Roger ball, *Rhino*…workin' fifty-five knots, axial."

As Elmo showed Wilson a centered ball, the Boss came over the 5MC: *"Get outta the landing area! Low state Rhino on the ball!"* The deck status light in front of Elmo glowed red—foul deck. He glanced at the winds—starboard and out of limits.

The Air Boss called him over the 5MC so all could hear.

"Put him on the ace, Paddles; the number 4 is damaged."

Keeping his eyes on Wilson, Elmo nodded his understanding, moving his head enough so the boss could see from the tower. He perceived his deep and rapid breathing. He'd try to set the admiral down right next to him on the pitching, heaving, and rolling deck.

"*Fuck*," he muttered to himself, shaking the tension from his shoulders.

Wilson eased across the wake, concentrating on the "ball" the LSO showed him. As light loaded as he had ever been for a carrier arrestment, he was working his left throttle close to the idle stop to keep it on speed…a setting that was not helpful to his FUEL HOT situation. None of that mattered now…again his peripheral vision sensed the *Sierra* hovering near the starboard quarter before he put that thought aside.

The deck appeared low and flat as *Valley Forge* fell into a trough, but the LSO showed him on glideslope. For a second time, he saw the carrier's outboard screws broach the surface. *Ignore it.*

As the ship wallowed in a Dutch Roll, he found himself lined up right and corrected, gripping the stick tight as he fought to keep on speed. He had to trap now, not trusting that the jet wouldn't flame out in close if he couldn't get aboard.

As the ramp fell away, a laconic and emotionless feminine warning in his headset from *Tammy* jolted him. *Engine left, Engine Left.*

Sonofabitch!

"Did you see that puff?" Craze shouted.

"Yes, he's still comin', and he's high!" Elmo shouted back. He keyed the handset.

"You're high, bring it down…power to catch it."

The phone talker, nervous as the jet neared the still foul deck, shouted in rapid fashion, "Foul deck! Foul deck!"

Elmo was at sensory overload, showing Admiral Wilson where he estimated him to be on glideslope as the ramp gyrated in front of him. The deck was foul; every instinct and his years of training had conditioned him to wave off a jet in this situation. At that moment, when he most needed it, the Air Boss helped him.

"Take him, Paddles. Disregard the deck status light. Take him."

The talker continued to sing out; *"Foul deck!"*

"We're taking him!" Elmo shouted as he dropped his arm, then forced himself to relax as he transmitted. "You're on glideslope, going a lit-tle flat…"

The carrier's ramp was down now, and for a moment stayed there as Elmo waited for it to come back up. In this condition, Wilson *looked* high, and from his cockpit Elmo knew he saw nothing but steel. If he had Wilson go for it now, with the ramp coming up to meet him, a blown gear or even collapsed strut was a real possibility.

He had to…

"You're high, bring it down, you're *high!*"

Wilson corrected as the ramp began its journey up.

"Holy shit!" Craze shouted.

Elmo saw the flight path the *Rhino* was on as it neared the rapidly rising ramp, held in place by the gale force winds. The jet was coming down like a safe. *Now!*

"Power back on! *Power!* Wave off!" Elmo bellowed into the handset, gripping the black out of it as Wilson's one engine howled at military power. The rate of descent had just started to shallow when he slammed into the deck next to the LSOs, his hook grabbing the one wire as Wilson rolled out with his engine in afterburner.

The force of the trap painfully compressed Wilson's spinal cord as his unsecured kneeboard was hurled forward to fall onto his right foot. Ahead of him was blue water as the *Rhino* strained against the wire that lassoed it to a stop. Stevenson, the Air Boss, took over.

"Keep your power up, power up, we got'cha. Nice job, four-zero-zero."

Wilson kept the power up as he waited for the blue shirts to chock him and ordies to dearm him. A tractor made a tight turn in front of him and backed up as blue shirts attached the tow bar. While the Boss directed the airborne pattern traffic, Wilson raised his flaps and folded his wings on signal. Along the foul line, dozens of sailors waited for him to be towed clear, with *Raven* troubleshooters he recognized hovering near the jet but unable to tend to it yet. The yellow shirt signaled him to shut down the left, and as it wound down, the tractor towed him clear of the foul line.

Admiral Jim Wilson rode the brakes under tow as he was brought underneath the island. He looked up into the bridge and Pri-Fly windows and spotted Olive. He gave her a thumbs-up, but she had already turned away.

He was chocked and chained on the foul line, with Comet and much of the *Raven* maintenance department waiting for him to deplane. *What did he have to do to fly a routine hop?* Wilson gathered his helmet bag and descended the ladder. Comet met him.

"Welcome back, sir, great job!"

Wilson nodded but didn't have time. He spoke to the troubleshooters.

"Got a simultaneous HYD 2A and 2B caution and shut down the right engine. Tried to get the probe out with any residual pressure but I was late and that didn't work. And blowing it out didn't work. Then after blowing the gear down here, I got an unsafe left main, but it obviously held. Probably popped a hard landing code."

The troubleshooters nodded. *Raven* 400 was hard down and would be on the first elevator run to the hangar bay. Complete, Wilson motioned to Comet. "Let's go below."

A sailor held the hatch open as Wilson and Comet entered. Wilson led them down the ladder without removing his helmet. Once on the O-3 level, he removed it and faced Comet.

"I'm sorry, Admiral."

Wilson raised his hand. "Shit happens. Has the jet been a problem?"

"No sir, four-zero-zero is a solid flyer."

"Okay—hydraulic failure over an hour into the hop, and I was late to get the probe out, that's on me, but then the emergency probe switch doesn't work; is that an electrical or pneumatic issue? Then the unsafe gear indication for good measure."

"Do you think sabotage, sir?"

"I think it's something we must consider. We're headed into who knows what and people are scared or upset or both."

"Sir, you just got here…the satellites are down."

"What?"

"Washington believes the Russians have crippled several of our GPS and SATCOM birds; I heard about it before I went up to the tower. CAG and the captain scrubbed ops for the rest of the day."

Thunderstruck, Wilson stood, trying to make sense of it. *The Russians just crossed the Rubicon.*

"Whoo boy; let's go."

Wilson took in the gravity of the situation. *Combat.* What is Mark Meadows doing? How is the strike group dispersed? *I shouldn't have taken that double cycle!*

Walking with purpose, he brushed past and into the flag spaces. Entering, he saw Mark, Olive, Weed, Skweez, and Shane, all waiting for him.

"Okay, what'cha got?" Wilson snapped, all business.

Mark answered. "Admiral, it looks like the Russians have nudged five satellites out of orbit and Washington expects more over the next 24 hours."

"Have we blinded them in return?"

"Don't know, sir. Trying every net to find out."

Wilson unzipped his torso harness and peeled it off. "Northern Fleet?"

Shane answered. "Still above the GIUK gap, sir. Moving south at roughly 20 knots. Will be able to cross between Iceland and the Shetlands tomorrow if they want to."

"The *Oscar?*"

"Still unknown, sir. Last datum south of the gap."

"Okay. Mark, does the strike group know?"

"Yes, sir, and everyone is just short of general quarters in anticipation of action."

"Subsurface action that will ruin our day. Olive, are we breaking out ordnance for SuCAP and alerts?"

"We are, sir, and my staff will get me a detailed action plan in 20 minutes."

"They have ten…alright, what have we heard from Sixth Fleet?"

"Nothing yet, sir," Mark answered. "However, Admiral Johnson called for you an hour ago."

Wilson frowned as he unzipped his last g-suit zipper. *I never should have taken that tasking, dammit.*

"Did you tell them I was flying?"

"Yes, sir."

"Good. Okay…War Room, twenty minutes, and I want Huey there too. Call Naples and pull info from them, including you, Shane. Wait, *can* we get through?"

"So far we've been able to, sir," Mark replied.

Wilson nodded. "Great; okay, ready, break."

As the group departed to make calls and check with their staffs, Wilson motioned to Weed, who stepped toward him.

"Who do you know in Norfolk?"

"Well, Naval Air Force Atlantic, *his own self*."

"Tim Matson! Perfect; if you can get a connection, see what Admiral Matson will share with you, then join us. *You are invited*."

"Wilco…have you come down, yet?"

"You mean from my pitching deck double emergency on fumes, to the hardest landing I've ever had, to the opening of hostilities with a peer competitor?"

"Yeah, I guess you've picked a bad day to quit sniffing glue."

"Ha," Wilson said. "Yes, and between you and me, I fucked up. Taking the double cycle tasking *and* mishandling the emergency."

"What?"

"I was late to get the probe out. HYD 2 failure at the ship…*that's the first thing you do*! And I was behind. And the unsafe gear…" Wilson stopped himself short. *Don't let on yet*.

"Not your day," Weed deadpanned.

"Yeah, but more like somebody's trying to tell me something."

"At least you got 300 *Happy Valley* traps."

Wilson grinned and shook his head. "Yes…they can't take that from me."

"See you in twenty minutes, Kemosabe."

"Thanks, man. Glad you're here."

Chapter 28

War Room, USS *Valley Forge*, 1300 June 15, 2024

Wilson entered and surveyed the room. Mark Meadows, Huey, Olive, Smoke, and Shane were at the table with Commodore Braud. Weed sat along the bulkhead, one that creaked as *Valley Forge* took a roll. Wilson felt their eyes on him as he took his seat and got right to business.

"Okay. GPS and comm satellites down, and essentially shot down. Everything the Russians could put to sea from the Kola Peninsula still moving toward the GIUK gap, with a wild card *Oscar* attack boat that could be anywhere in the North Atlantic. No tasking or even updates from the beach, and I don't know if that's due to the satellites or if they are fighting a closer alligator. Weather picking up, which will affect flying, refueling, station-keeping, and more. Norfolk has cleared out the waterfront and sent everything north. NATO mobilizing. That about right?"

Mark spoke first.

"Yes, sir, that's pretty much it. We do have unsecure comms with SIXTH Fleet, and they know we want tasking or updates on the high side, but they aren't going to send us anything until we get secure comms back."

Wilson nodded, then turned to Olive. "Olive, can we get an airborne radio relay to the beach?"

"Yes, sir, we can get an E-2 up and turn it toward Lajes with a *Rhino* ahead of it as a relay. As long as we have tankers we can keep them on station, and my recommendation is to triple cycle the *Hummer* and keep one up for the rest of today. But we are moving away from Lajes and Lisbon into a dead area of the ocean. Keeping that radio relay and link picture will be a lot tougher to maintain this time tomorrow."

"Roger, that. Huey, are your people—and yours, Olive—ready for 24-hour ops in these conditions?"

Huey considered the question.

"Sir, we'll make it happen, of course, but the deck is moving like you read about and that means longer launches and recoveries and a reduced PIM as we transit northwest."

Olive nodded and jumped in. "Expect hard landing codes on the *Rhinos* and *Growlers* with this pitching deck, which will require inspections—and elevator runs."

"Yes…can you waive the inspections?"

Olive nodded. "Yes, sir, wartime conditions, and we'll take it case by case, but we're still going to beat up the airplanes. I concur with Huey, the boarding rate is going to suffer, and staying off the radio is going to make everything harder."

Wilson held her gaze. "Are your crews ready for this? We need no-shit, double-secret EMCON for the foreseeable future."

"Admiral, we're talking about it, and the squadrons are on the step…but I cannot guarantee us *perfect* EMCON, and I don't believe any of us can. We just saw last recovery that sometimes we need to talk on the radio."

Olive regretted her last comment. Wilson ignored it.

"Huey, what kind of PIM do you think you can get us without trashing the jets and beating in your hull plates?"

"Twenty knots, sir. Now, I'll give you what you want, but twenty in these current conditions—which will probably change in an hour, then change again. Regardless, sir, I think we're gonna have this pitching deck for as long as we're up here."

Wilson nodded and turned to Bert for the surface warfare assessment. "Bert, what are you thinking?"

"Admiral, we keep *Manila Bay* next to us in shotgun, and the two BMD shooters we just got from Rota, *Lloyd Childers* and *Michael Estocin*, in the vicinity for inner-ring defense. I'd like to place *O'Hare* and *Lindsey* ahead of our PIM as scouts and to sanitize our track. Station them one to two hundred miles ahead."

"Is that enough? And how do we communicate with them?"

"Two hundred will give us the option to engage or avoid a threat, and their *Romeos* can scout even further ahead. Communication? Well, sir, we send a helo from here with our latest guidance that we can deliver upon deck recovery or drop with a beanbag. To me, Admiral, it's all about keeping this flagship in the fight, and since we're the only Atlantic Fleet carrier at sea…we need early warning and defense in depth to allow the air wing to do what they need to."

Wilson held his fingers to his lips for a moment. "Let's talk about scouting. What do you consider scouting?"

"Simple search…detect to engage or report back. Get the weapons we have in range, classify contacts, target them, and employ before the other guy can, or flank him if we want/need to remain undetected. The kill chain takes time, sir, the time it takes to get you the information and act on it and deliver a weapon. In that time a missile or even torpedo—if a sub gets through the ring of steel—could be inside of our decision matrix. Right now, sir, it's all about scouting and driving that kill-chain time down."

Wilson nodded. "Olive, what are your thoughts on scouting?"

"Admiral, we can fly armed recce ahead of and around us and we're standing by for tasking, but we must be as passive and covert as possible, coming up on the net only when there's something to report. We don't want an emission to help the Russian effort."

"How far do you want to send the *Rhinos*, single or in section?"

Olive thought for a moment.

"Not significantly farther than Bert can place the small boys with a *Romeo*... assigning them a couple/three hundred miles on our flanks buys us some range with a reasonable fuel cushion for them to find their way back in EMCON conditions. I'd be comfortable with that and we can explore extending that. Keeping them section as opposed to a single jet is my preference."

"Okay, thanks," Wilson said. All waited for his last word.

"We must *navigate*...without GPS. Huey and Bert, are your ships ready to navigate with sun lines and star sightings?"

Both men nodded. "Yes, sir," Huey said. "We practice celestial and DR nav and we still have INS, which is fine for out here."

"Okay, we can navigate. How about communicate? It's been what, three, four hours since we learned the satellites were downed and nothing from the beach?"

Olive took that one.

"Admiral, we can keep a *Hummer* and helos up in the short term, with some *Rhinos* to radio relay line of sight, but an MQ-4 *Triton* to help would allow us to schedule our assets better and give us a better link, big picture. If I may, sir, recommend we send a section of *Rhinos* to Lajes and call Sixth Fleet on a secure line for tasking and to send them our SITREP and outlook, plus your intentions."

"Do it. Send a section of *Foxtrots*, led by Deputy CAG or the squadron CO. I want them to talk with Admiral Johnson or the vice commander and pass everything we have—and get their intentions/tasking for us. Let's see...if you shoot them in three hours, they'll get there at night. I want them to make the calls, get some food and a nap, then launch before sunup to avoid visual detection from any spies in the hills. Lights out coming and going. Co-vert."

"Aye, aye, sir," Olive nodded.

"Smoke, get a SITREP from everyone and draft me an intentions message for Admiral Johnson. Want a memory stick and hard copy to go in both cockpits. And no personal calls home or mail drops. And no beers in town...they're coming right back. That's all your tasking for now, and I need it in five minutes."

"Aye, aye, Admiral," Smoke answered, smiling.

"Shane—what have we found on that merchant I rigged?"

Shane handed him an open folder with imagery.

"Admiral, we believe that ship is the MV *Captain Korbutskiy*, which sailed from St. Petersburg on June 3rd and is bound for Caracas. It's an old—about 40 years old—general purpose cargo vessel, originally with an icebreaker bow, and carries dry cargo, bulk, vehicles and machinery, and people, about 25 passengers. At the time and location you intercepted it, it was on a track for Caracas, no deviation."

"The drone I saw?"

"Yes, sir, we have it on your FLIR tape but cannot identify it."

"Okay, send everything you have on this in the package Smoke is sending to the beach, along with a list of your questions. Smoke, this will be a priority for Sixth Fleet intel to get us answers before our *Rhinos* launch back here."

"Aye, sir."

Wilson wrapped it up.

"Okay...for now I intend to scout north-northwest and to do what I'm told, so I ask for guidance and intentions. Ask for assets: a *Triton* and P-8s. And subs; I want to know where they are and if any are supporting me. What's happening in Norfolk, what are the Brits doing, French, Norwegians, who is supported and supporting, all of it."

All at the table scribbled in their notebooks as they listened to Wilson, who continued.

"Bert, signal the combatants by flashing light to put together their SITREPs and needs and have their helos deliver them here in two hours. Shane, I want international open-source news, opinion, just a data dump of anything from the beach, all the order-of-battle info on everything in the Northern Fleet, so a list of websites to search and phone numbers to your counterparts at Sixth Fleet and Norfolk that the aviators can contact once they are in Lajes."

"Yes, sir."

"Okay—move out, and let's regroup in two hours, ready, *break*. Olive, remain please."

As the room broke up, Wilson motioned for Weed to remain too. Weed's wry smile betrayed him.

"What a great combat meeting! And no briefing slides…the war is won!"
In no mood, Wilson exhaled.

"What am I forgetting?" Wilson asked no one.

Weed frowned. "There's so much going on that we don't know, but it's *started*. Downing the satellites is the opening shot, and anything we come across now that's not a friendly must be considered a threat."

"Concur. We're steaming half blind into the open ocean full of merchant hulls, COMAIR above, and the Northern Fleet getting closer by the minute."

"Flip, you've got to get a *Hummer* up ASAP and run helos throughout the night. And the *FireScout* UAVs on the Rota ships. That's going to be your picture until you launch the *Rhino* and *Growler* scouts in the morning, betting on the come for a steadier deck and help from CONUS and answers from Sixth Fleet."

Wilson nodded. "We'll be lucky to have a *Triton* in 24 hours, but maybe they are already working it."

"May be," Weed said.

"Weed, let me have a moment with Olive."

"You got it," Weed said, and departed into the passageway.

As the door closed shut, Wilson turned to his CAG. "I made mistakes this morning."

Dispassionate, Olive waited for him to continue.

"Comet is going to get back to me about the jet. Sudden HYD 2 failure, both circuits. Then I can't blow the probe out, then an unsafe gear indication. Disparate malfunctions and emergencies…why? Let's just say I have my suspicions. While his maintenance department is checking the jet, I need to own up. Taking the extra cycle was a mistake, my biggest, and not getting the probe out at the first sign of trouble was a mistake too. So…I'm done flying this deployment."

"Admiral, concur that we're going into combat, and you can do more aboard…"

"No, I wasn't thinking straight. I've flown my last hop this cruise."

"Admiral…"

"It's okay, Olive," Wilson said with a grin. "I can live with my decision."

While she was inwardly relieved, Olive left Wilson an out. "Open invitation to reconsider, sir, when the situation allows."

"Thanks, but I'm good. Time to command this strike group."

Chapter 29

Bridge, RFS *Admiral Alekseyev*, Norwegian Sea, 2300 June 15, 2024

Petrov looked at his watch; approaching midnight and the sun still hovered on the southern horizon, the glare causing him to squint. He needed his sunglasses.

After two days of keeping station 150 meters from *Vitac*, all his watch officers showed signs of fatigue.

Petrov himself hated the miserable scow, forced as he was more than most of his officers to gaze at him, assessing the slightest motion, evaluating how he rode in these seas, observing every stain of running rust on his hull plates and the welds that held them together. Each morning, a fat crewman with a beard like St. Nicholas—maybe the kapitan?—doffed his shirt and took in the sun on the weather deck aft of the bridge, drinking his coffee in the brisk sea air and oblivious to Petrov's sailors watching him as if they were across a street. Coffee probably spiked with vodka. Petrov would not allow it on his bridge, even for himself, and, with his crew, held the slovenly civilian master in contempt.

Nothing from St. Petersburg. Surely the fleet vanguard had split, with some on course for the Denmark Strait and others to enter the gap between the Faroes and Iceland. Or maybe the main body would transit the strait. Maybe all of the fleet would. He didn't know, didn't even know where *Vitac* would transit. The Faroes-Iceland gap provided more sea room, but a Denmark Strait passage would limit the NATO air threat. On the other hand, one *Amerikanskiy* nuclear submarine could block the strait. Neither option was "good." The Officer of the Deck brought him back to the present.

"Kapitan, a dispatch from Fleet Headquarters."

Petrov held his arm outstretched as the *starshey-leytenant* handed the computer print to him. He checked the date time group: one hour ago.

So, it had already started. The Yankees had attacked two ocean reconnaissance satellites in outer space. Soon the comm and navigation satellites would be targeted and destroyed. Regardless, they had initiated hostilities! Petrov finished the message. No orders, no summary of Russian actions or intentions, if any. Unforgiveable! Just steam as before under the midnight sun with this rust-bucket and head somewhere to do something. And expect to lose all space assets in the next 24 hours.

He scanned the crisp southern horizon as the sun hid above it, covered by a shelf of overcast. Bright rays broke through, illuminating the distant sea off his bow. With his binoculars he scanned the sharp line ahead of him, trying—and failing—to find anything resting on it.

What is going on? When will they direct me? And when will NATO appear?

Petrov watched as the Officer of the Deck took a call on the sound-powered phone. The *leytenant* raised his eyebrows and looked across Petrov to the south, which Petrov then did instinctively. Nothing. The OOD then hung up and turned to him.

"Kapitan, Combat reports an IR contact bearing 192 degrees, classified airborne contact."

Electrified, Petrov took the glasses and scanned, unable to see anything below the broken layer. It must be a NATO patrol plane, he was sure of it, and low on the horizon to reveal its heat signature under the layer. *Fools!* But if the plane detected him, it could climb into the clouds that offered concealment. That his ECM gear had not sniffed anything yet on that bearing did not surprise him; NATO was good at managing their emissions.

A glint of sun caught his eye. *Ah!* Petrov studied the speck: straight wing and painted a light color. Yes, a patrol plane! Probable *Orion*, but what nationality?

"Airborne contact, estimating 20 miles. OOD, get abeam of *Vitac* at 30 meters."

"Yes, Kapitan, port or starboard side?"

Petrov exploded. *"Starboard* side—away from the threat!" *Must I do everything?* he thought.

As the OOD maneuvered his ship closer to *Vitac*, Petrov called Combat. "This is the Kapitan. The airborne contact bearing one-nine-zero is enemy, probable P-3 *Orion*. Sound action stations! And do not radiate—DO NOT radiate! Optical guidance only!"

Seconds later, his order-to-action stations blared over the ship's loudspeaker, followed by the footfalls of hundreds of men rushing to their stations. Petrov again picked up the ASW airplane, now arcing to the south and east. Kuzmin appeared next to him.

"Can you see it, Kapitan?"

"Yes, moving opposite us, probably 20 miles, just a speck. Wait. It's turning."

With the binoculars held firm against his eyes, Petrov watched the plane change shape—a turn. But away or into? Impatient, Petrov waited for it to reveal itself.

"He's turning into us! Mister Kuzmin, supervise the deck watch and hug *Vitac* at 30 meters. Signal him not to change course and that we may have been spotted. Nothing rash."

"Aye, aye, Kapitan!"

On the bow, the dual 100mm gun mount trained out to port—pointing toward *Vitac* as the DDG eased up on her beam. Petrov frowned but it couldn't be helped. *Vitac* was his first line of defense.

He ignored the shouted *action station* reports that came into the bridge, keeping his eyes locked on the P-3. He could now see a black dot, not moving on the horizon, coming at him.

We've been spotted!

Petrov picked up the sound-powered phone to Combat. "Combat, this is the Kapitan: P-3 inbound 250 relative, *constant.*"

The watchstander answered. "Aye, aye, Kapitan! No ESM indications on that bearing!"

"Very well; keep me informed once he radiates."

Kuzmin stepped to his chair. "Kapitan, I can remain here if you wish to go to Combat."

Petrov shook his head. No, he needed to see for himself if his *camoutint* worked for him. And bark the order to engage as an eyewitness.

The *Orion* did not budge from its bearing, holding *Vitac* on its nose as it closed. At ten miles Petrov no longer needed the glasses, but he had a new problem; *Vitac's* superstructure and loaded containers obstructed his view.

"Mister Kuzmin! Open up on him and bring us forward so I can see!"

Kuzmin barked orders, and the helmsman turned away from *Vitac* by one half degree as Kuzmin ordered increased turns to move *Admiral Alekseyev* forward to maintain Petrov's line of sight. Petrov still could not see the plane, and his 100mm gun line of fire remained obstructed by the plodding merchant next to him.

"*Blast!*" he growled, and yanked up the dog-bar to the port bridge wing door. Stepping outside, he shouted at Kuzmin. "Drive him from here, I'm heading to the signal bridge to see!"

Petrov raced up the ladder and pulled himself onto the signal bridge. Still unable to see, he found a handhold and, with the superhuman strength borne of adrenaline, pulled himself up to the radar director platform. The P-3 continued in, the four engines visible. Kuzmin watched his kapitan from the bridge wing.

"Kuzmin, hold us here! He's five miles inbound. Visual firing solutions for missiles and close-in weapons system!"

Petrov assessed the image the two Russian ships presented to the enemy. His bow stuck out in front of *Vitac*, and his wake was much heavier with his twin screws. He studied the P-3 as it bore in, unable to discern if it had anything on its wings or if the bomb bay was open. His breathing fast, the indecision gripped him. Even if not attacked, he could be *sighted*, even with his pink overcoat, ruining the disguise *Vitac* provided. And Platonov's secret plan.

Fine then! Discover me! Shoot something at us now *so I may blow you out of the sky and fight this ship as the Motherland designed him to be fought, at speed, radiating and detecting and killing.*

The *Orion* banked left—easy—not alarmed. Petrov had seen them veer away much sharper. It flew parallel to their course at three miles, level at what Petrov estimated was 100 meters.

"Kuzmin, take turns off and slide back! Can you see him now?"

Seconds later the DDG responded, hiding as much as it could in the lee of the containership. Petrov remained on the director platform, the strong wind biting into him as he watched the plane fly ahead of them a few miles before banking left again, headed home to the North Cape of Europe. Did Norway still fly them? Petrov could not recall. The plane could be American or German or Spanish—or Canadian. He and the Red Banner Fleet were up against the whole world and their damned *Orions*.

As the patrol plane receded from view, Petrov came down and reentered the bridge. At once he noted his men as they took furtive glances at him. None had ever seen *that* before, the kapitan giving orders from the radar mast! He maintained a stoic calm as picked up his espresso cup, but when he turned to fill it, the bosun of the watch stopped him, and with a smile, took it to fill the cup himself.

Through the containers and latticework of *Vitac* he could still make out the P-3 as it flew away. "Mister Kuzmin, secure from action stations, but topside lookouts maintain a sharp, *sharp*, eye."

"Aye, aye, Kapitan! Secure from action stations, set the normal under-way watch!" Kuzmin faced Petrov, and when Petrov glanced at him, the exec smiled—what passed for a pat on the back to his kapitan.

As word was passed and the ship exhaled, Petrov relived the episode. How he wished for darkness now, the bane of sailors that made the simplest of seafaring tasks harder. Except celestial navigation—and he would not even have that bene-fit until well past the gap. He knew that he and *Admiral Alekseyev* had just gotten lucky. Could he avoid detection until the gap, holding hands with the cursed merchantman next to him? He studied *Vitac's* bridge, and through the windows detected two figures. Two! He noted the men studying him, and he knew what they were thinking. The pink warship alongside would be their death.

After a sip of espresso, Petrov motioned to the OOD, directing him to fall back into place on *Vitac's* dirty and rust-lined quarter. Deliverance. Exhaling as the stress ran out of him, he slumped in his seat...until his OOD cried out.

"Kapitan, visual contact off our starboard bow, zero-three-zero relative!"

Petrov bolted to the bridge window, taking the binoculars from the OOD. A trawler, and surely Norwegian. Ten miles! *Damn!* No ESM warning and no lookout warning—his bridge team was the first to detect it! And if he detected the trawler, it meant that—if the fishermen were paying attention—they could have detected the Russian merchant—with something next to it—and warned NATO.

His frustration with his crew overflowing, Petrov exploded. "Officer of the Deck, place me on the port side of *Vitac* but keep me within 150 meters of him at all times! Now!"

"Aye, aye, Kapitan!" the fearful OOD responded as tension on the bridge shot through the overhead. As the DDG slowly slid aft of *Vitac*, Petrov, fuming, yanked the sound powered phone out of its cradle.

"Combat, have the XO report to the bridge at once!" he snarled, slamming the receiver back into its housing.

He was not done. With his bow abeam *Vitac's* fantail, the irritated Petrov acted.

"This is Kapitan Petrov and I have the conn! Belay your reports! Helm, left two degrees rudder, make turns for fifteen knots! Now!"

The petrified helmsman, more afraid of Petrov's ire than to question that he was to *turn into* the ship next to him, repeated the order and complied as all on the bridge held their breath. *Admiral Alekseyev's* screws bit into the North Atlantic; the DDG's prow slid precariously close to *Vitac's* stern as one astonished merchant sailor aboard it watched, frozen in place.

Kuzmin arrived. "Reporting as ordered, Kapitan!"

Petrov raised his hand, ignoring him for the moment as his bow pointed clear on the merchant's port side.

"Helm, shift your rudder to right two degrees, reduce turns for 12 knots!"

Now on *Vitac's* port quarter, Petrov was shielded from the trawler. He assessed relative motion using seaman's eye as he crept forward.

"Rudder amidships!" he bellowed.

"Kapitan, my rudder is amidships!"

"Very well, reduce turns and hold us here!"

Still seething, Petrov turned to the hapless OOD. "Officer of the Deck, can you hold us here?" Petrov roared.

"Yes, Kapitan…"

"Then do it! You have the conn! Mister Kuzmin, come with me!"

Petrov pushed open the watertight door and stepped outside onto the port bridge wing as he shouted, "Close it!" Kuzmin complied, helpless to avoid his dressing down.

"Stand here!" Petrov snarled. Kuzmin stood against the rail with his back to the sea as he faced his kapitan, who seemed to regain control as he kept his own face from the bridge team while he spoke in a low tone.

"Yevgeny Sergeevich, I am now going to rip you for the benefit of this crew, who must learn that we are in combat and can be attacked from any direction—to include above and below—at any moment. Do you understand?"

"Yes, Kapitan," Kuzmin, answered, his grimace set for the blast he was about to receive. Petrov nodded his acknowledgement…and wound up.

"Mister Kuzmin! We may have been spotted by a fishing trawler on our track—inside ten miles! *I* was the one to make the sighting report, from inside the bridge, not the lookouts, and not anyone in Combat monitoring the emissions around us. They have a radar that's probably rotating, and a damn fish-finder sonar that's probably pinging, and I received no reports of it! Unacceptable!"

Kuzmin nodded. "Yes, sir, Kapitan."

"You will ensure that this does not happen again, because it may be our death!"

"Yes, Kapitan."

"We will see our families again *only* by remaining alert—for days or weeks or however long it takes! We will now return inside, and you will remain on the bridge until the trawler is out of sight, then put us back on his starboard side."

"Yes, Kapitan."

"Follow me."

Petrov turned and opened the bridge wing door, his frown evident to all as Kuzmin followed.

"And vodka rations for all hands are cut off until we can properly detect and report contacts!"

"Yes, sir, Kapitan," Kuzmin answered, his sailors understanding what had just happened.

Chapter 30

USS *Valley Forge*, North Atlantic, 1000 June 16, 2024

From his stateroom chair, Wilson watched the *Rhino* grow in size on the PLAT screen as it neared the deck. The first of two back from an overnight to Lajes, he expected it to have communications from Norfolk, Washington, Naples, and Lisbon. Unable to turn away, he watched as it touched down and rolled out into the centerline camera, the view changing from the centerline to the island camera as the *Spartan* FA-18F was wrestled to a halt. His stateroom vibrated from the thundering roar of the two F414's at military power one deck above him as the carrier rolled in moderate seas.

The previous night had been a long one, he and his strike group practically blind without the benefit of satellite comms and downlinks, steaming northwest toward Iceland in anticipation of tasking that he hoped was inside this jet and the next one. Wilson and his ships moved at 15 knots, tentative, watching with his airborne helicopters and single E-2, listening with his sonars, sniffing with his shipboard ECM gear. They moved across the water like a man in a darkened room with hands outstretched, listening, feeling for obstacles, wary of the dangers he might find at his fingertips.

After the second jet trapped, the yellow shirts parked it on the foul line next to the first one. Skweez waited there to lead the crews to Wilson, anxious for their full story. Mark, Huey, and Olive—plus Weed—waited in the War Room for Wilson to arrive, as the aircrew was led there after their two-hour flight.

All stood as Wilson entered. "Seats, please, and enough of that, I'm good for the deployment. We've got work to do...what's happened since I saw you last?"

Mark spoke first. "Admiral, our helo encountered a contact fifty miles to our north, a crude tanker heading west, and that's all that's near us as we head into an open area of the North Atlantic away from the main Rotterdam-Northeast U.S. sea lane. We should have roughly four hundred miles of open water until we reach the next sea lane, which is U.S.-North Cape...to include the Kola Peninsula ports."

Wilson nodded.

"Good, but I still want to search ahead of us. Olive, are you ready?"

"Yes, sir. We've got crews ready to brief and jets loaded with air-to-air and air-to-surface weapons, with a division of jets loaded with anti-ship LRASMs and alert crews identified. We're ready with our best guess of the tasking we may receive when it arrives."

"Good. Huey?"

"Admiral, my concern is about taxiing airplanes and running elevators in these seas. Right now isn't too bad, but we know the weather can and will change, and within hours. And sir, we have to think about operating in these northern latitudes. Tonight we are going to have only four hours of night, and if we proceed north at this rate, tomorrow night we won't have anything but a few hours of astronomical twilight, which is almost night, but still a faint horizon. Three hundred miles south of Iceland, about 57-degrees north: four hours of nautical twilight, which is a pink horizon. And from the GIUK gap north, nothing but daylight, 24-7."

"Launch the commanders!" Wilson joked, succeeding only to elicit a sympathetic snicker from the War Room. He looked at Olive. "What are you thinking?"

"Admiral, we're all going to be tired in a few days if we aren't already, and of course daytime is safer and more expeditious, but we *own the night*, we train to it, and we're not going to have it, *any of it* north of the GIUK gap if we go up there. We are going to be seen, the ship and the airplanes."

"They can be seen too. Do you want to wait for them in the dark latitudes?"

Mark, now energized, spoke up.

"Admiral, once they pass the GIUK gap, a hard problem becomes a lot harder. We can't let them run free in deep and open water south of it."

"Okay, but can *we* operate the ship south of 57 degrees, in open water away from the sea lanes, and still cover what we must in the gap?"

Olive answered.

"Sir, we'll tank as required, giving the ship four to five hours of darkness a night to hide in, but that doesn't really help my crews fighting in daylight. Now look, who doesn't love daylight, but the reality is that we will soon lose the covert capability night brings us. And—I can't believe I'm saying this—it won't get "better" with significant darkness up here for months."

Wilson glanced at Weed in time to see him suppress a grin. He returned to Olive.

"Okay, we'll consider this once we get tasking. Where are those guys?"

Outside they heard a knock, and Skweez poked his head in.

"Yes, bring them in," Wilson said. Skweez opened the door and the *Spartan* aviators, still in their flight gear with matted hair and mask lines on their faces, entered, led by their skipper, Bill Sizemore. One WSO carried a folder stuffed with paper.

"Size, welcome back. How was your time on the beach?" Wilson asked.

"Busy, sir, and we return with guidance."

"Good, and I know you are hungry and tired, but let's have it. First, did you converse with Admiral Johnson?"

"Yes, sir, and bottom-line up front: we are to move to a position 400 miles southwest of Keflavik and await further tasking. As we proceed, we are to consider any Russian naval vessels found south of the Arctic Circle as hostile and engage upon detection."

Referencing a chart, Huey did the math. "Admiral, that assigned position is 650 miles south of the Arctic Circle."

Olive nodded. "We can cover either side of Iceland from there, pretty much daytime ops with our own tankers."

Eager for more, Wilson remained focused on Size. "Have hostilities commenced, other than the satellites?"

"Yes, sir. The Russians opened fire on a Norwegian trawler one of their surface combatants encountered last night about 200 miles west of Vestfjord, gunfire only, and just straddled it—no hits. Drove it off though. The admiral said their intel is that the Russians want to engage merchant shipping they encounter, and the coalition has yet to respond...at least as of five hours ago when I was on the secure phone with him."

"Why is that? What more does NATO need since the shooting has already started?"

Weed jumped in.

"They're squabbling about what to do. What is it, a unanimous 32-to-nothing vote? If anyone, Turkey will veto a unified response, at least now anyway. And besides...inaccurate naval gunfire and no one dead yet. My guess is that NATO blood must be spilled before we're cleared hot." Wilson listened, waiting for more.

"Flip...forgive me, Admiral...we are already in the fourth Battle of the Atlantic, and have been for years, with Russia probing our defenses and identifying our undersea cables. They've just cleaned out the Kola Peninsula, sending everything they have toward the GIUK gap, a hostile act in my book even without the satellite downings, and their surface force is a side show, a decoy for their submarine force. Ships and airplanes can sink merchants and garner headlines, but the real threat is economic, to our undersea cables, and strategic once these guys get into launch windows."

The room was silent for a moment until Wilson answered. "Can't disagree; I could see NATO or a NATO merchant on the high seas absorbing the first hit for the public relations benefit...been done before to initiate combat...but *we* are not going to absorb anything. Size, have we executed an operational plan?"

"Yes, sir, Admiral: OPLAN 6602, Defense of the North Atlantic, and Admiral, it's a *coalition*, not NATO, led by EUCOM. Operation *Northern Security*."

Wilson shook his head as he chuckled. "That'll strike fear into their hearts. Okay, so who are the players? Brits, Norwegians...who else?"

"Sir, the Netherlands and France also have forces underway, but not Denmark, they are not playing. Canada signed on, and we can expect a *Hornet* and a P-3 squadron, er, *Aurora* squadron in Goose Bay or Gander. Sweden, Poland, and Finland are putting their navies to sea in the Baltic. Germany is on board...but not expecting much."

Wilson pulled on his chin. "So, *Denmark* is opposed, or just not motivated," he said to no one. "And they control the Baltic Straits...and Greenland. Maybe we were too quick to beat up on the Turks. Okay Size, what are *we* doing?"

"Admiral, he told me everything seaworthy is already underway from New London, Norfolk, and Kings Bay, and moving in this direction. *Tinian* got underway yesterday with at least one full squadron of F-35Bs, as many *Romeo* and *Sierra* aircraft and crews that Norfolk could spare, and extra *Ospreys*—Navy *Ospreys*—to help with logistics. P-8s are flowing to Keflavik and Gander, Newfoundland."

"Good, and who's commanding all this force?"

"According to Admiral Johnson, he is, sir, but there's discussion that Second Fleet, Vice Admiral Coleman, is going to move his staff to Iceland and take over the Atlantic fight."

"He's a submariner," Weed said. "That tells me this is going to be submarine centric."

"Around the GIUK gap for sure, and we'll probably chop to him at some point. Anyone know him?" Wilson asked. None did.

"Okay. Thanks Size, we'll go over this package of paper you brought us, but how do we communicate? Did he give any orders on that?"

"Yes, sir, and it's through a classified program that they are implementing tonight or tomorrow called HAVE SHARP. U.S. flag airliners on established oceanic route tracks will transmit burst communications at intervals mid-ocean. It's a black box they must carry to be certified."

"Well, well. All the U.S. major carriers involved?"

"Admiral Johnson told me just two for now, sir."

"Okay then, we'll get tasking and updates. Pushing back on any of it will be more of a challenge, but I'm sure we'll find a way. Size, anything else?"

Size reached into his g-suit pocket. "Admiral Johnson transmitted a P4 message for you, sir. The comm people put it in this sealed envelope."

Wilson took the envelope.

"Thank you, *Spartans*, well done, and please get some food. Skipper, we know where to find you."

As the *Spartan* aviators took their leave, Wilson opened the envelope and read the contents while the others waited.

```
FROM: COMSIXTHFLT
TO:   COMCARSTKGRUEIGHTEEN

SUBJ: PERSONAL FROM JOHNSON FOR WILSON


1. FULL SPECTRUM KINETIC HOSTILITIES ARE IMMINENT.
   RU NAVAL AND AIR FORCES HAVE MOVED AT SCALE INTO
   THE NORTH ATLANTIC AND SEA OF JAPAN AT NEVER
   BEFORE SEEN NUMBERS. CURRENTLY THREE RORSATS,
   FIVE GPS, AND FOUR SATCOM BIRDS (THREE U.S. ONE
   FR) HAVE BEEN NUDGED OUT OF ORBIT/KINETICALLY
   DESTROYED IN AN UNPRECENDENTED EFFORT THAT WASH-
   INGTON EXPECTS WILL CONTINUE. SPACE FORCE RETAL-
   IATION RESPONSE UNDERWAY BUT LAGS RU CAMPAIGN.
   BOTH SIDES EXPECT SPACE ASSET C4ISR OPERATIONS
   TO BE SEVERELY DEGRADED IF NOT COMBAT INEFFEC-
   TIVE WITHIN 48 HOURS.
```

Holy shit, Wilson thought. *This is really happening.*

```
2. RU SSBN AND SSN OPERATIONS BELOW GIUK GAP IS AN
   EXISTENTIAL THREAT - REPEAT - EXISTENTIAL THREAT
   TO U.S. HOMELAND AND MUST BE STOPPED. THIS IS
   PRIMARY MISSION FOR U.S. FORCES.
```

Existential threat—with emphasis. Ho-lee shit.

```
3. RU SURFACE AND AIR FORCES INTEND TO CONDUCT IN-
   TERDICTION OF NON-ALLIED MERCHANT AND NAVAL SHIP-
   PING WHERE FOUND. LOCALIZED SEA LINES OF COMMUNI-
   CATION TO IS AND NO THROUGH NORTH SEA AT HIGHEST
```

RISK. SHORT TERM INTERDICTION OF NORTH AMERICA –
EUROPE SLOC IS STRATEGIC DEFEAT FOR UK, DE, AND
NL WITH SEVERE POLITICAL INSTABILITY EXPECTED.

4. NATO HAS NOT AUTHORIZED OFFENSIVE ACTIONS FOR
ALLIANCE DEFENSE AND WE DO NOT ANTICIPATE IT.
COALITION OF US, UK, NO, DE, NL, FR, ES, PT, SE,
FI, PL, LT, LV, EE ESTABLISHED FOR NORLANT/BALTIC
AOR UNDER THE COMMAND OF EUCOM.

*Okay, Brits, Norwegians, Germany, Netherlands, France, Spain, Portugal, Sweden,
Finland...and Poland and the Baltic states. No surprise, but why not Denmark?*

5. IS HAS PROHIBITED US/NATO OFFENSIVE OPERATIONS
FROM THEIR TERRITORY. THIS CHANGED IN PAST 24
HOURS; EFFORTS TO RECONSIDER ONGOING. DK RUFUSED
TO JOIN COALITION FROM THE OUTSET AND/OR HOST
COALTION FORCES IN GREENLAND (GL) AND FAROE IS-
LAND CHAIN (FO).

*Iceland wants us to keep their sea lanes open but won't help? Expected more from
Denmark...guess Russia got to these guys first.*

6. DESPITE IS RESERVATIONS REGARDING OFFENSIVE HOST-
ING COMSECONDFLT EXPECTED TO MOVE FLAG TO LO-
CATION IN THEATER WITHIN 24 HOURS AND COMMAND
COALITION NAVAL AND AIR FORCES IN GIUK GAP TO
INCLUDE CSG-18 ONCE NORTH OF 57N. COMSECONDFLT
TO REPORT TO NAVEUR/EUCOM AS LANTFLT NAVAL COM-
PONENT COMMANDER.

Damn...no more top cover from The Big Unit.

7. US POLITICAL SITREP. WALL TO WALL COVERAGE OF RU
ACTIONS IN BROADCAST MEDIA. OPEN-SOURCE REPORT-
ING IN SOCIAL MEDIA IS EXTENSIVE AND ACCURATE.
BIPARTISAN SUPPORT FOR MILITARY ACTIONS IN CON-
GRESS.

8. EXPECTED RU GOAL. RU SEEKS TO SINK COALITION
AND ALLIED MERCHANTS AND COMBATANTS IF THE CON-
DITIONS ARE FAVORABLE IN ESCALATE-TO-DEESCALATE
STRATEGY TO ELIMINATE NATO/EU/COALITION SUPPORT
OF UKR. RU USE OF TACTICAL NUCLEAR WEAPONS IN A

WAR AT SEA SCENARIO IN SUPPORT OF THIS STRATEGY
CANNOT BE DISCOUNTED. TRUSTWORTHY I&W THAT THESE
WEAPONS ARE CURRENTLY DEPLOYED WITH RED BANNER
FLEET. CONSIDER – REPEAT – CONSIDER STRONG POSSI-
BILITY OF RU NUCELAR USE AT SEA. KREMLIN RESOLVE
ESTIMATED STRONG.

Mother of God! Wilson thought as he exhaled through his nose, reading the last sentence a second time while his insides tightened. What could hit him with a nuke? He answered his own question…*everything.*

9. COMMANDERS INTENT. UNTIL FURTHER ORDERED AND
   WITH POSITIVE ID DETECT AND ENGAGE RU AIR, SUR-
   FACE, AND SUBSURFACE MILITARY UNITS. HALT/BOARD/
   DISABLE RU CIVILIAN MERCHANTS ONCE POSITIVE ID
   CRITERIA MET. DO NOT ENGAGE ANY CIVIL AIRCRAFT TO
   INCLUDE AIRCRAFT ORIGINATING FROM OR ENROUTE TO
   RU. CONSIDER IS AND DK FORCES, SHIPPING, AND CO-
   MAIR AS FRIENDLY. RU AVIATION ASSESSED ABLE TO
   INTERDICT MERCHANT TRADE AND ENGAGE COALITION
   NAVAL FORCES IN VICINITY OF GIUK GAP. CONSIDER
   IMPERATIVE THAT RU FORCES AND ESPECIALLY SSBN
   FORCES DO NOT BREAK OUT SOUTH OF GIUK GAP.

Wilson considered Johnson's intent. *I must attack* and *defend at the same time.*

10. USS TINIAN IS ENROUTE FROM NORVA WITH 15 F-35B
    AND TWO DDGS MAKING BEST SPEED. EXPECT ARRIVAL
    TO YOUR EXPECTED POSITION IN 48 HOURS. I AM
    MAKING CASE FOR YOU TO ASSUME COMMAND OF THIS
    ACTION GROUP INTO A TASK FORCE UPON ARRIVAL.
    VALLEY FORGE MUST REMAIN OUTSIDE RU THREAT RINGS;
    RISKING THE CVN IS UNACCEPTABLE. SCOUT WITH DDG
    AND CVW ASSETS. HAVE SHARP TRANSMISSIONS WILL BE
    ONE WAY UFN. USE EMCON TO THE MAXIMUM EXTENT.

Yes! I want those F-35s.

11. SAR CONSIDERATIONS. GIVE HEAVY CONSIDERATION TO
    RISKING SURFACE UNITS IN RESCUE OPS IN AN AC-
    TIVE WEAPON ENGAGEMENT ZONE AND WHAT THE LOSS
    OF THEIR MISSILE TUBES WOULD MEAN TO YOUR COMBAT
    EFFECTIVENESS.

Wow—abandoning our sailors in these waters. The unthinkable is now authorized...or is it?

    12. IS ALLOWING USE OF KEFLAVIK FOR LOGISTICS.

Nice of them...

    13. COMNAVEUR HIMSELF LEADING VOICE FOR THE INCLU-
        SION OF THREE FREEDOM CLASS LCS INTO YOUR COMMAND
        TO BOLSTER SCOUTING WITH OFFENSIVE ANTI-SHIP CM
        CAPABILITY. EXPECT IN 48-72 HOURS.

What? Buffington is still pushing Littoral Combat Ships on me in this blue-water fight? I need VLS missiles, flight decks, and attack boats.

    14. THIS GUIDANCE IS PROVIDED TO SHAPE YOUR TAC-
        TICAL THINKING. YOUR ON-SCENE ASSESSMENT AND
        INITIATIVE PLUS THAT OF YOUR STRIKE GROUP IS
        CRITICAL TO SUCCESS. YOUR MINDSET MUST BE ONE
        OF ENGAGEMENT OF RU MILITARY UNITS AND AUTHO-
        RIZING/EXPECTING YOUR COMMANDERS TO TAKE FIRST
        SHOT WHEN ID CRITERIA MET. HESITATION IN THIS
        ENVIRONMENT PUTS YOURS AND COALITION UNITS AT
        RISK AND PLACES OUR HOMELAND IN EXTREME DANGER.

Message received, sir. But will you and Big Dick have my back?

    15. SHARING THIS P4 MESSAGE WITH YOUR WARFARE COM-
        MANDERS AUTHORIZED.

    16. CONTACTED MARY AND SHE'S HOLDING UP WELL; SENDS
        LOVE AND NOT TO WORRY. GOOD HUNTING, MY FRIEND.

When Wilson finished reading, he handed the message to Mark.

"Okay...that was a war warning and it's at best three hours old. Twelve friendly satellites down and more to follow—on both sides. Expect the Russians to engage anything that they come across, and it is imperative that we keep them north of the GIUK gap. Engage with positive ID any Russian military we encounter, disable Russian merchants encountered, and if they fire first, sink them. Do not engage Russian airliners. We're going to 57 degrees north and not above until further notice, and we'll probably be under the operational control of Second Fleet. Iceland and Denmark not playing, but most everyone else in this neighborhood is. *Tinian* loaded with F-35s and spare helos and accompanied by two escorts is enroute and Admiral Johnson's pushing for us to take operational control of them. They are also sending us three LCS."

Wilson looked around the room.

"This is now classified top secret, and I mean it. Not outside this bulkhead. I cannot emphasize this enough."

Huey nodded as the others waited for him to continue.

"Admiral Johnson warns of the strong possibility of Russian tactical nuclear use in a war-at-sea scenario. We won't ask questions; anything in the Russian military we come across and can ID, we shoot down or sink. If one of their merchant ships even makes us think twice—engage."

"Whoa," Mark muttered.

"That's what I said. Okay, everyone read this P4, and…"

Without knocking, Smoke burst through the door. "Admiral, Flag Plot reports transoceanic airliners are transmitting about the Russians sinking a Norwegian frigate with a missile."

"Where?"

"Between Iceland and Norway, sir."

No one spoke as they waited for the reaction of Admiral Wilson.

"Okay…Shane, without transmitting, do what you can to verify this. That said, it's believable to me."

All remained silent as they continued to absorb the news; the Russians fired first, with casualties likely. Wilson spoke again.

"Looks like we've got ourselves the high-end fight we've read about. I consider us at war."

CHAPTER 31

NORWEGIAN SEA, 1045 JUNE 16, 2024

At the time Wilson learned of the Russian attack on the Norwegian frigate—an *Akula* boat torpedoed it along the coast southwest of Bodo with the loss of nearly half the crew—a formation of four Tu-22M *Backfire* bombers floated high above *Admiral Alekseyev* as they headed southwest to attack Western shipping.

Each bomber carried one giant Kh-32 anti-ship cruise missile in its recessed fuselage housing. With a range of 540 miles, the bombers' plan was to launch the modified *Kitchens* at merchant ship targets identified through commercial tippers and all-source reconnaissance when overhead the Navy vanguard, now 300 miles west of Norway's Lofoten Islands. Protected by the SAMs carried on the *Udaloy* DDGs ahead of them, the bombers entered a "sanctuary," free to expend their weapons unmolested from NATO fighters who could be surprised by a missile from below while running an intercept on a bomber. For added protection, four naval aviation Su-33 *Flanker D* fighters patrolled outside visual range of the bombers in a moving barrier combat air patrol to block any Norwegian interceptors from the southeast.

Only two of the bombers entered targeting parameters into their weapons, one on a coastal tanker heading south 250 miles west of Trondheim and the other a containership bound for Norway. One *Backfire* experienced an INS system dump that prevented them from entering accurate data, and the remaining bomber crew could not manage the target-to-missile handoff software.

From 30,000 feet, the first bomber released its missile that fell clear before the rocket motor ignited. The deep thunder of the powerful burn echoed in the cockpit as the weapon roared away, in seconds reaching Mach 3.5 as it arced above the *Backfire* formation and the Russian combatants scattered on the Norwegian Sea in a line 200 miles across. The second *Kitchen* released five seconds later and veered right to find its assigned target as the bombers turned back to their base at Olenya.

A four-ship of Norwegian F-35 joint strike fighters from Orland Main Air Station had been vectored to the Russian formation while the cruise missiles were still on their bomber fuselage stations. Without early warning, the Su-33s were not aware of the JSFs on the eastern horizon until their RWRs went off, alerting them to missile radar locks. Shocked by the tones in each cockpit, they instinctively broke left into the threat, their thumbs pumping out expendables as fast as they could. The lead pilot spotted a small white puff floating alone against the blue sky before the AMRAAM that targeted him exploded on top of his jet, transforming it into fiery pieces of aluminum that fluttered down to the ocean four miles below.

The remaining three *Flanker* pilots, now panicked, pulled hard for the undercast layer that covered the surface, their eyes desperate to pick up an invisible missile targeting them as they rolled and pulled and expended to get the enemy electronic snare off them. As the undercast loomed up, two of them initiated recovery while the third remained supersonic in a vertical dive, still trying to pick up the threat. Once inside the layer, he pulled *hard*, overstressing his jet in horror at the realization of his altitude. Too late to recover even before he entered the undercast, he tensed and screamed once he broke clear to see the dark gray water rush up to meet him, realizing he was about to die. In terror he snatched the stick back in reflexive fear, spiking the jet to a crushing 11 g's that narrowed his final second of vision to a soda straw before it went black, the pilot still holding the pull as he slammed into the water at 400 knots.

The Norwegian fighters—falling prey to a SAM trap they had briefed yet ignored in the excitement—received a sharp reminder when RFS *Severomorsk* lit them up and launched two SAN-9 *Gauntlets* at near maximum range. The surprised JSFs, not expecting that the Russians had a sensor at sea that could track them, defended as singles and dove to the deck, saving themselves as they avoided the missiles, which went stupid when they could no longer hold a lock.

Meanwhile, the two airborne Kh-32's, like kestrel falcons, remained high above their intended targets before nosing over in their terminal dives, their radars locking on to the vessels as the guidance system controlled them to hit center mass. The first missile impaled the 615-foot tanker amidships, igniting the cargo of refined gasoline. The massive explosion ripped through the deck plates and clawed out a chunk of the double hull from the main deck to the keel, which soon snapped under the mammoth strain of the single screw still pushing the vessel forward.

The second missile bore down on the containership and entered a stack of containers just forward of the bridge and continued into the engineering spaces under it, killing twelve men and starting fires in the cargo and superstructure that the nine dazed survivors could not control. Without a functional bridge or engine room, the containership slowed to a stop. Both Filipino and Indonesian survivors, separated by ninety miles as their broken ships listed in the Arctic water, entered their orange lifeboats.

The four F-35s, their RWR displays clear and alerted to the Russian ship hidden under the cloud deck, pitched back into the fight, climbing west to attempt another intercept of the bombers. Checking left and with one monitoring the sea surface with radar, the 4-ship followed a shore radar vector to the *Backfire* division, now heading northeast on their egress.

At forty miles, the Norwegians saw the four long silhouettes cross their nose from left to right, holding their locks until well inside a no-escape range. The bombers flew on, oblivious as the JSFs continued in, practically joining on their right bearing line. With each F-35 sorted visually, the lead gave the signal to fire and three AMRAAMs leapt off their rails; the fourth one hung up.

Fired well inside no-escape, the missile rocket motors still burned as each one tore into its target with devastating force. Two of the missiles entered their respective fuselages just forward of the intakes that obliterated each airplane, and the third impacted a bomber on the right-wing root, from which it entered a tight roll.

The JSFs now pounced on the remaining *Backfire*, the fighter pilots transfixed by its bright burner cans as the terrified bomber pilots dove to safety on the surface. Out of radar missiles, the F-35s unloaded at max power to obtain closure on the escaping bomber that jammed their radars, causing drop lock. Behind him at his seven o'clock, one Norwegian pilot noticed four chutes float to the surface.

With all five airplanes low on fuel, the fighters had to break off their pursuit once the bomber entered the undercast, their *Sidewinders* unable to catch the supersonic jet as it fled for its life at Mach 1.6. After three minutes, the bomber pilot turned right 30 degrees to check if he was pursued, then right again. Nothing. He rolled out north and climbed for home, keeping a safe distance from the continent and returning three hours later to Olenya with only eight minutes of fuel remaining.

At Northern Fleet Headquarters, Admiral Platonov read the report from the surviving bomber in shock. Five jets out of eight lost—three of four bombers! He considered holding them back—but how could he? No, the Red Banner Fleet was the Kremlin's giant mace to force the West to back off—before the plump and kerchief-covered babushkas marched on Red Square to demand an end to the bloodshed of their sons on the killing ground of Ukraine.

For now, Russia *hoped* that the fleet could push the Western capitalists and the grieving mothers of *their* dead sailors to capitulate before reaching a pain level that could generate an even greater response. A delicate balance, and Platonov was unsure of his force's effectiveness; hours ago he learned of the loss of a Norwegian combatant through Western media, a loss that he could not yet attribute to his aviation, surface, or subsurface forces. Unable to communicate effectively with them as they approached the gap, he depended on the initiative of his individual ship and aircraft commanders.

Platonov did have another option that he could control, one he thought of constantly, and as he walked to the wall chart to study the Norwegian Sea he estimated where *Vitac* should be...and thought of Petrov. He glanced again at the clock; it was scheduled takeoff time from Olenya. How many more young widows would shriek tonight when they learned the news of this day? Under *his* orders. But what choice did he have? His fleet was the only thing that stood between Strategic Rocket Force Armageddon and Western surrender in his government's perilous gambit. Another minute passed as Platonov thought of his sailors—and soon the aircrews—moving south to engage the enemy.

Dasvidaniya and go with God.

CHAPTER 32

NORTH ATLANTIC, 300 MILES SOUTH OF ICELAND, 0615 JUNE 17, 2024

Glancing over her right shoulder at her wingman, Lieutenant "Otter" Engelsen, Olive noted him stabilized in position as she passed 20,000 feet in a gentle climb into a clear sky, the brilliant sun high to the southeast. Led by Comet—with Gigs on his left wing—the *Raven* division had topped off from the tanker that dragged them northeast of *Valley Forge* to a position east of Iceland from which they could prosecute any Russian bombers that dared to penetrate that deep into the Norwegian Sea, over 1,000 miles from their base in the Kola Peninsula. As the four FA-18E's continued their climb to 35,000 feet, the tanker sprinted back to the ship to recover, refuel, and meet the *Ravens* on the back end in two hours.

Underneath them was a white blanket of broken overcast that rested on the sea with a ceiling below 2,000 feet, obscuring their FLIRs from identifying any linked contacts from the *Knight* E-2D. Her armed SSSC scout sections had already searched the waters she flew over, finding them devoid of maritime traffic as the two naval elephants neared. Through breaks she saw whitecaps, no different from the high winds that whipped the waters around the carrier when she had left 40 minutes earlier.

Last night Russian bombers—reaching out almost 1,000 miles from the North Cape—had sunk a small chemical tanker fleeing in vain to Fuglafjordur in the Faroes, hitting it with another ancient yet effective *Kitchen* that took its bow off. The 12-man crew survived and were soon rescued by Danish forces, fortunate that the attack occurred inside 12 miles of the islands, with many eyewitnesses on the shore recording it with their smart phones. Maybe Denmark would change its position and join the coalition if the public outcry became loud enough, but that was not on Olive's mind now. Russian bombers could hit targets in the gap, and further south if they pushed hard enough.

Passing 31,000 feet on the way up, the four *Super Hornets*, each armed with two wingtip *Sidewinders* and two AMRAAM, began to mark in the sub-zero air, revealing themselves to anyone observing from miles around. Comet stopped

212

the climb and descended below the contrail altitude; 31 grand would be close enough.

Olive scanned the northeast horizon. Inside her right canopy bow, a white smudge floated above the cottony horizon, with another small smudge mark at her two o'clock. She correlated them to the datalink display: comm air from Europe heading west and conning, probably wide bodies. Designating the northernmost bogey on her helmet-mounted display, she commanded the FLIR to track it: a dark dot generating a thick funnel of contrail behind it. Too far to identify the type, she looked north and spied three volcanic peaks of Iceland that pushed above the layer some 200 miles away, clothed in white. Olive and the others continued to scan the horizon and monitor their cockpit displays in this manner as the four *Rhinos* sped to their station at 300 knots indicated. On Olive's link display, the graphics of two *Spartan* FA-18Fs carrying *Harpoon* anti-ship missiles also flowed northeast toward the gap, scouting ahead for the enemy underneath the broken layer.

Just before Olive walked, she learned that observers in Vardo, Norway had spotted a large formation heading west over the Barents Sea, a formation assessed as bombers in what was becoming a predictable Russian pattern. This word was passed among the aviators as they suited up: big game was coming to them—*if* they could get up there in time—and Comet pushed it up to give them a chance at bagging a *Backfire*.

"*Raven* one-one, *Knight*, picture clean, single group reported ROCK zero-four-zero four hundred, heading two-two-zero, high, hot, probable SWING-TIME."

Olive expanded her map. With ROCK as the bullseye reference waypoint, both the *Ravens* and the probable *Backfire* formation—codeword SWINGTIME—were each 400 miles from it and closing. *Well, well!* At this speed, Comet would get them there in 45 minutes, with shots off before then, once the group was positively identified. Near ROCK, and even north of it, Russian DDGs could potentially out-stick Comet's division with their SAMs if the Americans stumbled upon one. Yesterday the Russians had done a good job of cloaking themselves and limiting emissions to avoid detection. As CAG, Olive was mindful of this SAM-trap threat, as was Comet. The Russians would have to depend on this tactic after the heavy losses their air superiority fighters had taken yesterday at the hands of the Norwegians.

Comet took charge.

"*Knight*, *Raven* one-one, committing on the group ROCK zero-four-zero four hundred...break...*Ravens* deploy."

Taking their cue from the briefing, each pilot moved into a wall formation, with Comet and Olive in the middle and their wingmen on the ends. They also had near-far, left-right, and high-low sorting responsibilities on whatever formation the Russians approached them with, but that could wait for the link picture to build as the 800-mile range between them melted with over 1,000 knots of closure. Comet again keyed the mic.

"Smoker, one o'clock low."

Peering over her nose, Olive saw a pall of black smoke rise above the white undercast some twenty miles away. Something was burning down there, but why, and who? On her navigation display, she visualized an imaginary line from Iceland to the Faroes. This mystery smoke was south of it, south of the gap in open water. Had the Russians already penetrated it and hit something else? No surface contacts on the link. Could it be a sub attack? An "innocent" merchant with a *Klub*-in-a-box? Whatever it was, she and the others in the formation studied it as they approached.

"*Knight, Raven* one-one; we've got a pall of black smoke at our one o'clock about twenty miles."

"*Knight,* roger...*Spartan* three-three is enroute to investigate, no reports of enemy in the vicinity."

"*Raven* one-one...*Ravens* check left ten."

Olive and the others veered left ten degrees as the smoke—and cruising airliners—drifted down their right wings. She studied the smoke column, black and growing. No reports of enemy. Well, something had caused the smoke, and recently, as it had just popped through the layer. Stack gas? No, too heavy. Out-of-control shipboard fire, coincidentally in this combat zone? Maybe, but doubtful. She checked the range to the bogey group: 700 miles.

They continued north in the "gap" portion between Iceland and the Faroes, Indian Country for sure, not radiating to remain as convert as possible. The E-2 was behind but following as best they could, relaying linked information from an American E-3 *Sentry*, callsign *Warden* 42. The AWACS bird orbited north of Iceland to generate the radar picture, safe from Russian Su-33's that could not reach that far.

Keeping busy as the range between the formations decreased to 500 miles, Olive and the others monitored the cockpit displays, cleared each others' six, did endless fuel calculations in their heads, kept a wary eye on the Radar Warning Receiver display, and double-checked the combat checklist complete. On the link, a surface contact three hundred miles ahead—hostile! But what? A *Slava* SAN-6 carrier? One of their new frigates with a 60-mile missile? Soon they would be in the potential missile engagement zones of the longest-range Russian

SAM on the *Slava*, and they had to honor it. Things would happen fast now, and Olive fidgeted in the cockpit, impatient for a declaration from *Knight*. On the top of her nav display a line appeared, the Arctic Circle.

"*Raven* one-one, *Knight*, single group BRAA zero-three-five three hundred, high, hot, hostile. Cooperative engagement ready."

Hostile!

Olive decremented her display to break out the group, now showing two contacts in trail. She and Otter would target the trailers she estimated at five miles behind the lead group.

To stay out of the Russian weapon engagement zone as much as possible, the *Rhinos* would launch their radar missiles at near maximum range and reset south. Once on their way downrange, *Knight* would "grab" and guide each AMRAAM to their target, allowing the fighters to escape any surface combatant WEZ and potentially re-engage if a leaker got through. Olive and the others had no illusions about the complexity of this operation to guide each missile to each *Backfire*. Comet directed the action.

"*Knight*, *Ravens* are committing on the hostile group BRA zero-three-five three hundred. *Ravens*, *Armstrong*, let's bump it up."

Mirroring Comet, the wall of *Ravens* accelerated toward the bomber group, each pilot monitoring their assigned target as the lead-trail formation revealed itself on the AWACS-generated link picture from *Warden* 42, allowing each pilot to designate and target *their* bomber.

"*Knight*, *Raven* one-one flight is sorted...you ready?"

"*Raven* one-one, *Knight*, affirm, sweet timber."

Passing through the sound barrier—the only indication being that the Mach number increased from .99 to 1.0—and with the link connectivity suitcased, the *Rhino* pilots selected AMRAAM and passed their readiness to shoot the Tu-22 "archers" before the Russian bombers could release their anti-ship "arrows" at anything ahead of them. As airspeed continued to build, the shoot cue in each cockpit and helmet display illuminated, and Olive maintained a steady scan of Comet off her wing and her link display inside the cockpit with no indication the Russians were aware of their presence.

One mile to the left of Olive, an AMRAAM fell from Comet's jet and ignited, the bright rocket plume pushing the missile ahead and into a gentle climb.

"*Raven* one-one, Fox-three on the lead group."

"*Raven* one-three, Fox-three on the trail group," Olive transmitted as she pulled the trigger, her AMRAAM accelerating ahead with a deep WHOOM heard in the cockpit.

Seconds later Gigs and Otter also fired on their respective targets, and four white plumes each led by a fiery dot slowly climbed into the clear sky.

"*Ravens*—crank left—*go!*"

On Comet's call, the division checked hard left and descended slightly nose low, monitoring their missiles' travel on the link display as the plumes receded from view. With another AMRAAM at the ready, they waited for direction from *Knight*, who now had the hostile group on their own radar.

"*Raven* one-one, *Knight*, your birds are captured, guiding."

"*Raven* one-one, copy, *Ravens* reset south."

With the E-2 controlling the four missiles, Comet and the others turned hard left to south and rolled out, monitoring their link pictures and radar warning receivers. Olive checked the progress of her missile: another minute to go.

Boop

Surprised by the aural tone, Olive's eyes shot to the RWR display. On it, an indication at her seven o'clock for a naval SAM—an indication she had to consider their longest-ranged naval SAM.

Deeedle, deedle, *deedledeedledeedledeedledeedledeedle!*

Oh crap!

Olive slammed her stick to the left as she pushed the throttles to military, craning her neck to pick up a plume coming out of the thick undercast.

"*Raven* one-three, mud spike seven o'clock defending! Chaff!"

"Roger, one-one's naked; *Ravens* break left!" Comet replied, keeping an eye on Olive and also checking northeast for a white plume against a quilted blanket of white.

The four *Rhinos* descended as they broke into the threat and unloaded for knots, Olive doing all she could to break lock. Pulling hard, she saw a shadow on the cloud deck far to the north as a white plume broke above the horizon.

"*Raven* one-three, tally on the bird, my ten o'clock long—beaming!"

Aided by her call, the formation put the missile on their right shoulders as they continued down. In Olive's cockpit, the missile guidance indication extinguished, with the SAM indication remaining.

"*Raven* one-three's naked."

Just then, a surprise from *Knight*.

"*Knight*, new picture, two groups azimuth! Bomber group continuing south, new group stripping west-southwest toward *Warden* four-two!"

The four *Rhino* pilots glanced at their link displays and saw it immediately.

"*Warden* four-two, *Knight*, scram west: bandit group high, hot."

"*Knight, Warden*, we're in the turn now!"

Olive checked her link page as Comet reversed them right to the northeast. The bombers continued in, unaware they were targeted by the AMRAAMs inside 30 seconds from going active. But this new group! Breaking off right toward the AWACS and *fast*. How? More *Backfires?* She watched in horror as the range between them decreased—no bomber could accelerate that fast.

The E-3, orbiting unescorted north of Iceland in open water, was clear of the bomber's route to the surface targets between Iceland and Norway. When the surprised controllers saw the radar contact split, they studied it as a potential anomaly before cold realization hit them. Now running for its life, the big four-engine jet did the best that its airframe and engines could deliver. In the *Rhino* formation, Comet took control.

"*Raven* one-one, *gate*, reference three-zero-zero! *Knight, Ravens* are committing on the threat group to *Warden*; get a tanker up here now!"

As the four *Ravens* devoured fuel in burner, they accelerated in a gentle climb, in what all foresaw was a doomed attempt to cut off the hostile group running down the AWACS in their desperate attempt to survive. Olive realized the group must be fighters, fighters that hid in the radar resolution cell of the bombers. *Bastards!* she thought, though she had to give them credit.

And big Russian fighters were fast, carried lots of fuel, and carried radar missiles with big rocket motors. The latest AA-10 *Alamo* variant had a range of over 100 miles. Comet keyed the mic again.

"*Ravens* radiate!"

Good call, Olive thought as she energized her APG-79 radar and opened up the display. Though cutting the corner to intercept the Russians, they were still 100 miles away as the bandit group beamed them. Popping the radar mode into AUTOACQ, Olive fished for a lock, a challenge at that aspect. An American radar lock—with a spike—would alert the Russians to their presence and maybe end their pursuit of the AWACS.

Maybe.

Holy crap! Olive thought, as the link display showed the Russian threat group at a staggering Mach 2, more than twice as fast as the E-3 on its best day. Looking through her windscreen toward Greenland, she searched for the AWACS inside her helmet-mounted cue box and saw it in a slight dive, beneath her altitude.

"Timeout on the lead missile, eastern group."

Olive whipped her head right, hoping to see a puff or flash in the distance. Two seconds later she saw one near her linked designation box, followed by a growing dark smudge.

One down.

Olive's radar got a lock—the AWACS—and she bumped the castle switch to reject it and find a Russian pursuer. Inside 80 miles she decremented her radar display and checked her fuel: down to 7,500 pounds and going fast. She groaned in frustration, knowing they were too far to help the E-3 and without fuel to pursue their potential executioner.

"Checkin' left ten," Comet transmitted to sweeten the intercept as the ragged formation sprinted to help. Olive detected that his voice was resigned, knowing as they all did that the range between the AWACS and the Russians was closing at too fast a rate.

Seconds later, she saw a faint light trailing a plume.

"Missile in the air!" she cried. "*Warden*, check left or right!"

Now, thirty miles from the E-3, she observed it in a shallow dive to the southwest as the plume behind it disappeared—rocket motor burn-out. Could the big jet escape? It did not appear to turn as she watched it in her MFD target designator box. She locked her FLIR to it.

A puff appeared next to *Warden* 42. *No!*

Another flash, and the big jet began to trail smoke. A laconic voice transmitted, "We're hit."

Olive's jet hummed at 1.15 Mach as she and the others raced toward the AWACS and its hunters. In the high teens, and despite her pressing the throttles to the stops, that was all her combat-loaded and drop-tanked *Rhino* was going to give her in level flight.

Horrified, Olive watched *Warden* 42 roll 90 degrees, the left wing fire generating a sheet of black smoke. She could only imagine the terror-stricken crew inside and bump-locked again to find the Russians. A disembodied voice transmitted.

"I can't hold it."

The E-3 continued its roll as Olive and the others watched, transfixed. She took charge.

"Comet, break off and pursue the bandits! *Knight, Warden* four-two is hit and going down. Launch the SAR!"

"Mayday, mayday!" the voice cried.

"*Raven* one-one, wilco!" Comet responded.

Olive, with Otter in trail, ramped down as they headed for *Warden* 42, trailing heavy smoke as it slowly cork-screwed down in its death throes.

"Rudder! Full power!" the radio transmitted, followed by silence.

Unloading to the deck as the AWACS rolled out of control in front of her, Olive's radar picked up the bandits to the right of her screen, egressing away to the northwest at forty miles and opening. No way Comet could run them down.

On her FLIR, she saw the four-engine jet steepen its dive as the large radar disk was torn from it. Sickened, she and Otter watched the flaming wing come off and flutter behind the fuselage as it plunged into the undercast. She keyed the mic.

"Mayday, mayday, mayday, *Warden* four-two is going in. *Knight, Raven* one-three, *Warden* is off my nose two-six-five at twenty-five."

On comm 2, she directed her wingman. "Otter, take trail and follow me through, we're going underneath for a visual."

"*Raven* one-four, wilco."

Olive needed more SA. "Break, break, Comet, what luck?"

"*Raven* one-one is forty miles in trail and they're pulling away. My state six-seven."

Olive figured as much, and brought her throttles out of burner to military as she slowed. She was at 6,300 pounds, below joker fuel with the nearest tanker over 200 miles away, a tanker that had to tank four thirsty jets just to get them to the ship another four hundred miles further.

An invisible force pushed her against her straps as the jet slowed inside the transonic wall, just above the white cottony deck. Her engines stabilized, she retarded the throttles as she pushed into the goo at 4,000 feet, bore sighted on where the black plume entered the undercast.

Punching through, she noted that faint smoke marked a spot on the sea ahead, and as she approached it, she searched the spot for any debris. Did AWACS jets have chutes? Olive doubted it, and scanning the horizon, she didn't see any.

She slowed and took a cut to the left to avoid the smoke and keep eyes on the disturbed ocean surface. Finding a piece of debris, she studied it...a flight control surface. No signs of survival for the 15–20-person crew. On the southern horizon, a fishing trawler headed south. Another fishing boat rested on the horizon far to the west. Comet called.

"*Raven* one-one, no joy, resetting."

After obtaining a visual on Otter behind her, Olive entered an easy right hand turn over the dissipating North Atlantic froth with nothing but a trailing edge flap and small pieces of cabin wreckage to indicate that *Warden* 42 ever existed. Unable to stay longer to direct the SAR as her fuel state dwindled to a critical level, she marked the spot and—with Otter joined—accelerated into a climb to punch through the goo and find Comet. Their next task was to find the tanker, successfully plug, successfully transfer, then find the ship in EMCON after a transit of hundreds of miles, then hope for a ready and relatively steady deck to trap.

All had to go perfectly, for the four of them, and *Knight*, and the SSSC birds. And again for Air Wing FOUR events this afternoon, this evening, tomorrow, and the next day.

CHAPTER 33

RFS *ADMIRAL ALEKSEYEV*, NORWEGIAN SEA, 1005 JUNE 17, 2024

Petrov lay in his cabin and stared at the ceiling, frustrated and feeling guilty. Though midmorning, he had to rest…but how could he with his inexperienced yet equally exhausted *leytenants* keeping station on that hell-ship next to him? He always felt *Vitac's* presence, no respite, even in his sleep. Colliding with him dominated his thoughts. What would happen? Petrov's port bow would tear against the containership hull plates, ripping out *Admiral Alekseyev's* forward lifelines and maybe the anchor, leaving a gash of stove-in steel on the plodding merchant five meters above the waterline. In a moment of clarity, it struck him…so *what* if they collided? Platonov put him here to do what no kapitan had ever done, not even one of the vaunted and pampered Yankee kapitans: maintain a football pitch distance from a civilian ship and together transit the length of the undulating and white-capped Norwegian Sea!

Screw him—and them! he thought. *What are they going to do to me that they haven't done? Make me fight the* Amerikanskiy *Navy?* Just then, in his next moment of clarity, he was reminded of his port side anti-ship missile tubes, and Tube 2 in particular. No, he could never allow such a collision, even minor. Light leaked into his stateroom from his lone porthole. He hated standing watch in the gloomy darkness of winter in the northern latitudes, but now craved it like the restful sleep his body yearned for. With his arm over his eyes he tried…before he heard two knocks on his door.

"Enter."

Kuzmin poked his head inside, then opened the door and entered.

"Forgive me, Kapitan, but a dispatch from home just arrived." Kuzmin walked to Petrov's rack and handed it to him.

Petrov checked the originator—Platonov—and the date time group: two hours ago. The message was to *Admiral Alekseyev*—and no others in the task force. His heart rate increased.

```
FROM: COMMANDER NORTHERN FLEET
TO:   RFS ADMIRAL ALEKSEYEV
```

```
SUBJ: OPERATIONAL ORDER 005
```

```
RMKS: MUTIPLE AMERIKANSKIY ARLEIGH BURKE CLASS SUR-
FACE COMBATANTS DETECTED IN GIUK GAP ALONG LINE CEN-
TERED N06430 W00800 ORIENTED 300-120.  COMBATANTS
OBSERVED OPERATING IN COMPANY WITH UNITED KINGDOM
AND NORWEGIAN COMBATANTS TO PROTECT WESTERN MER-
CHANT SHIPPING AND PROSECUTE RFS SUBMARINES BREAK-
ING OUT INTO OPEN ATLANTIC.
```

```
REMAINING ALONGSIDE VITAC TO MAXIMIZE COVERT POS-
TURE, MAKE BEST SPEED TO VICINITY N064 30 W008
00.  RENDEZVOUS ENROUTE WITH FLAGSHIP RFS MARSHAL
YERMOLOV FOR COORDINATED MISSILE ATTACK ON AMERIKAN-
SKIY ARLEIGH BURKE CLASS COMBATANT AS DIRECTED BY
FLAGSHIP. USE OF AVIATION ASSETS FOR SCOUTING AND
TO AFFECT SURFACE ACTION GROUP RENDEZVOUS IS ENCOUR-
AGED. DO NOT ENGAGE ENEMY OR WHITE MERCHANT TRAFFIC
ENCOUNTERED. DETACH FROM VITAC AT COMMANDING OFFI-
CER DISCRETION WHEN CONDITIONS WARRANT.
```

```
WHEN DIRECTED BY FLAGSHIP ENGAGE WITH SINGLE SALVO
OF THREE - REPEAT - THREE P-270 MOSKIT ASCM ON DESI-
GATED ARLEIGH BURKE CLASS COMBATANT IN CONCERT WITH
FLAGSHIP DIRECTED SURFACE ACTION GROUP. RENDEZVOUS
WITH FLAGSHIP NO LATER THAN 172300Z JUN. SUGGEST
ACTION STATIONS SOUTH OF N067 00.
```

```
FOR PETROV: DISPLAYING THE STERLING QUALITIES OF
RUSSIAN WOMANHOOD, MRS. ARINA PETROVA IS IN GOOD
SPIRITS AND SENDS WELL WISHES TO THE GALLANT CREW
OF YOUR FINE SHIP.
```

Petrov froze, then looked away. ARINA. Catching himself, he continued as
Kuzmin watched.

```
WHEN THIS OPERATIONAL ORDER IS RECEIVED AND UNDER-
STOOD, RESPOND VIA MESSAGE FORMAT TO ACKNOWLEDGE
RECEIPT. INCLUSION OF PERSONAL MESSAGES FOR FAMILY
MEMBERS OF YOUR CREW IS AUTHORIZED.
```

```
THE MOTHERLAND STANDS IN AWE OF HER BRAVE SONS IN
OUR DEFENSE OF OUR CHRISTIAN RELIGION AND NATIONAL
SOVEREIGNTY. GO WITH GOD.
```

Petrov handed the message to Kuzmin and paraphrased it.

"There it is, Yevgeny. We are to turn—with *Vitac*—to the latitude/longitude in this message and at best speed join with *Marshal Yermolov* and the rest of the Red Banner Fleet to attack an enemy *Arleigh Burke* class spotted in the gap. We are to launch a salvo of *Moskits* at the target the flagship assigns us with salvos from the others. And we need to get there by 2300Z—thirteen hours. What can *Vitac* make in these seas?"

"Nineteen knots on a good day, Kapitan," Kuzmin answered, then asked the question that kept *him* up at night. "Tube two, Kapitan?"

Expecting the question, Petrov nodded slowly. "Yes, read down to the end."

Kuzmin read, soon exhaling audibly through his nose as he did. "Mrs. Arina Petrova."

"You do not know what it is like to read your wife's name in such a message, Yevgeny."

Kuzmin held Petrov's gaze, then nodded his understanding and acceptance. "Nineteen knots, Kapitan."

"Very well. Message him with the course you plot from this and demand *twenty* knots. No excuses about fried engine bearings either, this is it. Oh, yes, wake up the pilots. I want them airborne to scout ahead of us. Do not fire on anything without my authorization. I want scouting to avoid fishing boats and merchants and sightings of the fleet ahead of us. Get everyone a hot meal; Borsht and one ration of vodka. After this operation we'll go back to normal rations, but *only* once complete with a successful salvo and a sinking of an *Amerkanskiy* ship. We'll run for home to refuel and celebrate then."

"Aye, aye, Kapitan."

Petrov's mind returned to their secret mission as he spoke in a deliberate tone. "And the *Moskits*…tubes one, two, and four. I want to shoot a *salvo of three* just inside max range."

Kuzmin held Petrov's gaze as he nodded. *Nuclear attack…from this ship.*

"Kapitan, we have five *Moskits,* and the crew will want to know why we don't launch all.

Petrov concocted a cover story. "The flagship will coordinate salvos from all his available ships. Once this salvo is downrange, he may want another on the target or flow to another target if nearby. He must husband his available missiles—three from us is the right number."

"Yes, Kapitan," Kuzin answered with a knowing nod.

"I want our *Helix* loaded with a war shot torpedo; their *Virginia* boats could be watching us—or *Vitac*—now. Go, and I'll be up there shortly. Oh yes…

Medvedev's wife is expecting. Did I hear him say in the wardroom yesterday that he wishes for the boy to be named Alexandr?"

"Yes, Kapitan."

"Good. I'll include that in my response, our cover story. Another *Sasha* among the children of *Admiral Alekseyev.*" Petrov smiled at the thought of it, as his mind returned to what *Sasha* meant.

"He'll appreciate that, Kapitan...thank you," a shaken Kuzmin replied.

"Are you prepared for this, Yevgeny Sergeevich?"

Kuzmin remained silent as he locked unhappy eyes with Petrov, then nodded before he whispered, "Yes, Kapitan."

"Good, but before you go, this is what we've trained for, combat with the West. Do not let the crew see you discouraged. They must be *energized*, especially these next 24 hours. You and I will carry this burden. Dismissed."

Kuzmin forced a smile and left with the message for the navigation bridge while Petrov drafted a response. Today...or tonight. Less than 24 hours. It was happening...and his own hand would initiate it.

He thought of Platonov's targeting plan. Missile salvos from multiple ships to overwhelm the enemy defenses, some likely the new hypersonic wonders. And with his salvo mixed in with the others, who would know who delivered the killing shot...once the horizon turned white. He glanced at the calendar on his desk: 17 or 18 June. Dates that future humanity would not ever forget.

Petrov scribbled a draft response for the signalmen, thinking about Arina and Sasha as he did.

After four hours airborne, an exhausted Olive—with mask lines on her face and still wearing her flight gear—entered the War Room and joined the strike group leadership to figure their next move. Wilson offered Olive a seat next to him. Mark, Smoke, and Weed were already seated as they waited for the CAG to join them.

"Did you see it go in?" Wilson asked.

Her eyes downcast, Olive nodded. The tormented look on her face from the memory of *Warden 42's* final moments was description enough. She turned to Wilson.

"Sir, any intel? How did they do it?"

"Two Su-33's flew the whole way inside the radar resolution cell of the *Backfires.* Once the bombers launched their *Kitchens* with tipper info from their DDGs in the area, the fighters peeled off for the AWACS. The Air Force is shocked; they kept the jet on the edge of radar coverage—nothing from the Kola Peninsula could hit it from that range and it would be seen if they tried—but not if they stayed in res cell."

"Gotta hand it to them," Smoke said, before adding, "They must have been slick and accelerated to Mach 2 before they launched an edge-of-the- envelope missile, probably a late-model *Alamo*. A fighter could have escaped, but not a 707 airframe."

"Did we get a bomber? I think we did," Olive asked. Wilson answered.

"You got one. Don't know if it was you, but only one confirmed."

"Did they get a ship?"

"They got a fishing boat," Smoke said. "Actually it was a 200-foot ocean-going trawler; we hear they put two missiles on it and blew it away with the loss of all hands."

Olive nodded. *Another failure.*

Wilson moved on.

"The SSSC players on your event detected the lead of their surface action group now south of the Arctic Circle, six that we've found, a *Sovremenny* DDG, some *Udaloys*, and a few of their new frigates. Expect that their *Slava* is in there, too. Their attack boats are probably nearby the SAG with their boomers, and their plan appears to be running the gauntlet between Iceland and the Faroes. The Brits and our own P-8s flying from Lossiemouth are shadowing the Russians while they are trying to pin down and prosecute the subs. Mark, give Olive the run down on our DDGs."

The surface warrior pointed to the chart. "We've sent the Rota BMD ships *Michael Estocin* and *Lloyd Childers* up there. *Childers* has our only defensive laser, and while we'd like it to help defend us, it can do more good up there defending salvos once the Russians get into surface-to-surface missile range. Both can use their SM-6s in the gatekeeper or attack roles, and both have two *Romeos* aboard to help the patrol planes with the ASW problem. Two *Romeos* working together is a buzzsaw for the Russian boats, and if a P-8 can help them, it's a killing field."

Wilson spoke next. "And while they are dealing with the undersea threat, I want to hit them hard with the LRASMs we have. Take out one or two missile shooters. Smoke, how many do we have again?"

"Only twenty-two, sir, and we're asking for more from any source we can get them. NAVEUR is working to get some out here on an *Osprey* from Keflavik."

"Just don't tell the Icelanders. And speaking of Kef, STRATCOM is sending two E-6s there to help us with the command and control, keeping one airborne over the island to maintain line of sight with us. Expect Admiral Coleman to be inside it most of the time."

"We still need early warning," Olive said.

Wilson agreed. "Yes, and until the Air Force finds a way to escort their AWACS, it's going to be the *Knights* and our BMD ships that provide the picture. Ask Norfolk for some *Hummers* for basing at Kef but for the time being it's just us. Smoke, where's the *Tinian* ARG?"

"About 600 miles from us, sir. We could task their F-35's tomorrow."

"Great. Olive, we need a self-escort LRASM strike for tomorrow, and I'm inclined to shoot our wad to bag at least one of their missile shooters and bet on the come that Admiral Coleman or Johnson will get us more missiles. Get connectivity with *Tinian* and work in F-35s into the strike package."

"Aye, aye, sir," Olive replied.

Smoke continued with his report. "Admiral, three LCS are set to join us tomorrow. What would you like to do with them?"

Wilson exhaled. "Not really what we need for this fight, but last time we spoke, Buffington was adamant we use them. My sense is to keep them in company with us."

Mark objected. "He wants them up in the gap, sir, to act as missile shooters. They left Norfolk with full loads of Naval Strike Missiles."

"I know, but they've got, what, ten NSMs, no missile defense except for a little pop gun on the bow?"

"We could use the firepower sir…thirty missiles…"

Wilson shook his head. "No. Expendable is one thing, but suicidal is something else. Keep them nearby and employ them the best you can. He didn't tell me that explicitly, so…plausible deniability."

All at the table nodded in agreement, then Smoke added, "That early season hurricane in the Gulf of Mexico is supposed to go ashore in the panhandle today. It's a Cat 1 storm and it will weaken, but it's still a major system on a northeast track and it will be a factor here in less than a week."

Wilson looked at Mark for his assessment.

"Admiral, the weather here changes minute to minute and the seas are sporty all the time, but yes, if we get even a tropical storm or a bad gale up here, our *destroyers* are going to have a tough time in that. The LCS…I'd send them to port to ride it out."

"Which one?"

"Faslane, Scotland comes to mind. About a day-and-a-half transit at 20-knots from here."

"Okay, we'll keep Faslane in our back pocket."

The desk phone buzzed. Mark answered it, then turned to Wilson.

"Admiral Buffington is on the line for you, sir."

Wilson smiled. "Speak of the devil…okay, everyone stay and I'll take it here."

Wilson took the receiver and waited for Buffington's staff to connect him.

"Wilson, Rick Buffington."

"Good morning from the North Atlantic, sir."

"Wilson, the Air Force is living in my ass about that AWACS you lost today. Why didn't your people down the Russians first?"

Back on his heels again, Wilson answered.

"Admiral, my CAG was on that flight and is here with me now filling us in. She…"

"Put her on speakerphone."

Wilson punched in the speakerphone and responded. "Admiral, the Air Wing Commander Captain Kristin Teel is here, with my Chief of Staff and Ops Officer."

Savoring the audience, Buffington ignored the niceties.

"CAG, why didn't you get between the Russians and that AWACS? We cannot live this way, losing high value units to fighters we can see coming for miles."

Breathless at the implication, Olive caught herself and formed an answer. Wilson nodded for her to speak freely.

"Admiral, we had tipper and link info on the bombers, which we engaged cooperatively with the E-2. We shot at near-max range to avoid any missile shooters underneath us that we didn't have solid positioning on because of…"

"I don't buy that, Captain!" Buffington snapped. "You should roll back that threat with LRASMs first while you get missile shooters up there to defend from their cruise missiles! And regarding this res-cell excuse, you are paid to think about this known tactic!"

Wilson fumed as Buffington ripped his subordinate officer in front of him, in public, and was angrier still that the resolution cell tactic had made its way from the ship to Buffington. With a throat-slashing motion, he ordered her to stop and took over.

"Admiral, we are assessing all the intel we've collected and will honor this threat in future ops. If we had two extra missile shooters, we could move them north of Iceland as a sanctuary for AWACS and other big-wing ISR assets…"

"Wilson, we just gave you two DDGs! BMD shooters, fully loaded with SM-6's! What more do you want?" Buffington growled.

"Sir, we have them between the Faroes and Iceland, but I need some defense-in-depth around me. If we had two more, we could bolster the Denmark Strait for ASW and establish a WEZ to defend against any more incursions."

The line was silent, and Wilson wondered if Buffington was still connected. He was.

"Admiral Wilson...you have a chief of staff and a Commodore who are *career* surface warriors and can advise you on the optimum placement of units in your beefed-up strike group. I *suggest*...that you follow their recommendations. I will further *suggest*...that you place the LCS you just got in the Iceland-Faroes gap. That's over thirty Naval Strike Missiles to plug that gap and free up your DDGs to knock down their bombers, their damned *archers*, before they launch their *arrows*, and at the same time defend the Air Force, which is there to help *you*. Now, before I contact my fellow joint force commander to promise perfect execution of this meat-and-potatoes Navy mission, do I have your understanding of my intent?"

Before he answered, Wilson glanced at Weed, who suppressed his disgust. *Vintage Buffington.*

"Yes, sir," Wilson answered in the uncomfortable silence.

"Good. Carry on, no more fuckups like this morning, and shoot the damn archers and defend the damn merchants. Attrition is the mission. Out here."

Mark hit the button to disconnect. "Admiral...it's not as easy as he makes it." The room remained silent.

"I know," Wilson answered, his insides churning with rage.

"Sir, after we refuel them, the two LCS could be on station in 24 hours. Shall we send them?"

All waited for Wilson to answer.

"Refuel them. Olive and Smoke, I want the LRASM gameplan after lunch."

"Aye, aye, sir," both replied.

Without a word, Wilson got up and departed the War Room through his stateroom door. Weed's eyes met Olive's. Both had seen Flip like that before.

Chapter 34

RFS *Admiral Alekseyev*, Norwegian Sea, 2340 June 17, 2024

Vitac labored in the growing swells as an impatient Petrov checked the time. *We're late,* he thought. His *Helix* had found something far down the horizon, a verification of a tipper broadcast from Headquarters transmitted from a bomber. How many bombers were left at Olenya? Petrov felt little for his lost country-men; he needed the Yankees to be distracted, by them, the attack boats, or the rest of the destroyer division. *Anything* to allow him with his miserable escort to stalk their prey, showing his hand at the last moment. The bridge status screen showed eighteen knots. *Can't he go faster?*

His reliable Officer of the Deck, *Leytenant* Nikitin, approached his chair. "Kapitan Petrov, request permission to recover the *Helix*."

"Granted," Petrov answered. His other helicopter, the *Katran* attack bird, was enroute to the datum to maintain contact and find the flagship *Marshal Yermolov*. While the *Helix* refueled, the pilots grabbed some food before heading back out.

His helicopter ranging 100 miles ahead of their track should have found the flagship before now. *Blind,* with *Vitac* holding him back as he had for days. They'd be over the horizon now if the bastard could make 20 knots, and well over 100 miles closer if Petrov could sprint ahead on his own. But closer to what? American- and British-guided missile destroyers lying in wait, with *Virginia* class underneath and a swarm of *Super Hornets* with missiles above? Nothing from Fleet HQ, nothing from the flagship. Does the flagship know I'm coming, *and what I'm carrying?* As Petrov stewed at the time, the two ships continued on, each one believing that they were being escorted by the other. Nikitin interrupted his thoughts.

"Kapitan, surface contact sighted zero-one-five relative, estimating fifteen miles."

From his chair Petrov used the starboard anchor capstan as a reference point and scanned the horizon with his glasses. There, a dark shape resting on the sharp line between sea and sky. He studied it. Yes, a combatant...but what type?

"Mister Nikitin; Sound action stations."

As the call-to-action stations echoed throughout the ship and his crew rushed to their stations, he remained locked on the object. It turned to present its silhouette.

"Kapitan, lookout reports *Slava* class cruiser zero-one-seven relative, fifteen miles."

Petrov studied the shape. Yes, a *Slava*...must be *Yermolov*. Next to it, he saw another shape that formed a combatant, probably one of the *Udaloys*. They had finally caught up to them.

"Very well, contact him by blinking light. Send him our identification and availability for tasking."

Nikitin and the signalmen complied as Petrov considered leaving *Vitac*. No, not yet.

Petrov's *Helix* raced toward him, and he watched as the pilot flew down the starboard side before turning tight and slowing to a hover as it approached his bow. *He has a message for me*, Petrov thought as the downwash kicked up spray on his bridge windows. With the wipers energized, the bridge team watched the helicopter stabilize over the forecastle and drop a beanbag before the pilot pedal-turned right and accelerated away to set up his landing approach aft. Two sailors moved forward from the superstructure to retrieve it, and minutes later it was delivered to Petrov by Kuzmin.

"Well, well," Petrov said when he finished reading the sighting report. "An *Amerikanskiy* ESM cut on our nose for 200 miles. They also saw a P-8 in the vicinity but do not believe they were spotted by them. Well done to our aviators, Mister Kuzmin, and send this report to the flagship by blinking light."

"Aye, aye, Kapitan," a glum Kuzmin replied.

"Is all in readiness, Yevgeny?" Petrov asked in a hushed tone.

Kuzmin held his gaze. "Yes, Kapitan."

"Very well."

Kuzmin left Petrov alone with his thoughts as he scanned the southern horizon. *The enemy is down there.* He did not know if the Yankees were aware of the Russian presence...but they had to be. If his bucket-of-bolts *Helix* got a sniff, surely their capable *Seahawks* could too. Four hundred miles east of Iceland...Petrov was amazed that they had made it this far. He again scanned the horizon around *Marshal Yermolov*. Two escorts. Where were the others?

From the flagship Petrov observed a blinking light. His signalmen would have it to him shortly, and, while he waited, he wondered what the flagship could see of him at this range. Maybe all they could detect was *Vitac*, but regardless, Petrov assumed that this message was a firing order, *the* firing order. He checked the time: almost midnight. June 18 would be the day. From the depths of his memory it hit him. June 18—*the Feast of St. Constantine, Metropolitan of Kiev and all Rus.* Petrov considered the irony of the date. *We are striking for Kiev and all Rus.*

The message was delivered to him.

```
TAKE STATION 7 ATTACK METHOD C5. REFERENCE HEADING
175, SPEED OF ADVANCE 23. WITH VALID IDENTIFICATION
AND TARGETING INFORMATION EXPECT LAUNCH SEQUENCE 3.
EXPECT TIME HACK FROM FLAGSHIP OVER HF.
```

There it was, Petrov thought. The drills, the discussions, the tests. His entire career at sea for this moment. *War at sea* with the Americans, now, *here!* The fleet would soon send a barrage of missiles south—what would come over the horizon back at them?

Launch sequence three meant Petrov would fire his salvo one minute after the launch time given from the flagship. Another scan of the horizon revealed another combatant, a *Udaloy*. With his orders to station, it was time for him to leave *Vitac*.

"Mister Nikitin, detach and take station seven, attack method C5. Get me there quickly."

Electrified as all the watchstanders were, Nikitin gave the orders, clear and with meaning. Seconds later they felt the deck vibrate beneath their feet as *Admiral Alekseyev's* gas turbines whined at full power, her bronze screws biting into the sea to propel the DDG past *Vitac* and to his station.

Petrov stepped out to the port bridge wing, and, using his arms, sent a semaphore signal to *Vitac's* master...*retire north.* He then saluted the merchant as his ship surged ahead of it and returned inside the pilothouse.

After four days alongside *Vitac*, Petrov and his crew felt it at once. *Freedom,* and as the destroyer rose and fell in the long swells, each man on board also sensed that action was coming, action they had trained for, had dreamed of. All felt it, through the soles of their feet if standing on engine room boilerplate or through the seat of their pants if seated in front of a screen in CIC. Petrov recognized their excitement, their *purpose* of service to the Motherland they loved that sent them south to do battle. The Americans, the British...*whoever* was over that horizon, the Red Banner Northern Fleet—arrayed on the sea such as none had ever seen!—would vanquish them with the giant missiles *Admiral Alekseyev* and the other division combatants carried.

Soon, Russian steel would rip into the thin hull plates of the enemy, tearing off their superstructure and cutting their ships in half. Petrov caught Nikitin and the helmsman trying to hide their faint smiles, anticipating action that they would one day tell their grandchildren about. Kuzmin stood next to the bosun with hands behind his back, his eyes searching one thousand miles ahead as he contemplated the future.

Petrov watched as the fleet units hurried to their stations. *Admiral Alek-seyev's* assigned station was on the left wing, the furthest east as the formation sped south. At this speed, Petrov estimated ten minutes to it. Satisfied with Nikitin's course—and after taking a last look at *Vitac* in his wake—he stepped toward Kuzmin and nodded for them to go below. Resigned, Kuzmin followed him down the ladder.

In silence they walked to Petrov's cabin. Once inside, Petrov closed the door behind them, and Kuzmin's heartbeat increased as he watched his kapitan manipulate the combination to the bulkhead safe. Once they heard the safe *click*, Petrov opened the door, and without looking at Kuzmin, spoke in a whisper.

"Take it."

When Kuzmin didn't move, Petrov snapped his head and looked at him without emotion. "We knew this day could one day come, Yevgeny Sergeevich. We pledged we would do this, and we received a valid order from the Fleet Commander. The *Motherland*...commands you to take it."

As if a prisoner next in line to be executed, Kuzmin stepped to the safe and reached inside, retracting a small key chained to a wooden placard with a female clasp. As Kuzmin stood aside, Petrov reached in to take his key and then attached his male clasp to the clasp on Kuzmin's key. Both men held their ends of the key as Petrov closed the safe door and opened the stateroom door to the passageway.

Each holding their end of the joined keys, they walked aft to a ladder, climbed, and walked forward to CIC. Petrov lifted the quick-opening dog bar, and they entered the darkened space, waiting for a moment as Kuzmin closed the door and dogged it shut behind them. Inside, the radio speaker blared a transmission from the flagship. "Thirty seconds to mark, time 2400."

Conversation stopped when they entered the red-lit compartment, the men realizing at once what this meant as Petrov and Kuzmin shuffled inside while holding their keys. *Nuclear weapons...the kapitan and Mister Kuzmin have the actuation keys!* Under their feet, *Admiral Alekseyev* rolled and pitched on the Norwegian Sea as the steady whine of the gas turbines permeated the space. This was no drill.

"Ten seconds to mark time..."

All remained frozen at their stations as the countdown from the flagship continued. Petrov noticed the wide-eyed Federov near the chair reserved for the kapitan, his lower lip quivering in fear.

"Five, four, three, two one, *mark*, time 2400."

Petrov spoke.

"Men, the Motherland has assigned your kapitan and executive officer a valid order. We will carry it out. Mister Kuzmin, detach and stand before your station."

Kuzmin opened the clasp, and, with his key, stepped to his station next to the air-search radar console. Petrov stepped to his station next to the P-270 control panel.

Inside the dark and chilly space, the HF radio speaker crackled. "Commence attack method C5 at time 0010."

Petrov had to get them back to the mission at hand.

"Watchstanders! Monitor your consoles! Mister Federov, control your watch or *you* will be relieved!"

Breathing through his mouth, Federov gagged a response that Petrov ignored. "Mister Kuzmin, insert your key!" he ordered.

Kuzmin complied, the sailor next to him paralyzed with fear and foreboding.

Petrov inserted his own key, and, like Kuzmin, held it in place as they had done through the many drills they had participated in.

"Mister Kuzmin, on my count...*right detent*. Three, two, one..."

Both men turned their keys 90-degrees right at the same time as their spellbound shipmates held their breath. The special weapon control panels illuminated in front of Petrov and Kuzmin.

As the nuclear-armed *Moskit* held in station 2 woke up, Petrov selected weapon option A, followed by the fuzing: INST. Kuzmin did the same on his panel, then checked the time: 0002. After a short delay, green lights illuminated on the panel, with one amber light also illuminated.

Taking his hand off the key, Petrov turned to Kuzmin. "Mister Kuzmin, I have green light logic, weapon safe."

"I have green light logic, weapon safe, Kapitan," Kuzmin replied.

Satisfied, Petrov raised his voice so all could hear. "Very well, Mister Kuzmin... you may rest at ease as you remain at your station. Inside Combat, this is the kapitan: prepare *Moskit* launch tubes one, two and four in three-missile salvo, minimum spacing. Mister Federov, contact the bridge for time to station."

Fumbling for the sound-powered phone, Federov stammered his kapitan's request, then turned to Petrov. "Five minutes to station, Kapitan Petrov!"

"Very well," Petrov replied as he again checked the time. Once on station, he'd have three minutes to launch.

"Kapitan, may we radiate?" Kuzmin asked.

Petrov considered it for a moment. Every man in Combat wanted to energize their search radars and *see*, despite the risk of detection.

"Not yet!" Petrov answered, all business.

The speaker blared a transmission from a *Helix* belonging to one of the division ships. "Enemy sighted, bearing one seven two, estimating twenty miles from my position...*Burke* class! No—two *Burke* class!"

Petrov did not know how far south the helicopter was, hugging the waves and using its sensors to identify the Americans and relay their finding back. *Arleigh Burke* class! He had boarded one as a midshipman when one of the American destroyers had visited St. Petersburg some twenty years ago. He was astounded by how *clean* the American ship was. And *women* went to sea on it, even the officers! He then thought of the night he met Arina along the same waterfront. Simpler times. *Arina...be well, my love.*

Launch on bearing; just send it downrange and hope that the missile, like a rabid dog, would lock on to one of the American missile destroyers. He would have to depend on the flagship to put his salvo within range. Petrov wanted to be on the bridge *and* in Combat at the same time. *And* on the flagship bridge, *and* his weapons space. His helicopter, the *Katran. Recall it!*

"Mister Federov, recall our helicopter at once. No delay."

Federov stood before the radio console, unsure. A *michman*, annoyed at Federov's never-ending incompetence, punched in the frequency and handed him the R/T handset as an impatient Petrov glared at his *leytenant*.

"*Katran* helicopter...*Katran* helicopter...return to *Admiral Alekseyev* at once. *Katran* helicopter...*Kat*—"

Petrov lunged at Federov and ripped the handset from his grasp. "You *do not* identify this ship name on voice radio! Go below, you are relieved! *Michman*, you have the watch! Contact and recall our bird at once!"

As the *michman* transmitted the recall order, a fearful Federov looked at Kuzmin expectantly. Kuzmin glowered at the man and signaled him with a sharp tilt of his head—*go below!*

Federov fled the space as if he'd been shocked, leaving Petrov to scowl at Kuzmin. *You've failed with him...no more chances!*

The bridge intercom interrupted the tension. *Combat, bridge...we are on station.*

"Very well," the *michman* answered as Petrov nodded his understanding. Kuzmin did not take his eyes off his kapitan.

Combat, bridge...flagship sends cleared to fire on timeline!

"Very well," the *michman* answered back. Without energized radar consoles, each watchstander focused on the red LED symbols of the clock counting down.

Petrov and Kuzmin had held this burden inside of them for days. With reality only minutes away, Petrov considered how his missiles would be integrated with the salvos of six ships in the formation. His missiles would arrive *second* after an initial barrage, followed by smaller terminal attacks that his three *Moskits* would be part of. The missile in tube two, serial number 31917186-S, would arrive second in his three-missile sequence. If it worked, his third missile would not continue to impact—*it would be vaporized.*

Kuzmin thought of how he would be judged by God.

Petrov checked the time: two minutes to launch. One last step.

"Mister Kuzmin, this is the kapitan...activate final arming on my count, acknowledge!"

"Standing by to activate final arming on your count, Kapitan," Petrov's dispirited exec replied.

Kuzmin and Petrov returned their hands to their activation keys. None of the watchstanders could breathe as they did.

"Very well...three, two one, *activate!*"

Both men twisted their keys another 90-degrees right, the amber light on their consoles turning green.

"Mister Kuzmin, this is the Kapitan. I have green light logic, weapon armed, activation key released."

"Kapitan, I have green light logic, weapon armed, activation key released," Kuzmin rasped back, barely able to stand as *Admiral Alekseyev* pitched in smooth rhythm underneath him.

Petrov remained fixed on the LED clock display. At one minute to go, the flagship and others in the formation should have launched their missiles. He punched in the bridge intercom.

"Bridge, Combat...report sightings of formation missile launch."

The response was immediate.

"Combat, Bridge...birds away from the flagship and two others in the division! Heading downrange!"

As per doctrine, Petrov thought. It's happening. June 18. Under his hand. Maybe others in the division, but his for sure.

A dejected Kuzmin shuddered as adrenaline coursed through him, his chest tight, his mouth dry. He could stop it...*he should stop it!* A lunge at Petrov to prevent the launch order, smash his console with a battle lantern, rave hysterically. He had a duty! *To obey!* He was read in—by Admiral Platonov himself! This order was from Moscow. The President! His judgment…his order. How would history judge him—and Petrov—and himself? God would judge him…*I was only following orders.*

Thirty seconds, twenty-nine, twenty-eight. Kuzmin made peace with himself then. An American ship…just like the one he stood on. An American ship—or ships!—would soon die with hundreds of men. Husbands, fathers, sons, brothers, boyfriends…men, such as those who had died horrible deaths on the high seas over the millennia. *These Yankees today would not know, or even feel.* Kuzmin lowered his head and prayed that they would not.

Two meters next to Kuzmin stood Petrov, resolute. Young Sasha would know that his father did his duty to save the Motherland. Arina could handle whatever the future held. Their father and husband was a warrior, no less than a Cossack cavalryman leading a charge into the Crimea.

At fifteen seconds, Petrov, his jaw set as he inhaled through his nose, boomed the order.

"This is the kapitan of *Admiral Alekseyev*! On my order, *for the Motherland*, prepare to launch missiles from tubes one, two, and four!"

"Tubes one, two, and four are in readiness, Kapitan! Doors open!" the *michman* bellowed back. Outside on the weather deck, under the pilothouse, alarm bells sounded, bells heard inside CIC.

"Very well…five, four, three, two, one—*FIRE SALVO!*"

The men turned to the grinning fire control technician, who pulled the console triggers.

Admiral Alekseyev shuddered as the first *Moskit* roared out of tube one, rattling the bridge windows and covering the forward part of the ship in white smoke that soon drifted aft as the ship bounded ahead at full power. They heard men in adjacent spaces cheering as the rumble of the rocket motor subsided. Kuzmin stood like a statue, comprehending, yet as if watching from afar. *Please God, no.*

The second missile tore out of its launch tube and accelerated away, rocket motor echoing across the water. *"For Mother Russia!"* Petrov cried as he pumped his fist, overcome with a crazed bloodlust he did not know he was capable of. "For the brave martyrs of *Moskva*!" another sailor cried out, eliciting cheers.

An involuntary sound came out of Kuzmin that was unfamiliar to him, a stark realization that the die was cast. The sound was a wail more than a whimper, a sob-like bleat that signaled the finality of what was happening, and not caring if anyone heard. Next to him, Petrov beamed like a man possessed, arms clasped around his chest as he balanced himself on the heaving deck. Kuzmin stared at him in disbelief. *Who is this man?*

The final missile in the salvo burst out of tube four and rocketed over the waves to follow the first two to their assigned target as other cruise missiles from the division formation shot ahead of their ships in fiery arcs.

Petrov gave new orders. *"Michman,* radiate the air and surface search radars. Contact our helicopter—signal, *expedite!"*

As CIC returned to order, dozens of Russian cruise missiles sped south, their terminal guidance radars seeking prey as they climbed through the overcast into clear air under radiant midnight sun. The historic naval action was one for the ages, but this action and this date would be remembered by humanity forever.

Like the other world-changing action from some 2,000 years earlier, Russia had just crossed another Rubicon.

Serial number 31917186-S, NATO codenamed SS-N-22 *Sunburn,* followed its lead missile as they integrated with missiles fired from the other division ships toward a point roughly 100 miles south of the Russian SAG. The four ramjets attached to the five-ton missile held it at Mach 2.6 as it reentered the low ceiling on its flat trajectory, descending to a cruising altitude of 20 meters.

Four minutes after launch, the active terminal radar began to sweep, and within seconds captured a surface contact three degrees right of its nose. The missile eased right to center the contact as it descended to 7 meters over the waves. Ahead, two fiery plumes lifted from the surface contact's forward hull as it transited right to left in front of 31917186-S. Two more lifted, each targeted at a large salvo of cruise missiles in the terminal phase of flight along a spectrum of arrival within 120 degrees of the contact's port side.

With 25 seconds to impact—and unseen and unknown to 31917186-S—the surface contact engaged the Russian missiles ahead of it with a combination of rounds from the Close-in Weapon System aft of the aftermost stack and a self-defense laser, knocking down incoming weapons as the frantic operators in the Combat Information Center prioritized the multiple incoming contacts on their screens. Dense clouds of chaff trailed the ship as the swarm of *"vampires"* bore in, and unseen waves of RF energy permeated the air.

Ahead of 31917186-S as it ripped over the waves, cruise missiles only thousands of feet from the surface contact exploded once engaged by the contact's defenses, showering the sea with swaths of debris that pointed to—and in some cases hit—the contact. The SPY-1 fire control system phased array aft of the surface contact's port bridge wing was riddled with several pieces of supersonic debris, rendering it inoperative.

As fire control technicians and operations specialists reacted by human reflex to a piece of flaming debris that had punctured the port bulkhead of the surface contact's CIC, missile 31917186-S entered the contact just above the main deck adjacent to the forward marine gas turbine stack of the contact, detonating as it contacted the thin steel plate.

The surface contact—USS *Lloyd Childers*, an American guided missile destroyer with a crew of 363 men and women—was vaporized by the equivalent of 115 kilotons of TNT. The blast—over five times that of Nagasaki—cleared the sky of the low overcast layer some 10 miles around it as the flash dome transformed from a giant luminescent bulb to a growing mushroom cloud that rose into the sunlit sky. Her MH-60 *Romeo* helicopter, with a crew of four, was airborne prosecuting a subsurface contact by laying a buoy field five miles east of the blast. After experiencing a blinding flash and before the aviators and aircrewmen could comment on it, the aircraft was crushed by the shock wave, its crew knocked unconscious and then killed when the mangled fuselage slammed into the ocean at over 100 knots.

On the horizon twelve miles to the southeast, two officers and one sailor on USS *Michael Estocin's* bridge watch were blinded by the explosion as the DDG raced to the aid of her sister under attack. In CIC, operations specialists listened to *Childers* fight in what were her last moments before a shock wave shook *Estocin* as she absorbed it head on, blowing out two bridge windows, damaging the forward SPY-1 arrays, knocking the SPG-62 fire control radar off its track, and frying or destroying numerous radio antennas on the yardarms. As his corpsmen tended to the wounded and without any radios, the captain ordered his hangared MH-60R airborne to deliver the news to the coalition ships to the south; USS *Lloyd Childers* was nuked and no word of survivors, with USS *Michael Estocin* combat ineffective and retiring south.

His detachment pilot looked at him in disbelief.

"Yes, *nuked*," the captain snarled at the still-shocked lieutenant. "And we may be next. Get airborne, *right fucking now*, and run south to drop a bean-bag message on the first ship you see. Tell them.

"*Tell everyone!*"

CHAPTER 35

USS *VALLEY FORGE*, 0030 JUNE 18, 2024

Nobody in flag plot observed him as Wilson entered TFCC from the aft door and quietly sat in a metal chair next to Smoke on the raised platform of the red-lit space. Tense watchstanders—wearing jackets or pull-over sweaters to ward off the chill of the electronics cooling—buzzed among themselves as they tried to analyze the surprise missile attack on the DDGs up north. Their four consoles monitored information from numerous sources into flag plot to allow Wilson and his staff to direct the actions of the Strike Group ships and aircraft. Wilson tried to pick up the action from the urgent radio transmissions coming in on the overhead speaker. On the forward bulkhead, two large flatscreens displayed linked information from the E-2 and an AWACS that orbited over Iceland. On the Common Operational Picture screen, linked symbols showed a strike of twelve *Rhinos* accompanied by two EA-18G *Growlers* and three F-35B's from *Tinian* headed toward the LRASM launch window of the last known vanguard of the Russian surface action group. The second screen displayed the status of a sonobuoy field that his MH-60 *Romeos* were working northwest of the Faroe Islands.

Wilson's eyes went at once to the common operational picture screen. The COP showed merchant traffic had all but evaporated from coastal Norway to the North Sea to Iceland, with only one defiant fishing trawler left in the Denmark Strait. Air traffic avoided the area as well, with transoceanic traffic from Scandinavia and the Middle East crossing no further north than the Western Isles off Scotland. From his position south of Iceland, Wilson had, for the most part, an unobstructed battlespace to his north with operational control of five Norwegian, British, and French surface combatants working in concert with two of his DDGs, *Lloyd Childers* and *Michael Estocin*. Hundreds of miles south, the CVW-4 strike package converged on the last reported Russian position.

The strike *had* to go; it was Wilson's one shot to overwhelm the Russian SAG with all the LRASMs *Valley Forge* held in her magazine. Knocking out the missile shooters would allow his *Romeos* and P-8's flying from the UK and Canada to operate unmolested as they prosecuted the Russian boomers and attack boats that could be entering the gap now. Wilson and the coalition concentrated their assets to close the widest door for the Russians to break through, the 300 miles of open water from the Faroes to Iceland. Each *Super Hornet* striker carried two LRASMs, but only one of the 2,400-pound weapons could be recovered back aboard the carrier.

The lieutenant monitoring the link console sang out. "Tracks lost on *Lloyd Childers* and *Estocin.*"

Smoke glanced at the link picture, then noticed Wilson next to him. "Sir, the Russians just launched a large salvo of missiles from multiple ships and two bombers that we've tracked for the last hour. Looks like they targeted those guys."

Wilson pulled on his chin as he studied the screen in acknowledgement. Smoke continued.

"Admiral, *Childers* with the laser weapon is the northernmost asset, acting with *Estocin* as a goalkeeper for their *Romeos* and the coalition ships to work the ASW problem. They are within visual sight."

"How'd the Russians get into a launch position?" Wilson asked.

"Sir, it looks like they turned and sprinted south/southeast once they got a tipper on our task group. We didn't have a scouting flight to cover it, and it was during a seam of AWACS coverage."

Just then, an ashen Commodore Braud joined them from his watch station in Combat.

"Bert, what's up?" Wilson asked.

"Admiral, *Childers* and *Estocin* have been hit."

Wilson turned back to the screen as he waited for Braud to continue. *The first report is always wrong.*

"Sir, the Russians swarmed them with *vampires* at ranges we haven't seen before. Our goalkeepers were operating on the edge of their range rings as we are prosecuting what we think are two boats west of the Faroes."

"How many missiles, do you think?"

"Roughly fifty, sir, in a coordinated attack."

Wilson shook his head in amazement. His surface ships were out-sticked by the Russians in range, and his two missile shooters up there—despite their capability to include a defensive laser aboard *Childers*—would have their hands full with that number of missiles inbound.

"What kind, do you think?"

"*Onyx* sir, they shot at range, and probably some *Sunburns* as well."

Wilson nodded again. "All Mach 2, plus…were they close enough for *Sunburn?*"

An ashamed Braud nodded. "Yes, sir, we believe so."

As Wilson struggled with the news, Braud added.

"We fucked up, sir."

Wilson did not react as he considered this news. The fog of war and scenarios none had ever trained for, including him.

Shane then stepped out of SUPPLOT, her worried eyes locked on Wilson as she approached. *Uh-oh.*

"Admiral...airliners are talking about a flash and large cloud formed on the horizon far to the north of their flight paths."

Wilson knew it at once. *They used a nuke.* He studied the tracks of *Childers* and *Estocin*, frozen on the COP at their last reported position.

"Extrapolate the possible launch range from these last-known positions. Smoke, how much on-station time does the package have to engage the Russians missile shooters?"

"Sir, thirty minutes. Maybe we could squeeze forty minutes. We could keep a division out there an hour if we run a dedicated tanker to them, and we can have one airborne in thirty minutes."

Both men knew that would mean two dozen now-priceless LRASMs jettisoned safe into the sea, silver bullets he could not waste.

"And sir, we'll lose waves of missiles to overwhelm them—like they've done to us."

Wilson nodded. "Shane...get a transcript of the airline pilot voice chatter. Get it to me and send to the beach."

"Yes, sir."

"Where's Olive?" Wilson asked.

"She's in Combat, sir," Smoke replied.

The phone buzzed and Smoke answered.

"Flag plot, Captain Offenhausen."

Wilson waited as Smoke said, "Yes, sir." *Who is he saying* yes, sir *to?*

Smoke handed the receiver to Wilson. "It's Admiral Coleman, sir."

Surprised, Wilson took the receiver. Coleman, the fleet commander, orbiting south of Iceland in an E-6 command plane. "Admiral Wilson, sir."

"Jim, Warren Coleman...*Childers* and *Estocin* just got nuked."

Wilson exhaled as Coleman let him absorb the news. *Confirmation* and from credible higher authority. After a few seconds, Coleman continued.

"Jim...get out of there. *Move south.*"

Quick on his feet, Wilson took a moment to answer. "Admiral, we have a strike package airborne, and soon we expect they'll be in a position to launch and pick some of these guys off, and..."

Coleman wasn't having it. "No, Jim. Both of us are paid to make smart decisions. We need to run, regroup and assess, and plan our next move. Recall your planes and move everything south. The Brits and French are recalling their forces."

"Admiral, if I recall them, we jettison about a dozen LRASM in the water...I can't bring them all back."

"Why not?" the submariner snapped, impatient.

"Max weight for a carrier arrestment, sir, and I'm not going to waive the restriction, especially in these seas."

Coleman was silent for a moment before he answered. "Then we'll get you more. I'm sorry, but the world just changed."

Dismayed, Wilson could only comply. "Yes, sir." With Coleman listening, Wilson turned to Smoke. "Recall the strikers now. Recall. Jettison the missiles safe and buster back. Do it."

Incredulous, Smoke could only nod and motion his assistant to contact CIC to recall them. The strike was off, only 45 minutes away from an expected launch position.

Wilson went back to Coleman. "Sir, how do we *know* it's a nuke?"

"The AWACS crew some three hundred miles away saw the flash; the pilot is experiencing flash blindness and co-pilot is bringing the jet back. And *I* saw it from our position south of Iceland, a mushroom cloud to the northwest. Are you monitoring the airlines chatter?"

"Yes, sir," Wilson said, still trying to fathom what had taken place with the flimsy evidence, but knowing that air sniffers would be deployed soon.

"It looks and sounds like a duck, Jim, so we're regrouping to live and fight another day. Okay, I've got Washington, Norfolk, Colorado Springs and Brussels all wanting their hand held—and I want *my* hand held—but get your people aboard and head south until I tell you to stop. I'll coordinate refueling. Gotta go, out here..."

"Sir, *what about my DDGs?*" Wilson interjected before Coleman could hang up.

"We're trying to find that out ourselves. Will be in touch, Jim. Out."

CHAPTER 36

Around the world, first millions, and then *billions* of human beings froze when they learned of the news from the North Atlantic, none of them ever forgetting where they were when they heard it.

A *nuclear weapon*—exploded in naval warfare in the North Atlantic between the continents. Receiving the news in the early morning darkness, Europeans woke up family and friends to tell them, and throughout the rest of the world, the news spread at lightning speed.

Learning of it late at night on June 17 as tens of millions of Americans tuned into the evening news, the Washington government establishment absorbed the report in a state of shock. The cabinet and congress were all notified, and the Secretaries of Defense, State, Energy, and Transportation, along with the administration National Security Team, rushed to the situation room with the President and Vice President for what all knew would be days of debate, planning, and reassurance to the nation and the world. Websites crashed and phones rang off the hook all over Capitol Hill as fearful Americans looked to their government for answers.

Frantic citizens took to their automobiles and descended on the open-all-night big-box stores, the grocery stores, convenience stores, and gas stations to stock up and fill up, cleaning them out as they filled carts that many did not even pay for as they rushed the doors, the outnumbered employees not even trying to stop them. Before dawn on the 18th, the roads along the Eastern Seaboard of the United States were clogged with travelers who moved south and west to rural America, away from the big cities, especially the Washington Capitol Region, their vehicles filled with staples and family heirlooms in a desperate attempt to escape from the nuclear Armageddon that would surely follow. Preppers with property in the countryside took their sleeping kids out of their beds, and with their go-bags and weapons, loaded them in minivans, abandoning suburban neighborhoods to their fate, while city dwellers who knew they lived in ground-zero looked to them as their only option as society broke down with breathtaking speed.

In Moscow, foreign ministry officials prepared for an army of international reporters that stormed the Kremlin in the twilight of early morning, each of them risking their freedom to demand answers. A perfectly coifed and made-up spokeswoman was ready for them:

> *The Russian Federation denies responsibility or involvement for the incident that has occurred in the North Atlantic Ocean, but we must point to the repeated provocations of the West and NATO that have resulted in the confrontations and illegal actions against our forces in international waters and airspace. The Russian Federation is free to conduct naval maneuvers at any time we wish, no different than that of Western militaries who, for decades, have routinely conducted offensive military demonstrations in waters belonging to us and our allies. We join with the international community in regretting the reported loss of life from such a needless and undeclared escalation of hostilities, but we also demand an end to the military encirclement of the Russian Federation, and end to the economic sanctions that starve our citizens and are themselves an act of war, and an end to the Western military support of a break-away republic that, under its fascist regime, is an existential threat to the Russian Federation.*

At STRATCOM in Omaha, NORTHCOM in Colorado Springs, INDOPA-COM in Honolulu, and Fleet Forces Command in Norfolk, staff officers rushed to work as many of their families fled to rural areas without them, all knowing that they were targeted by Russian intercontinental and submarine launched ballistic missiles. Personnel at Barksdale, Dyess, Ellsworth, Minot, Offutt, and Whiteman Air Force Bases, plus Vandenberg Space Force Base, were recalled to set an immediate strategic alert posture, as Navy vessels that could get underway on short notice in New London, Norfolk, Mayport, San Diego, Bremerton, Pearl Harbor—and especially Kings Bay and Bangor—put to sea on the next tide, joining naval forces already underway to avoid a follow-on strike...and potentially deliver a response.

The world, tense if not terrified, held its breath.

With the aircraft of Air Wing Four chocked and chained, *Valley Forge* and her strike group escorts moved southwest through moderate seas in a low mist. Through the gloom the assault ship *Tinian* plowed through the swells in company with the carrier as the nine-ship task force made twenty knots. Hundreds of miles ahead, the oilers USNS *Perdido* and USNS *Gene Cernan* raced to meet them for an assigned rendezvous in ten hours. As his ships took turns alongside, Wilson and his pick-up team of combatants would have time to regroup and respond to the next steps from Admiral Coleman once Washington decided on a course of action.

USS *Estocin*, damaged and radiated by the blast, headed to Faslane, Scotland with a Royal Navy escort for the ship to be surveyed and the crew treated. Eyewitness accounts of the Russian missile salvo told of an overwhelming and well-timed attack on USS *Lloyd Childers*, one the ship valiantly fought until it succumbed to an unknown missile type. Could the missile have detonated on a magazine? While possible, analysts discounted that theory. The guided-missile destroyer *Lloyd Childers* was *gone*—without a trace—with 367 missing and presumed dead, leaving only a massive mushroom cloud that could not have been produced had all the ordnance inside her cooked off at the same time. Sniffer aircraft deployed from the United States and Great Britain would arrive at the area within hours to confirm it. Meanwhile, a *Virginia* class attack boat had scored twice, reporting two Russian combatants sunk northeast of Iceland.

As Wilson studied the war plans Smoke and Shane had brought to him from their files, Olive knocked on his stateroom door.

"Come in," Wilson said, loud enough to be heard.

Olive poked her head inside, then entered.

"Hey, glad you're here. Have a seat."

Expressionless as usual, Olive took a seat on the couch.

"So CAG…how is Air Wing Four doing?"

"Doing okay, considering. All the strikers saw it, too far away to be blinded, thank God. They knew what it was right off."

Wilson waited for more.

"The range is, 'let's get those SOBs now' to 'is my family going to be okay?' to 'I didn't sign up for this.' The aviators and most of the chiefs are in the first group."

"Is your chaplain making the rounds?"

"Oh, yes…had a visit with him myself."

Wilson studied Olive as she looked away, then back at him.

"When was the last time you heard from Chris?" he asked.

"Before we went River City…what…four days ago?"

"What's the latest with little Margaret?"

"Enjoying her summer break…fourth grade next year."

"Hard to believe," Wilson said as a smile formed on his lips, thinking of Derrick and Brittany during those days, long ago now.

Olive smiled as she again looked away, missing her husband and daughter, and contemplating the dark future ahead of them…and her air wing…and humanity. She turned back to Wilson.

"You know, when we got the message from Admiral Johnson…nuclear war possible…I was skeptical. It's…it's just too unthinkable that they would do this, knowing they are going to receive a response."

"Maybe they don't think we will," Wilson said.

"Oh, we will," Olive answered, pursing her lips as she nodded to herself. Wilson changed the subject.

"You heard we bagged two Russian ships?"

Olive nodded. "Yep…and maybe the guy that triggered Armageddon."

"Moscow triggered it, but do you think it's going to go to that?"

The CAG rubbed her eyes before answering. "Yes, I do. We have to respond, and probably with a bigger bomb than they used. All that *mutually assured destruction* talk in the War College seems quaint now, doesn't it? Deterrence has failed, and I'm sure they are already chanting *Remember the Childers!* in the streets. And I would too. People will demand retribution, and we must send a message back. We have no choice."

Wilson nodded, then asked, "What would you do?"

"If I were you?"

"No, the President."

Olive considered it for a moment. "I'm not sure the President—any President—has thought this scenario through like we would, but…sinking every ship in their navy comes to mind, Atlantic and Pacific. Tell them we're going to do it, then do it."

"Looks like the bubbleheads are taking it for action," Wilson said.

"Yeah, get some," Olive responded as she shook her head in disgust. "Maybe Weed has an idea."

The conversation paused as they each considered the ramifications of such an action. Would the intended message be understood or misconstrued? Both sides faced the strong chance of miscalculation of enemy intent. The fog of war—similar to the mist that enveloped the strike group at the moment—could lead to overreaction and a strategic exchange. Wilson studied her for a moment. Smooth and steady Olive…she could break like any of them.

They heard two raps at the door, and Weed poked his head inside. Wilson motioned him in.

"Mister Hopper. Our own strike group political advisor; please join us. We were just talking about you."

A somber Weed entered. "Just heard." He pulled out a seat at the table and sat.

Wilson contemplated his friend. "Thoughts?"

Weed exhaled. "We have to respond."

"In kind?"

"No, I think more."

"A city with a ballistic missile?"

"They'd see it coming and launch a counterstrike of dozens. No, a bomber… which they would see coming out of our bomber bases. They have spies, or any number of Americans who would camp outside Knob Noster, Missouri and tip them off every time a B-2 got airborne."

"A city? Moscow?"

'No, that's Armageddon, but something that hurts. Their sub base at Polyarny comes to mind. Isolated and sparsely populated. Maybe an Arctic radar site along the Kara Sea near their oil rigs; that would freak them out. But three hundred and sixty some Americans are dead. We have to respond, and I think on land."

Olive spoke next. "Why not sink every ship in their navy and tell them we're going to do it? Then do it. They can fight or they can surrender and we'll take the crew off, but their ships are going down."

Wilson watched the exchange as Weed answered her.

"Reasonable…and proportional…but not the crew part. Find them and sink them where they are. Americans will want those deaths avenged."

"And justice must be swift," Wilson added. "Not an ICBM from Wyoming swift, but I think within a number of days. Ten days? Wonder what the Russians will do if we do nothing for a while."

"Evacuate their cities as I'm sure we're doing," Olive said.

Weed nodded. "We are. I just saw Shane and she told me. Also riots in London and Paris, demanding the Brits and French stand down."

Olive shook her head but said nothing as she studied the bulkhead, thinking of her little girl in Virginia Beach. Wilson broke the silence.

"Look, we're going to refuel and regroup tonight as we wait for tasking, which we'll probably get soon. I've directed Huey to continue south into the shipping lanes and summertime darkness. Mark and Smoke are working to reload us with as much as Norfolk can send us. With us and *Tinian* full up, I believe we'll be back at it tomorrow with the air wing striking them from long range. My sense is that they are going to retreat back to the Kola Peninsula. Just hope they can get some LRASMs to us."

"We've got plenty of SLAMs and *Harpoons*," Olive said, then added, "and we can still stay outside of any known threat."

"Yep…have the planning teams plan some options with them and everything else we've got in the magazines."

"They are now, sir…should have something to you in a few hours."

"Great…thanks."

"Roger that, sir," Olive replied.

"And Weed," Flip said as he turned to him. "What can the Council for Naval Studies do for Strike Group Eighteen in our hour of need?"

"Well, if Shane can help me with connectivity, maybe I can reach back to Norfolk and get some studies or papers on a notional nuclear war at sea."

"Yes, doctrine for us to deviate from," Wilson quipped.

"Exactly. Crisis management is our Navy's greatest strength, and the enemy knows it. Who knows how the crazy Americans will respond."

Wilson nodded. "Concur…let them twist for a while. Meanwhile, I've got some letters to write. Did either of you meet the CO of *Lloyd Childers*?"

Both shook their heads no.

"He heloed over here when they joined us for a meeting with Bert. Upbeat guy, smiling; he looked like a damn lieutenant."

No one spoke as they contemplated the loss of so many, mourning them despite not knowing them.

"Okay, I've got some writing to do. Both of you please join me for dinner."

"Thanks, sir. What's for dinner tonight?" Olive asked.

"Filet mignon, I'm told."

Weed smiled to himself and shook his head. "Eve-of-nuclear-combat dinner?"

"You may decline the invitation if you wish," Wilson said with a grin.

"No, I'll be there! Maybe that's standard flag officer fare around here. No lobster?"

"Shall I ask?" Wilson said, playing along.

"No, I'm good!"

Wilson glanced at Olive, who ignored them with her eyes on the bulkhead, her mind thousands of miles away.

Chapter 37

USS *Valley Forge*, North Atlantic, 1900 June 18, 2024

Two span-wire refueling rigs that connected *Valley Forge* to USNS *Perdido* pumped aviation fuel from the oiler to the carrier as one MH-60 *Sierra* lifted pallets of stores from *Perdido's* flight deck to the carrier's fantail in a familiar pattern. USS *Manila Bay* maintained position on the replenishment oiler's starboard side as she took on fuel and lube oil. Two miles to the west, the dry cargo ship USNS *Gene Cernan* transferred pallets of stores to a strike group guided missile destroyer via highline as another *Sierra* transferred ammo pallets from her to the carrier on a hoist. The ships had been alongside for hours, and behind *Valley Forge* steamed *Tinian*, her narrow flight deck crammed with F-35Bs as she waited her turn to fuel.

Seated next to Olive, Weed dug into the cheesecake the culinary specialist served to all at the admiral's table. Wilson turned to the young sailor.

"My compliments, Petty Officer Shugart. Excellent meal," Wilson said as he lifted his coffee cup. All at the table murmured their concurrence.

"Thank you, admiral," the proud sailor replied, basking in the attention.

At the table with Olive and Weed were Wilson's available staff officers, including Mark, Smoke, and Shane. Skweez was in TFCC monitoring the communications from the E-6 orbiting south of Iceland to maintain line-of-sight. In the eighteen hours since the nuclear detonation, Washington had set DEFCON 2, not set since the Cuban Missile Crisis some sixty years earlier. With the *event*, DEFCON 1 could have been set, but the Americans did not want to go straight to the highest level, avoiding a Russian nuclear overreaction and increasing allied nation unease. While Western nations condemned the Russians in the strongest terms, most of Africa and Asia remained silent, with the exceptions of Iran and North Korea...to the surprise of no one.

At that moment, the routine underway replenishment formation in the middle of the North Atlantic was one of the few untroubled human activities on Earth. Trans-Atlantic air travel had ceased, and with it the HAVE SHARP communications that could burst transmit large files of data. Hundreds of millions of workers in Europe and North America had called in sick, either hunkering down at home or continuing to clean out what was left inside retail stores. Most gas stations on the continents had already run out of gas, the tanker trucks themselves not coming to restock underground tanks pumped dry within hours. Refugees by the millions continued to flock to the continental interiors, away from the cities and away from critical infrastructure.

In the United States, thousands upon thousands of campers pulled their trailers onto available dirt roads and set up camp, unsure of how long they would need to, and praying to survive the first exchange. Urban and suburban neighbors who had never spoken a sentence to one another suddenly became friends and contemplated what would come, while local churches and synagogues were jammed at all hours with the newly faithful.

Others knew the truth: society would devolve into factions and be at each other's throats in a matter of days—a small number of days. The networks continued reporting news but with reduced staff as many of them had fled. Without an audience—and with no one believing what was reported anyhow—they saw little point in staying, as did utilities workers, supply-chain workers, corporate farmers, and many, many more.

The men and women of CSG-18—those not on watch—met in their berthing spaces and discussed their future. Several had friends on *Lloyd Childers*, but the sudden and violent loss—*the ship utterly gone!*—weighed on all. *What will the heavies do now?* Was *Childers'* loss—and their own potential end-of-life within hours—worth it? Huey and Olive had their work cut out for them, as did all the ship captains...and most of all Wilson. In an hour he would sit for a videotape message to his strike group ships, and later talk directly to the crew of *Valley Forge* on the 1MC, still not sure of what he would say.

Skweez burst through the door leading to TFCC.

"Admiral, an *Osprey* is inbound sir."

Wilson looked puzzled. "I thought we were done flying for the night?"

"It just showed up sir, not one of ours...and probably from Keflavik. It's squawking friendly and is talking to Strike. Asking for Charlie on arrival...we think it's a message or a VIP delivering a message, sir."

Wilson glanced at the PLAT screen over the scullery door. "The angle looks clear—if they are ID'ed friendly, let's recover them. What's the range?"

"Inside fifty miles, sir. Will be here in about five minutes."

Wilson looked at Mark. "What's your take?"

"Something or someone important, sir."

Wilson nodded.

"Concur...okay, I believe our evening plans just changed. Mark, get your float coat and let's meet at the Admiral's hatch. Skweez, stay with me. CAG and Weed—Mister Hopper—please finish your cake and then join me in the War Room. We'll be back shortly with something big—or not."

The room broke up as the staff went to their stations. Wilson ducked inside his stateroom to retrieve his float coat and cranial. *An unscheduled Navy* Osprey *from the beach.* He and Mark met in the passageway and with Mark leading, went up one deck into the island and lifted the dog bar to a hatch that opened to the flight deck.

The big rotors of the CMV-22 *Osprey* whirred as the aircraft slid over the carrier's port side as the pilots followed the orders of the yellow-shirt who signaled them to lower and land. Blue shirts with chains draped over their shoulders ran under the heavy rotor wash to chock and chain the tilt-rotor as the loading ramp aft was lowered. In seconds, Wilson noted khaki legs with black shoes descending it. *Yep.*

Amid the kerosene-scented turbulence of the spinning rotors above him, Vice Admiral Warren Coleman stepped off the ramp and headed to the island with three staff officers following. Wilson waited with Mark and Skweez. The surprise visit of COMSECONDFLEET was less of a surprise now. The old man himself would deliver to Wilson—a younger old man—his commanders' intent. As Coleman exited the rotor arc, Wilson stepped toward him.

Shouting to be heard, Wilson extended his hand. "Welcome aboard, sir!"

"Thanks, Jim, we've got work to do," Coleman replied, and with Wilson leading the way, they entered the island and went below to the flag spaces.

Inside Wilson's flag spaces, the fleet commander doffed his float coat, as did his staff. Skweez collected the items from the admiral, two captains, and Coleman's aide as the culinary specialist brought out a cheese plate and glasses of water. After Wilson led everyone into the War Room and made introductions, Coleman got down to business.

"Ladies and gentlemen, Washington is evaluating response options for what happened last night, and the one I'm about to discuss involves you. The nuclear threshold has been crossed, and one option—of many—is to respond in kind."

Coleman stopped as he spied Weed seated along the bulkhead.

"Who's he?"

Wilson answered him. "Sir, that's retired Captain Mike Hopper. He's with us from the Council for Navy Studies."

Coleman remained doubtful. "Are we cleared Top Secret?"

"We are, sir."

Weed remained expressionless as Coleman studied him. Satisfied—or unwilling to delay any longer—the submariner continued.

"Options: We can blow a *Udaloy* out of the water and kill roughly the same numbers in crew. We've got conventional munitions to do that, and they are *nasty*. But they are conventional...the Russians obviously aren't afraid of them, and the goal of our response is to dissuade/deter them from any more nuclear events. So, an option is to respond with a nuclear weapon, but which one? Bombers with gravity bombs are an option, but we've gotta think they have people outside our bomber bases and probably with sniffers. If we do launch a bomber strike, we telegraph our punch and incentivize them to act before we arrive. Missiles are another option, but if they see a missile or two climbing over the pole, they have only moments to act and I'm convinced they will, with a 'first-strike' counterstrike which will cause *us* to escalate, followed by the mutually assured destruction scenario. Same with submarine-launched missiles from the boomers, with the added wrinkle that they won't know if they're American, British, or French. They could involve those allies in a counterattack that would soon escalate, and the Brits have already told us *don't even think about it.* So, if we launch bombers or missiles from our strategic triad, they are tipped off and they are scared and they react. They overreact. We overreact. Mutual destruction."

All were riveted on Coleman, and Wilson expected his next option would involve them.

"We want an option that forces them to react to as we are reacting, one that hits them hard...but not *too* hard, one that is in kind and can deliver the limited message we want delivered. An option that passes for proportionality, if you can call it that. *You guys* let the genie out of the bottle, *you* fucked up, and we are avenging our sailors and letting you know that we are even, and you can stop the escalation—or not. We are on a hair trigger to DEFCON One and an exchange, and they need to know that we are serious. It must be nuclear, and it must be limited."

Wilson and the others waited.

"A manned nuclear option, recallable...from this ship."

After an uneasy silence, Wilson spoke.

"Admiral...we don't have that capability."

"I know...and I was surprised to learn it, actually. Funny what I've learned or been disabused of in the past eighteen hours. One thing I once thought is that an airplane is an airplane and a carrier-based fighter is a carrier-based fighter, and I've learned that's not necessarily true. What I learned is that your *Super Hornet* fighters cannot deliver a nuclear weapon."

"That's correct, sir, unless there is something I—we—don't know about. And even if our jets had that capability, we don't have aircrews trained in the delivery of these things."

"Correct on all counts, Admiral Wilson. So we are going to send you airplanes that can deliver them: FA-18 *Hornets*."

Doubting, Wilson thought Coleman was mistaken. "*Super Hornets*, sir?"

"No. FA-18 *Hornets* that we used to fly...I imagine that all of you aviators did in the last decades. They have the required wiring because they were built during the Cold War, when this was a much bigger deal. After the Soviet Union dissolved in 1991 and the Cold War ended, we took this tactical capability off our carriers and the rest of our fleet and got out of this business."

Wilson remained unconvinced. "Sir, our legacy *Hornets* haven't been operating in the fleet in what, Olive, five years?

"Sounds about right," she said before she caught herself. "But the Marines have been flying them, as have the reserves."

"Whatever," Coleman said. "You can expect two FA-18 *Hornets* to fly to you here in the next 48 hours. You can also expect an air-dropped tactical nuke to be flown out here too. It's an Air Force bomb, and an arming crew will accompany it. And a security team."

Wilson grew uncomfortable at the growing number of new requirements— not to mention who had custody of the airplanes and weapon.

"Admiral, the devil is always in the details. We don't have parts for the older *Hornets* aboard, and airplanes break with regularity. Who has custody of them? Who has custody of the weapon, when and where will it be loaded, how is security maintained, who gives the final launch order? How is it released? What is the target? That will determine our launch position. Who recalls the aircraft if it comes to that? And my first question...who is going to fly these jets on such a mission? You said two jets and one bomb?"

"Jim, I do not have ready answers to your questions, but here goes. One bomb, one mission to a target to-be-determined, but expect the Kola Peninsula. Two airplanes, and if one breaks down, you have a spare. Air Force loading and security teams. We have yet to devise the launch authentication procedure, but we'll have it in less than 24 hours and it will be flown out here and delivered to you personally. With that guidance, do what you must."

"Admiral Coleman, that's great...but I foresee a challenge."

Coleman gave Wilson a knowing look. "Just one? Go ahead."

"An Air Force security team unfamiliar with us, the ship, and this environment will generate friction. How about SEALs or marines, *senior* marines, who can provide all the security we need while speaking our language?"

"The Air Force insists that they control the weapon until it's launched. I hear you, but it's going to be a fight. They want to send a colonel to oversee the operation."

Wilson shook his head. "Sir, how many cooks do you or Washington want in this kitchen? A subject-matter expert to advise is fine, and please send that person out here, but unity of command is my concern. When disagreements arise, somebody must rule on them and that should be the embarked flag officer. Will you fight it, sir?"

"I'll fight it…what else?"

"Who's going to fly the jet on the mission? Is the pilot carrier-qualled and trained in dropping this thing? What kind of delivery? What kind of support package, if any? Overflight rights. Rules of engagement. Go/no-go criteria. Recall procedures. Many, many more questions, sir."

Coleman nodded his understanding.

"The pilots are TOPGUN instructors from Fallon, and the planes belong to TOPGUN. The plan is to take off tomorrow night, in-flight refuel over the continental U.S., and land in Virginia Beach. The airplanes will be hangared out of sight for the day, then take off at night—refuel over the Atlantic—and arrive here at night. Regarding any waivers: it's waived by me; do what you must, and I'll back you. Consider the airplanes yours and the pilots yours. At the same time, we'll fly the weapon and expertise out here on *Ospreys*, and they'll just show up, so be ready and I'll fight the security fight with the Air Force. What we need is a viable and covert option that surprises the Russians, hits them proportionally, and makes them rethink with time, not react in minutes. I'll give you wide latitude to do what it takes to make this happen when this gets called away, and it's going to get called away."

Wilson nodded. "Yes, sir." All at the table remained silent.

"And Admiral, I am leaving Commander Chuck Maynard—an aviator on my staff—here as my liaison. Use him as you wish, please, and consider him your personal manservant." Maynard, sitting next to Coleman, smiled.

Wilson also smiled. "Thank you, sir."

"Don't mention it. Now that *Osprey* I see on your little TV screen is waiting for me, so I'm heading back now, but before I do, let's talk about our current fight. We need to keep attriting them. Our P-8s with the Brits are doing great work in the gap—they bagged a *Delta* boat this morning—but the Russian tactic is to make us fight their surface action group that we believe most of their boats are hiding under…the boomer got too far ahead of them and was caught. After you finish refueling, turn around and head back where you were this morning. You now have OPCON of the tanker and stores ship. Bring them with you as far as you can and fill up with all they have aboard. We are flying LRASMs to Kef and you'll get the first batch tomorrow on an *Osprey*. Keep *Tinian* with you and use their jets. Keep *Manila Bay* in shotgun with you and the DDGs you need to defend yourself, but send the extra combatants north to fight the ASW fight. I've got control of the attack boats and you'll be hearing from them soon; they've probably bagged a Russian surface combatant since I've left the beach. You sink ships with missiles and submarines with your helos. And…this ship cannot—*cannot*—be lost. Losing *Tinian* would be bad, but losing this carrier is unacceptable. Attrite them but stay out of their reach. Clear?"

"Yes, sir," Wilson said, and then addressed the elephant in the room.

"Admiral, who do I report to?"

Coleman exhaled as he considered how to answer.

"You are still in the NAVEUR area of responsibility…but you are soon coming to mine under NORTHCOM, and if this mission that we discussed goes, it will be under *NORTHCOM*, not EUCOM or NATO. Not coalition. It will be *us* if it happens…and I think it's going to happen."

Wilson needed more. "Sir, do you see us chopping to your AOR in hours or days? And…does Admiral Buffington know you are here?"

"First answer—within 48 hours. Second, he does not, and he *will* not. You have your brain trust here—that's it. NORTHCOM will tell Admiral Buffington when you come to us, and there will be no arguments from him; SECDEF himself will handle it, so don't worry."

Wilson wasn't sold, knowing that once he finished refueling, Buffington was going to task his strike group *and* command it. Checking his watch, Coleman grew impatient.

"Okay, I've gotta get back. Expect a team to come out there, and Chuck here will be with them as my liaison with authentication procedures. Finish refueling and get back in the fight."

All stood as Coleman rose, but Wilson had one more question. "Admiral, before you go…what's going on back home? In Washington?"

Coleman shook his head. "The country is pretty much going ape shit, and Washington is struggling to contain it. This potential mission is probably their most coherent response now. People don't know what they want, really…they want to go back to how things were two days ago."

Just then, the 1MC blared. *"General quarters, general quarters! All hands man your battle stations!"*

Chapter 38

USS *Valley Forge*, North Atlantic, 1937 June 18, 2024

All in the War Room froze as to the meaning of this "surprise" GQ. "Oh, fuck," Coleman muttered. Each one considered what it could be—another nuke.

Then, as if shocked by electricity, the room exploded into activity as Huey, Olive, Smoke, and Mark bolted for the exits, leaving the two admirals, Maynard, and Weed behind. Coleman motioned to his staff—*let's go!*—before turning back to Wilson, who, like all of them, did not know the extent of this sudden threat.

"Jim, we're getting on that *Osprey* and back to the beach, if there's a beach left. You fight the strike group and deal with whatever this is, and you'll hear from me shortly."

The 1MC intoned again. *"Emergency breakaway, emergency breakaway!"* Outside, six short blasts from the ship's horn reverberated through the carrier's steel hull plates.

The footfalls of dozens—and then hundreds—of sailors crowding the passageways rumbled through the bulkhead as the crew rushed to their stations. Coleman and his staff nervously donned their float coats and fastened their cranial helmets.

"Jim, I know the way! Will be in touch!"

After they left, Wilson stood for a moment as his mind raced.

"May I join you, Kemosabe?"

Having forgotten for a moment that he was not alone, a surprised Wilson whipped his head to Weed.

"Yes, come with me," Wilson said. He then noticed Maynard, unsure of his battle station, and added, "You, too."

Wilson led them to CIC, entering through the forward door as the watch team shouted orders and reports in the red-lit space. A junior officer recognized Wilson, but before the man could sing out, Wilson raised his finger to his lips, his message to ignore him and fight the ship. He then approached the anxious Tactical Action Officer, who had the 1MC microphone near his mouth.

"This is the TAO! *Vampire* inbound, bearing zero four one!" He picked up the sound-powered phone.

"Bridge, combat; turn left one-one-zero! Engaging with *Sea Sparrow.*"

Whoa! A nervous Wilson thought. A *vampire*, a missile? Here, over 500 miles from the gap? *Are they in the gap? Is it nuclear tipped?*

"*O'Hare's* engaging with 5-inch! *Vampire* heading for *Tinian!*"

Above them, the *Osprey* rotors changed pitch as the aircraft lifted into the air. *Get out of here, sir.*

The watch captain turned and noticed Wilson. Before the lieutenant commander could speak, Wilson shook his head. "Ignore me and fight the ship."

The Watch Captain complied. "Engage visually, port side *Sea Sparrow* and RAM. Do you have a lock?"

"Trying, sir!" came the reply from the console. Next to him, a man blessed himself as he breathed through his mouth in fear.

Keeping the sound-powered phone to his ear, the officer filled Wilson in as both were glued to the COP.

"Admiral, this is an infrared pop-up contact on the horizon. Moving slow—we estimate four-fifty. Can't get a radar lock."

"Can you engage?"

"Trying to, sir…okay, *Tinian* engaging with CIWS and 50 cal!" The TAO then turned to the watchstander behind him. "Tell me when our 50 cal is manned! Now!"

The PLAT monitor showed the horizon aft of *Valley Forge*, with flashes and puffs of gun smoke from a DDG as *Tinian* fled behind the carrier. As if juggling snakes, the TAO fought the ship. Aboard all the ships in the strike group, thousands fought their growing panic. *What if this is a nuke?*

"Forty-eight radar, keep looking for more! Manual search northeast!"

The 1MC blared: *"Set condition Zebra throughout the ship! Close all watertight doors and hatches!"*

Amid the shouts of harried watchstanders, Wilson and Weed let them do their jobs, knowing that their performance separated them from a hit on an enemy missile or impact and the loss of the entire strike group. Unable to do anything, Wilson could only wait. A thought came to him: *Mary.*

"Tinian's bracing for shock!"

On the PLAT, two streams of tracers from the amphib's port side weaved skyward to down an inbound threat only seconds away. Wilson then saw an object pitch up and rapidly down into the LHA, and knew it was too late.

"Brace for shock!" the TAO cried, and Wilson instinctively bent his knees in a crouch, giving himself a chance if the *vampire* carried a low-yield warhead. None in CIC could take their eyes off the object on the PLAT screen, and someone yelled *please, Jesus!*

The explosion flared bright from near *Tinian's* port deck-edge elevator, soon turning to a column of black smoke as she heeled hard in a port turn.

"Thank God," Wilson muttered to himself, and hoped that casualties were few and that *Tinian* could still fight. He needed those F-35s.

"Bridge, combat, reverse course, starboard two-one-zero, when out of turn, all ahead flank! Scope's clean."

The strike group ships maneuvered hard to escape southwest as they each tried to make sense of what had happened. A pop-up contact, *here*, in what was thought to be a sanctuary. Weed leaned in to Wilson.

"What did that look like to you?"

"A small airplane that pulled up, rolled on its back, and pulled down. Kamikaze."

"Concur—drone, I'll bet."

Mark entered from the Surface Module.

"Admiral, we could *not* radar-lock that *vampire*. It must be an older system of less than 500 knots, but it's more than low observable, it's stealth."

Wilson needed more.

"Manila Bay couldn't lock it? All our SPY-1 combatants?"

"Sir, we'll find out who saw what when, but this is a new one, sir. And unexpected." Wilson saw that Mark was truly dumbfounded.

Holding his thumb and index finger an inch apart, Wilson's eyes seared into his Chief of Staff. "Mark, we were *this* close. We've gotta station a picket ship—or two."

"Will do, sir," Mark answered, himself coming down from the specter of eminent death.

They studied the COP as the tension level subsided. Wilson thought of Coleman—*do not lose this carrier.*

"Watch Captain, find me the *Osprey* that just departed here."

The junior officer moved the mouse and highlighted the CMV-22 on the screen, ten miles west of them in a right turn to north.

"Admiral, I've talked to the bridge; we're pretty much topped off and have only four pallets left from *Gene Cernan*. Recommend we get those, get the report from *Tinian*, but continue southwest for now until we find out what that was and what the beach has on the Russian vanguard."

"Concur, but what do you think that was?"

Mark studied the COP as he formed an answer.

"I think a *Sunburn* sir, older and slower, but unless they've modded it big-time, it doesn't have the range, and the warhead was much smaller than I expected. Regardless, their ability to hit us here was unexpected, sir."

Wilson nodded, watching *Tinian* smoke on the PLAT before the carrier's turn to starboard obscured the camera view. His strike group needed direction.

"Alright, when we come out of GQ, finish the UNREP, then continue southwest to buy us some more time, but do not get into the sea lanes. Set an Alert Five of two fighters ASAP, then find out what that was and how to defeat the next one. And get me a damage report from *Tinian*."

"Will do, Admiral," Mark answered as he returned to the flag spaces.

As the tension and commotion in combat receded, Wilson tried to make sense of it. Standing behind him, Weed reminded Wilson of his two pressing needs, each requiring the opposite action.

"So, what's the closest alligator? Coleman's visit or avoiding another face-shot from whatever that was? And given yesterday, we just dodged a nuclear bullet."

Wilson frowned as his eyes remained on the COP. "Don't know yet, but how about if I give you an hour to tell me?"

Weed smiled. "Flag tasking, and a chance for the slimy CNS analyst to earn his keep. Wilco; see you in an hour."

Wilson then shook the hand of the relieved TAO and returned to his stateroom, thinking about how to respond. *What* was *that...and they're going to send me a nuke.* He felt as if he had lived a year in the last day. And he felt the burden weigh on his shoulders.

This game just changed.

Once back in his spaces, he phoned the bridge.

"Captain," Huey answered.

"Huey, Admiral Wilson...did you see it?"

"Yes, sir, low on the water and did a little pop-up in the end game? Just talked to the CO bridge-to-bridge and no reports of casualties."

"How big, would you say?"

"Umm—fifteen, maybe twenty-foot wingspan, and the fuselage about that length."

"Big...maybe it's not a missile."

"May not be, sir. Will get the PLAT tapes and maybe we can do a PLAT analysis and get the dimensions. Sure didn't expect it here, about 800 miles from the Iceland-Faroes line."

"And no one picked it up until it was on us? With all of our sensors?"

"Yes, sir, I think it was a lookout on one of the DDGs that sounded the alarm. I couldn't track it, and neither could Bob Dolan. Stealth or low observable; whatever it is, we're in their launch acceptability region and I'm accelerating through twenty-nine knots and going to whatever the plants can give me to get out of Dodge."

Wilson considered the fuel in his escort ships; at least they were topped off...except *Tinian*.

"Alright, Huey, thanks...and I want to address the crew on the 1MC tonight."

"Roger, sir, what time do you prefer?"

"Right before the evening prayer."

"You got it, sir. See you then."

At 2145 hours, Wilson and Skweez stepped onto the bridge, lit red but illuminated by the low sun that sat on the southwest horizon. *Valley Forge* had moved south into what passed for darkness in an effort to cloak themselves from whatever had attacked them hours earlier. A DDG next to them had a "bone in her teeth" as the strike group moved in moderate seas at full speed. Wilson looked aft on the port quarter and saw *Tinian* ten miles away with another small boy accompanying her, the sun reflecting off their hull plates in a pinkish tint.

On the flight deck, a *Rhino* and *Growler* were spotted on the waist cats in preparation for the 2200 launch to maintain the CAP north of them. Behind the raised JBDs, two more *Rhinos* waited their turn, the whine from their idling engines permeating the bulletproof window glass. As Wilson walked up to Huey someone yelled, "Admiral's on the bridge!"

Huey turned to greet Wilson. "Good evening, sir."

"How thing's going, Huey?"

"All's well, sir. Launching soon...would you like to speak to them now?"

"Yeah, let's do it."

Huey led Wilson past the helm to the bosun station. Next to the bosun, Father Campbell—on the bridge, waiting to deliver the evening prayer—greeted Wilson.

Huey nodded to the bosun, who then took the 1MC microphone and blew the familiar notes calling the crew to attention. The sailor then said, "Now standby for a message from Commander, Carrier Strike Group Eighteen." Once the bosun finished, Huey took the mic from him and handed it to Wilson. "All yours, sir."

The yellow sun rested on the sea under a layer of cloud as Wilson began, the bridge bathed in soft light.

"*Valley Forge*, this is Admiral Wilson." After a short pause for effect, he continued.

"The strike group is moving south while we maintain a defensive combat air patrol and await our next tasking. The entire strike group, and you aboard *Valley Forge* in particular, have performed magnificently over the past week since we left Gibraltar. However, more, much more, will be asked of us.

"The Russian Navy is north of us and trying to get into the open Atlantic. We and coalition nations are holding them up, but the strike group led by this ship, plus *Tinian*, are needed. While we can and will engage the enemy from this position, we need to refuel at intervals, to regroup, then reengage when it is most advantageous to us and can deliver decisive combat power to defeat the enemy.

"We find ourselves in what we call a high-end fight against a peer competitor. We send a round downrange at them, and can expect that one will come back at us. Hours ago, we saw that—a missile or a 'kamikaze' drone that hit *Tinian*. We're still not sure which it was yet. Fortunately, *Tinian* suffered no casualties, but did receive damage, thankfully not critical, and while she can still fight, the ship is in a degraded state of combat readiness."

Wilson paused as he thought of his next point, knowing that 5,000 sets of ears were waiting.

"This is a reminder to us, that we *must* be ready for action…and I do believe that there will be more action."

Wilson let that point resonate before he rose to his culmination.

"Hostile Russian naval forces in the open Atlantic…are an existential threat to our nation…our homes and families. We have not experienced this as a nation since World War Two, almost eighty years ago. Right now it is naval and air forces from the United States and our coalition allies that are preventing them from 'breaking out,' as we say, and while we have shot down a number of enemy airplanes and sunk several enemy ships and submarines, they too have had success. To those of you who have friends aboard USS *Lloyd Childers*, I can confirm to you now that they gave their lives in the service of our country, and please accept my sincere condolences. I can also confirm to you what our families and the rest of the world knows…*Childers* was hit by a Russian nuclear warhead that destroyed her instantly."

From a nearby compartment, Wilson heard a shriek of grief...or fear. He paused again as the ship absorbed the news, now official.

"*Valley Forge*...we may be in World War Three and not know it, but we *are* in a new Battle of the Atlantic, and this time it is nuclear. Avoiding their arrows while we shoot ours into their forces to destroy them is what the game is now. It is a war of attrition, and how well you monitor the plant in the reactor spaces, direct airplanes, maintain our sensors and defenses at peak readiness, or make meals for the crew day and night...will determine the outcome of this battle. We cannot lose it, and we *will not* lose it. Once we reengage the enemy in strength—and we will respond to the Russians, I assure you—the safety of our nation...and the world...depends on our ability to defeat them on the high seas and prevent further attacks, nuclear or otherwise. Each of you must do your utmost—here and now—to win decisively and restore peace."

Wilson paused again to let the message sink in and gather his thoughts.

"Your leaders, all supported by me and my staff, will ensure that you have all you need to win, which includes adequate food and rest. However, each of you will be tested in combat, and will have to dig down into your own reserves, and look out for one another, and perhaps pick up the flag and lead should you be called to do so. There may be times in the coming days—or weeks—that we cannot provide all that we need. In *those* times...it will be your own personal fortitude and courage that will see us through."

Caught up in the moment, Wilson gazed off the bow as the last sliver of orange slipped below the horizon.

"Shipmates, as I now hand this microphone to Chaplain Campbell to deliver the evening prayer, let us all thank the Almighty for His grace to us, and ask Him to bless us and our homes as we do what our good nation charges us with here on Earth. Take care of each other, get rest when you can, I'm proud to be your shipmate, and God bless each of you. That is all."

Wilson handed the microphone to Chaplain Campbell, who offered his approval. "Well said, Admiral."

Nodding his appreciation to the chaplain, Wilson returned to Huey's chair as the captain pointed to a message he had received on the classified message screen while Wilson spoke.

"Admiral, we just got an overhead message: two legacy *Hornets* arriving here from Oceana at 0430 local. We are directed to an expected recovery position 100 miles southwest. That's six point five hours from now, and we'll have a ready deck."

Wilson raised his eyebrows. "Did you say *legacy Hornets?*"

"Yes, sir, FA-18 Charlies."

"Wow, that's a hike for them. How far is that?"

After checking his Nav screen, Huey answered him. "Twenty-two hundred miles from here as the crow flies, sir, if Canada gives them overflight." From behind the helm, the bosun spoke into the 1MC mic.

Now stand by for the evening prayer...

As Chaplain Campbell called the ship to pray, Wilson stood in silence and contemplated the skies to the southwest. *Two old jets, but jets that can do the job. What else are they sending me?*

Listening but not listening, Wilson remained silent as he thought of Oceana, and Virginia Beach, and Mary...and Admiral Coleman.

Chapter 39

RFS *Admiral Alekseyev*, North Atlantic, 0320 June 19, 2024

Vitac plowed through the swells as the merchant again led Petrov and his ship steaming close alongside through the North Atlantic, this time on a northerly heading at a steady 13 knots. The Red Banner Fleet was under orders to withdraw to open water north of Iceland as Moscow assessed the American response, and to give their crews an opportunity to prepare.

As before, Petrov sat in his chair with one eye on *Vitac* and another on the dispatches from fleet HQ. A nuclear-tipped missile—his, or a different one from another ship?—had gotten through to sink one American DDG and severely damage another, with hundreds of American sailors dead. The report also stated that all the Western navies had fled the waters of the gap as they too assessed their next moves. The news had already travelled around the world, but had it made it to Severomorsk? Did Arina know? What news had she learned since he left her only one week ago?

He scanned the horizon. Two of the Anti-submarine Division ships rode its sharp line to the east under the low clouds. To the west, nothing. Petrov considered that beyond it was Greenland, and for the moment, safety. Anything the Americans sent north through the Denmark Strait would be detected, and the desolate waters of the Greenland Sea up to the edge of the polar ice cap offered him and the fleet a haven to consolidate and defend from an American response that would surely come.

Most of yesterday, and before the rendezvous with *Vitac*, Petrov had slept, which Kuzmin was doing now before he relieved the watch in a few moments. Petrov slept soundly, but could see his exec was shaken by the action and reported confirmation of success. *It may not have been ours, Kuzmin!* Alas, Petrov's attempts at encouragement fell short. Kuzmin's depression—and Petrov's own exuberance after the nuclear attack—surprised him. The *Moskit* in Tube 5 dominated his thoughts.

He still had two *Moskits* in his tubes—one of them nuclear—some 30 SAMs, all his torpedoes, plus the helicopters. And his gun. If he could get close to an enemy on the horizon with *Vitac* as a cover, he'd employ the 130mm rounds. At this point *anything* that popped up on the horizon was enemy until he could confirm that it was not, and he would ensure *Vitac* stayed within visual sight of the division to minimize the chance of fratricide...unless he was given another mission from the flagship—or Platonov. Startled from his daydreaming, he noticed a slow drift toward *Vitac*, and snapped at the OOD to correct it.

"Good morning, Kapitan."

Petrov turned to see a haggard Kuzmin, his eyes bloodshot, his jaw set.

"Mister Kuzmin, how did you sleep?"

"Quite well, Kapitan." Studying him, Petrov detected the lie, told for the sake of the bridge watchstanders.

"Let's conduct our turnover outside."

As the DDG sailed into a rare light wind, the port bridge wing was mildly pleasant as Petrov led them outside so they could enjoy the last days of spring—and clear the air. Kuzmin dogged the hatch and took his place next to Petrov as they both studied—in silence—*Vitac's* hull plates 100 meters away. Petrov spoke first.

"Yevgeny Sergeevich, what's on your mind?"

For a long moment Kuzmin said nothing, before finally inhaling.

"Kapitan, we are in a nuclear war...one that we initiated...and under my hand."

Petrov had his answer already prepared. "We are professional warriors following valid orders, Kuzmin, in the service of the Motherland. We've both known throughout our careers that this day could come and have both known what this ship carries and why. To be frank, I expected more from you. Fine, pray for the lost American souls, and pray for our souls on the day we meet God, but we did our job, *did it well*, and we will again if the Motherland orders us. Just one of our *conventional* torpedoes could sink an American submarine and leave no survivors. Hundreds and maybe thousands have yet to die on the high seas in an instant...this is *naval warfare*, Yevgeny Sergeevich, the stakes are always high, and you are the executive officer of this warship and *you must lead*."

Kuzmin absorbed Petrov's words, unflinching, before he answered. "The *Amerikanskiy* dead are the fortunate ones."

Petrov turned to Kuzmin, his jaw clenched. Mindful of the bridge team observing them anytime they were together, he turned back to *Vitac*.

"Be *very, very* careful of what you say to me, Kuzmin. If you cannot or will not fight this ship, then you tell me now. I could relieve you for that, and would, except for *him*, that bastard scow over there, and I need you on this bridge when

I am absent so that these schoolboys don't hit or *get* hit by him. Those inside must know that we will do our utmost to fight this ship so they can survive. *Will you do it?*" Petrov growled in suppressed fury.

Kuzmin answered at once. "I will serve and die alongside them. They are brothers to me."

Petrov struggled to control his breathing. "And me, Yevgeny Sergeevich? Will you serve and die alongside of me?"

Kuzmin waited a count for effect. "Yes, Kapitan…and when we return to base, I will request reassignment orders."

Stung, Petrov paused, then snarled his answer through clenched teeth. "Know that I will write them myself before we throw the first line over."

Again they stood in silence with their arms on the rail, observing *Vitac* as their minds raged. A long minute passed before Petrov spoke. Both knew their relationship, what for Petrov passed as his only friendship aboard, had changed irrevocably.

"Why, Kuzmin? Why *now* do you abandon me? I—we—need you, and I always must trust you. *We are still armed!* Why now?"

Kuzmin ignored the drop of spray that lashed him, then countered.

"You loved it too much, Kapitan, the lust for blood. It surprised me…and has actually shocked me. We need you, *Kapitan*, to fight this ship smart, to kill when necessary, of course, but not to place us at high risk when seeking *vengeance*. Why do you seek vengeance? May I ask you that?"

Petrov didn't answer, didn't *have* an answer, but thought better of making one up. Kuzmin was right, though. When the second *Moskit* tore out of tube 2, he was filled with exhilaration, and much more so than the first missile. His name would be in the history books alongside those heroes of the Great Patriotic War. He *felt* that, that unforgivable thought. *Esteem. Position.* Command of the Baltic Fleet would one day be his!

He *felt* that when focused on the rocket motor burning bright as it roared away to the south. He wanted that enemy ship, a prize, *his* prize, to vanquish the rich and cocksure Americans in their gleaming ship and *show* them. And deep down, he wanted to experience that feeling again. Was he guilty of what Kuzmin had accused him of? Pride? Jealousy? Ruthlessness? Vengeance? And what of Yevgeny Sergeevich, like a brother to him only days ago, *hours* ago. What happened to him?

"You will remain here on the bridge, Mister Kuzmin, while I go below."

"Aye, aye, Kapitan," Kuzmin acknowledged, keeping his eyes on *Vitac* as the guilty kapitan of the combat-proven RFS *Admiral Alekseyev* stepped inside and went below.

Wilson rolled over and checked the LED readout on the bulkhead next to the PLAT monitor: 3:54. Four hours of fitful sleep, what he knew was a luxury for many aboard *Valley Forge*. Feeling the roll of the ship and the hum of machinery all around him, he realized that he was awake…and alive. At once his mind went back to yesterday. *Vampire inbound!* Thinking back, he was surprised that his life didn't flash before his eyes as a nuclear detonation two miles astern was only seconds away. Would the PLAT screen have turned white for the nanosecond before the blast arrived, and would Wilson's brain even have been able to comprehend it in its last firing synapse?

The hit on *Tinian* damaged the port elevator track and fragged the tail of a JSF parked over the water. An inoperative elevator and one "down" jet, but no casualties. It was an older missile for sure—a *Zircon* at Mach 4 would have traveled the beam of the ship and exited the starboard slide in a swath of destruction no one could imagine. How did the shooter get in range? To prevent another surprise, Mark positioned two DDGs aft of the strike group as it transited southwest, away from the threat—and the gap it was ordered to plug. The air wing had maintained a CAP of fighters up since the attack. Grabbing the remote on the nightstand, he checked the ship's position: N56:21 W38:45 and heading southwest at 20 knots to catch the legacy *Hornets* from the beach. Clicking to the OPS screen, he noted they were roughly 300 miles from the southern tip of Greenland. He heard the sounds of the flight deck and clicked to the PLAT, seeing a *Rhino* led to cat 3 as the JBD rose behind it, signaling another day of nuclear combat in the North Atlantic.

Slowly waking up, he sat on the edge of his rack and looked at his desk, the picture of Mary catching his eye, the same photo of her that had adorned his desk for the past twenty years. Her megawatt smile. He thought of her for a moment before the *Rhino* on the waist went into tension, and soundwaves from the twin F414's less than 200 feet away vibrated the steel bulkheads of his cabin.

After the *Rhino* cleared the angle and climbed into the darkness, he went back to the image of Mary. What would she say to him now? The whole ship was on edge, dreading what lurked over the horizon, thinking of their fearful families back home and unable to help them as they literally headed for the hills of Appalachia. How could he allay their fears and get them to concentrate here? The extreme roll of the ship brought him back. *This is significant.*

He dressed, and after helping himself to a cup of coffee in the mess, he walked into Air Ops, where Olive waited. The time was 0407.

"Good morning, sir."

"Good morning, CAG…what's the latest?"

"A *Rhino* and two *Hornets* just checked into Marshal."

"A *Rhino*? Thought we were just getting the *Hornets*."

"He's a tanker from the beach, sir, FA-18E. The *Hornets* launched out of Oceana lights-out with three *Rhino* tankers on a night section takeoff, so nobody monitoring the action in Virginia Beach can count them missing. After they topped off from two *Rhinos* off Long Island, two returned to Oceana and this one stayed to give them an extra drink as they rounded Cape Race. All part of the cover story. The legacy *Hornets* are about six point five, and they've been airborne close to five hours."

"Varsity stuff," Wilson said, then added, "Deck's movin' a lot now."

"Yes, sir, but at least it's not a black night. Faint horizon still visible."

As *Valley Forge* turned into the wind, Wilson and Olive waited in Air Ops to observe. Soon the first *Hornet* checked in, using a *Raven* callsign for cover.

"Approach, *Raven* four-one-four with you passing two for one point two, state five-three."

"*Raven* four-one-four, radar contact, clean through ten."

"*Raven* four-one-four."

Wilson and Olive saw the familiar twinkling external lights of an FA-18C *Hornet* low on the PLAT screen, a sight they had not seen since their time on *Hancock* some six years earlier. On the status board, a *Rhino* tanker orbited overhead if the *Hornets*—flown by TOPGUN instructors who were not carrier qualified in the older jets—needed them.

The carrier rolled hard to port, then back to starboard as Wilson steadied himself. He picked up the phone and called Huey.

"Huey, this is the admiral in Air Ops. What's your assessment of the seas?"

"Pickin' up sir, and with this wind, the seas are on my starboard beam. Speeding up or slowing down won't make much of a difference."

"Okay, thanks—let's get them."

The LSO on the platform keyed the radio microphone. "Working twenty-eight knots, slightly axial."

Olive spoke low so only Wilson could hear. "Hope these guys remember how to trap at night…and on a rolling ship."

Wilson nodded. "If they've ever done it. Doubt these jets have been to a carrier in years…they'll be hand-flying them the whole way."

The second *Hornet*, followed by the *Rhino*, checked in on approach, the three jets forming a line of pulsing lights behind the ship that the PLAT deck camera recorded. The line meandered from centerline as the carrier rolled, each pilot fighting to get back on centerline. The final approach controller took charge.

"*Raven* four-one-four, three miles, begin descent. *Raven* four-one-five, dirty up."

"Olive, who's going to take care of these guys?"

"The *Ravens*, sir. They've got a bunch of chiefs that served in *Hornet* squadrons, and they're excited to recover them. One of them is up there with tie-down chains around his neck as plane captain. Comet did a cruise in them as a nugget, and that's what passes for *Hornet* experience around here."

Wilson smiled. Things would go wrong in the coming days, with these jets and who knew what else. *Whatever.* Far from support, the ship and air wing would just deal with it.

"Four-one-four slightly right of course, slightly above glideslope, three-quarter mile call the ball."

"Four-one-four, *Hornet* ball, four-two."

"Roger ball…deck's movin' a little, you're high."

Mesmerized, Wilson and Olive watched the *Hornet*, one that they had seen on a PLAT a thousand times but not since their days aboard *Hancock*, float above the PLAT crosshairs. *Talk to him*, Wilson thought.

"You're high…power to catch it…come left…"

As the *Hornet* neared the ramp, Wilson detected the three drop tanks it carried. Good. When the ship rolled to port, the LSO jumped in.

"Power."

The FA-18C slammed down on a 2-wire and drifted left on the roll out, the pilot throwing the throttles into burner as he did. Olive was stoic as her eyes remained locked on the PLAT and the second *Hornet*.

"*Raven* four-one-five, on-and-on, three quarter miles, call the ball."

"*Raven* four-one-five, *Hornet* ball, three-nine, auto."

"Roger ball, *Hornet*, auto…twenty-six knots."

Olive commented. "An auto flyer…wonder if he's ever flown a *Hornet* aboard with it."

The *Hornet* grew larger in the PLAT crosshairs as the ship took a roll to port. When the pilot corrected for lineup and settled, the LSO was on it.

"Don't settle…go manual."

"Manual!"

Nervous with the jet below glideslope, Wilson shifted his weight. *Get back up there...*

"Power," the LSO transmitted with inflection.

Now in close, the *Hornet* overcorrected and flattened out, heading for a bolter. With no warning, the jet then lowered its nose and picked up a huge rate of descent.

"Get rid of him!" Wilson commanded to no one, fixated on the PLAT.

"Power! Attitude!" the LSO shouted into his handset, but too late. The *Hornet*, with engines close to military, pulled its nose up as it dropped its right wing, driving the right main into the deck as the nose soon followed, slamming and twisting the airframe in a shower of sparks as the hook grabbed a wire and wrestled the jet to a halt...at idle power.

"Power in the wires!" the LSO screamed, well after the fact.

"Did he just blow a tire?" Olive exclaimed. All in Air Ops waited for the jet, camouflaged in a TOPGUN livery, to taxi clear. When it didn't, and deck personnel appeared around it, they knew.

"Yep. There are those that have and those that will," Wilson said. "Can't blame him after flying from Nevada to here with a short pit stop in Oceana. Okay CAG...after you meet with your new pilots and they get some food, bring them by so I can welcome them aboard."

"Wilco, sir."

"And if they have a message for me from Admiral Matson, bring that ASAP."

"Yes, sir."

Smoke entered Air Ops and walked to Wilson. Even in the night-adapted space, Wilson noted his grave look as Olive waited.

"Whatcha got, Smoke?"

"Tasking, sir...from Admiral Coleman."

Wilson nodded, knowing what it was.

They really mean it.

Part III

Far-called, our navies melt away
On dune and headland sinks the fire
Lo, all our pomp of yesterday
Is one with Nineveh and Tyre
Judge of the Nations, spare us yet
Lest we forget—lest we forget!

– Rudyard Kipling

CHAPTER 40

RFS *ADMIRAL ALEKSEYEV*, SOUTH OF JAN MAYEN, 1530 JUNE 19, 2024

Through the glasses, Petrov studied Jan Mayen, a lonely dark-gray lump of an island adorned with two white peaks twenty-five miles to the north. Uninhabited for most of the year, Petrov's *Helix* helicopter had just finished scouting it and rushed back to the ship to inform their kapitan, who ordered *Vitac* to heave-to along the volcanic island's western shore.

Northern Fleet Headquarters had pulled the division—what remained of it—north of the gap for two reasons. To regroup for a planned coordinated push through the Denmark Strait, and to give the West—and the United States, in particular—time to think. Would the Americans risk Armageddon and civilizational destruction with millions lost for the lives of mere hundreds?

Word had come down from HQ that one ballistic missile boat and an *Akula* had been lost in the gap, but the reported loss of the frigate *Admiral Nasorin*—and especially the destroyer *Severomorsk*—from their own anti-submarine division hurt Petrov and the entire crew, all of whom had friends aboard the ships in the close-knit network on the isolated Kola waterfront. The submariners kept to themselves up in the Sayda Inlet, but their loss also hurt...the missile boats were what would bring the West to their knees and victory to the Motherland.

Petrov thought of Kulakov, the rakish and fun-loving kapitan of *Severomorsk*. Did he know what hit him? Did he land a blow on the enemy? Not knowing anything about the loss of the DDG gnawed at Petrov...the terse message from Headquarters reported the ship lost with no further information. Were there survivors? Is Kulakov alive? Petrov suspected he was not, and as he contemplated Jan Mayen, he imagined his friend's last moments. Was he on the bridge? Combat? His rack? Was he in the wardroom? *Torpedo inbound, all hands brace for shock!*

Kuzmin. They had not spoken at lunch, and he suspected the officers knew... and soon the entire crew would. *The Kapitan and Kuzmin are fighting each other! Who will help us fight the Yankees?* Petrov needed an XO, and Kuzmin had proven himself competent. He was also trusted...by the crew. Petrov would have to settle for that and find a way to be seen engaging with Kuzmin to allay their fears. But would Kuzmin respond?

Flight quarters, flight quarters!

In a wide circle, the *Helix* flew down Petrov's starboard side and slowed for his approach as *Vitac* and *Admiral Alekseyev* steamed north in the mirror-like sea. Once the aircraft recovered aboard, the pilots headed to to the bridge where Petrov waited. Before they arrived, Kuzmin entered the bridge and busied himself with something away from Petrov, who turned to see the aviators enter.

"*Leytenants*, is this deserted island ahead of us actually deserted?"

Before the senior pilot answered, he looked at Petrov with trepidation.

"It is not, Kapitan. We found a small trawler of about 15 meters anchored along the western shore. The camps on the island showed no sign of life, and we did not see anyone on the trawler's deck, but it is probably inhabited."

Damn, Petrov thought. A Norwegian fisherman as witness to him as they approached, perhaps with an HF radio aboard or access to an undersea landline on the beach.

"Did they spot you?"

"We do not know, Kapitan. We came upon it suddenly...it surely heard us."

Petrov looked away in disgust. *Joyriding pilots...just bursting into the next bay without any idea of what could be in it. What's done is done.*

"Show me on the chart."

The pilots compared their charts to the marine chart on the navigation table. The trawler was spotted in a protected bay along the isthmus connected to the abandoned settlement on the island's eastern shore, separated by a range of low hills.

"Kapitan, we avoided the meteorological and old LORAN stations on the east. Once we rounded the northern tip of the island, we looked south, saw nothing, and then backtracked along the western shore."

"So they saw you a *second* time?" Petrov countered, suspicious.

"Kapitan we had our speed up, over 200 kilometers per hour."

Not buying it, Petrov pondered the chart. Any halfway competent trawler crew anchored near such a barren outpost could identify a Russian helicopter at twice the speed. He noticed Kuzmin hovering behind one of the aviators, and then glanced at *Vitac*.

"Mister Kuzmin, attend to station keeping."

"Aye, aye, Kapitan," Kuzmin replied before he turned.

Petrov devised a plan. He could not risk being seen or spotted near the island. The trawler crew saw a helicopter reconnoiter the island but did not know from where it launched. By now the Norwegians—and Americans—knew at least that but did not have to know any more. Without looking at the pilots he gave an order.

"You are dismissed, but summon the attack helicopter pilots to the bridge at once."

Once the aircrew saluted and left, Petrov remained at the chart in contemplation. Sensing a presence, his head swung. *Kuzmin.*

"What are you thinking, Kapitan?"

Petrov kept his voice low as he returned to the chart. "Whoever is on that island is alerted. Sink the trawler, destroy the LORAN antenna, and destroy any structures that humans could live inside."

"And any humans we find outside?"

Petrov turned to face his XO. "Yes, Yevgeny Sergeevich, and without remorse."

"Sounds reasonable—we are at war, after all."

"Oh, *thank you,* executive officer, for your swift concurrence and unwavering support!"

Kuzmin ignored Petrov's sarcasm. "No prisoners, Kapitan?"

"*No,* dammit! We will anchor and refuel from our rusty friend, and hope that the Fleet has orders for us." Petrov returned his gaze to Jan Mayen in the distance.

"Signal *Vitac* to take some turns off before we get within visual range of the shoreline, and bring us west twenty degrees. I'll brief the pilots on their mission. Once we drop the hook this evening and rig the hose from *Vitac,* double ration of vodka for the crew not on watch. We will rest in the bosom of Jan Mayen, obscured from prying eyes and defended from radar missiles."

"I will ensure it happens, Kapitan."

"Yes, Yevgeny Sergeevich...ensure it without delay."

"Enter," Wilson barked.

Olive opened the War Room door and saw Wilson at the head of the table with Shane seated on his left and Weed on the couch. She introduced the pilot with her.

"Admiral, this is Lieutenant Commander Kendall 'Mag' North from TOP-GUN."

Wilson stood and extended his hand. "Mag, welcome aboard—Jim Wilson. This is our Intel Officer, Lieutenant Commander Duncan, and retired Navy Captain Mike Hopper."

Mag said good afternoon to all as they exchanged handshakes. Mag took the seat he was offered on Wilson's right, with Olive next to him.

"Where's your wingman?" Wilson asked. Olive answered.

"Sir, he's med down in sick bay. That hard landing may have broken a vertebrae; he's in pain and can barely walk. Doc says he's down."

"Whoa…and the jet?"

"Blown tire, which is easy to fix…*if* we had a tire for a legacy *Hornet* aboard. And a busted planning link; same thing. We've sent a message to the beach to get the parts out here. The jet landed hard and probably popped some hard landing codes, but we can't read them with our *Rhino* software."

Wilson nodded at the logistic realities. But he still had one good *Hornet* and its pilot.

"Roger that…okay, Mag. What do you know?"

Puzzled by the question, Mag struggled for an answer. Wilson helped him.

"Did they tell you why you guys flew out here, why we need the *Hornets?*"

"Well…we thought it's because you were shorthanded and needed the jets… and TOPGUN expertise."

Wilson smiled. "Yes, we do need the jets, and you. But we expect to be assigned a mission that only you—and the *Hornet*—can accomplish out here." The blank look on Mag's face revealed that he had no clue.

"Back in the Cold War, some 40 years ago, the *Hornet* was designed to carry weapons that we don't train with anymore."

Mag nodded. "Yes, sir, I get it now. We've got some war reserve *Walleye* glide bombs, a shaped charge with decent standoff. Great for war-at-sea, and…"

Wilson stopped him. "No, that's not the weapon."

Stumped, Mag waited, hoping he would not have to guess again. Weed broke the silence.

"Have you ever heard the term *bucket of sunshine?*"

Mag held his gaze as he considered the question. After a moment, his eyes widened.

"Yep," Weed said, nodding. Wilson then laid it out.

"Mag, we've been tasked to be ready to deliver a tactical nuke. We've got the airplane and delivery pilot aboard…once the weapon arrives, it's an option for Washington."

Shocked into silence, Mag could only take it in, searching the eyes of the senior officers in the room for deliverance. *A nuke! Me!*

"Against a Russian ship, sir, like *Childers*? I mean…is this a bomb or a missile?"

"Maybe a ship…and maybe not," Wilson answered.

"When was the last time you flew a timed low-level?" Olive asked.

Mag considered the question. "It's been a while, ma'am. I'm probably out of qual."

Wilson raised his hand and made the sign of the cross. "You are now in qual."

"When's the last time you took a cat shot?" Olive asked, all business.

"Been a while, ma'am, not since the fleet about two years ago."

"You're qualled," Wilson said, unblinking.

Weed jumped in. "Like riding a bike, I'm told. Been over five years for me and I'd take any hop I could get if the admiral here would let me. You did a nice job in the wee hours this morning, your first night trap in what, two years?"

"First trap of any kind since then, sir." Mag kept his gaze on Weed. *Who the fuck is this guy?* He felt the gaze of the woman across the table from him and turned to her. Her expressionless face remained still, her eyes unblinking.

Wilson resumed.

"Mag, you are one of our finest tactical aviators who's current in the jet we need you to be current in. Did you fly the *Hornet* in the fleet?"

"Yes, sir, nugget cruise before my squadron transitioned to the *Rhino*."

"Good then. You're current, and you have muscle memory in the jet that only a few of us old guys have out here. But we are has-beens, and no longer tactically sharp. We need your tactical abilities and knowledge of enemy defenses and weapon delivery knowledge. We may need you to drop a nuke…on a target Washington could assign us in hours. This is new to all of us."

Wilson studied Mag, and sensed more than unease.

"Will you do it? You seem…uncertain."

Mag opened his mouth to answer. *Damn right I'm uncertain, sir.*

"Admiral…I'm here to serve. Just…trying to wrap my head around this. Never considered it until now."

"Neither had we until two days ago. What is the mood back home?"

"People are freaking out, sir. Highways are jammed and most gas stations are empty, people are pulling their money out of banks and the stock market. Store shelves empty—looting going on in the cities. It's bad, sir."

"Do people want retribution for the destruction of *Lloyd Childers*?"

"Some do, sir, but most…are clueless. Washington has no answers; my uncle has a friend there who says Congress is heading for the hills, too."

Wilson nodded. The nuclear event was ripping the United States apart. Could an effective response prevent a total unraveling?

"Mag, do you have some buddies aboard?"

"Yes, sir. In the *Bucs* and *Spartans.* One guy in the *Ravens.* Skipper Halley was one of my department heads, good guy."

"Yes, he is. Good. I want you to hang out with them…however…I want you to join us for lunch here shortly. What we have talked about is *Top Freaking Secret.* It is of grave importance, and you need no convincing of that. We need you here and nearby—this *cannot* get out of this space. Do you understand?"

"Yes, sir, Admiral."

Wilson gestured to Shane. "Commander Duncan."

Opening the folder in front of her, Shane turned it and pushed it toward Mag, who studied it as Wilson resumed.

"Please review and sign this document. The operation that is contemplated does not yet have a name, but consider yourself read in. And Mag…"

As if jolted by electricity, Mag snapped his head toward Wilson.

"No matter what happens, you and all of us will take this to our graves. Copy?"

"*Yessir.*"

"Very well. Continue and sign."

Mag took another thirty seconds to review the document as all watched him. He then took the pen and signed his name. Shane took the folder and placed it in her lap.

"You are excused now; take a right out the door and you'll see a lounge area. Take a seat, and tell anyone who asks that I've directed you to wait there."

"Yes, sir," a shaken Mag said as he got up to leave. After he closed the door behind him, Weed spoke first.

"He's scared shitless."

"Wouldn't you be?" Wilson shot back. "Summoned into flag spaces and informed that you are going to be dropping a nuke in a matter of hours?"

"Kemosabe, I detect more than that. He's thinking of reasons not to do it."

Olive shook her head. "He's a TOPGUN instructor, for cryin' out loud. If that isn't commitment to the mission, I don't know what is."

"Even TOPGUN bros are human…believe me," Wilson added while he stared at the bulkhead in thought. Weed continued.

"That guy is a superstar, of that we can all agree. He knows the TAC manual by heart and can beat you one-circle, two-circle, defensive, you name it. But we can also agree that the world just changed, and from a standing start we are asking him to be Paul Tibbetts."

Olive disagreed. "Colonel Tibbetts never dropped a nuclear bomb until he did in combat. I'm sure he was kept in the dark until a day or two before."

"Maybe he was," Weed replied, "But he had made peace with the fact that he might be called to deliver something game-changing, and when the order came down, he was prepared mentally. We just sprung this on young Mag, and unlike Tibbetts, he's seen pictures of Hiroshima, and this is more than twice that. He knows. That's my point; he needs time to process this. I mean, the whole world could know the name Kendall North by this weekend."

"How much time can we give him?" Wilson wondered. "We probably don't have much."

In the silence that followed, Shane excused herself. This conversation was about airplanes and pilots.

Olive brought them back to reality. "Well, we have one 'up' *Hornet* pilot aboard to fly one 'up' *Hornet*, and he's the best the Navy can give us right now. If this goes down, it's him, and we'll have to prepare him as best we can."

Weed nodded his concurrence. "Yes, and you know, we—I mean you, sir—should reach back to the beach and talk to one of the old guys that used to do this mission in the eighties. Admiral Smith comes to mind; he's retired in the Virginia Beach area."

Wilson smiled. "Admiral Smith...think he'll remember us from the *Raven* days?"

"Oh, he won't remember me because I didn't help myself to my buddy's kill so I could bag *two* bandits on the biggest combat hop of the year, but he'll remember the guy who did, who is you, Flip! And you've caught up to him with a star on your collar, and after this imminent red-letter day in world history, more stars to follow!"

Wilson could only shake his head. "Mea culpa, already! A Navy Cross, and what?—four dollars these days?—will get you a cup of coffee."

"All in the past, Kemosabe! Here to serve once again on the Good Ship *Valley Forge*, and with our kid sister Olive here as CAG. Allow me to coordinate the call so I can do something more than keeping you grounded, *Admiral*."

"Yes...please do," Wilson replied. Both men then looked at Olive for her reaction and noticed her again staring at the bulkhead, lost in thought.

Chapter 41

Jan Mayen, 1700 June 19, 2024

Bursting over the ridgeline, the Ka-52 *Katran* overbanked down the backside of the island's southern peak, the trawler at anchor in the calm bay before them, just as the *Helix* crew had reported. The copilot in the left seat of the *Hokum B* slewed the aiming reticle on the trawler's pilothouse and designated it.

"Target designated! Range six kilometers!"

"*Ponyal!*" the pilot acknowledged. "Rocket pod selected, ripple fire!"

The attack helicopter bore in on the trawler, its crew now alerted to the rapid *whup whup* of the six counter-rotating rotor blades. At three kilometers, the IN RNG cue illuminated.

"Fire rocket pod!"

Holding the aiming reticle steady, the pilot pulled the cyclic trigger and held it, rippling twenty S-8 rockets from a pod on the aircraft's right wing. In less than four seconds the pod was empty, with the first of the rockets only seconds from impact.

Less than one second after the rocket motors burned out, the big 80mm projectiles ripped into the wooden trawler and the water next to it, killing the two crewmen in the pilothouse, one smoking a cigarette on the foredeck, and one who jumped overboard in desperation, only to be sprayed with shrapnel from the high explosive frag warheads before he hit the water. The boat heeled hard to port and caught fire despite the misting shower of water that fell around it, settling fast in its death throes.

With the trawler transformed before them into spray and smoke, the helicopter pulled off west over the water to set up for another run. After they extended for a mile, they armed the second pod and turned in, only to see the burning vessel lift its bow into the air. Selecting the 30mm gun, the pilot moved in to finish it off, the rounds punching big holes in what was left of the hull above the water before it sank below it.

Hugging the desolate western shoreline of Jan Mayen, the Northern Fleet *Katran* sped south and back to *Admiral Alekseyev*, full of success at their summary execution of the sitting-duck trawler.

After five minutes, the sound of the rotor blades was replaced by the whistling of the winds that rushed through the rocks and rustled the small plants that clung to them. It was then that Deckhand Hedda, stunned at what she had seen, stood up from her hiding place behind the rocks in disbelief. Too shocked to cry at the carnage, she dropped the wildflowers she had come ashore to collect—now crushed from the grip of her tightly clenched hand during the attack. Stumbling as if in a trance to the shoreline, she inspected the tip of one forlorn outrigger that remained above the surface.

"Henrik? Anders!"

Wallowing in denial, the sobs came, and through her tears she searched the bay for any sign of life, hoping against hope. As acceptance set in, she realized she was alone—and in danger. Retrieving her parka and water bottle from the dinghy, she set out up the hill on what she estimated would be a two-hour hike over the saddleback to the outpost on the other side of the island, a place from which she could shelter and possibly contact the outside world, anyone.

The helicopter looked like one of Russian design. Of that, she was sure.

With foreboding, Wilson read the message a second time.

```
FROM: COMSECONDFLT
TO:   COMCARSTKGRUEIGHTEEN

SUBJ: OPTASK MSG 401 24/019/JUN

1. A2/PERIOD/200900ZJUN24-210900ZJUN24

2. A3/ADMIN/PROCEED WITH CSG-18 ASSIGNED UNITS AT
   CSG DISCRETION TO TRANSIT DENMARK STRAIT TO MOD-
   LOC N6835W1755 NLT 210900ZJUN24 AND AWAIT FUR-
   THER TASKING.

3. B1/CONDUCT/MAINTAIN COMBAT ALERT POSTURE ENROUTE
   AT CSG DISCRETION. OVERFLIGHT OF IS (ICELAND)
   AUTHORIZED. MAINTAIN 12 MILE STANDOFF FROM GL
   (GREENLAND). THE POSSIBILITY OF RU SURFACE AND
   SUBSURFACE ASSETS ALONG EXPECTED ROUTING CANNOT
   BE RULED OUT.
```

Yep, Wilson thought. *Will I have any help?*

4. EXPECT ASW AND MARPAT ASSETS STATIONED IN VICIN-
   ITY DENMARK STRAIT UNDER OPCON OF C2F DURING
   CSG-18 TRANSIT WINDOW.

Good. Lots of them, please.

5. ATTRITION OF RED BANNER FLEET AND NAVAL AVIATION
   HAS SLOWED RU ADVANCE INTO GIUK GAP. ASSESSMENT
   OF RU NAVAL CAPABILITIES REMAINS FORMIDABLE. RU
   AIR ASSETS ASSESSED MARGINAL. RED BANNER SAG
   HOLDING NORTH OF ICELAND-FAROES GAP IN PROBA-
   BLE COORDINATED REATTACK. RU SUBSURFACE UNITS
   EXPECTED TO FOLLOW SAG AND BREAKOUT INTO OPEN
   WATER.

6. ASSESSMENT: STRONG I/W THAT THE NUCLEAR ATTACK OF
   18JUN24 APPEARS TO BE A ONE-TIME ACTION. COALI-
   TION GOVERNMENTS ARE NOT EXPECTED TO RETALIATE
   IN KIND. RU SEEKS END TO COALITION SUPPORT OF
   UKR. DIPLOMATIC ACTIVITY STRONG; COALITION NAVAL
   FORCE STRATEGY IS TO SECURE GIUK GAP IN A DEFEN-
   SIVE POSTURE AND RESTORE NORTH ATLANTIC SLOCS.

BT
NNNN

Wilson handed the message back to Mark. "Operational deception."

"Given what Admiral Coleman told us, yes, sir, but maybe…"

Wilson shook his head. "No. I'm thinking this message is going to be inter-cepted and cause the Russians to lower their guard a bit…and placate the EU, who have been clutching their pearls this whole time. I think we're going to strike them, and that's the mind set all of us must have."

"Yes, sir. Admiral, we're about twelve hours from the Denmark Strait, and with the forecasted seas we'd better head up there now and transit sooner rather than later."

"Yes, and I want to fly *hummers* and *helos* and a section of *Rhinos* as we do, with alert thirty set for all of them. Want *Tinian* to have alert thirty *Cobras* and JSFs. Get the word to Huey, Olive, and Bert. People need to get rest where they can because I believe the next ninety-six hours are going to be intense."

"Aye, aye, sir."

"More than the last ninety-six if that's possible. And ensure we have solid comms with the ASW assets—we cannot have blue-on-blue."

"Will do, sir."

After two knocks on Wilson's stateroom door, Skweez poked his head inside.

"Admiral, two unscheduled *Ospreys* from the beach are ten minutes out."

"Coleman?" Wilson asked.

"Don't know, sir, but they didn't send a code."

Wilson checked the time. An unscheduled late-afternoon logistic hit. Two aircraft.

"If Admiral Coleman is aboard one, I want to know one second after you find out. And get Commander Maynard up there, too."

After Skweez left and Mark followed him out to inform the strike group leaders, Weed popped his head inside. "What's up?"

"Come in. Two unscheduled *Ospreys* from the beach will be here in minutes, and we just got tasking to transit the Denmark Strait."

"Do you know who or what's aboard them?"

Wilson shook his head. "No. What do you think?"

Weed lifted his eyebrows. "I think a bucket of sunshine."

Wilson considered it. "Yeah, could be. No heads up."

"Standard operating procedure," Weed quipped.

Wilson turned on the PLAT and saw that the angle was clear. *Good.*

"What about the Denmark Strait?" Weed asked.

"Second Fleet just tasked us to get up to a point northwest of Iceland after transiting the strait in the next twelve to thirty-six hours. Mark says we gotta go now with the weather picking up from that hurricane that's off the east coast."

"Furthering the Eastern Seaboard bug-out gridlock."

"No doubt. Coleman's going to have an unknown number of attack boats and P-8's helping us as we blast through. The Russians were last located north of the Iceland-Faroes line, but you never know."

"I just saw Shane. That thing that hit *Tinian* was a suicide drone. An unmanned airplane, about thirty feet long. It had a warhead, but it was a dud. Thousand-mile range."

Wilson nodded. "A thousand miles, wow. Does she know how it launched or what launched it?"

"Not yet."

The inbound *Ospreys* now appeared on the PLAT as dots, and both men watched them approach. Above on the flight deck they heard the 5MC: *Stand clear of the waist cats, taking two* Ospreys *on spots three and five.*

In lead-trail, the aircraft approached the ship in a hover, the first one sliding over the deck on signals from the yellow-shirt LSE. Once it touched down, blue-shirted deck crewmen ran out to chock and chain it as the next aircraft slid over spot five and soon settled on to *Valley Forge's* heaving deck.

Once the second CMV-22B was on deck, the ramp from the first aircraft was lowered. Ten soldiers with M-4 carbines jumped from it onto the flight deck and ran to the trailing *Osprey*, taking up defensive positions.

"What the hell!" Wilson exclaimed. He lunged for the phone to call Huey while watching the scene on the PLAT, stunned at what he was witnessing.

"HUEY! What the fuck's going on?"

"Admiral, I'm not sure either. I'm sounding a security alert," Huey answered as both watched another soldier carrying a briefcase walk from the first aircraft to the second.

Wilson slammed down the receiver and grabbed his float coat and cranial. "You stay here," he told Weed before shouting at his aide. "Skweez, flight deck! Now!"

The 1MC intoned: *Security alert, security alert! Security alert on the flight deck. Away the security alert team. Away the backup reserve force. All personnel not involved stand fast.*

Fuming, Wilson ignored the 1MC instructions as he bounded through the passageways with purpose, sailors bracing against the bulkhead to allow him passage. *They just sent me a nuke with no warning!*

Inside the island, Wilson yanked up on the dog-bar and shoved the hatch open to step on to the flight deck, pushing his way through a throng of sailors as wind whipped through the parked helicopters over the reverberating cacophony of the four sets of idling *Osprey* rotors. At the foul line he stopped and waited as a large weapon canister was lifted aboard the second tilt-rotor. He spied the lone soldier that monitored the off-load and headed toward him. As Wilson approached, a security force airman holding his weapon at low-ready darted toward him.

"No further! Back off!"

"Get him, NOW!" Wilson boomed, pointing at the soldier he could see was in charge.

"No, YOU back the fuck off!" the airman shouted back. At the island hatch, the first security team masters-at-arms burst through the hatch and toward the turning aircraft.

The officer soldier in charge saw the confrontation and moved toward Wilson. *"What's your problem? Back off!"* he shouted at Wilson.

Beyond incensed, Wilson saw the man's rank tag was that of a colonel, and realized his camo was Air Force.

"I'm Admiral Wilson! *Who the hell* are you?" Wilson raged, loud enough to be heard throughout the flight deck.

"I'm Colonel Ethan Clapp, deputy-commander of the Sixteenth Bomb Wing. I have orders to deliver this here cargo to Navy Captain Morrison. Where is he? Hey! Tell your men to stand down!"

Dumbfounded, Wilson stood there under the beating rotors, unable to speak. As the carrier security team came up behind him, the Air Force personnel tensed up, and Wilson could see that he had no control over the airmen, and with them not expected to make decisions, things would escalate quickly. He turned to the leading chief.

"Chief, stand down! Return to the island and wait by the helicopters."

"Admiral, we have orders…"

"I JUST COUNTERMANDED them, Chief! Go, all of you, now!"

As the Navy security alert team withdrew to the island, Wilson returned his attention to Clapp. Both stared each other down as the thunderous sound and rotor wash swirled about them.

Wilson turned away first. Looking up to the bridge, he saw Huey observing them. Wilson pointed at him, then emphatically pointed to the flight deck next to him. Huey got the message and disappeared from the window.

With the weapon canister on the bomb cart, Wilson noted the crewmen carry a second cannister off the cargo ramp. Two weapons. *Whoa.*

Amid the chaos of the flight deck, Clapp remained focused on Wilson. "I have my orders to coordinate with Captain Morrison for the storage of this cargo. Who are you?"

"I'm Admiral Wilson!" Wilson raged. "What is that cargo?"

"That's need to know, sir."

Boiling with anger, Wilson controlled his temper and held the man's gaze as the two stood nose-to-nose on the foul line in their Mexican standoff. Having flown down five ladders, Huey appeared next to them without wearing a float coat. Armed with this backup, Wilson turned to the colonel.

"Okay, here he is: Captain Morrison! The *Valley Forge* Commanding Officer! What you tell him, you tell me!"

Noting the eagle on his flight suit shoulder, Clapp studied Huey. "Need to see an ID."

Before Wilson could react, Huey pulled it out of his billfold and handed it to Clapp, who studied it.

"Okay, Colonel. I'm Colonel Clapp, deputy commander of the Sixteenth Bomb Wing. I'm to escort these weapons to your magazine and remain in custody of them until directed by higher authority."

Huey picked up at once what was happening and took a breath before he unloaded.

"It's *captain*, and you are on *my* ship next to *my* admiral. You aren't going to direct *shit* here. You are going to *request*. *Do you copy?*"

Clapp was having none of it.

"My orders are from STRATCOM himself, and I'm escorting these weapons to your weapon storage area. And sir, you've gotta move all these people and planes back at least five hundred feet."

As the *Osprey* rotors continued to beat the air above them, Wilson and Huey both saw that they were dealing with a self-important idiot. Taking this cue, and prioritizing the weapon stowage in the magazine, Wilson took the lead back.

"Yes, I see now. Captain Morrison, bring the Ordnance Handling Officer up and introduce him to Colonel Clapp. Colonel, our weapons magazine is below this deck. Captain Morrison, do you believe we could lower these weapons on elevator two?"

"Yes, sir, we'll escort the colonel and his people to El 2, and place the weapons as far from the deck edge as possible."

"And you need to move these people back," Clapp added.

Wilson stepped in again. "We'll do the best we can, Colonel, because this ship is only 250 feet at its widest. Captain Morrison, please supervise this elevator run personally, and see to it that the colonel joins me in my in-port cabin upon completion."

"Aye, aye, sir," Huey responded, playing along.

Under Clapp's wary eye, Huey introduced him to the Ordnance Officer, and the Air Force detail moved the weapons toward elevator 2. Wilson, fighting to calm himself, returned to the island and went below with Skweez following. In the passageway, he dictated his message.

"Message, personal-for Admiral Coleman. Two CMV-22B's arrived, all is well. That's it."

"Will do, sir."

"Then get with the ship and find berthing for our Air Force friends. Put Clapp in the visitor's stateroom on frame 88 under the cat 2 JBD that Captain Hopper vacated."

Skweez grinned. "You got it, sir!"

Inside his stateroom, Wilson changed out of his flight suit and into khakis. *Who did this? Coleman? No warning, no coordination? Or Buffington? Truer to form.*

With the stars on his collar and the top row of ribbons clearly visible, Wilson's uniform made a statement. His staff assembled in the War Room, he waited to be called as the rotors of a single *Osprey* turned on the steel deck above him. Skweez knocked twice and entered.

"He's here sir, with Captain Morrison and CAG."

"Very well. What did you find out about our new shipmate?"

"Commissioned Air Force Academy 2003. B-1 pilot…twenty-five hundred hours with over half of them combat hours. Iraq and Afghanistan. Bronze Star, one individual Air Medal, five strike-flight. Five Meritorious Service Medals."

"Wow, he's got some big-time green ink. A regular twenty-first century Curtis LeMay…but he's still a prick. I'll be there in five minutes.

"Yes, sir."

After allowing sufficient time for Clapp to cool his heels, surrounded by higher-ranking strangers, Wilson entered.

"Ladies and gentlemen, the admiral."

All rose to attention.

"Seats, please," Wilson said, and took his seat at the table head. He noticed Clapp eye his single row of ribbons; *Navy Cross, Silver Star, Legion of Merit.* After a pause, Wilson began.

"Ladies and gentlemen, this is Colonel Clapp of the Sixteenth Bomb Wing. Colonel, you've met Captain Morrison, and this is Captain Teel, Commander, Carrier Air Wing Four, and Captain Braud, our Commodore. The rest of the officers are on my staff. My job is Commander, Carrier Strike Group Eighteen and Task Force Twenty-two. Before we proceed, Commander Duncan will provide you a non-disclosure agreement to sign."

"I'm cleared to up to Cosmic," Clapp growled.

His path clear, Wilson rolled in.

"You can be cleared up to anything you want, you sanctimonious son-of-a-bitch, but if you don't put a 'sir' at the end of anything you say to me, you'll be taken bodily and placed on that *Osprey* turning above us—that I have held for just this contingency—and sent back to Keflavik in five minutes. Before you even land, STRATCOM and every four-star from here to Hawaii will know what a pompous ass you are. So, my advice to you, Colonel, is to shut the fuck up, sign that NDA, and answer my questions."

Clapp, bristling with indignation, narrowed his eyes at Wilson as he picked up the pen to sign. Before he did, he studied Weed with a mixture of disdain and unease at the civilian. Wilson spoke again.

"He's here because *I* want him to be. Sign that now or make my day."

Controlling his fury, Clapp held Wilson's gaze for a moment before he signed. Wilson nodded to Skweez, who picked up the phone and said a single word. Sitting back in his chair, with his fingertips forming a triangle, Wilson kept his focus on the bomber pilot.

"Now Colonel, what exactly did you bring us?"

Clapp inhaled and replied. "Two shapes."

"Please continue."

"Plus electrical cannon plugs and connections for the FA-18 *Hornet.*"

"Anything else?"

"A loading manual, two cockpit switch boxes, and five checklists. I'm told you have the proper hoists."

"I'm sure we do; Captain Morrison, please provide a list of all we have aboard. Now Colonel, where do we get an FA-18 *Hornet?*"

Taken aback, a puzzled Clapp searched the room full of poker faces. Above, the sound of an *Osprey* at full power receded as it took off on the return trip to Keflavik.

"Sir…I was informed that you had them."

"Who specifically told you?"

"STRATCOM sir…the general himself."

Wilson waited before he answered.

"Well then, it seems you are up to speed. We were in the dark about your unscheduled arrival, so when you arrived and started to command what you do not own with your sword drawn, you can see why we reacted as we did. Now, going forward, you—and your arming team—are going to assist us with whatever mission we are assigned, but your control of those weapons has come to an end. You are relieved, Colonel Clapp, of responsibility for those weapons. Huey."

Huey pushed a folder in front of Clapp as Wilson explained.

"You will sign over custody of those two serial numbers. Please read and sign."

"Gen—I mean Admiral, my orders are to maintain custody until they are loaded, and—"

"Clapp, knock it off!" Wilson growled, leaning in for effect. "I'll bring that *Osprey* back here and put you and your team on it, it's easy to do. You support *me* now, and have zero authority on this ship. Zero. You answer our questions and help out, or your career ends."

"Admiral, a *four-star* told me it ends if I relinquish control before those jets are loaded. I'm sorry, but he outranks you."

"Then he should have sent you a letter authorizing it. I'm done. Huey, recall him."

Wilson's bluff called, Huey got up to call the Air Boss. Clapp remained resolute as Wilson studied him.

"I'm taking the hardware back with me, *sir*."

"Oh, no, you aren't."

"You can't load them without our expertise."

"They'll send us someone else that is not you. Huey, your Masters-at-Arms can escort the colonel to the flight deck."

"Admiral…"

"Too late, Clapp. This meeting is over."

CHAPTER 42

JAN MAYEN, 2330 JUNE 19, 2024

As the quarterdeck relief arrived to assume the midwatch, Petrov stepped onto the abandoned bridge. In the isolated bay on Jan Mayen's western shore, *Admiral Alekseyev* rode at anchor while tied next to *Vitac,* which pumped two hoses of gas turbine distillate and diesel fuel to top off his bunkers. With his aviation fuel at over 80%, he would soon be ready for another run to the south. Alone with the midnight sun, he realized that tomorrow would be the first day of summer. Without a breath of air and the outside temp a pleasant 6 degrees C on the mirror-like water, he'd let the crew enjoy the scene with glasses of vodka on the helipad. With their sleep cycles upturned due to the pace and constant sunlight, it mattered little. With rain forecast for midday, a short moment was all he could give them.

Footsteps on the bridge ladder interrupted his enjoyment of the serene bay. *All I wanted was two minutes.* He turned to see who it was. *Kuzmin.*

"Kapitan, a dispatch from Fleet HQ." He handed the sheet to Petrov.

```
FROM: COMMANDER NORTHERN FLEET
TO:   RFS ADMIRAL ALEKSEYEV

SUBJ: OPERATIONAL ORDER 008

RMKS: AMERIKANSKIY AIRCRAFT CARRIER AND ESCORTS MOV-
ING NORTH TO TRANSIT DENMARK STRAIT ETA 201400ZJUN.
HEAVY ENEMY AIR ACTIVITY OBSERVED FROM UK, ICELAND,
AND CANADIAN AIR BASES. LARGE ENEMY SURFACE ACTION
GROUP OPERATING SOUTH OF FAROES COORDINATED WITH
LAND-BASED AIR BLOCKADING EFFECTIVE RUSSIAN PUSH
INTO OPEN WATER.

REMAINING ALONGSIDE VITAC TO MAXIMIZE COVERT POS-
TURE, MAKE BEST SPEED TO VICINITY N6700 W01700.
RENDEZVOUS ENROUTE WITH FLAGSHIP RFS MARSHAL YER-
MOLOV FOR COORDINATED MISSILE ATTACK ON AMERIKAN-
SKIY AIRCRAFT CARRIER AS DIRECTED BY FLAGSHIP. USE
```

OF AVIATION ASSETS FOR SCOUTING AND TO AFFECT SUR-
FACE ACTION GROUP RENDEZVOUS IS ENCOURAGED. DETACH
FROM VITAC AT COMMANDING OFFICER DISCRETION WHEN
CONDITIONS WARRANT.

WHEN DIRECTED BY FLAGSHIP ENGAGE WITH SINGLE SALVO
OF ALL REMAINING – REPEAT – REMAINING P-270 MOSKIT
ASCM ON DESIGNATED AIRCRAFT CARRIER COMBATANT CO-
ORDINATED WITH FLAGSHIP SURFACE ACTION GROUP. REN-
DEZVOUS WITH FLAGSHIP NO LATER THAN 201200ZJUN. SUG-
GEST ACTION STATIONS SOUTH OF N68 00.

FOR PETROV: MRS. ARINA PETROVA IS LEADING THE GAL-
LANT WIVES OF YOUR CREW IN CONFIDENT ASSURANCE OF
YOUR ULTIMATE VICTORY.

Petrov nodded to himself. *As expected.*

WHEN THIS OPERATIONAL ORDER IS RECEIVED AND UNDER-
STOOD, RESPOND VIA MESSAGE FORMAT TO ACKNOWLEDGE
RECEIPT. INCLUSION OF PERSONAL MESSAGES FOR FAMILY
MEMBERS OF YOUR CREW IS AUTHORIZED.

THE MOTHERLAND DEPENDS ON YOUR SPLENDID SHIP IN
THIS VITAL EFFORT TO OPEN THE SEAS TO FREE NAVI-
GATION. THE PRESIDENT JOINS ALL IN THE RED BANNER
NORTHERN FLEET WISHING YOU SUCCESS AND GODSPEED IN
YOUR VICTORIOUS ENGAGEMENT. GO WITH GOD, AND GOOD
HUNTING.

His eyes met Kuzmin's. "How far from here?"

"Just over three hundred miles, Kapitan."

"Blast…how much longer from him?" Petrov asked, motioning at *Vitac*.

"Five minutes ago it was ninety-one percent distillate, eighty-three diesel."

"We'll take it. Inform *Vitac* and set the sea-and-anchor. Cease refueling. No vodka ration until we are in transit. Draft a response for me. Go."

As Kuzmin descended the ladder with his tasking, Petrov considered the barren shoreline. *Three hundred miles in twelve hours!* He couldn't do it tied to the plodding *Vitac*. He'd plead for more time in his message response, explaining the time/distance realities. He thought of Arina and Sasha. In little more than twelve hours, he'd be inside the range of enemy planes and missiles, hanging on to deliver his remaining silver bullet. At an American carrier! How could he miss such a monster! If Kuzmin could be trusted. And if they could rendezvous with the flagship to launch a coordinated salvo. So many variables. He studied the shoreline.

All I wanted was two minutes.

High on the ridge overlooking the bay, Hedda took another picture with her mobile phone as she hid behind a rock. She had never seen such a thing; two large ships touching while at anchor…and one painted pink! The pink ship had the lines of a warship, but she had difficulty making out detail as it seemed to blend in with glassy sea behind it. Regardless, she knew a Russian tri-color flag when she saw one.

Having hiked up the saddleback and down to the eastern shore, she had broken into the radio hut and turned on the radio transmitter to call out a Mayday in the blind, not knowing if anyone heard her transmissions. Frustrated, she filled up on some canned food she scavenged in the shack before she hiked an hour back up the saddleback to survey the bay, surprised at the two ships less than a mile offshore. Yes, Russians. *The Russians killed Henrik!*

Unknown to Hedda, her in-the-blind short-wave transmission was picked up in Svalbard to the north, relayed to Oslo, then EUCOM. *A helicopter attack of an anchored trawler in Jan Mayen.* An American P-8 *Poseidon* from Keflavik was scrambled to investigate.

Five hundred miles south of Jan Mayen, *Valley Forge* labored in heavy seas as she pounded north. The seas had slowed the strike group's PIM, now two hours behind. Gale force winds on their beam hindered their ability to fly while maintaining their track. Wilson had to fly his *hummers* and helos, and hoped that the seas would soon abate so Huey and the rest of the group could kick it up.

Unable to sleep, Wilson donned his flight suit and poured himself a cup of coffee from the flag mess urn the culinary specialists always kept fresh. Stepping into TFCC, the watch captain brought him up to speed: one *hummer* and two MH-60 *Romeos* airborne, *Manila Bay* in shotgun, five DDGs in an ASW formation. Steaming as before.

On the COP flatscreen display, Wilson noted the two LCS holding trail positions in the formation.

"How are our LCS doing in these seas?" he asked the surface warrior watch captain.

"Hanging in there, sir, no complaints."

"Ever serve on one?" Wilson asked

"Yes, sir. I'm sure they're hatin' life, and with these beaming seas they're struggling."

"Did you ever operate in one in seas like this?"

"No, sir...bet they haven't either."

Wilson nodded. To use their twenty naval strike missiles, he'd have to move them up, way up, to engage any Russians encountered north of the strait—or even in the strait. He sipped his coffee and asked another question.

"What's our PIM to the narrowest part of the strait?"

The lieutenant commander manipulated the track ball and did the math in his head. "Seven, maybe eight hours, sir. And the weather is following us...we'll be in this for the next twenty-four hours plus."

Wilson nodded again. Unable to control it, they'd do the best they could.

In the red-lit passageway, abandoned at this early hour, Wilson headed forward 20 frames before he ducked into CVIC, the ship's intel center. The normally full space was devoid of activity, until Wilson turned the corner to see Olive, alone over a chart.

"Anyone ever tell you that CAGs need sleep too?"

Olive looked up. "Good morning, sir. Yes, I've heard that said before."

"There's truth to it. What are you doing here alone?"

"The planning team knocked off for the night about twenty minutes ago. I'm just studying the geography around the strait...scheduled to fly with the *Spartans*...Irish has the lead on this alert sixty, war-at-sea strike."

"What's the latest you've heard?"

Olive pointed to the chart. "Their main body is thought to be here, two to three hundred miles northeast of Iceland. Led by their *Slava* cruiser, with a handful of *Udaloys* and frigates. Still no indications that their attack boats or boomers have transited the gap. Have you heard about the attack at Jan Mayen?"

"No."

"Got word that yesterday a military helicopter attacked and sank an anchored Norwegian fishing trawler off Jan Mayen, here."

Wilson studied the small pork chop-shaped island, isolated in the desolate Greenland Sea.

"They launched a P-8 to check it out; we should get a report in about three hours," Olive added.

Wilson nodded. "What about these seas? I hear they're going to pick up."

"Have no choice but to fly in them, sir. We're probably going to get some outer bands and squall lines later today…at least we don't have to operate at night, but we're going to have big-time pitching deck for the next several days."

Wilson folded his arms. "I'm worried about the small boys flying—and especially—recovering their *Romeos*. What do you think about bringing them all here?"

"I'd support that, sir, and make a game-day decision if we have to send a DDG off on a contact."

Wilson steadied himself as the carrier took a roll. Just then a member of Wilson's battle watch team arrived with a message.

"Admiral, just got this. Second Fleet is coming here at 1000."

After Wilson took the message and read it, he dismissed his lieutenant. Turning to Olive, he smiled. "Expect that this visit concerns our Air Force visitors."

"And maybe more," Olive surmised.

"Yes. Delivering the order in person is what I would do too."

In silence, Wilson and Olive contemplated the chart of the North Atlantic and what Coleman's visit could mean.

"When is your brief?" Wilson asked.

"Zero-nine hundred."

"Get some sleep."

"Aye, aye, sir."

Hours later, *Vitac,* with *Admiral Alekseyev* close aboard, cruised south at twenty-one knots, all that *Vitac* could muster. On his bridge, Petrov sat with his feet up, not minding that his bridge team saw him in such a state of relaxation in the all-business pilothouse. *They must wait as I did*, he thought. *They'll command their own ships one day.*

Petrov contemplated the southern horizon, knowing that by the end of this day his ship could again be engaged in combat. *Nuclear* combat—and a once-in-a-lifetime opportunity to bag a Yankee carrier. His name would be alongside those of Nelson and Togo, Spruance and Halsey. Russian schoolchildren would know his name as they did Peter the Great.

But what of Kuzmin? His executive officer had avoided him since the message from Fleet HQ arrived. As he searched the southern horizon, he thought back to the *Moskit* that burst out of Tube 2. One more. Just one more.

"Kapitan, lookouts sight an enemy airplane, bearing two-one-five, altitude high!"

"Sound action stations!" Petrov bellowed as he jumped from his chair and bounded to the starboard bridge wing. *Should I radiate? Take him with a missile or anti-aircraft?*

As his crew scrambled to their stations, Petrov craned his neck up to search the breaks in the clouds. "Where away?" he shouted to the lookout on the signal bridge.

"There, Kapitan!" the lookout pointed.

Petrov looked to the spot through a break and saw it, an airliner body banking away to the west. An American P-8, what else could be up here? If he saw the American, the American could see him. Or could it? *Vitac* for sure, but was he identified? He checked aft and noted his wake was distinct from *Vitac's*. A sharp-eyed observer from four to five miles away might see that.

Petrov knew he was not *invisible* from radar, IR, or even EO, but so long as he stayed next to *Vitac* his coatings degraded the enemy EO and RF sensors. A human eye close enough, however, could identify him as a combatant. No, he needed *Vitac* for another 200 miles, then he'd detach for his rendezvous with destiny! He'd sink the damn scow himself if it would help.

Every instinct spurred him to radiate and shoot. *It's right there, and turning away!* With a mix of indecision and gut feeling, Petrov held his fire as his antiaircraft battery acquired and tracked the patrol plane visually. He called to Combat through the voice tube.

"Combat, bridge, status!"

"Enemy ESM hit, Kapitan! He's transmitting!"

Transmitting *what*, Petrov seethed, realizing that it was no use. The bastard Yankee had spotted something: *Vitac* or *Vitac* and a combatant. Shooting it down now would confirm the presence of a combatant. He tried to track the jet himself through the cloud breaks. If it swooped in low, he'd shoot it at once. So long as it stood off and flew away, he liked his chances. If unmolested, he still had hours of lonely transit ahead. He decided against the Vodka ration—too dangerous now. After the attack. Yes. A victory toast to long life for the Motherland.

Unknown to him, the P-8 observed and reported a single merchant ship heading 194 at 21 knots—the reciprocal course pointed back at Jan Mayen. The *Poseidon* crew then headed to Jan Mayen and circled it, finding no evidence of any vessels. Flying south along the eastern shore, an observer saw flashes of light from a ridge on the middle of the island. Identifying it as a signal mirror distress signal, the P-8 did a 270 and came in low, seeing what appeared to be a woman waving her arms and jumping up and down in wild desperation.

Chapter 43

USS *Valley Forge*, 150 miles SW of Keflavik, 0945 June 20, 2024

Stunned, Wilson looked at Olive in disbelief. "What?"

"Yes, sir. He turned in his wings. Refuses to start World War III and end life on Earth."

Wilson shook his head. "You gotta be…"

"That's what I said."

"In a way I can't blame him, but…where is he now?"

"In his stateroom…told him to stay there until I tell him to come out."

Wilson exhaled as he looked at the PLAT. With his only medically up *Hornet* pilot refusing to fly, it mattered little if Admiral Coleman arrived with tasking and weapons expertise. One up FA-18C and zero qualified *Hornet* pilots with Lieutenant Mag North's action.

"Get him in here, then," Wilson said, resolute in what he had to do.

On the flight deck, a war-at-sea strike led by Comet was fifteen minutes from launch. Wilson was inside an envelope for any Russian thousand-mile drones, but with his escorts positioned ahead and Air Force F-15Cs from Kef, he felt well defended. His strike group had to draw blood on this strike to allow the P-8s and ASW helos freer rein on both sides of Iceland. He glanced at the PLAT and checked his watch.

Damn. Mag turning in his wings was an irrevocable step. But he needed him to fly the jet on what could be a nuclear mission! Washington would just have to wait until he was supported better. Especially with trust lost…who knows what Mag might have done.

They should have briefed the pilots before they flew out here. What were they thinking?

Five minutes later Olive returned with Mag, who appeared shaken. Wilson directed them to take a seat. When Mag raised his eyes, Wilson began.

"CAG just told me. Why?"

"Admiral, I can't drop a nuke on a city. I mean…I've never considered it…"

"You don't know that. And neither do I. Now, we have a combat-ready *Hornet* aboard that we need in this fight, and I may need it. You are the only qualified *Hornet* pilot aboard and one of the finest tactical aviators in the Navy. And when your country needs you, you quit?"

Mag's lip trembled as he looked away.

Wilson didn't know how to handle this. Did a coward sit in the chair next to him, or one of the bravest aviators in history? He wished he could go back an hour in time. A week in time. Mag turned back to him.

"Admiral, I haven't slept since I've been aboard. First, if such an order were to come, how would I know it's valid? Second, though I feel for the guys on *Childers* and their families…"

"Lieutenant, we all do, but this is above even them. If they go nuclear with no reaction, it invites more. They need to know. Now, I doubt that your target would be Moscow, if you could even make it from here one way, but a proportional response is an option the President must have, and it falls to you. Fate chose you."

Mag listened in the awkward silence, as Olive waited for Wilson to finish with lowered eyes. Skweez knocked twice and stuck his head in.

"Admiral, the *Osprey* has checked in; the admiral's aboard."

Wilson motioned him inside, and after Skweez closed the door, the silence returned. Wilson stood.

"Mag, please stand."

Mag pushed himself out of the chair and stood before Wilson, who continued.

"Give me the wings on your flight suit."

Resigned, Mag hesitated before he found his courage. With his right hand he reached up and pulled the Velcro patch off and handed it to Wilson.

"And the TOPGUN patch."

Mag's eyes narrowed in contempt. Keeping them on Wilson, he reached up with his left and pulled the patch off his shoulder, again handing it to a resolute Wilson.

"You're getting on that *Osprey* right now. When you go back to Fallon, tell them whatever you want, so long as it's unclassified. And if I find out that you've compromised what you've been read in to—and I'll check—it will be bad for you, copy?"

"Yes, sir," Mag replied, as the weight of what he had done increased the pressure inside his chest.

"Skweez, please ensure he gets on that *Osprey*, and escort the admiral back here. Dismissed."

As Skweez escorted the humiliated junior officer away, Flip turned to his CAG. "Now what?"

"Admiral, there's about ten pilots aboard who have any operational experience in the *Hornet*. Us of course, Comet and Irish, and a handful of squadron XO's and department heads."

Wilson nodded. Old guys—like him.

"Do you know who is the most current?"

The *Buccaneer* XO was a department head on the last *Hornet* cruise about four years ago. Comet last flew them in 2018. Roughly the same for the others, late teens."

Wilson nodded as he rejected the idea in his mind. Four years since the last time a pilot touched a FA-18C? Just this side of suicidal to send him or any of them into combat with that long a layoff. The jets *were* similar, but they were also different. If only he had a week to refresh them...but who? Who would he—or Olive—pick for this likely one-way mission? A squadron CO? Unless the Navy got them a qualified pilot in the next 48 hours, he had no options. The 1MC blared.

Ding ding, ding ding, ding ding, ding ding...Second Fleet, arriving.

"Stay here, Olive. This is an air wing issue."

"Do you think he has tasking?"

Wilson nodded. "That's why he's here. Hopefully in days, not hours."

On the PLAT they watched the *Osprey* land at the top of the angle, the 1MC sounding a single *ding* as it did. Coleman and two of his staff exited the ramp. All about the flight deck, the *Rhinos, Growlers* and *Hawkeyes* that were on the war-at-sea strike taxied to the catapults under the direction of the yellow shirts. Wilson watched one figure in a flight suit, escorted by the Air Transport Officer, board the *Osprey*.

"What have I done?" Wilson muttered to himself.

"You had no choice, sir. He turned in his wings."

Wilson nodded. Olive was right...but what would *he* have done as a JO? *Nuclear delivery pilot* was something from the old days...even before Cajun's day. At least those old guys could contemplate it in theory. He gave Mag only hours to decide amid a de facto nuclear war.

Wilson and Olive moved to the passageway entrance to greet the fleet commander, who followed Skweez as officers braced up against the bulkheads to allow them to pass. Coleman wasn't smiling.

Wilson offered his hand. "Welcome aboard, Admiral."

"Jim, CAG...let's go," Coleman said as he led the way to the War Room. Mark, Smoke, Charlie Maynard, and Shane were already there, and perfunctory greetings were exchanged.

"Are you launching a strike?" Coleman asked.

"Yes, sir, in about five minutes."

Coleman nodded as he surveyed the room. "Are we cleared TS-SCI?"

"We are sir." Wilson nodded, as did Shane.

"Very well. Thirty-six hours," Coleman said, his eyes locked on to Wilson's, who waited for him to continue.

"And to here," Coleman added as he placed an open folder in front of Wilson. Wilson saw an image of the Kola Peninsula with a black square along the coast. He leafed through to the next black-and-white satellite image. The graphic at the bottom contained the lat/long plus elevation, and a name: VARDA NOS.

"Varda Nos?" Wilson asked.

"It's their boomer base. You can see the large overwater shed where they refuel and reload them and several auxiliary piers. They can put two boats inside that shed, but we don't believe any are inside now."

Wilson continued to study the image, then the accompanying chart. "Severomorsk and Murmansk are nearby."

"And Polyarny. Yep. The drop will be a low-yield surface burst, and the topography of the fjord plus prevailing winds will mitigate damage to adjacent facilities. It's this one that we want destroyed. Time on target will be 2355 Zulu time, which makes it 0255 in Varda Nos…roughly thirty-six hours from now."

Wilson nodded. "Five minutes till midnight."

"The irony is not lost on you, Jim. Yes, this is from the Secretary himself; I was on a conference call with him three hours ago. This will send a message: cease hostilities now and return to base."

"Are we sure it will send that message, sir?"

Coleman's eyes narrowed on Wilson. "With the diplomatic cable we'll send at 2356, it will be clear."

Olive took the folder and pulled out the chart of the North Atlantic. She measured a distance with her thumb and forefinger, then moved them along the chart. "Over fifteen hundred miles from here. The *Hornet's* combat range is well less than half that."

Wilson sat back in his seat. "Can we expect Air Force tanking, Admiral?"

"No."

Wilson nodded his understanding. He'd have to move *Valley Forge* close to the North Cape of Norway, or launch multiple tankers, or both.

"And covert. EMCON the whole time."

"Recallable?"

"Absolutely, up until the airplane crosses into Russian airspace, and while Washington and Moscow *are* in touch, it's bad, and this is probably going to go."

Wilson studied the chart. "Finland?"

"No overflight," Coleman answered.

In the uncomfortable silence, Olive kept her eyes on Wilson to get his attention. When their eyes met, Wilson knew he had to speak next.

"Admiral, we've had a development. Our one healthy *Hornet* pilot sent from the beach just turned in his wings. He passed you on the flight deck and he's in that *Osprey*." At that moment they heard the rotor beat increase to full power and watched on the PLAT as the aircraft became airborne and slid left to clear the deck for the launch.

Frustrated, Coleman absorbed the news with a frown, and waited for Wilson to continue.

"Sir, we now have one up jet, no pilots, two weapons in the magazine, a cockpit black box with associated wiring, and some technicians to help us load and arm it. The no-pilot part is the limiting factor, and we'll need one—and a backup—from the beach."

Coleman surveyed the glum faces in the room. "Not sure that I can just shit you a fighter pilot in the next 48 hours, much less in the 24 you'll need him to be aboard and prepare him. What do you recommend, Admiral?"

Before Wilson could answer, Olive jumped in.

"We've discussed this sir, and I have about seven or eight pilots who have flown the legacy FA-18 operationally. They are carrier qualified, tactically proficient, and…it's like riding a bike. We'll identify one of them, sir."

Wilson leaned forward. "Or postpone, sir. Can we have 96 hours? Even 72 will help."

Coleman shook his head. "No. It's already been three days since we lost *Lloyd Childers*, and the country is tearing itself apart. People want action and an end to this before it escalates further. Justice must be swift as well as certain, and if we are seen as wavering or weak, we invite more."

Wilson glanced at the PLAT. Both waist cats were loaded with *Rhino* tankers. One minute to launch. Coleman continued.

"I didn't say this, but…we have a plan for their Pacific Fleet…I've heard."

Wilson looked at the fleet commander for more.

"After…your strike," Coleman added. "They'll see it coming, giving us credibility."

"Will they see *my* pilot coming?" Wilson asked with an edge.

"Not unless your pilot highlights himself. You have overflight of Norway, and my staff tells me it'll be less than an hour till Varda Nos. We want as covert as possible, to surprise and shock."

"Do the Norwegians know, sir?"

"No, but they will one minute before your plane enters their airspace," Coleman answered with a reassuring nod. Wilson found it anything but.

The *Rhino* on cat 3 then went into tension, reminding all of the significance of the moment. Wilson needed this strike to draw Russian blood, lots of it, to put most or all of their combatants on the bottom, to *end this*. Or would sweeping the seas of the Russians actually end this? Russia crossed a line, unthinkable last month or even last week. Did it require a response in kind? And a strike on their soil? Escalation, big time.

The room vibrated as the speeding catapult shuttle pulled the howling *Super Hornet* down the track. The *Rhino* leapt into the air with a *boom* as the shuttle slammed into the water brake.

Turning away from the PLAT, Coleman faced Wilson. "When do you expect them to be in launch positions, Jim?"

"Depends on where we find them, sir, but my sense is that the first missile will come off in roughly ninety minutes. From there, it could be 20, maybe 30 minutes of flight time. They have Icelandic overflight, and are going at the last datum, which is about one-fifty miles north-northeast."

Coleman glanced at Olive, then back to Wilson. "Who's in charge?"

"Our top CO, sir, Comet Halley."

Coleman smiled and shook his head as he muttered. "Aviators and their call signs."

"Yours would be *Cooler*, sir," Wilson offered with a smile.

"I'll take it…but let's get back. CAG, tell me more. Can your pilots really do this?"

Olive nodded. "Yes, sir. They are veteran aviators. We'll get the right one."

Coleman studied her. "Knowing nothing about the aviator who just quit, I'll imagine that your veteran aviators have families."

The Air Wing Commander nodded again. "I'd say that yes, sir, all have families." Olive kept her eyes on Coleman.

Another *Rhino* roared down the angle and banked left. Wilson spoke next.

"Admiral, I'd say that many, if not most, of the aviators launching now have young families. Olive and I will talk to those with *Hornet* time, including some of these guys like Comet when they come back. We'll have a pilot, sir. When do you think we'll get tasking?"

"I'll get you an update in twelve hours. What else do you need?"

"Sir, do you know Admiral Smith? He was our strike group admiral sixteen years ago when Olive and I were JO's here in VFA-64."

"Sure, Vice Admiral Jim Smith. He's part of the retired graybeard crowd in Norfolk. I see him on occasion."

"Sir, I'd like to speak with him. With his background, he may have some insights into this mission."

Coleman considered it. Smith would have to be found, brought to the Second Fleet compound, read into a program, then put on a secure line in a questionable electro-magnetic environment.

"Maybe. What do you want to ask him?"

"Sir…I'm not sure, but I think his insights will generate specific questions. I mean…what did he think about when he was flying this mission as a lieutenant, and what questions should I ask as an admiral now?"

Coleman frowned. "I'll see what I can do. Can you scribble down some questions? It may be that I can only get you written answers over a secure line and have them hand-delivered here."

"We'd appreciate it, sir, and we'll get you something before you depart." Wilson pointed to Smoke, who nodded his understanding.

Another *boom* shook the ship as the last of the strikers was shot off the bow.

Wilson checked his watch. "Admiral, would you like to join us for a quick snack, then monitor the action with me from TFCC?"

"Considering the time, yes. My deputy can handle things in Keflavik. Seems like the action in Second Fleet is right here."

Wilson got up and motioned Coleman to the door, as he and the rest of the aviators imagined themselves as *Tomahawk* lead climbing to meet the tanker with the coast of Iceland ahead.

Chapter 44

Raven 401, 75 miles SW of Keflavik, 1025 June 20, 2024

Comet backed out of the tanker basket and slid to the right of the formation, coming up in parade next to his Maintenance Officer "Bone" Kouvaris in 404, who, over his shoulder, signaled his CO to take the lead. Comet tapped on his helmet and motioned ahead; *I have the lead.*

As he flew formation on the *Buccaneer* tanker, he assessed the formations around him. Four *Rhino* tankers dragged four divisions of strikers, each loaded with two LRASMs per jet, northeast toward Iceland. Off his nose was Keflavik, where a 4-ship of F-15C *Eagles* was scheduled to take off five minutes ago and push out ahead of them as a sweep north of the island, to kill any bandits in their path. Following in a long trail, Comet and the strikers would then get into launch positions for their missiles...once the *Knight*, holding high over Iceland, sent them the latest targeting info.

None of them had ever dropped a LRASM, much less in anger, but this strike called for them to drop them in a coordinated manner, to overwhelm the Russians with inbound missiles from all points of the compass. With the ranges involved, they had to overfly Iceland and risk that any number of spies—or even innocent gawkers—could see them and report what they saw. For the moment the island was shrouded in a blanket of cloud with only three volcanic peaks in the east protruding. Comet wasn't too worried, but undercast layers did have holes. They would have to deal with being spotted and get their missiles off in the most quick and efficient manner once *Knight* passed the enemy datums. The radio crackled.

"*Iron.*"

"Two."

"Three."

"Four."

"*Knight, Iron* seven-one's up as fragged."

"*Iron* seven-one, *Knight*, roger, *Tomahawk* also up as fragged. Picture clean."

Comet noted the *Eagles* pop up on his link screen and slide onto the course line of his NAV display. Intel had assessed the likelihood of Russian fighters nearby as low, but if the *Eagles* didn't shoot down a Sukhoi they could tickle the radars of the Russian SAG—*if* the Russians were radiating in the cat-and-mouse of naval warfare.

Far to *Comet's* left, four F-35Bs from *Tinian* tanked off a *Super Hornet* in company with two *Growlers* from the VAQ-146 *Rickshaws*. Once topped off, one *Rickshaw* would join with a section of F-35's to take up orbits north of the island, first to find the SAG, then to electronically attack it when the LRASMs were inbound.

All the strikers but Comet's #4 wingman were tank-complete, and after *Raven* 411 disengaged and retracted his probe, Comet moved acute on the tanker and motioned for him to retract the basket. Once the basket retracted inside the buddy refueling store, Comet gave the pilot a thumbs-up followed by a kiss-off detach signal, as well as signals to his wingmen to accelerate and climb. Before it disappeared under his leading-edge extension, the tanker banked left with the others to RTB, and, on timeline, Comet held his fuel dump switch open for a second. The small white cloud that blossomed behind Comet's jet was visible to all in the group spread out over several miles. *Here we go.*

Accelerating in a ragged wall formation, the twenty-two Navy and Marine Corps jets ramped up as twenty-eight pilots and NFOs fiddled with their displays and double-checked their combat checklists complete. In each division, the lead popped out a bundle of chaff—which bloomed and disappeared behind them—watching over his shoulder as the wingman mimicked him.

Comet checked the time. The first step in the kill chain was to find them, and *Knight* had linked nothing to his display yet. With the undercast, the strike depended on the E-2 and/or AWACS to find them, and preferably both. Fuel drove everything, and as the lead, Comet had a window to first find and fix, then track as he deployed his formations to engage and deliver their weapons on multiple axes to arrive at a certain time. If the Russians were careless, the F-35s might detect them. All Comet could do was lead the formations into the most likely release positions, and flex quickly when the Russian SAG was found.

Floating high over a sea of white, with the *Eagles* ahead and the F-35s with their lone *Rickshaw* deployed on either side of the gaggle of LRASM shooters, the Americans got their first sniff.

"*Raven* one-one, *Knight*, fly your timber."

Comet opened up his display to see the symbol for an enemy combatant illuminated some three hundred miles off his nose. *Yes!* He checked the time and determined that he had a fifteen-minute window to deploy his outrigger formations to the east and west.

"*Spartan* and *Buccaneer*, action. TOT base minus five."

The outboard formations veered away and accelerated to their stations. They would launch their missiles first, allowing their LRASMs to fly programmed tracks on the enemy flanks and converge close to when Comet's *Ravens* and the division of VFA-62 FA-18E's, callsign *Arrow*, launched their weapons head on. With time as the only real constant, the aviators in each cockpit calculated their time to launch and expected fuel state.

Now feet wet north of Iceland, the Americans encircled their prey...but how many? *Knight* only showed one contact. Where were the others? East? West? North? Already sunk? Comet doubted it. As he fed the linked data into his missiles, the show began.

"*Iron* seven-three spiked zero-two-zero, notching southeast!"

Comet checked the position of the *Irons* on his link then glanced up at the horizon off his nose. The linked contact was 025, almost 030, but 020 was slightly left of his nose. Something there that the early warning aircraft hadn't yet seen. But *Iron* 73 got a RWR hit and honored it as he must. He called a warning to the *Spartans* who had the western side of the pincer.

"*Spartan* two-two, that's on your side!"

As Comet transmitted, another enemy symbol popped up. By his estimation it was 25-30 miles west of the first. Less than 200 miles ahead; if the Russians had shot a SAM through the layer, it was still too far to pick up visually. However, by radiating, they had flinched, and the ELINT sections shared via link what they were collecting real time.

Another symbol illuminated on his MFD. The surface action group was spread in an east-west line, at least three contacts—big game for the 32 LRASMs in his strike. He checked the time; with ten minutes till his launch, he had to pump once to not enter their SAM launch acceptability region.

"*Ravens*, in-place-left, *go*, saunter."

Comet rolled left and pulled hard, watching his western wingman Bone and Bone's wingman do the same. Out of the turn they would throttle back, essentially "holding" in the middle of a weapon delivery to save gas and not drift too far away.

"*Spartans*, Kraken, op-away!"

"*Cutlass*, Kraken."

Within seconds, sixteen LRASMs fell from the wing pylons of eight *Super Hornets*. After one second of fall, the missile wings extended and jet turbofan engines lit off as their guidance computers flew them on a pre-programmed track to converge on the target each *Rhino* pilot designated. Aware of each other, the missiles depended on inertial navigation to get them to the end game, where their passive radar and ESM homing and their IR and EO seekers would scene match and guide the missile into the most vulnerable spots of the targeted combatant.

"*Irons*, beam right, shackle!"

Comet checked his link for the action some fifty miles north of him. The F-15s had tickled the Russian defenses far enough and, with no bogeys, had no reason to push further.

"Missile in the air! Nine o'clock long!" an anxious *Eagle* pilot sang out.

Comet craned his neck left and looked to the northern horizon along his left wing. Nothing, and the link confirmed it. The Air Force fighters were at least sixty miles away, the Russians well beyond that.

"*Arrows* turning in."

Comet checked the time. *Now.*

"*Ravens*, in-place-left, *go*, Armstrong."

With eight Navy jets off to the east and west as their missiles flew their assigned tracks, the *Ravens* and *Arrows* pulled around back to the north and accelerated in their weapon release runs. Rolling out, Comet designated his assigned target as the others did, now heads down and working the speed/distance problem to get to their individual launch baskets on time.

The *Ravens* and *Arrows* accelerated to the linked contacts on their nose in a wall of eight, the *Spartans* and *Bucs* were out Winchester and flowing away, with the *Rickshaws* and their F-35 escorts holding high to the east and west collecting and disseminating all the RF trons that they could.

"*Irons*, reset south." Comet checked his link: *Oh great.*

"*Iron, Knight*, group on your nose one nine five, fifty-three, hot, FRIENDLY! *Raven* one-one."

"*Iron* seven-one, copy."

With the F-15s resetting, Comet and the others would be nose-to-nose with the resetting *Eagles* in their weapons release, though separated by at least 20 miles. He put the geometry out of his mind. *Big sky, little airplane.*

Armed and designated, Comet neared the release point level at 480 ground, the small triangle symbols of their targets on the undercast ahead through his helmet-mounted sight. The release cue floated down, and *Comet* mashed down on the pickle.

His jet shuddered as 2,400 pounds fell from his left wing, and shuddered again as the second missile released two seconds later. Comet overbanked left and transmitted *"Raven* one-one, Kraken," as he looked down at his LRASMs that lit off in order and sped ahead.

Thirty-one missiles (one malfunctioned) raced along their assigned tracks and profiles to their targets as the *Rhinos* egressed south. This strike was designed to attrit Russian combatants that could molest the maritime patrol aircraft and helos sent to prosecute the submarines that were yet unable to penetrate the Faroes gap. The massed Northern Fleet task force would push through the narrower—yet less defended—Denmark Strait, accept losses, and free up at least some of their missile and attack boats to enter the open Atlantic to hold Western shipping, undersea cables, and population centers at risk.

The Russian flagship admiral was furious when one of his frigates radiated—and then shot two max-range SAMs that could be easily defeated—without authorization. Now highlighted, the Russian SAG radiated everything they had to counter an expected inbound strike. The admiral, fearful of being attacked before he could inflict damage, quickly ordered six of his twelve SS-N-33 *Zircon* hypersonic missiles from three ships to attack Keflavik, the logistics and C2 center-of-gravity for the Americans. One frigate was unable to launch the new missiles because of crew unfamiliarity and poor training, but the flagship and another frigate launched a salvo of four. In fiery bursts, they shot from their vertical launch tubes and into the overcast layer, nosing over to the southwest as their scramjets lit off on their semi-ballistic profiles.

Their launches detected by the F-35s, the information was linked back to the JAOC at Keflavik, who assessed it as an anti-ship attack on one of the American DDGs in the Denmark Strait. When the missiles went hypersonic and disappeared from radar, none guessed that the real target was them.

While the American carrier planes were still feet-wet on the egress with their LRASM noose tightening, the Mach 9 *Zircons* nosed over in their lethal dives, slowing to allow their sensors to identify their assigned targets as they dove into and through the overcast just as the Americans could again "see" them and sound the alarm—but too late.

Three tons of red-hot kinetic energy slammed into the volcanic soil near the fuel farm pump house, excavating a gigantic crater and tearing into the tanks themselves, which caused a massive secondary explosion with ejecta that travelled hundreds of yards in all directions. As the JAOC personnel bounced in their seats from the explosion, the next hypersonic missile hit alongside their building and vaporized it, with dozens of watchstanders killed instantly and all communications with Keflavik obliterated.

As the frag continued to fall, another bolt from above clipped the wingtip of a parked E-3 on the airfield ramp, demolishing it and the parked E-6 next to it while pelting three adjacent P-8s with massive clusters of ejected earth and killing exposed flight line personnel. The final missile slammed into the asphalt along the edge of Runway 10-28 near the intersection of Runway 01-19, blowing out a massive crater that cut both runways, limiting their use until repairs could be affected that would require hundreds of dump trucks and mixers to return them to full service.

Stunned passengers in the airport terminal regained their feet after being knocked to the floor by the impacts, and roiling clouds of black and brown smoke enveloped Keflavik and rose into the overcast. Twenty miles away, Icelanders in Reykjavik believed they had just experienced a massive earthquake with three sharp aftershocks, and the vital American installation known to all as "Kef" was effectively put out of the fight.

With their eyes glued to the COP in TFCC, Wilson, Coleman, and all the watchstanders observed the LRASMs envelop the enemy surface combatant tracks.

"Time to impact," Wilson demanded.

"Four plus forty, sir," the watch captain responded.

Wilson turned to Admiral Coleman. "Admiral, we're out of the known ranges of any missiles they've got, and those have missile profiles, not the slow-speed drone that hit *Tinian*. I think they are going for *O'Hare* in the Denmark Strait, and they're at GQ."

"Heaven help them. Hypersonics...how do you defend?"

Wilson didn't have a confident answer. Navy knew about the *Zircon*, a game changer for sure. Coleman leaned toward him and spoke in a low tone.

"Nuclear tipped, Jim?"

"Could be, sir. *O'Hare* is a good ship, and they are alerted. They have a chance to knock them down in the terminal phase."

"We just lost Kef," the operator on the forward console sang out.

Wilson and Coleman ignored the comm glitch. The team would soon reestablish contact with Keflavik, but the real show was about to begin. Wilson had to disable or sink most of the Russian SAG with this one strike, an all-in gamble with every LRASM he had in the magazine. He could pick off survivors later with his air-launched SLAMs and *Harpoons* and surface-launched missiles that could close the range tonight. He could then concentrate on the ASW effort. The LRASM symbols converged as they dived in unison for their terminal run-ins, and the console operator opened up the screen.

"Uh-oh," the watch captain said.

Wilson turned to him. *"O'Hare?"*

"No, sir. Just got a high-side text that Kef got waxed by hypersonics. Nothing from the JAOC or my buddy in Second Fleet."

Coleman perked up. "How about the AWACS orbiting overhead?"

"Connected with him, sir, but Kef is dead...I've been texting and no answer."

"Email?"

"I'll try, sir."

At that moment, the first sea-skimming LRASM entered a slight pitch up to avoid a stream of close-in AK-630 gunfire, then pitched back down to the *Udaloy* DDG and entered it at the starboard main deck behind the wheelhouse. The blast ripped away the superstructure forward and killed all in the forward main propulsion room. The ship heeled over almost on its beam before it righted itself and coasted to a stop, just as another missile entered at the waterline under the helo hangar, blowing the stern off.

Wilson and Coleman, neither of them surface warriors, could only imagine the carnage inflicted on this ship, now just a computer symbol, and then another on the eastern side of the formation.

"What do you hear from *O'Hare?*"

"No report sir...they're not under attack."

Shane entered TFCC from SUPPLOT.

"Admiral...Keflavik got hit hard. We think hypersonic *Zircons*. We've got social media video from airport passengers and highway cameras. It's bad, sir."

A shocked Coleman groaned in despair as he followed Wilson and Shane into SUPPLOT, seeing the video played over and over in a loop.

"Get me Norfolk, Fleet Forces Ops," Coleman ordered. "And NAVEUR. I'll talk to whoever comes up first."

On the COP, more LRASM symbols faded away, either downed by the Russian defenses or finding their marks.

One of those marks was the flagship, *Marshal Yermalov*, the only *Slava*-class guided-missile cruiser in the fleet. Observing the action to the west from high on his bridge, the panic-stricken admiral gave empty orders to shoot down the inbound missiles as the frantic radar operators in Combat and gunners in the 130mm mount forward did the best they could in a scenario they had never experienced before, even in training.

The first LRASM hit amidships starboard on the after-most SS-N-12 missile tube, ripping a giant hole in the superstructure and igniting adjacent missiles in their tubes, tearing away massive chunks of the topside spaces and the starboard half of the wheelhouse. Sailors were lifted into the angle-iron overheads and knocked unconscious, falling in heaps on deck as blood poured from multiple lacerations and deep wounds. The forward engineering space was soon unhabitable as a fuel line burst, soaking the sailors who scrambled out of the space, only to be ignited by the flames along the main deck.

As the admiral pulled himself up and looked through the bridge window, another LRASM entered the hull under the forward gun mount, the explosion spraying shrapnel aft that the bulletproof windows could not withstand. With a mangled bow and no one driving, *Marshal Yermalov* plowed ahead at the most speed the remaining turbine could provide as smoke billowed from his wounds, the aft gunners trying—and failing—to pick up and shoot more inbound missiles. With the loss of the flagship and his admiral, the Red Banner Northern Fleet was leaderless while more red-and-black explosions of Russian warships broke the sharp horizon.

CHAPTER 45

USS *Valley Forge*, 100 miles SW of Keflavik, 1200 June 20, 2024

Despondent, Vice Admiral Warren Coleman sat in Wilson's stateroom, staring at the bulkhead and thinking of his staff at Keflavik. How many dead? He had to fight the fleet—but who would fight it? Chances were that some of his staff survived, asleep in their rooms as part of the night watch. But *who?* In his mind, Coleman scanned the faces of his officers and petty officers as they did their jobs on the watch floor. Like him, they did their duty, while in the back of their minds thinking of their loved ones home in Norfolk preparing for or evacuating from the specter of a nuclear strike. He thought of his OS chief and her infectious smile, a mother of four. Is she on the night watch team? He couldn't recall. Word would come soon, and with it, the horror. Wilson stepped inside, a welcome interruption.

"Admiral, we just got word: This morning's strike sank four combatants, including the *Slava*. Two frigates are withdrawing north, and my people tell me one of them may have been hit but the warhead didn't detonate. The Brits may have sunk an attack boat, too, awaiting verification. Sir, the jets are recovering soon and we'll get more from their debrief, but for the time being sir, my stateroom is your stateroom, and my staff is yours. You can fight the fleet from here, Admiral, and for as long as you need."

Coleman nodded. "Thanks, Jim, and well done to your aviators. What about the SAR effort?"

"Two Brit P-8s out of Lossiemouth are enroute sir, but no plan yet on how we'll recover survivors. With Kef down, our P-8 effort is to sweep the Denmark Strait with jets out of Gander, about a four-hour transit. We can expect coverage of one over the strait 24-7, and we're asking for more. Commander Maynard is doing great work coordinating it, sir."

Coleman nodded again as he summoned the courage to get back in the fight. "What do you hear from Buffington?"

"Nothing yet."

"Wow, I'm surprised. This is Big Dick's big chance—eliminate the middle-man who no longer has a staff."

Wilson remained expressionless.

Regretting his disparaging barb, Coleman recovered his professionalism. "You didn't hear that. Okay, getting through the strait is job one. Brief me in an hour on your plan. Finding out about Russian survivors north of Iceland and American and NATO survivors at Kef is job two. And your plan for an expected nuclear response—all of that in the next hour."

"Roger that, sir," Wilson answered with a wan smile that conveyed his understanding. Above them, the 5MC blared.

Rhinos *in the break, make a ready deck!*

The reality of combat had returned.

Petrov couldn't believe his eyes. *Sunk!* The flagship, a DDG, and two frigates, with another frigate limping north to escape the next American onslaught. Sunk in minutes from a coordinated salvo of missiles delivered by carrier planes—*while our own naval pilots play chess in Severomorsk!* Petrov thought of their "aircraft carrier," the pride of the Red Banner Northern Fleet, rusting away at its moorings for *years* after its last underway.

Contempt filled him for its crew, but most of all for the Moscow and St. Petersburg apparatchiks who constructed and had delivered a broken, casualty-plagued ship that could not sail, so far gone it could not even be repaired. Even if it could get underway, the Americans would pounce on it and probably sink it as soon as it rounded the North Cape—*but at least we could exact some enemy losses!* Anything was better than that carrier and the vaunted but broken-down nuclear-powered cruiser along the pier beside it, sitting out the greatest Russian naval action in over 100 years!

Kuzmin approached his chair. "I've heard, Kapitan."

Not responding, Petrov held his gaze for a moment. *Can I count on you for anything now, Kuzmin, or must I fight the American Navy myself?*

"The crew also knows, Kapitan."

Petrov turned away and nodded to himself with a frustrated smile. "What else does the crew know that I do not, Mister Kuzmin?"

"Kapitan, they are still processing the shock of it, but they are ready to avenge their deaths."

"And you, my trusted Executive Officer? Will you too fight to the death for the Motherland?"

Keeping his voice low so the helmsman could not hear, Kuzmin nodded his sincerity in a way Petrov could not mistake. "Yes, Kapitan. I'm ready."

"With *everything*, Yevgeny? Because this is everything. We will not hold back."

"Will we receive orders, Kapitan? At least the cover of orders?"

"I don't know. As I see things now, we—no, *I*—am the senior officer underway that is engaged in combat. Moscow and Platonov are wringing their hands with indecision as Washington targets their very bedrooms with a nuclear holocaust they'll deliver in minutes. We must strike again, and this time harvest more than an expendable destroyer, a mere escort ship to them. If we bag a carrier and the thousands aboard it, the Yanks will see we are a capable force and sue for peace. They won't sacrifice New York for the Donbas."

Kuzmin listened, unsure that an angered Washington would not rain one hundred or even one thousand warheads on the Motherland if an aircraft carrier and the thousands aboard the giant ship were blown out of the water. Unlike the Czar's seamen of the last century, who had never heard of a place called Tsushima as they sailed with expectations of glorious victory, he had come to grips with his own death the moment *Admiral Alekseyev* had cleared the sea buoy. None of them were coming back. There was no hope of defeating the Americans and NATO at sea, but they could be bloodied. He and his shipmates would give their lives for each other, not the bastard Platonov, and especially not the perfumed princes in Moscow who—with the wave of their soft, fleshy hands—sent the Red Banner Fleet to do the impossible. He—and his immortality-seeking kapitan—would do the men's work knowing—as did the kulaks of old—that they were going to their deaths in the service of a state that would not mourn them.

"What is your plan, Kapitan?"

Petrov glanced over at *Vitac*. "I am going to leave him, sprinting to the Denmark Strait as fast as our shafts can propel us. I'm going to shoot anything in our way and launch our last salvo when the Yankees are sighted. Any sighting...even another destroyer. A carrier cannot be too far from it, and better to shoot at something than hold back for perfect and be sunk in the process.

"The engineers are ready, Kapitan."

Petrov turned to Kuzmin and took his measure with a penetrating look.

"Are *you* ready, Yevgeny?"

"I am, Kapitan."

"You know what will be expected of you, of us?"

"Yes, Kapitan. I've made my peace."

Petrov smiled. "Very well, Mister Kuzmin. Once we leave our old uncle and are established, vodka for the crew. I estimate ten hours till we get into a firing position. And cigarettes, our special supply of *Amerikanskiy* cigarettes. A pack for each man. When victory is assured, another ration."

"Standing by for your course, Kapitan."

Petrov glanced at his digital screen, considered it for a moment, and pointed at a lat/long. "Here, Kuzmin. North sixty-eight, west eighteen. Give me a course."

Kuzmin manipulated the display and entered a range circle for thirty knots.

"Two-two-four, Kapitan. Ten hours at thirty knots."

"Very well. Give me thirty-one...to remind the Yankees of their history."

"Aye, aye, Kapitan. Shall you give the order, or I?"

"You may take the honors, Yevgeny Sergeevich, and lead the Red Banner Fleet to its final glory. Please proceed."

"Aye, aye, Kapitan," a solemn Kuzmin replied. He then turned toward the helmsman, took a deep breath, and bellowed.

"In the pilothouse, this is the Executive Officer and I have the conn! Belay your reports! Helm, right standard rudder to new course two-two-four! When steady, engines ahead flank, make turns for thirty-one knots!"

Electrified, the bridge team repeated the orders, turning the wheel and ordering a flank bell, at last breaking free of the hated merchant. When Kuzmin informed all that the smoking lamp was lighted for an American cigarette ration, they beamed their good fortune. Word raced around the ship—*we're going to attack the Americans again!*—and as the DDG bounded over the long swells the men toasted their upcoming victory.

Petrov watched *Vitac* recede as his ship pulled away to the southwest. He had left him without so much as a wave, done with him after a full week alongside. *We will now see what the eggheads in Moscow have given us,* he thought. *Admiral Alekseyev's* paint and RF and IR signatures would be put to the test in single combat with an enemy strike group only hours away.

Chapter 46

War Room, USS *Valley Forge*, Greenland Sea, 2200 June 20, 2024

"What the hell is *that?*" Wilson asked out loud as he studied the jpeg image. The merchant in the foreground was clear, but the strange object on the far side of it resembled a combatant. But was it? Was that a gun mount forward or a crane? He needed analysis, and his Intel Officer Shane sat across from him with answers.

"Admiral, we believe it's a *Udaloy II*, the only one in the Russian Navy, RFS *Admiral Alekseyev*. The merchant is *Vitac*, with a length of 460 feet. Comparing the length of the hull shape in the background to *Vitac*, we get a length of 535 feet—and the *Udaloy II* is 535 feet. The pinkish color is camoutint, a low-observable color that's been around since World War II. We believe they painted the entire ship with it just before they sortied."

"Who took this?"

"A Norwegian girl with her phone, sir. She was ashore at Jan Mayen when attack helicopters that we believe came from this ship sank her trawler and killed all aboard. The Norwegians rescued her about six hours ago."

Wilson studied the faint image of the *Udaloy II* DDG. Yes, that could be a gun mount, and the superstructure mast looked like it could belong to a combatant. Details were difficult to determine, but Shane had more.

"Admiral, if you look just in front of the merchant's superstructure, on the other side is what looks like a smudge. That is the hull blast-deflector for the starboard SS-N-22 *Sunburn* quad pack. The discoloration indicates that one or more missiles have been fired from it."

Wilson nodded. "So, the merchant ship is cover, hiding in plain sight?"

"We believe so, sir. Norfolk has it for analysis and we should be getting a report from them in another hour."

Wilson turned to Mark. "Can we get an attack boat up there? He must have an acoustic signature, at least the merchant. Find the merchant and find him."

"Will ask, sir, but that's a 600-mile hike from here even if we had a boat assigned to us, and NAVEUR has them plugging the GIUK gap from Russian intrusion and helping to defend us in ASW."

Olive spoke next.

"Sir, we've got a bunch of stand-off missiles and laser weapons. We'll have to work in close to get the *Harpoons* off and at least disable it, then put it on the bottom with some 2,000-pound GBUs."

Wilson considered it. Flight ops in the restricted waters of the strait, then 600 miles up to Jan Mayen and back. If they could detect, track, and target it. What other defenses did it have from American sensors?

"Mark, we've got to get a rough position first. Is there a *Triton* up that we can vector toward Jan Mayen?"

"There's one in Lossiemouth, sir. Will contact NAVEUR and ask for a mission."

Wilson frowned. *Buffington is going to jump into my cockpit again.*

"Okay. Get a *Triton*, P-8, attack boat. We need scouting."

"We'll send a section of *Rhinos* too, sir, with a *Growler*," Olive added.

"As soon as we can, *and* one or more F-35s from *Tinian*. All the airborne ELINT sensors we can. This guy might be the only capable surface combatant they have left."

Mark took the cell-phone image and found the spot Shane identified. "With that blast scar he probably was part of the missile strike on the 18th."

"*Sunburns* are postulated to have a nuclear capability, sir," Shane added. The room went silent as they considered the implication. This ship could have attacked *Lloyd Childers*...and could attack again.

"Find it and sink it," Wilson muttered as he rose from his chair. He motioned to Olive. "And, CAG, we must talk. Flag bridge, let's go. Mark, Shane, back here in an hour—with your answers."

Wilson led Olive up to the O-8 level. With the midnight sun illuminating the gray clouds that hovered low on the horizon, they entered the flag bridge. Wilson walked to the windows and stood looking out over the forward flight deck crammed with jets parked along the edges in familiar fashion. *Manila Bay* steamed in company on the western horizon, with *Tinian* shrouded in mist to the east. Strike group escorts rode in assigned positions along the perimeter of the formation, and multiple MH-60 *Romeos* buzzed about as they searched and listened for threats below. The carrier creaked as it rolled in a beam sea that had worsened.

"We have to find and sink this *Udaloy*, job one, but I expect that we'll have a more important mission in about twenty-four hours. What do you propose we do for a pilot?"

Olive faced Wilson before she answered.

"Me."

Emphatic, Wilson shook his head. "*No.* Olive, you are the Air Wing Commander, and you are not going. You must lead, and you must assign. Nice try, but who? Any volunteers?"

"Haven't asked for any."

"That's up to you, but who?"

"I am taking it, Admiral."

Livid, Wilson pounded the windowsill. "Olive, *enough!* We don't have time for this shit! You're not going; now knock it off and tell me who is, *now!*" he snapped.

Undeterred, Olive set her face and stood her ground. "Yes, Admiral, I know I'm the Wing Commander, and as Wing Commander it is my job to identify aircrew and assign missions. There is no pilot aboard who is more qualified in the jet and mission and who understands the strategic stakes better than I do. I'm taking it, sir."

A furious Wilson looked away, breathing through his nose as he fought to control his anger.

"It's me Admiral, and it's my call…unless you relieve me, which, of course, is your prerogative."

"I should! I expect more from my CAG, who should know that *any* CAG is too valuable to fly on such a mission."

"You mean like the Fiery Cross mission *CAG*? The one where you earned your Silver Star?"

Caught short, Wilson's mind raced. "This is different!" was all he could blurt out.

"How so, sir? You led from the front as CAG, when I and the other COs could have led that strike just as well—and, you know in your heart, better—than any CAG, even you. So, I learned from you. I know the jet and this mission."

"By that logic, I should take it."

"Don't be ridiculous, sir. We both know your best flying days are behind you."

Stung, Wilson narrowed his eyes. Olive was right, but to hear it from her! Despite the gray flecks in her hair and the eagles on her shoulders, she was still

Lieutenant Teel to him, a fact she knew and resented. Olive had never defied him before, and both realized she had crossed a line.

"Olive, you are a *mother*." Wilson regretted saying it as soon as it came out of his mouth. Olive paused to acknowledge Wilson's mistake before she spoke.

"Comet and Irish are fathers, with more kids than I have. One of the *Buc* department heads with time in the *Hornet* is married with four kids. Must I send the junior pilot, a father of four, to his death on what we all know is a one-way mission? *You* wouldn't…and didn't."

"At Fiery Cross we all had mutual support, suppression, and a fair chance of coming back. This…*is different!* A single jet, covert, overland…and who knows what's going to happen after the detonation. EMP will fry your cockpit, even your watch, and you'll have nothing but a turn-needle and ball that works."

"You're making my point, Admiral. It's a one-way mission for the human being that's going to fly it, and I've made *my* point. I'm taking it, sir."

Wilson was furious. "I forbid it!" he snarled.

Embarrassed by Wilson's outburst, Olive looked away, emitting an amused giggle that Wilson thought was the most feminine—and sarcastic—sound Olive had ever made. As Olive suppressed a smile, Wilson held firm. "I mean it Olive, you're not going. As CAG you are too important to risk."

Olive walked behind the admiral's chair to contemplate the angled deck, cluttered with *her* airplanes that she was responsible for. After a moment, and with her back to Wilson, she answered in a clear voice.

"No."

Olive turned back to Wilson and continued.

"Sir, I'm the commanding officer of Carrier Air Wing Four, and this is *my* call, not yours. If you don't like it, you can relieve me and run the airwing yourself, just like Admiral Buffington wants to run this strike group for you. I admit there's no one better to run Air Wing Four than you…after all, I've only recently started my CAG tour. However, sir, I am the CAG until you relieve me for cause. And know, sir, that I want to return home to my family as much as anyone aboard, but the world just changed…and this responsibility falls to me if Washington orders it."

Both knew Olive had just crossed another line with her contemptuous personal attack, and Wilson could relieve her on the spot for that alone. Her Deputy CAG, or even a senior skipper like Comet, could run the airwing almost as well. Wilson would not have tolerated it from anyone else…but this was unlike Olive, stressed as they all were but volunteering to face death more than Wilson or anyone else aboard. Despite his past glories, both also knew that at this moment

Olive was a better tactical aviator, and she made a strong case that professionally—and personally—she was the right aviator at the right time for the job.

In the silence that followed, Olive's eyes softened. "You've been here before, haven't you, sir?"

"What do you mean?"

"You put your career on the line with Saint that night in CVIC. Did you know he would back down?"

Wilson considered Olive's question. "No...but it was worth it."

"Well, that's how I feel now. I don't know what action you are going to take, but I'm right about this one, and it's worth it."

Wilson nodded his understanding as he looked off the bow. "First...I'm not going to relieve you. But I am going to think about this. My gut tells me no, that I need you as CAG, and how I'll be second-guessed if I relent, but I'll think about it for now."

Skweez burst through the flag bridge door, panting from his sprint up five ladders.

"Admiral...Admiral Buffington is on his way out here."

Wilson shook his head in disbelief. "When?"

"His *Osprey* checked in with Strike about five minutes ago."

"That gives us ten to fifteen minutes, sir," Olive estimated.

"Does Admiral Coleman know?" Wilson asked.

"Yes, sir," Skweez answered, "and so does Captain Morrison."

"Good. Okay, I'll meet him on the flight deck with rainbow side boys. Let's go below and get the latest from TFCC."

Skweez stopped him. "Sir, the Russian merchant. They think they've got a track on him, about 250 miles north of Iceland and heading toward the North Cape."

"And home," Wilson figured. "With the DDG in company?"

"No, sir."

"Okay, let's go."

With Skweez leading, the three of them descended the ladders for flag plot. As Skweez flew down the rails ahead of them, Olive warned her admiral.

"Regarding our conversation and your decision, sir, it would seem you have minutes, not hours."

Wilson continued down the steps in silence, knowing that she was correct.

CHAPTER 47

RFS *Admiral Alekseyev*, Greenland Sea, 2300 June 20, 2024

With a fresh cup of espresso, Petrov walked into the chart room to check their track. Finding the young *starshy matros* quartermaster asleep in a chair, Petrov feigned ignorance and dumped the steaming liquid in the man's lap. Howling in pain, the sailor leapt to his feet in anger followed by shock at seeing his kapitan scowl at him.

"You clumsy fool! Watch where you stand and fill this cup back up at once!"

The sailor, his face white with fear, said, "*Yes, sir, Kapitan, at once,*" as he took the cup and left the space to Petrov, who smiled. The man could be summarily thrown into the brig, only to be beaten by the *michmen* when he was released. Petrov needed him and all his men in the coming hours. The vodka would flow again when they were victorious.

He plotted the INS position on the chart—only three miles behind PIM. He'd live with it to save his shaft bearings for what he knew would be a long sprint north once his missiles were downrange. Launch them all in a desperate shotgun blast, hoping that his *Moskit* in tube 5 could take out an entire American strike group. But where? He hoped for a transmission from headquarters, an ESM hit, anything to detect them, and prayed quietly to the fleet's patron, St. Fedor Ushakov, Victor of the Black Sea, for deliverance. The klaxon sounded, followed by an announcement.

"*Action Stations! Action Stations! All hands man your action stations!*"

Petrov flew out of the chart room to the wheelhouse. "Where away? What?" he shouted.

Kuzmin had the binoculars to his eyes as he scanned south. "Enemy aircraft, Kapitan, low on the horizon, just a speck."

"Has it detected us?"

"Does not appear to, Kapitan. It's moving off to the west."

"What type?"

"I'd say carrier-based, accustomed to flying low over the sea."

Petrov grabbed a pair of binoculars. Yes, an airplane beaming them, well over ten miles, a dark speck against the gray horizon. He scanned around it to find a mate but could not.

"I'm going to Combat; sing out the moment it closes us."

"Aye, aye, Kapitan."

Petrov slid more than stepped down the ladder and entered the dark and cold CIC, the men putting on flash gear as they sat buckled in their console seats.

"This is the Kapitan! Do you have an IR track?"

Petrov recognized the voice of Leytenant Medvedev in the darkness. "Yes, Kapitan! Estimating twelve miles bearing two-two-six, and it appears to be opening!"

"Very well, Mister Medvedev! Continue to track passively, do not radiate."

Petrov studied the IR screen. The speck moved left-to-right against the cloud backdrop before it flashed a planform silhouette.

That's a fighter.

"The contact appears to be turning, Kapitan!" Medvedev cried.

Petrov concentrated on the turning fighter, little more than a speck. Was it turning into or away from him? He felt the eyes of Medvedev and the *michman* on him. Petrov detected aspect, and went with his gut.

"Radiate and track! Mister Medvedev, at max engagement range shoot two *Tor* SAMs with AK-130 rounds, then look."

"Aye, aye, Kapitan! Acquire and track contact bearing two-three-one!"

The *michman* had a lock in seconds. "Target acquired! Nine miles and closing!"

Petrov studied the IR screen. No objects had been released from the fighter, but he had tipped his hand. He cursed that he only had three SAMs in his magazine, but he had no choice.

"Maximum range!"

"Shoot two!" Petrov bellowed.

"Missile control, shoot two on targeted track!"

Seconds later the first SAN-9 *Gauntlet* burst from the vertical launch tube, soon followed by another. Petrov remained glued to the IR track monitor.

The fighter turned hard, and Petrov saw flares separate from it. *He knows he's targeted!*

"Time to impact!"

"Twenty seconds, Kapitan!"

Damn, Petrov thought. A nimble fighter could escape in that time. *Dammit!* As the missiles streaked to their target he second-guessed himself. *Should I have fired? He could have been targeting me. Is something coming at me? Is he sending a radio warning now?*

The IR contact bloomed brighter as it changed shape. *He's escaping with his afterburners!*

"Contact beaming east!"

"No, Mister Medvedev, he's withdrawing."

All in CIC watched the digital clock count down the seconds.

"Is he transmitting?"

"Yes, Kapitan!"

Blast! They had been discovered.

As the contact on the screen receded away, Petrov watched the seconds count down, hoping to see a missile fall on the enemy jet from the top of the screen.

"Time out!" Medvedev cried.

The dot on the IR screen continued away. Both missiles had missed. Petrov then went with his backup plan.

"Break lock but stay in search. Prepare to launch both helicopters immediately, armed or not. Get the pilots up to the bridge at once. Bridge, turn right heading two-five-zero, ahead full. Mister Medvedev, analyze the IR tape and tell me what that was!"

As Petrov returned up the ladder to the bridge, he thought of Platonov. *Where are my orders?* His eyes met those of Kuzmin, and the two retreated into the chart room.

"What was it, Kapitan?"

"I think a *Super Hornet* scouting ahead of its carrier. It has certainly called a warning, knowing that something shot at it. Now they know a threat is in this vicinity and will attack it in hours if not minutes. So, we must strike first. I want the helicopters to scout the Denmark Strait, the *Katran* to the east near Iceland and the *Helix* to the west. They must find the enemy strike group, and search for it until they run out of fuel. I want us to run toward Greenland, to avoid Iceland and give us the widest view of the Denmark Strait when it's time to launch."

"Do you want the aircraft to radiate and transmit, Kapitan?"

"Yes, and once clear of us I want them to call the fleet on any channel to obtain any direction. We are standing by for orders, but in the absence of orders, Yevgeny, we will act."

Keeping silent, Kuzmin exhaled hard through his nose.

"No time to discuss, Yevgeny Sergeevich, we must do what we must *now*, for the Motherland." Outside, they heard a pilot inform the OOD that he was summoned.

Petrov opened the chartroom door and summoned them in. The senior pilot was *Kapitan-leytenant* Denisov, who flew the attack bird. His fellow *leytenant* Tereshchenko was the aircraft commander in the *Helix*.

"Mister Denisov, there's no time to waste because the Yankees have likely discovered us. I want you to skirt Iceland to the west but stay low and outside thirty miles. Once clear of the Vestfirdir Peninsula turn south. Report all you see, but I want the position of the *Amerikanskiy* carrier *Valley Forge*. Avoid their surface combatants and keep working south to find the carrier using all your sensors. Tereshchenko, same thing but you head toward Greenland here at this bay—Helheim Glacier—then turn left to roughly two-one-zero. Stay outside visual range. Radiate and report, no limits."

The shaken pilots nodded their understanding of their mission and what it was—a suicide last gasp attempt to detect and target the Americans. Denisov spoke.

"Kapitan, where will you be—when we return?"

"We will work to the west southwest here, until we are at a position to launch at anything in the strait."

The pilots said nothing. Petrov perceived their unease.

"Sons of Russia...you *must* detect and report them. The success of the Red Banner Northern Fleet, of the Motherland in this conflict, depends on it. If your fuel becomes exhausted, abandon your craft and signal an enemy ship for rescue. Launch at once, there is no time to spare! If you detect them soon come back and we will toast to your aviation skills and great valor. However if we do not see you again this day...*please forgive me*...and go with the utmost respect of your shipmates."

Tereshchenko stared hard at Petrov, a condemned man saying nothing but conveying everything. Even if the Americans didn't shoot his ancient *Helix* out of the sky he and his crew would freeze to death in their rafts on the icy surface of the Greenland Sea, despite the summer sunshine—*if* they could escape the fuel-starved helicopter's deadly blades in its death throes, and *if* the rafts even inflated.

Petrov kept his composure as Kuzmin looked away in disgusted embarrassment, unable to face his mates in their last minutes before they launched from the last ship in the decimated Red Banner Fleet.

Denisov shook hands with Petrov. "Pray for our success, Kapitan."

"All of us will, as will all of Russia, Mikhail Ivanovich." He then pulled the pilot close in a bear hug.

Tight-lipped, Tereshchenko offered his hand to Petrov, who squeezed it hard as he held it for a long moment. *"Prashai*, Sasha. We need you."

The young aviator nodded and followed Denisov out to return to the helicopter hangar. Once they were gone, a downcast Petrov clasped his hands before him. *Sasha...only twenty years older than my Sasha.* He then realized that Kuzmin had not spoken.

"I know, Yevgeny Sergeevich. It is one of the many burdens of command to order brave men to their deaths."

Kuzmin nodded in silence before he replied. "Yes, Kapitan, and there will likely be more of that as this night unfolds."

Lieutenant Junior Grade "Gigs" Gigliotti in *Raven* 402 was lucky to be alive.

Just as he turned to inspect a strange vessel or object off his nose, a missile launch indication on his RWR gear froze him for a moment before he reflexively broke right. He had the presence of mind to record his FLIR and hit MARK as he lit the cans and popped out chaff and flares. Jinking on the egress, he put the radar indication at his six as he twisted in his seat to pick up an inbound missile that would come out of the low overcast. After harrowing seconds that seemed like a lifetime, the indication disappeared, and he transmitted to *Knight*.

"*Knight, Raven* four-zero-two! I just had a missile launched at me!"

The word was passed back to the ship and within minutes to Wilson, who was with Buffington and Coleman in the War Room.

Wilson read the sighting report.

"Gentlemen, one of our scouts just got lit up and potentially shot at northwest of Iceland. He's okay and coming back, but the position is about 200 miles north."

Buffington threw up his hands. "This makes my point. You could have had the LCS up in front of you on point and they could have taken this guy out. Regardless, sink this mofo and get through the strait because we have bigger fish to fry."

Coleman shifted in his chair. "Admiral, we have to find out what this guy is before we get any closer. We don't want to be in his launch acceptability region."

"Warren, what could it be? A half-dead destroyer or frigate? Whatever it is, Second Fleet is ordered to sink the damn thing. Put your best people on it and do it, now. My tasking is from Washington and *you* are supporting."

Coleman looked to Wilson for help, as the air-surface fight was not part of his career background. Wilson rescued him.

"Admiral Coleman, we've laid on a quick reaction strike; it's on alert sixty and the crews have been briefed. It's a *Harpoon* strike and it'll go once we track and target what this is. I've ordered *Tinian* to launch two JSFs to investigate."

"Can't the JSFs just sink it?" Buffington asked.

"Sir, *Tinian* does not have the anti-ship weapons aboard."

Buffington shook his head in disgust as Coleman jumped back in.

"Thanks, Jim. Admiral Buffington, where do you want us and when? We've got the capability if this goes down."

"And I think it's going to. The diplomats are on the phone, but the American people are losing it and demand action. Washington is not sure the country can stay together if we don't respond in kind."

"Sir, is the goal to punish or deter?"

"Warren, I don't give a fuck what it is. I have a warning order and I'm not going to fuck it up, which means both of you aren't going to. You tell me where you need to be to hit Varda Nos."

Wilson raised his hand.

"Admiral, what is the weapon profile?"

Buffington gave Wilson a quizzical look, then scowled.

"Wilson, I don't need a bunch of aviator jargon. I don't freakin' know…You're the aviator and I'm not going to tell you how to suck eggs, just when to hit the target, so when can you?"

Wilson stepped to the wall chart.

"Admiral, we've looked at this, and we can launch on this circle here, tanking the jet twice on a low-low profile. Covert ingress through Norway and Finland…"

"Not Finland. They don't know about this, but I just have a feeling. No overflight."

Wilson frowned. Sparsely populated Lapland was a preferred ingress route. They'd have to find an alternate through the villages of Norway's north cape.

"Aye, aye, sir."

"What's this place?" Buffington growled.

"That's Jan Mayen, sir. Norwegian."

"Can you hide there?"

"We could, sir," Wilson answered. "But getting there in these seas may be a challenge."

Buffington stopped and stared at Wilson, who held his gaze.

"Admiral Wilson, I am really getting tired of your chicken-shit excuses. Are you telling me this nuclear-powered aircraft carrier cannot manage heavy North Atlantic seas? Solve your problems! Deal with it, and I'm tired of excuses."

Buffington stepped to the chart and measured off a distance.

"Six hundred miles from here, which is near your circle. Now I'm a four-star, and four-stars don't navigate and mission plan, *one* stars do that, so do your fuckin' job Admiral, and tell me what you are going to do—and I want to know in five frickin' minutes! Warren, come with me."

Buffington flung the door open as Coleman followed, leaving Wilson alone with his chart—and his unanswered questions.

"Okay then, Big Dick. We'll do it my way," he muttered to himself.

Chapter 48

RFS *Admiral Alekseyev*, Denmark Strait, 0040 June 21, 2024

"Kapitan to the bridge! Kapitan to the bridge!"

Laying awake in his rack, Petrov bolted upright and depressed the lever to the intercom box.

"What is it?"

"Enemy aircraft detected in attack formation, Kapitan!"

The next moment, *Action Stations* sounded throughout the ship.

Petrov raced up the ladder in his slippers and entered the bridge, noting the midnight sun low to the northwest and a ridge of purple cloud to the south as the ship labored in the white-capped swells. He stepped to the air-search radar repeater and saw multiple contacts along the southern arc.

Shit!

"What have we heard from our aircraft?" he shouted. It had been over an hour.

"Nothing Kapitan, from either one."

Petrov couldn't believe it. The *Katran* should have at least rounded Vestfirdir by now...if it wasn't already shot down. The Americans could have easily downed it on its way.

"I'll be in Combat. Maintain this course and speed. Bosun, have Mister Kuzmin lay to Combat on the double!"

Gripped with fear, Petrov focused on controlling his breathing. With only a glance at the radar repeater, he saw at least six returns. If they didn't have a lock on him, the Americans knew he was nearby, and multiple contacts like this indicated to Petrov that they were armed and aiming to kill him.

One SAM left, practically worthless tactically! With too little range to down an airplane, he'd have to use it to intercept an inbound cruise missile only seconds from impact. *If* his inexperienced fire control team could track and target it. But what of the other missiles that would surely follow, from multiple axes of arrival? Deck guns, his 130mm shells and 30mm bullets, would have to do.

And what about his passive defenses? If the Yankee cruise missiles could not identify their targets, would they go stupid before they got into 30mm range? Petrov didn't know, but he *needed* to know, now.

Kuzmin arrived, and lifted his flash hood over his face. Petrov grabbed his arm and pulled him aside.

"Yevgeny, we must launch all we have down the strait now before the Americans hit us. We cannot allow ourselves to be destroyed with offensive firepower still aboard."

"We should have heard from the pilots by now," Kuzmin replied.

"Yes, Yevgeny, and why haven't we?"

And at that moment, deliverance. The radio loudspeaker blared:

"*Amerikanskiy* ships! Sixty-six north! Twenty-six west! Engaging!"

Petrov and Kuzmin rushed to the chart. "It must be Denisov in the *Katran*," Kuzmin surmised. "But what kind of ships? What course and speed?"

"No matter!" an impatient Petrov answered before he turned to his watch officer. "Mister Medvedev! Enter the coordinates for a *Moskit* firing solution. Launch on bearing! Take me west, and fast! I want a clear firing lane! Salvo of two!"

With no time to spare, Petrov motioned Kuzmin to follow, and, as they had on the Feast of St. Constantine, took the *Moskit* launch keys out of the safe. Away from the crew, Petrov spoke.

"We launch the *Moskits* and run west to Greenland to hug the icepack as we withdraw."

"The American planes, Kapitan? What of them?"

"Defend with all we have, but we have got to get these missiles off. Come!"

Returning to Combat, they saw that the Americans had closed the noose.

"Fire control! Report status!"

"Kapitan, firing solutions entered for *Moskit* tubes three and five, launch bearings one-eight-five and one-nine-zero!"

Petrov glanced at the radar screen to assess the American aircraft to his south. "Very well! Mister Kuzmin, insert your key!"

With his kapitan's eyes on him, both officers inserted their actuation keys. The unthinkable only days ago, now familiar. Petrov assessed their position in relation to the strait and made his best guess.

"Mister Medvedev, assign the *Moskit* in tube five bearing one-nine-zero."

"Aye, aye, Kapitan, *Moskit* tube five assigned bearing one-nine-zero!"

Satisfied, Petrov began the sequence.

"Mister Kuzmin, on my count...*right detent*. Three, two, one..."

Both men turned their keys to the right. Just then the radar operator screamed.

"Radar separation! *Amerikanskiy* missiles released!"

Medvedev was on it. "Very well! Compute missile and gun firing solutions! Time of arrival!"

"Estimating four minutes, Leytenant!"

Petrov nodded to himself, knowing that his last cruise missiles would be aloft in two.

As the nuclear cruise missile in station 5 woke up, in familiar sequence, Petrov again selected weapon option A, followed by the fuzing: INST. Once again, a single amber light illuminated the weapons panel.

"Kapitan, I have green light logic, weapon safe," Kuzmin stated.

"Green light logic, weapon safe," Petrov responded, then continued.

"Inside Combat, this is the kapitan: prepare *Moskit* launch tubes three and five, in two-missile salvo, individual bearings. Mister Medvedev, inform the bridge to come left to launch heading one-nine-zero!"

"Three minutes and fifteen seconds to first missile impact!"

Petrov saw them now, missile tracks on his radar, all converging on him. *Admiral Alekseyev* heeled to starboard as he began his turn, and the closest enemy missile crossed the twenty-mile ring. How he wished for targeting, a confirmed position. As before, all he could do was launch and hope the rabid dogs could find prey. With 45 degrees of turn left and the missiles closing, he could wait no longer.

"Medvedev, rudder amidships! Mister Kuzmin, activate final arming on my count, acknowledge!"

"Standing by to activate final arming on your count, Kapitan," Kuzmin responded.

With hands on their activation keys, they waited for Petrov's countdown as the watchstanders held their breath.

"Very well...three, two, one, *activate!*" All green lights returned to the weapons control panel.

"Mister Kuzmin, this is the Kapitan. I have green light logic, weapon armed, activation key released."

"Kapitan, I have green light logic, weapon armed, activation key released," Kuzmin answered, his face expressionless as the deck steadied underneath them. With seconds till impact, Petrov could not delay.

"This is the kapitan of *Admiral Alekseyev*! On my order, prepare to launch missiles from tubes three and five!"

"Tubes three and five are in readiness, Kapitan! Doors open!" Medvedev shouted back as warning bells sounded outside the thin bulkhead.

"Very well… *FIRE SALVO!*"

The *michman* fire control technician pulled the console trigger, and one second later the missile in tube three roared away as the space shook from the blast. Men in the adjacent radio room cheered, as did all aboard the pride of the Red Banner Fleet.

Kuzmin could only stare at the radar display of the converging tracks, paralyzed at what he had done again, in what would likely be his last minute of life. If Petrov had similar feelings, he did not show them.

"Saint Fedor, pray for us!"

The *Moskit* in tube 5 burst away from the ship with a metallic shriek none had heard of before and accelerated away from the ship as it gently climbed and turned south. Petrov and the crew had no time to spare.

"Engage inbound missiles! Fight the ship! Yevgeny, remain here!" Petrov boomed to his XO as he flew out of the space and raced up the ladder to the bridge, picking up the white exhaust of the tube 5 missile as it entered the overcast.

Dasvidaniya!

A split second later a *Dagger* surface-to-air missile burst from its vertical launch tube, momentarily covering the bridge windows in white smoke.

As the ship broke clear, the bow-mounted 130mm gun, trained to port, fired its first round, a deafening hammer blow that shook the ship to its keel, followed by more antiaircraft rounds every two seconds. Amidships, chaff bundles fired from their mortars, and wispy clouds of gossamer metal floated aft as *Admiral Alekseyev* bounded through the swells.

"There!" the OOD cried.

Petrov picked it up, a tiny object trailing a dirty mist. By the launch ranges he suspected he was being attacked by *Harpoons*, an older system, but effective in a swarm. And here was an example of something he had studied for years, growing larger. An object entered his field of view from above and exploded on top of the cruise missile, turning it into a careening fireball that plunged into the sea, lifting a thin curtain of spray. *One down!*

Petrov was now out of missiles, and looked to his guns to save him.

Shell casings littered the foredeck as the 130mm continued to fire. Petrov followed its barrel downrange and saw splashes, as the OOD shouted orders to the helm from Combat. Suddenly the gun swiveled right and opened up on a new threat, as more rounds jumped from the barrel with the sound of Thor beating his hammer on a giant steel drum.

"Look!" the OOD cried.

Petrov's heart sank. Off their port bow a missile bore in—and drifted right! Amazed, Petrov and the astonished bridge team watched it pass left-to-right in front of their jackstaff and continue on.

"Ha! The bastards missed!" the bosun exclaimed.

It didn't see us, Petrov thought. The paint, the passive RF defenses, the IR coating—*they really can't see us!*

But the American missiles saw something as they continued in, and the frantic OOD gave orders to the helm to unmask the 30mm and bring the 130mm to bear on new threats.

Nothing more from his helos, nothing from Severomorsk or the task force! The last gasp of the Red Banner Northern Fleet, Petrov and his crew fought alone with all they had as their two silver bullets continued over the horizon downrange, their wild-eyed targeting sensors programmed to glom on to anything they could.

At that moment, a Standoff Land Attack Missile—Expanded Response opened up its IR seeker toward the linked target. Launched from a *Spartan* FA-18F, the WSO noted flashes of return on the right of the screen. He slewed to it and discerned periodic returns with evidence of solid returns next to it. As the missile closed, he attempted a lock, but the seeker would not hold it and drifted off, forcing him to manually slew it back. A faint outline then appeared between the flashes, return that the seeker head could lock onto. The WSO was surprised when the range indicated 1.5 miles—right on top of it!—and before the missile flew into the return he could make out the lines of a surface combatant.

The missile guided on the port side aft stack, tearing it off before it plunged into the adjacent starboard aft stack. *Admiral Alekseyev* lurched hard to starboard from the blow, which also loosened the footings on the aft tripod mast, which soon fell back under the strain of its weight on the pitching and rolling support beams, carrying Petrov's main air-search radar with it.

Petrov was catapulted into the overhead and fell bleeding onto the deck as the ship staggered under the force of the impact. Regaining his senses, he got to his feet before the rest of the dazed bridge team while the 130mm continued its thunderous fire, adding to their sensory overload.

As blood flowed down the side of his face, Petrov looked aft to see smoke and flame—and one 30mm still spitting its defiance with a tongue of flame and accompanying chainsaw-like sound. *At what?*

He faced out to sea in time to see it, a phantom apparition that approached in silence, ghostly white, registering its identity and purpose in his brain as the howl of its engine reached him.

The missile entered the hull just below the main deck under the *Moskit* blast deflector, ripping out the superstructure above it, incinerating all in the forward main machinery space, vaporizing the Combat Information Center and Yevgeny Kuzmin, who died as he helped a wounded man stem the flow of blood from the first impact.

Petrov was blown out of his shoes and thrown across the bridge, again slamming into the overhead lagging as his mortally damaged ship rolled to starboard almost on its beam. Momentarily knocked unconscious, he awoke to the sound of screeching metal and snapping electric cables. Someone cried *abandon*, forcing Petrov—despite an arm that hung limp at his side—to gather his energy and stand.

The aft part of the bridge was open to the sky as a torrent of black and white smoke poured from *Admiral Alekseyev's* gaping wound amidships, the forward mast gone as fire lapped the deck underneath his feet. Through the smoke he heard the mournful chainsaw of the 30mm aft—defiant to the end.

Abandon...abandon...

The deck tilted up, and with his good arm, Petrov held onto the compass repeater as his field of view became flame and smoke that slowly approached him. On the far side of the pilothouse a man—without a uniform as it had been blown off him—cried as he slid off the tilted deck and into the cauldron of fire and steam. Through the burning chasm that no one could cross, Petrov saw a sailor, a non-rate, flash burned with his hair gone and crying for his mother as he himself clung to the derelict that moments ago was a deadly surface combatant. *A goner*, Petrov thought, about both the young sailor and his ship.

Though dazed, Petrov's first thought was of saving himself. *Arina!* He then realized, *No. I cannot. I must not.* With no more commands to give and no one to give them to, a resigned Petrov held on as he and any remaining survivors aboard the forward half of his ship were fed into the burning maw. *Saint Fedor, I commend my soul.*

Admiral Alekseyev's bow lifted high out of the water before it settled back and slipped into the frigid Greenland Sea, taking forty-two Russian sailors with it. The aft half of the ship floated, only to receive another sea-skimmer that clipped the roof of the hangar bay, spraying shrapnel to port that killed men blown from the forward half who were struggling in the water. Thirty-five surviving crew released the clamshell life rafts and clambered in, huddling together to conserve body heat as the remains of the finest guided missile destroyer in the Red Banner Fleet raised its stern high, bronze screws glistening in the Arctic sun as they slowly disappeared below the surface.

Two hundred miles south, the airborne *Moskits* continued their assigned mission.

CHAPTER 49

CUTLASS 306, DENMARK STRAIT, 0130 JUNE 21, 2024

Through a break in the clouds, Lieutenant Tim "Debbie" Walsh saw it.

A sea-skimming missile, white, and ripping over the waves at a blinding speed. By reflex, he overbanked down as he slammed the throttles into burner. From 20,000 feet he needed all the altitude advantage he had to turn it into airspeed just to keep sight.

"Strike *Cutlass* three-zero-six, tally one *vampire* inbound, Mother's zero-two-zero seventy, on the deck!"

"Roger, *Cutlass* three-zero-six, cleared to engage!"

Locking the missile with his helmet system as he eased out of his diving turn, he got a single-target track as the white dot pulled away. The airspeed of it stunned him—*2.1 Mach!* He lagged it while he armed up, holding zero g to gain as many knots as he could in a desperate tail chase with over 700 knots opening. He selected AMRAAM and got a momentary SHOOT cue before it disappeared, the supersonic sea-skimmer pulling away. At only sixty miles from Mother, Debbie realized at once that he could be in burner all day and never catch this deadly specter, heading right for Mom. In desperation he squeezed the trigger anyway, and seconds later the AMRAAM rocket motor ignited with a deep *WHOOM* Debbie heard in the cockpit as it arced ahead in a shallow dive to catch its prey.

"Strike, three-zero-six, it's out-of-LAR. Steady heading one-eight-five, on the deck!" By the geometry, he could see it wasn't headed directly toward *Valley Forge*, but close enough.

After several seconds, Strike answered. "*Cutlass*, maintain contact. Engaging with birds."

Debbie didn't like this one bit. *Those birds are going to guide on me!* He wasn't worried about the carrier's shorter-range defenses, but those of *Manila Bay* and the strike group DDGs with SM-2s or 6s that he'd never be able to escape from. Blue-on-blue, but what choice did they have with this howling guided bullet bent on killing any ship it came across? If they could track Debbie, they had a chance at acquiring the missile he was chasing. *Fuck this!*

His intakes hummed at 1.48 Mach as he passed four thousand feet, veering toward a narrow hole in the deck to remain in the clear. His radar remained locked on the *vampire*, burning a hole in it, but the missile wasn't going to catch it.

In the clear under the layer, he looked right and saw it down his wing line. *Another missile!*

Maintaining his lock and still in full blower, Debbie eased right toward the pop-up contact, almost as big as a fighter, his eyes padlocked on this new screaming banshee. He watched it drift ahead as it raced along, and knew he had to act soon.

The AMRAAM timed out far behind the first *vampire—fuck!—*but that allowed Debbie to break lock and target the newcomer. Maintaining his intercept heading, he designated the target with his Helmet Mounted Cueing System and locked it; three miles and opening. *Damn!*

"Strike, three-zero-six, pop-up *vampire* BRAA two-four-eight, three miles, on the deck heading one-niner-five."

"*Cutlass*, Strike, engage!"

Debbie selected his remaining AMRAAM as the *vampire* slid in front of him. He was maxed out at 1.5, the fastest he had ever been down low. With the strike group ships in the gloom someplace fifty miles to the south, he had to get this one.

With a lock and flashing SHOOT cue, he squeezed to the trigger a second time. Frustrated after several seconds with no airframe jolt from the missile release, he punched in the STORES page.

HUNG

"*Sonofa!*" he raged. With his radar missile unable to fire, he selected *Sidewinder* without thought. His headset was rewarded with a screaming tone, but at an edge-of-LAR range with opening velocity. Now!

Rolling a few degrees left to center the dot he squeezed the trigger hard. The AIM-9X whooshed off the rail and porpoised ahead before it settled down. Guiding on a steady bearing line, Debbie watched it disappear as the rocket motor burned out. *C'mon...Come on!*

Debbie was about to fire his last missile when a puff appeared next to the *vampire* that continued ahead. He squeezed again just as the *vampire* pitched up and suddenly disintegrated against the sea-air barrier it traversed at Mach 2, a spray of misting white fingers reaching toward its quarry to the south. The second *Sidewinder* guided on a small piece of flaming debris tumbling toward the water and exploded on it just before it slammed into the dark waters of the Denmark Strait.

"Splash one *vampire! Cutlass* three-zero-six, splash one *vampire!*"
Strike acknowledged him. "Roger *Cutlass*…we're at GQ here."

Wilson watched the action from Flag Plot with Coleman and Buffington. All the admirals could do was observe the kids in their ships and aircraft defend from this missile attack, missiles no doubt launched just before the air wing cornered and reportedly sank an unidentified combatant north of the strait. The COP showed a *vampire* intercept by *Cutlass* 306 to the north. Were there more? Seconds counted down, and the first known threat was at the edge of the group formation.

Missile symbols came off *Manila Bay* and *Eugene Lindsey*. To Wilson, the *vampire* seemed to be heading toward his cruiser only five miles away. Coleman was thinking what Wilson was thinking, and spoke in a low tone.

"Do you feel lucky?"

The watch captain sang out the latest status.

"Birds away from *Manila Bay* and *Lindsey! Tinian* engaging inbound *vampire* with RAM. *Valley Forge* has a lock!"

"What are they tracking, dammit?" Buffington growled. "Another *Sunburn?*"

In what many sensed were the last seconds of their lives on Earth, the watch team viewed the COP in silence, focused on the missile symbols and nothing else.

"Splash the *vampire!* Splash the *vampire!*"

A whoop went up in the space, grins of relief under their flash gear, as Wilson's staff slapped each other's back and hugged. They'd *live*—for a little while longer at least—but soon returned to their duties as they noticed the stone faces of the two guest admirals.

"Well done," Wilson said aloud. "Watch captain, please send my compliments to the TAO. But we're still in Indian Country and will be for the foreseeable future, so stay alert. SUPPLOT, we need your I and W more than ever, and pass the word ASAP."

Buffington muttered to Wilson, "Let's go," and turned to exit the space. Wilson and Coleman followed before Wilson led them back to the War Room—where Mark Meadows waited with a troubled look.

"Tasking sir. The Varda Nos mission is on—for tonight."

"Give me that," Buffington growled as he grabbed the message out of Mark's hands. Coleman clasped his arms across his chest as he waited with Wilson.

"It's from Tom Garcia at STRATCOM. Varda Nos at zero two hundred Zulu tomorrow."

"That's twenty-four hours from now, sir," Meadows offered, looking at his admiral.

"How do we know it's from Admiral Garcia?" Wilson asked. "Is the message authenticated?"

"It is, sir," Mark answered.

"Weapon specified?"

"Yes, sir."

Without acknowledging him, Buffington handed the sheet back to Mark and turned to Wilson.

"Wilson, you and your people better make sure that every letter of this OPORD is followed exactly as written. This weapon must go 'boom' on the proper target at precisely the time specified, to the second. Who is going to fly it?"

Wilson swallowed hard and answered.

"Captain Teel, sir."

"Who's he? Get him in here."

"It's she, admiral. She's my Air Wing Commander."

"A woman?" Buffington asked as he raised an eyebrow. "Why a woman? Can she handle it? Anyway, I'm not sure of the optics. Get someone else."

Wilson paused a moment before answering. "We'll see who else is available, sir."

"Good. Now, I want the route of flight, attack profile, dip clearances, voice reports, all of it, and I want it in an hour. And recall procedures. And contingencies…what if the jet is shot down? What if the pilot is captured? Weather. All of it."

Wilson himself wasn't sure about all those details, but he was aware of the time. "Admiral, I request postponing until zero-eight hundred so I can ensure all is in order. That's over twelve hours before launch time, allowing us time to flex and address any contingencies."

Buffington made a face as he exhaled his annoyance. "Zero-*seven* then, and not a moment after."

"Yes, sir, zero-seven, thank you sir."

"I'm going to bed. Where's you in-port cabin?"

"Just next door, Admiral, and it's ready for you. Captain Meadows will escort you. We'll see you here at zero-seven hundred."

After Mark escorted Buffington away, Coleman faced an expectant Wilson.

"Never knew that Strike Group Command was this exciting."

"Admiral, as much as I don't want to send my CAG on this mission for a variety of reasons...I'm hard-pressed to find a better pilot. And she's adamant...it's her Air Wing until I fire her."

"Are you going to? Buffington has given you an out. If there are other available pilots, and the four-star doesn't want the woman...seems cut and dried."

Wilson knew Coleman was right. He didn't want Olive to go...but he didn't want Comet to go either. Someone had to—*in about twenty hours from now!*—and the responsibility fell to him, to identify and assign a pilot to fly a probable one-way mission just this side of suicide, and which could lead to a full-blown nuclear exchange.

"Olive—Captain Teel—wants to go, she's mentally ready to go, and she does have more *Hornet* hours and carrier experience than the others. She's a test pilot, and I know the mission will be suitcased."

"Suitcased?"

"Ready to go, sir, fully prepared with answers for any contingency."

"Jim, Buffington doesn't want a woman. Select one of the men."

Wilson looked away, lost in thought as he considered his options.

"Admiral...the admiral...or you, sir, can fire me. Captain Kristin Teel is my choice for this, and I can back it up with solid rationale."

Coleman held his gaze for a moment before he spoke.

"I can't help you."

"I know, sir. I know."

CHAPTER 50

USS *VALLEY FORGE*, GREENLAND SEA, 0250 JUNE 21, 2024

Wilson steadied himself as the carrier rolled hard to starboard. With the Denmark Strait and seas north of Iceland clear of the Russian SAG, Huey had run north at a hard 27 knots, the most he dared in the heavy sea state. In fifteen hours—if they could maintain PIM—*Valley Forge* would be in a position south of Jan Mayen from which to launch the single *Hornet* to Varda Nos, the pilot of the jet still unclear. Escorting the carrier was *Manila Bay*, barely able to keep up as both ships pounded through the building waves.

After Buffington turned in, Wilson woke Olive, Comet, and the other experienced *Hornet* pilots aboard and had them report to CVIC. There, with Shane, he read-in the aviators and handed them the mission folder on Varda Nos. All but Olive were taken aback at the notion of a nuclear retaliatory strike, but soon focused on the mission, planning it as long-range covert strike that one of them would fly that night. As the aviators planned, Wilson pulled Olive aside.

"Buffington doesn't want you to fly it."

Olive held Wilson's gaze as she absorbed the message.

"Because I'm a woman, right?"

"Correct."

Olive frowned as she contemplated the bulkhead. "Sir, I could understand if it was because I'm the CAG. What did you say?"

"I told him we'll get a pilot among those available and he dropped it."

"Who then?" Olive asked, her anger building.

"I want you to trust me."

Impatient, Olive looked away as she fought to maintain control.

"Admiral, I won't be able to live with myself if I send Comet to his death when I know that *I* should take this. I'm the closest thing you have to a volunteer, I'm qualified, and it's *my call*."

"Not anymore it isn't, and I expect Comet to come back. You are the backup, and I want you to be versed in every aspect of this strike. We're going to tell—no, *you're* going to tell Comet that he's the go pilot. He might freak out like Mag…"

"I highly doubt that, sir."

"He might, so we have a contingency for that, which is you."

Ensuring the others at the planning table could not detect it, Olive controlled with rage and answered in a low tone.

"If you won't fire me, I'll resign, because you and the admiral don't trust my judgment."

"Olive, enough of your whiny shit! I get command judgment in this too, and you just got overruled, by me and *four fucking stars*. Now, I want you to compartmentalize, run the Air Wing, and trust me, dammit."

Unsold, Olive closed her eyes to calm herself. When she reopened them, Wilson had already turned and walked away from her.

As the strike group sped north to the planned launch position near Jan Mayen, the effects of Tropical Storm Belinda, losing strength south of Iceland, had caught up to Carrier Strike Group Eighteen.

Escorted by two attack boats safely submerged and 24-hour P-8 coverage, the surface ships—rigged for heavy weather—labored in the high swells and gale force winds. Torrents of white water lifted by her bow slammed into the tall superstructure of *Manila Bay* as she held position on *Valley Forge*. Heavy spray wafted over the forward flight deck of the carrier each time her bow dug in, dousing the *Rhinos* parked on cat 1 several times per hour. In her hangar bay, Aviation Boatswains Mates slowly moved the "go" *Hornet* aft to Hangar Bay three, a real-life game of Rubik's Cube in the cramped space. Bringing the jet up on an elevator would be dicey—if not dangerous—for the men standing by with tie-down chains. When the time came, the brake-rider in the cockpit—an airman young and invincible—would be watched closely by the chiefs, who knew he would be in much more danger than he realized.

The stormy North Atlantic seas paled in comparison to what was happening on the adjacent continents.

Vast crowds of angry protestors jammed the streets of Brussels, London, and Paris, calling for an end to the Western military actions and demanding no counterstrike to the Russian nuclear attack. Violent mobs blocked the entrances to bases in the UK, especially RAF Lakenheath and HMNB Portsmouth, with replacement protesters filling the ranks of those carted away by the beleaguered police. At the same time, in Western European churches that had been all but abandoned for decades, prodigal believers filled the pews, confessed their sins, and prayed for deliverance.

In the United States, both sides of the political aisle made their voices heard, the left protesting in the manner of their European fellow travelers, and the right demanding retaliation and an end to Russian aggression. Cries of *"Remember the Childers!"* and *"Nuke 'em back to the stone age!"* resounded from coast to coast.

As Americans continued to flee the cities and stock up, a spontaneous general strike—because no one showed up to drive the trucks or fly the planes—crippled the nation. Fear-fueled unrest broke out everywhere, and Washington cracked down in the National Capital Region, the only area of the country that they could in a desperate struggle to keep the United States united, while faithful in the rest of the country jammed the churches as they had not been since Sunday, September 16, 2001.

In the flag War Room, six bells sounded. Wilson stood before the head of the table in front of the briefing screen, as Buffington and Coleman sat at the far end with Huey, Olive, and Wilson's senior staff. Along the bulkhead, the admirals' aides and staff strap-hangers, ready with answers, took notes. Among them was Weed, who stayed out of view of the senior admirals as much as he could. Wilson began:

"Admiral Buffington, this is Commander Halley, Commanding Officer of Strike Fighter Squadron Sixty-Four, who is the go-pilot for this strike. He is an experienced carrier pilot and prepared to deliver this weapon on target and on time. He will now brief you on the route of flight and the attack profile, and will address contingencies followed by answers to your questions and concerns. Commander Halley."

As Wilson took his place on Buffington's right, Comet began. Behind him, a digital map of the Norwegian Sea and North Cape of Norway, with the route of flight designated in black, appeared.

"Good morning, Admiral. Tonight's mission is a single-plane strike supported with enroute tanking, launching from a position…"

Comet stopped when a grimacing Buffington waved his hand.

"Jim, why are we flying over Norwegian airspace? They've got a fifth column of greens all over that country who are going to see your guy coming and get right on the phone, probably with a picture. Why would you not stay off the cape and out of sight?"

Comet stood in silence as Wilson answered for him.

"Admiral, two reasons. One is time and distance; we must top off this older model FA-18 with fuel just to get him to a position to go right at Varda Nos overland. Second, most of the route is over uninhabited territory. While no one can guarantee that he won't be spotted by a hiker once feet dry, fishing boats are all along the coast. An arcing route along the North Cape keeps him in and among those boats that have crew with cameras and comm links, to include Russian boats."

"Does Norway know?"

"Yes, sir."

"Prove it."

Wilson motioned to Stretch. After a moment of quickly leafing through papers in his folder, he pulled out a sheet and handed it to Wilson. Before he could point out the passage, Buffington grabbed the paper out of his hand. After a cursory glance, he handed it back to Wilson.

"Proceed," Buffington growled, followed by Wilson's quick nod to Comet.

"Sir, we'll rendezvous overhead with the tanker and proceed to Waypoint One..."

Buffington shifted in his chair to Wilson. "Enough of this! Does this man know how to find the target and hit it on time?"

Wilson remained a statue as he answered with a terse, "Yes, sir."

"Fine! I don't have all day to absorb all this fly-boy minutiae. Send your airplane out and hit the damn target, but what's your defensive posture up here? What's the comm lash-up? What are the Norwegians and the Brits doing, if anything? Where are my Combat Logistics Force ships and when are you going to refuel your force after running at a flank bell in these seas? *That's* the stuff we need to talk about, and that's my expectation for this brief! What is the latest from State? What's the commander's intent from NORTHCOM and STRATCOM? Who is supported and supporting? Do you even know?"

Wilson turned to his staff. "Strike Group staff, except Chief of Staff, depart. CO and CAG, stay."

Buffington's eyes narrowed at Wilson as the embarked staff stood and filed to the door. Comet stood stunned, unsure of his next move. Wilson nodded to him to exit, and he followed Weed out as Skweez closed the door behind them. The aides of the guest admirals also remained.

Buffington glared at Wilson. "Admiral Wilson, *we* have work to do, and *we* don't have time to waste with low-level bullshit."

"Admiral, to your question, I am the supported commander. We can get an airplane—with the weapon—to the target and back. But I need help with

NATO and the State Department *after*—we enter Norwegian airspace. I need defense-in-depth, I need a solid radio relay with the strike aircraft to recall it if Washington directs, I need a follow-on course of action, I need final approval to launch, and I need to know your thoughts and direction to us. I need a lot of support, Admiral, and we would get to all of it in the brief we've prepared and address the detailed questions you have. But now, sir, I'm going to take the brief alone with my exhausted staff, and once complete, we will provide your staff a comprehensive list of requirements and recommendations." Once Wilson finished in the shocked silence of the War Room, the only sound was of creaking frames and deck plates as the carrier rolled to port.

Seething, Buffington responded with a broadside he had mentally loaded as Wilson spoke.

"Wilson you are an arrogant bastard, and if you think that that Navy Cross you wear for just doing your job is going to save you now, you're wrong. This is the big leagues, *Admiral*, and you work for *me*. Once this is over tonight, you will be off this ship by lunchtime, relieved, *for cause*, because I no longer have confidence in your ability to command. That's a great all-purpose out we have, isn't it, Wilson, that a commander can relieve another commander if he doesn't like the way he parts his hair, or his smug condescension, or his whiny bullshit. Any reason I want, and I *want*, Wilson, for you to be gone, and I cannot wait to talk to SECDEF, the CNO, Flag Matters, and all who know you that in flag command, and tell them that you are an overrated baby who can only fly an airplane—and you can't even do that well anymore. Oh, yeah, Wilson, I heard about that flight last week where you almost crashed. Here, in this junior billet, you are the embodiment of the Peter Principle, and have risen to your level of incompetence at only one fucking star. You're out—now *get out*."

Keeping his eyes on Buffington, Wilson sat back in his chair. With a nod to Coleman, he responded. "I work for him, and I've not been relieved by him."

An evil smile formed on Buffington's face. "You don't know shit, do you, Wilson? *Vice* Admiral Coleman here is *so close* to four stars and what that will mean for the rest of his life, long after retirement. Do you think, Admiral Wilson, that he is going to jeopardize that…even for you?"

To Wilson's surprise and gratitude, Coleman laid his stars on the table.

"I don't have reason to relieve him, sir, and I need his aviation expertise."

"No, you don't, Warren! His Chief of Staff here—a surface warrior who knows three-dimensional warfare!—can run this strike group just fine." An embarrassed Mark looked down, wishing this moment would end.

At her limit, the Air Wing Commander spoke next.

"Gentlemen, what I know is we have a time-on-target in eighteen hours, and after witnessing this flag-officer shit-show, *I* do not have confidence in sending my people on this mission. I demand unity of command, and I, and I'm sure Captain Morrison, don't see any of it for tasking that absolutely demands it."

"Concur," Huey added. "And each hour we steam closer to the enemy shore, risking the 5,000 on my ship and hundreds on the others. As a CO, are we going to do this or not?"

Buffington sat grinning with his arms crossed. "You do not know who you are dealing with. Warren, you've hit your terminal rank, and the rest of you insubordinate assholes are going down at Admirals Mast. Now that that is out of the way, we have tasking, and I still don't know how the final approvals will come down and how they'll be communicated, so let's begin with that. Captain Meadows, you have background with comm circuits and an understanding of the chain of command, so I'll task you with that, and I need it in five minutes. Carrier CO—where's the launch posit? Air Wing CO—return to force procedures; does your pilot know them? Chop, chop—we've gotta move."

With all eyes on Buffington, no one moved.

Buffington looked at his watch, then at each of the motionless officers at the table who stared back at him with blank faces, which filled Buffington with contempt. He spoke slowly.

"Maybe you didn't hear me. We have been tasked by Washington—the President—to respond to the unprovoked nuclear attack that killed over three hundred of our shipmates. We have hours—and you have minutes—to get me answers to my valid questions so we can prevent *fucking World War Three* from escalating. Warren, if you want to retire with three stars or *any*, you and your people had better get moving."

Coleman had waited 37 years, since he was a youngster at Annapolis, for this moment.

"Dick, this is how it's going to go. I am the supported commander, and you are supporting. I will work with my people inside the chain to accomplish this tasking, and I've got it. You have access to the comm center, Admiral Wilson's in-port cabin, the flag mess, and flag bridge…and that's it. If I see you in here or in Flag Plot or Combat or the Intel spaces, or anywhere fucking with my people, we're done."

"Dammit, Warren, what about State! What about NATO! You're just gonna nuke Russia without giving them a heads-up?"

"I'm not saying shit to State or NATO, and neither are you because it's not your job, Admiral. In fact, you just lost your comm center privileges. As far as

I'm concerned, you are ashore. You can read the messages I release, and once this is over, I'll go right to SECDEF myself—I was his aide when he was Assistant Secretary for Acquisitions fifteen years ago. Remember that? You go to him about me or my people, and he's going to get a full report about what really happened out here from his trusted aide and friend. Now, Admiral, if you'll excuse us, we have work to do, and I'll call you if I need you."

Red with anger, Buffington—his face contorted—didn't move.

"Five seconds Admiral Buffington, or we're done, and I'm on the phone before you."

Scowling at Coleman, COMNAVEUR pushed away from the table.

"And take your kid with you," Coleman added as he motioned to Buffington's aide. "Don't want to see him either."

With a head nod to his aide to follow him out, the brooding four-star stood and departed, slamming the door behind him.

Coleman exhaled. "He's not done with me, or us, far from it, but we can breathe and accomplish this mission."

An incredulous Wilson responded. "Admiral Coleman, I've never seen that before. Are you sure we want to do this now, sir, with NAVEUR just this side of house arrest?"

"Yes, we need to. Washington is depending on us, and we must respond. It's proportional and sends the right message. And—it's a valid, signed, and authenticated order. I once commanded a boomer. We don't moralize over this; it's a mindset—my mindset—and my tasking to you. Yes, Varda Nos, tonight as ordered from SECDEF."

Wilson nodded. "Aye, aye, sir." Next to him Huey nodded his assent, while Olive remained still.

"Okay…can you get your pilot back in here? I want to know the details of how he's going to deliver this and what his considerations are.

"Wilco, sir," Wilson answered, and Olive got up to retrieve Comet. Sitting back in his chair, Coleman exhaled the tension out of his body.

"And coffee, black, and lots of it."

CHAPTER 51

USS *VALLEY FORGE*, APPROACHING JAN MAYEN, 1330 JUNE 21, 2024

Pounding hard in the increasing seas, *Valley Forge* continued north with her escorts. The DDG *Eugene Lindsey* had experienced an engineering casualty and had fallen back ten miles aft of the carrier, no longer visible from it in the misting haze that had turned a darker shade of gray by the hour.

High above the flight deck, Wilson sat at his at-sea cabin desk studying the route of flight for the nuclear mission. Who to send, Olive or Comet? Both were capable—and both had spouses and children. Whoever went tonight would be alone on a near one-thousand-mile strike, in an ancient short-legged *Hornet* topped off after launch and enroute on a covert ingress. What would the Russians do if they detected one jet inbound toward the Kola Peninsula? Launch a first strike of ICBMs and the SLBMs that they could?

Defending their installations from the intruder was a given, and Wilson surmised that everything on the Peninsula was at high alert. SAMs, tactical and strategic. All calibers of triple-A, especially around Varda Nos. ECM, jamming, maybe directed energy. And alert fighters, the Naval Aviation Su-33s and land-based *Flankers*, maybe Su-34s and even the fifth-gen Su-57 *Felon*. Olive and Comet's only defense would be covert surprise…but what about the egress? What would EMP do to the enemy—and his *Hornet*? With way too many unknowns, Wilson felt rushed and overwhelmed.

A knock on the door returned him to the present.

"Come in."

Olive entered. "You wanted to see me, sir?"

"Yes, let's go outside."

They stepped onto the open flag bridge and to Wilson's chair command post, from which they could monitor the COP, navigation, weather, and more. Wilson stood near the chair and called up the navigation screen.

"How're you doing?"

"Fine—livin' the dream."

Wilson gave her a look. "And Comet? How's he?"

"He's ready. Just visited the Chaplain, and I told him to get some sleep. Brief is at 1700 in the War Room."

"How's the jet?"

"In Hangar Bay Three. Systems check good. The corrosion guys painted it with *Raven* markings. Looks pretty good."

"The weapon?"

"Won't be loaded until brief time. Once it is, they'll take it to the roof and spot it near the island with a perimeter around it."

Wilson nodded. "Okay. Let's see where we are." Wilson checked the ship's speed on the inertial navigation display and, with a mouse, ran a course line ahead.

"Eight hours at 25 knots should put us here, southeast of Jan Mayen. Will that work? What's the ingress game plan?"

Olive referred to the screen. "That's the vicinity of our planned launch point. He'll launch as part of a normal event, one that includes two dedicated tankers for him and scouts on a vanilla surface search hop. Comet will top off immediately and stay at roughly 2,000 feet or in the layer as much as possible to avoid detection. The tankers will be pathfinders and comm relay keeping him topped off until here, when he'll detach, punch off his wing tank, and accelerate. The coast-in point is here at the mouth of this fjord, where he'll bump it up and bring it down to the deck."

Wilson saw that the overland route was clear of settlements. "Where does he enter Russian airspace?"

"Here, sir, and he'll take a jog down this valley, over the ridge, and into Varda Nos. He should be able to see it at 15 miles once he pops over."

"You know this route cold, don't you?"

"I planned it, sir. Know it better than Comet."

"How about off target?"

"Continue out to sea, clear Russian territorial waters with a jog north, then sprint west to the Norwegian coast. Once back in Norwegian airspace, climb VFR to the same ingress point and enroute descent to here, about three hundred miles off the coast where a *Rhino* tanker should meet him."

"*Should* meet him. What if they can't rendezvous?"

Olive pointed a coastal airfield.

"He can duck into Andøya, sir, a former Norwegian P-3 base. It's abandoned, but the concrete's still there."

"Landing unannounced in Andøya may be as dicey as dropping the weapon."

"We'll let Admiral Buffington deal with that, sir."

Wilson smiled. "Indeed. What else will Comet be carrying?"

"Two tanks, two 'winders and an AMRAAM, an AARGM, and bullets—and a pistol."

"Alone and unafraid...okay...what's the comm plan?"

"He'll be assigned a discrete freq. to monitor, but we don't expect any transmissions until he joins with the tanker on the RTB. Once feet dry inbound, he'll give us five quick mic clicks. We'll have a *Rhino* orbiting high here, so we'll have line of sight comms—until he enters Russian airspace, not sure we can maintain it after that."

Wilson considered the narrow and tenuous recall window. "How can we recall him if that comes down?"

"He'll have a script, and after we transmit the order through the radio relay, he will authenticate it and RTB."

"Okay...everything suitcased."

"It is here. The rest of the world has lost its mind, but we're ready."

"How about you Olive, are you ready?"

Unsure of his meaning, Olive studied a pensive Wilson and waited for him to continue.

"Do you want it?" he asked.

Olive looked out to sea, to the east. She turned back to Wilson.

"Yes."

"Are you ready mentally?"

"Yes, and more than Comet."

"I'd give you a fifty percent chance of coming back."

Olive smiled as she emitted a feminine chirp, more sarcasm than amusement.

"You are generous, Admiral. I told Comet one in four."

"Have *you* made your peace?"

"Yes. I've written what needs to be written. And...I visited the Chaplain last week.

"After *Lloyd Childers*?" Wilson asked her.

"No. Well before that."

In the silence, Wilson gathered his emotions and decided.

"Okay...I want you to take it."

Olive nodded as she suppressed a smile. "Thank you, I guess."

"I don't want to, Olive."

"I know, nobody *wants to,* but I must take it...and was going to anyway behind your back."

Shocked, Wilson lifted his eyebrows.

"Could not have lived with myself—this hop is *mine*. I would have been at the jet when he manned up—first one in the cockpit. Besides, everyone else around here has torched their careers."

"Come back, Olive. Fly the hop of your life."

"I will, sir. I'll come back," she replied, not convincing either one.

The door to the passageway opened, and Weed entered.

"Hey guys."

"Weed, what have you heard?"

"Well, Buffington wants to go over to visit *Manila Bay*...if you can find a helo pilot dumb enough to fly in this weather. And I've heard of rioting and demonstrations in Moscow to join the rest of the Western world. Hear what happened in Washington? SECDEF resigned...or was fired."

"There goes Admiral Coleman's poker hand," Olive said.

"He has plenty more cards," Wilson responded. "But wow. Maybe we'll get a stand-down order."

"Maybe," Weed answered, then added, "Pentagon is on skeleton manning, Command Centers only. Most of the rest have taken their families and headed west, where they are now marooned on the interstates with no gas."

"I'm going to Admiral Coleman. We've got to get verification and know that Washington has someone in command."

Olive stepped toward the door. "Sounds great, sir, but we've got a launch to prepare for. Excuse me, gentlemen...unless you have more for me, sir."

Wilson shook his head. "No, we're complete. Go." Their eyes locked for a moment, saying nothing, yet confirming their understanding.

After Olive left, Weed spoke. "You know, even when she was a JO, I always thought Olive would be CAG if she stayed."

"She's doing well," Wilson said, lost in his thoughts.

"She's gonna take it, isn't she?"

Wilson nodded.

"Yes. Heaven help me."

Chapter 52

War Room, USS *Valley Forge*, 1815 June 21, 2024

Comet advanced the last slide, a stock photo of a *Hornet* launching off the bow. "Admiral, this concludes the brief, are there any questions?"

Coleman brought his fingers to his lips as he thought.

"Commander, thank you. I've not experienced a flight briefing like this, notwithstanding this moment in history and what you are going to deliver. My question is, at what point can we not recall you?"

"Admiral, so long as I'm in radio communication, I can be recalled. It will depend on line-of-sight and atmospherics. If we have a radio relay high off Norway, I expect that you can at any point."

"What about the Russians, if they try to trick you with a recall transmission?"

"This script sir, while clear voice, is unique and customized. It has a word-for-word prompt and word-for-word response."

Unsure, Coleman could only listen. Seemed like a lot for one pilot in an airplane who had to fly it, navigate it, and defend it from threats. Then read a word-for-word response on the radio—after listening, copying, and authenticating the recall transmission word-for-word? Wilson broke in.

"Admiral Coleman, the go-jet is loaded and spotted on the flight deck above us, as part of a twenty-plane launch. Commander Halley is going to need to meet with the tanker pilots and get some food before he mans up in about two hours, sir."

Coleman agreed. "Yes, okay, go. Well done, Commander. All I can say is good hunting—and Godspeed."

Coleman stood and strode to Comet to shake his hand. Nodding his appreciation to the admiral, Comet and three of his *Raven* pilots waited for the senior officers to depart. As the room cleared, Wilson and Olive approached him.

"Comet, good brief. I want a word with you. Let's go to CAGs stateroom."

Olive led them out of the flag spaces and across the passageway to her stateroom. After they entered, Olive closed the door behind them.

"Comet, take a seat," Wilson told him. "We want to discuss the mission with you."

In puzzled silence, Comet took a seat across from Olive, sensing something bad was about to happen. Olive spoke next.

"Comet, you are ready, willing, and able to take this hop, and we have every confidence...but I'm taking it."

Comet glanced at Wilson, then back to Olive.

"CAG...why? I can take this. My guys and I have been planning it since last night. I'm a squadron CO. I'm on the step, and it falls to me."

"No, Skipper, it falls to me. This one is mine for the reason you just stated. I'm the senior here, and I have more deployed *Hornet* hours than you. I've monitored the planning with you and am intimately familiar with the routing and target area. So, I'm taking it, and—"

"CAG, this is—"

"*No*, Comet. I'm taking it and the admiral here is backing me. It's settled, but—"

Wilson interrupted her.

"We received tasking from above. Admiral Coleman and the chain thinks you're flying it. You go through the motions, but CAG is going to take this one."

"Why, sir? I can do this! I just planned and briefed it to a three-star! I'm prepared with the right attitude."

Olive answered him.

"Comet, I'm CAG and you're not going. I'm going because I'm not going to live with regret sending you on a hop I should take."

"CAG, I'll come back..."

"And so will I, I have every expectation, but we are wasting our time, what little time I have to get a bite to eat and..."

Wilson broke in, ending it. "Comet, you're not going, and not a word to anyone, do you read me? You're dismissed, and if I were you, I'd lay low. I'll contact you when I need you. Go."

A stunned Comet shook his head in frustration and left, closing the door with a little too much force.

"He'll never forgive me," Olive said.

"Or me, but that's not our problem," Wilson replied. "*You* are my problem. I'm hanging it out for you, against my professional and personal instincts."

Olive paused for a moment before answering. "Then why are you, sir?"

Wilson's eyes fell to the table, then back at her.

"You make a good case, CAG. You are the most experienced *Hornet* pilot aboard, and you lead from the front...like I did."

"And Annie did."

"Olive, she did what she had to in the moment, with only seconds to decide."

"Yes, sir, and though my moment has lasted days...so am I."

Olive waited for Wilson to answer, and when he couldn't, she changed the subject.

"Sir, I'll have the PRs bring my flight gear down here and walk at about 2000. For now, I'm going to grab a bite of lumpia in the dirty shirt wardroom, go over the route and target area, and...get ready to go."

Wilson stood. "Won't you join me in the flag mess? I'll get Petty Officer Shugart to make anything you want."

"No thanks, sir. I do appreciate that, but I'm good...and I need to move quickly."

"Okay. I'll escort you to the flight deck when it's time."

"That will be nice, sir."

With foreboding, Wilson turned and opened the stateroom door.

"Flip?"

Wilson snapped his head back to Olive, who smiled a grateful smile.

"Thank you, sir. For everything. You are the finest officer I've ever served with or will ever serve with."

Wilson nodded his appreciation, and with his own forced smile, closed the door behind him.

From his at-sea cabin, Wilson checked his watch: 1955. Time to go.

He stepped out onto the flag bridge and noted the formation of his strike group ships under a dark gray overcast and white-capped seas. From his cabin, he had noted their position southeast of Jan Mayen; Huey had almost made up the distance to the planned launch point. With the wind just off the bow they wouldn't have to turn to a launch heading.

The demonstrations in Europe—including Russia—had not let up, but the coalition Ministers of Defence and their leadership had held firm in their support, material and tacit, of the American push into the Norwegian Sea. Shane had briefed him an hour ago; the Russians were aware *Valley Forge* was above the Arctic Circle and of the length of its long air arm and missiles.

Nothing yet from Washington.

He trundled down five ladders and strode through a small maze of blue-tiled passageways to flag country—and Olive's stateroom. He knocked twice.

"Come in," Olive said from inside.

Wilson opened the door to see Olive suited up, her helmet bag in hand—and a 9mm attached to her torso. The black rubber neck of her dry suit reminded Wilson of the cold-water conditions here, hundreds of miles from Norway.

"Ready to go, CAG?"

"Yes, sir."

Wilson held the door open for Olive as she exited and turned aft. He glanced at the photo of Olive's husband and daughter on her desk before he closed the door behind him.

Olive turned at the blue tile passageway to ascend the captain's ladder to the flight deck. Alone, Wilson peppered her with questions.

"Do you have everything?"

"Yes, sir."

"Arming checklist?"

"Yep, triple checked in my kneeboard."

"Authenticator?"

"Affirm."

"Comm plan."

"Yes, sir...and I've got a combat watch and all the charts."

"ID card?"

"Yep...and some spending money."

"*Hornet* pocket checklist?"

"Yes, sir, and it's updated. I'm ready, Admiral. You know, I checked the bureau number and we've flown this jet. It was in the *Firebirds* with us twelve years ago."

"Wow...so it's gotten you home before."

"Yes, sir," she answered as she continued to the flight deck.

Olive led them up the ladder to the O-4 flight deck level inside the island. She stopped to don her skull cap and JHMCS helmet as Wilson donned his cranial helmet. Lowering the helmet visor over her game face, Olive heaved up on the hatch dog bar to open it and stepped onto the familiar flight deck.

A brisk forty-knot wind whipped around them and the helicopters parked along the island. Stepping over the aircraft tie-down chains, Olive and Wilson turned aft to where her *Hornet* waited, parked by itself forward of the four-wire and resplendent in its new *Raven* livery.

Olive's callsign for this mission was *Raven* 11 to blend in with *Valley Forge* radio traffic...not that Olive would make a single transmission from here to the target. Around the jet, security personnel maintained a perimeter as several Air Force technicians waited near the weapon. Huey greeted them, surprised to recognize Olive.

"Olive? You taking it now?"

"Yes," Wilson said. "And no need to inform anyone else."

"Aye, aye, sir," Huey answered.

Olive extended her hand. "Keep this deck steady for my trap, shipmate."

"We will, CAG, and we'll run hard to you and be ready when you show up."

"Thanks," she said as they shook hands. She then turned to Wilson and saluted.

"By your leave, sir."

Wilson returned the salute, then extended his hand. They shook hands, and Wilson held it for effect. What could he say to her now? Olive was going to get in that jet and fly hundreds of miles over Arctic water, enter Russia, and nuke it. Chances of her success were far from certain, and the chances of her returning to the ship in five hours much less so. Regardless, Olive's life would either end or be changed forever, her name alongside that of Tibbetts.

"Olive—may God be with you."

"Thank you, sir. See you soon."

With that, she turned to her plane captain, a *Raven* chief who had a tour in *Hornets*. He saluted her as she stood before him, and Olive returned it.

"Jet's good to go, CAG."

"Great, thanks Chief. Be right back."

As Wilson watched, Olive climbed the familiar boarding ladder and stowed her gear before returning to the flight deck and her preflight. All business, she conducted it as she had almost twenty years earlier when she was a young pilot in the *Ravens*, one that Wilson had trained to be a combat wingman and later a capable strike lead. He watched her inspect the jet as she manned up for the most consequential hop of her career—the most consequential hop in the history of naval aviation and one that would be remembered the world over.

Without acknowledging Wilson, Olive bounded up the ladder again and dropped herself into the seat, with the chief following to help connect her fittings and strap her in. Complete, Wilson watched them shake hands as the chief said something to her. Olive nodded and smiled, and for a brief instant her gaze fell to Wilson. She then began her ritual of readying her familiar— yet unfamiliar— cockpit after almost a decade away.

Wilson turned to Huey. "What's up ahead?"

"Heavier seas, sir. Not expecting a lot of precip, but we'll be moving a lot and going in and out of low vis. We're in the Gulf Stream…the water temp is a balmy 55 degrees now."

Wilson nodded. The weather over the continent was reasonable, low overcast with good visibility underneath.

"We will do all in our power to get her aboard once she returns, Admiral."

"Ask the Chaplain to help."

"Have him on speed dial, sir."

The rest of the air wing aviators manned their adjacent aircraft in the same manner, the only sound the whistling of the wind.

Wilson checked his watch. "Let's leave her alone—engine starts in about ten minutes."

The men exited through the security perimeter and reentered the island. Wilson led them up, stepping onto the flag bridge as Huey continued to his chair in the pilothouse.

After Wilson checked in with Mark for the latest—nothing new from Washington—he stepped behind his chair to take another look at Olive.

She sat motionless in the cockpit with her head up and eyes closed, resting physically and mentally for the task ahead, her face illuminated by rays from the evening sun that broke through small crevices in the overcast. Wilson watched her as he contemplated her courage and determination. Just under Olive's shoulder, the weapon hung ominously on its wing station. *I cannot believe that we're doing this.*

The door opened and Stretch entered, followed by Weed.

"Admiral, care for some company?"

"Yes. Where's Admiral Coleman? And Buffington?"

"Buffington is in the flag mess, sir. Admiral Coleman said he's going to TFCC—Mark is with him."

"Good. I'll join him, but I want to be up here for this," Wilson replied.

"There she is," Weed said as he studied Olive in the cockpit.

Wilson nodded. "Doubt we'll ever see more courage than what she's displaying now. Stretch, what's the latest on Varda Nos?"

"No CAP up at the moment, and no I&W that we're comin,' sir."

Wilson nodded again.

"The Moscow protest—if you can call it that—is going full speed," Weed added. "Reminds me of when Yeltsin stood on the tank."

"Any government officials standing on tanks now?" Wilson asked.

"Didn't see any."

"Anyone standing on a tank in Washington?"

"Nope."

The men returned their gaze to the flight deck and Olive, who was now head down in the cockpit. At that moment, the 5MC sounded as the Mini-Boss prepared the flight deck crews for another launch:

On the flight deck, aircrews have manned for the 2100 launch. Time for all personnel to get into the proper flight deck uniform...

While the Mini continued with the pre-start litany, Weed asked a question all of them had pondered for days.

"Flip—what do you think her chances are?"

As Stretch held his breath, Wilson waited to answer.

"Of getting there and delivering it...sixty percent. Of delivering it and getting back here...twenty."

Outside, the launch continued as all three observed Olive waiting for the plane captain to signal her to start the APU. From Pri-Fly, the Mini wrapped up the starts call with a flourish.

Start the go aircraft, start 'em up!

CHAPTER 53

FLIGHT DECK, USS *VALLEY FORGE*, 2058 JUNE 21, 2024

Olive released the parking brake and goosed the power. Tapping the brakes once, she added power to turn left as the ship rolled right. Sitting in a cramped *Hornet* cockpit on a carrier flight deck after so many years away felt to Olive as if she had never left.

Valley Forge labored in the heavy seas, barely making steerage in the gale force winds. Streaks of white cap foam lined the dark water under gray skies. Airmen that could huddled near the idling jet exhausts of the "go" jets to keep warm as they waited for the launch to begin.

Olive was led behind the cat 3 JBD as the *Rhino* tanker ahead went into tension. She watched the bow lift high as the *Super Hornet* remained at full power; the catapult officer—topside for this launch—also watched and waited for the right time. *Valley Forge* buried her bow, and as the deck started back up, the shooter touched it and pointed forward. One second later, the *Rhino* surged ahead to flying speed over the wet flight deck, trailing billowing spray kicked up from the thundering exhausts.

Olive was then motioned forward as the *Growler* on cat 4 went into tension, the howling cacophony bombarding her Plexiglas cocoon as her jet vibrated and bounced in place. Once the EA-18G roared down the track, the yellow shirt straddling cat 3 directed Olive to spread her wings as she continued to follow his directions to align her jet.

Heavy catapult steam clouds enveloped Olive's *Hornet* as it crept forward, reducing visibility to zero before she emerged to see her yellow shirt motion her forward again. Troubleshooters—more squadron chiefs that had *Hornet* experience and who demanded to final check their CAG on this epic launch—checked for secure panels and proper flap configuration. Once she locked her wings, the yellow shirt transferred control to the ordies, who armed her missiles and gun while she held her hands above the canopy rail.

Despite the high and bone-chilling winds, hundreds of onlookers on deck and in Vultures Row watched every move of their wing commander in the old museum piece. A photo mate who had recorded Olive man the jet and taxi continued to take photos for the historical record.

Dark water ahead of the track filled her view as Olive felt the tug of the holdback bar and goosed the power under the yellow shirt's command to get the launch bar properly seated in the shuttle. She looked over her left shoulder and saw the *Rhino* tanker that launched in front of her nose on as it approached the carrier's port side. *Yes.* On her game, she reached down and hit MARK on the Nav display, a position over 70 degrees north of the equator.

On the Flag Bridge, Wilson watched the flight deck in silence. He considered that the old strike-fighter airframe had not experienced a cat shot in years. That it was from a carrier's pitching deck on the Norwegian Sea at near max catapult weight only added to the concerns of Wilson and those experienced enough to worry about it. To the north, two *Sierras* hovered on top of a Norwegian fishing boat that had ignored the Notice to Mariners that covered the entire North Atlantic. Taking no chances, Huey directed them to drive the boat away, and the helicopter rotor wash kicked up a spray around the boat that shielded the carrier from prying eyes—and cameras.

Coleman entered the bridge and pointed at the *Hornet*. "Who's in that airplane?"

He knows, Wilson thought.

Remaining calm, he answered truthfully. "Captain Teel, sir."

A wary Coleman looked at him in shock. Wilson stepped toward him to make his case.

"She's the best pilot for this mission, Admiral. It's my call."

Now angry, Coleman wasn't buying it. "What? After the express orders of Admiral Buffington?! Why wasn't I informed? I've backed you here."

"You have deniability, sir. My call, and I'll take the heat."

"You mean we'll *both* take the heat…you've gone too far, Jim."

"Admiral, she delivers what Washington wants and comes back, all will be forgotten."

"And what if she doesn't?"

"Then nothing will matter anymore, sir. Actually, even if she is successful, nothing may matter. Regardless, Admiral, we are launching this mission as ordered, and it's on schedule."

Both men peered down from the flag bridge and waited.

On signal, Olive slammed the throttles to military and cycled the controls. Engine readings good, no flight control anomalies. Ahead, the bow pointed toward a gray sky.

She looked back to see the catapult officer, and once their eyes met, he opened his upraised hand wide. In response, Olive pushed the throttles into burner, hearing the booming sound behind her, feeling it in her spine, and seeing the nozzles open on the engine display. Turning to the catapult officer, she raised her right hand into a salute and held it for a count before dropping it. The catapult officer returned it and looked forward as the bow fell below the horizon. Olive used the opportunity to check over her left shoulder. The tanker was inside a half-mile. *C'mon!* She waited for the shot, sensing all on deck watching her.

The bow finished its downward motion and stayed there for a moment before it slowly lifted. Olive gripped the canopy towel rack harder in expectation.

The sudden g force of the cat firing pushed her back into her seat, and the deck edge raced up as the catapult track lifted into clear sky. Once the shuttle released her and she was launched into the gale, her HUD display disappeared.

"Dammit," she muttered to herself while banking left and cleaning up. She knew instinctively that the Heads Up Display cannon plug must have come loose from the force of the stroke. Her backup HUD display on the DDI worked fine, and despite the loss of her primary flight instrument—a downing gripe—she would not abort this mission.

She turned to parallel the base recovery course and saw it, the *Rhino* tanker who had positioned himself perfectly at her 10 o'clock, 500 feet. She joined on the right wing of *Spartan* 105, who checked easy right on a heading of 085. Uncharacteristically, Olive twisted her body to look back over her shoulder in time to see *Valley Forge* wallowing amid an angry sea.

CHAPTER 54

NORWEGIAN SEA, 2130 JUNE 21, 2024

Stabilized behind the bouncing basket, Olive added a touch of power to drive the refueling probe home. Connected, she was rewarded with a green light as she settled in to fly form on the tanker that pushed through a faint wisp of cloud at 3,000 feet. Fighting the gusty winds, Olive held her position on the *Rhino* that led them on a course to the coast-in point at the mouth of the Lyngen Fjord...some 400 miles away.

Staying just above the tops of the marine layer, the two jets—and another *Rhino* tanker flying wing on them—did not radiate or check out with the ship. Remaining undetected was critical to mission success. *Knight* fed them linked data to see another surface contact roughly 200 miles ahead of their track. Taking peeks inside her cockpit as she remained plugged, Olive was satisfied that the tanker pilot leaned right enough to avoid the "white" surface traffic to the north, most likely another fishing boat. Also ahead of their track, *Rhinos* searched the sea and airspace for traffic while a *Growler* and two JSFs from *Tinian* collected what ELINT they could, passing it all to the E-2 and back to *Valley Forge*.

Topped off for the moment, Olive slid out and joined on the tanker's right wing, signaling the pilot to retract the basket. Once retracted, Olive gave them a thumbs-up that the WSO acknowledged. As she eased out into tac wing, *Spartan* 105 joined up with the second tanker to top off. While Olive burned down fuel over the course of the next hour, she would top off from 105 again as the pathfinder led her to the coast in. This was the easy part. Finding the mission recovery tanker on the post-strike egress over open water would be more of a challenge.

She checked the Nav display: 270 ground speed with a slight quartering tailwind. A headwind on the way home...and she would be up high on the egress with a *serious* headwind.

The bomb on station three dominated her thoughts. She accomplished the early parts of the weapon release checklist and did her combat checklist. She glanced again at the bomb, firmly attached to the wing pylon over her left shoulder.

She was going to deliver that weapon, the fourth combat nuclear attack in history. What were the Russians thinking? Nuclear escalation, and the United States not respond in kind? Today was the first full day of summer. Would it be *her* last day? Would tomorrow be the last day for hundreds of millions in Eurasia and North America?

She thought of Chris and her little girl, Margaret. A letter placed on her desk as she walked would suffice to say goodbye—she had poured her heart out writing it days ago, *knowing* that she would be in this cockpit. She had to! Like a captain who must go down with the ship, as CAG she had to do first what she expected of others. But…who could have imagined *this*, a Cold War throwback to when nuclear weapon delivery was the very *raison d'être* of carrier aviation. *Like decades earlier, Washington shrugs off the human risk and gives orders, and ours is but to do.*

Buffington and his optics! Olive chafed as she thought about it, as she thought about the flag officer shouting match in the War Room. Unbelievable. Too much high-level churn…why didn't she just refuse then, for her or any pilot in her air wing? *Are we ready for this?* Flying wing on the tanker, with 105 plugged and receiving over the gray cotton of the undercast layer, she thought about it. *No…Coleman was right, and he had given the matter great thought as a career submariner. We had to respond, and reasonably soon, with a manned and* recallable *strike.* She checked the time…about two more hours until that option would have passed.

In TFCC, Wilson, with his staff and Admiral Coleman, watched and waited.

No word from Olive or the tankers was a good thing…they assumed that Olive's jet was up and the tankers sweet. Now halfway to Norway, Olive was scheduled to tank again, then, once her drops had transferred, punch off the wing tank to lessen her drag count. Huey kept *Valley Forge* into the seas to close where Olive would recover; saving one hundred miles of transit out here on the top of the world mattered. Shane exited SUPPLOT and her excited eyes met those of Wilson's. *Uh-oh.*

"Admiral, you need to see what the broadcast and cable networks are showing."

"Put it up."

On the large flat screen next to the COP, Shane brought up the feed from a European cable network, relayed to the ship from a P-8 relay orbiting high north of Iceland. The grainy image was of Red Square, jammed with tens of thousands.

"Those are protestors, sir, and they've been there all day. The police just opened fire on them near the Kremlin, but they're still coming, and we've received reports that some police are refusing to fire into them. Pretty much unprecedented for Russia, sir."

All in the space watched the scene in Moscow unfold with mobs of rioters running through clouds of tear gas. Wilson kept one eye on the COP—and Olive. Coleman and Weed joined them as Wilson questioned Shane.

"Okay, what do you hear from the American media, including social media?"

"Military social thinks it's a coup, and it's more than just conspiracy theorists. DNI confirms that the Russian president is holed up outside the Kremlin in his dacha."

"So who is speaking for the Russian government?"

"Don't know yet, sir. The protestors have some Duma ministers and generals in their ranks. Right now, it's like some generals are fighting others with the soldiers they control as the civilians mass around the Kremlin."

"Like the Bastille," Weed quipped. "Storming the Kremlin."

"Commander, what is the Washington media reaction?" Coleman asked Shane.

"They're all covering it sir, and the State Department is reported to have a statement at 6pm Washington time. Congressmen and senators are all running to the cameras."

"That's in about 30 minutes," Weed said.

"What about the White House? And the Deputy SECDEF? What's the latest from them?" Coleman demanded.

"Will keep monitoring, Admiral, and let you know as soon as it comes across."

After Wilson excused her and Shane returned to SUPPLOT, Wilson turned to Coleman.

"Sir, are we sure of who is in charge in Moscow, and with SECDEF out, who is really in charge in the Pentagon?"

Coleman nodded. "My thoughts exactly, but we haven't received direction to stand down yet."

"Shall we remind them, sir, that we have roughly two hours to recall my pilot?"

Weed jumped in. "Gentlemen, as the CNS guy...the situation in Moscow is much more tenuous post-strike. I mean, who holds the nuclear keys now or in the next few hours, and who will they answer to tonight or over the next few days? That answer will shape our diplomatic message post-strike and what we can expect from them in response."

"Concur with all," Wilson said, "But we need our comms with Washington to be more than just one-way to us."

Buffington entered TFCC.

"Coleman, you are operating in my AOR, so what the fuck is going on, and don't give me any bullshit." Buffington kept his eyes locked on Coleman, ignoring Wilson. Coleman remained calm.

"Admiral, there's unrest in Moscow, big time. Most of the Western world capitals are in turmoil, but Moscow could be experiencing a coup."

"A coup? Did that come from Washington?"

"It's from SUPPLOT, Admiral," Wilson answered. "Supplemental plot of media reports, social media."

"Screw that Mickey Mouse bullshit!" Buffington sneered. "Coleman, we have what, just over two hours till impact?"

"Yes, sir, and there she is," Coleman replied, pointing to the COP.

Here it comes, Wilson thought.

"She? Did you say *she?* A woman is flying the airplane?"

"The Air Wing Commander is flying it," Coleman admitted.

Buffington leveled his gaze at Wilson. "After my direct order!" Around them, all the TFCC watch-standers were spellbound by the display.

Ready to explode, Coleman spoke next.

"Admiral, I made the call, because she's the most qualified pilot for this mission, and *that's the way it fucking is,* so please excuse us, *sir,* and depart from here!"

"Both of you are dead men!" Buffington roared. *"Dead!"*

Coleman snickered back. "I work for NORTHCOM, and he's supported—*sir."*

"And my people work for *me,* Admiral," Wilson added. Next to him, Mark stood resolute.

Shane reentered TFCC, ending the drama as the flags waited for her update. Her large glasses accentuated her deer-in-the-headlights look as all waited expectantly. Unsure at first, she faced Wilson, her immediate boss.

"Admiral...the Russian president has been captured by the military."

"Then who's in charge?" Buffington snapped. "A military coup, *now,* of all times! Who's in charge of the Strategic Rocket Forces? Do they have control of them? And the Northern Fleet—and Pacific Fleet—boomers? We need to know, and now, young lady!"

Coleman turned to Wilson. "Get Colorado Springs and the Pentagon on the horn now; I'll talk to whoever answers first. Where's your pilot?"

Wilson referred to the COP screen for Olive's tanker as he checked the time.

"There, sir, *Spartan* one-zero-five. They're just over 200 miles to the east and probably still tanking."

Buffington wasn't finished. "Where's that Russian boomer near the Faroes? Warren, why haven't you sunk it yet? And why are the LCSes down there when they need to be up here? They can hide in the fjords, collect intel, and shoot if the Russians come at us." Finished, Buffington glared at Wilson, who stood firm, wishing that he had an *Osprey* to take the four star away.

Having had enough, Wilson answered. "Admiral, we're nuking the Russians now! We don't need those ships up here! What we need is answers from the beach."

Coleman, at his limit, stepped toward Buffington.

"Admiral, I've got it, *we've* got it! Noted, and please include it in your report, but I don't work for you and I need help from above, above you! This is your last professional courtesy, sir; please allow us to fight this strike group or secure, *sir*."

The phone buzzed and a watchstander answered. "It's NORTHCOM, sir." Coleman took the receiver as Wilson picked up on another line.

"Admiral Coleman, sir."

"Warren, Sam Green. How are things on your end?"

Coleman glanced at Buffington. "All well here, sir, and the mission is proceeding."

"When is the drop-dead for recall?"

Coleman looked to Wilson, who mouthed *twenty-three*.

"Twenty-three hundred our time, sir, about an hour."

"Okay, Warren—they've stormed the Kremlin, and we don't know who is in control. We believe it's the commander of the VVS, their air force. He's got the local district army commander with him. No indications that the Russian navy is with them, but the Northern Fleet could be while we have indications that the Pacific Fleet is remaining in port. Clear as mud?"

"Social media reports that the president is captured, sir," Coleman replied.

"We've seen that, but it's not verified yet. Regardless, we need to get that missile boat near the Faroes while we make a decision on your mission."

"I've got two attack boats, a destroyer with two *Romeos*, and a bunch of P-8s in the vicinity of it, sir. The Brits are on it as well. He's cagey, but we'll keep him down and I expect we'll sink it in the coming hours."

Wilson considered what that meant: another hundred souls lost in a hideous death.

"Warren, keep this line open while I check with Washington. If we don't know who's in control of the nukes, there's a good possibility we'll turn this off."

"Please tell us as soon as possible, sir."

"Will do, I'll be back in a moment."

Coleman turned to Wilson. "They might send a recall signal. You have the recall procedures here?"

"Yes, sir." Wilson pointed to the folder.

"Authentication?"

"Yes, sir, and Olive—Captain Teel—has a card. It's challenge-response."

"NORTHCOM cannot be serious!" Buffington growled. "If we don't respond to fire with fire, it's over for the U.S. The people demand it!"

"Enough, Admiral!" Coleman exploded. "We don't know who has the nuclear keys over there, and with SECDEF out, I'm not all that sure who does on our side! Regardless, I'm in touch with my boss and standing by. You may secure, sir, and I'm done talking with you."

The unhinged squabble between the two fleet commanders shocked all inside TFCC, and Wilson realized it could spread among his staff, who were as emotionally drained as anyone aboard.

He checked the COP. Olive should detach from the tanker soon.

Three hundred miles to the east, Olive backed out of the basket.

Topped off and almost to the detach waypoint, she slid to 105's right wing as the WSO watched her. She tapped the top of her helmet and gave him a thumbs-up. The WSO understood she was topped off on fuel and gave her a thumbs-up back. He took a photo with his smart phone of Olive in her jet, the bomb on her wing pylon. For posterity, Olive thought.

After the tanker pilot retracted the basket, he glanced at her, pointed ahead, and gave her the take-lead signal. Olive tapped her visor and pointed ahead, taking the lead on course to the coast-in point another 300 miles away. The *Rhino* eased away as both men contemplated Olive, knowing where she was going—and what she would do when she got there in less than two hours. In unison, they saluted their CAG.

Olive returned it, holding it to convey meaning before she dropped it, followed by her open-hand kiss off signal. *Spartan* 105 banked away as the WSO waved to her one last time. Accelerating to cruising speed, she took one last look back at them, a dot now against the cloud deck. Returning to her cockpit, she set the power and autopilot, settling in for a lonely hour transit over cold, open water.

Other than her HUD not working, the jet was fine, and at only 3,000 feet, she flicked off a bayonet fitting on her mask. She figured that this transit to the coast-in would be the most difficult of the hop, an hour for her mind to wander. On the common frequency, she heard the P-8 make a routine transmission in the blind. Good. He's there, a lifeline to home. If a recall came, who would send it? The ship? Washington? With all the flag-officer drama of the past 48 hours, she was unsure. She pulled out the arming checklist and delivery procedures. The recall was a gibberish phrase that she had all but memorized:

COLLIE FAIRWAY MARINA GRILL

After authentication by the P-8, the phrase would be relayed, and Olive would authenticate it, then respond back with her own scripted response before she turned for home, safed the switches, and brought the bomb back. Once she coasted in and accelerated on the low level, line-of-sight radio contact would be spotty—if not completely severed—until she climbed high over the North Cape of Europe off target.

The bomb. Weed's *bucket of sunshine*. She studied it, her first time "alone" with the bomb on her left wing. *What did they say? How many Hiroshimas?* Whatever yield was set by the Air Force ordnance men, *one* Hiroshima was too much to fathom. Whatever...she would deliver it, betting her life on the escape maneuver. If she could get to the target through the SAMs and strip-alert fighters, if they could track her. Staying low in the valley fissures, she could avoid radar detection. Could she, all the way to Varda Nos?

With her jet flying itself, Olive pulled a granola bar from her g-suit pocket and checked the fuel.

In the twilight of the longest day of the year, the hundreds of thousands who had crowded Red Square since morning showed no signs of dispersal.

Here and there violent clashes with the police broke out. One overzealous water cannon truck driver who got ahead of his escort was pulled from the cab and beaten, while pops of gunfire were heard at the far end of the square. At several Kremlin access points jeering mobs confronted the guards—many of them petrified conscripts fumbling with their weapons—and demanded entry. A coterie of generals who knew the building entered it with their own fierce FSB plain-clothes security detail from the street opposite the square, the sentries granting entry. Meanwhile, on the Square, Russian kids pleaded with their fellow kids in uniform to put the tear gas away and end the nuclear madness. TV cameras from all the major world networks recorded the scene.

Ignoring the chaos outside, the Army and Air Force generals moved briskly through the building and established control. At the communication center, when the sentry on station stood to confront a general who demanded entry, he was summarily shot by one of the rebellious agents. At the nuclear hardened command post, the leader, a tall and distinguished Air Force *Leytenant General* with two stars on his dress uniform, entered with his usual access code. Surprised by the general's sudden entry and the entourage with him, a colonel on watch demanded to know his intentions—and was summarily shot by an FSB agent as the horrified watchstanders knew at once who was now in charge.

Though the president was not in the building, the coup was moving as the plotters had planned. Despite the severing of Kremlin communications to them, control of the Strategic Rocket Forces was still in doubt.

Meanwhile, outside Platonov's quarters that overlooked Severomorsk, two cars drove up. Having sent his family to St. Petersburg for safety, Platonov was alone in the kitchen as he gazed upon the empty docks of his Red Banner Northern Fleet. Expecting the cars at this late hour, he was dressed in his winter blue uniform with full medals, the uniform he wished to be buried in. His fleet defeated—the details of which he learned from Western news reports! —and with thousands of his fine sailors resting on the bottom of the cold ocean, he would join them as a warrior. As the men pounded on his door, he bit into the capsule.

Please forgive me, God.

Chapter 55

Approaching the North Cape of Norway, 2305 June 21, 2024

Selecting the 80-mile scale, Olive saw the digital map coastline that marched down on her Nav display, aiming for the northern tip of a jagged island at the mouth of Lyngen Fjord. Finding that tip of shoreline and flying directly over it was vital to update her Inertial Navigation System. She estimated the visibility at maybe five miles. She energized the TACAN to see if anything was radiating. Nothing from Andøya—or Tromso. *The Norwegians aren't fools.*

Twelve minutes and forty-two seconds ahead. She wanted to cross the coast-in-point at the island's north shore at precisely 2318 shipboard time, at which point she would accelerate. Locally, it was after midnight, June 22.

The Nav display had her on course, but who knew how far the system could have drifted. Without GPS and not radiating her ground mapping radar to avoid detection, she had to eyeball it as the island came into view—in marginal vis. According to the route timer, she was ahead of schedule, and retarded the throttles a hair to correct while the jet flew with altitude hold engaged at 500 feet.

She had topped off from *Spartan* 105 an hour ago and had jettisoned her tank on station 7—as planned—some 200 miles back. Detecting peripheral motion, she saw a sea bird fly past her right-wing line—*a puffin!*—and instinctively scanned ahead of her nose for more. Nothing, but the bird was a sign of land ahead.

No word from the ship, though at times she heard routine transmissions from the P-8. Good. She would transmit at the coast-in point: five mic clicks…in about five minutes.

She entered a wisp of cloud. The weather had lowered, and she eased down to 200 feet over the water. Decrementing to 40 miles, the HSI display showed her on track for the coast-in point. How she wanted to radiate her radar and peek! No, too dangerous, even here in Norwegian waters. She had to hope for a tight system after two hours of open water in an ancient *Hornet* that hadn't operated from the ship in years.

With the weapon data entered, the combat checklist items were complete except for the steps saved for the final run-in. Master-ARM…she could arm-up now, could have once she left the tanker. For a reason she could not explain, she held it, in spite of the fact that anything military she encountered, including Norwegian military, could show hostile intent.

If you're gonna do it, you'd better recall me now, she thought. Once she accelerated on the route, time would fly by at eight miles per minute. Despite the missiles she carried, stealth and speed were her primary weapons. Covert ingress, and from a range not considered likely from a carrier airplane.

Using heading hold, Olive shifted the autopilot one degree left. Figuring her fuel remaining for the umpteenth time, she scanned the gloom around her and waited as her *Hornet* approached the rugged coast of Norway.

Placing his hand over the mouthpiece, Coleman turned to Wilson. "They're recalling her!"

Wilson's eyes went to the COP screen. Though almost feet dry, Olive was past the planned recall window, but close enough.

"The P-8 on station south of her should be making the call now," Stretch offered.

Wilson found the P-8, *Tiger* five-three, and nodded. "We've got twenty minutes to recall her. Are we monitoring the discrete freq.?" he asked.

"Yes, sir," Mark answered. All in TFCC waited expectantly for the P-8 transmission on the loudspeaker. After thirty seconds, Coleman spoke.

"What's the delay?" he barked.

"Can we get *Tiger* five-three?" Wilson asked the watch captain.

"Yessir, we've heard him. *Cutlass* three-zero-two is the relay."

"Move three-zero-two east and have him climb to forty grand, we need as much range as possible."

Finally, the radio crackled.

"*Raven* one-one, *Raven* one-one, *Tiger* five-three."

Good, Wilson thought. *This madness will end.*

Seconds passed, and Olive did not transmit a reply.

"Why doesn't she acknowledge? Coleman asked.

His eyes locked on Olive's link display, Wilson didn't have an answer for him.

Emerging from the marine layer, Olive saw the rocky shore of Ormø-Smøla some three miles ahead. Realizing she was headed to the mid-section of the green island and not the rock at the northern tip, she pulled hard left to fly along the shoreline. Ahead, she saw it, the last and northernmost rock, the update point, and taking a cut to the left before she reversed right, she flew over it in knife-edge, looking down her wing line as she designated.

The error was 2.3 miles—a drifty system, but what could she expect with this ancient jet? —and she accepted it as she rolled out to skirt a larger island ahead and enter a wide bay. She shoved the throttles to military to increase her speed by another mile per minute, on course and fifteen seconds late, time she would easily make up in the final run-in. Olive allowed herself a smile. She had *found* it, after transiting hundreds of miles of open water. From here in, navigation would be visual using major features.

Thirty minutes to target.

As she skirted the island's northern shore, the glassy water touched the sheer granite wall without even a ripple. The stillness of the water that opened into the broad Norwegian Sea struck her, as if it somehow knew why she was there, and with what.

"*Raven...*"

It hit her: *the mic clicks!* With her thumb in slow, deliberate motion, she keyed the Comm 1 mic five times. *Feet dry and on time.*

"One, authenticate golf, li...ov."

Easing down to the deck, she reset the radar altimeter while wondering what the garbled transmission meant. She heard *Raven* and one and authenticate. The relay P-8 was calling her...a possible recall! But she had to authenticate it, and waited for them to try again.

"Ra...one, one, your signal coll..."

Desperate to hear the full transmission, Olive turned the volume up to full.

"Marina, gr..."

They're trying to recall me! C'mon!

"'Thenticate golf lima."

The visibility opened as Olive came upon a high peninsula that bisected two fishing villages she wished to avoid. Adding power to enter a gentle climb, she thought about the radio call. Was it from the P-8 radio relay? Maybe, maybe not. Could the Russians be on the discrete frequency? Norwegians? Do they know I'm coming? Needing to know, she transmitted.

"Calling *Raven* one-one, repeat your last."

Olive waited as she put pressure on the stick to cross the ridgeline at 200 feet. Out from the deep fjord, the radio reception was loud and clear.

"*Raven* one-one, *Tiger* five-three, you signal collie, fairway, marina, grill. I authenticate golf lima….foxtrot."

That's it! Olive thought as she reached down to pull the authenticator out of her g-suit pocket. On the back side of the ridge, she steadied herself in a three-degree dive, set attitude hold, and looked up golf lima.

She found it. *Kilo.*

Flying the airplane as she leveled over rolling terrain, she checked again. Kilo.

The P-8 called again. "*Raven* one-one, I authenticate golf lima as foxtrot."

Olive's blood ran cold. *The Russians are on this freq!* Kilo was the proper authentication for this day, June 21, *not* foxtrot. The codewords must have been compromised! She keyed the mic.

"*Beadwindow.*"

With the terrain rising, she added power to climb, on course, and checked the time as she crossed the tip of a mountain pond. Only nine seconds late, she banked 30 degrees and rolled out on her new course.

In desperation, the P-8 called again. "*Raven* one-one, *Tiger* five-three, recall! Repeat, recall! Collie, fairway, marina, grill—acknowledge!"

Over 500 miles to the west, Wilson listened to the comms as he watched the COP in disbelief.

Coleman, fighting to maintain control, turned to his aviator. "Jim, what's going on? What'd she say? *Beadwindow?*"

"Yes, sir, means unauthorized transmission."

"What? That's the damn script! What's she doing?" Both looked at the time: 0229 in Murmansk. Twenty-six minutes till time on target.

Wilson felt the eyes of his staff on him as he thought.

"Get me an authenticator, now!"

The befuddled staff looked around their consoles, in folders.

"Now! You've got one minute to get me one!" Wilson roared. On the COP, Olive continued deeper into Europe, on course and on time.

"Holy fuckin' shit," Coleman muttered, as fear gripped him.

Chapter 56

North Cape of Norway, 2330 June 21, 2024

Unable to tolerate flying blind any longer, Olive energized her radar while still over Norway. Staying out of the rocks and scanning around her for threats, she castled right into AUTOACQ, not expecting an airborne lock at this hour and over this sparsely populated territory. She had held from radiating as long as she could stand it, but inside thirty minutes to Varda Nos and with her Radar Warning Receiver clean, she risked it.

The transmission from the "P-8" gnawed at her. How did the Russians obtain the codewords but not an authenticator? Maybe they didn't expect it. The enemy sure *sounded* authentic, with no trace of an Eastern European accent, but Olive had to honor the checklist. Codewords from an *authenticated* source. The late ploy made sense…but did they know she was inbound?

With a clean radar picture Olive zipped over the rocks and down the backside of the rolling ridgelines. On time, on course. Weapon ready, baro altitude entered. She'd arm up once in Russian territory—on the final run-in to Varda Nos.

She crested a ridge and overbanked down, encountering a long lake carved by a glacier thousands of years earlier. The southern tip was easily visible, and she overflew it as the computer gave her steering to the next waypoint.

Twenty-three minutes to go, and her breathing increased. Washington was going to do this. The Russians "escalated," as Weed said. How could they have been so mad? Sink an American ship—with a nuke! *This*, however, an overland surface burst…would *this* end the conflict, even after the Northern Fleet was all but destroyed?

Fly the jet! she told herself, searching ahead for the next waypoint as snow-capped mountains loomed in the distance, their peaks covered by the overcast sky. *Concentrate. Fuel. Time. Distance. Look for threats. Stay out of the rocks. Fly the jet.*

She turned left on the next leg, a long one of over 90 miles. Ahead, the overcast broke up, and splotches of midnight sun illuminated patches of the valley pine forests and green rolling meadows as Olive flew toward a distant horizon of dark-gray and rocky mountains. To the south toward Finland, a large raincloud soaked the tundra and filled the numerous lakes.

Boop.

Alerted by the aural tone in her headset, Olive's eyes flashed to the RWR. Surface search radar to the north. Norwegian. Olive considered the threat to the south (Finland) and east (Russia) and maintained most of her scan there as she managed the navigation and terrain-masked while the seconds and minutes counted down.

Sensing that the opportunity for a legitimate recall had passed, she resigned herself to the low level and attack, making sure that this route and this weapon delivery would be the best she had ever flown.

Shane burst through the door. "Here it is, Admiral."

Wilson took the daily authenticator and found golf, then cross referenced lima. The letter was foxtrot.

"What day is this for?" Wilson snapped.

"Today, sir, twenty-one June."

Weed spoke up. "Maybe the P-8's are on twenty-two June—that's local time in Varda Nos."

Wilson groaned in frustration and turned to Shane. "I need twenty-two June!"

"Yes, sir!" Shane replied as she spun to retrieve it.

"You gotta be…" Wilson muttered before catching himself. Seconds counted. *Screw the authenticator, we can't wait.*

Wilson stepped back and picked up the UHF handset as he gazed at the COP of Olive's synthetic route progress. His staff—with a nervous Coleman—looked to him for deliverance, a last-chance radio transmission to convince the CAG to accept the recall and abort.

"*Raven* one-one, this is CSG-Eighteen actual. Olive, it's me, Flip. Acknowledge!"

Silence permeated the space as all listened for anything to come over the speakers. Wilson didn't have time for guesswork.

"*Tiger*, five-three, *Tiger*, five-three, this is CSG-Eighteen actual, how do you read?"

More silence, and then, an answer.

"CSG-Eighteen actual, *Cutlass* three-zero-two has you weak but readable."

A lifeline! Wilson looked at the synthetic track of 302 on the COP, some 350 miles east of the carrier as he depressed the transmit button.

"Three-zero-two, CSG-Eighteen; your signal is *buster east!* Climb as high as you can—clean off your tanks. Launching a *Texaco* now." Wilson nodded to Smoke, who responded with a thumbs-up as he picked up the phone to Air Ops.

"*Cutlass* three-zero-two, wilco, continuing my climb, bustering east."

On the open frequency that Olive was briefed to monitor, Wilson squeezed the handset again to relay through 302 and the P-8 his message to Olive almost 1,000 miles to the east.

"Olive, it's Flip calling in the blind. Disregard the damn authenticator, your signal is recall! Collie, fairway, marina, grill. Recall. Olive, this is no shit."

With gentle pressure Olive eased the jet up in rising terrain as a weak and scratchy signal sounded in her headset.

...it's Flip...the blind. Dis...damn auth...recall!...fairway, mar...call. Olive this...

Was that Flip? Olive thought. The transmission sounded like him, and satisfied the jet was out of the rocks for a moment she ran the Comm 1 radio volume up to full blast and pressed the sides of her helmet to her ears. *He'll try me again.*

Olive, Flip calling in the blind from TFCC. Re...repeat, recall. Collie...way, marina, gr...acknow...

With her hands back on the throttles and stick, she veered left a little to correct for course, thinking about what she had just heard. That sounded just like Flip...but AI generators could do that too. Olive checked the clock: 19:45 left to go. Enroute to her waypoint, she saw that her current best course along the rising terrain of the next mountain peak would take her into Finland. *Screw 'em,* she thought. *Won't matter tomorrow!*

Recall, repeat, recall. Olive, collie, fairw...na, grill! RTB, Olive, now!

Her tension and indecision had reached a boiling point, and Olive screamed into her mask. *That sure fucking sounds like Flip!* she thought as she squirmed in her seat, her breathing heavy. What to do? *Is it really him or do the Russians have a SIGINT capability that we can only imagine?* She thought it the latter. "Flip" and "Olive" were well-known callsigns in naval aviation, everyone knew CSG-18 was aboard *Valley Forge,* and the codewords were obviously compromised. But not the authenticator, a routine step in the multi-step security protections? Thank goodness! All he had to do was authenticate.

Olive, we were in the Ravens! With Cajun! Quoth the Raven!

Olive shook her head. *Not today, Ivan!* That combat cruise with Flip Wilson and all who served in VFA-64 was another well-known piece of naval aviation history. Everyone knew that *Quoth the Raven* was the squadron battle cry, just like *Tonight We Ride!* and *Here's to Us!* were to other squadrons at Oceana. Tempted, she placed her fingers on the Comm 1 volume knob, needing to concentrate now in the end game. A sudden bird ahead caused Olive to jerk the airplane up and away to avoid collision. Clear, she overbanked down and rolled out two hundred feet above the moss-covered tundra as she continued toward the empty northern corner of Finland.

Wilson noted *Cutlass* 302 moving east on the COP screen. He checked for the pilot's name and recognized it. A nugget. A nugget pilot relaying his radio signal as far as possible was the thin thread upon which thousands—and perhaps millions—of lives rested. He checked the time.

"Seventeen minutes, Flip," Weed reminded him.

"I know! She's not responding. Not even sure that she's hearing me."

"What would only you know about Olive? Not '*Quoth the Raven*;' everyone knows that. Something only you would know?"

Wilson fought to control himself. "Like what!"

"The karaoke bar! That night in Dubai when she dressed up and sang *Zombie*. Psycho was with her."

"I wasn't there!"

Weed pressed him as he shook his head. "But you know of it, that bit of *Raven* liberty lore. What was the name of that place?"

"The Highlander!"

"That's it! Tell her!"

Buffington burst through the aft door. "What the fuck is going on?"

Before Admiral Coleman could answer, Weed rolled in.

"Hey, Dick! We're fighting a war here!"

Buffington froze, his eyes at first blinking in disbelief, then bulging in white hot anger at the disrespect from this retired...*pissant.*

"You..."

Weed walked toward Buffington. "You know, *Dick*, since I'm from the Council for Naval Studies and here to help..."

"Warren, get this man away from me!"

Ready for him, Coleman shot back. "Admiral, we're at a critical juncture here, so *shut the fuck up* very respectfully, sir! Jim, go!"

Wilson had already keyed the mic.

"Olive, it's Flip. Your signal is RECALL! My authentication is that night in Dubai on the 2008 cruise, you and Psycho at the Highlander. You sang *Zombie* in a dress. Saint and the soybean field. Your mom met you at the Oceana fly-in with the big hat. Recall, Olive. Acknowledge and RTB!"

At that moment, Olive, flying a low level at treetop height, hadn't heard a thing.

With one minute to the turn, Olive maintained 200 feet in gently rising terrain. Nothing more from the Russian "P-8." Or were the Russians still transmitting? She was on the deck, but not so much that that radio line of sight was lost. If they had her going feet dry, they should easily have her now.

She brought up the stores page. Station selected. Should she arm up now? No. She'd hold off unless threatened. On station 8, her AARGM launcher swayed under its suspension hooks as Olive's jet was buffeted in the dense Arctic air. No emitters yet, but the chances of her being lit up would increase after this turn.

Resigned, she prayed for strength. *Please God, help me do this.* Olive wanted more than anything to be recalled, but the authentication was bogus! She had to proceed, the very reason she didn't slough off the hop to a subordinate. Olive didn't screw up and she made correct decisions. She knew the jet, the route, the threat, the delivery. And the stakes. Screw this up after thinking about nothing else for the past two hours? No.

Coming up on it, the turn point was the southern tip of a pond, hidden by pine trees. Olive peered over her nose—*there*—and seconds later flew over the deserted pond in a knife-edge right turn to the next point—a leg that would take her over the neutral country Finland. Below her on the pond's surface, startled birds took flight.

The border was easy to see, the dark Karasjohka River. On the Norwegian side a road ran along it. In this deserted land at this late hour Olive didn't expect to see any traffic. All she had seen were a few huts in this untamed and open country; only scattered radio towers and power lines provided any evidence of human habitation. Nestled in another valley, she approached the river and the handful of houses at the bend. Couldn't be helped, and if someone was outside now, a FA-18 *Hornet* was not that uncommon, as they remained the mainstay of the Finnish Air Force. At over 400 knots, Olive would zoom past before they got a chance to point their cell phone.

As the river disappeared under her nose, she entered a gentle climb to clear the ridge ahead. The land was rocky and rugged with no wildlife visible, not birds, nothing. Far to the south, she spied a radio tower, more thin evidence of humanity in this desolate and unforgiving landscape.

She checked her fuel: under the ladder but passable. She'd put it down at a Norwegian airfield or eject inside Norwegian airspace if she had to.

Suddenly, a faint radio transmission.

Olive, it's Flip...you and Psy...Highlander! You...Zombie! Your signal...now! Acknowledge! Acknow...Recall! Your...call!

What?

With both hands, Olive pressed her helmet to hear the transmission, now garbled gibberish through two radio relays. She heard Highlander...and Zombie! That night in Dubai! The voice sounded like Flip and she definitely heard the word *recall*. But no script, no authentication. She flew the jet over the rocky surface and waited for him to call back. Transmitting now could alert the Russians, just over the horizon.

The Nav display showed the border approaching, and in seconds she would be back inside Norwegian airspace...but only for five minutes before she entered Russia, accelerated, and delivered the weapon. *They know my callsign, and that's an AI voice of Admiral Wilson.* Instinctively, Olive scanned the southeast sky for fighters, and her AESA radar picture remained clean.

Back inside Norway, she chanced it, and transmitted on the discrete freq.

"Flip, Olive, say again?"

Nothing.

"Flip, Olive, say again."

"Flip, Ol..., say ag...."

A cheer went up inside TFCC as they heard Olive's transmission over the loudspeaker.

"Knock it off!" Wilson boomed, returning the handset to his lips.

"She's about to make the turn into Russia," Weed said to no one.

Wilson nodded as he concentrated on the COP.

"*Raven* one-one, Olive, it's Flip. Signal Recall. Collie, Fairway, Marina, Grill. I authenticate the Highlander in Dubai, the black dress with Psycho, Zombie. That's all I got! Recall, signal recall! Acknowledge!"

Wilson and the others listened for a voice almost one thousand miles away.

Coll...way, Marina, Grill. I authen...Highlander in Dubai...ack dress, Psyc...zombie! That's...got! Recall...call! Ack...

It's Flip!

Olive allowed the jet to climb as she fumbled for her authenticator—which slipped out of her hands! Reaching down between the seat and right console she fished for it. *C'mon!*

Fair...Marina, Gr...

"*Screw it!*" Olive shouted to herself in frustration and keyed the mic in response.

"Flip, Olive, roger, signal recall. *Tiger,* five-three, *Raven* one-one in the blind, acknowledge signal recall. RTB."

Relief washed over Olive like a breaking wave as she pushed the throttles to military and picked the jet up in a gentle wingover climb as the entirety of the North Cape opened before her. She shallowed the turn and looked right over her LEX—the Kola Peninsula and Varda Nos. She thought of the people there, unsuspecting of what could have—and would have—happened in minutes. Before she turned away she saw something, a black speck on her canopy. Her sixth sense alerted, she detected another dark "dot" near it. Five miles.

Those are no dots!

Olive snapped the jet right and pulled hard as she slammed the throttles into afterburner. With her helmet mounted sight, she locked the first "dot," a fighter from the growing shape and exhaust plume as she reefed her nose to it. The AIM-9 tone screamed into her headset at the same time her RWR came alive with a radar spike.

And a white plume that grew under the jet, nose-on.

Crap!

Olive centered the SHOOT cue, unloaded for a nanosecond, and pulled the trigger. As expected, time slowed as she overbanked down to the rocks only 1,000 feet below and brought the throttles to idle, popping out chaff and flares.

Her Sidewinder hadn't come off!

Her mind working overtime as she defended from the enemy missile that was still burning, it dawned on her. *Shit! MASTER ARM!*

Unloading as she entered her dive recovery, she practically ripped the arming switch out of the housing to arm herself. Her forward quarter shot lost, she yanked the jet up to defend against the missile that pitched down into her. It was big, rocket motor still firing, and beyond it were the two fighters she identified as *Flankers* from their silhouettes.

The missile dove on Olive as the motor burned out, and, leaving the throttles in idle, she pulled all she had to make it overshoot. With her nose parked high and slowing below 200, she saw it, a white tube with X-fins mid body. *An Alamo!* The missile tried to make the diving turn but crossed her wing line and slammed into the rocky surface 500 feet underneath. Her two assailants flew in a loose tac wing across the circle as Olive wavered on the edge of stall.

"I'm engaged, two *Flankers!*" Olive cried out on the radio, pushing the throttles and stick forward to regain precious airspeed as she cranked her neck left to keep sight. The Russians split, with the lead continuing his arcing left turn as the wingman reversed right up into a graceful wingover, extending away from the fight—in front of her. *Yes!*

She saw a shot develop as her nose crossed the extending fighter's path, selected AMRAAM, and, with her helmet sight, locked it. On the edge of the envelope, she eased her pull and squeezed the trigger.

With a deep WHOOOMM, the AMRAAM roared away, going ACTIVE almost immediately. With the lead *Flanker* approaching ninety off, she had to honor the powerful Sukhoi and reengaged with it, hoping to jam his shot and keep his missiles on the rail. Inside two miles, the *Flanker* pulled hard into her, giving everything away. With 300 knots, Olive matched him before her *Hornet* mushed down below 250, and both jets crossed each other with 1,000 feet of separation in a slow-speed Lufbery.

Glancing at the HSI, she noted their position: over Norway, just north of the Finnish border. *These guys aren't supposed to be here!*

Her jet groveled on the deck as it clawed for airspeed with the added burdens of the bomb and an AARGM. Olive kept her lift vector as close to the lead as she could while arcing herself to gain maneuvering airspeed. She had a feeling that she had never left this cockpit, fighting the *Hornet* as she had earlier in her career. She checked over her left shoulder and saw a dark column to the west that led to a fireball on the ground. Nearby floated a single chute. *One down!*

At the merge, the Sukhoi rolled level and went up, riding his two giant cones of fire.

Yes, Olive thought, keeping her turn in while nibbling for an extra fifty knots. She heard a call on the radio but ignored it, concentrating and going for the spot the Russian entered his pull as he attempted to redefine the fight. Missing the sheer power of the *Rhino*, she had one advantage—a superior roll rate.

The Russian continued to extend in the vertical, giving Olive some time, but also gaining turning room. If he were smart, he wouldn't let Olive come up, and just as she leveled her wings to follow him, he pivoted in the sky 5,000 feet above her. Olive realized that he was smart.

Olive rode her cans up in a gentle pull to oppose him as he pounced, his nose dropping to a lag position behind her. Unable to loop with him, Olive kept her nose tracking up as she watched his with every fiber in her body. When the big jet squatted, she knew a gunshot was coming. *Not yet, not yet...*

When she saw the bottom of his jet, she acted. *Now!*

Olive rolled left and pulled with her available airspeed as the Sukhoi hosed a burst of 30mm, missing her low. With the gun's slow rate of fire from a single barrel, the pilot had to be judicious, and holding her high angle of attack, Olive rudder-rolled to keep her lift vector on as she watched him reset. The Russian pulled *hard* to stop his downrange travel and keep Olive in front of him.

With her rudder all the way left, Olive held her nose up as she swung the top of her *Hornet* toward the blue jet, now fewer than 500 feet distant. On the nose, she made out two big numerals painted red, and in the cockpit, the white helmeted pilot, locked on Olive underneath his dark visor. Getting *here* was a success. *We're neutral now, buddy!*

Olive kept her roll in, as did the Russian, entering a rolling scissors that could not last long at 2,000 feet above the granite surface. Olive could fly her jet slow, but the big Saturn engines gave the *Flanker* a true one-to-one capability if light on fuel, which he probably was. By the progress of the fight, the Russian was smart enough to take advantage of it.

Glowing yellow in the midnight sun, two columns of fire from the huge tailpipes held the *Flanker* in place as Olive inched forward, flushed out ahead, both fighters slowly descending toward the rocks.

Olive was in big trouble, and she knew it.

Holding her AOA as high as she could to remain in this airborne wrestler's embrace, Olive had a moment. Her left hand shot to the right outboard push tile, followed by SELECT JETT to jettison her AARGM. She felt the heavy missile fall away, gaining her a little more airspeed with which to fight as she continued her scissors with her lone assassin.

Knowing that she was devouring fuel, she checked it and was shocked to see 5.9! No matter—the nearest alligator was hundreds of feet behind and above her.

Holding her nose at max AOA she ruddered to keep sight and keep the *Flanker* treed above her, also unable to reposition unless he got impatient—or got help, an option Olive did not have.

She glanced at the fuel: 5.1 *Dammit!*

Something—or somebody—had to give.

Both jets had their noses parked high as they held position on one another, both unable to redefine the fight without ceding an advantage. The Russian had the altitude advantage, but with her superior slow-speed ability and turn rate, Olive could avoid another snap-shot and gain an offensive position.

Olive glanced underneath her and saw it, a narrow gorge cut into the granite dome. Acting immediately, she stepped on her right rudder at full extension to knuckle below the horizon and scoop out into the space with maneuvering airspeed only 100 feet above the bottom, with narrow canyon walls on either side.

Once Olive went, the Russian followed, but his big jet lagged, allowing Olive to pick up knots before the *Flanker's* nose could come to bear. Looking over her shoulder as she extended on the deck, she speculated that the pilot was uncomfortable maneuvering in this low-altitude regime, as his lift vector remained above her.

With his nose still off but closing on her, Olive pulled into him hard to force an overshoot. Unable to overbank down into her lest he scrape himself off on the rocks, the Sukhoi turned level as Olive reversed underneath. Now with a 90-degree cut, she eased back into him as he held his turn and arced left, his burner cans bright yellow. *He's lost sight!*

Selecting *Sidewinder*, she designated him on her sight, pulled her nose to him, and squeezed.

The missile came off with a *whoosh* and followed his flight path as the *Flanker* turned planform in the clear sky. At the last moment he broke into it, but too late as the back of his jet exploded into flame. Olive reversed west, and after she rolled out saw that the Russian had already ejected. As she watched his chute blossom, she accelerated to 300 knots and climbed west.

Her state was four thousand, four hundred pounds.

Chapter 58

USS *Valley Forge*, Norwegian Sea, 2355 June 21, 2024

"*Tiger* five-three, *Raven* one-one is RTB. Four point two."

A loud cheer went up in TFCC as they heard Olive's faint transmission relayed from far over the continent. The big screen next to the COP showed a Sky News report from Red Square, with simultaneous celebrations and protests happening the length of it.

Wilson stood resolute. "What's her fuel? Four point two? Relay it."

As the question was relayed to *Cutlass* 302, Wilson noted the E-2 some 200 miles to the east. He wasn't done.

"Move *Knight* six-zero-one east and launch the alert tankers, all of them. We need gas in the air hundreds of miles from here if we're gonna catch her, and we are *going to catch her.*"

Their attention to task restored, Wilson's staff picked up handsets and sound-powered phones to accomplish their admiral's orders. Get assets airborne and move them east ASAP, and move *Valley Forge* and the strike group escorts east at best speed.

Coleman stepped toward Wilson.

"That was a close one, Jim."

"Yes, sir, and it's not over."

"We're going to pay, you know."

"*After* we get her back, Admiral, and until we do, that's my focus."

"I know...okay, I'm going to get on the horn with Washington and NORTH-COM. What are the chances of getting her and that bomb back here?"

"Fifty-fifty, sir. Norway would be a better option if you could work it."

"No," Coleman protested as he held up his hand, an answer Wilson expected.

"Then we need to move if she only has four thousand pounds, sir, especially since we expected she'd have almost twice that off target. Now she's got maybe an hour and a half, if she manages it well before flameout, and she needs three hours of fuel to get here, all over open fifty-five-degree water."

"Flameout?"

"Empty tanks, sir. In that case, she ejects, and hopefully we can put a helo on her within an hour."

"And the bomb?"

"Stays on the jet…and both go into the ocean."

Coleman nodded. "Fifty-fifty?"

Wilson held his gaze. "I *hope* for fifty-fifty, sir."

Olive climbed on a bingo profile high over the North Cape, and from 35,000 feet could see all of it, from the Lofoten Island chain to the southwest to the Kola Peninsula and Varda Nos behind her. After midnight local time, the sun shone low on the northern horizon, a sight she found fascinating.

On the way up she punched off the centerline and reduced drag, which would save her 200 pounds. She still carried an AMRAAM, unneeded weight and drag she would jettison once feet wet. The single *Sidewinder* on her right wingtip would help the drag aerodynamics—a little.

And she needed every little bit. *Valley Forge* was roughly 800 miles away, too far away even with a full bag of gas. She needed fuel to get there—part of the plan from the beginning, but the unexpected 1v2 fight had gobbled thousands of pounds. She had forgotten how little fuel the *Hornet* carried internally, and now she was down to just over three thousand pounds. She would level at 40,000; even with a slight headwind, she'd maybe squeeze 400+ miles from her two F404 engines, but that still left her three hundred miles short—a *long* way on what was essentially the open and frigid Arctic Ocean.

She leveled off and set the power to hold 248 calibrated…410 knots ground-speed. At this fuel setting, she'd go another 200 miles then bring the throttles to idle—*with only 1,000 pounds remaining!* —puckering the exhaust nozzles as *Hornet* pilots had for generations in their efforts to get the maximum range out of every drop of fuel. If she held a gentle ramp-down of 1,000 feet per minute as the engines all but windmilled, she could go 30-40 minutes before she hit the water or flamed out. Feeling the cockpit cold in her tension-filled joints as she floated over the top of the world, she turned the cabin heat up higher.

Off her nose to the left was Andøya, the abandoned Norwegian P-3 base. An option for her once the weapon had been delivered, it was no longer. She had to bring the bomb back aboard or die trying.

The P-8 called her on the UHF.

"*Raven* one-one, *Tiger.*"

"Go ahead," Olive answered.

"Yankee Six Delta passes *Texaco* enroute."

"*Raven* one-one copies. My state three point one, please pass."

"*Tiger* five-three, wilco."

Olive expected that the ship—identified by the P-8 as Y6D—would have tankers enroute, a key part of the return-to-force plan. But Olive was now in extremis, had been since she turned at the merge with the *Flankers*, and the tanker rendezvous point needed to be hundreds of miles east. Like a trapeze artist leaping blindly from the bar, Olive had to trust that the refueling store-equipped "catcher" would be there, stabilized with the basket ready to plug.

In unknown Arctic weather, that could change in minutes.

Padlocked on the cockpit fuel and engine displays, she coasted out, watching Andøya float past under her left wing. She could land there, unannounced, and with her sidearm, guard the weapon with her life. Despite the insubordinate disobedience of orders, at least she would still have a life. The hell with the Norwegians, and NORTHCOM, and Washington. She had to risk her life because of diplomatic niceties. She added The State Department and NATO to the mix. None of them cared for her.

But Flip cared, and she knew that hundreds of miles to the west, he would lay his stars on the table to get her back safely.

She had about an hour to join up on a tanker out there in the blue abyss—or die trying.

Flip picked up the phone to the bridge. "Huey, kick it up, flank. Even after we tank her, she'll have hundreds of miles left before we can bring her aboard."

"Admiral, wilco, sir, but in these seas we're going to trash the jets on the bow with salt water and run ahead of our escorts."

"I don't care if we lose everything up there, go. I'm contacting the rest of the strike group, and if we outrun them, I'll take the heat. Get some *Romeos* ahead of us, too. Get the whole airwing up—we've gotta catch her."

"Sir, in this state—with all we've got—we'll be able to give you twenty-eight knots, maybe."

"Make it happen!" Wilson barked as he slammed the receiver down. On the PLAT, he saw the first alert tanker taxi to one of the waist catapults. It had to sprint 400 miles to catch Olive and transfer 4,000 pounds just to get her to the ship to plug again or trap on fumes. The E-2 needed gas; *Cutlass* 302 needed gas. The tankers themselves would be low-state after the high-speed transit and transferring the minimum to Olive. He needed lots of gas in the air and the carrier as east as Huey could run it or he'd have more than one airplane in the water. Watching Wilson from his perch off to the side, Coleman approached his anxious one-star.

"What's your plan?"

"Sir, we need to get tankers out there and run east even faster than we've been doing. We're going to outrun our escorts, especially in these seas. The cruiser will keep up for a while, but all of them will be in our wake in an hour."

"Can you risk it? We're deep in the woods, here, Jim, and if everyone is at a flank bell, in these seas...they could have an *Akula* lying in wait on our track. We can't outrun our coverage in a headlong sprint."

Wilson nodded.

"Yes, sir, I've thought of that...but if we've got to get that weapon back aboard, and I can save the pilot doing it, then yes, sir. We can sprint-and-drift our attack boats, and I'm placing an overwatch of *Romeos* ahead of us."

Coleman studied him.

"You'd sacrifice your pilot in these waters if it weren't for the bomb?"

Wilson focused on the COP as he formed his answer. Looking down, he nodded with regret and said, "Yes."

Above them, the first *Rhino* tanker went into tension on cat 3.

Olive adjusted her throttles as she added clicks of nose-down trim. From 40,000 feet she was now committed, and in some thirty minutes she would either be plugged and receiving or make a MAYDAY call before she pulled the handle as her jet flamed out.

She established a shallow rate of descent as she tweaked the throttles, closing the variable exhaust nozzles from full open at idle to slightly closed. The FUEL LO light had been on for almost thirty minutes, and now, at 1,000 pounds remaining, she could coax maybe another forty minutes of idle thrust from the engines and another 200 miles of range to the waiting trapeze catcher as Olive descended on her blind jump.

On the surface, she saw a contact that her radar had discovered twenty minutes earlier, a lone fishing trawler. If she had to get out at the end of this descent, she hoped there would be one nearby. Taking one last look behind her, the peaks of the Lofoten chain were barely visible 200 miles away in the white band where sky met sea.

Her lifeline, *Cutlass* 302, himself approaching low state, orbited some 200 miles ahead. Olive's TACAN searched air-to-air for 302…for now, she would have to settle for the human voice of a nugget pilot she barely knew as both floated high above the desolate and inhospitable ocean.

"*Cutlass* three-zero-two, *Knight*."

"*Knight*, three-zero-two, go ahead."

"Squawk one-one-four-two and IDENT."

Olive doubted that the E-2 could see her yet, but if they could see *Cutlass* 302 on radar, that increased her chances.

"*Cutlass* three-zero-two, *Knight*, radar contact, say state."

"Three-zero-two's five point eight."

"Roger, *Cutlass*, *Texaco's* inbound—break—*Raven* one-one, *Knight* calling in the blind. *Texaco's* inbound, and we're looking."

"*Knight*, *Raven* one-one copies, state one point oh. Enroute descent on my outbound track."

"*Raven* one-one, *Cutlass*, got you loud and clear and I'll pass your state."

Olive rogered 302 as she held her rate-of-descent and adjusted her heading for winds. Right now, her outbound track was the way home, and she hoped the tanker crews had it.

Four hundred miles to her west, the *Super Hornet* tankers were just under the number as they sprinted east at .95 Mach. The lead tanker, *Raven* 401, was flown by the skipper, Comet. *Hobo* 204 was the wingman, flown by Fuji, the squadron Ops Officer.

At 25,000 feet and close to military power, Comet did some math on his kneeboard card. CAG Teel was probably 4-500 miles east, with *Cutlass* 302 and *Knight* 601 in between. At their high fuel flow and distance back to the ship, both tankers could only give 4,000 pounds each. CAG needed 4K just to get back to the vicinity of the carrier on fumes. And the E-2 did not yet have CAG's *Hornet*. All the carrier jets raced toward each other in the blind.

In *Raven* 11, Olive's TACAN still did not have a range to *Cutlass* 302, the nugget whose voice she did not recognize. Now passing 30,000 feet and reading 800 pounds, she held what she had, falling through space after letting go of the trapeze.

The radio boomed loud in her headset.

"*Raven* one-one, *Knight* six-zero-one, squawk one one five six."

Yes!

Olive punched in the numbers on the Up-Front Control and waited.

"*Raven* one-one, *Knight* radar contact, say state."

"*Raven* one-one point eight, descending."

"Roger *Raven*, eight-oh."

"*Knight* from *Raven* one-one, negative. Eight hundred pounds."

Three *Valley Forge* airplanes were in extremis four hundred miles east of the ship, and, once they transferred fuel, the two tankers would join them in carrier aviation hell. First, a tanker had to find Olive, and Comet took that responsibility upon himself.

"*Knight*, *Raven* four-zero-one, snap to *Raven* one-one."

"Four-zero-one, fly heading zero-niner-three to intercept."

"Range?" Comet asked. A relieved Olive recognized his voice.

After a pause, *Knight* responded. "Estimating three-six-zero."

In her cockpit, Olive did the math. She could squeeze 140 miles from her fuel if she held this rate of descent and fuel flow to the wavetops. Maybe 150. It was up to Comet, who flew his buddy-store-equipped *Rhino* just under the number to catch her.

Ahead of Olive rested a blanket of white undercast. *But how high is it? And how thick?* She'd enter it to grab the lifeline of *Raven* 401, but felt it would be a factor in the rendezvous.

She considered shutting down an engine but rejected it, needing the range the added airspeed of two engines would give her as much as the fuel. Comet would have to fly in front of her with the basket out for this to work perfectly, which at only 700 pounds, it had to.

The FUEL LO caution mocked her as she continued down into the unknown. She had never been this low on fuel before, certainly not hundreds of miles from anything. A left or right FUEL HOT caution would pop up any minute now, the first indication that her thirsty *Hornet* would soon die unless it received a life-saving drink in the next twenty minutes.

"*Knight*, *Raven* four-zero-one, intercept heading to *Raven* one-one."

"Four-zero-one, fly heading zero-eight-six, *Raven* one-one bears one-zero-one, one-thirty miles."

"Comet, Olive, I'm up yardstick, twenty-nine."

In his cockpit, Comet entered the air-to-air TACAN freq. Soon he got a range.

"Gotcha, *Raven* one-one, say angels and state."

"Passing angels sixteen on my way to the deck, state point-seven, cherubs seven. Solid undercast ahead. Gate."

"Roger *Raven* one-one, and I'm whippin' the ponies. We'll get'cha."

In both cockpits Olive and Comet calculated their rendezvous point and fuel remaining. As they did, *Knight* vectored *Hobo* 204 to *Cutlass* 302 as the *Knight* pilots also converged on the source of their only hope.

"Comet, do you know what the bottom of that undercast layer is?"

"Negative, *Raven* one-one."

Now in heavier air, Comet was in mid-range burner to catch Olive, who refined the intercept altitude, figuring that she would be entering the solid undercast just as Comet arrived. She shallowed her descent as much as she dared, careful not to get too slow as tension coursed through her body. Comet transmitted.

"*Knight Raven* four-zero-one contact, single only, zero-eight-nine, seventy-five miles, niner thousand."

"*Raven* four-zero-one, *Knight*, that's *Raven* one-one."

Olive saw Comet's radar return march down her own screen and bump-locked him, pleased to see him scream transonic out of 15,000 feet. She'd let him make the stern conversion intercept to roll out in front of her with only gallons to spare.

"Three-zero-two's plugged and receiving."

Good, Olive thought. At least the nugget will be okay.

On her FLIR she saw Comet, a speck at range as he raced to her in what would be an aggressive rendezvous. Ahead of her, the solid clouds of the under-cast showed visible outlines, and Olive anticipated that she would be in them when Comet arrived. What to do? Dump the nose and hope they didn't go to the deck? Come up on the throttles to level off in the clear above it, with only two minutes of fuel to spare? She had nothing, airspeed or fuel, from which to maneuver. It would be all up to Comet. Far to the west she noticed a jagged horizon, indicative of convective weather. Was the ship inside it?

Engine right, engine right

A shot of cortisol exploded inside her heart as the aural warning sounded in her headset, Olive's eyes flashed to the new—but not unexpected—trouble, an oil overtemp on her right engine airframe mounted accessory drive, which could soon lead to electrical and hydraulic problems as her jet's internal organs began to shut down from lack of fuel cooling. Unable to add power to increase fuel cooling, she had to wait another five minutes to fill her parched engine feed tanks.

She continued down as her fuel passed below 600 pounds. By her estimation, she had two minutes till she entered the clag underneath her. She designated

Comet on her helmet-mounted sight, noticing a tone in her *Sidewinder*. To her horror, she realized that she was still armed, and quickly safed up, her breathing deep under her oxygen mask.

Olive estimated Comet entered his conversion turn with 500 knots as he rolled into her, just as the first wisps of the cottony quilt they were settling into reached up to them. At that moment, a small crevice opened underneath her jet, and she saw the gray- and white-capped sea surface. *Oh, thank you!* If Comet couldn't get aboard now, she'd push through the thin layer to give him a Hail Mary attempt once in clear air.

The top of Comet's *Rhino* turned white as he pulled hard to join on Olive's left side. However, with too much smack on his jet, he overshot Olive's six as she twisted in her seat to see him roll out at her five o'clock 1,000 feet behind. When she noticed an arm of cloud whip by, she turned her head forward in time to plunge headfirst into the goo.

Once inside, Olive popped the stick forward and reset her attitude. Seconds later the clouds opened as she eased herself down, now showing 500 pounds at 4,000 feet.

Comet appeared behind her at her four, coming up fast but controlling his closure. She saw him yaw right as he cross-controlled to slow himself as he slid forward on her right wing.

"You've got the lead," Olive radioed.

"I've got it," Comet answered.

"Keep a slight rate of descent for me," Olive added, which Comet followed with two mic clicks.

With Comet stabilized next to her, Olive brought the throttles up to fly formation on him, the refueling store basket extending from the centerline station. Not waiting to be cleared in, Olive pulled a little power and eased back.

She extended the probe, and relief washed over her when it moved into her slipstream.

Four hundred pounds.

She stabilized behind a basket that swayed in the turbulent wind, forcing herself to remain calm. *"Slow is smooth"* she said to herself, trimming the stick forces out and holding the sight picture. She added power to plug, and the basket bounced right, her probe lipping it and causing it to sway violently away and then back into her as she pulled power to avoid it.

Three hundred!

Stabilized again, she watched the basket oscillate as she eased up behind it. *Now.*

Olive added a shot of power and lunged at the basket, driving her probe into it as she pushed it forward, her entire being now focused on the amber transfer light. After an eternity, it changed to green.

"Good transfer," Comet transmitted. "And I can only give you four."

His CAG rogered him. *Whatever.*

After hours of tension and over five hours strapped into the seat, Olive's entire body ached. The ship was somewhere ahead, unknown to her, but probably 300 miles. She'd have to tank again, or roll into the groove with mere gallons. Exhausted, she flew formation as life-giving fuel flowed into her rickety jet. *Whatever.*

The light on the buddy store changed from green to amber. *That's it?* It was, and Olive showed 3,700 pounds, her engine and fuel cautions gone. She joined on Comet's right wing as he retracted the store, giving him a thumbs-up when the basket stowed and exchanging states. Comet didn't have much more than she did.

Comet pointed ahead of them and showed Olive two fingers, then five, then a fist. Olive understood immediately: *Valley Forge* was 250 miles ahead.

Resigned, she nodded, expecting that she would see the FUEL LO and engine accessory cautions again on this hop. She moved away from Comet as both of them babied their jets ahead at max range cruise fuel settings.

CHAPTER 59

USS *Valley Forge*, Norwegian Sea, 0040 June 22, 2024

Wilson steadied himself as he checked the COP for the hundredth time. Olive, three *Rhinos*, and a *Hummer* that had been up for over five hours were all low-states returning to *Valley Forge* some 200 miles away. The weather had worsened as Huey charged ahead to the east, the ship transiting bands of sleet while the heavy seas pummeled the jets parked on the bow with white water, including two critical tankers they could not get to.

An hour earlier one of his buddy-store equipped *Rhinos* had landed hard on the carrier's pitching deck, blowing a nose tire and fodding the right engine. And his last "up" tanker was down with a sudden hydraulic leak. Without recovery tankers, the ship had no choice but to take the low-states aboard when they arrived, some of which—most importantly Olive, with her cargo on station three—would be in extremis with only hundreds of pounds, mere *minutes* left.

On the PLAT he noted a helo being towed to the angle to launch and join the three other *Seahawks* already airborne. With no gas overhead and the deck pitching out of limits, Wilson expected to lose an airplane in the next hour. He watched as dozens of squadron maintainers spread the rotors on the MH-60S in the gusting 60-knot winds. More than one of his helicopters had a chance at a rescue this night.

The Battle Watch Captain held the phone handset for Wilson. "Captain Morrison, sir." Wilson took it at once.

"Huey, talk to me."

"Admiral, this is as fast as we can go, sir, without washing all the jets off the bow and knocking everyone down on the flight deck. I'll also have to turn right about forty degrees to put the winds down the angle."

"We've gotta have a ready deck when they arrive. What do you think?"

"Sir, we can take 302 and 204 first—they're about five minutes in front of the others. Comet, the E-2, and CAG are going to get here at about the same time."

Wilson had thought hard about the question he was about to ask. "We've got to get the *Hornet* and the weapon. She'll be on fumes when she gets here; what do you think about a barricade?"

Wilson waited for Huey's answer.

"Admiral, even with the heads-up we'll need five minutes to rig it, and if they all arrive at pretty much the same time, somebody's not going to get aboard. Maybe if he can run ahead we could take Comet, then rig the barricade for Olive, but that leaves the E-2 waiting, and I'm not sure he can wait that long."

"How long would it take for you to clear the landing area after the barricade?'

Wilson could almost hear the captain form his response.

"Like everything else, it depends, sir, but minimum five minutes. And we'll have the added security for the weapon as we pull the jet out, and the combat FOD walkdown will take time."

"Screw the FOD walkdown. Okay…keep it in your back pocket."

"Admiral, we barricade low-state planes that only have one look at the deck, but we can't barricade *three* low-states."

"Understood. What's the status on another tanker?"

"Sir, we're running a buddy store up the forward weapons elevator, taking a chance it gets doused with white water, then rolling it back to three-zero-six parked on the foul line. Thirty minutes if all goes well."

"Roger," Wilson responded, cradling the receiver and again studying the COP. His flagship, now ahead of the strike group with all four screws churning hard in the raging seas, was exposed to an undersea threat in a part of the world known for them. If he broke EMCON now, other threats could triangulate on him. He wasn't tracking any, but they could still be there. And if Olive boltered on her one look at a deck now moving like a San Francisco rooftop during the great earthquake amid a hurricane, she'd eject before her jet and the weapon it carried pancaked into the sea. A barricade arrestment—if she could fly into the moving nylon wall—would catch her, but could they clear the deck in time for the E-2, with five souls aboard and maybe only five minutes of flying time remaining? Wilson checked the PLAT clock. On the big screen, next to the COP, ran the news feed from Red Square.

Weed stepped into TFCC from behind him. "Kemosabe…we going to get her?"

"Are we going to get *them* is the question. Five low-states with nine souls inside—and a nuke on a wing. Huey can't go any faster in this sea state. We can probably trap the three *Rhinos* okay, but Olive and the E-2 will be getting here at about the same time."

"You've got a decision to make," Weed deadpanned.

"And we're outside the ring of steel, lost visual on the escorts, threat waters."

"Sounds like the Philippine Sea all over again."

"What?"

"You know, the Battle of the Philippine Sea, 1944. The 'mission beyond darkness' when all the *Hellcats* and *Helldivers* returned to the Fifth Fleet. In submarine infested waters, Admiral Mitscher said, 'turn on the lights,' giving his aviators a chance."

Wilson nodded. "I've thought of this. One submarine would have had a field day then, and today, if there's one ahead of us."

Weed smiled. "You've already outrun your coverage, and why? To get everyone aboard, especially Olive with that weapon. What holds you back?"

For Wilson, the equivalent of blazing lights to guide his aviators back was RF energy that the Russians could detect at much greater range. If *Valley Forge* radiated her search and approach radars to help guide the low-states to their most efficient approaches, that would help them conserve fuel and give them the best chance to get aboard in these conditions. The airplanes were going to be aboard or in the water in an hour, and minutes saved meant fuel saved.

Weed watched his friend consider his options. "You going to ask Coleman?"

Wilson waited, then shook his head. "No. Will have Huey radiate and transmit. Launch a CAP to deal with any surface threats and get every *Romeo* airborne. And get at least one tanker up."

Olive noticed the FUEL LO caution again illuminate on her DDI. She had about 25 minutes as she continued west to meet a waiting tanker or a ready deck.

Ahead, two miles to her left, Comet nursed his jet home as both flew a sea-level, fuel-conserving "bingo" profile toward the unknown location of *Valley Forge*, with *Knight* providing a general heading. Steady at 1,000 feet, Olive noticed the ceiling lower, the gloom darker on their flight path. She was not flying form on Comet, but did not want to be within even a full mile of him in instrument conditions. The other *Rhinos* and the E-2 were also on their own programs, all converging on the same spot with the same needs. Suddenly, *Knight* transmitted to all of them.

"Ninety-Nine, *Tomahawk*, check in with Strike."

Olive switched up Strike Control on Comm 1, hearing *Knight* passing their fuel state. On a hunch, Olive switched to the ship's TACAN frequency and was surprised and relieved that she had a lock-on just inside 100 miles.

Flip's radiating, she thought, knowing that he was risking the flock to recover five lost lambs. Just then, the ship called to her.

"*Raven* one-one, Strike, you up?"

"*Raven* one-one's up, state one-point-seven."

"*Raven* one-one, roger, radar contact. Expected final bearing one-three-one. Check in with Marshal."

Comet's jet became more difficult to see as bits of sleet bounced off Olive's windscreen in the lowering weather. After she switched Marshal and checked in, she learned it was worse ahead.

"*Raven* one-one, Case Three recovery, CV-1 approach. Expect vectors to expected final bearing one-three-one. Mother's weather, five-hundred overcast, two miles in rain and sleet, altimeter 29.82, fly heading two-six-two."

"Marshal, *Raven* one-one, roger. Pass no HUD on the ball."

"Roger, *Raven* one-one, will pass."

Five hundred feet and two, Olive thought, knowing that a pitching deck and high gusty winds would accompany the low ceiling and vis. Whitecaps covered the surface below her, giving little comfort knowing that the weather was worse ahead.

Tension gripped her at the next transmission from the ship.

"Ninety-nine, marshal, recovery *Texaco* is unavailable, repeat, *Texaco* is unavailable.

Holy crap. No tanker—*for anybody!*—with five low states all going for the same ramp at the same time. The carrier would manage it, but did she and the others have the fuel to allow the ship to untangle this knot?

After all the airplanes had checked in, she had a picture in her mind. *Hobo* 204 and *Cutlass* 302 would arrive and be taken aboard first. After them, Comet, the E-2, and she would arrive at the same time. She took charge.

"Comet, Olive, can you bump it up a little."

"Affirm."

Comet added some power as he continued to open away from Olive, providing them a landing interval.

Finding herself in the thin ceiling, she pushed her nose down a degree and held it with attitude hold as she reset her radar altimeter to 450 feet. She'd normally drop her hook for landing but held it, wanting to keep her jet as drag-free as possible.

Alone, Wilson climbed the ladder to the flag bridge. Buffington could be there—unwanted company—but watching from that vantage point was better than hovering over the crew in Air Ops and Pri Fly. Outside on the flight deck, a CAP *Rhino* went into tension on the waist. On the O-5 level he noticed the chapel, a small space he had passed countless times. He felt a voice inside and ignored it, but the voice pressed him. He opened the door.

He was alone, with ambient light from behind the altar. Stepping into a pew of folding chairs, he kneeled.

What to pray for? Only a few hours ago his pilot—his friend!—was going to rain unspeakable fire on a Russian town, a valid military target, but with women and children just outside the gate in their soulless apartment buildings on a joyless military outpost. Washington's orders…but also his. He folded his hands.

Please God, forgive us, forgive me. Please…bring them back aboard safely, I pray.

After saying the Lord's Prayer, he got up to go, then, inexplicably, sat down in the seat. He had to go, had to command. Buffington and even Coleman would want to know where he was. *Where the hell is Wilson?* Huey needed his guidance, Mark, Smoke. The whole ship needed him to be on his game and fight the strike group. For a moment, however, he could not move as he contemplated the altar, hearing the activity on the flight deck outside but not reacting to it. He needed a moment as he thought of Olive and Comet, the nugget in 302, and the crew of the *Knight* who couldn't even eject if they had to escape, all of them now in peril in the air.

Along with the hundreds of kids on the flight deck and thousands inside the ship, now in the open with radiated RF energy shouting their position to all.

The chapel bulkheads creaked as *Valley Forge* pitched down and buried itself into yet another swell. The 5MC sounded: *Spinnin' a Rhino on the four wire, heads up.*

Please God…

As the din of a *Super Hornet* at military power reverberated and penetrated the thin steel superstructure, the jet roared down the track and leapt into the air. Once the shuttle slammed into the water brake, Wilson heard another voice. *Go.*

He got up, bowed to the cross above the altar, and stepped outside to continue up the ladders to the bridge.

Chapter 60

Raven 11, Norwegian Sea, 0105 June 22, 2024

Inside fifty miles of Mother, Olive shifted in her seat. She had been strapped into it for what seemed like days. Once again in extremis near 1,000 pounds, the FUEL HOT caution would soon return. Low on the water, she conserved her fuel at max range cruise at only 400 feet to remain in the clear, her only company the whitecaps below.

She had helped build this box she was in, unable now to climb into clear air to tank even if the ship could get a tanker airborne. The horizon around her was nothing but gray as the gloom met the sea. She bounced in her seat from the turbulence as another band of sleet lashed her, and knew she would get one look at the deck—if all went well.

She monitored Comet on her radar, now three miles ahead. Listening to the marshal directions, she guessed the E-2 was to her right and descending, also with only 1,000 pounds. The turboprop could manage it better, but not much better. Some twenty miles ahead 302 and 204 received vectors to the final bearing.

She had to keep her power up. Slowing to max endurance could keep her airborne a few minutes longer but short of the ship. She had to get behind the ship, hold her dirty-up till the last second, and trap.

With no HUD! She especially wanted it in these semi-instrument conditions. She had landed on carriers without a HUD before, but they were rare occurrences, and she knew she would miss it most in the expected weather ahead.

"*Raven* one-one, fly heading two-seven-zero, check in with approach on button one."

Olive rogered the call but declined the vector, knowing it was to give her a long ten-mile, straight-in approach, requiring seven miles that she didn't have. She would take charge.

"Approach *Raven* one-one, checking in, state nine hundred. I'll need a two-mile turn to final. No HUD."

The First-Class Air Traffic Controlman knew at once what she needed. Assessing the relative motion of the ship, the winds, and Olive's low-fuel state, he vectored her right at the ship to allow the separation to build between Olive and the E-2.

Approaching twenty miles, the weather lowered further, and Olive climbed to 800 feet to give herself the best chance for a good approach start. She reset the power and, once stabilized, noted 700 pounds. Seconds later she got an *engine right* aural warning as her right AMAD oil temperature increased once again. With only five minutes till landing, she reduced the right throttle setting and compensated with the left, planning to bring the right up and trap with both engines. Once her power stabilized, she received another caution: INLET ICE.

In frustration, she swatted the engine anti-ice switch on and vented her tension into her mask. *Stay with me, bitch!*

"Thought you'd be up here," Coleman said as he stepped onto the Flag Bridge. "Where's Buffington?"

Wilson pointed to the at-sea cabin. "Think he's inside, sir."

"Good. Okay...are we going to make it?"

Wilson turned to the sleet pelting the bridge windows, then back to Coleman.

"Five airplanes, including CAG with the weapon, are in extremis, and these conditions are the worst I've seen—daytime."

"You didn't answer my question."

"We'll work to get them all, sir, but I'm steeling myself for the worst."

"What is the worst?"

"Loss of the E-2, sir. A low altitude bailout in this stuff...five souls and we'd be lucky to rescue two."

Coleman nodded his understanding. "I hear you—but disagree. Their lives are precious, but getting that weapon back aboard is paramount. Can't you prioritize your CAG?"

"Sir, we expect to get two *Rhinos* aboard in the next few minutes, then a third. Olive—CAG—and the E-2 are next and they're both on fumes. The ship is doing their best to sequence them, but the way this deck is moving...going to be tough."

"Can't you rig that flight deck net to ensure you stop them?"

"We can, sir, but we lose five minutes and, very important, once we catch someone, the deck will be closed for some time before we can clear it."

"You've got to, Jim. A tough call and people might die, but we've got to get that weapon back."

Wilson pursed his lips as he looked down. Outside, the heavy swells were streaked as the gale force winds lashed them.

"Admiral, imagine being in that 50-degree washing machine..."

"Jim, don't give me that! Is it worth the loss of airplanes and personnel to the United States to get the bomb back? Yes, it is! I've been under the ice and in harbors I'll never admit to having been in, risking one hundred and thirty souls because it was in the interest of the United States that I be there. Damn dangerous, and no one's ever heard about it. And no one's going to know about this mission either, Jim. We came close, and the world got lucky, but we're not going to come back up here in their backyard and retrieve a fucking nuke on the seabed and let the world know what almost happened. Now, save who and what you can, but I *suggest* you use all means to get that bomb back aboard."

When Wilson didn't answer, Coleman exhaled in disgust.

"Admiral Wilson, I've helped all I can. You had better be right."

"I'm not going to do that, sir," Wilson responded.

"I know, dammit!" Coleman shot back as he stepped toward the door.

"You could relieve me, sir," Wilson said quietly.

His anger gone, Coleman turned and looked at him. "I know," he said.

Coleman opened the door and left, leaving Wilson alone as the 5MC sounded outside.

Rhino at four miles, make a ready deck!

Olive listened to Elmo call to the airborne aircraft from the LSO platform. "Ninety-nine pattern, little squall here, landing lights on...workin' fifty-two knots, MOVLAS recovery, MOVLAS recovery."

Olive expected Elmo to guide them in manually in these conditions, but she wasn't fooled by his calm cadence. *Valley Forge* was moving big time and hidden in visibility down to inside a half mile.

Cutlass 302 called the ball first, with Elmo talking to him the whole way. When approach called to 204 who was next, Olive knew that the nugget was aboard. One down, four to go.

"*Raven* four-zero-one, five miles, intercept the final bearing one-three-one, dirty up."

Olive waited for Comet's answer. "Four-zero-one, roger, holdin' my dirty."

Good, Olive thought. More interval between she and Comet gave the deck more time to get Comet out of the landing area and ready it for her...or the *Hummer.* She did not know who they would take first, and depended on the Tower and Air Ops to handle it. Approach called to the next jet in line.

"Two-zero-four, three-quarter mile, slightly right of course, call the ball."

"Clara," Fuji responded.

"Paddles contact, you're lined up right...fifty-four knots slightly axial."

Olive—and all on the circuit—could only listen.

"Ball!" the pilot barked once the MOVLAS came into view.

"Roger ball, don't settle...right for line up, easy with it, *easy* with it, POWER!"

Following a short silence, approach called Comet to begin his approach, a signal to Olive that 204 got aboard. The Air Boss then called to her.

"*Raven* one-one, Tower, what's your state?"

Olive answered immediately. "Seven hundred, if the reading is correct."

"Roger," the Boss replied.

What are they thinking? Olive thought. *If they are taking Comet, they'll have to take me normally, no time to rig the barricade.* There was no time to barricade everyone, only one, and the ship had made their decision. *Flip* made the decision to radiate, to transmit, and to allow everyone a chance at survival.

"Workin' fifty-six knots, slightly axial," Elmo informed everyone. Her LSO's calm voice could not hide the real message. *Fifty-six freakin' knots!*

Specks of sleet continued to pelt Olive as she continued in, locked on the ship and listening to the approach controller for situational awareness. Fifty-six knots of wind was uncharted territory for everyone.

"*Raven* four-zero-one, three miles, begin descent."

"Four-zero-one," Comet answered.

Inside ten miles, Olive slowed to 225. She'd drop the flaps to half as she neared the final bearing, and would lower her gear once on it, using every trick she could to conserve fuel.

"Four-zero-one, below glideslope, three-quarter mile, call the ball."

"Clara."

"Paddles contact, keep it coming...Paddles contact, you're low."

"Ball!"

"Roger ball, you're low...deck's movin' a little, you're on glidepath...little power, little right for lineup...POWER!"

After Elmo had talked to Comet the whole way, Olive waited in the sudden silence.

"*Raven* one-one, final bearing now one-two-niner, say state."

"Six hundred pounds," Olive answered.

"*Raven* one-one, Paddles."

"Go," Olive replied.

"Understand you're no HUD, I'll be talkin' to you. People are breaking out at a half-mile but we've got a lot of wind, so stay energized. Landing light on."

"Wilco," Olive responded as her breathing deepened. This was it, her one chance, and the first challenge was intercepting the final bearing and dirtying up in a turn at 800 feet. She couldn't break the jet with a hard landing and foul the landing area either, as the *Hummer* with five souls aboard was sequenced behind her. However, the deck would do what the deck was going to do, under the control of no one.

"*Raven* one-one, unable ACLS lock-on, fly your bullseye three miles."

"Roger, good bullseye," Olive answered.

"Roger, *Raven* one-one, recommend left turn to intercept."

Only three miles from the ship, in the goo at 800 feet and with non-precision glideslope and azimuth, Olive brought the right throttle up and turned to intercept the final bearing, dropping her gear and hook as she did. Concentrating on her HUD on the left DDI display was better than a partial panel scan, but not much better and the challenge would come in seconds once she broke out and saw the ball. She breathed a sigh of relief when the gear indications turned solid green and illuminated the landing light. In two seconds, she accomplished a quick landing checklist that she knew by heart.

Elmo keyed his handset. "Fifty-seven knots, *dowwwn* the angle." As he transmitted, Olive overheard the LSO platform bell warning of an out-of-limit deck cycle.

Holding a steep angle of bank, she rolled out on course as rapid waves of heavy sleet bounced off her windscreen. She energized the windshield anti-ice and flew the jet, tension coursing through her as she squeezed the stick to hold the jet steady in the violent winds. She checked her fuel: 400 pounds.

"*Raven* one-one, three quarter mile, call the ball."

Ahead of her, Olive only saw murky precipitation illuminated by her landing light.

"Clara, point five, no HUD."

"Paddles contact, *Hornet*, deck's moving a little, roger no HUD, okay gotcha, you're going high."

Still unable to see the ship, Olive popped the nose and reset it.

Engine right, engine right

Olive glanced at the left DDI and saw the expected R FUEL HOT caution. *Screw it!*

"Power back on to catch it, don't settle."

Through the murk she saw the green MOVLAS datums, surprisingly close. Elmo showed her a low. 'You're going low, power, fifty-five knots."

Olive jammed on some power to correct, too much. "Easy with it!" Elmo called as he raised the handle to show her a high ball in close.

At that moment the deck cycled, the ramp falling to its nadir as the deck pitched in its ponderous rhythm. To Olive, she was now flying into a steel wall. Nevertheless, a lifetime of training forced her to correct off the high Elmo showed her, and once she pulled power in her light jet, the deck heaved back up to meet her.

"Power back on! Power! POWER!" Elmo cried as he ran the MOVLAS handle down to the red. Olive shoved the throttles into afterburner in reaction to Elmo's calls and the white round down rising up just under her nose.

She came down hard on her main mounts next to the LSO platform, her nose gear slamming onto the one-wire from the whipsaw effect, blowing one of the two nosewheel tires. As twelve tons of FA-18C teetered on one wheel, the *Hornet's* tail lifted, carrying the hook over the one, two, and three wires as Elmo and the other platform LSOs watched in horror.

In her cockpit, Olive reefed back on the stick…

Her hook picked up the four-wire on the fly, and Olive was thrown forward in welcome realization as her engines staged into burner. *Yes!*

Engine right, engine right

Unknown to Olive, bright flame shot from the right tailpipe as the *Hornet* was wrestled to a stop at the end of the angle, her eyes darting from the dark gray water ahead of her to the R FLAMEOUT caution that appeared on her DDI as the RPM rolled back. *Shit!*

"*Raven* one-one, looks like you blew a tire on the trap!"

"Roger, Boss, and I just lost my right engine—unable to taxi," Olive replied. She realized the danger of the situation right away: *the E-2!*

"Roger, standby, we'll pull you, keep the power up for now," the Boss advised her.

Olive rogered him

"*Knight*, six-zero-one, three miles begin descent."

"Six-zero-one."

Waves of sleet rolled across the flight deck as the crew surrounded Olive's jet, her left engine still turning as they placed chocks on her main mounts. Without the right-side hydraulics, she couldn't taxi, had no brakes, and couldn't even raise the hook or fold the wings. With *Knight* 601 sucking fumes only a little more than a minute behind her, they had to hook her up to a tractor fast as Olive remained in the cockpit with only the hook attached to the cable. To her right, a gaggle of security personnel and Air Force ordnance men waited. The tension released, she smiled to herself as one of the airmen looked on the flight deck scene as if he had seen a ghost.

A tractor pulling a towbar drove in front of her, then backed up to her nose as sailors maneuvered the towbar in place. Outside, she heard the Boss on the 5MC. *We've got a low-state* Hummer *at two miles, chop chop!*

As an Air Force Master Sergeant gesticulated with the yellow shirts about the unauthorized personnel crawling all over the *Hornet* with their bomb attached to it, Olive monitored the approach frequency.

"Workin' fifty-two knots, axial. *Knight*, say state."

"Six hundred pounds, if we can believe the gauge."

"Roger, got a little raindrop here, landing light on."

With the towbar attached, the yellow shirt had Olive shut down the left engine. Now unable to hear the drama on approach, she turned her radios and displays off but kept her canopy closed and seat armed. Olive felt a tug as the yellow shirt motioned the tractor driver forward and right to exit the landing area. *Valley Forge* rolled to port as the tractor struggled to pull the FA-18 up the steel incline, and with her hand on the emergency brake handle, Olive felt the main mounts slide to the left behind her.

She twisted in her seat to look over her shoulder. The great carrier bucked in the swells, showing the sea behind it before the ramp rose high, revealing nothing but heavy sleet and fog. She could no longer hear the action on the radio, but when she picked up the *Hawkeye's* landing light, she doubted they could pull her tail clear before the big turboprop could trap. Would be close.

Through her canopy, she heard the 5MC, this time Huey.

Paddles, this is the captain. Take him, drop your arms, take him, my call.

With her bow down, *Valley Forge* rolled right, forcing the driver to stomp on the brakes. Olive was now on the right ladder line…with another forty feet of airplane behind her fouling the landing area. Huey was going to take 601 now, their only chance, if Elmo could get him aboard.

The E-2 emerged from the gloom behind the island as the ramp fell once again. The airplane twitched as the pilot fought lineup and the high winds. *"Get that* Hornet *clear,* Hummer *on the ball!"* the Boss barked over the loudspeaker.

Olive could only watch the scene unfold as the E-2 flew down to the swaying deck and right at her.

From the flag bridge, Wilson watched the action from behind his bridge chair, powerless to help. Olive was aboard with the weapon but trapped at the end of the angle, tied to a tractor as the largest airplane in the air wing was seconds from touchdown. If the pilot and LSO could not trap the E-2, both it and Olive's *Hornet*, the six souls inside them, and an untold number of deck crew would be lost in the ensuing fiery collision.

Leaving his people to manage the problem, he had heard Huey make the call. *Take him.* With that call, the captain placed all the responsibility for what could happen on his shoulders. However, Wilson had made the call to get *everyone* back, and Olive's blown tire and ruined engine that put the aviators and deck crew in this situation did not absolve him of that responsibility. From the LSO platform, Elmo talked the *Hummer* aboard as Wilson watched and listened.

"On glideslope...*onnn* glideslope, fifty-three knots."

"There's a jet in the landing area!" the *Knight* co-pilot cried on the radio.

"We know, six-oh-one, she'll be clear, you're high...a little power to catch it, right rudder."

Wilson's head snapped from the E-2 at the ramp to Olive, the tail of her *Hornet* still over the ladder line. *C'mon!*

At the ramp, the E-2 approached the ship in slow-motion as the turboprop struggled against the tropical storm-force winds. Elmo still had him lip-locked.

"You're goin' high...*easy* with it...little right for lineup."

Knight 601 settled on the one wire, exactly where Elmo wanted to place him. With Olive's jet still fouling the angle ahead, the E-2 rolled to a stop 150 feet short of the FA-18C, just crossing the ladder line.

Yes! Wilson whispered to himself as he pumped his fist. On the 5MC, he heard Huey's voice again: *Great job, Paddles!*

As Wilson picked up the phone to call the bridge, a voice from behind surprised him.

"Wilson, you are one lucky son of a bitch."

Admiral Dick Buffington glared at him.

Transiting southwest through the Denmark Strait, *Valley Forge* ran at twenty knots with her screen ships arrayed in an ASW posture. High overhead, two P-8s flew overwatch for the strike group as it left the dangerous waters north of Iceland on its way to a hero's welcome in Norfolk.

Over the past 36 hours, the coup leadership in Moscow consolidated their hold of the Russian government, going to great pains to allay the fears of the West, stating that Russian naval and air forces, and especially the Strategic Rocket Forces, had stood down. Nevertheless, American and NATO navies remained at sea and on high alert, soothing the nerves of allies and shipping companies who wanted to resume business as before. Hours earlier, a commercial airline flight from Rome to San Francisco had transited north of Iceland once the airspace was declared free of combatants.

Admiral Buffington had departed that morning, on an *Osprey* that took him to Reykjavik where he could board a flight to Washington. There he would make a full report of the action and his key operational leadership aboard his flagship under fire to the Secretary before they together visited the White House. Like Halsey and Spruance, Buffington would take his place in the annals of naval history as a four-star who commanded at sea.

The world, especially the Western world in Europe and North America, remained on edge as shocked citizens returned to their homes and tried to make sense of what had happened, looking with suspicion on their governments, who had brought them to the brink. Americans who never gave the dull inanities of foreign policy any thought now spent more time thinking about the unthinkable.

One hour after Buffington departed, Coleman asked to meet with Wilson alone in his at-sea cabin before dinner. Expecting it, Wilson stood on his flag bridge when Coleman arrived.

A tight-lipped Coleman stepped onto the flag bridge and saw Wilson standing alone next to his chair. "Jim."

"Good afternoon, sir."

"We alone?"

Wilson nodded.

Coleman walked to the front of the bridge, and together they surveyed the strike group around them, steaming as one in brilliant sunlight. Here and there, helicopters darted about in execution of missions required of a working task force in a combat zone.

Not wanting to start yet, Coleman asked Wilson a routine, professional question.

"When do you refuel?"

"Tomorrow at dawn. We'll rendezvous with *Chattahoochee*, scheduled for four hours alongside."

Coleman nodded. "As a submariner I'm always amazed by it. Over one hundred and fifty thousand tons of ships only two hundred feet apart."

Wilson smiled in the awkward silence. *Yes, it is amazing, almost as amazing as attacking a nuclear superpower with a nuke.*

They stood admiring the scene, both knowing what was next.

"Jim, Buffington was on the horn last night with Fleet Forces. I'll be frank with you...he's not a fan of yours and told Admiral Woods chapter and verse about what a poor job you've done running this strike group."

"Do you concur with that, sir?" Wilson asked.

"No. However, I was disappointed with your judgment yesterday morning, and...you can't just tell your bosses in so many words to go screw themselves and ignore the direction they suggest. You *know* that, but you did it anyway."

"And everyone's alive."

"Yes, Jim, in hindsight you made the right call, but you hung it out there, risking the ship, risking getting that bomb back, and..."

Wilson waited for Coleman to continue. *Get on with it, sir.*

"Jim...you are going to get orders tonight, and after the replenishment tomorrow, you can expect a C-2 to pick you up and take you to Gander. From there, a plane will take you back to Norfolk."

"With my staff?"

"No."

In the uncomfortable silence, both men stared off the bow at the horizon.

"I'm sorry, Jim, but you'll get another command. Kirk Kalstad is retiring as Navy Region Mid Atlantic, and I recommended to Buffington—and will to Fleet

Forces and anyone else who will listen—that you roll into that job, do it for a year, and then...retire."

Wilson remained silent.

"If I were you, Jim, I'd...oh, I don't know what I'd do."

Through clenched teeth Wilson nodded. Fired. *We don't want you. Get out.*

"Who will relieve me?" he said.

"I'll stay aboard until Norfolk, and your Chief of Staff can keep things together until another guy assumes command."

Wilson nodded again. *I did all that you dickheads asked me to.*

He then changed course.

"Admiral, Olive Teel deserves a Navy Cross. She *deserves* a Medal of Honor, but a Navy Cross is realistic. I've already started writing the citation—"

Coleman shook his head. "No. I'm sorry, but no medals or recognition that what happened two days ago even happened. She, and all of us, can live with the satisfaction of accomplishing the mission. I know how you feel; I've got sea stories I can't even tell you, but...no medal. All of your aviators can get medals for the other actions, but not that one."

Wilson thought of Annie Schofield, who gave her life in another undeclared war. That it was considered a police action made no difference to her family, who received nothing but a flag.

"Jim...you do understand all this. They told us at baby flag school: All of us are expendable and at any time. You also know that it's cutthroat up here, and we serve at the pleasure...I'm sorry, Jim."

Wilson chafed at Coleman's condescension, holding his tongue as he exhaled tension through his nose. Buffington's disdain for aviators was well known, and no aviator in his chain was high enough to save Wilson. Big Dick Buffington was a four-star, after all, with much more credibility than a baby flag officer. Coleman wrapped it up.

"I've been invited to dine with the XO in the Wardroom tonight, which allows you to spend the evening with your staff. You can tell them that Fleet Forces wants your after-action debrief, those are your orders. Once we go pierside and everyone goes on liberty, I imagine an announcement will be made. We'll keep it low key...unless you..."

"Go vertical."

"Vertical?"

"Yes, that's what we aviators say. Go vertical in a fight and you have everyone's attention."

"Heh, yes, of course…vertical. An option for you aviators, to quickly go in any direction. Just don't be impulsive."

His face set, Wilson turned to the three-star and nodded. "Yes, sir. Going vertical is an option…and there are times to use that option."

Coleman's face fell as Wilson's cold gaze embraced him. He took a step back in reaction to a conversation that had taken a sudden turn.

"See me before you get on that airplane, Jim. Good night."

Coleman turned and departed the bridge, leaving Wilson to contemplate his strike group—and the end of his career.

That night, Wilson packed up his stateroom office in preparation to leave the ship. The cover story was that Fleet Forces in Norfolk, followed by the Pentagon, wanted an after-action debrief. They did, and Wilson kept it from all but his closest staff that he would not be returning, ever.

CHAPTER 62

FLIGHT DECK, USS *VALLEY FORGE*, NORTH ATLANTIC, 1030 JUNE 24, 2024

Dressed in khakis and his flight jacket, Wilson stepped out of his stateroom office with his overnight bag and briefcase. To his right, the flag mess was deserted of officers. He smiled to himself. Not unusual at this hour, and no need to make a big production. *The admiral has been summoned to brief the heavies* was one of the truer cover stories among the lies necessitated by combat…and the political expedience of the flag officer corps to keep their public laundry always clean.

Only the culinary specialist, Petty Officer Shugart, was present, arranging the table. Wilson stepped toward him.

"Petty Officer Shugart…I'll be taking off here shortly, but you've done a great job during my short time aboard. Look forward to seeing you soon."

"Thanks, Admiral, and safe travels. Have a beer for me, sir."

"Will do," Wilson said as they shook hands.

Skweez, who would accompany Wilson, entered from the passageway with the Air Transport Officer, who carried a flight deck life preserver and cranial for Wilson to wear on the *Greyhound*. In silence, Wilson donned the "float coat" and cinched down the cranial strap as he had for 30 years, wondering if he would ever wear one again. Skweez could tell his admiral was preoccupied. Both wanted this part to be over.

"Let's go," Wilson said.

The ATO led the way through the blue tiles to the captain's ladder and up. There, Olive met him, while Skweez went out with the ATO to the turning C-2 parked abeam the island. She handed Wilson a letter.

"Admiral, may I ask you to deliver this to Chris when you get home?"

"Happy to. Mary and I will deliver it ourselves."

Olive, not one to show emotion, looked away with a trembling chin as the gravity of the moment hit her. "Sir, thanks for all you've done for us…and for me."

"You're a trusted shipmate in the truest sense of the word, Olive, and a damn fine CAG...better'n me."

At that moment, the 1MC sounded: *Carrier Strike Group Eighteen, departing.*

She tried to smile, upset at the injustice Wilson was now experiencing and would experience again and again in the four-star offices of Norfolk and Washington. Wilson offered his hand and Olive took it, both of them unable to look the other in the eye after almost twenty years together at sea, in combat deployments, in wardroom and ready room conversations and shared squadron forced-fun activities, in family events that bonded them and all their shipmates for life. The end of it—by their choice or the Navy's—would one day come, as it would for all, as they knew it would, yet now they stood in the flight deck vestibule, shocked that it actually had.

In a moment neither could explain, they both embraced in a tight clutch, the only time they had ever hugged, saying nothing yet conveying everything, holding each other past what society viewed as a friendly clasp, expressing the love for one another that only combat veterans would ever know. Outside, the C-2's turboprop engine droned in wait, reminding both that the hour had come. Wilson squeezed Olive one last time and released her, and, with a wan smile, reached down to lift the flight deck hatch dog bar up.

He was met by the low rumble of a turning eight-blade propeller and a light sea breeze as he opened the door. What he saw next was unexpected.

At parade rest, eight rainbow side boys in their multi-colored float coats stood alongside a ceremonial red carpet with bullet piping, coming to attention and then saluting as Wilson strode between them. Wilson returned their salutes. At the end, Wilson's strike group staff stood in wait: Mark, Smoke, Shane, the watch captains, the yeomen and more. Mark saluted and offered his hand, shouting close to Wilson's ear to be heard over the din.

"Safe travels, Admiral. We've got it here; you've done the hard part."

Wilson smiled as he clasped his arm, then waded through his staff, exchanging handshakes as he made his way to the waiting COD.

Free of the group, he walked toward the lowered ramp as the 5MC sounded.

"On the flight deck...*attention on deck!*"

Hundreds of sailors aboard *Valley Forge* stopped what they were doing and came to attention as Wilson continued to the airplane. As the 5MC intoned again, he recognized Huey's voice.

"*So long, Admiral...honored to be your shipmate.*"

Wilson raised his thumb high in acknowledgement before he turned and saluted the bridge. He then walked to the ramp and hopped aboard.

"Here's your seat, Admiral."

The ATO directed him to a seat with a window, the only passenger seat that had one on the right side. Sitting at the left-side window was Weed, who smiled and mouthed *'Kemosabe.'* Behind Weed sat Skweez who was already asleep in his chair.

Wilson strapped himself in and listened to the loadmaster give the safety brief. Outside the cavernous ramp opening he saw that sailors had returned to their duties among the jumble of airplanes parked on the bow and forward elevators. *The one-row. The point. The corral. The foul line.* Jargon that he and everyone else on the flight deck knew, that gave him a sense of belonging. Wilson had been walking on this deck to combat loaded jets since many of the sailors outside were learning to walk themselves. For now, these sailors only experienced another grueling day at sea, days that would continue long after Wilson retired, a date he now measured in months.

The ramp began to close, and Wilson followed it up, as all inside did, the world of the flight deck closing on him—forever. He watched the scene until the ramp finally swallowed it shut, relative silence filling the austere cabin of exposed wiring and airframe ribs covered in dingy lagging. The characteristic hum of the engines permeated the spartan cocoon.

Peering through his grimy window, he saw a blue shirt run underneath the airplane. Soon the aircraft lurched, free now as it taxied under the direction of a yellow shirt. On the horizon, Wilson glimpsed *Manila Bay*, still technically *his* ship. He was responsible for it, even now. *The bastards.*

With Wilson twisting in his seat to observe the progress, the C-2 taxied aft and turned as it was led to cat 3. Wilson sensed sailors in the forward seats watching him look out his little window while they had none. *Unseemly. Just look down or into the back of the seat aft, as they all sit facing aft, and act like an admiral, not a cashiered has-been unfit for advancement, clinging to a last glimpse.* He felt the airplane twitch and lurch as it lined up on the cat.

Fired. He had been fired.

Wilson felt the airplane hook up to the catapult holdback and shuttle, and, as the others, braced himself forward in his straps in anticipation. With a jolt, the C-2 went into tension, and the crewman twirled two fingers over his head as he shouted, *"Here we go, here we go, here we go!"*

The engines at full power created a steady hum inside the dark and dank cabin as 21 passengers braced and waited. Wilson glanced at Weed, who braced with his head down, hands on his shoulder straps. Wilson did the same, head down toward the scuffed seat back in front of him, fogs of condensation pouring from the vents in this surreal tube, in anticipation, waiting, realizing. *Our last cat shot.*

The cat fired, creating an instantaneous force of four g's that held Wilson firm against his straps as the *Greyhound* raced down the track. The C-2 leapt into the air with a lurch that sprung Wilson and the others back into their seats as the invisible grip on them was released. He immediately looked out the porthole to see the carrier's bow, jets parked on the 4-row that receded away into nothing but gray water as the COD turned and climbed. He watched the water as they sped over it at 500 feet. He had never really noticed the water before, preoccupied with flying his jet and managing his cockpit during the hundreds of carrier launches he had logged. As an aviator, he was intimately familiar with the water, knew it, had seen plenty of it, but at this moment, he contemplated it for the first time.

He turned away to stare at the back of the seat again, checking his watch to mark the time. Three-plus hours in this thing until Gander. He removed his cranial and glanced at Weed, who was already asleep. Good idea, Wilson thought.

Over the next three hours, he fidgeted in his seat to get comfortable, but his mind would not let him doze, holding him in its grip the entire way.

For cause...

Wilson had finally drifted off when the engine pitch changed, and he felt the airplane descend. He glanced outside to see the gray/green tundra of Labrador far below. Checking to his right, he found Weed still asleep. *How does he do it?*

Over the next twenty minutes, he thought of the ship, Buffington, Olive, Coleman. He soaked in his wounded pride as tension built in his gut. *Saint.* Saint Patrick had taken the COD off *Valley Forge* 16 years earlier after CAG sent him home. For cause. Maybe this COD. Maybe this seat. Wilson considered the irony of it.

He donned his cranial for the landing, and after it landed, the C-2 cleared the runway and taxied to the parking apron, lowering the cargo door just as it pulled in front of the FBO entrance. A pleasant summertime temperature greeted them, and Wilson surveyed the scene. A sign next to the FBO read WELCOME TO HAPPY VALLEY. He thought of the ship again, knowing that Huey and the crew of *Happy Valley* steamed as before, as all aboard her focused on the tasks at hand, accomplishing them just fine without Flip Wilson.

First off the COD, Wilson was met by a Royal Canadian Air Force Colonel who led him inside and offered food and refreshment. A Navy C-40 waited on the ramp, parked next to three American P-8s. While Skweez made phone calls and coordinated with the C-40 crew, Wilson listened with polite disinterest as the colonel went on about his experiences during a patrol of the Denmark Strait in one of the CP-140s parked outside. Wilson smiled when he needed to, his mind already over 1,000 miles away.

Soon the American sailors were led to the C-40 that would take them home to Virginia Beach. Modeled on the 737 airliner, the *Clipper* offered the comforts of a passenger plane for their next three-hour flight. Per custom, and after thanking the Canadian officer, Wilson boarded last and took a seat next to Weed. In minutes, the pilots started the engines and taxied for takeoff.

"Does Mary know you're coming?" Weed asked.

Still brooding, Wilson nodded. "How about Karen?" he asked.

"Yep. She'll be at Oceana to pick me up. Just like the old days."

"When we flew home in glory."

"Flip, if glory is what you want...you've got it. Defeat of the Red Banner Fleet. Everyone has all their fingers and toes."

"Not aboard *Lloyd Childers*."

"You waged nuclear war at sea, and those guys at Fleet Forces can't even carry your helmet bag—so they must destroy you."

Instinctively, the pilots grew silent as the C-40 took the runway and accelerated to flying speed. Wilson looked out the window as the bleak landscape rushed past and then fell below. *Airborne.*

After they passed 10,000 feet, Weed began again.

"What did Coleman tell you? Not enough style points in your win?"

"Buffington and his LCS fixation," Wilson replied. "He didn't want Olive to fly the strike, and Coleman wanted me to bring her aboard first. I expected to have them reach into my cockpit from a data link or SATCOM call, but not to have them literally over my shoulder."

"Two too many cooks in a one-cook kitchen," Weed murmured.

"I didn't follow their suggestions, and I'm a problem child who can't be trusted, so I'm out."

"Even though all is well."

Wilson looked outside at Newfoundland to the southeast. He had always wanted to visit it, and now with his career soon ending, maybe he would.

Weed continued.

"You know, you've got what, 4,500 hours, over a thousand traps? Four air-to-air kills. Well, three if you don't count that F-4 you stole from me at Yaz Kernoum, but four technically. Your chest full of *the choicest* fruit salad, the honor of men, and flag retirement benefits out the wazoo."

"I'll buy you a cup of coffee with it," Wilson deadpanned.

"Yeah, it's over, Flip...and not on your terms. We love them for a thirty-year career, and they drop us like a hot brick after we delivered just want they wanted."

"Thought I could beat the odds."

"Join the fuckin' club," Weed answered. His answer had an edge.

Ashamed, Wilson recoiled in the awkward silence. Did he lay his eagles on the table to defend Weed after the Maug Island strike? No. Weed was re-moved—*for cause*—and Wilson stood and said nothing as his friend departed the ship in a COD.

"I'm sorry, Weed."

Weed didn't look at Wilson as he nodded his response, fixed on the window next to Wilson as he stared blankly at the Atlantic skies.

The loadmaster appeared in the aisle.

"Admiral Wilson, the aircraft commander requests your presence on the flight deck."

Weed got up to let his friend out, and an embarrassed Wilson rose to graciously accept another perk of his rank. Leading him forward, the loadmaster rapped on the cockpit door and entered.

The left-seat pilot, a senior lieutenant commander, turned to greet Wilson.

"Welcome aboard, Admiral. Great to meet you, sir."

Wilson and the pilots exchanged small talk as Wilson observed the cockpit and scene outside. Some 35,000 feet below them, the rocky coast of Newfoundland gave way to the broad Atlantic, shimmering in the afternoon sun.

After ten minutes, the aircraft commander offered. "Admiral, would you like to sit in the left seat?"

Wilson's answer surprised even himself.

"Sure, thanks."

With the airplane on autopilot, Wilson eased into the empty left seat. Excited to show their transport to their legendary guest, the C-40 pilots explained their cockpit gizmos and navigational toys to Wilson, who nodded his understanding with interest.

"We'd let you hand-fly it, sir, but we're not allowed to take it off autopilot at altitude. Would you like to make a frequency change to Moncton Center in about ten miles? We can let you do that if you'd like."

Wilson laughed. "No, you guys manage it, all yours."

The aircraft commander twisted the knob to change heading. "We've got a good gig, sir. Taxiing at Atlanta Hartsfield is about our biggest challenge."

"I'm sure you embellish. What did you fly in the fleet?" Wilson asked him.

"MH-60 *Sierras*, sir."

Wilson nodded. "How about you?" he asked the second pilot.

"*Hornets* and *Rhinos*, sir...I got to the *Ravens* four years after you left."

"*Quoth the Raven!*" Wilson responded.

"*Quoth the Raven*, sir!" the smiling pilot said.

Under the tutelage of the pilots, Wilson learned about the C-40 and chatted about flying. The pilots changed frequencies and monitored the fuel as the transport jet flew high over the Canadian Maritimes.

"Yes, sir...this is pretty much our lives up here at altitude. Wish we could let you fly it, but the FAA and then our admiral would have a cow...I mean, sorry, sir."

Wilson smiled. "I have no doubt."

In the silence that followed, Wilson looked out the left window toward the horizon. Arrayed before him, the peaceful blue Atlantic Ocean rolled eternal. How many times during a quiet stroll on a carrier flight deck had he contemplated it, searching toward the horizon at the sunlit tops of cumulus clouds over 100 miles distant, knowing that the nearest land in a certain direction was *thousands* of miles beyond what he could see in the unlimited visibility. *The vastness.*

Wilson took in the moment, savoring distant cloud buildups hovering like sentinels low over the sea, the jagged white edges of them that he had explored, pulling hard against a white and cottony pylon, rolling through a misty cave before bursting into the clear on the other side, then pulling down in a dive to run along the surface of the sea. *Alone* over the ocean like no one except carrier aviators could fathom, climbing and rolling and diving on a whim, the *freedom*, if only for ten minutes before the recovery, and the knowledge to experience this exhilarating moment of human existence. *Thank you, God!*

Cruising off Nova Scotia and down the rocky coast of North America, Wilson sat motionless as he viewed the ocean far below—and far away. Beautiful...and dangerous. Calm one moment, and a lethal killing ground the next. Suddenly he realized that where once, as a younger man he belonged out there, now he was a spectator and always would be. It hit him then, and he didn't know how to react to it.

He had overstayed.

"Guys, thanks, but I'll let you have your cockpit back. We'll see you on deck."

"Anytime, sir. We'll park in front of Base Ops in about two hours, sir."

Wilson returned to his seat and noticed Weed had moved across the aisle. When he sat down next to him in the middle seat, Weed turned to him.

"Weed, I owe you an apology. For remaining quiet six years ago, and for thinking only of myself now."

"Kemo, *I'm* sorry. You just got sent home, and you needed to vent. If not to me, then who? I should have let you."

Wilson nodded his understanding. "I owe you a beer."

"Then I accept your apology. Now, what is it like to fly a C-40?"

"Wouldn't let me touch it…the jet flies itself and they just change the radio freqs."

"Really? While you were up there, everyone in the cabin was screaming and I almost got airsick. You sure you weren't flying?"

Wilson smiled. "Hope you feel better soon; we've got about two hours to go."

"Good, time for sleep."

Both men looked out the window as Nova Scotia drifted down their right side. Weed spoke next.

"You know, Saint got sent home, but he didn't have a Mary to meet him."

Wilson remained silent for a moment before he answered. "I think about him a lot." Silence returned as they scanned the western horizon, lost in their thoughts. Weed broke it.

"Did he love the Navy, expecting it would love him back? All of us get jilted at some point, but we can fly into the arms of our families and in no time the sea, the jet, the Navy…the "other woman" …is forgotten. And we are forgiven."

Wilson said nothing, knowing his friend was right.

"So, what are you going to do, man? Go quietly, or go high and right?"

Wilson remained silent as he stared outside at the western horizon.

"Not sure yet."

CHAPTER 63

NAVAL AIR STATION OCEANA, 1700 JUNE 24, 2024

Through his passenger seat window, Wilson studied the column of contain-erships plodding their way toward Cape Henry. He counted five of the be-hemoths, each stacked high with *thousands* of the colorful 40-foot rectangu-lar boxes bound for Norfolk, Baltimore, or Philly. Unabated by the action in the North Atlantic, they ended their three-to-four-week journeys carrying the goods that Americans wanted…or a hidden cruise missile that America's ene-mies wanted.

The C-40 descended toward the ocean surface, and Wilson observed the wing spoilers extend and flaps lower as the pilots slowed the jet. With a sudden rumble, the landing gear extended, and he figured they were on final to Runway 23L at Oceana. He knew it well.

Small craft darting in and out of Rudee Inlet came into view, as did the resort hotels and beach condos of Virginia Beach. He'd take the family out to dinner there tonight at a favorite seafood place on the strip, straight from Base Ops. There he could finally relax—and from the table contemplate the North Atlantic Ocean that had bewitched him for decades.

As the jet touched down and pilots pulled the thrust reverser levers, Wilson detected a small gathering of colorful clothes outside of base ops. Mary and the kids were in there. It had only been three weeks since Naples! A lifetime ago.

During the long taxi up to Base Ops, Wilson thought about how he would tell Mary. Should he tell the kids, too, tonight at dinner? Maybe one night, just one night of not being in the Navy. Could he do it? As the jet turned to its parking spot, he doubted that he could.

At once he recognized Mary, Derrick, and Brittany among the gaggle of families. Karen Hopper stood next to them. Yes, he and Weed were lucky to have families to return home to.

A young father who hadn't seen his newborn daughter—who was born after *Valley Forge* deployed—was the first off the airplane. Wilson allowed the others to depart ahead of him as the sailors rushed headlong into the arms of squealing families. Skweez stepped up to a leggy blonde and lifted her off her feet as they kissed.

"Go ahead, Weed."

"Home from the sea. Never gets old."

Weed descended the boarding stairs, while Wilson stopped to thank the pilots. At the door, the stifling summertime heat and humidity of the Tidewater region enveloped him. *Home.*

Wilson strode to his family. Years earlier, the kids ran ahead. Now adults, they waited for their mother.

"Welcome home, James," Mary said with a reserved smile.

She knows.

He kissed and embraced her, then hugged his children. "Let's go to Jack's Catch for dinner, on me."

Mary smiled. "Jack's Catch? Well. Spend all your sea pay in one night?"

Wilson smiled as he led his family out. *Home.*

Hours later, as they prepared for bed inside their flag quarters in Little Creek, Mary stopped and waited for Wilson to notice her.

"What?" he said.

"I know why you're here."

Wilson looked away. "I know you know. The girls always know first."

"The spouses..."

"Yes, the spouses!" Wilson snapped. Mary recoiled, and Wilson recovered. "I'm sorry, Mary, I'm sorry—"

"You've been fighting World War Three. You're entitled, this once," she said.

"When did you learn?"

"It's all over our little flag officer ghetto here. All our neighbors know."

"Leaked," Wilson said out loud to himself. *Harder to reinstate.*

In bed, Mary drew close to him as he stared at the ceiling.

"What are you going to do?"

"They're going to give me the Region job."

"I know," she whispered.

Wilson chuckled. "Okay, then *you* tell me what to do."

"Well, what is the Region job?"

"Make sure the base utility bills are paid, go to the new Exchange gas station grand opening and make a speech, that kind of stuff."

"Sounds easy."

"Figurehead…civilians run it."

"Then what?"

Wilson exhaled. "Retirement."

"Our goal for the past twenty years. Where will we live?"

"Where I can get a job."

"Like Consolidated?"

"Yeah, a defense prime like them. *Acme Defense*…we can solve your every warfighting need with our latest high-tech hammer."

"Do you want to do that?"

Wilson exhaled again. "Yes…no…not really."

"Why don't you fight?"

"Fight what? Tired of fighting, the Russians, the admirals…and now you."

"James, you'll never forgive yourself if you don't fight back. Why did they fire you, really?"

Wilson could not tell her everything.

"They suggested I take certain actions, I defied them, and we won the war anyway. My flagship and all aboard it are okay."

"Was the *Childers* yours?"

"Yes. I lost a ship in a nuclear war."

"What's the real reason?"

"I defied them, and it only takes one time…and I'm an aviator."

"Now we're getting somewhere."

"And jealousy. I'm the only guy on active duty with a Navy Cross. They hate that."

Silence returned as they each waited for the other to resume.

"James, if an injustice has occurred, or they are being unfair, you have to confront them."

Wilson looked at her. "I can't believe you. I'll get a cushy shore job and have a band at my retirement ceremony in a year. What we've wanted for years is finally here."

"No, I don't want the next decades full of your grumbling and resentment. They're marginalizing you and you know it. Fight back. You may lose, but you'll die with your boots on, and we can put it behind us."

"What if I win?"

"Then I want to live in Hawaii, or at least San Diego."

Wilson pulled her close. "I'll demand that as a condition."

"I mean it. I want out of here, too, and away from them."

Wilson considered her words as the silence returned.

Mary nuzzled closer to her husband. "Well, are you going to make love to me now, or lose me forever?"

"Isn't that from a movie that shall not be named?"

"I can quote that line anytime I want, *Admiral*. And I can quote this line; '*I feel the need.*' And these lines; '*Tell me about the MiG some other time…ya big* STUD.'"

Wilson smiled and turned out the light.

Chapter 64

NSA Hampton Roads, 1340 July 1, 2024

Wilson drove down Terminal Boulevard past the Breezy Point Golf Course, rehearsing again what he was going to say to Admiral David Woods, Commander, Fleet Forces Command. He had met the four-star aviator once but had no relationship with him. A train carrying cars of containers from the Port of Norfolk inched along the track in the opposite direction. *Containers.* Wilson considered them, *millions* of them, that clogged all the oceans of the world with stuff for human consumption.

The world had slowly returned to normal since the moment on June 18th that had changed it forever. Churches that were packed to overflowing on June 23 had room for all in the pews the following Sunday. A televised Memorial Service for *Lloyd Childers* that Wilson attended in Norfolk competed with economic and political news in cable broadcasts. He felt the eyes of family members on him, parents and siblings who blamed him for the loss of their loved ones. More than one father with a full beard and gray ponytail stared at him with contempt. One mother cried, "*You* should be out there, not my girl!" In his white uniform, Wilson stood and took the invectives, said and unsaid, in silence.

Finger pointing on Capitol Hill over who had brought the world to the brink of destruction raged over defense appropriations that many believed should surpass the one trillion mark. Social media platforms—with one exception—retained heavy censorship over world geopolitics, feeding more loveable-dog videos into the algorithm than ever before.

Turning into the gate, Wilson saluted the sentry and followed his smart phone directions to the CFFC building. Arriving early, he drove past the horseshoe parking area to see if they had a sign out for him. They did.

Dressed in summer whites, Wilson drove another lap to kill time and parked in front of the sign that read RDML J. WILSON

Retrieving his cover from the seat next to him, he exited and strode to the entrance, where a Navy lieutenant dressed in green camouflage greeted him.

"Good afternoon, Admiral. Admiral Woods sends his regrets that he cannot meet with you this afternoon as the luncheon with the Chairman and NATO Secretary General went long."

"I can wait," Wilson answered.

"Ah…he won't be back, today, sir. Taking a flight to Colorado Springs at 1600. Our Deputy, Vice Admiral Korson, is here, sir, and she'll take your meeting."

Wilson's poker face did not twitch at this news. Korson was a surface warrior and the first native American woman to command a Navy warship. Where the aviator Woods could lend a sympathetic ear, he was unavailable. Korson was an unknown whom he had never met.

Wilson could only nod as he followed the lieutenant inside the modern glass-encased quarterdeck and up the stairs to the Deputy Commander office.

He was directed to a chair and offered coffee or water, which he declined. As the office personnel went about their duties, Wilson waited. Noticing his nervous rotation of his combination cover in his hands, he forced himself to stop and sit and wait as one-stars were forced to do.

As the minutes passed, sailors went in and out of Korson's office, bantering with one another and sharing office gossip as if Wilson were not even present. Fifteen minutes passed as Wilson sat expressionless, a recalcitrant schoolboy waiting outside the principal's office, the nonchalant staff unimpressed with him.

Five more minutes passed, the intended message to Wilson loud and clear. Looking down at his shoes for a moment, he allowed himself to be surprised as Korson walked up to him in silence.

"Jim, welcome, come on in."

Wilson stood to shake her offered hand and followed her inside the large office, furnished with a conference table and small sitting area adjacent to her desk, with floor-to-ceiling glass behind it. The door remained open.

"Please, have a seat. Coffee?"

"Yes, ma'am, thank you."

"Black like a sailor, or do you put stuff in it?"

"Black's fine, ma'am."

She called for the yeoman, and soon a tray of steaming coffee in china cups and saucers appeared. Korson picked hers up and held it in her hands as she took a tepid sip. All business, she got to the point.

"Jim, last month was a devastating loss, I can't call it anything else. Losing *Lloyd Childers* was an absolute body blow. I mean, Americans don't know how to process the loss of hundreds at a time, and it will take us a *long* time to recover.

That a nuke got in among your screen is something that we must address, with training and hardware. Then there's *Tinian*. If we had lost her to a nuke, and your carrier and Lord knows what else, I don't think we'd have a country anymore. People are just...spun up, out of control. We took a bullet and dodged another one that would have really ruined our day, and we'll learn from it, but we must take action when warranted or we lose faith and trust."

Wilson knew where she was going with this. Remaining stoic, he waited for her to continue, giving her the rope to do so.

"Look, Jim, you know that we are promoted for the *next* job on sustained superior performance. The hiccups that occurred during your tenure in CSG-18 are, well, not insignificant. A warship and 300 souls...on your watch, not to mention ignoring the suggestions of a four-star on scene. What were you thinking? So, we must act. The public demands it for the ship alone."

Wilson took her measure. "So, Admiral, after three weeks in the job and a nuclear war-at-sea, the Navy has already decided on my fitness for further command?"

"Jim, you know that's true! If the minute after you say *I relieve you, sir!* a fire starts in the main machinery space, it's *your* responsibility, and if your people are found negligent, *you* take the fall. You *know* this, all of us have since we were lieutenants, and I'm sorry, but this has now happened to you. Look...we're going to make it right. We'll keep it quiet, out of the public eye, and have you take the Region job next month. It's an important shore command, and you can make a difference there and retire next year with any number of civilian opportunities. Our graybeard network is going to place you, and you and your family will be *well* taken care of, Admiral."

Wilson detected the bribe as Korson sat back, smiling. He'd play his cards.

"Admiral, you don't know who you're dealing with."

Incensed, Korson's face flushed with anger as she lunged forward in her seat and pointed at him as she growled.

"No, *you* don't know who you're dealing with, Mister! You *fucked up* out there, Wilson, tactically and politically. That Navy Cross on your chest for something you did as a JO doesn't mean *shit* up here! We warned all of you when you first became a flag that you had better play ball, and that we can move you at any time to any place we want. And that network goes away the minute we want it to go away. All it takes is a phone call."

"What are you going to tell me next, Admiral, that I'm never going to work in this town again?"

Enraged, Korson unloaded loud enough to be heard in the outer office.

"Yes, Wilson! I'll spell it out for you; you're finished! And we can bring you to mast and retire you as a captain! What does it take to get it through your skull? We *own* you!"

Wilson pursed his lips as he nodded his understanding.

"Admiral Korson, it appears that this meeting is over, so I'll be leaving now for my 1600 appointment at the Virginian-Pilot. Good day, ma'am."

Korson's eyes widened in surprise.

"Wilson, you stay right in that seat. What do you mean?"

"Admiral, we just fought and won a nuclear war, and I was the strike group commander. I'm sure the paper would love to do a feature story on my experience, and the publicity will likely lead to a book deal that, I imagine, will more than compensate for retiring me as an O-6."

"What are you saying?"

"I'm saying that I have receipts, ma'am, from the Med to the Norwegian Sea…to Fleet Forces Command."

"Wilson…if you…"

"If I what, ma'am?"

"What happened last month is classified. Any word of it and you'll be charged and sentenced. Your family will receive the retirement benefits of an ensign if they're lucky."

"I'm not talking about that, to anybody, ever. Do you think I'm a traitor? You insult me, ma'am."

Korson smiled nervously. "Wilson, *that* would be bad for you. Look…you've won this battle, this high-end fight with a peer competitor. You need a break at the Region, and it's a two-star billet. We'll fast-track your second star and get the secretary to sign off on a two-star retirement next year. No need to come out of your chair, especially now with world and domestic tensions as they are. Two-star command, Jim, with the post-retirement network. I'll forget I heard anything to the contrary."

"Admiral, I want three stars and command in San Diego, specifically the Third Fleet."

Stunned, a broad smile crossed Korson's face as she studied him. "You can't be serious!" she scoffed, chuckling at the notion of it.

"Third Fleet, Admiral, with a move this fall. And with you as guest speaker. You can say that I commanded during a momentous time in our national history, that I shouldered responsibility. As you said, when things go bad, commanders are blamed, and when things go well and the United States wins a nuclear war, commanders are promoted…quickly…ahead of their peers."

"Sluggo Compton is slated for that job. I'm sorry, Wilson, no freaking way."

"Admiral, I commanded that strike group that delivered the combat effects it was asked to. The bullshit style points you and Buffington demand after the fact are just that, bullshit, because as an up-and-coming aviator I'm a threat to you. Now I know Admiral Compton, nice guy, but I'm sorry, *I* want that job, now…so you tell him."

"Only the commander can direct that."

"Then get on the horn with him, ma'am. You've got twenty-four hours, and if I don't hear from you or Admiral Woods, my meeting with the military-beat reporter will be rescheduled for Wednesday afternoon…right before the national holiday celebrating our independence from tyranny."

Her bluff called, Korson sat up straight, not sure what to say or do next, and showing fear.

"He loves writing hit pieces on the brass, Admiral. He's experienced at it."

A deflated Korson could barely murmur her response. "I'll talk to the boss."

"Thank you, ma'am, and please extend to him my warm regards. I'll see myself out."

Leaving Korson seated, Wilson took his cover and stepped to the door. He turned.

"Orders, in writing, twenty-four hours. Good day, ma'am, and I look forward to your inspirational remarks in San Diego."

Without acknowledging the staff as he strode out of the office, Rear Admiral Flip Wilson departed the Fleet Forces building and drove home to his wife Mary.

That evening, he opened a bottle of red and poured two glasses. Together they relaxed on their lanai to plan their next Navy adventure.

Mary opened the map on her smartphone.

"So, where would we live again?"

Wilson took a sip. "The house on the beach at North Island. Sweeping view of the Pacific Ocean from Point Loma to Mexico. You could walk to the golf course."

"Oh yeah…with a runway running through the front yard. And it's so isolated! We'd have to live there?"

Incredulous, Wilson smiled. "It's Coronado! You're turning down the most awesome quarters in the Navy?"

"No…but. Anyway…"

"A complaining sailor is a happy sailor."

"And a complaining wife is a problem, for you."

They both took a sip from their glasses. Mary changed the subject.

"Are you sure you want this? They'll be gunning for you the whole time."

"They're not going to mess with me, and it's harder three time zones away."

Unconvinced, Mary took another sip.

"The peaceful Pacific," Wilson added. "Will be a fun tour."

"Yes, love Coronado, and everyone will come to visit. Two years will go fast. Then what?"

"Retire."

She took another sip.

"James, why? If you've gone this far, why not go all the way? You can be frenemies with the Washington crowd, but I know you love it. No guarantees, but why not try?"

"You want to go back to Washington?"

"I wouldn't mind. We have real friends there too. What holds you back?"

Wilson set his glass down.

"It doesn't look fun. We've known some great people in those jobs, and God bless them, but after fleet command, in my mid-fifties…why not do something else while I can?"

"Like what?" Mary asked.

"Travel the country in an RV, like other retired people."

Mary laughed. "So long as you drive *and* cook. But no, we're too young for even that."

"Then I just want to be home with you."

"Home from the sea?"

Wilson smiled. "Yes, after this one last tour, then really."

He walked over to Mary and kissed her.

"Really, Mary. Then I'll be home."

Mary drained her glass. "I'll drink to that. Now refill this and let's talk about that trip to Hawaii."

"Sure, that would be fun after we settle in."

"No, Admiral Wilson, I mean next month!"

At that moment, under moonless skies more than 5,000 miles to the east, Burak observed the ketch through his night vision device. The two-masted boat—over twenty meters in length—sailed steady at five knots on a course of west some thirty miles south of Chrissi Island. With the crescent moon scheduled to break the horizon in another hour, he had to go in the next fifteen minutes.

With running lights blazing as *Konya K* overtook the ketch two miles to the north, deckhands lowered the inflatable on the starboard side to remain hidden as Burak and the coxswain descended to it via the Jacobs ladder. Once seated, Burak snarled, *"Git."*

This op was a gift to Burak, the take-down of a Swiss financier—Hans—on holiday along with two prostitutes. The financier, almost sixty, was part of the Davos crowd of climate activists who eschewed so-called fossil fuels while flying the world in their private jets. Money for "green" industry projects had made him a fortune while crippling the Turkish energy sector, whose efforts to drill in the Eastern Med were underfinanced on purpose. Because of Hans, Turks suffered, and tonight Burak would alleviate the suffering of his people while he enjoyed every minute of it.

He would terrorize the women as the quivering Hans watched helplessly, crying, *begging* for mercy and his life. Would the weakling sacrifice the girls to spare his own life? Burak would find out how fast.

Clear of *Konya K's* wake, the inflatable skimmed over the smooth sea under an unusually clear sky, the luminous band of the Milky Way comforting Burak as it always did at sea. The coxswain would drop him off on the transom. If the swine were outside, he'd disable the man and toy with the women before he threw the shrieking whores overboard. He would then bind the man in the same way and deliver him into the arms of *Mare Nostrum*.

As they neared, he studied the boat's cockpit. Empty. Inside the forward cabin, a faint light burned.

"Stand off until you see me return," Burak said to the coxswain, who eagerly nodded his understanding.

Easing over the gunwale, Burak drew his knife. Clad in black, his sinister appearance inside the cabin would maximize their terror. Tingling with excitement, he hoped they were in the forward cabin, exhausted from their lust, yet awake enough to see him enter.

He peered into a dark galley window as he listened. Nothing. Slowly he descended into the well to open the cabin door. Grasping the door handle with his left hand, he turned it slowly until it could turn no more. *Open.* The door opened to the inside, and once he took a deep breath, he exerted pressure and entered, his right hand gripping the knife like a hammer.

Filling the door frame, his sixth sense alerted.

Phtttttt!

A spear fired from a spear gun impaled him through his right lung as he fell back into the cockpit. Dropping the knife, he grabbed the spear as blood oozed from the wound while he grunted from the searing pain.

Pain exploded into his brain when a woman kicked him in the groin, following with a crushing stomp that broke his left arm. Gasping and desperate, Burak felt for his pistol when a rifle butt crashed down on his jaw, breaking it.

The women screamed for a reason the delirious Burak did not know as a man—a younger man, not Hans! *How?*—took the knife and without fanfare jammed it under Burak's chin.

Burak's assailant rose to his full height as the women sobbed and begged for their lives. In unaccented Turkish the man called to the coxswain standing off 50 meters.

"Would you like to see these two? Come, come, get a good look!"

The coxswain gunned the outboard and drew close to the port quarter, the women still wailing. Illuminated by the glow of the stern light, the coxswain slowed and stood to get a better look at the two Greek sirens who would soon be dead.

The man raised his rifle and fired, knocking the coxswain back into the engine, dead. The boat continued ahead and caressed the ketch as one of the women grabbed a line and secured it. The man placed an envelope inside Burak's vest, and together they maneuvered his lifeless body over the gunwale to fall into the boat in a bloody heap.

Casting the inflatable adrift, the ketch turned to the east along the southern shore of Crete. *Konya K* dared not follow.

With dead eyes wide in shock, Burak lay in a pool of his blood under a starlit sky as the boat bobbed on a gentle sea in waters claimed by multiple nations, just as other nations had competed and fought upon these ancient waves over the millennia. On the eastern horizon, the rising crescent moon began its journey across the heavens, mute witness to it all.

About the Author

Captain Kevin Miller, a 24-year veteran of the U.S. Navy, is a former tactical naval aviator and has flown the A-7E *Corsair II* and FA-18C *Hornet* operationally. He is the author of the *Raven One* series of contemporary carrier aviation fiction, and the multi-award winning *The Silver Waterfall: A Novel of the Battle of Midway.*

Contact the author at kevin@kevinmillerauthor.com

I hope you enjoyed reading *High End* as much as I enjoyed writing it. Whether you found it good or "other," I'd sincerely appreciate your feedback. Please take a moment to leave a review on Amazon or Goodreads.

Thanks and V/R,
Kevin

FIGHT FIGHT

Chapter 1

Waters west of Scarborough Shoal, South China Sea, November, 2018

Liao Chang stepped to the starboard side of the pilothouse and peered through the binoculars. *There they are*, he thought. A smile formed on his lips, and his body shivered from excitement.

Today was the day.

Finally, exactly 1,400 years since the time of Tang Dynasty, and after more than 100 years of foreign humiliation, China—under the Red Banner of the People's Republic—was going to once again exert control over what belonged to it. Beginning today, and in these waters, the Han people, weak no longer, would unify all under heaven and return *order* to her ancient seas. Liao smiled again when he thought of the military history books that would have *his* name written alongside the names of Sun Tzu, Admiral Zheng He, and Chairman Mao himself.

The 34-year-old Liao, a peasant fisherman from Hainan, had spent his life on the waters of the South China Sea, on trawlers like the one he now captained. At twenty meters long, *She Kou* was a seine trawler with a blue hull and the characteristic high spoon prow of Asian vessels. The boat was modest compared to the *hundreds of thousands* of ocean-going trawlers the PRC sent worldwide in search of protein for its 1.3 billion people. Most mariners would call it a rust bucket, but *She Kou*, at this moment, was the most powerful warship in the South China Sea.

A woman. Liao's eyes were drawn to his sister on the bow. Li Ming was two years younger, but her weathered face and her hands, calloused from a lifetime on the boats, made her look two decades older than she was. Li's sad eyes were focused on the task before her, one she could do in her sleep. The years ahead would be filled with more drudgery and grime, and the smells of diesel, rotting fish, and salt. She ignored the spray that lashed her, as it had thousands and thousands of times in her lifespan, and continued to work the block and tackle of the nets. Now considered a dried-up old maid, she had no way to rise above her deckhand status. Liao watched her from the bridge, and, as the wind blew her long frizzled hair about her head, he noticed the streaks of gray.

Liao would be rewarded by the Party with a woman, and not a hag from the Hainan docks like Li Ming. His woman would be a young beauty from Hong Kong or Shanghai, like the girls who read the news on television with their smooth skin and shiny hair. And silk dresses that hugged their curves, adorning a strong body that could bear him a son. For the service he was about to render to the People's Republic, he would ask for *two* sons, and he would get them. Liao Chang would ensure they were educated and ready to attain their leadership positions in the Party. His reward would be great for his actions this day.

Liao lifted his binoculars again to study the wooden banca boats one mile off the starboard bow, six of them in open water northwest of Huangyan Island. They were within hailing distance of each other as they moved northeast dragging lines for tuna. Or grouper. These big fish could feed dozens and dozens of hungry mouths on the mainland, and the mouths were insatiable. The mongrel Filipinos were stealing them from Liao and the People's Republic right before their eyes—in Chinese waters! A frown formed on Liao's face when he read the message painted in poorly formed characters on the colorful banners flying above the decrepit and dirty bancas: *The Western Philippine Sea is Ours!*

We'll see about that, Liao thought as he turned the wheel left to open the distance a bit. He grunted at the mere thought of the body of water they called the Western Philippine Sea. Even the Western barbarians called this the South *China* Sea. And the islands were the Zhongsha Islands, not the Filipino name Ku-lumpol ng Panatag and certainly not the western Scarborough Shoal—whatever a "Scarborough" was. The sea and the territory was *Chinese,* and the Chinese people, through the ancient construct of *yi* integrity, named things that belonged to them under heaven.

A stiff breeze from the north formed whitecaps on the one-meter seas, and visibility had fallen to under two miles in gray mist. *Perfect,* Liao thought, and he nudged the throttle ahead a hair to ensure this opportunity would not pass if the unpredictable bancas were to turn away. Pinned as they were against the shallow bank of Huangyan a few miles to their right, he knew he had them trapped.

From his position at the helm, Liao twisted his head right and peered through an aft-facing window. He saw the technician Xia who stood beside the generator in full foul-weather gear and unusual facemask. When their eyes met, Liao showed two fingers, his estimate of when *She Kou* would be in perfect position. The plan was to engage the generator when they were one mile upwind; at the moment, the winds were out of the north-northeast, holding steady at 15 knots with an occasional gust to 20. A big deck hand they called "Fatso" worked on a fouled net and hovered nearby. He was not briefed, nor was Li Ming. Both were wise enough not to ask about their landlubber passenger as they went about their tasks. Liao hoped they were up forward when the time came—in two minutes.

The wooden bancas bobbed in the sea, their half-naked deck hands oblivious to the raw conditions as they heaved in lines across gunwales of peeling paint. He saw one of the filthy boats pull in a large fish, and through the binoculars, he could see the Filipinos looking at him from across the water. One sent a gesture of contempt his way before returning to haul in another big fish, one that Liao surmised to be a tuna. Filipinos in their flimsy boats caught the large fish on lines—the barbarians cared about such things! Powerful Chinese boats like *She Kou* could drag nets and catch fish in the bulk needed to feed the vast multitudes on the mainland that did the People's work, Western sensitivities be damned.

With gentle pressure on the wheel, Liao turned into them 10 degrees and steadied on a heading of northeast. The pathetic little flotilla was falling off down his starboard rail, and he craned his neck right to keep them in sight. Spray flew over the port side when the protection of the boats' high prow was lost. Li Ming now worked in even greater misery on the rolling deck under the bridge.

Liao whipped his head left and scanned the horizon. The lead seiner *Le Peng* 4220 was in position two miles off his port quarter, a gray silhouette in the mist, a single light showing from the mast. *Good.* The militia vessel provided Liao mutual support and would serve as witness to the service *She Kou* would render to the People's Republic on this momentous day.

Liao again checked the winds and with his seaman's eye assessed the Filipino position as they fell further aft.

Now.

With exaggerated movements of his head, Liao pointed at the clueless bancas and signaled to Xia who nodded in return. Xia threw a switch on the generator, and it cranked to life. Fatso was too close and oblivious to the danger. He watched the machine sputter as Xia moved away from it.

Get back to work, Fatso! Liao thought. *Curiosity killed the cat!*

Beyond the generator's single exhaust tube, Liao saw *something* cause the sea in the background to appear out of focus. He knew the substance was clear and odorless and was surprised he could detect it. Xia motioned for Fatso to get away, but the big deck hand ignored him.

Liao grabbed the deck loudspeaker microphone, *"Do as he says!"* he bellowed.

Fatso suddenly fell to his knees. Then, on all fours, he gasped for breath. Fatso looked up at the pilothouse in agony, uncomprehending. *Why can't I breathe?*

With a cry, Li Ming appeared from the port side. Liao warned her, *"Stay away!"*

It was too late. As soon as Li put her hand on Fatso's shoulder, she, too, dropped to her knees in agonizing convulsions. With Fatso motionless on deck, Li gasped for air before she then collapsed next to her already dead crewmate.

The machine sounded like a gasoline-powered grass mower and continued to run as Liao shook his head in regret and double-checked the winds. After several minutes, the machine sputtered and stopped. Taking great care to ensure he was upwind, Xia stepped to it from his position under the pilothouse by stepping over the dead. Xia crouched and grasped the wooden stocks it rested on, and using the strength of his legs and hands, pushed up and out. The machine tumbled over the side and into the South China Sea.

Xia then looked up at Liao, who nodded to give permission for what must be done. Xia grabbed Fatso's ankles, and, with all his strength, dragged him to the deck edge. He then pushed him under the rail with his foot. The splash was visible to Liao from the pilothouse as Xia turned to Li Ming's lifeless body and grabbed her wrists. After he dragged her to the rail, he rolled her thin frame underneath and pushed her over the side without ceremony. Liao shook his head in contempt. *She should have listened to me!* Xia found a hose and washed off the deck, gunwales, and railings of *She Kou* before they turned to Hainan and home. As the vessel chugged ahead through the waves, Liao saw Li Ming's body floating in their wake. *Dammit*, he thought. *Xia should have weighted the body first.*

Keeping his eyes on the banca boats, Liao pulled the throttles back to slow the trawler… He wanted to see this firsthand.

He saw a crewman move aft on the easternmost boat but did not detect further motion. The boats in the lee appeared normal, and then began to turn in different directions. One collided with another, but Liao saw no signs of fishermen hauling in lines or otherwise trying to avoid further damage. Another boat turned away to the west, and Liao studied it for signs of movement. Seeing none, he scanned the other bancas. The only sign of life he saw was on one of the two boats that hit each other: a man waving a single arm while on his knees. Liao scanned again, dwelling several seconds on each boat, but could not discern any further movement.

Mission accomplished! They had done it!

The intruding thieves had been executed for trespassing on the Zhongsha Islands, and Liao had captained the vessel that ensured the rights of the People's Republic were upheld—even here at this faraway outpost on the very edge of heaven. There would be more crimes to avenge in these waters, and Liao was honored to lead the effort. In payment, he would acquire power and wealth and would rise in the Party hierarchy. And he would soon choose, as a bride, a beauty not unlike the women he saw on television. Any girl he wanted would be his.

Beyond the drifting bancas, now under no one's command, he grew concerned when a shadow came into view on the gloomy horizon. He studied it, and saw it was a ship of an unusual shape and standing into potential danger. His first impression was that it was an oilfield servicing vessel, and he hoped it would navigate clear of the invisible cloud that the winds were carrying toward it.

Get out of there! he thought. Then his eyes widened in alarm, and his heart rate increased.

It was a warship.

At her watch station between the two main engine rooms of the guided-missile cruiser, USS *Cape Esperance*, Ensign Isabel Manning was bored out of her mind.

After two hours of working on her quals as Engineering Officer of the Watch under instruction in the cruiser's Central Control Station, Isabel had checked and rechecked all the gauges and readings of the LM 2500 marine gas turbine, monitored the log entries, conducted a walk-around inspection with the chief, and even helped Fireman Apprentice Williams with his personal qualifications standards. She could trace the gas turbine "steam cycle" in her sleep; air was drawn from the downtakes, compressed, fuel and spark combusted to drive the turbine and auxiliaries and draw in more air for compression.

It was a never-ending cycle. *Suck, squeeze, bang, boom,* the snipes called it. And exhaust through the uptakes. Hell, it was a jet engine, an actual airliner engine adapted for a ship! Aboard this cruiser no one could escape the constant background whine of the rotating turbine blades. But here, she was mere feet from it, and all of the watch team wore foam earplugs to protect their hearing from the relentless din.

However, it wasn't the noise that drove Isabel up the bulkhead. No, it was the soul-crushing monotony of pipes and pumps and dials and trunks and lagging and fire mains and circuitry that made up the engineering spaces of this, and any, ship. No windows, everything painted white, and only the gentle rolling of the deck to indicate they were on a ship underway. She was the only woman on this watch, and around her the male sailors seemed fascinated as they tended the machinery, took readings, and inspected fittings. Ensign Manning, on the other hand, was dying of boredom, and if she had to spend her whole *career* down here as Chief Tobin had, she would slit her wrists.

What was worse, she was *missing it*, missing the close-aboard passing of Scarborough Shoal on this freedom-of-navigation operation up the South China Sea. She hovered in the background during the navigation brief and saw they were going to transit inside five miles of the shoal. This would be a target-rich environment of surface traffic and probable Chinese Coast Guard, or intelligence collectors, with plenty of fishermen and merchants to add to the problem. Above her, in the ship's Combat Information Center, analyzing threat emitters and playing electronic warfare cat-and-mouse as the two navies collected intel off one another was another challenge.

For junior officers like her, opportunities to handle *Cape Esperance* in the SCS surrounded by surface contacts and under the captain's watchful eye, to learn and make good decisions under pressure, were rare. And once past the shoal, the plan was to transit around Luzon into the Phil Sea and open water—fewer challenges, more boredom. Right now, the action for an aspiring Surface Warfare Officer was topside on the bridge, and in CIC...anyplace but *here* in Central Control, her ear-splitting personal hell. She lamented that she wasn't scheduled on the bridge watch team. *Damn XO!*

Four bells sounded on the 1MC: 1400. Two hours of the afternoon watch complete with two more to go. *Ugh.*

Returning to CCS, Ensign Manning made a log entry: "Answering all-ahead one-third bell for 7 knots; steaming as before." *Sigh.*

Eight decks above on the busy bridge, Captain Ron Thompson studied the boats he saw off the starboard bow as they emerged from the mist. *Bancas by the look of them,* he thought. He focused his eyes. *What are they doing?*

He grabbed the binoculars by his bridge chair and found the boats. If they weren't just wallowing in the swell, they were maneuvering in an unusual manner. He then saw two of the bancas collide. *Who the hell are these guys? The Keystone Cops?*

Thompson turned to his Officer of the Deck, Lieutenant Hal Wagner, a mustang with lots of shiphandling experience. "Hal, look at these knuckleheads…I don't know what they're doing." Thompson picked up the phone and dialed his XO in the Combat Information Center below.

"XO, sir."

"Mike, do you have the contacts zero-four-five at about 4,000 yards?"

Lieutenant Commander Mike Eddins answered him. "Yes, sir, looks like a nest of fishing boats about 2,000 yards off the bank. North of them are a few bigger boats that we think are Chinese. Trying to get a positive ID on all."

"These banca boats off our bow are all over the place, and I just saw one run into another. No real factor but we're gonna come left a few and give them a wider berth. Yeah, I see the boat to the north, a trawler. Have you got emissions on him?"

"Yes, sir, and another is north of that contact."

"Roger, can't see him yet with this mist. We're gonna come left now, but please recommend a heading to stay 3,000 yards from the larger boats, especially if Chinese."

"Aye, aye, sir, I'll send it to the OOD."

"Very well," Thompson said as he cradled the receiver and called to his OOD. "Mister Wagner, let's come left ten degrees, please."

"Aye, aye, sir, coming left ten degrees," Wagner replied, and then repeated the orders to the Conning Officer who then repeated them to the helm in a familiar and ancient seafaring ritual of verbal command, verbatim acknowledgment, and physical action.

"What're they *doing?*" a young Quartermaster standing near Thompson asked himself. Thompson saw where he was looking and followed his eyes. Forward of the forecastle, both sailors standing force protection watch on the .50 cal mount were down, one rolling on the deck and the other kneeling next to a bollard. Both appeared to be in great pain.

"*What the fuck?*" Thompson muttered, and he turned toward Wagner to find out.

Just then, an alarm squealed and the stunned bridge team looked at each other in confusion. *The Chem/Bio alarm? Is this some kind of drill?*

Thompson looked back at the sailors on the bow, one of whom was no longer moving.

"Sound general quarters! Activate the emergency countermeasure water washdown system!"

As soon as the words left Thompson's mouth, he felt headache pain worse than any migraine he had ever experienced. And he couldn't catch his breath.

Others on the bridge were convulsing and struggling, falling to their knees and gasping for air, their eyes showing confusion—and fear. Thompson grabbed the sound-powered phone to Combat in an effort to have them conn the ship out of this unseen danger. He could only croak out the words "left full..." before he was overcome with excruciating pain. He thrashed about on the deck under the Captain's Chair in agony, exerting great effort to take just one breath, thinking about nothing else.

Below the bridge in Combat, the watch team members who huddled over their scopes in the darkened and cool space seemed to seize up in unison as the ventilators delivered the deadly vapor into the ship. At least the washdown system was activated. Inside the ship, hundreds of sailors going about their normal duties were gripped by a sudden sensation of pain and drowning. They noticed one another as they fell but were unable to help each other or even blurt out a warning as their survival instincts drove them to somehow take *one more breath*.

Chief Tobin, who had come up as a Gas Turbine Technician, was speechless when the garbled order to activate the emergency water washdown system was received from the bridge. Conditioned by his training, he activated it at once. His bored and preoccupied ensign was now focused.

"Ma'am, emergency countermeasure washdown system activated on orders from the bridge. I don't know why—unless it's the real thing."

Isabel put down her smart phone as Chief Tobin monitored the gauges. With the chief expecting an answer, she picked up the sound-powered phone to the bridge. She heard no answer. She tried to call them on the bitch-box. Nothing.

She then tried Combat where her roommate Abby was on watch, having all the fun. She waited longer than usual for an answer. Hearing no response, she turned to Tobin in concern.

"No answer from the bridge or Combat," she whispered, careful not to alarm the others.

Cape Esperance drove ahead at 7 knots on her assigned track, a gentle spray now covering the ship as the washdown system bathed it in seawater to remove whatever agent she had encountered. However, no humans on the bridge or in Combat controlled it, and over eighty percent of her crew was dead or dying. There were pockets of safety deep inside the ship, and one of them was Central Control where Ensign Manning was the senior member of the watch team.

"Ma'am, something's not right up there," Tobin said in an effort to prod his ensign into action. With a realization born of fear and concern, Isabel gave her first order. "Secure ventilation. *Secure ventilation!*"

"Secure ventilation, aye—ventilation to Engine Rooms One and Two secured. Securing habitability zones forward, midships, and aft."

"Nobody leaves this space. Check this space for MOPP gear or masks. How many watchstanders do we have here?"

"About six, ma'am, including us, and ten each in the main engine rooms, including the rovers."

"Call and check on them, and check if anyone answers in aft steering."

"Aye, aye, ma'am." The chief turned to his leading petty officer as Isabel checked the engine indications and rudder position. Still set for 7 knots and both rudders were left 5-degrees after a small course correction a few minutes earlier. On the Voyage Management System she noted *Cape Esperance* passing through 350. Checking the time, she knew they were in the vicinity of the shoal, and it dawned on her that the ship may not be under command.

Minutes passed and there were no 1MC announcements, no new orders to the helm, and no answer. Isabel's thoughts were of Abby. *Is she okay? Did we really get slimed? With what? Do we have enough antidotes aboard? Who? Why?*

Chief Tobin returned with his report.

"Ma'am, we have CBR suits for everyone, some SCBAs and plenty of EEBDs. We can outfit a runner to check topside, but recommend we maneuver clear of any contamination before we breach the space. And Petty Officer Brister is on station as helmsman in aft steering, just him. The others are down."

Tobin stepped closer to Isabel and spoke in a low tone. "Ma'am, you are the only officer in engineering and maybe the only one aboard that's alive... standing by for your orders to the helm."

Isabel blinked at him as it sank in. *Cape Esperance* was steaming into the unknown at 7 knots and not under command, but she and the snipes in engineering could control her from CCS as long as required, and Brister in aft steering could turn the rudders. She knew the ship was heading north. To her east—right—was shoal water... But who knew what was around them? She formed a plan.

"Okay, Chief, we're gonna get out of here. Get me comms with Petty Officer Brister."

Chief Tobin grabbed a sound-powered phone set and handed it to Isabel, who spoke into the transmitter. "Aft steering, Central Control."

"Aft steering, aye," Brister answered at once.

Isabel took a breath. "Petty Officer Brister, this is Ensign Manning—and I have the conn. On my mark I want you to take steering control."

"Aye, aye, ma'am," Brister answered. Isabel sensed he was unsure.

She looked at the bulkhead clock and saw the sweep second hand approach 12 and again depressed the switch. "Three, two, one, mark! Rudders Amidships!"

"Rudders amidships, aye," Brister answered, and after he manipulated the rudder controls, he called. "Ma'am, my rudders are amidships."

"Very well," Isabel answered.

"What's your plan, ma'am?" Tobin asked.

"We're gonna pivot west, then sprint for five minutes. Get ready."

"Aye, aye, ma'am."

On her computer screen Isabel pulled up the VMS and, after a quick review of the track, saw only minor course changes since before the afternoon watch.

With the sailors in CCS waiting, she took a breath. *"All back full!"*

At that, Chief Tobin and the others swung into action.

"All back full, aye! Engines making turns for back full!"

Isabel and the other braced themselves as the deck pitched forward from the sudden decrease in momentum. She watched the VMS speed readout count down, and at one knot gave her next order.

"Right engine – ahead full!"

With one shaft backing and the other pushing, the cruiser pivoted in the sea like a teen maneuvering a skateboard. The gyro repeater arced to the right, and Isabel assessed the rate of change. *Now.*

"All ahead flank!" she boomed, and the ship shuddered as both screws bit into the sea and propelled it forward. The compass settled on 265, and Isabel ordered Brister to maintain 280. She hit her wristwatch stop feature, and realized she hadn't been logging her own orders to the helm. The turbine engine whine permeated the compartment.

Are we heading into passing traffic? Is there a bank or shoal to the west we could run aground on? Isabel did not know and could not know as Chief Tobin tried in vain to get anyone topside to answer on any circuit. She had to get the ship clear, and her *best guess* was all *Cape Esperance* had at the moment by way of navigation.

Cape Esperance was now on an even keel and accelerating blind to the west at over 30 knots inside a South China Sea that was always choked with surface traffic. The deck below their feet steadied out to a gentle pitch as the ship bounded through the waves.

Isabel sensed on her the uneasy eyes of the young snipes, no older than she was, as they waited. Theirs was a desperate run to what they *hoped* was clear air, and they still didn't know the situation of the crew—their friends—on the decks above them. And she, Isabel Manning, was in charge, less than a year from her commissioning.

She watched the VMS, as they all did, in their high-pitched metallic cocoon, for the moment safe from whatever evil was on the other side of the bulkheads. She knew what she had to do, and turning to Chief Tobin, she lowered her voice.

"Chief, after we finish this run, I'm going topside, and I want one man with me. We'll go dead in the water and put on the two chem/bio suits. Want a guy, a big guy."

"I'll go with you, ma'am."

"No, Chief, want you here and in charge. We'll have everyone don a gas mask before we go through the hatch, and you can dog it down after we leave. We'll either call you when all clear or come back."

"Won't you be contaminated?"

Isabel considered his words. He was right. It would be a one-way mission.

"Yeah, well, we'll go to the bridge and assess, and get a radio call off to…. I don't know. Who should we call?"

Tobin gave her a hard look. "Ma'am, that topside stuff is all yours, I just keep the engines running."

Isabel nodded as she realized the truth in his words. While she knew enough to be dangerous, none of the snipes around her had ever spoken on a radio frequency. She had wanted to be back in navigation and operations, and she had gotten her wish. Both were now her show.

"Okay, I'll figure it out. Williams…he's a big guy, and I may need some muscle power. I want to take him."

"You gonna ask him, ma'am?"

"No, you are going to order him," Isabel answered, her eyes locked on her chief, both knowing what she was asking.

Tobin nodded, turned to the group, and bellowed, "Williams! Break out a chem/bio suit and get in it. You're going topside with the ensign. Salazar and Bennett, help him."

As the sailors set about their tasks, with a wary Seaman Williams not sure why he was chosen for this, Isabel noted the time. One minute to go.

They had been steady on their present course and speed for the past two minutes—the equivalent of a mile—and the initial acceleration and deceleration after she had given the order would account for another mile. Close enough, and once on the bridge, she could at least steer *Cape Esperance* clear of additional dangers. She gave the order.

"All stop."

Chief Tobin manipulated the throttles a second time. "All stop, aye… Ma'am the engines are at idle, prop pitch neutral."

"Very well," Isabel replied as the turbines' rotation slowed and the cruiser coasted to a stop. She fought to remain calm as she donned the chem/bio suit, wondering what she and Williams would find topside.

SUPERSONIC CARRIER AVIATION FICTION FROM
KEVIN MILLER

The Unforgettable Raven One Trilogy

www.braveshipbooks.com

**FROM TODAY'S MASTER
OF CARRIER AVIATION FICTION**

KEVIN MILLER

A NOVEL OF THE BATTLE OF MIDWAY

THE SILVER WATERFALL

KEVIN MILLER

Midway as never told before!

www.braveshipbooks.com

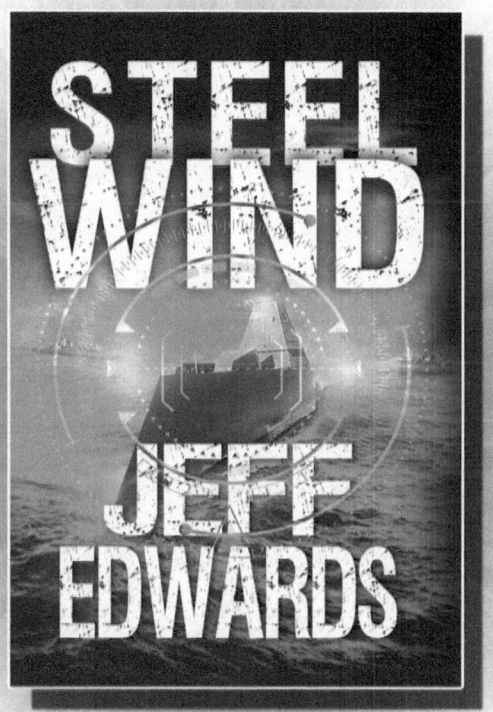

WHITE-HOT SUBMARINE WARFARE
BY
JOHN R. MONTEITH

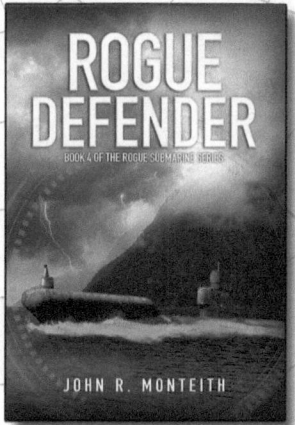

www.ingramcontent.com/pod-product-compliance
Lightning Source LLC
Chambersburg PA
CBHW020501020726
47493CB00001B/129